Fanny Hensel

FANNY HENSEL

The Other Mendelssohn

R. LARRY TODD

John Michael Cooper
Georgetown, Texas
23 October 2009

OXFORD
UNIVERSITY PRESS

2010

OXFORD
UNIVERSITY PRESS

Oxford University Press, Inc., publishes works that further
Oxford University's objective of excellence
in research, scholarship, and education.

Oxford   New York
Auckland   Cape Town   Dar es Salaam   Hong Kong   Karachi
Kuala Lumpur   Madrid   Melbourne   Mexico City   Nairobi
New Delhi   Shanghai   Taipei   Toronto

With offices in
Argentina   Austria   Brazil   Chile   Czech Republic   France   Greece
Guatemala   Hungary   Italy   Japan   Poland   Portugal   Singapore
South Korea   Switzerland   Thailand   Turkey   Ukraine   Vietnam

Copyright © 2010 by Oxford University Press, Inc.

Published by Oxford University Press, Inc.
198 Madison Avenue, New York, New York 10016

www.oup.com

Oxford is a registered trademark of Oxford University Press.

Library of Congress Cataloging-in-Publication Data
Todd, R. Larry.
Fanny Hensel : the other Mendelssohn / R. Larry Todd.
p.   cm.
Includes bibliographical references and index.
ISBN 978-0-19-518080-0
1. Hensel, Fanny Mendelssohn, 1805–1847.   2. Women composers—Germany.   I. Title.
ML410.H482T63 2009
780.92—dc22   2009003999

Music examples (marked in text with ●) are available online at
www.oup.com/us/fannyhensel.

1 3 5 7 9 8 6 4 2

Printed in the United States of America
on acid-free paper

For Nancy and Jim, in deep appreciation and admiration

Daß du nicht enden kannst, das macht dich groß,
Und daß du nie beginnst, das ist dein Los.

(That you can never end, that makes you great.
That you cannot begin, that is your fate.)

—Goethe, "Unbegrenzt," trans. John Whaley

Art is thus for individuals; dilettantism, for the crowd.

—J. P. Eckermann, *Goethe's Aphorisms* (No. 290)

Preface

Who was Fanny Hensel? This volume attempts to answer that question, even as it doubtless poses many others. Only a few decades ago, she was principally remembered as the talented sister of Felix Mendelssohn who wrote songs published under his name. We were aware that in Buckingham Palace Queen Victoria sang Fanny's sensuous Grillparzer setting, *Italien*, under the impression that her brother had composed it, that Fanny produced well-crafted songs and short piano pieces (though few were in print), and that she was a more than estimable pianist (some accounts claimed she was her brother's peer). Occasionally, her piano trio surfaced as a chamber work by a nineteenth-century woman composer. But hardly anyone had an inkling of the full scope and depth of her music. Most of it was sequestered in inaccessible archives, and the narrative of her life was inevitably linked to the international celebrity in her family.

The conventional wisdom began to change with the accelerating revelations of the 1980s and 1990s, continuing to this day—the sudden release of unknown compositions such as her String Quartet, Overture, cantatas, concert arias, partsongs, and the piano cycle *Das Jahr*, along with the publication of her letters, diaries, and other documents. As of this writing, we are in the midst of a full-scale Fanny Hensel discovery and revival, on both sides of the Atlantic, so that it is now timely to offer a fresh account of her life and music. Today, she is widely regarded as the most significant female composer of the nineteenth century, even though for most of her forty-one years she practiced her art privately among a circle of family and friends, and semiprivately in the brilliant Sunday concerts she supervised at her Berlin family residence, accessible to the artistic and social elite of the day but closed to the general public. Her only three documented public performances, at Berlin charity concerts, featured none of her own music, but a concerto and piano trio by her brother, whose meteoric career dominated Anglo-German musical life of the 1830s and 1840s.

Though largely removed from public view for most of her life, Fanny was driven to compose and remained fully dedicated to her art, which she practiced faithfully for nearly thirty years. Composition was her constant companion, evidenced by her prolific output, which we now know exceeded 450 works, principally songs and piano pieces, and also extending to chamber, choral, and orchestral works. Fanny composed neither for the glare of public concerts nor for the scrutiny of the press, but to answer her own inner drive, and to offer new compositions for the musicians who performed on her concert series. Though she received little official recognition during her lifetime, her brother ranked her songs among the very best German examples of the time,[1] and one critic who compared the siblings' music found that Hensel allowed fantasy "a freer reign" and applied form "with broader brush strokes."[2] Because she usually composed with no foresight of publication, only rarely did she refine and polish her compositions with the firm intention of seeing them through the press. Many of her manuscripts impress as first drafts; indeed, several were left unfinished. Fanny's music is largely diary-like, and we are now like so many eavesdroppers, entering into the private creative space of a musical genius all too long ignored, and all too long hidden from fame.

Why did history forget the music of Fanny Hensel? She is a cogent example, as Virginia Woolf suggested on the eve of the Second World War in *Three Guineas* (1938), of how women were denied their own creative space—of how, in effect, history erased their voices, their identities. In Fanny's case, the rigidly stratified society in which she lived effectively restricted her authorial voice. Fanny's earliest surviving composition, a congratulatory birthday greeting for her father, Abraham Mendelssohn Bartholdy, dates from 1819, four years after the Congress of Vienna and the year of the Carlsbad Decrees, the beginnings of the post-Napoleonic conservative reaction in Germany. Her final composition (*Bergeslust*), an Eichendorff setting, was written the day before her death on May 14, 1847, less than a year before barricades went up in Berlin, signaling the Revolution of 1848. Her creative career of not quite three decades thus spanned the political reaction and restoration known in German realms as the *Vormärz* (the period before March 1848), a time of Biedermeier sensibility and political stability, but also of occasional tremors that presaged the impending social cataclysms of midcentury. As a member of a prominent well-to-do family that mingled with the highest echelons of Berlin society, Fanny was expected to observe the circumscribed, domestic role of genteel women.

Thus, as early as 1820, when Fanny was fifteen, Abraham began limiting the scope of music in his daughter's life: though Felix, aged eleven, might someday build a public career upon a musical foundation, Abraham instructed Fanny to hang "musical ornaments," that is, to produce modest piano pieces and songs, genres associated with domestic music making. Since she was a lady of leisure, there was no consideration that she would ever work as a professional composer or musician. (Indeed, even Felix, as a young gentleman of leisure, initially deferred to the social code of his class. When at age twenty he made his London debut at the Philharmonic, he was announced as a musical amateur, not a professor, since he could not accept remuneration.)

History forgot the exceptional case of Fanny Hensel, too, because of the paradoxical position of the Mendelssohn family in Berlin society. Though among the heirs to the great fortune of Fanny's great-grandfather, Daniel Itzig, court banker of Frederick the Great, her family figured among nineteenth-century Jewish Prussians who sought full assimilation into the dominant culture by embracing the Protestant creed. It was an uncertain process. On the one hand, by virtue of their wealth, the Mendelssohn Bartholdys had easy access to the highest layers of Prussian society. The music concerts over which Fanny presided were a meeting place where nobility and commoners, Jews and Christians, could comfortably mingle, and where musicians, poets, and artists could exchange ideas. But beyond this venue, the Jewish ancestry of the family—Fanny's grandfather, Moses Mendelssohn, had arrived in Berlin in 1743 from the ghetto in Dessau and then risen from poverty to become an eminent philosopher and man of letters—marked them in some circles as outsiders.

Thus, in 1850, three years after her death, Richard Wagner published his scurrilous article "Das Judenthum in der Musik" ("On Judaism in Music"), which began by denigrating the Jews as a foreign race that could only imitate the masterpieces of German music. Writing under cover of anonymity, Wagner observed that Fanny's brother "has shown us that a Jew can possess the richest measure of specific talents, the most refined and varied culture, the loftiest, most tender sense of honor, without even once through all these advantages being able to bring forth in us that profound, heart-and-soul searching effect we expect from music."[3] Fanny herself was spared this insult in print, though had she, like Felix, enjoyed a successful public career, her reception in mid-nineteenth-century Germany might well have been equally problematic.

History forgot Fanny Hensel because of straitened nineteenth-century views of women's artistic creativity, attitudes, ironically, sometimes reaffirmed by talented, creative women themselves. Through much of her adult life, Fanny remained deeply conflicted about publishing her music, and when, late in life, she began to proceed, she felt obliged to assure her brother that she was no *femme libre* and that she would not disgrace her family.[4] Such self-effacement also visited women considerably more established in the public view. Thus Clara Schumann, who did enjoy international fame as a pianist and composer, confided to a diary these sobering reservations about her Piano Trio in D Minor, op. 17 (1846), which she planned to dedicate to Fanny: "There are some nice passages in the Trio, and I believe it is also fairly successful as far as form is concerned, but naturally it is still woman's work, which always lacks force and occasionally invention."[5] And in 1859 George Eliot, whose identity as Mary Ann Evans was just being discovered with the release of her first novel, *Adam Bede*, offered the pessimistic assessment that "with a few remarkable exceptions, our own feminine literature is made up of books which could have been better written by men."[6]

Finally, history forgot Fanny Hensel because her musical identity was overshadowed by the very public fame of her brother, whom Goethe and Heine had likened to a second Mozart. To the extent Fanny Hensel's compositions were known, they were deemed dependent on the Mendelssohnian style, a style imitated by any number of admirers of Felix, from Robert and Clara Schumann to Charles Gounod, William Sterndale Bennett, Niels Gade, and Arthur Sullivan. Her few published compositions were thought to be derivative; her piano pieces were heard as imitations of her brother's *Lieder ohne Worte* (*Songs without Words*); and her struggle to approach the larger musical forms (and thereby escape the stereotype of the songsmith) contrasted with his easy mastery of chamber music genres, the symphony and concerto, and oratorio.

Hensel's life story might be regarded as an example of the tribulations of an artistically gifted, nineteenth-century woman to fulfill herself as a composer; but what lends her life even greater poignancy is that, like her brother, she was an extraordinary musical prodigy and genius. Reports of her pianism compare favorably with those of Mendelssohn, one of the fabled virtuosi of the nineteenth century, and her musical memory matched her brother's acute powers of recall (at age thirteen, she was performing for her father from memory large portions of J. S. Bach's *Well-Tempered Clavier*). Her composition teacher, Carl Friedrich Zelter, who promoted the career of his prize pupil Felix, informed Goethe in 1824 that Fanny had completed her thirty-second fugue and judged some of her Goethe settings worthy enough to be shared with the poet, who the following year sent greetings to Felix and to "your equally gifted sister."[7] Not without reason did Felix liken her to his Minerva, with whom he habitually shared his compositions before releasing his music to the world. Indeed, one of Fanny's letters to Felix from 1834 reveals just how close their relationship was. Reminiscing about their former lives together in Berlin, she recalled how she would offer suggestions to bolster Felix's inspiration while he composed, so that when he finally overcame his habitual self-doubt and finished the work, she felt that she had collaborated in its creation.

What has dramatically changed Fanny Hensel's historical estimation in recent decades, what has allowed her finally to emerge in full view, is that now, for the first time, we can examine the large bulk of her music, begin to assess critically the complete range of her art—one of the primary goals of this book—and admire its manifold beauties. If she was in her element as a miniaturist, a composer of epigrammatic songs and lyrical character pieces for piano, she also ventured into a variety of other genres. The formal freedoms of her String Quartet offer a refreshing perspective on the quartets of Beethoven and his late style, a repertory that preoccupied Mendelssohn, Robert Schumann, and their generation of German composers. The large-scale

Cholera Cantata, her most substantial choral work, reveals her to have been just as zealous a disciple of J. S. Bach as her brother, and demonstrates that she was capable of grappling successfully with issues of large-scale form and tonal organization. Hensel was among the first composers to set portions of the second part of Goethe's *Faust*. Her part-songs, largely clustered in the last year of her life, are choral gems that readily bear comparison to the finest examples of the genre, including those of her brother, Robert Schumann, and others. And her piano cycle *Das Jahr*, an autobiographical musical calendar of the months of the year, is a substantial work that dwarfs anything her brother wrote for the instrument and should now take its place beside the great large-scale piano cycles of Robert Schumann.

This biography seeks to plumb the rich depths of all this music, much of it still relatively unfamiliar, and to present a full narrative of Hensel's life drawn from the evidence of her letters, diaries, and manuscripts. The primary sources are vexingly incomplete, at times rendering the biographer's task especially difficult. While Felix's letters number in the many thousands—we have some 5,000, balanced by a comparable number of *Gegenbriefe* addressed to him—Fanny's survive in the hundreds, written to a small, intimate circle of family and acquaintances. Because she lived at the Berlin family residence with her parents and husband, the court painter Wilhelm Hensel, and because she traveled but rarely, relatively few family letters have come down to us. Of these, by far the most significant portion was addressed to her brother, who left Berlin in 1829, traveled widely, and was undoubtedly the most important correspondent in her life.

These two sibling prodigies were like musical twins who had uncanny abilities to intuit each other's musical thoughts, inspirations, and frustrations. Mirrorlike, Hensel's music often seems to reflect significant stages in her brother's development. Thus, her early Piano Quartet of 1822 can be seen to respond to his piano quartets, her String Quartet of 1834 to his String Quartet op. 12, her cantatas of 1831 to his chorale cantatas, and so on. After he left Berlin, she became, in effect, his foremost representative in the Prussian capital. Nevertheless, to perpetuate the idea that Hensel was simply an epigone of her brother would be a gross distortion. Granted, Hensel's music is fraught with allusions to Mendelssohn's music. But an equally valid view suggests that Hensel herself contributed to the formation of the Mendelssohnian style. Thus, there is evidence that Mendelssohn's *Lieder ohne Worte* originated in a musical game the siblings played together during the 1820s; it is not farfetched to imagine Hensel actively involved in the preparations for Mendelssohn's landmark revival in 1829 of J. S. Bach's St. Matthew Passion; and it is clear that Mendelssohn, who composed several significant works for her birthday (among them the *Fair Melusine* Overture and Piano Trio in C Minor, op. 66), valued her critiques of his music throughout his career.

What emerges from Hensel's diaries and letters is a woman of strong character and sharp intellect more than able to hold her own in conversations about politics, poetry, painting, and, of course, music. She read Greek up to Xenophon, was fluent in French, and was well enough versed in English to advise her brother about German translations of Byron. Her knowledge of Italian was sufficient to allow her to set Ariosto and Metastasio. She eagerly attended the public lectures of the scientist Alexander von Humboldt and mingled with other brilliant, in her words, "clever men," though women were not allowed to matriculate at the University of Berlin. She read with great interest reports of the July 1830 Revolution in Paris, and held liberal political views that could clash with those of her husband, a monarchist. One of her last diary entries concerned the famine in Prussia in the early months of 1847 that accelerated the outbreak of revolution there a year later.

Hensel's passion about the music of J. S. Bach, a trait shared with brother, was reinforced by three other remarkable women in her family—her maternal grandmother, Bella Salomon, who provided Felix with his copy of Bach's St. Matthew Passion, the work with which he effectively launched the modern Bach revival; her maternal great-aunt, Sarah Levy, an active, skilled musician who had direct ties to two of Bach's children, Wilhelm Friedemann and Carl Philip Emanuel; and her mother, Lea, who made a practice of playing through the *Well-Tempered Clavier* at a time when Bach's encyclopedic masterpiece was still relatively little known. With Felix, Fanny also shared a zeal for improving musical standards. Her private letters are filled with criticisms of vapid performances, whether of sensational virtuosi, of her teacher Carl Friedrich Zelter's maladroit attempt to direct the St. Matthew Passion, or of his assistant's decision to add to her brother's oratorio *St. Paul* a tuba, an effect Fanny likened to the antics of inebriated brewers. Fanny reserved in her musical pantheon places of honor first of all for J. S. Bach and Beethoven, followed by her brother, and it is no coincidence that she named her son Sebastian Ludwig Felix Hensel.

If Fanny was devoted to her art, she was equally devoted to her family and friends. She was a significant influence on the young Charles Gounod, who owed his first impressions of Bach and Beethoven's keyboard works to Fanny's performances at the French Academy in Rome; Gounod, it seems, was smitten by her. Fanny's diary reveals her heartfelt grief after the deaths of her parents in 1835 and 1843, and early in 1845, in the depth of winter, she hastily departed with her husband and son for Florence, in order to nurse back to health her sister, Rebecka, pregnant and suffering from jaundice, and brother-in-law, the mathematician Gustav Dirichlet, ill with typhoid fever. Fanny was the mainstay in the rearing of her son and an irreplaceable support for her husband, a painter and portraitist who lacked business acumen and periodically succumbed to self-doubt. Not endowed with physical beauty, she suffered from astigmatism and a slight orthopedic deformity inherited from her paternal grandfather, Moses Mendelssohn. But all who met her were impressed by her cultured taste and sheer musicality—the force and depth of her playing as a soloist and chamber musician, and her skill as a conductor of a choral repertoire that included major works by Bach, Handel, Gluck, Mozart, her brother, and, of course, herself.

Fanny's stage and principal creative outlet was the music room of her residence, the spacious *Gartensaal* that accommodated an audience of some 200, who during the warm weather could spill out onto the lush lawns and gardens of the family estate. From the piano, she directed her fortnightly series of Sunday concerts, which offered a blend of solo, chamber, and choral works, with a strong preference for German music. Because these concerts took place in a private, exclusive setting, and because they were not open to the public, they have been compared to the salons, literary and musical, that flourished in Berlin, Paris, and other cities in the early decades of the nineteenth century.

One is indeed tempted to regard Fanny as a salon musician and to compare her to Chopin, who made most of his appearances not on the public stage but in the fashionable residences of the Parisian aristocracy. But important qualifications remain. As Petra Wilhelmy-Dollinger has observed, in European salon culture music was never an aesthetic end in itself but rather, with conversation and poetry readings, often improvised on the spot, an integrated part of the social intercourse of the upper class.[8] In the case of Fanny's concerts, one has the impression instead that they were just that—dedicated concerts with announced programs in a private setting for the edification of the invited guests.[9] Fanny was the organizing force of this institution, and her piano, the instrument at which she composed her music, its central symbol. Be that as it may, the concerts were undeniably brilliant social affairs that gradually attracted, in the words of W. A. Lampadius, an early biographer of Mendelssohn, "all the culture of Berlin": "men of eminence in all departments, musicians, painters, sculptors, poets, actors, scholars."[10] During Fanny's tenure the guests included countless nobility, Liszt, Robert and Clara Schumann, the violinists Ernst, Vieuxtemps, and Joachim, the sopranos Clara Novello and Wilhelma Schroeder-Devrient, the painters Cornelius, Ingres, and Vernet, and the Danish sculptor Thorwaldsen, among many others. Invitations to these concerts were highly coveted, and Fanny's accomplishments, despite efforts to safeguard the family's privacy, were widely known, so that after her death in May 1847 Ludwig Rellstab eulogized her as having "attained in music a level of refinement that not many artists professionally devoted to their art could claim."[11]

In considering the extraordinary case of Fanny Hensel, we need to resist the too-long-engrained view of her as a composer overly dependent on her brother, an issue that ultimately bears on the question of her own style. As a Mendelssohn biographer, I must confess that my initial impressions of her music formed during the 1980s and 1990s were conditioned by its undeniable similarities to her brother's music. Quotations and allusions to Mendelssohn seemed to leap off the pages of her scores, like so many thinly disguised debts, and the reader will indeed find several detailed in this volume.

Nevertheless, initial appearances proved deceptive, and further examination revealed the complexity and nuances of the sibling relationship. Thus, for each borrowing, one could also cite distinctive passages in Hensel's compositions that asserted stylistic distance from her brother. Hensel's larger compositions—for example, the piano sonatas, String Quartet, Piano Trio, and *Das Jahr*—exude a formal freedom and spontaneity not characteristic of her brother, who tends to adhere to classical forms. Fanny's lieder, finely crafted, jewel-like miniatures, reveal an intensity of expression conspicuously at odds with the surface equipoise of Mendelssohn's songs, such as the quintessentially Mendelssohnian *Auf Flügeln des Gesanges* (*On Wings of Song*). And in comparison to her brother, Hensel betrays a more adventuresome approach to key relationships and harmonic progressions, and in particular explores a broader harmonic palette, further traits that separate her style from her brother's. To hear Hensel's own voice, one need only compare Mendelssohn's *Venetian Gondellied* in G Minor, op. 19, no. 6 (1830), once a popular mainstay of nineteenth-century parlor-room piano music, with Hensel's exquisite *Notturno* in the same key (1838). While Mendelssohn establishes a modest accompaniment of gently lapping rhythms to support a doleful, duetlike barcarole, Hensel paints with a considerably broader brush and produces a harmonically more colorful composition, twice the length of her brother's, that uses the full range of the instrument, with softly dappled, blurring harmonies and widely spaced arpeggiations reminiscent of Chopin.

Hensel's musical life was a journey toward artistic self-actualization and independence, marked by several important way stations. For example, her periodic turn from small-scale songs and piano pieces to larger genres in the early 1830s, her culling of ten piano pieces to form a coherent, substantial collection in 1837, and her painstaking preservation of *Das Jahr* in a fair copy illustrated by her husband and prefaced with an "official" title page were all signs of her steady approach toward official authorship. She finally attained this goal in the last year of her life, when she began publishing her music under her own name and then tragically died before she could emerge fully in public view as a composer. Her story is one of metamorphosis from "amateur" to a professional composer with a distinct authorial profile and individual voice. Her life celebrates the power of an artistic genius that did transform the "other Mendelssohn" into Fanny Hensel, a composer we should now recognize and celebrate.

Acknowledgments

This book would not have been possible without the pioneering efforts of scholars who have preceded me in raising our awareness of Fanny Hensel. Now widely regarded as the most important European woman composer of the nineteenth century, she is emerging fully from the recesses of history that shrouded most of her music for well over a century after her death in 1847. Serious research into her life and work actually extends back just a few decades, so that we are only some twenty-five years or so into the modern rediscovery of Fanny Hensel, a phenomenon that continues to surprise many who rather prematurely viewed the nineteenth century as an all too well tilled field. In the United States, signal contributions were made to Hensel research during the 1980s and 1990s by Victoria Sirota, Marcia Citron, Camilla Cai, and, in recent years, by Marian Wilson Kimber. In France, Françoise Tillard was the first to write a substantial Hensel biography, which appeared first in French in 1992, at a time when much of the composer's music was still unavailable. In Germany, the center of Hensel research has been and remains the Mendelssohn Archiv in Berlin, where the vast majority of her manuscripts are housed. I have drawn liberally on this material, and on the work of several German scholars who have mined its treasures—Renate Hellwig-Unruh, who released the first systematic catalogue of Hensel's music in 2000; Rudolf Elvers and Hans-Günter Klein, who published her diaries in 2003; Cecile Lowenthal-Hensel and Jutta Arnold, who produced the first biography of the composer's husband, the court painter Wilhelm Hensel, in 2004; and Hans-Günter Klein, who completed several critical studies of Hensel and editions of her letters in the years surrounding the 2005 bicentenary. In addition, other scholars have edited important collections of essays devoted to Hensel, including Martina Helmig, Beatrix Borchard and Monika Schwarz-Danuser, and, most recently, Susan Wollenberg in *Nineteenth-Century Music Review*, all of which have advanced the field considerably.

This critical mass of Hensel scholarship informs the pages that follow, but I would also like to acknowledge several colleagues and friends who over the years have kindly shared with me their insights into Hensel. They include Anna Harwell Celenza, J. Michael Cooper, Ann Leo Ellis, Therese Ellsworth, Claire Fontijn, Giuseppe Gerbino, Roger S. Gilbert, Ken Hamilton, Sheila Hayman, Monika Hennemann, Paula Higgins, Dorothy Indenbaum, Hans-Günter Klein, Harold and Sharon Krebs, Joan Kretschmer, Thomas Leo, Wm. A. Little, Angela Mace, Kerry McCarthy, Roberto Prosseda, Nancy Reich, Sarah Rothenberg, Douglass Seaton, Jeffrey Sposato, Suzanne Summerville, Christian Thorau, Jacqueline Waeber, Peter Ward Jones, Janet Wasserman, Ralf Wehner, Susan Wollenberg, and Susan Youens.

I am indebted to the staffs of the Mendelssohn Archiv, Staatsbibliothek zu Berlin–Preussischer Kulturbesitz; Duke Music Library, Durham, N.C.; Bodleian Library, Oxford; Pierpont Morgan Library, New York; Bibliothèque Nationale, Paris; and Library of Congress, Washington, D.C., for facilitating my research, and remain especially grateful to Roland Schmidt-Hensel of the Mendelssohn Archiv for permission to publish illustrations. To Sheila Hayman a hearty thank you for providing a reproduction of the Julius Helfft painting that graces the dust jacket.

For smoothing the production process I am obliged to my editor at Oxford University Press, Suzanne Ryan, and to her able staff, including Madelyn Sutton and Norman Hirschy, and to the production and copy editors at the press, Liz Smith and Karen Fisher. For help with the index and proofreading my best thanks to Angela Mace, and to Karen Carroll of the National Humanities Center, who expeditiously read an early version of the manuscript and disentangled many of its more intractable aspects. Interminable thanks to Dan Ruccia for ably dispatching the task of setting the musical examples. Completion of the volume was considerably accelerated by release time provided by fellowships from the Guggenheim Foundation and National Humanities Center (William J. Bouwsma Fellowship), where I enjoyed stimulating conversations with fellows from across the humanities in 2007–2008. This book is much the better for their advice and illuminations.

Once again my family has endured with good humor the unpredictable trials of a biographer—to Karin and Anna, my heartfelt thanks for their patience whenever the author succumbed to a very Mendelssohnian "revision illness." And to Karin, for any number of suggestions and improvements to the manuscript, my eternal gratitude. Finally, to my sister- and brother-in-law, Nancy and James J. Yoch, Jr., of Norman, Oklahoma, to whom this volume is affectionately dedicated, I am indebted for their unflagging encouragement.

Contents

The Itzig Family

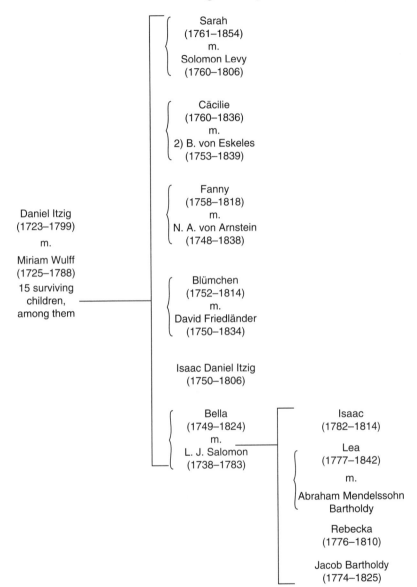

Daniel Itzig
(1723–1799)
m.
Miriam Wulff
(1725–1788)
15 surviving
children,
among them

Sarah
(1761–1854)
m.
Solomon Levy
(1760–1806)

Cäcilie
(1760–1836)
m.
2) B. von Eskeles
(1753–1839)

Fanny
(1758–1818)
m.
N. A. von Arnstein
(1748–1838)

Blümchen
(1752–1814)
m.
David Friedländer
(1750–1834)

Isaac Daniel Itzig
(1750–1806)

Bella
(1749–1824)
m.
L. J. Salomon
(1738–1783)

Isaac
(1782–1814)

Lea
(1777–1842)
m.
Abraham Mendelssohn
Bartholdy

Rebecka
(1776–1810)

Jacob Bartholdy
(1774–1825)

The Mendelssohn Family

Nathan
(1782–1852)

m. _____

Henriette Itzig
(1781–1845)

Abraham
Mendelssohn
Bartholdy
(1776–1835) _____

m.

Lea Salomon

Henriette (Jette)
(1775–1831)

Moses
Mendelssohn
(1729–1786)

m. _____

Fromet
Gugenheim
(1737–1812)

10 children,
of whom 6 survived
to adulthood

Joseph
(1770–1848)

m. _____

Henriette (Hinni) Meyer
(1776–1862)

Recha
(1767–1831)

_____

m.

Mendel Meyer
(d. 1841)

Brendel (Dorothea)
(1764–1839)

m. _____

1) Simon Veit
(1754–1819)

2) Friedrich Schlegel
(1772–1829)

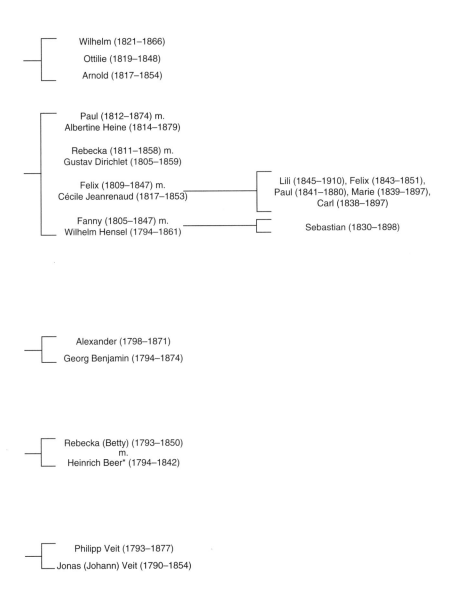

Wilhelm (1821–1866)

Ottilie (1819–1848)

Arnold (1817–1854)

Paul (1812–1874) m.
Albertine Heine (1814–1879)

Rebecka (1811–1858) m.
Gustav Dirichlet (1805–1859)

Felix (1809–1847) m.
Cécile Jeanrenaud (1817–1853)

Lili (1845–1910), Felix (1843–1851),
Paul (1841–1880), Marie (1839–1897),
Carl (1838–1897)

Fanny (1805–1847) m.
Wilhelm Hensel (1794–1861)

Sebastian (1830–1898)

Alexander (1798–1871)

Georg Benjamin (1794–1874)

Rebecka (Betty) (1793–1850)
m.
Heinrich Beer* (1794–1842)

Philipp Veit (1793–1877)

Jonas (Johann) Veit (1790–1854)

* Brother of Giacomo Meyerbeer

About the Companion Web Site

www.oup.com/us/fannyhensel

Oxford University Press has created a Web site to accompany *Fanny Hensel: The Other Mendelssohn*. Here readers will find forty-four musical examples to supplement those that already appear in the book and to illustrate further the discussions of Hensel's music. Examples occur throughout the text and are signaled with OUP's own symbol, ☻, for easy access. In addition, it is the author's intention to add to the Web site from time to time recordings of selected works by Fanny Hensel, in an effort to make her music more readily available.

List of Illustrations

Fanny Hensel

CHAPTER I

Fugal Fingers

(1805–1818)

There are in all religions only one God, one virtue, one truth, one happiness. You will find all this, if you follow the voice of your heart; live so that it be ever in harmony with the voice of your reason.

—Abraham to Fanny Mendelssohn Bartholdy, April 5, 1819

September 1805—Europe was again at war. Less than a year before, at a coronation validating an imperial reign through contrived analogies to Charlemagne, founder of the Holy Roman Empire, Napoleon had stirred crepuscular memories of the old Frankish dynasty. Now England joined Austria, Russia, and Sweden in a third coalition to oppose French expansionism. To answer, the self-proclaimed emperor dispersed the army massed at Boulogne in preparation—whether feigned or not, historians would debate—for invading England. After forced marches, some 200,000 troops, divided into seven corps to facilitate lightning-like advances, crossed the Rhine near Strasbourg and reconstituted, an imposing spectacle of uniforms and accoutrements—blue-coated chasseurs in kolbachs; carabineers with red-plumed headgear; grenadiers with tall bearskins; lancers and hussars in plumed shakos; green-coated dragoons with tiger-skin turbans; cuirassiers with gleaming metal breastplates and helmets; and horse artillerists in dark-blue uniforms trimmed in red. Allied with the French were Italian conscripts, Germans from Bavaria and Württemberg, Dutch from the Batavian Republic, and a company of exotically clad Egyptian Mamelukes astride Arabian horses. Seerlike, Napoleon predicted his forces had already won the campaign with their legs.

Hastening to engage General Mack's Austrian army before Russian reinforcements could arrive, the French wheeled south and, maneuvering deftly, enveloped the enemy, forcing them to surrender without resistance at Ulm on October 20. Though war's fortunes shifted momentarily as word came of the crippling defeat of the French fleet at Gibraltar, the *grande armée* now yearned for future glory. Vienna was defenseless, and on November 14, 1805, Napoleon established his headquarters at Schönbrunn, one day after the French vanguard marched into the Imperial City, with battle flags unfurled and ceremonial music sounding. Within a week, French officers were attending at an eerily half-empty Theater an der Wien the premiere of Beethoven's rescue opera *Fidelio*, based upon a French libretto and resonating, ironically enough, with the republican theme of freedom from tyranny. Only days before, the straggling remnants of the Austrian nobility, including the empress and several of Beethoven's patrons, had fled—no more, according to Napoleon's estimate, than 10,000 aristocrats among the general population of 250,000.[1]

As these dramatic world events were playing out, in the "free" city of Hamburg Fanny Mendelssohn was born at 6:30 A.M. on November 14, the very day of Napoleon's triumphant entry into Vienna. She was the first of four children of Abraham (1776–1835) and Lea (1777–1842) Mendelssohn. In December 1804 they had married in Berlin, where Abraham founded with his elder brother, Joseph, a banking firm destined to become a thriving nineteenth-century German financial house. Renamed in 1805 Gebrüder Mendelssohn & Co., the firm expanded to accommodate a second branch in Hamburg, where the brothers resettled with their families. Their primary residence was a three-story edifice, no longer extant, on Grosse Michaelisstrasse (no. 14), not far from the Mendelssohn business (no. 71a) and just behind the Michaeliskirche (St. Michael's Church), in the vault of which Carl Philipp Emanuel Bach had been laid to rest in 1788. Consecrated in 1661 and rebuilt in the eighteenth century, this landmark afforded commanding views of the city from its tower; still, in 1820 St. Michael's impressed one English traveler as a "second rate building, in which all the faults of Italian architecture" were "carried to a ridiculous excess."[2]

Grosse Michaelisstrasse no. 14, which Abraham and Lea shared with Joseph, his wife Henriette, and their two sons, offered somewhat cramped surroundings for Lea, who was accustomed to considerably more commodious quarters in Berlin. The residence would be the birthplace of two of Fanny's siblings, Felix (1809–1847) and Rebecka (1811–1858), and of the violinist-composer Ferdinand David, who later became the concertmaster of the Leipzig Gewandhaus Orchestra under Felix's baton. In 1869 the Swedish soprano Jenny Lind installed a marble tablet above the doorway to commemorate the celebrity among the Mendelssohn siblings—Felix—though at the time, no recognition of Fanny was made.[3] There the marker remained until its removal in 1936 by the Nazis, who were intent upon blotting out traces of the Mendelssohns in German culture and finance.

i

Joseph and Abraham Mendelssohn were two of six surviving children of Moses Mendelssohn (1729–1786), the eminent Jewish philosopher-belletrist who in 1743 had followed his rabbi to Berlin from the ghetto of Dessau, capital of the small duchy of Anhalt-Dessau some eighty miles to the southwest. At that time, the Prussian state rigorously controlled the Jewish population, denied it citizenship, and compelled it to pay onerous concessions in exchange for the right to coexist in the capital. A few years before, in 1737, the elector Frederick William I had expelled more than half of the Jewish families. Those who remained, tolerated because of their wealth, soon experienced the discriminatory preferences of a new monarch, Frederick the Great, who acceded to the throne in 1740 and regimented his Jewish subjects into six categories. At the apex of this social pyramid were a few unusually prosperous families, dominated by a handful of bankers and minters who financed Frederick's military campaigns and received special dispensations as "protected Jews" (*Schutzjuden*). At the base were common laborers, permitted to remain so long as they were employed or sponsored. Moses fell into this latter category, as he paid a toll to enter Berlin through the Rosenthaler Thor, the only gate through which he could legally pass.

Short in stature, disfigured by a hunchback, and prone to stuttering, Moses worked as a tutor and bookkeeper before he became a partner of a prosperous silk manufacturer. His impressive intellectual gifts—Moses was a Talmudic scholar and polyglot who valued mathematics as "the best exercise in rigorous thinking"[4]—facilitated an intimate friendship with the playwright-critic Gotthold Ephraim Lessing and the colleagueship of the philosopher Immanuel Kant. A disciplined autodidact, Moses rose from obscurity to become an eloquent spokesman for the German Enlightenment. His writings, including *Phaedon* (1767), a modern gloss on Plato's dialogue about the immortality of the soul, and *Jerusalem* (1783), a spirited defense of religious tolerance, reached broad audiences, and turned *le juif Moses* into an improbable international celebrity, a distinction attained by few earlier Jewish scholars, such as Maimonides in the twelfth century and Spinoza in the seventeenth. Moses Mendelssohn's son Joseph later contextualized his father's achievement thus: "That a living Jew could write German philosophical tracts, in a classical style surpassing in clarity and elegance everything previously published in Germany—this phenomenon was completely new."[5]

Resting his faith squarely on reason, Moses became a beacon of enlightened thought. Optimistically promoting the assimilation of German Jewry into the Prussian state, he believed that without forsaking Judaism his coreligionists might yet grasp the elusive goal of emancipation by adopting modern German language, dress, and manners. To that end, he translated the Psalms and Pentateuch into German, and thereby sought to strengthen the dual identities of German Jews, who for centuries had preserved their minority culture as a separate "nation" within a nation. If Orthodox Jews viewed Moses's work as sacrilegious—some rabbis banned the translations as heresy (*Ketzerei*) and inveighed against "newcomers" who learned German[6]—influential Christian writers probed a different extreme.

The Swiss mystic chiliast Johann Caspar Lavater, for instance, compared Moses to Nathaniel, recognized by Jesus as "an Israelite in whom there is no deceit" (John 1:47). Imagining that the mass apostasy of Jews would presage the Second Coming of Christ, Lavater called upon Moses to convert and resorted to the pseudoscience of physiognomy to fuel his proselytizing zeal. For Lavater, Moses possessed a radiant soul within an Aesopian casing; his silhouette projected a noble forehead, his eyes a Socratic depth—traits desirable enough for a convert. But Lavater's enthusiasm prompted Moses to reaffirm his Jewish faith. Still, after the philosopher's death in 1786, Lavater persisted in pondering the silhouette: "Yes, I see him, Abraham's son, who—together with Plato and Moses—will surely recognize and worship the crucified Lord of Splendor!"[7] Lavater was not the last to seek to integrate members of the Mendelssohn family into mainstream German culture, a process that would affect directly the lives of Moses's children and grandchildren, including Fanny Hensel.

If Fanny's paternal grandfather overcame considerable barriers to achieve international renown as the German Socrates, her maternal relatives enjoyed lifestyles of ease and luxury. In 1755 her great-grandfather, Daniel Itzig (1723–1799), won the lease of the Prussian state mints and began profiting handsomely from coining currency, much of it evidently adulterated with impure alloys. By 1761, he was one of few Berlin Jews granted the "general privilege"; eventually, the monarch Frederick William II conferred on Itzig's family the rights of Christian citizenship. This extraordinary status further consolidated Itzig's fortune, recently estimated as equivalent to some ten million euros.[8] He purchased several exclusive Berlin properties—a mansion overlooking the Spree River, a house near the Royal Palace, and the Bartholdy *Meierei*, a summer country estate near the Schlesisches Thor (Fanny's family would later add Bartholdy as a second surname). Itzig also acquired the Luisenhof, also near the Schlesisches Thor but within the city walls.[9] Its celebrated garden in Dutch style was landscaped by the royal gardener and contained an open-air theater adorned with sculptures of subjects drawn from Greek mythology. The garden was a favorite haunt of Fanny's mother, Lea Salomon, who later recalled her childhood, passed in its "comfortable little country house, buried in vines, mulberry and peach trees," in which she occupied a "neat but very simple little room with my piano, bookcase, and desk as furniture.... Here my feelings developed, here my youthful mind ripened,...here I read my favorite poets with a higher enjoyment,...and I even fancy that the weak notes my unskilled fingers produced [were] here more melodious and pure."[10]

The sparse accounts we have of Lea's youth testify to her cultured mind and intellectual acumen. Fanny's son, Sebastian Hensel, preserved some reminiscences by a family friend, among which we read: "Lea was not handsome, but her eloquent black eyes, her sylph-like figure, her gentle, modest behavior, and the power of her lively conversation, full of accurate judgment and striking but never malicious wit, made her most attractive. She was acquainted with every branch of fashionable information; she played and sang with expression and grace, but seldom, and only for her friends; she drew exquisitely; she spoke and read French, English, Italian, and—secretly—Homer, in the original language....Her taste, formed by the classic authors of so many languages, was exact and refined, but she seldom ventured to pass a judgment."[11] Nevertheless, later in life her intellect and bearing made quite an impression; in 1875, the physician G. F. L. Stromeyer recalled that she had such "sharp features" (scharfe Züge) that "initially one stood in fear of her" (figure 1.1).[12]

According to the music theorist A. B. Marx, Lea "had made the acquaintance of Sebastian Bach's music, and in her home she perpetuated his tradition by continually playing the Well-Tempered Clavier."[13] Musically Lea was quite sophisticated. The mother of Giacomo Meyerbeer, Amalie Beer, found that Lea possessed "much musical knowledge,"[14] and Marx detected in her resonances of Johann Philipp Kirnberger, the bookish music theorist employed by the Prussian princess Anna Amalia with whom Moses Mendelssohn had had some lessons. In a formidable treatise, The Art of Pure Composition (Die Kunst des reinen Satzes, 1771–1777), Kirnberger had summarized the didactic method of his own teacher, none other than J. S. Bach. Lea was only six years old when Kirnberger died, so it is unlikely that she studied with him. Still, she must have been familiar with his writings, including some elucidations of Bach's fugues, which were of consequence for Fanny's and Felix's musical studies. And Lea's playing of the Well-Tempered Clavier familiarized her children with the complexities of Bach's music, at a time when the Thomaskantor's historical significance was not at all widely appreciated, even within German realms, where only a handful of connoisseurs perused his ineffable scores.

If Lea was a musician of some accomplishment, Abraham was a dilettantish music lover, albeit a discriminating one (figure 1.2). In a self-effacing witticism, he described himself as formerly the son of his father and then the father of his son, as if to minimize his role to that of a hyphen linking two

FIGURE I.I. Lea Mendelssohn Bartholdy, pencil drawing by Wilhelm Hensel, 1823 (Berlin, Mendelssohn Archiv, BA 2)

greater intellects, and to confirm Samuel Butler's observation that often the grandfather's spirit is "refreshed by repose so as to be ready for fresh exertion in the grandson."[15] Still, Sebastian Hensel maintained that Abraham was a "vigorous character" who "had nothing of the epigone in him";[16] like the madcap Mr. Shandy in Lawrence Sterne's *Tristam Shandy*, partial not to repose but to disputing, Abraham willingly defended weak fortresses.[17]

As a young man, Abraham spent his early career in Paris, where he lived and worked for several years between 1797 and 1804 as a bank clerk at Fould, Oppenheim & Co. En route to France, Abraham had paused in Weimar to meet Goethe, who asked if he were a "son of Mendelssohn," the first time, Abraham later recalled gratefully, that he had heard his father's name mentioned "without an epithet."[18] Much of Abraham's Parisian sojourn coincided

FIGURE 1.2. Abraham Mendelssohn Bartholdy, pencil drawing by Wilhelm Hensel, 1829 (Berlin, Mendelssohn Archiv, 408)

with Napoleon's consulate, a period that reaffirmed the egalitarian principles of the revolution, including religious tolerance, and enacted the Civil Code. In 1791, French Jews had received the right of citizenship, and after observing firsthand this measure of civic freedom—in Prussia, citizenship was not bestowed upon Jews as a class until 1812—Abraham became an ardent Francophile. Thus, he was quite content to eat dry Parisian bread (*manger du pain sec à Paris*),[19] and to develop his refined taste for the neoclassical operas of Gluck and the more contemporary fare of Cherubini, until his sister Henriette introduced him to Lea Salomon, prompting him to return to Berlin. The new Mendelssohn bank found a financial supporter in Lea's mother, Bella Salomon, willing to commit her daughter's dowry to the venture, but otherwise hesitant to embrace Lea's marriage to a modest bank clerk, albeit a son of Moses Mendelssohn.

ii

Of Fanny's other relatives, four women in particular merit attention for their musical and literary interests. Three were maternal great-aunts; one, a paternal aunt. The sturdy nonagenarian Sarah Itzig Levy (1761–1854), sister of Lea's mother, married the banker Solomon Levy in 1783 and maintained a vibrant musical salon in Berlin from 1800. Her habitués included Fanny and Felix's future composition teacher, Carl Friedrich Zelter, the poetess Bettina Brentano, philosopher J. G. Fichte, theologian Friedrich Schleiermacher, and writers E. T. A. Hoffmann and Fanny Lewald. The last-named found in Sarah "a rather unbecoming masculine aspect,"[20] a reaction either to her homely appearance—unlike the sylphish Lea, Sarah was physically unattractive and habitually squinted from astigmatism—or her fascination with the cerebral music of the Bachs, a curiosity not associated with ladies of leisure, whom society generally encouraged to pursue relatively undemanding songs or keyboard pieces.

Composers no less than Mozart and Haydn visited Sarah, though her chief musical devotion seems to have been to the instrumental scores of the Bach family. She nourished relationships with two of Bach's sons—W. F. Bach, with whom she studied harpsichord in Berlin, and C. P. E. Bach, of whom she became a significant patroness. When in 1791 the composer C. F. C. Fasch established the Berlin Singakademie to promote sacred German choral music, Sarah was among the first to join. And when in 1800 the directorship passed to Zelter (who seven years later founded an affiliated Ripienschule for performing older instrumental music), Sarah actively participated in that ensemble. She frequently appeared as a soloist in keyboard concerti of the Bachs, including J. S. Bach's Fifth Brandenburg Concerto (ca. 1721), the first concerto to feature a written-out, virtuoso keyboard cadenza. Though by 1807 Bach's high, contrapuntally charged, baroque style had long been obsolescent, the chesslike permutations of its parts still intrigued Sarah. No doubt her diligence in collecting and preserving this music facilitated the later Bachian pursuits of both Fanny and Felix, including, of course, Felix's watershed 1829 performance of the St. Matthew Passion, the event generally recognized as triggering the modern Bach revival.

From all available evidence Sarah was an estimable virtuoso and connoisseur, traits that passed on to her niece, grandniece, and grandnephew. She was also an inveterate bibliophile who amassed a considerable music library, much of it eventually donated to the Singakademie. Though now scattered by the vicissitudes of time, many manuscripts and printed editions bearing her stamp of ownership still survive in European and American libraries.[21] A cursory review reveals her highly specialized, eighteenth-century tastes, centered on J. S. Bach and composers active in Berlin. Among the extant portions of her library are manuscript copies of Bach's *Well-Tempered Clavier* and French Suites; fantasies of W. F. Bach; keyboard works, concerti, and orchestral works of C. P. E. Bach; and—recovered most recently—flute quartets of J. J. Quantz, not in the popular, *galant* style typical of that composer, but in severely contrapuntal idioms approaching the austerities of J. S. Bach.[22]

A few manuscripts from Sarah's library certify her patronage of C. P. E. Bach, for nearly thirty years the accompanist of Frederick the Great, who, when not redrawing the European map through his military campaigns, advanced his skills as a flutist; Emanuel Bach later served for twenty more years as the director of sacred music in Hamburg. Sarah possessed autographs of several experimental works from Bach's very last year, 1788, presumably commissioned for her Berlin salon. The three Quartets (H 537–39) featured solo parts for flute, viola, and keyboard (harpsichord or fortepiano, increasingly popular since the 1770s); a cello doubled the bass line of the keyboard and thickened the trio texture to a quartet. This unusual scoring enabled Bach to test varying combinations of instrumental colors and to enrich the middle register of the ensemble by assigning independent material to the viola. But an even more singular work was the Concerto in E-flat Major for harpsichord, fortepiano, and orchestra (H 479), in which two musical sound worlds collided—the elegant, baroque finery of the harpsichord and the graduated dynamics and undamped sonorities of the new piano. Like the quartets, the concerto illustrated the quirky, mannered style for which Emanuel Bach became celebrated, with its impulsive, angular leaps in melodic lines and unpredictable excursions to distant keys that tested the limits of eighteenth-century functional harmony.

Sarah's sisters Fanny (1758–1818) and Cäcilie (1760–1836), the two great-aunts after whom Fanny Cäcilia Mendelssohn was named, were also highly trained musicians. All three sisters subscribed to Emanuel Bach's series of keyboard works published in six volumes between 1779 and 1786 for "connoisseurs and amateurs" (*Kenner und Liebhaber*). Here, in expressive three-movement sonatas offering sharply delineated and contrasting moods, in fantasies impressing as unpremeditated improvisations, and in lighthearted rondos designed for a more popular audience, the sisters could explore the full range of Emanuel Bach's art.

Relatively little is known about Cäcilie and Fanny's Berlin years, but they numbered among the connoisseurs in Sarah's circle. Cäcilie's library included a copy of J. S. Bach's Concerto for Two Harpsichords in C Minor (BWV 1060), and we might easily imagine her joining Sarah to perform Emanuel Bach's double concerto. In 1776 their sister Fanny wed Nathan von Arnstein and moved to Vienna; after a failed first union, Cäcilie followed suit in 1799 by marrying his brother-in-law Bernhard von Eskeles and thereby strengthened an endogamous financial enterprise. These two court bankers, among the first Viennese Jews to hold patents of nobility (Fanny and Cäcilie would both attain the rank of baroness), founded the house of Arnstein & Eskeles, which rose to prominence during the Congress of Vienna (1814–1815). Advisors to the Austrian emperor, they also counted among their less well-to-do clients Beethoven, who invested in their bank shares[23] and composed for Cäcilie's album a short Goethe setting. Befitting a woman of her status, Cäcilie kept a salon, but considerably more visible among the aristocracy was her older sister Fanny. She attended Mozart's concerts and committed her time and resources to philanthropy; among her benefactions was a charity concert in 1812 that led to the founding of a Viennese concert society, the high-profiled Gesellschaft der Musikfreunde.

During the Congress of Vienna, Fanny's salon counted among the most illustrious, where one might encounter Wellington, Talleyrand, the Prussian minister Hardenberg, and other allied potentates assembled to erase memories of Napoleon's empire, and celebrities in the arts and letters, including the Schlegels, Madame de Staël, and Wilhelm von Humboldt. Decidedly anti-French and pro-Prussian, Fanny celebrated Christmas in 1814 by introducing at her residence a Berlin tradition, a tree adorned with gifts for her guests. Metternich's secret police eavesdropped on her conversations and Cäcilie's, and found the ladies "scandalously Prussian" (*scandaleusement prussiennes*). When Fanny von Arnstein died in 1818, her niece Lea Mendelssohn eulogized her as "the most interesting woman in Europe, a miraculous phenomenon in our stupid, egoistic times."[24]

A considerably less extravagant lifestyle was enjoyed by Dorothea Schlegel, a paternal aunt of Fanny Mendelssohn. Born Brendel Mendelssohn (1764–1839), she was the eldest of Moses Mendelssohn's children to survive to adulthood. Groomed intellectually by her father, she developed her mind, as Sebastian Hensel later observed, "to a higher degree than usually falls to the lot of her sex."[25] But her education proved a "dangerous gift" after her marriage at age eighteen to the banker Simon Veit, a match prearranged by Moses, following Jewish custom. Enduring a loveless relationship, she bore two sons, the painters Jonas and Philipp Veit, who later became members of the brotherhood of German Nazarene artists in Rome, so named because they wore their hair in imitation of Christ.

Talented as a writer but afforded little public recognition of her authorship, Brendel found artistic and intellectual stimulation instead in the Berlin salons of the 1780s and 1790s, which enjoyed a remarkable florescence until the artificial caesura imposed by the French defeat of Prussia in 1806. Their significance requires a brief digression. Based on French models, the salons recalled as well the informal gatherings at the home of Moses Mendelssohn, at which Lessing, the publisher Friedrich Nicolai, and others had discussed philosophy, literature, and the arts. But the new salons differed markedly in their social inclusiveness and areas of interest. First of all, their organizers were Jewish women, notably the first of the Berlin *salonnières*, Henriette Herz (1764–1847), and their most celebrated proponent, Rahel Levin (1771–1833), who held her salon in the garret of her parents' residence, where she served her guests tea.

Henriette, wife of the physician and amateur philosopher Marcus Herz, was an intimate friend of Brendel and of Alexander and Wilhelm von Humboldt, with whom she founded in 1787 a "league of virtue" (*Tugendbund*). While Marcus, a former pupil of Immanuel Kant, discoursed in one room about science and philosophy, Henriette promoted introspective literary conversations in another, where she explored the highly subjective world of the German preromantic *Sturm und Drang*. Rahel's salon drew nobles and commoners alike, and several early romantic writers, including Friedrich Schlegel, Ludwig Tieck, de la Motte Fouqué, and Rahel's sister-in-law Friederike Robert. Unmarried and idolized by the nobility, Rahel took many lovers, and in the opinion of many Berliners qualified as a *femme libre*. Her letters, of which thousands survive in an informal style blending Yiddish and German, suggest a deliberate withdrawal from the sweeping political events of the day into an inwardly romantic realm of feelings. Rahel yearned for full assimilation into mainstream German culture and for separation from her Jewish identity. Changing her surname to Robert, she was baptized as a Protestant, an act that cleared the way for her marriage in 1814 to the diplomat Karl August Varnhagen von Ense. Three years later, at the urging of the theologian Schleiermacher, Henriette Herz accepted baptism into the Lutheran Church, but only after the death of her mother, an Orthodox Jew.

In the rigid, hierarchical society of late eighteenth-century Berlin, the new salons afforded a semipublic/private escape where Prussians of different religious persuasions and social standings—Jews and Christians, nobility and commoners, conservatives and liberals, the wealthy and the middle class— could freely mingle, unencumbered by class, gender, or religious distinctions. Here, in a Prussia that denied Jews citizenship, ideas of interfaith tolerance and assimilation germinated. For Brendel Veit, Henriette Herz's salon offered relief as well from an increasingly untenable marriage. Here, in 1797, Brendel met her soulmate, a brilliant if impecunious literary critic, Friedrich Schlegel (1772–1829), younger than her by some eight years and about to propound a radical theory of modern poetry as a romantic art form that tended toward the "universal." By late 1798, Brendel had left her husband and moved to the outskirts of Berlin, where she enjoyed assignations with Schlegel. A divorce followed early in 1799, and Brendel was finally free from the "long slavery" she likened to a shipwreck.[26] Salvaged from its flotsam were her writing desk, piano, and custody of her younger son, Philipp.

The same year two other events profoundly influenced Brendel's new life. First, Friedrich published his sensational novel *Lucinde*, a thinly veiled, allegorical account of his relationship with Brendel, and of their perfervid spiritual and physical love. *Lucinde* was roundly condemned—by Schiller as unnatural and formless for its experimental mixture of literary genres, by Hegel as an immoral attack on the institution of marriage, and, later, by Kierkegaard as "naked sensuality."[27] Second, Friedrich, Brendel, and Philipp moved to the small university town of Jena, the epicenter of early German romanticism, where they joined Friedrich's brother August Wilhelm Schlegel and other writers, including Tieck and Novalis, and the philosopher Schelling. In this circle Brendel found new freedom for her literary muse. The novel *Florentin*, now understood as her response to or reading of *Lucinde*,[28] appeared anonymously in 1801 under Friedrich's "editorship," for, as Brendel observed, in her prose "the devil too often governed where the dative or accusative should have."[29]

Amalgamating, like *Lucinde*, a variety of genres to create Schlegelian "romantic confusion," *Florentin* nevertheless projects a clear narrative, though its characters remain "indeterminately developed."[30] The novel treats the moral development of the young, wandering artist of the title and his relationships to the fifteen-year-old Julianne, daughter of a count whose life Florentin has saved, and to her mysterious aunt Clementina. Likened to St. Cecilia, she performs annually a requiem of her own composition and has trained a choir to read "magnificent old pieces which one otherwise would never hear."[31] There are some suggestions that Clementina is Florentin's mother, but her identity is never revealed, and ultimately Florentin simply disappears, leaving the novel open-ended. In Brendel's unpublished dedication to Friedrich, whose literary theories privileged the fragment, she addressed this issue through a simile: "Usually, though, one finds no ending of a novel satisfying unless the person in whom one is most interested gets married or is buried, and people will complain that here neither of the two options brings us completely to rest....I am like those little girls who prefer to play with a naked doll which they can dress differently every hour and to which they can give a totally different appearance, than with the most splendidly and most perfectly dressed doll that has her clothes—and, with them, her final destiny—sewn permanently into place."[32]

There is evidence that Brendel conceived new variants of the doll's game in a sequel to *Florentin*. Left among her papers were incomplete drafts of a novella titled *Camilla*, possibly intended for insertion into *Florentin*, a technique recalling Cervantes's digressions in *Don Quixote*, one of Friedrich's favorite novels. The *Camilla* fragments are noteworthy, too, for what they reveal about Brendel's evolving spirituality. In contrast to the anti-Catholic stance of *Florentin*, the title character of *Camilla* is a devout Catholic, paralleling Brendel's own remarkable spiritual trajectory that included not one but two conversions. In 1804, after accompanying Friedrich to Paris, Brendel was baptized as a Protestant, whereupon she took the name Dorothea, married Friedrich, and became Dorothea Schlegel. Then, four years later, after a peripatetic lifestyle that led them to Cologne, the couple converted to Catholicism. For Friedrich, Protestantism had remained tethered to the rationalist Enlightenment of the eighteenth century; the Catholic faith, in contrast, beckoned him to tap into the emotional roots of Christianity. For Dorothea also, the second conversion symbolized a further removal from the Enlightenment and from her father's values and Jewish upbringing.

As a writer, Dorothea subordinated her creative role to that of her husband. Apart from *Florentin*, she contributed translations, essays, and critical reviews to Friedrich's journal *Europa*. She translated Madame de Staël's novel *Corinne* and an Arthurian romance about the magician Merlin, only to see both appear under Friedrich's name and several of her other writings subsumed into his collected works. For much of her life she remained estranged from her relatives, including Fanny's father, Abraham, whom she once described as a "barbarian without feeling."[33] Though ultimately the siblings reconciled (her brothers supported her financially in her declining years), Dorothea's sensational life story did not at all accord with the genteel existence, free from want, of Abraham and Lea. And yet there are familiar parallels between Dorothea's and Fanny Hensel's creative worlds. Like Dorothea, Fanny was largely denied an authorial identity. Until the last year or so of her life, Fanny composed the vast bulk of her music with little thought of publication. The few works she released before 1846 appeared either anonymously or under the aegis of the dominant masculine influence in her life, her brother Felix, who appropriated six of her lieder into his first two song collections. Like Dorothea, Fanny discovered her own creative space within a domestic setting well removed from the glare of officialdom. As we shall see, Fanny's solution would be to supervise during the 1830s and 1840s a salon-like institution at the Berlin family residence, not a literary type modeled on the precedent of Dorothea's friend Henriette Herz, but a brilliant series of musical gatherings recalling the refined tastes of Sarah Levy. At the family residence Fanny explored a semipublic/private space in which her own music and music making found expressive outlets.

iii

Remarkably little is known about Fanny's early years in Hamburg. The first notice about her is a letter, written by Abraham to his mother-in-law the day after Fanny's birth, reporting the difficulties of Lea's labor but also her prophetic maternal observation—their daughter had "Bach fugal fingers."[34] Some three years later, Felix's arrival on February 3, 1809, prompted more comparisons: the son, Lea informed her Viennese cousin Henriette von Pereira Arnstein, promised to be "more pretty" than Fanny, an allusion to a slight orthopedic deformity inherited from her grandfather Moses. At age three and a half, she was reading her letters plainly and purposefully fabricating phrases with clarity and coherence.[35] We then lose sight of Fanny and her siblings—Rebecka was born in Hamburg on April 11, 1811, and Paul in Berlin on October 30, 1812—for several years, allowing us to trace the fortunes of the Mendelssohn bank, the family's decision to leave Hamburg in 1811, and the rise to prominence of the Berlin firm.

When Abraham and Joseph established Gebrüder Mendelssohn & Co. in 1805, Hamburg was a free, "neutral" city of about 130,000 residents as yet unscathed by the Napoleonic campaigns. A centuries-old member of the Hanseatic League, Hamburg had prospered as a north German center of shipbuilding and commerce. Among its entrepreneurs plying the banker's trade was Salomon Heine, uncle of the poet, who amassed a fortune of forty-one million francs and described himself as Abraham's "best friend."[36] Though the Mendelssohn brothers moved in Salomon's social circle, their business began as a comparatively modest concern. Still, by 1806 they were attracting clients from Amsterdam, London, Paris, Riga, Warsaw, and Vienna; and Lea Mendelssohn, who had inherited a share of the Itzig fortune, maintained an account that alone generated an annual income of 7,000 thalers.[37]

Supporting Hamburg's neutrality was a stalwart municipal government that might be described as a democracy for its 3,000 to 4,000 propertied Lutheran burghers, ruled by a senate and administrative colleges. To maintain its independence, Hamburg had successfully rebuffed claims on its sovereignty by the German *Reich* and, since the middle of the eighteenth century, had thwarted the aggrandizing interests of Prussia. Hamburg's neutrality was challenged too by Denmark, which in 1640 had acquired Altona, just one mile north of Hamburg on the Elbe River. Here, in a bustling merchant city that by 1800 was rivaling its neighbor, duty-free wares were readily available, and, through the enlightened policy of the Danish monarchy, French Huguenots, Dutch Mennonites, and Spanish, Portuguese, and German Jews enjoyed religious freedom. In particular, Jews could worship openly, in contrast to Hamburg, where synagogues were suppressed. Perhaps this measure of freedom explains why Abraham's mother, Fromet, spent her final years in Altona, and why Abraham and Lea decided to purchase Martens' Mill, a "country cottage with a balcony" near Altona,[38] to serve as their summer residence from 1805 to 1811.

Hamburg's vaunted neutrality had encouraged one unusual political enterprise: between 1796 and 1803 members of the United Irishmen used the city as a base to forge a Franco-Irish alliance, a futile escapade that exposed Hamburg to belligerent diplomatic exchanges between France and England. Then, about a year after the Mendelssohns' arrival, Napoleon decisively compromised the city's neutrality. In July 1806 he established the Confederation of the Rhine, an artificial alliance of sixteen German states that opposed Prussian interests, and aroused the usually lethargic monarch, Frederick William III, to abandon his policy of neutrality in favor of mobilization. But the outmoded, oblique formations of his military—the novelist Theodor Fontane likened them to the "valedictory parade of the Frederickian army"[39]—were no match for Napoleon's flexible tactics. At Jena he outflanked and routed the Prussians, while at Auerstädt Marshal Louis Davout crushed a numerically superior enemy. With Frederick William in full flight, Napoleon entered Berlin, seized as a spoil of war the quadriga atop the Brandenburg Gate, and established the Continental System late in 1806 to blockade English trade with Europe. In retaliation, the English began interdicting vessels bound for ports under French control.

The new economic sanctions were catastrophic for Hamburg; fortunes dependent there upon free trade now vanished. A succession of *gouverneurs*—beginning in November 1806 with Marshal Mortier and culminating in February 1811 with the dreaded Duke of Auerstädt himself, Marshal Davout—imposed repressive measures leading to the formal annexation of Hamburg as a French territory. English goods were seized as contraband, and citizens faced arbitrary conscription into the French navy. But there was one unintended consequence: Hamburg became a smuggler's haven, where blockade-runners practiced a thriving trade, tacitly supported by venal French officials. Resorting to subterfuges that strained credulity, the smugglers conveyed English and colonial goods from Altona to Hamburg under the very eyes of customs agents, in thinly disguised, sugar-filled gravel carts, and in interminable funeral processions with caskets bearing coffee, vanilla, and indigo instead of cadavers.

For about four and a half years, the Mendelssohns experienced firsthand the French occupation, which tempered Abraham's Francophilia and converted him into a German patriot. At some point in the first half of 1811, the brothers evidently ran afoul of the authorities, so that, Sebastian Hensel informs us, their families were "obliged to flee the town, and in mist and darkness they escaped one night in disguise, turning their steps toward Berlin."[40] Hensel's intriguing statement arouses speculation about the brothers' illicit activities: were they, for instance, blockade-runners or even agents of Frederick William? We shall probably never know for certain, though recently released Prussian archives from 1811 and 1812 allow us to flesh out some parts of Hensel's sketchy account.[41] Titled "The Arrest of the Mendelssohn Brothers," the archives indeed document a different sequence of events, even as they raise new questions.

Here we learn, first of all, that Joseph's family departed Hamburg in May and Abraham's separately in June 1811, so that the brothers probably did not flee incognito under cover of darkness. But they did bring to Berlin their account books, enough to raise the suspicions of French authorities in Hamburg that they were attempting to evade a debt owed to the customs office, the grand sum of 200,000 francs. And so, in July 1811 the French ambassador to Prussia requested the brothers' immediate arrest and the surrender of their accounts. There followed weeks, then months of diplomatic exchanges and procrastination from the Berlin authorities, as they determined that the

Prussian government had a vested interest in not granting the French access to the bank's documents. Since Napoleon's regime meanwhile had seized the Hamburg firm, Joseph and Abraham formally dissolved Gebrüder Mendelssohn & Co., owing to "changed circumstances," and reorganized the Berlin branch as the business J. & A. Mendelssohn. To placate the French, the Prussian police interrogated the brothers, placed them under house arrest, and confiscated their books. Protesting their innocence and invoking their legal rights as "protected Jews" of the Prussian monarch, Joseph and Abraham nevertheless agreed to raise a security deposit of 200,000 francs, and in October their account books were dispatched to Hamburg, where officials examined them under the watchful eyes of the Prussian legate. Early in January 1812 the French finally released the accounts, but not until April did the Prussian foreign ministry exonerate the brothers and close the matter.

At age six, Fanny was innocent enough of these worldly affairs, though she evidently was beginning to correspond with her aunt Henriette in Paris, who described the child's writing as "really the 2nd edition of all the maternal talent."[42] By this time, political events had taken a dramatic course. On March 11, 1812, the Prussian monarch issued a decree emancipating, or so it seemed, Jewish subjects through the grant of citizenship. Now essentially a vassal state of France, the government extracted harsh levies from its citizenry to support a momentous turning point in European history—Napoleon's invasion of Russia. But after the emperor's forced retreat—only one-sixth (100,000 men) of his *grande armée*, the largest military force yet assembled, managed to return in December to Paris—bellicose Prussian voices clamored for freedom from the French yoke. In March 1813 Frederick William struck an alliance with the tsar and again declared war on France. J. & A. Mendelssohn—assessed, one year before, tens of thousands of thalers for the Russian campaign—now actively supported the War of Liberation. For the next several months, Abraham divided his time between Berlin, Breslau (where the Prussian court had reconvened), and Vienna, where he oversaw shipments of Austrian arms to the Prussian army.

Because of fears that the French would march again on Berlin, Lea and the children fled in June to Vienna and took refuge for several months at the residence of Fanny von Arnstein,[43] whom Lea likened to a "second mother," even if Vienna was a "veritable Sodom" of vanity and superficiality. In Vienna Abraham donated 500 gulden for the care of wounded Austrian soldiers;[44] also around this time he acquired the unlikely nickname of Septimius Severus, after the Roman emperor (193–211 A.D.) who had persecuted Jews and Christians alike. Fanny Mendelssohn's earliest surviving letter, penned in Vienna on July 12, 1813, when she was seven, captures a rather absurd moment during a time of great anxiety and uncertainty: "Meanwhile one of the ladies disguised father and named him Emperor Septimius Severus; a shawl represented his cloak, a wreath of pear foliage his crown, and a parasol his scepter. He assumed completely the imperial manner; when Uncle [Jacob] entered and didn't doff his hat, father took his scepter and knocked it off his head."[45]

The final defeat of Napoleon at Waterloo on June 18, 1815, accelerated the rise of the Mendelssohns' bank. In the reactionary aftermath of the Congress of Vienna, Prussia joined the allies in imposing punitive war reparations upon France. A consortium of banks, led by the Rothschilds of Frankfurt and including the Mendelssohns' firm, managed the lucrative enterprise of overseeing the payments; for J. & A. Mendelssohn, the receipts amounted to 5/32 of the profits from the transactions.[46] Exploiting the new business climate, Joseph Mendelssohn established a *bureau* in Paris, where he took up residence with his family in October, and began managing the fund transfers from Paris to Berlin. Meanwhile, the Berlin branch expanded its operations from a new location on Jägerstraße, in the center of the city's business district, where it remained until 1938, when the Nazis finally "Aryanized" its assets and liquidated the bank.

iv

On March 21, 1816, coincidentally or not the birthday of Lea's favored composer, J. S. Bach, Lea and her husband witnessed the baptism of their children by Johann Jakob Stegemann, Reformed Protestant minister of the Jerusalemskirche near the Gendarmenmarkt. According to most accounts, the ceremony took place in the church, but it may well be that the sacrament was administered at the family quarters at Markgrafenstraße no. 48, owned by Pastor Stegemann, and not far from the Mendelssohn bank on Jägerstraße.[47] The parents, who chose not to convert that day, were well aware that their action would cause a schism within the family, and so they took special pains to withhold the news from Lea's mother, an Orthodox Jew. In the baptismal record, the children appeared with the second surname Bartholdy, and Fanny with the name Cäcilia, so that she became Fanny Cäcilia Mendelssohn Bartholdy (Felix became Jacob Ludwig Felix; Rebecka, Rebecka Henriette; and Paul, Paul Hermann).[48] The addition of Bartholdy followed the example of Lea's brother Jacob Salomon, who, upon converting in 1805 to the Protestant faith, had adopted the name of the dairy farm owned by his grandfather, Daniel Itzig. In the case of the Mendelssohn children, their new identity also may have been in response to the Emancipation Edict of 1812, by which the Prussian monarch had directed Jewish subjects to adopt fixed family names. Indeed, as early as that year, Abraham began using Bartholdy; in a list of the Berlin Jewish congregation, he appears as Abraham Mendelssohn Bartholdy.[49]

The question of religious identity, so influential for the music of Felix and Fanny, animated a new phenomenon in late eighteenth- and early nineteenth-century Berlin: middle- and upper-middle-class Jewish families pursuing the elusive goal of assimilation now became increasingly attracted to conversion. Thus, of Moses Mendelssohn's six children, only two remained faithful to Judaism; two, including Abraham, became Protestants, and two, including Brendel, became Catholics. The willingness to convert was in part opportunistic, in part motivated by genuine spiritual conviction, and in part impregnated by the idea circulating in the salons that the gulf separating the Jewish and Christian faiths was narrowing and indeed might disappear altogether in the future. And so, in 1799, David Friedländer—a maternal great-uncle of Fanny, disciple of Moses Mendelssohn, and leader of the Berlin Jewish community—made a startling proposal: German Jews might join the Protestant Church through a rapprochement based upon common moral values instead of the formal recognition of Christ's divinity. Friedländer's assumption was that Judaism and Christianity would merge into a "confederated unitarian church-synagogue" and that so-called dry baptism would advance acculturation and assimilation.[50]

Though Friedländer's optimism was not commonly shared, the wave of Berlin conversions continued to wash over the Jewish community, so that some historians later likened the apostasy to an epidemic of baptism. In the case of Abraham and Lea, the decision to convert was no impulsive act, but one influenced by family history and their status in Prussian society. In 1763, after repeated petitions, Frederick the Great had reluctantly granted Moses Mendelssohn a letter of protection (*Schützbrief*),[51] subsequently extended by Frederick William II to Moses's widow and children in 1787, the year after the philosopher's death. In contrast, since 1761 Daniel Itzig had enjoyed the exalted general privilege, at the time granted only to three Jews. Then, in 1791, the Prussian monarch took the unprecedented step of naturalizing Itzig's family, including on the maternal side his children and grandchildren. In short, the Itzigs acquired the rights of Christian citizens, though they remained free to continue worshiping as Jews. But the king placed a provision on his largesse: the rights were revocable if the Itzig issue "should fall into the Jewish petty dealing that is still common among a great part of the Jewish nation."[52]

As far as Abraham and Lea were concerned, the royal edicts protected them (by marrying Lea in 1804, Abraham had become a citizen), but not their issue. They therefore faced a dilemma: should they raise their children in the Jewish faith and risk the whims of the Prussian government, or should their children at some point convert to Christianity and thereby embrace the dominant culture? The evidence establishes that early on the parents favored the latter course. A Jewish register of male births in Hamburg and Altona between the years 1781 and 1811 contains no entry for Felix; what is more, in 1821 C. F. Zelter claimed to Goethe that Abraham had made the "considerable sacrifice" of not having his sons circumcised,[53] a statement confirmed in Lea's correspondence with her Viennese cousin Henriette von Pereira-Arnstein—there, Lea revealed the distress of her mother, Bella Salomon, that Felix "was not made a Jew" (*nicht zum Juden gemacht war*).[54] In a concert review published just months after Abraham and Lea converted in October 1822, an anonymous critic averred that Felix "was born and raised in our Lutheran religion"[55] and thus helped disseminate the image of the Mendelssohn Bartholdys as upstanding Protestant burghers. As Zelter put it, Felix was "the son of a Jew, but no Jew."

The precedent of Jacob Bartholdy weighed heavily on the parents' deliberations about their children's spiritual upbringing. When Jacob Salomon changed his faith and name in 1805, Bella Salomon summarily disinherited him. Nevertheless, Jacob continued on the path of assimilation. A patriot, he fought against Napoleon in the Austrian campaign of 1809 and later served as the Prussian consul to Rome, where he resided in the Casa Bartholdy overlooking the Spanish Steps. An art connoisseur, Jacob commissioned the German Nazarene painters (among them Dorothea Schlegel's son Philipp Veit) to prepare frescoes for his drawing room. Jacob believed strongly in the correctness of his decision to become a Christian and sought to overcome whatever ambivalence Abraham had about conversion. An undated letter from Jacob gives a glimpse of the earnest discussions of the brothers-in-law:

> You say *you owe it to the memory of your father*, but do you think you have done something bad in giving your children the religion that appears to you to be the best? It is the most just homage you or any of us could pay to the efforts of your father to promote true light and knowledge, and he would have acted like you for his children, and perhaps like me for himself. You may remain faithful to an oppressed, persecuted religion, you may leave it to your children as a prospect of life-long martyrdom, as long as you believe it to be absolute truth. But when you have ceased to believe that, it is barbarism. I advise you to adopt the name of Mendelssohn Bartholdy as a distinction from the other Mendelssohns.[56]

In 1816, Abraham took Jacob's advice and separated his children from the "other Mendelssohns." As we shall see, Fanny later applied her musical talents to reconcile her uncle with his estranged mother and alleviate the distress caused by their religious divide.

From all appearances, Fanny and her siblings before their baptism were nonpracticing Jews. One intriguing question remains: why did Abraham and Lea delay their children's conversion until 1816? Prussian history perhaps provides some answers. Between the defeat of 1806 and resumption of war in 1813, Frederick William's monarchy, stripped of considerable territory and depleted financially, was reduced to a puppet state of France. During this period Napoleon's decisive rout of the Prussian military emboldened some reform-minded civil servants, including the minister Karl August von Hardenburg (a friend of David Friedländer), to press for equality for Jews. Perhaps the prospect of full Jewish citizenship held out by the 1812 edict induced Abraham and

Lea to defer their children's conversion. But, as was often the case with royal promulgations, appearances were deceptive. The ambiguous wording of some clauses encouraged the perpetuation of certain discriminatory aspects of the status quo; thus, after 1812 as before, Jews were barred from government and university positions.

The successful prosecution of the War of Liberation in 1813 in fact did little to advance the cause of Jewish emancipation. On the contrary, the conservative restoration of the Congress of Vienna encouraged a political backlash, as Prussia and the hodgepodge of German states experienced a surging nationalism that stamped an indelible image of a homogeneous, Christian *Volk* on their common cultural identity. At one extreme, patriotism asserted itself in burgeoning student societies through a crudely appropriated, medieval Christian zealotry. Jews had willingly volunteered and sacrificed for the war, but they were increasingly unwelcome in the intolerant post-Napoleonic political order. Though the king never annulled the Edict of 1812, he essentially rendered it ineffective by circumventing some key provisions. Restoration Prussia thus did not meaningfully advance social equality for Jews, and Abraham and Lea's apprehension about the future was probably a significant factor that led them in 1816 to have their children become Protestants, in order to ensure their rights as Prussian citizens.

v

Regrettably, we know little about Fanny's early formal education beyond her son's statement that "at first the parents themselves undertook the scientific instruction of their children."[57] According to Sir George Grove, author of the entry for Felix in the pioneering *Dictionary of Music and Musicians*, the parents routinely roused their children at 5:00 A.M. and insisted upon a strict regimen of studies.[58] Some idea of parental involvement is evident in the letters Abraham sent home during his business travels. One letter to Fanny, dated Amsterdam, April 5, 1819, reveals a concern for his daughter's Christian upbringing, even as the unconverted father espoused a deistic, unitarian position, probably not far removed from the faith of his father:

> You are now old enough to find subjects to write to me about, not only in the daily events, but also in your thoughts. I should like to hear now and then what ideas your occupations awaken in you. As long as I was at home, for instance, mother told me much about your lessons with the clergyman. You should do that yourself now; so that I may see by your letters, now that I cannot personally watch it, what influence his teaching has on your heart and mind. Above all, let it be that of more and more strengthening your endeavor to please your loving and revered mother,

and to arrive through obedience at love, through order and discipline at freedom and happiness. That is the best way of thanking and worshipping the Creator, the Maker of us *all*. There are in all religions only one God, one virtue, one truth, one happiness. You will find all this, if you follow the voice of your heart; live so that it be ever in harmony with the voice of your reason.[59]

If Fanny's parents played the dominant role in her early education, Felix followed a different course. By 1816, Abraham had enrolled him in a private elementary school, where at age seven his impressive memory was attracting attention. That year, he was already studying piano and with Fanny examining the complexities of opera piano-vocal scores, gifts from his grandmother. His passion (*Leidenschaft*), according to Lea, was to read the plays of Goethe and Shakespeare—to that end, his parents established a "small theater," which Fanny provisioned with puppets. Here, on this domestic stage, Felix discovered Shakespeare's *Midsummer Night's Dream*, which, Lea revealed, became the child's favorite reading (*Lieblingslectüre*), a disclosure that might well raise our eyebrows, until perhaps we remember that only ten years later the precocious adolescent would compose his celebrated concert overture to Shakespeare's comedy.[60]

In 1818, Abraham engaged a history docent from the University of Berlin to tutor Felix and Paul. Then, in 1819, the classical philologist C. W. L. Heyse (father of Paul Heyse, the first German Nobel laureate in literature) was retained as the Mendelssohns' tutor, and, according to Paul Heyse's memoirs, for seven years groomed Felix to prepare his matriculation at the University of Berlin. Undoubtedly, Fanny and Rebecka's education was far less systematic. In their case, there was no prospect of advanced studies, for the university was then not an option for women. Instead, young, leisured ladies were inculcated with the "ideology of domesticity," predicated upon the idea that "the home should be the source and repository of all affections and virtues and woman its guardian angel."[61] Thus, domestic arts and subjects—the skill of conversation, foreign languages, ethics and religion, music, drawing, painting, and dance— were encouraged, while practical and traditional subjects were introduced only to the extent that they promoted the efficient management of a household. Nevertheless, the Mendelssohns were highly cultured and intellectually curious, and Fanny and Rebecka did benefit, to some extent at least, from Heyse's tutelage. One of Felix's letters reveals, for example, that in 1821 he was sharing with Fanny each week two hours of history lessons, two of arithmetic, one of geography, and one of German conversation,[62] and, according to family friend Julius Schubring, Felix was tutored "partly with his sisters and partly alone."[63] Supporting Fanny was the unusual example of her mother; the young Lea Salomon had developed her mind to a high degree, and there is every reason to believe that Lea Mendelssohn Bartholdy encouraged her daughters to do so as well. Behind the façade of social reserve and domestic femininity, Lea had delighted in exploring the fugal peregrinations of the *Well-Tempered Clavier* and perusing Homer in the Greek. Perhaps not surprisingly, Fanny's personal library included a copy of Herodotus's *Persian Wars*,[64] though there is little hard evidence that she advanced very far in Greek, unlike Rebecka, who by the late 1820s was comfortably dispatching Aeschylus, or Felix, who occasionally embellished his letters with pithy quotations from Homer.

Of course, music formed the strongest bond between mother and daughter. On account of her Bachian "fugal fingers," Fanny no doubt explored her musicality to an extent far greater than was customary for women. Her first instructor, naturally enough, was Lea, who began with lessons of only five minutes, which she gradually augmented and molded into systematic instruction; she employed the same approach for Felix.[65] At some point, Lea entrusted the siblings' keyboard studies to leading Berlin pedagogues and secured first for that purpose the Moravian Franz Lauska,[66] who had served as a proofreader for Beethoven in Vienna and promoted himself as a pupil of Mozart, though that tutelage is questionable. A composer of piano sonatas that taxed amateurs but not virtuosi, Lauska was a familiar figure at the Berlin Singakademie and salons; his pupils included the young Giacomo Meyerbeer and members of the Prussian royal family.

Around April 1817, the highly regarded virtuoso Ludwig Berger replaced Lauska. A former student of the versatile pianist, composer, music publisher, and piano manufacturer Muzio Clementi, Berger had pursued an unusual career that never reached its full potential. Following his teacher in 1804 to St. Petersburg, he had developed a Russian market for Clementi's pianos and formed a friendship with another expatriate Clementi disciple, the Irishman John Field, the first composer of piano nocturnes. Napoleon's Russian campaign of 1812 prompted Berger to flee for England, where he became a founding member of the Philharmonic Society and celebrated Napoleon's defeat at Waterloo by emblazing the name of Wellington's ally, the Prussian General Blücher, before his residence.[67] Safely returned to Berlin, Berger gave a successful concert in 1814, but an arm injury forced him to abandon his virtuoso career in favor of teaching. Despite suffering too from hypochondria, Berger was a highly sought-out pedagogue who commanded the highest fees in Berlin. Among his many successful students were Fanny and Felix, who, according to Ludwig Rellstab, became "independent virtuosos" under Berger's tutelage.[68] His life overlapped significantly with the Mendelssohns until the latter part of 1819, when Carl Friedrich Zelter emerged as Fanny and Felix's composition teacher.

Whether Berger offered Fanny instruction solely in piano or also in composition is a question neither much explored nor answerable. Though Fanny's first surviving composition dates from late 1819, when she was fourteen, is it far-fetched to imagine her notating musical musings a few years earlier? If she did, Berger may have played a significant role (in 1822, embittered over Zelter's success with the children, Berger did claim credit for shaping Felix's compositional development[69]). Berger himself specialized in two genres to which Fanny later devoted most of her creative energies: the solo, texted art song (lied), and the short character piece for piano, which could take the form of a lyrical, songlike miniature or an athletic etude designed to address some aspect of piano technique. Though most of Berger's music is now forgotten, two compositions deserve mention. In the Piano Sonata in C Minor, op. 18 (1801), he set for himself an unusual challenge: all three movements spring from the same taut six-note motive, which infiltrates the work and lends it an unrelenting thematic concentration. Something reminiscent of this strategy is detectable in Fanny's piano sonata in the same key (1824, H-U 128;[70] see p. 81); its first movement avoids thematic contrast in favor of a compact head motive, insinuated into numerous guises throughout the movement.

The composition for which Berger is usually remembered, though, is his 1819 song collection *Die schöne Müllerin*, published a few years before Schubert's famous cycle on the same subject. A product of Berlin salon culture, Berger's work has an unusual tie to Fanny. In the winter of 1816–1817, presumably not long before he began instructing Fanny and Felix, Berger frequented the salon of Elisabeth von Stägemann, a gifted singer, former daughter-in-law of the composer C. H. Graun, and wife of a privy councilor. Berger joined an artistic circle forming around Elisabeth's daughter Hedwig, which included the poet Wilhelm Müller, writer Clemens Brentano, portraitist Wilhelm Hensel, and his sister Luise, a Catholic convert later known for her mystical Catholic verse.

Their pastime was a novel form of entertainment known as the *Liederspiel*, a narrative play broken up by interspersed songs. Initially they improvised one example on a subject familiar from folk poetry, of the seductive miller-maid pursued by a series of suitors, including a miller-lad, played, appropriately enough, by the namesake Müller, and a hunter, played by Fanny's future husband, Wilhelm Hensel. (In real life, the alluring Luise Hensel considered marriage proposals from Berger, Müller, and Brentano, but rejected them all in favor of a claustral life of Catholic charities.) Using an ingratiating folk style, Berger composed a cycle of ten settings, of which five were on poems by Müller, who in 1820 then reworked his verses into a "poetic monodrama" told from the viewpoint of the miller-lad.[71] In turn, Müller's anthology served as the source for Schubert's immortal 1823 cycle. In 1817 Fanny was too young to participate in the *Liederspiel*, but she came to value Berger's music; six years later, after setting Müller's text *Die liebe Farbe*, in which the jilted miller-lad requests a burial in green, she critiqued her effort with the comment, "Herr Berger understood this better" ("Das hat Herr Berger besser verstanden").[72]

Though Fanny's musicianship first blossomed in Berlin, in 1816 (and possibly again in 1817) her musical horizons expanded considerably when the

Mendelssohns visited Paris. If the Prussian capital remained a bastion of conservatism in politics and the arts, Paris evinced a more cosmopolitan outlook, notwithstanding the autocratic rule of the restored Bourbon, Louis XVIII, who had reentered post-Napoleon Paris rather ingloriously in the "baggage of the Allies." The documentation for the Mendelssohns' Parisian sojourns is meager, but we can trace their itinerary in April 1816 from Berlin to Weimar, where en route Abraham brought a letter to Goethe from Zelter. "He has lovely, worthy children," Zelter informed the poet, "and his eldest daughter can let you hear something by Sebastian Bach."[73] But on this occasion Goethe did not meet the children; instead, the family proceeded to the French metropolis, where Abraham relieved his brother Joseph of his banking duties. While there, the parents had copies made of the earliest surviving portraits of their children, taken at some point by the Mecklenburg miniaturist August Grahl. Here Fanny, shown at about age eleven, strikes a self-possessed pose— she wears earrings and has her hair gathered in a chignon.

In Paris Fanny met her aunt Henriette, the youngest, unmarried daughter of Moses and director of a boarding school for girls. Among her familiar circle were Madame de Staël, expelled from France in 1810 for *De l'Allemagne*, her book about German manners, which Napoleon's censors judged too subversive, and Helmina von Chézy, who provided opera libretti for Schubert and Carl Maria von Weber. In 1812, Henriette had converted to Catholicism and become the governess of Fanny Sebastiani, daughter of one of Napoleon's generals. When not tutoring her pampered charge in an opulent *hôtel* overlooking the Champs Elysées, Henriette might be found attending the new chamber music concerts established in 1814 by the violinist Pierre Baillot, who offered opera-sated Parisians an alternative—string quartets of Boccherini, Haydn, Mozart, and Beethoven. Probably through Henriette, Fanny and Felix were introduced to the French virtuoso, a disciple of Viotti and one of the first faculty members of the Paris Conservatoire, which had opened its doors in 1796. Baillot now coached Fanny and Felix in ensemble playing. "You know Baillot's face," Henriette wrote to Lea after the Mendelssohns' return to Berlin in November 1816; "this expression remained as long as he spoke of Fanny and Felix, and we spoke of no one else."[74]

One of Baillot's colleagues was the Alsatian pianist Madame Bigot de Morogues (née Kiéné), who gave lessons to Fanny and Felix. Through her husband, the librarian of Beethoven's patron Count Razumovsky, Madame Bigot had gained access in Vienna to Haydn and Beethoven, who was so impressed by her rendering of the *Appassionata* Sonata that he gave her his nearly illegible manuscript. Bigot made a specialty of interpreting Beethoven's more difficult piano works, and she may have instilled in Fanny and her brother a healthy curiosity about the composer, whose music was still relatively unknown in Paris (as late as 1825, Felix would decry the Parisian ignorance of *Fidelio*). According to the Belgian music critic Fétis, Bigot's playing possessed a nuanced expression and charm unsurpassed in her time. But she also offered Fanny practical advice about strengthening the weak fourth and fifth fingers—slow and arduous practicing of J. B. Cramer's etudes, for Bigot a sure way to achieve digital independence.[75]

One of the Mendelssohns' way stations between Berlin and Paris was Frankfurt, where they visited Dorothea and Friedrich Schlegel. Fanny and Felix performed works by Bach and Handel for Dorothea, who was dumbstruck by their "energy, skill, precision and expression."[76] In April 1817 the Mendelssohns were once again in Frankfurt, presumably about to repeat their Parisian experience, though exactly how many family members accompanied Abraham on this trip is not clear. In any event, for the occasion Friedrich inscribed some paternalistic verses for his niece, who preserved them in her album:

Lebe heiter, denke milde,	Live happily, ponder gently,
Schwebe still im sanften Gleise,	Move quietly over a soft path,
Blühend nach der Blumen Weise	Blooming like flowers,
Wie sie duften im Gefilde.[77]	Fragrantly wafting over the fields.

Friedrich's idealized image of Fanny did not exactly accord with her reception then taking hold in Berlin, where Rebecka Meyer described her cousin in 1818 as the least pretty of the Mendelssohn children but strikingly precocious (*altklug*); Rebecka rated the "angelic" Felix a "true musical genius."[78] Indeed, Felix's musical maturation now accelerated at an incredible rate. At age nine, in 1818, he appeared in a public concert of the horn virtuoso Heinrich Gugel, which received a notice in a Leipzig music journal. There is evidence too that he performed that year a piano concerto by Dussek.[79] For Fanny, there was no public debut, but at least one compelling private demonstration of her talent. Her son informs us that in 1818, at age thirteen, she performed from memory for her father twenty-four preludes from Bach's *Well-Tempered Clavier*. Since Fanny turned thirteen on November 14, this display of filial affection must have occurred in November or December, perhaps on December 11, Abraham's birthday. When Henriette Mendelssohn received the news in Paris, it provoked wonderment but also remonstration: "Fanny's wonderful achievement…and your perseverance, dearest Lea, in superintending her practicing, have made me speechless with astonishment, and I have only recovered the use of my voice to make this great success generally known. But with all the intense admiration I feel both for you and Fanny, I must confess that I think the thing decidedly blamable: the exertion is too great, and might easily have hurt her. The extraordinary talent of your children wants direction, not forcing. Papa Abraham, however, is insatiable, and the best appears to him only just good enough."[80] As a governess, Henriette had definite enough views about how to rear a young lady from a respectable Berlin family. For Henriette, the mores of the leisured class trumped the fugal fingers that would explicate Bach's encyclopedic masterpiece.

CHAPTER 2

Musical Ornaments

(1819–1821)

Music will perhaps become his profession, whilst for *you* it can and must only be an ornament, never the root of your being and doing.

—Abraham to Fanny Mendelssohn Bartholdy, July 1820

History has remembered Carl Friedrich Zelter (1758–1832) first as Felix Mendelssohn Bartholdy's prickly composition teacher and then as Goethe's musical advisor, who in a protracted correspondence over three decades exchanged perceptive but at times commonplace, even crass confidences about German cultural life. To the extent that Fanny figures in Zelter's biography, she receives only a token acknowledgment as his student. To date, few scholars have assessed her work with the musician whom Lea described as not particularly sensitive, and the actress Karoline Bauer, bristly as a shoe brush.[1] Zelter's efforts as a musical pedagogue stood in inverse relation to the relative insignificance of his own music, which for the most part has not withstood the passage of time. As an educator, his influence was considerable: his other pupils included the opera composers Giacomo Meyerbeer and Otto Nicolai, the songwriters Bernhard Klein and Carl Loewe, the choral musician Eduard Grell, and the music theorist A. B. Marx, though admittedly Marx decried Zelter as a book-bound pedant. Zelter's vision was to elevate Prussian music from its incidental role as a court entertainment to a central, durable element of his countrymen's lives. Ideally, music would seep into their cultural awareness, advance ethical development, and promote *Bildung*, that untranslatable German concept that allied culture with self-improvement. To this end, Zelter developed the Singakademie into a venerable institution for preserving sacred choral music; founded during the French occupation a *Liedertafel* for disseminating patriotic part-songs; drafted a position paper on the civic role of music in Prussia; established singing schools in Königsberg, Dresden, and Berlin; and served as an august professor at the Berlin Academy of Fine Arts.

The son of a stonemason, Zelter showed early on no irrepressible aptitude for music and discovered his preferred vocation only after attaining the status of master mason in 1783. Upon the death of Frederick the Great three years later, Zelter produced an ambitious memorial cantata. Nevertheless, J. P. Kirnberger remained skeptical of the aspiring composer's prospects and pointedly inquired, "Do you wish to build houses and then compose, or do you wish to compose and then build houses?"[2] Undeterred, Zelter sought out the composer Carl Friedrich Christian Fasch, Frederick the Great's former musical valet, for lessons. When Fasch accompanied the king to Sanssouci during the summer, Zelter rose early, trudged the several miles on a dusty road to Potsdam for his lesson, and returned the same day to Berlin in order to supervise his construction projects. Among Zelter's clients were the Itzigs and their friends, through whom he met Moses Mendelssohn and his son Abraham.

Like Johann Sebastian Bach, Zelter's teacher Fasch descended from a line of Lutheran musicians. In his time a well-respected composer, Fasch specialized in sacred choral works that blended chorales and complex, high baroque counterpoint with traces of a lighter, more modern *galant* style. A perfectionist who burned works he deemed substandard, Fasch produced a quantity of cantatas and psalm settings, including one of Psalm 30, for six-part chorus and organ continuo, which rejected the standard Lutheran translation in favor of Moses Mendelssohn's rendition. Fasch's magnum opus, from 1783, was a Mass for sixteen voices (in four four-part choirs) and continuo, a tour de force of counterpoint and part writing that revived the polychoral tradition of the seventeenth century. As a teacher, Fasch followed a methodical course progressing from chorale harmonizations to rudiments of counterpoint and canon, and then the composition of short character pieces and French dances before a culminating treatment of fugue. Not unlike the pedagogical method of the Bachs, Fasch's approach indoctrinated Zelter with a love of counterpoint and a respect for the traditions of the German baroque, predilections he in turn passed on to Fanny and Felix.

Another significant part of Fasch's legacy touched the lives of Zelter and the Mendelssohns. In 1789 Fasch had begun supervising rehearsals of sacred choral music, including the motets of J. S. Bach. Eventually the ensemble coalesced as the Singakademie, and by 1800 expanded into a 150-strong amateur chorus that executed "the most difficult polyphonic vocal works with a purity and precision beyond all belief."[3] Its success attracted the attention of the young Beethoven, who visited Berlin in 1796 and entertained the ensemble with a piano improvisation on one of Fasch's fugal subjects. Upon his death in 1800, Zelter became the new director; his first deed was to perform for his teacher's memorial a work then unknown in Berlin, Mozart's Requiem. As we have seen, within a few years Zelter organized the Ripienschule, which supplemented the chorus with performances of eighteenth-century instrumental works and secured among its roster the eager participation of Fanny's aunt Sarah Levy.

Though Zelter tried his compositional hand at various instrumental and vocal genres, his strength lay in lieder, German art songs, of which he crafted some 200 examples and published between 1796 and 1828 about 100 in collections designed for the growing market of amateur domestic music making. Zelter's lieder contributed only modestly to the process of harnessing the rich expressive potential of the modern piano to German lyrical poetry. His experiments were far less demanding than the seventeen-year-old Schubert's pioneering 1814 setting of Goethe's *Gretchen am Spinnrade* (*Gretchen at the Spinning Wheel*), in which a rotating piano figure, established with cyclic regularity before Gretchen's entrance, becomes a mesmerizing symbol of the wheel and an indelible part of the listener's reading of the poem. In contrast, Zelter's song aesthetic routinely viewed music as ancillary to poetry. The ideal song was strophic (the composer simply reused the same melody for successive stanzas), and the vocal lines were relatively undemanding and easily singable, as if a concession to their amateur audiences. Elaborate word repetitions and melodic flourishes were kept to a minimum, and the piano accompaniment was mostly restricted to a backdrop of chords that merely supported the metrical and rhythmic patterns of the poem.

Zelter's preferred poet was the reigning figure in German arts and letters—Goethe. Fully one-third, or about sixty, of Zelter's songs set Goethe's verses, including many of his most celebrated poems, such as the Harper songs and the ineffable *Wanderers Nachtlied*. Goethe reciprocated by recognizing Zelter as the ideal song composer, whose music faithfully reproduced the poet's intentions and elevated the poetry into the listener's consciousness, like a balloon lifted heavenward by invisible gas.[4] But Zelter's unassuming settings could conceal considerable art. A case in point is his rendition of Goethe's *Um Mitternacht* (*At Midnight*), composed in 1818, about a year before Fanny and Felix became Zelter's pupils. Here he relaxed a repetitive strophic design to capture musically Goethe's three vignettes of a frightened boy turned passionate youth and reflective old man, who, illuminated by the stars and moon, recalls his experiences of midnight stretched over a lifetime. While the piano part, unaltered for each stanza, establishes the diurnal cycle through slowly pulsing chords broken only by an occasional arpeggiation, the vocal line undergoes subtle retouches from stanza to stanza, invoking the passage of time and creating, in effect, a series of variations upon a common theme.

"Every note contains a thought of you," Zelter wrote Goethe, "as you are, as you were, and as mankind should be."[5]

This, then, was the mason turned composer who on June 12, 1819, inscribed Fanny's album as her teacher.[6] Presumably, formal lessons had commenced somewhat earlier, for on May 1, Lea reported to her Viennese cousin that Fanny and Felix were already attending the Ripienschule at the Singakademie, where they heard the "most serious things"—instrumental works of J. S. Bach, Handel, and other eighteenth-century composers.[7] By July, having observed several lessons, Lea was assessing Zelter's tutelage as mediating between the sublime and mundane: "He weaves so much spirit, taste, meaning, humor, even genius into his discourses everywhere, that I often regret not having jotted down the best of it. In his case the belief of the ancients that man has two souls seems to be true, for I cannot deny that the same man who charms us with inspiration of an artist, touching seriousness of thought, and jokes à la Jean Paul, can also be downright insipid and prosaic."[8] In the summer of 1819, the instruction reached a hiatus when Zelter departed Berlin for Weimar to visit Goethe, and then proceeded on to Vienna, where he found Mozart's "nemesis" Salieri still spinning out compositions like a silkworm, and Beethoven, imprisoned by deafness, beginning to create the abstract works of his late period.

During Zelter's absence, Fanny diligently completed exercises in an eighteenth-century style and by August 18 had written twelve gavottes.[9] This stylized baroque dance, typically in a moderate tempo and duple meter, with occasional telltale, caesura-like breaks in the middle of the measure, seems to have held a special position in Zelter's composition method. In 1825, his voice student Gustav Wilhelm Teschner had survived a heavy dose of chorale exercises only to have to churn out for his next assignment baroque dances—minuets, polonaises, and no fewer than twenty-four gavottes.[10] Lest Teschner stray too far from the straight and narrow path, Zelter had him copy model gavottes from the keyboard suites of J. S. Bach and Handel. In August 1819 Fanny followed the same routine and learned to compose by emulating Zelter's historical exemplars. In effect, Zelter became a musical hyphen, connecting Fanny's nineteenth-century sensibilities to august, eighteenth-century musical traditions. Meanwhile, her brother, not as far advanced, was negotiating figured bass exercises[11] in preparation for his own tutorial in chorale harmonizations, which began in October 1819.

None of Fanny's gavottes has survived, so gauging her progress under Zelter in 1819 is nearly impossible. How far the creative ambitions of the thirteen-year-old exceeded the antiquated realm of baroque dances is not clear, though there is evidence she was exploring free composition. Her letter to Zelter of August 18 mentions not only gavottes but an unspecified musical effort she dismissed as a "shoddy effort" (*musikalisches Machwerk*), as well as some songs that were proving difficult for her to finish. As for her brother, Felix seems to have enjoyed considerable creative latitude, even as he was negotiating a thicket of figured bass lines and devising tenor and alto parts to harmonize dozens of chorale melodies Zelter notated. In a letter of November 1, 1819, the ten-year-old referred to a recently finished double piano sonata.[12] The English scholar Peter Ward Jones has located an unsigned, undated manuscript that may transmit this work and lay claim to being Felix's earliest surviving composition.[13] In three movements, all in D major, this early effort shows influences of Mozart, Haydn, and Clementi but betrays the neophyte in awkward harmonic progressions and handling of sonata form, as if the boy's creative muse chafed at the rigor of Zelter's instruction. Almost certainly, Felix's sonata was intended for performance with Fanny; by 1819, the siblings were becoming the talk of Berlin society and a source of delectation for the Mendelssohns' circle. Thus, at a dinner party hosted by Zelter in May 1819, guests including the philosopher Hegel and Goethe's daughter-in-law Ottilie heard the two perform duets with "unbelievable skill, precision, and knowledge of art."[14]

Though Fanny in 1819 was certainly the more advanced pianist of the two, around this time her parents made the decision to promote Felix's musical training. Thus, on Lea's initiative, in May, Felix began violin lessons as a surprise for Abraham, then in Paris, and in August, Aunt Henriette sent word from there of some special presents he was bringing home for the children— for Fanny a necklace of Scottish jewels, but for Felix writing implements with which he might compose his first opera.[15] There is no mention of similar encouragements for Fanny. Instead, in 1819 we begin to see the parents' expectations for the two divide: if Felix's musical world might encompass the very public realm of the opera house, Fanny's domain would remain relatively private, centered on domestic, intimate forms of music making—piano pieces and songs.

i

As if deferring to her parents, Fanny's earliest surviving composition indeed is a song, created for her father's birthday on December 11, 1819. The quatrains of this *Lied zum Geburtstag des Vaters* (H-U 2) are anonymous, but surely someone close to the Mendelssohns, if not a family member, contrived them. Invoking vibrating strings to celebrate filial love, the poem contrasts the security of a domestic family setting with the wintry outdoors, where a "dim veil covers the colorful splendor of the fields." There are allusions, too, to a paternal figure who "presides over our circle" as the "worthy refuge of our house." Conveniently enough, Felix set the first strophe of the same poem and thereby afforded a comparison with his sister's effort.[16] His creation is much less assuming, just twenty-six bars in length. Throughout Felix's lied the piano has elementary chords that occasionally double a rather square-cut vocal part but never test the modest limits of Zelter's strophic settings. In contrast, Fanny's supple melodic lines show the gift of a natural songwriter. And she indulges in some interpretive word painting: the strings (*Saiten*) of the poem resonate in arpeggiations throughout the accompaniment. What is more, Fanny's sixty-nine bars accommodate four more stanzas of the poem, set in a considerably more complex, through-composed arrangement, with subtle alterations in the vocal line for the second strophe, and a series of key changes and melodic departures for the third and fourth before the reconfirmation of the original key for the fifth.

If Fanny's festive offering projects an image of untroubled domestic life, contemporary external events suggest that the Mendelssohns' Berlin existence may not have been completely harmonious. In August 1819 the Hep-Hep Riots erupted in Bavaria and began spreading through central Germany and further north. Jews were harassed and attacked and their property vandalized; in Hamburg, the persecuted found temporary haven by fleeing across the neighboring Danish border. The slogan "Hep! Hep!," derived from the Latin *Hierosolyma est perdita* (Jerusalem is lost), recalled the distant fanaticism of the Crusades. Though Berlin was spared the rioting, and though the Mendelssohns' social standing partially insulated them, Abraham and Lea could only have viewed with apprehension the flaring up of civic unrest in the German states. According to Karl August Varnhagen von Ense, an unnamed royal prince "jovially shouted 'Hep, Hep!' after the boy Felix Mendelssohn in the street,"[17] though if and where this alleged incident occurred and whether Fanny was affected remain unclear. Perhaps the family was then traveling, and encountered some difficulty en route, away from Berlin (Fanny mentions in her letter of August 1819 an imminent trip to Dresden). Around this time, Abraham pondered moving his family to Paris, for he found Berlin oppressive, and vented in no uncertain terms to his sister Henriette, though without revealing the particular nature of his distress: "Why did my mother not bring me into the world in Bernau or Buxtehude—then I wouldn't have to seek excuses for finding my paternal city wretched [*erbärmlich*]."[18]

Be that as it may, the Mendelssohns did remain in Berlin, and early in 1820 settled into new quarters at Neue Promenade no. 7, a fashionable residence owned by Lea's mother, Bella Salomon, in the Spandauer Vorstadt near the eastern edge of Unter den Linden.[19] Here Fanny kindled her muse: between March 1820 and June 1821, at ages fourteen and fifteen, she began preserving her compositions in a musical album, filled with no fewer than thirty examples, but including also several piano pieces, possibly an attempt at a sacred choral work, and, as we shall shortly see, the beginning of a dramatic scene.[20] In the songs Fanny set a range of eighteenth- and nineteenth-century German poets, as well as the "wizard of the North," Sir Walter Scott. But what first captures our attention in her album are its thirteen clustered French settings of Jean-Pierre Claris de Florian (1755–1794), the eighteenth-century writer of

Arcadian stories, pastorals, and fables. Now remembered for the poem "Plaisir d'amour" ("Pleasure of Love"), he enjoyed celebrity during the waning years of Louis XVI's reign as one of the most widely read Parisian literary figures.

Florian was a great-nephew of the *philosophe* Voltaire, who after falling out with the French and Prussian monarchs lived from 1754 near Geneva, where he wielded his trenchant pen to espouse cases of religious and civil freedom.[21] Florian achieved literary fame first with his comedies and then the escapist pastoral *Galatée* (1783). Written in imitation of Cervantes, with occasional verses interspersed through the prose, *Galatée* was an immediate best seller and ran to four editions within a year. A series of six stories on French, German, and exotically tinged Spanish, Greek, Portuguese, and Persian subjects followed in 1784, before the French Academy feted Florian with membership in its august ranks. But his ties to the ancien régime compromised his position—like many compatriots, Florian had viewed Louis XVI as a "model of virtue, goodness, and justice"[22]—so that after the outbreak of the revolution the author was briefly imprisoned before his death at age thirty-nine.

It is difficult for postmodern readers to grasp the eighteenth-century allure of Florian, who peopled his literary world with unabashedly idealized shepherds inhabiting a semipristine natural state. Their irenic innocence shielded them from the corrupting influence of civilization and assorted ills of preindustrial urban life, an idea, of course, that had shaped the philosophy of one of Florian's favorite authors, Rousseau. Now the adolescent Fanny would have come to Florian through her Francophile father, who, it seems, was quite taken with the Frenchman's utopian visions, once again in vogue during the post-Napoleonic restoration of the Bourbon monarchy. In 1820 Abraham's favorite song by Fanny was the romance "Les soins de mon troupeau" (H-U 7) on verses from Florian's *Galatée*, which she set down early in April. Elicio, a shepherd who frequents the banks of the Tagus River in Spain, loves Galatée, daughter of a wealthy landowner. Nature, Florian explains, has endowed Elicio with many gifts, but fortune and love have not treated him as well. Meanwhile his rival for Galatée's affection, Erastre, has a good heart and knows more how to feel than to express. As for Galatée, she is "simple as the flowers of the fields" and beautiful, though she does not realize it. Love is far from her mind, for she is devoted to her flock:

Les soins de mon troupeau	The cares of my flock
M'occupent toute entière,	possess me entirely,
C'est de mes seuls agneaux	My happiness depends
Que depend mon bonheur.	On my lambs alone.

Fanny captures this naive sentiment in an unassuming strophic setting in C major, with a tuneful soprano line falling comfortably into a range barely exceeding an octave, a modest piano part buoyed by octave leaps in the bass, and scant, scrupulously regulated dissonances. In July 1820, during one of his business trips to Paris, Abraham came to know the piece well and praised his daughter's effort as "cheerful" (*heiter*) and "flowing naturally" (*fliessend natür-lich*), traits he urged her to emulate in her future efforts.[23]

Not as prepossessing for Abraham were Fanny's other Florian settings, which reveal for us considerably more sophisticated approaches to songwriting but in his paternalistic estimation were "too ambitious for the words." For example, in "Arbre charmant" (H-U 11, May 1820), on poetry from the pastoral *Némorin*, the piano emerges from its conventional, ancillary role to depict an enchanting tree that draws the narrator to its shade with memories of his lover Estelle, whose name he had carved into its bark. Somewhat as Schubert would achieve eight years later in *Der Lindenbaum* (*The Linden Tree*) in *Winterreise*, Fanny conjures up the rustling of the leaves through a fleeting piano figure in the treble that establishes the mood in a framing prelude and postlude. And, like Schubert, Fanny plays on the contrast between the major and minor modes: at "O souvenir cruel et doux" ("O cruel, sweet remembrance"), the dynamic level drops to *piano* as the music briefly dips from A major into A minor. There are additional major-minor dichotomies in her setting of "Plaisir d'amour" (H-U 8, April 1820), on verses from the Spanish *nouvelle Célestine*. Fanny's rendition of the timeless refrain, "Plaisir d'amour ne dure qu'un moment, chagrin d'amour dure toute la vie" ("The pleasure of love lasts but a moment, the pain of love an entire life"), offers nuanced readings of the text. First, she divides the music into two unequal phrases, one of four bars to encapsulate the transitory moment, the other extended to eight for the enduring *chagrin* (example 2.1). Rests interrupt this second phrase to create the effect of a prolonged melodic line. And the piano mirrors "chagrin d'amour" with a transient chromatic inflection that briefly touches on C minor before returning to the major.

In May 1821 Fanny undertook a more ambitious, though ultimately unfulfilled, project that would have capped her reading of eighteenth-century French poetry: she attempted to recompose "J'ai perdu tout mon bonheur" ("I have lost all my happiness"), the opening air of Rousseau's *Le devin du village* (*The Village Soothsayer*).[24] This was the celebrated *intermède*, or operatic diversion, that had rendered the philosopher-composer fashionable in 1752, so that, as he recorded in his autobiography, "no man in all Paris was more sought after."[25] Performed at Fontainebleau before the French monarchs (courtiers later overheard the tone-deaf Louis XV humming its repetitive yet ingratiating strains), *Le devin du village* had triggered the Querelle des Bouffons (1752–1754), the literary "war of the clowns" then raging over the merits of Italian versus French opera. Drawing on the Italian intermezzo, a short, comic work typically performed between the acts of a serious opera, Rousseau crafted the text and music of his composition fully bent on reform—to turn French music away from the Cartesian, scientific harmonic theories of the composer Jean Philippe Rameau and toward the supple, melodic attributes

EXAMPLE 2.1. Fanny Mendelssohn, "Plaisir d'amour" (1820)

of Italian opera. For Rousseau, the subjective, emotional powers of melody and language were essentially inseparable; indeed, the very origins of language lay in music. What was needed to regenerate French music was a return to an elemental vocal style drawn from the Italian recitative, carefully "timed to the speaking of the words."[26] Not surprisingly, the author of *La nouvelle Héloise* (*The New Héloise*) and *Du contrat social* (*The Social Contract*) favored in his musical subjects the celebration of an uncompromised rural life, as if to recapture something of a primordial state of grace.

For Fanny, Rousseau's score was not far removed from Florian's pastorals. In place of Elicio and Galatée, *Le devin du village* centers on the estranged shepherd and shepherdess Colin and Colette, eventually reunited through the intervention of the soothsayer. In Colette's opening air, she bewails her lost happiness, caused by Colin's straying. The scene inspired from Rousseau an artless melody in F major for Colette, accompanied by strings and winds, that dominates the texture. There is no distracting contrapuntal detail in the orchestra, which supports the melody with routine, uncomplicated harmonies. The syllabic vocal style, with one note per syllable of text, also underscores the preeminence and unadulterated simplicity of the melody.

A close student of Rousseau's score, Fanny nevertheless found her own path to the text. Casting her scene in F minor,❂[27] she began with a brief introduction for string orchestra that outlined a new, affecting melody for Colette, still conceived in Rousseau's restrained, syllabic style, as if to confirm that "the simplest tune could be the most compelling."[28] But after eighteen or so bars, Fanny struck a good portion of this effort and drafted a replacement. This time, for "Colin me délaisse" ("Colin abandons me"), she brought the minor-hued music to a pause, and to capture Colin's fickleness abruptly shifted tempo from Lento to Allegro, and key from F minor to F major. Now Colette delivered "Hélas, il a pu changer! Je voudrais n'y plus songer, j'y songe sans cesse" ("Alas, he could have changed! I no longer wish to dream of him, I dream of him endlessly") in a more animated, florid style, with characteristically two notes per syllable. A Da capo of the F minor Lento then rounded out the whole. Still not satisfied, she began afresh on the next page with yet another setting of the text, this one in D major, but was able to complete only its opening section before abandoning the project.

Fanny's work on "J'ai perdu tout mon bonheur" marks her first, albeit modest, effort at writing for orchestra and at approaching the world of the opera house.[29] But the unrealized fragment contrasts strikingly with an incredible feat of Felix, who in ten short weeks between September and November 1820 completed his first full-length opera, with an overture and fourteen numbers in full orchestral score. *Die Soldatenliebschaft* (*Soldiers' Love Affair*) was performed first with piano accompaniment for Abraham's birthday in December 1820. (An autograph arrangement for piano duet of the overture, presumably used by Felix and Fanny for the occasion, has survived.[30]) Then, on Felix's twelfth birthday (February 3, 1821), Abraham and Lea underwrote a full-scale production of the opera at their residence before invited patrician guests, with the best members of the royal *Kapelle* engaged for the orchestra. Among the soloists was Fanny, who sang the role of the soubrette Zerbine, reminiscent of Susanna in Mozart's *Marriage of Figaro*. The proud mother recorded some impressions of the young composer for her Viennese cousin Henriette von Pereira Arnstein—Felix posing Raphaelesque among the stupefied older musicians, at the end the soloists carrying the shy boy out to acknowledge the audience, and the success of the whole evening prophesying his future "calling."[31] Lea disclosed one other remarkable—and revealing—detail. Abraham had stipulated that his son create the work in artistic isolation; other than Fanny, no one, not even Zelter, saw a single note until the opera reached rehearsal. In short, we are to imagine the eleven-year-old prodigy producing an orchestral score of 200 pages without adult assistance.

Fanny was his only companion in this solitary endeavor; she was allowed to enter his creative world and indeed may have played a significant role. According to Lea, as a matter of course Felix dutifully submitted his compositions to Fanny's critique, and "mercilessly" struck whatever passages she questioned.[32] Fanny became his Minerva, the goddess of wisdom and patroness of the arts, who in Roman mythology sprang fully developed from Jupiter's head. But there was no reciprocal license for Fanny to explore fully her own creative space.

And so, a few months later, Felix premiered his second opera, *Die beiden Pädagogen* (*The Two Pedagogues*), which brought even the hardened Zelter to tears; but Fanny was not expected to complete her aria for *Le devin du village*, let alone compose a dramatic work, and she would have no debut before high society. Meanwhile, Felix's musical horizons continued to expand. As early as May 1819, as a surprise for Abraham, Lea engaged the court violinist C. W. Henning to instruct her son, and in 1820 Felix began lessons with Eduard Rietz, protégé of the French virtuoso Pierre Rode. There is no mention of comparable instruction for Fanny. Similarly, when around this time Felix was permitted to study with August Wilhelm Bach, organist of the Marienkirche, Fanny could only attend the lessons[33] but not take up the instrument in any meaningful way herself. In short, her artistic space remained centered on domestic music making, as she channeled her creativity in part through the accelerating accomplishments of her younger brother.

Nevertheless, throughout 1820 and into 1821 Fanny continued to fill her album with songs and piano pieces, several of which bear corrections in Zelter's gruff hand. What is more, scattered among these efforts are exercises in harmony and counterpoint, then the fundamental, complementary disciplines of any aspiring composer.[34] Not surprisingly, Fanny's studies paralleled those of Felix, who was diligently dispatching his own exercises in figured bass, chorale harmonizations, invertible counterpoint, canon, and fugue,[35] all under Zelter's watchful eyes. Thoroughly grounded in eighteenth-century German theoretical traditions, Zelter based his conservative tutelage of the siblings on the treatises of Bach's pupil J. P. Kirnberger. Through Zelter, in short, Felix and Fanny found renewed confirmation of their family's attraction to Bach's music and its intricate mysteries.

Chorale exercises in four parts formed a central part of Bach's teaching, in which well-known Protestant melodies served as *cantus firmi* (literally, "fixed melodies") and provided the source for various contrapuntal elaborations. Against the chorale tune, usually positioned in the soprano voice, the student had to create alto, tenor, and bass parts in a straightforward, note-against-note style. The purpose of this exercise was twofold—first, to enhance the understanding of the harmonic (vertical) relationships between the four parts and of the rules of voice leading, and second, to generate independent lines that could have melodic profiles of their own, so as to explore the potential contrapuntal (horizontal) nature of the chorale texture. Once the student attained sufficient competence, Zelter then assigned the task of composing new chorale melodies and of fleshing them out with the requisite three additional parts.

To this end, in 1820 Felix set to choralelike melodies of his own invention several religious verses of the eighteenth-century Saxon poet C. F. Gellert,[36] and Fanny's album reveals that she undertook similar exercises. Thus, sometime in December 1820, she notated the opening of her own chorale melody in D minor on the text, "Der Seele Ruhe ist es, Gott! Zu Zion dich zu loben, Gelübde dort dir zu bezahlen" ("It is the peace of the departed, O God, to praise you at Zion, to pay homage to you there"). Following these thirteen bars, we find a short recitative drawn from the Requiem Mass ("Erhöre des Gebets, zu dir kommt alles Fleisch"; Exaudi orationem meam, ad te omnis caro venit"; "Hear our prayer, to you all flesh returns") that prefaces a very Bachian-sounding aria in G minor, the reassuring text of which reads, "Ist uns der Sünden Last zu schwer, die Missethaten, du verzeihest sie" ("If the burden of our sins is too severe, you pardon our misdeeds"). A cursory glance suggests the beginnings of a sacred cantata by Fanny (H-U 25), but after the aria a surprise awaits us: a chorale in A-flat major that reuses the preceding texts, now stitched together to form eight phrases of a newly manufactured chorale melody. At Zelter's directive, Fanny herself composed the melody for this exercise, as is confirmed by several revisions Zelter himself entered into the part.

Exactly when Fanny proceeded from chorales to the more cerebral realm of pure counterpoint is unclear, but that step may have occurred as early as April 1820, when she was fourteen. Around this time, Zelter was beginning to introduce Felix to the art of counterpoint, and, most likely, Fanny's instruction followed in tandem. After finishing her setting of Florian's "Plaisir d'amour" on April 17, she labored over a brief sketch that elicited the comment, "O du schlechter Kontrapunkt" ("O, you wretched counterpoint"), through which she commiserated with untold generations of neophyte contrapuntists. Several pages further on in the album we discover the cause of her exasperation— a series of innocent-enough-looking numerals in Zelter's hand:[37]

$$1\,2\,3\,4\,5\,6\,7\,8$$
$$8\,7\,6\,5\,4\,3\,2\,1$$

that summarize the principles of invertible (double) counterpoint at the octave. In invertible counterpoint, the student sets against a given melodic line— Zelter again typically employed a preexistent chorale melody—a second, newly devised part, conceived so that the two can be "inverted," or flipped (i.e., with one part transposed an octave above or below the other), without infringing the rules of voice leading and dissonance treatment. Zelter's rows of numerals conveniently illustrated for Fanny how intervals change when subjected to this type of inversion: the interval of the second (e.g., the pitches C–D), for example, became a seventh (D–C), the third (C–E) a sixth (E–C), the fourth (C–F) a fifth (F–C), and so on. Owing to the centuries-old prohibition against two adjacent fifths, this exercise precluded two adjacent fourths, since under inversion they would produce the dreaded parallel fifths. Invertible counterpoint was thus a test of the composer's facility to manipulate and recombine the horizontal parts of music. The most renowned contrapuntists had demonstrated an awe-inspiring command of this erudite art—for instance, J. S. Bach, who in *The Art of Fugue* (begun around 1742) explored not only double but the more recondite triple and quadruple counterpoint, and Mozart, who in a breathtaking display near the end of his *Jupiter* Symphony K. 551 (1788) amassed rich textures of quintuple counterpoint, with five different subjects rotating simultaneously in dizzying contrapuntal permutations.

Zelter seems to have relished the special properties of double counterpoint. After inscribing his numerical series, he filled the page in Fanny's album with chorale phrases, including the beginnings of well-known Protestant melodies such as "Machs mit mir, Gott, nach deiner Güt," and Luther's popular Christmas hymn, "Vom Himmel hoch." Against these *cantus firmi* in sustained half notes, teacher and pupil devised new supplemental parts in more brisk rhythms, all calculated to observe the laws of Zelter's stolid numerical rows. In one final application of the technique, he even appropriated the famous minuet from Act I of Mozart's *Don Giovanni* and used its delectable theme to generate an additional exercise. Here Fanny had to conceive a second part in double counterpoint above or below the preexistent line, now no longer a measured chorale tune but an animated dance melody with considerable rhythmic variety.[38] Her solution was to place the second line in a delayed, answering imitation of Mozart's theme, effectively creating a texture with two duetlike melodic strands and an example of what we now term imitative counterpoint (example 2.2).

The goal of these introductory exercises was to approach the summit of counterpoint—fugue. By the 1820s, many musicians viewed fugal composition as an obsolescent science. Thus, in Paris, Hector Berlioz resisted the pedantic rigor of his fugal studies at the Conservatoire, where during the yearly Prix de Rome competition secluded candidates strained to compose cantatas culminating in wooden fugues. Berlioz found this academic pursuit "an unpardonable offence against musical expression"[39] and exacted some revenge

EXAMPLE 2.2. Fanny Mendelssohn, contrapuntal study on the Minuet from Mozart's *Don Giovanni*, Act I

by caricaturing the genre in the cavorting witches' dance from the finale of the *Fantastic Symphony* (1830). But in German realms, the grand fugal traditions of Bach and Handel, of Haydn and Mozart, endured, as evidenced by the late works of Beethoven (including the austere fugues in his final piano sonatas and string quartets[40]). For Zelter and the Mendelssohns, the fugue, especially as perfected by J. S. Bach, was no less than an article of faith. Thus, fugal composition became a lifelong proclivity of Felix; what is more, we have it on Zelter's authority that in December 1824, Fanny completed her own thirty-second fugue.[41] Regrettably, little has survived of these compositions, but we may infer that they occupied her from 1821 to 1824. Among the evidence is a sketch Zelter notated after a chorale exercise Fanny completed on the last day of 1820.[42] Here he introduced her to examples of the *dux* and *comes* (Latin for "leader" and "companion"), that is, the subject and answer, the building blocks of a fugue. A few pages later, Fanny copied a florid example in baroque style that began with a subject in B-flat major, answered by a counterpart in F major that she placed beneath the subject's continuation, or countersubject. Whether she ever completed the fugue is unclear, but if she did, it may have numbered among the thirty-two undertaken for Zelter.

ii

If Abraham and Lea encouraged Felix to explore musical genres freely—by 1821 he was composing operas, string symphonies, concerti, choral works, chamber music, piano and organ compositions, and songs—Fanny's compressed artistic sphere revolved around two domestic musical genres associated with the feminine: short character pieces for piano and songs. A way station toward her artistic "freedom" was Zelter's directive to compose minuets in eighteenth-century style, a few examples of which appear in the closing pages of her album. But her notated music from 1820 and 1821 reveals her special gifts as a songwriter; in the romantic terrain of the art song she first found expressive outlets for her creative ambitions.

Apart from the Florian settings—as we have seen, a concession to Abraham's tastes—Fanny produced German lieder in 1820 and 1821, including seven on texts by Herder, Novalis, Grillparzer, Goethe (three), and (in translation) Sir Walter Scott. As it happened, of these settings no fewer than five also inspired Schubert between 1815 and 1825, allowing some profitable comparisons between Fanny and the leading early nineteenth-century practitioner of the lied. There is nevertheless little question of direct influence here, for hardly any of Schubert's music was known at the time in Berlin, where song composition was largely beholden to Zelter's conservative conception of the genre.

Generally Fanny's piano accompaniments, like Zelter's, remain subordinate to the texts, though occasionally a tension emerges between her music and the poetry, as when, for example, a vivid piano figuration momentarily captures our attention. Her charming rendition of Herder's "Die Schönheit nicht, O Mädchen," conceived in April 1820 (H-U 10), offers an example. Neither beauty, finery, nor wit, the eighteenth-century theologian opines, ultimately moves our hearts, but nature alone. Fanny opts for a modified strophic setting, in part to accommodate an illustrative change in the piano accompaniment—in the third strophe, the introduction of rapidly descending scale fragments to depict the errant arrow of wit ("des Witzens Pfeil") that misses its mark. In her rendition of Grillparzer's *Light and Shadows* (*Licht und Schatten*, H-U 22, October 1820), she strengthened the piano part as an afterthought. Initially, the Austrian poet's sensuous verses, alternating between feminine and masculine lines,[43] prevailed over the music, as Fanny restrained the accompaniment to a few discrete chords. But upon finishing the draft, she appended some new piano passages to serve as transitions between the three stanzas and as a concluding epilogue. Through this means she highlighted the role of the piano and began to rebalance the relationship between the poetry and music, a process that would bring her conception of song composition closer to the world of the Schubertian lied.

A more sobering task was the composition of "Wenn ich ihn nur habe" ("If only I have him," H-U 17), the fifth of Novalis's *Geistliche Lieder* (1800), devotional poems prized by Fanny's uncle Friedrich Schlegel near the turn to the nineteenth century. Here, again, the piano receded into the background as Fanny limited the part to a few judicious chords to support these fervent verses:

Wenn ich ihn nur habe,	If only I have him,
Wenn er mein nur ist,	If only he is mine,
Wenn mein Herz bis hin zum Grabe	If until the grave my heart
Seine Treue nie vergißt:	Never forgets his faithfulness,
Weiß ich nichts von Leide,	I shall know nothing of pain,
Fühle nichts, als Andacht, Lieb' und Freude.	I shall feel nothing but devotion, love, and joy.

Fanny set only this first stanza, though she likely would have reused her music—a compact eight measures—for the remaining four, along the lines of Schubert's strophic setting completed less than a year earlier, in May 1819 (D 660). Presumably the similarities between their openings—both begin with a steplike ascent in the vocal part, and both restrict the piano part to modest chords articulated by rests—are coincidental, but Fanny's conception reveals one original touch not contemplated by Schubert. In the opening line, she changed the word *ihn* (him) to the familiar *dich* (you) and thus intensified on a personal level the longing for communion with Christ.

What drew Fanny in July 1820 to Novalis's impassioned text is not known, but a significant event in her life around this time—her confirmation as a Protestant—may have encouraged her choice. As early as April 1819, she had begun preparatory lessons with a clergyman, attentively monitored by Abraham so as to gauge their influence on his daughter's "heart and mind."[44] Now, around July 1820, he wrote candidly from Paris of the parental decision to baptize the children, of the religious divide that separated parents from children, and of his own deistic sympathies:

> Does God exist? What is God? Is He a part of ourselves, and does He continue to live after the other part has ceased to be? And where? And how? All this I do not know, and therefore I have never taught you anything about it. But I know that there exists in me and in you and in all human beings an everlasting inclination towards all that is good, true, and right, and a conscience which warns and guides us when we go astray. I know it, I believe it, I live in this faith, and this is my religion....The outward form of religion your teacher has given you is historical, and changeable like all human ordinances. Some thousands of years ago the Jewish form was the reigning one, then the heathen form, and now it is the Christian. We, your mother and I, were born and brought up by our parents as Jews, and without being obliged to change the form of our religion have been able to follow the divine instinct in us and in our conscience. We have educated you and your brothers and sister in the Christian faith, because it is the creed of most civilized people, and contains nothing that can lead you away from what is good, and much that guides you to love, obedience, tolerance, and resignation, even if it offered nothing but the example of its Founder, understood by so few, and followed by still fewer.[45]

In confessing her faith Fanny had "obtained the *name* of a Christian," and Abraham now enjoined the *Neuchrist* to follow her conscience, in order to "gain the highest happiness that is to be found on earth"—harmony with herself.

The hallowed verses of Goethe—by the 1820s the Nestor of German arts and letters—brought Fanny into the creative space of Zelter, who had committed fully one-third of his own 200-odd lieder to the poetry of his cherished *Duzbruder*, all without encroaching musically upon the supremacy of the texts. Of Fanny's initial Goethean efforts, *An den Mond* (*To the Moon*, H-U 19), *Nähe des Geliebten* (*Nearness of the Beloved*, H-U 36), and *Erster Verlust* (*First Loss*, H-U 18), the first two impress as relatively reserved and well within the limits of Zelter's style, especially when compared to those of the eighteen-year-old Schubert, who in 1815 had responded to the same poems.[46] In *An den Mond*, for instance, Fanny seems not to have progressed much beyond the first stanza, and her subdued piano triplets in E minor do not reflect the mysterious sheen of Schubert's natural landscape bathed in moonlight. In *Nähe des Geliebten*, Fanny contented herself with strophic repetitions of a terse, nine-bar passage (again supported by a few piano chords) to achieve an epigrammatic intensity. Like Fanny, Schubert compressed his rendition into a miniature time frame; a bare ten measures had sufficed for him, when, five years before, he released his lied as op. 5, no. 2. There are too some similarities in the harmonic plan of the two settings: apart from a brief motion to the relative minor key, both composers adhere firmly to the tonic major, a tonal symbol of the perceived proximity of the loved one, about whom the narrator first reminisces, then senses in a variety of visual and auditory images. But Schubert adds one impressive, purely musical device—a series of *pianissimo*, pulsating piano chords that begin harmonically off-key before ascending step by step to the tonic as the voice enters, as if to affirm the approach and figurative presence of the lover. Schubert's stratagem transforms his miniature into a highly expressive composition in which music and text briefly interact, mirror one another in various ways, and indeed achieve a new equilibrium.

Fanny's 1820 setting of *Erster Verlust* (she would revisit Goethe's poem three years later) reveals a distinctly new compositional stance that moved her closer to this Schubertian aesthetic. Now for the first time, and apparently independently of Schubert, her song begins with a significant piano introduction, a meandering, drooping melodic phrase that wavers ambiguously between F major and D minor.◉ The play on the major and minor duality is a musical conceit that translates into sound the central idea of the poem—the nostalgic longing for lost love—and, further, exploits the piano as an interpretive agent of the poem. Just as Goethe frames his verses with the lines, "Ach, wer bringt die schönen Tage, / Jene Tage der ersten Liebe" ("Ah, who brings back those sweet days, / Those first days of love") and a slightly modified variant, "Ach, wer bringt die schönen Tage, / Jene holde Zeit zurück!" ("Ah, who brings back those sweet days, / That golden time"), so Fanny reuses her piano introduction as an instrumental postlude. The central section, a "lament" that mourns the "lost happiness," turns to D minor, replicating on a larger scale the harmonic oscillation of the prologue between F major and D minor, the keys associated with the past and present. Curiously enough, Schubert's version (D 226) also exploits a major-minor dichotomy to capture the sense of yearning, but there is no piano prelude, only an unexpected afterthought. After the singer completes a final cadence in the major, the piano adds a *pianissimo* comment, one bar that turns the music back to the minor and dispels the security of the perceived major-keyed tonic and the reverie of lost happiness.

In approaching the poetry of the "wizard of the North," Sir Walter Scott, Fanny succumbed to a craze that swept over nineteenth-century Europe, with pirated translations of the narrative poems and *Waverly* novels, and operas such as Boieldieu's *La dame blanche* (1825) and Rossini's *Donna del lago* (1819),[47] the latter based on Scott's *Lady of the Lake* (1810), in the third canto of which Fanny (and later Schubert[48]) found the interpolated *Ave Maria* in the German translation of Adam Storck (1780–1822):

Ave Maria! maiden mild!	*Ave Maria!* Jungfrau mild,
Listen to a maiden's prayer;	Erhöre einer Jungfrau Flehen,
Thou canst hear though from the wild	Aus diesem Felsen starr und wild,
Thou canst save amid despair.	Soll mein Gebet zu dir hinwehen.

Set in the Highlands during the early sixteenth-century reign of James V (father of Mary Queen of Scots), Scott spun in rhyming couplets a romantic tale of clashing Highland and Lowland cultures, and inadvertently helped transform the Trossachs into a tourist destination. Sequestered with her outlawed father on an island in Loch Katrine, Ellen Douglas is wooed by two suitors, one of whom, Roderick Dhu, chieftain of Clan Alpine, rallies his clansmen to oppose the king. Before his defeat at the hands of James, Roderick overhears Ellen singing the "Hymn to the Virgin," conceived as a series of petitions on the familiar Marian greeting. Like Schubert, Fanny treated the piano as a harp-like instrument with rippling arpeggiations, the upper pitches of which gently sculpt a melodic counterpoint to Ellen's vocal entreaty (H-U 20). Once again, Fanny encased her setting with a piano prelude and postlude, revealing that she closely read the poem, for Scott himself had employed the framing device. Thus, preceding the hymn we read: "But hark! What mingles in the strain? / It is the harp of Allan-bane, / That wakes its measure slow and high, / Attuned to sacred minstrelsy. / What melting voice attends the strings? / 'Tis Ellen, or an angel, sings." And, after the last refrain of *Ave Maria*, "Died on the harp the closing hymn." As with her other early lieder, in 1820 Fanny entertained no idea of publishing her setting; nevertheless, the Scottish musician John Thomson, who visited Berlin in 1829, was so impressed that in 1832 he arranged to print it with the English text in the periodical *Harmonicon*,[49] the first occasion when her music appeared under her own name.

As a pianist, Fanny had demonstrated her precocity in 1818 by memorizing sizeable portions of the *Well-Tempered Clavier* for her father's delectation. Three years later, Lea described her daughter as "musical through and through," an accomplished pianist whose technique won praise from the usually taciturn youngest son of Mozart, Franz Xaver Wolfgang (1791–1844), who concertized in Berlin in 1821 and privately played duets with her.[50] Still, Lea noted, Fanny lacked Felix's composure and confidence in performance; what is more, while Felix composed full-length piano sonatas in three movements, Fanny again dutifully confined herself to short pieces of relatively small proportions. For example, the piano works in her album include miniatures that resemble two-part inventions in an obsolescent baroque style and impress as rather studious exercises for Zelter.

A few other pieces betray a more practical purpose, as we learn from Abraham's letter to his daughter of July 16, 1820.[51] When Fanny complained of the lack of etudes to strengthen her fourth and fifth fingers, he consulted in Paris with Marie Bigot, who advised diligent practice of Johann Baptist Cramer's *Studio per il pianoforte* (1810), a pedagogical work admired by Beethoven. To address the need further, Felix dashed off some exercises for his sister, and Fanny herself notated a few in her album. One (H-U 37) has brisk, running figurations exchanged between the hands, while another (H-U 39) features broken chords in triplets that show she was capable of negotiating some wide leaps. Yet another, the last entry in her album, is a study in digital independence, with a persistently winding line in sixteenth notes that Fanny turned upside down in mirror inversion midway through the piece. The composer evidently prized this Allegro agitato in G Minor (H-U 40), for in contrast to its untitled companions, she labeled it *Übungsstück* (Etude) and, furthermore, designated it to be copied out (*abzuschreiben*).[52]

Fanny's miniatures could also approach the stylistic world of her songs, as she readily transferred to the keyboard her lyrical, melodic gifts. A memorable example is an untitled draft in E minor, with a poignant melody in a high tessitura supported by arpeggiated triplets in the bass (H-U 29).[53] The texture and effect anticipate Chopin's early Nocturne in E Minor (op. post. 72, no. 1, ca. 1829), another piano work that clearly alludes to a vocal model.◉ In Fanny's draft, one may easily imagine a song whose text has been deleted— a "song without words," as it were. Though we usually attribute this Mendelssohnian genre to Felix, who later published several volumes of *Lieder ohne Worte*, Fanny claimed that as children the siblings played a musical game of adding texts to piano pieces, a pastime that may betray the source of the new genre.[54] Fanny's role in its creation—Felix's earliest *Lied ohne Worte* dates from 1828—is unclear, but we should note that she later habitually referred to many of her own piano compositions as lieder. Songlike features are especially pronounced in the untitled E minor draft of 1821, possibly her first example of a piano lied.

One final piano piece from Fanny's album stands alone and reveals quite a different side of her creative imagination. It was written for the artist Karl Begas (1794–1854), who visited the Mendelssohns in June 1821 and painted Felix's portrait.[55] A disciple of Antoine-Jean Gros, a leading representative of Empire art, Begas was a musical amateur, and for the occasion Felix and Fanny composed piano pieces. Felix's offering remains unidentified, but Fanny's survives as an untitled character piece crafted, ingeniously enough, upon the letters of the painter's name (H-U 41).[56] As Fanny perceived, German musical nomenclature could readily accommodate "Begas" as the pitches B-flat [B], E-natural [E], G [G], and A-flat [AS], from which, in turn, Fanny derived the principal theme of her composition. Undoubtedly, she would have been aware of the esoteric tradition of musical cryptography practiced by J. S. Bach, who had a penchant for "signing" his music with the chromatic tetrachord B-flat [B], A [A], C [C], B-natural [H]. But Fanny's gift to Begas betrays a certain playfulness and whimsy. In particular, she noticed that the first two pitches of his name, B-flat and E, formed the unstable, dissonant interval of the diminished fifth, and established straightaway a harmonic tension she was able to manipulate by bending her music first toward the key of F minor, and then A-flat major (example 2.3). Fanny's tonally ambivalent experiment looks forward to the enigmatic "sphinxes" of Robert Schumann's piano cycle *Carnaval* (1834), with its shifting permutations of the musical letters of that composer's name (S [A-flat or E-flat], C [C], H [B natural], and A [A]). Indeed, one variant sphinx Schumann employed—A–E-flat–C–B—forms the transposed mirror inversion of Fanny's encoded Begas motive, a coincidence that might encourage enigmatologists to wonder if she embedded additional cryptographic conundra in her music.

iii

For all her remarkable talents, Fanny remained a young lady of leisure in the segregated Berlin upper class, and inevitably the social mores had a dampening effect upon her musical pursuits. Thus, as early as July 1820, Abraham began to temper his daughter's aspirations. At age fourteen, Fanny herself brought up the obvious comparison to her brother and his accelerating, ever more public successes. Regrettably, her written thoughts about this issue do not survive, though we have Abraham's reply:

EXAMPLE 2.3.   Fanny Mendelssohn, untitled piano piece on "Begas" (1821)

"Begas" represented by pitches

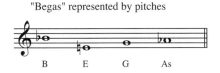

B   E   G   As

What you wrote to me about your musical occupations with reference to and in comparison with Felix was both rightly thought and expressed. Music will perhaps become his profession, whilst for *you* it can and must only be an ornament [*Zierde*], never the root [*Grundbass*] of your being and doing. We may therefore pardon him some ambition and desire to be acknowledged in a pursuit which appears very important to him, because he feels a vocation for it, whilst it does you credit that you have always shown yourself good and sensible in these matters; and your very joy at the praise he earns proves that you might, in his place, have merited equal approval. Remain true to these sentiments and to this line of conduct; they are feminine, and only what is truly feminine is an ornament to your sex.[57]

While conceding that had she been male, Fanny may well have "merited equal approval," Abraham nevertheless couched his paternal admonition in the condescending code of the time and reaffirmed a clear distinction between gender expectations. The feminine was decorative, the masculine, structural; the feminine was an ornament that embellished but did not challenge or supplant the male foundation. Ironically enough, Abraham's choice of metaphor contained some allusions to music. *Grundbass* was a term the theorist Kirnberger had used in the eighteenth century to designate the fundamental bass, the underlying, structural bass line of a composition; *Zierde*, or decoration, could be construed as well to apply to the various ornaments—trills, mordents, turn figures, and so on—that composers and performers added to adorn melodic lines. For Abraham, Fanny's musical activities operated at the surface level of decorations, while Felix's ambitions might well plumb the structural foundations of the art.

Despite this paternal clarification, a certain contradiction arose between the parents' expectations for Fanny and their willingness to expose her to the very best Berlin musical life had to offer. And so, in October 1820, Fanny and Felix together joined the Singakademie, where they sang as altos in the chorus and absorbed Zelter's conservative repertoire of eighteenth-century sacred music. What is more, both performed for the train of visiting virtuosi who concertized in Berlin and visited the Mendelssohn residence, including the pianists Carl Maria von Weber, who premiered his romantic opera *Der Freischütz* at the Berlin Schauspielhaus in June 1821, and another former wunderkind, Johann Nepomuk Hummel, Kapellmeister at Weimar; the French violinists Pierre Rode and Alexandre Boucher; and the French flutist Louis Drouet. Rode, among the few outside the Mendelssohns' circle to examine Fanny's songs, praised her Florian settings, though some he found "too French." Boucher, celebrated for the imperious Napoleonic poses he struck during his concerts, addressed her deferentially as "Cécile Mendelssohn," as if to compare her to Cecilia, the patron saint of music. Drouet, finding words too difficult to express his admiration for Fanny's *rares talen[t]s*, turned instead to the hardly less arduous task of writing a fugue for her.[58]

Increasingly, however, Fanny's musicality was subordinated to that of Felix, as Drouet discovered in a rather unexpected way. A little-known, recently rediscovered memoir of the singer Johanna Kinkel relates what happened when Felix, not Fanny, was asked to accompany Drouet in a composition for flute and piano:

> After the first chords it was observed that Drouet's flute stood in the Paris-Orchestra-Pitch, which was a semitone higher than the pianoforte, tuned in Berlin. Drouet excused himself now from playing, as he declared this impediment impossible to be overcome. Little Felix said, "Oh you want only to play your piece which is written in a, in a flat, then it will do." Drouet laughed at this proposal, which he took for a childish "naiveté" and said, a musician could not be expected to transpose a difficult piece in a lower key, because the whole fingering was to be changed. He was right in so far, as really in a piece which is written for the sake of showing brilliant passages, such a task would exact an immense ability. But Felix offered, if the composer could not conveniently manage to transpose the Solo a semitone lower, *he* Felix would transpose it [the piano part] in[to] a-sharp major, a higher key which would have 10 sharps, incl. x [i.e., double sharps].—This task the child overcame with perfect ease in a piece which he never had seen before.[59]

Was Fanny's sense of pitch as acute, and was she capable of such a remarkable feat? Lacking comparable documentary evidence, we do not know.

Be that as it may, Zelter did not hesitate to promote Felix's budding career. Writing to Goethe in August 1821, he mentioned a promising young pupil then deep in work on his third opera. Felix was "cheerful and obedient" and, Zelter added, the uncircumcised son of a Jew.[60] Late in October teacher and pupil, accompanied by Zelter's daughter, set out for Weimar, where Goethe, surrounded by musicians from the ducal court, examined the boy's musical prowess and concluded that he was indeed a second Mozart. Felix had brought along some of Fanny's lieder, which he shared with the poet's daughter-in-law, Ottilie, and Goethe himself heard a reading of Fanny's *Erster Verlust*, though his judgment has not survived.[61]

Fanny remained in Berlin, where she experienced Felix's first encounter with the German poet laureate vicariously through the stream of detailed letters he sent to Berlin. Adopting a mock parental tone, and momentarily usurping Zelter's role, she wrote: "How is your present Minerva—your Professor Mentor—satisfied with you? I hope (to put it like a tutor) that you acquit yourself *reasonably* and do honor to the training given by your *House-minerva*. When you go to Goethe's, I advise you to keep your eyes open and prick up your ears, and if you can't relate every detail to me afterwards, I will consider us ex-friends." In another letter, she addresses Felix as "my dear son." But despite the protective instincts of the elder sister, there is also a wistful sense in her letters of the growing separation between the siblings: "Adieu, my little Hamlet! Think of me when I turn 16.... Don't forget that you're my right hand and my eyesight, and without you, therefore, I can't proceed with my music."[62] Indeed, while the poet of *Faust* feted Felix, Fanny struggled to compose the first movement of a piano sonata in F major, but found the corrections arduous. No trace of the work, one of her first efforts to explore beyond the confines of songs and miniature piano pieces, has survived.

Though Fanny's music making remained restricted to domestic circles, in August 1821 she found an unusual opportunity to apply her creative talents. A favorite of her maternal grandmother, Bella Salomon, Fanny often played the piano during her visits, and on one occasion so impressed the declining septuagenarian that she asked Fanny to name a suitable reward. Remembering a distant though painful schism in the family—in 1805 the Orthodox Bella had cursed her son Jacob upon his baptism as a Protestant—Fanny requested forgiveness for her uncle. Bella agreed, and the two were reconciled "for Fanny's sake,"[63] as Bella dictated in a letter Fanny herself probably copied. In reply, Jacob thanked his niece for her skillful intercession and observed that in such matters the heart always ruled over the mind, even during those disputed occasions when one heard "much talk about the genius of great men." But then, lest gender lines become blurred, he clarified that he intended his comments to praise her feeling (*Gemüth*), not to tread too near her genius (*Genie*). And, indeed, in his next letter to Fanny, the "talk" was no longer about Fanny's musical mediations but Felix's triumphant visit to Weimar, for Jacob an omen that the boy would pursue a career in music.[64]

In Berlin Fanny's life was enriched by an expanding circle of friends. Among them was Therese Schlesinger, a soprano who sang with Fanny in the Singakademie chorus, studied with Zelter, and endured the drudgery of his figured bass exercises. After Therese successfully dispatched a role in Felix's *Die Soldatenliebschaft*, she became a daily visitor to the Mendelssohn residence, where, she reminisced, Fanny "displayed her beautiful, significant musical talent."[65] Though separated by class, Therese regularly attended the lavish Sunday musicales that the Mendelssohns began to organize around 1822, for which she played another, more familiar role: "Fanny once jokingly remarked that she desired to wear only jewelry I selected for her, and so I chose with conscientious rigor, and she regularly followed my advice."[66] To Fanny, Therese confided her secret engagement to the young baritone and actor Eduard Devrient, who also participated in productions of Felix's early operas and became an intimate of the family. Astonished by Felix's skill and precision at the piano, Devrient nevertheless found Fanny's playing still superior at this time.[67]

Of more momentous consequence was Fanny's introduction early in 1821 to a young painter then struggling to establish a career at the Berlin Academy

FIGURE 2.1. Wilhelm Hensel, self-portrait, pencil drawing (Staatliche Museen zu Berlin, Kupferstichkabinett, Hensel-Album 10/13)

of Arts. Wilhelm Hensel (1794–1861), son of Johann Jacob Hensel (1763–1809), a hapless Protestant minister who suffered reverses during the Napoleonic period, hailed from a small town in the contiguous March of Brandenburg. The novelist Theodor Fontane detected in Wilhelm an example of a vanishing Brandenburger characterized by "a combination of strength and beauty, of gaiters and toga, of Prussian militarism and classical idealism. The soul Greek, the spirit *altenfritzig* [resembling Old Fritz, i.e., Frederick the Great],...in Hensel everything remained in balance, none of these heterogeneous elements suppressed or conquered the others, and the new uniform of a regiment of the guards...interested him as much as the purchase of a Raphael"[68] (figure 2.1).

But this equilibrium contrasted with Wilhelm's childhood, when against his father's wishes he yielded to an irresistible longing to paint. Forced to become resourceful, the boy learned how to extract colorful tints from pressed berries and flowers, and painstakingly fabricated brushes from the hairs of calves.[69] Sent to Berlin to pursue engineering, after his father's death he resumed painting in earnest, studied anatomy and perspective, and as early as 1812 began exhibiting work at the Academy of Arts. One of his first efforts, *Der Engelssturz*, described as a "fantastic portrait painting," depicted a scene familiar from Revelations 12:7—St. Michael vanquishing Lucifer with a flaming sword. But the faces of the two combatants bore striking resemblances to Tsar Alexander and Napoleon, and in a Prussian capital still controlled by the French (Napoleon's *grande armée* was then marching through Russia), Hensel's allegory resonated as civil disobedience.[70]

When in 1813 Frederick William III called upon his subjects to rise up, Wilhelm volunteered to join a mounted troop of light cavalrymen. In a self-portrait he cuts quite the dashing figure: he wears a black beret that subdues a disheveled profusion of curly blond locks, sports a gallant Van Dyke beard, and musters himself in a uniform garlanded with a confusion of epaulets and cords.[71] Gripped with idealistic fervor, his sister Luise would have willingly accompanied him to the field, but, as she was compelled to care for her widowed mother, she offered instead patriotic verses.[72] Wilhelm saw action in several engagements and in 1813 experienced the Battle of the Nations in Leipzig, in which the Fourth Coalition dealt the French a significant defeat. Thrice wounded, Wilhelm twice marched in 1815 with the victorious allies into Paris, where his *altenfritzig* demeanor softened considerably before the treasures of the Louvre.

Though discharged from the army as a lieutenant and nominated for the Iron Cross, he faced dim employment prospects in an impoverished postwar Prussia. For the next few years, he made a meager living by illustrating calendars and almanacs and acquired considerable skill in the art of etching. Several of his illustrations appeared in volumes of fairy tales published by E. M. Arndt and Clemens Brentano, of whom the latter became an impassioned suitor for Luise Hensel's hand. But Wilhelm also tried poetry, his favorite avocation. In Fontane's judgment, Wilhelm was the purveyor of the "rhymed impromptu," who habitually decorated his letters with short poems and nimbly set down aphorisms of the moment, including these two quatrains, cleverly constructed, though probably failing to transport their readers:

Keinen Eindruck laß entschwinden,	Let no impression vanish,
Fürchtend daß die Zeit entweiche,—	Fearing the erasures of time,—
An den flüchtigsten der Striche	To the most fleeting strokes
Läßt sich die Erinnrung binden.	Memory lets itself be bound.

and

Vor des Künstlerblickes Tiefe	Before the artist's penetrating glance
Bleibt Natur nicht Hieroglype;	nature remains no hieroglyph;
Und was sein wird und gewesen,	and what will be and has been,
Weiß er aus dem Jetzt zu lesen.[73]	He knows how to read from the present.

Wilhelm's literary ambitions extended to writing a one-act comedy that reached the stage in 1817; what is more, as we have seen, he frequented the salon of Elisabeth von Stägemann, where the verses of his friend and fellow veteran Wilhelm Müller, the poet of *Die schöne Müllerin*, were read and sung. Utterly smitten by the alluring Luise, Müller counted himself with Brentano among her unsuccessful suitors.

At the Akademie, Wilhelm continued to display his work, including sepia drawings of scenes from the recent war and an allegorical painting titled *Knight's Struggle against a Sorceress*. Of the latter a brief catalogue description reads, "the sorceress, who might signify sinfulness, stands in dazzling, but upon closer inspection hideous splendor upon the back of a fire-spitting dragon."[74] Gradually Hensel's art came to the attention of the architect Karl Friedrich Schinkel, commissioned in 1818 to rebuild the royal theater (Schauspielhaus) after a fire had consumed it. Hensel in turn received the assignment of decorating an antechamber to its great concert hall, for which he painted scenes from Greek tragedy (e.g., Prometheus in chains, Elektra's recognition of Orestes), Shakespeare (Macbeth and the three witches), Goethe (Faust's compact with Mephistopheles), and Schiller (the death of Joan of Arc). By 1820, the artist Johann Gottfried Schadow, director of the Berlin Academy, was supporting Hensel's efforts to secure royal funding for further study in Italy. But before his departure in July 1823, his life was altered again when, early in 1821, he met Fanny.

The occasion was a state event, the visit of the heirs to the Russian throne, Grand Duke Nicholas and his Prussian wife, Grand Duchess Alexandra Feodorovna (the eldest daughter of Frederick William III, formerly Princess Charlotte). To regale his guests, the king ordered an entertainment on the subject of *Lalla Rookh*. This "Eastern romance" had appeared in 1817 from the pen of the Irishman Thomas Moore, best known perhaps for his *Irish Melodies*, including the poem "The Last Rose of Summer," set to a folk song and popularized in innumerable musical settings (in 1830, Fanny's brother would compose a piano fantasy on it). By the end of the nineteenth century George Saintsbury was reassessing *Lalla Rookh* as a "very remarkable poem of the second rank,"[75] and in the twentieth century Miriam Allen DeFord cautioned that readers could gather a few gems from Moore's romance only after "wading through vast stretches of scented mud."[76] Today, Moore's poetry is largely forgotten, but in the 1820s its perfumed exoticism created a veritable sensation in a Europe intrigued with a cultural "other," and in 1843 Robert Schumann found inspiration in Moore for his secular oratorio *Das Paradies und die Peri*.

The subject of *Lalla Rookh* (*Tulip Cheek*) is an Indian princess who travels—sometime during the sixteenth century, though we do not know exactly when, as Moore distorts the reader's sense of time—from Delhi to Kashmir to marry Akiris, the young king of Bucharia. Along the way, a young minstrel entertains her in verse with four escapist tales ("The Veiled Prophet of Khorassan," "Paradise and the Peri," "The Fire Worshippers," and "The Light of the Harem"), all stitched together with framing narratives in prose and accompanied by rather extensive annotations that impart a measure of pedantic erudition. The second tale, of the four the most sentimental and romantic, concerns a fallen Persian fairy who can reenter paradise only by discovering the gift "most dear to Heav'n." When, after two failed attempts, she succeeds by securing the tear of a repentant sinner, there falls a "light more lovely far / than ever came from sun or star," which the peri immediately recognizes as a bright angelic smile "from Heaven's gate to hail that tear / her harbinger of glory near!"[77] And so the peri reenters heaven, but not without some caustic commentary in the prose interlude that follows, where a chamberlain of the princess's train (perhaps the authorial voice of Moore) denounces the "lax and easy kind of meter" of the poem, and then pontificates, "If some check were not given to this lawless facility we should soon be overrun by a race of bards as numerous and as shallow as the hundred and twenty thousand Streams of Basra."

Perhaps midway through Moore's romance, the alert reader surmises that the minstrel is indeed the bridegroom Akiris, a conceit that proved irresistible to the Prussian and Russian royalty gathered in Berlin in January 1821 to celebrate their own matrimonial alliance. And so, to a festive march newly composed by the royal Kapellmeister Gaspare Spontini, a bejeweled assemblage of 168 nobility attired in Eastern costumes designed by Mountstuart Elphinstone, the governor of Bombay, processed into the Berlin palace, in living re-creation of the wedding party of Moore's fictive Indian princess. Of course Grand Duchess Alexandra, borne on a gold stretcher, played the part of Lalla Rookh, and her husband, the young minstrel. Convening before a stage with drawn curtains, the royals then viewed in succession twelve *tableaux vivants* designed by Wilhelm Hensel, depicting scenes from Moore's four verse tales, with aristocrats pressed into service to strike suitable poses.

For "Paradise and the Peri," Hensel selected three scenes—the peri seeking entrance into heaven; the peri offering in vain the last drop of blood from a dying soldier; and the peri securing the prize by presenting the tear of the repentant sinner. So impressive was the spectacle that a second performance ensued on February 11, this time before an invited audience of 3,000, when, presumably, Fanny and her family attended and made the acquaintance of Hensel. But the artist's son Sebastian later offered a different account. To preserve memories of the event, the Prussian king instructed Hensel to prepare a "drawing room book" with paintings of the *tableaux* he had designed. Executing his paintings *nach der Natur*, with the royals recalled to restrike their poses, Hensel then exhibited the results in his studio and there met Fanny, who had "come with her parents to admire his beautiful drawings."[78] And so began a relationship destined to unite, in the words of Sebastian Hensel, two Prussians of dissimilar backgrounds, one of a "Christian-Teutonic" type, the other of "pure Jewish descent."[79]

CHAPTER 3

Sibling Rivalry and Separation

(1822–1824)

Then they accompanied poor Felix's quartet. My only pleasure all the while
was to study physiognomy. Then I had to play something, and now, "bid me
not speak, bid me be silent."

—Fanny Mendelssohn Bartholdy, July 1822

If Wilhelm Hensel's appearance added a new layer of complexity to Fanny's life,
her brother provided continuing musical and intellectual sustenance. Strengthening the sibling relationship was a most rare, intimate bond of artistic communication. "Up to the present moment," she observed in 1822, "I possess his
unbounded confidence. I have watched the progress of his talent step by step, and
may say I have contributed to his development. I have always been his only musical adviser, and he never writes down a thought before submitting it to my judgment."[1] The occasion for this matronly comment is unknown, but she may have
recorded it in a biographical sketch of Felix begun around this time but now
unfortunately lost. According to her son, Sebastian, Fanny's document included
a year-by-year accounting of Felix's compositions, as if she intended to capture
for future biographers the breathtaking pace of his early development. But cataloguing her brother's music and recording his widening ambitions in opera, the
symphony, and other large forms must have reminded her of the gendered divide
separating them. If his compositions and performances drew increasingly public attention—in June 1822 Heinrich Heine, echoing Goethe, likened Felix to a

second Mozart[2]—her musicianship remained a guarded family secret while her musical aspirations were constrained within the domestic sphere.

One artistic outlet was open to Fanny: the private concerts given at the family residence on the Neue Promenade, which coalesced late in 1821 into a fortnightly Sunday institution that Lea referred to as *Sonntags Übungen*, or "Sunday practices."[3] Here we find the antecedents for the lavish gatherings over which Fanny later presided in Berlin during the 1830s and 1840s, though regrettably, information about her participation during the early 1820s is meager indeed. Clearly, the principal purpose of the concerts was to showcase Felix's precocity, to secure a sympathetic venue for readings of his compositions. Reports from the music theorists A. B. Marx and Heinrich Dorn reveal, for instance, that Felix directed from the piano performances of his string symphonies, of which he composed a good dozen between 1821 and 1823, with members of the ensemble engaged from the elite royal orchestra.[4] Whether Fanny routinely presented her own compositions to the invited guests is uncertain, but we do know that she contributed significantly as a piano soloist. Helmina von Chézy, librettist of Carl Maria von Weber's romantic opera *Euryanthe*, visited Berlin in 1822 and heard Fanny render many of Weber's piano works. She compared Fanny's execution to that of the composer himself and penned this gushing memoir: "[The music] streamed forth like woodland fragrances, like the morning hymns of forest birds at the rustling of the treetops."[5]

A letter from Lea to Henriette von Pereira Arnstein discloses the program of one musicale held on March 24, 1822, before an audience graced by Prince Antoni Henryk Radziwill, a brother-in-law of the Prussian king and the future dedicaté of Beethoven's *Namensfeier* Overture, op. 115. According to Lea, on this occasion the visiting Frankfurt pianist Aloys Schmitt made an appearance; Felix directed one of his string symphonies and at the prince's bidding improvised on a fugal subject of Mozart; and Fanny performed a piano concerto by Hummel.[6] Exactly which concerto is unclear, but it may have been the pensive Piano Concerto in A Minor, op. 85, then embedded in Felix's musical consciousness, for that very year he modeled his own virtuoso A minor piano concerto on Hummel's work and presented it to Fanny, among the first of many fraternal musical gifts to come. Conceivably, she then introduced it at the Sunday concerts.

The first half of 1822 was a relatively fallow period for her own compositions, but in at least three works she encroached, unwittingly or wittingly, upon the compositional space of her brother. In May she conceived a setting of Ludwig Uhland's *Die Nonne* (*The Nun*), a work that Felix eight years later silently incorporated into his second collection of published lieder as op. 9, no. 12. Fanny required only thirty measures in a dark, subdued A minor to capture the medieval aura of Uhland's sentimental verses about a young woman who, entering a convent to honor her deceased lover's memory, reveres him as an angel before she herself expires beneath a Marian image:

Im stillen Klostergarten	In the still convent garden
Eine bleiche Jungfrau ging	walked a pale maiden,
Der Mond beschien sie trübe,	the moon shone upon her gloomy figure,
An ihrer Wimper hing	on her eyelashes hung
Die Thräne zarter Liebe.	tears of tender love.

Fanny set Uhland's four stanzas strophically and devised a simple yet endearing melody with hypnotic pitch repetitions. Animating the music is a restless figure in the piano that connects the vocal alternations of long and short notes, as Fanny matches the poet's triple-stressed lines with regularly recurring patterns.[7] When Felix appropriated her song in 1830, it appeared intact save for one notable retouching—the piano postlude was fitted with an expressive crescendo and diminuendo and thickened in texture by the addition of a static, repeated pitch in the tenor, an evocative echo of the opening vocal phrase (example 3.1). Did Fanny contribute these revisions, or were they the creative afterthoughts of her brother, an example of the intuitive musical exchanges between the two?

Between January 29 and February 19, 1822, Fanny drafted a considerably more ambitious composition for piano solo. At first glance, the Allegro assai moderato in E Major (H-U 44) might not warrant much scrutiny, but on the inner cover of the autograph appears in her hand the terse comment *angefangene Sonate* (beginning of a sonata), marking it as her first surviving essay in the genre.[8] For Fanny the weighty traditions of the piano sonata, the male-dominated category of Haydn, Mozart, Clementi, Beethoven, and countless others, would have contrasted with the feminine "lightness and naturalness" Abraham had encouraged in her settings of Florian. At the center of the instrumental genre was sonata form, since the late eighteenth century the dominant structural paradigm for larger-scale instrumental compositions such as sonatas, quartets, and symphonies, all of which the young Felix was then producing in ever increasing quantities. By attempting a piano sonata, Fanny was thus expanding her compositional horizons into Felix's creative space and exploring a new measure of creative freedom, as she endeavored to develop a musical argument over a temporal span extending well beyond the relatively compact space of the lied and short piano character piece.

She approached her task with some reserve, for the opening theme in E major, fitted with an expressive turn and sixteenth-note roulades, suggests not so much a piano sonata as the instincts of a lyrical songwriter, a composer predisposed more to vocal ruminations than to sculpting large-scale harmonic blocks of sound, as Beethoven had accomplished in many of his piano sonatas. Further, Fanny's application of sonata form impresses as somewhat tentative— tentative, that is, if we judge her essay according to conventional expectations of the form. Tripartite sonata form typically entailed (1) an exposition that

EXAMPLE 3.1.   (a) Fanny Mendelssohn, *Die Nonne*, original version of the ending (1822); (b) final version of the ending, as Felix Mendelssohn's op. 9, no. 12 (1830)

presented the essential thematic material (often in two groups) and established a tonal polarity between two contrasting keys (in this case, E major and B major, the tonic and dominant tonalities), (2) a central development section that then elaborated the material through various techniques (e.g., thematic concision, fragmentation, or expansion) and explored a succession of keys further removed from the tonic, and (3) a counterbalancing recapitulation that reestablished the thematic succession of the exposition and concluded the movement in the tonic key. Fanny's Allegro is striking for its relative freedom

from this model. Thus, in the exposition, there is no discrete secondary thematic complex, and she minimizes the second key area (B major), so that it
does not appear until the last three bars of the section. Further, she devotes a
fair portion of the exposition to quasi-developmental techniques, with excursions to such distant keys as F major and B-flat major that enrich harmonically
the tonic-dominant tonal axis of E and B major. In contrast, Fanny does direct
the development toward a tonal goal, by centering a substantial portion on
the key of C-sharp minor. The material leading up to the recapitulation introduces one more unexpected interruption of the formal process—a prolonged
cadenza with spiraling turns performed ad libitum that again remind us of the
vocal origins of the opening theme.

In short, Fanny's Allegro evinces a tension between an irrepressible lyricism and the mechanical working out of sonata form, a tension encountered
not infrequently in her larger-scale instrumental compositions and, it should
be added, in some of the piano sonatas of another songwriter—Schubert.
That Fanny in 1822 did not produce a textbook example of sonata form could
betray her inexperience in venturing beyond the short character piece. But
one could also argue, perhaps, that she had no intention of replicating a conventional blueprint; since there was no prospect of publishing her composition, she may have designed the movement to explore the adaptability of the
sonata-form process to an essentially lyrical inspiration. Be that as it may,
she abandoned her effort; no additional movements survive, and her sonata
remained a fragment.

By far Fanny's most ambitious achievement of 1822 was the Piano Quartet
in A-flat Major (H-U 55), begun on May 1 but not finished until November 23.[9]
Here was another opportunity to explore a large-scale work far removed from
the miniature dimensions of her lieder and to gain further experience in handling sonata form, now through the medium of chamber music, albeit via
an unusual genre with few historical precedents. Fanny would have known,
of course, the two masterful piano quartets of Mozart (K. 478 and 493), and
examples by Louis Ferdinand, the gallant Prussian prince who had died in
combat at the hands of the French in 1806. But most likely there was another,
more immediate incentive for her foray into chamber music: in 1821, her
twelve-year-old brother composed a piano quartet in D minor and almost
certainly performed it that year in Weimar for Goethe. So we must consider
the possibility that the following year Fanny wrote her quartet in response to
Felix and that, as she continued after abandoning her piano sonata to explore
the larger forms, she was not only entering his compositional arena but, in
effect, competing with him.[10]

Though she does not seem to have commented on this topic, Felix later
did. In 1838 the English publisher J. Alfred Novello pressed the internationally
acclaimed composer of *St. Paul* to submit a composition to a prize competition. His refusal includes this revealing statement: "I cannot do it, if I would

force myself to it; and when I was compelled to do so, when a boy, in competition with my sister and fellow-scholars, my works were always wonders of stupidity—not the tenth part of what I could do otherwise. I think that is the reason why I felt afterwards such an antipathy to prize-fighting in music, that I made a rule never to participate in it."[11]

That sibling rivalry was a possible motivating factor for Fanny to write a piano quartet might explain some similarities between the slow movements of the siblings' compositions, both of which fall into a ternary *ABA* form, with a lyrical opening in the major followed by an agitated, contrasting middle section in the minor. On the other hand, the two quartets are in other respects conspicuously dissimilar. The key Fanny chose, A-flat major, is as far removed from D minor in the tonal system as possible, as if she intended to separate her work from her brother's. And the general character and layout of her first movement, by far the weightiest of the four, depart considerably from Felix's effort. Where he strove to integrate the piano, violin, viola, and cello into an ensemble that shared motivic and thematic material, she chose to distinguish the piano from the string complement, with brilliant keyboard passagework in the style of Hummel and Weber offset by relatively modest, reserved comments in the strings.❷ While Felix emphasized connections between the four instruments, Fanny underscored the *concertante* potential of the ensemble, which assumed more the character of a piano concerto with string accompaniment. What is more, her treatment of sonata form was again anything but conventional. True, the exposition now fell into two contrasting thematic groups, but instead of concluding the exposition with a strong cadence, Fanny paused on a dissonant chord and then launched her development with the second theme in the exotic key of E major, as if to interrupt the formal rigor of sonata form with an improvised fantasy. In the recapitulation, she omitted altogether the return of the second theme, and instead assigned much of the section to virtuoso display in the piano.

Less successful, but no less experimental, were the last two movements, a minuet with cross accents on the second beat reminiscent of a Beethovenian scherzo, and a highly condensed Presto finale that, for at least one scholar, leaves the listener somewhat at a loss, as it is "too weighty for a coda, but too compact for a finale and of too little importance."[12] That Fanny chose to link the two final movements shows that Beethoven's influence was beginning to assert itself. In 1808, of course, Beethoven had linked the third and fourth movements of his Fifth Symphony, and the device seems to have captured Fanny's attention in the Piano Quartet, as it would Felix's in two unusual chamber works of 1824 and 1825, his Piano Sextet and Octet.

Fanny struggled considerably to compose her quartet. In June she admitted to Zelter that her progress was tediously slow, and she feared that without his assistance the piece would founder.[13] Her autograph betrays signs of difficulties; far from a fair copy, it contains uncorrected errors and harmonic and rhythmic inconsistencies. Furthermore, no string parts appear to have survived, so the question remains open whether the work was ever performed before its first edition, delayed 177 years, finally appeared in 1989.[14] (Ironically, Felix's D Minor Piano Quartet, among many juvenilia he passed over, had to wait even longer, until 1997, for its publication.)

Still, the "competition" between the siblings took an incontrovertible turn in 1823 and 1825, when Felix responded to Fanny's effort by releasing in quick succession three new piano quartets in C minor, F minor, and B minor as his opp. 1, 2, and 3, with official, and of course public, dedications to Prince Radziwill, Zelter, and Goethe.[15] The publisher was the respected Parisian firm of Moritz Schlesinger, who in 1823 brought out Beethoven's final piano sonata, op. 111. Felix's compositional debut was thus an international event, one that garnered critical comparisons between him and Mozart, while Fanny's first chamber music essay languished in obscurity.

i

On July 6, 1822, a festive caravan of carriages bound for Switzerland conveyed the Mendelssohns, the children's tutor Carl Heyse, a Doctor Neuburg, and servants from Berlin at the beginning of a leisurely summer vacation. As it happened, July 6 was the birthday of Wilhelm Hensel, who had prepared for Fanny's departure by turning to poetry and confiding to her these lachrymose verses:

Lebewohl	Farewell
Wohl hab' ich dich, lieb' Angesicht	Well for the last time
zum letzten Mal gesehn,	have I seen your lovely face.
doch weine nicht, ach weine nicht	But do not cry, oh, do not cry,
und laß mich stille gehn.	and let me go quietly.
Ich weiß es nicht, wie mir geschieht,	I know not what will become
	of me
muß ich dein Weinen sehn.	if I must see your crying.
Ach weine nicht, ach weine nicht,	But do not cry, oh, do not cry,
und laß mich stille gehn.	and let me go quietly.
Dein Weinen mir das Herze bricht,	Your weeping breaks my heart,
ich kann nicht widerstehn,	I cannot deny it,
und lässest du dein Weinen nicht,	and if you do not cease,
so kann ich nimmer gehn.	then I can never leave.

Fanny responded by setting them as a song in a style of slow lament (H-U 48),[16] a compelling example of using music as autobiographical release—a diary translated into sound. Perhaps she conceived the distinctive initial harmonic gambit, which emphasizes the subdominant (C minor) at the expense of the tonic (G minor), to symbolize the impending separation by means of a harmonic break. It was a simple but effective device that looked ahead to the opening of the slow movement of Robert Schumann's Piano Quintet op. 44 of 1842.🅮 But in 1822 Fanny's music only served to arouse Wilhelm's passion, and so he recorded these verses in her album, two days before the family's departure:

Ein Liedlein hör ich rauschen,	I hear a little song murmuring,
das folgt mir überall,	that follows me everywhere,
die Englein selber lauschen,	even the angels eavesdrop,
es horcht die Nachtigall.	as does the nightingale.
Und wie der Mond die feuchten,	And as the moon disperses
tiefbraunen Schatten bricht,	the damp, deep brown shadows,
ergeht ein stilles Leuchten	there escapes a soft glow
vom lieben Angesicht.[17]	from a lovely face.

The "lovely face" of this poem is of course the *liebes Angesicht* of the earlier *Lebewohl*; and the "little song" that haunted the lovestruck Wilhelm is Fanny's lied, all of thirty-one bars in length.

Traveling "like princes—poets, artists, and princes all in one,"[18] the Mendelssohns proceeded to Magdeburg and the Harz Mountains before pausing in Cassel, the capital of the Electorate of Hesse, where they enjoyed "animated musical discourse" with the recently installed Kapellmeister, the celebrated violin virtuoso and composer Louis Spohr. Zelter had provided a letter of introduction, and Spohr arranged a chamber music party, in which he participated in reading a quartet by Felix, presumably the Piano Quartet in D Minor. Whether Fanny performed that day or remained a silent auditor is unknown, but at their next destination, Frankfurt, she played the contrasting roles of piano virtuosa and demure young lady of leisure. Here their host was the pianist Aloys Schmitt, teacher of the young Ferdinand Hiller, who recalled the event in his memoirs. Once again Felix's quartet was featured, but Hiller was "most struck by his sister Fanny's performance of Hummel's *Rondeau brillant* in A, which she played in a truly masterly style."[19] A bravura display piece, the rondo for piano and orchestra had appeared in 1814 as Hummel's op. 56; presumably, for the Frankfurt occasion, a string quartet or small ensemble replaced the orchestra.

Fanny remembered the event in a considerably less flattering light than Hiller, and indeed deprecated her own efforts by quoting the opening line of one of Mignon's plaintive lieder from Goethe's *Wilhelm Meister*: "Then they accompanied poor Felix's quartet. My only pleasure all the while was to study physiognomy. Then I had to play something, and now, 'bid me not speak, bid me be silent' ["Heiß micht nicht reden, heiß mich schweigen"]. The whole room full of strange people, pupils and friends of Schmitt's, the accompaniment very bad, I myself trembling all over. My failure was such that I could have beaten myself, and all the others, with vexation. To break down like that in the presence of twenty virtuosi!"[20] The disconnect between Ferdinand Hiller's and Fanny's account is remarkable indeed: what Hiller recalled as a masterly performance Fanny relegated to an unmitigated failure. It was not the first nor the last time that her insecurities about performing beside male virtuosi would get the best of her. But her insecurity masked her annoyance, even competitiveness. The musicians at Schmitt's gathering were not up to the task of accompanying "poor" Felix or Fanny, and she concluded, "I must quit the subject, or I shall grow angry again."[21]

After visiting Darmstadt, Heidelberg, and Stuttgart, the Mendelssohns reached Switzerland on July 28. While Felix, who, as Fanny reported to Zelter, could not remain idle for an hour,[22] sketched landscapes, she wrote letters. The family was amazed, she disclosed to her aunt Hinni (wife of Abraham's brother Joseph), to trace the origins of the familiar Rhine to a "chalky, colorless stream" that metamorphosed into green tints at Lake Constance and then became a veritable contest between blues and greens at the raging cataracts of Schaffhausen.[23] From Zurich the family made several excursions—to Glarus and Linthal, a *wildromantisch* area, Fanny wrote, hardly fit for human habitation, and to the Tellskapelle near Immissee, where William Tell had allegedly dispatched the tyrant Gessler. After observing snow-crested mountains from different proximities, the family joined a venturesome party of thirty-four intent upon ascending the Rigi. Fogbound halfway up for an entire day, they finally reached the summit and absorbed the sublime panoramas. "To wake up on the Rigikulm on a lovely morning," Fanny recalled, "is striking and highly moving. An hour before sunrise, when the heaven is clear, the Alphorn sounds, rousing all the residents of the house with its sharp, piercing tone. Now amid the darkness stirs the liveliest bustle in the narrow quarters,...and figures worthy of Hogarth's brush emerge....But no brush, no words capture the majesty of nature, how first the highest peaks of the Bernese snow-clad range turn red hot from the sun, then the lower, nearer mountains, and finally the lakes and valleys are illuminated. It is a sublime, divinely awesome sight to behold."

From Lucerne the Mendelssohns cruised across the shimmering Lake of the Four Cantons, experienced a driving hailstorm on the Urnersee, and pursued a road near Altdorf "worked into the rocks with the aid of gunpowder," for Fanny a "grand illustration of the power of human perseverance, which can even bend the will of Nature."[24] As they approached the St. Gotthard Pass, an intense desire to see Italy overpowered her, and she again turned to song, to Goethe's irrepressible verses of longing from *Wilhelm Meister*, "Kennst du das Land wo die Citronen blühen?" ("Do you know the land where the lemon trees bloom?").[25] Titling her setting *Sehnsucht nach Italien* (*Yearning for Italy*, H-U 50), she animated it with rippling arpeggiations to suggest the glowing fruit, tall laurel, and gentle breeze, and followed, probably unknowingly, the precedent of Schubert, who in 1815 had employed a similar device when he rendered the same verses as *Mignon* (D. 321). The restless answer to the poet's question—"Dahin, dahin möcht ich mit Dir, O mein Geliebter, ziehn" ("There, there I would like to go with you, O my beloved")—of course bore special meaning for Fanny, as she contemplated Wilhelm's impending departure the following year for five years of study in Italy. But in 1822 she was unable to fulfill her desire, when for lack of supplies her family had to turn back to Lucerne.

After visiting Thun, Interlaken, and Bern, early in September the travelers reached Vevey on Lake Geneva, where Fanny imagined the weather might yet allow an excursion to the Borromean Islands on the Lago Maggiore, so that she could experience Italy and, as she rhapsodized, be "carried on clouds to paradise."[26] But this idealized, romantic transport too was frustrated, and the family visited instead Voltaire's château at Ferney, then viewed Mont Blanc near Chamonix before beginning their return journey via Basel. By the end of September they were again resting in Frankfurt.

Refreshed, the siblings participated in more music making, this time before Johann Nepomuk Schelble, director of the Cäcilien-Verein, a choral organization founded in 1818 that specialized in Catholic sacred music and Handel. According to the musician F. X. Schnyder von Wartensee, Felix and Fanny performed in a masterly (*meisterhaft*) way Hummel's Sonata in A-flat Major for Piano Duet, op. 92,[27] but Fanny receded all too soon into the dumb-struck spectators who witnessed Felix improvise in a learned style on subjects from two J. S. Bach motets that Schelble had just rehearsed.

Then, in a private ceremony on October 4, Abraham and Lea closed the spiritual breach in their family by converting to the Protestant faith. Abraham Moses became Abraham Ernst, and Lea, adopting her sons' names, Lea Felicia Pauline.[28] What is more, the Mendelssohns now added the second surname Bartholdy, emulating the distant precedent of Lea's brother Jacob (see p. 21). Abraham and Lea's ultimate intent, it seems, was to separate themselves even further from the Mendelssohns. Just as Jacob Salomon had changed identities to Jacob Salomon Bartholdy and then to Jacob Bartholdy, so, presumably, in time would the Mendelssohn Bartholdys contract their name to Bartholdy and sever the final familial ligament to the enlightened Judaism of Moses Mendelssohn.

Details of the parents' baptisms are not known, but what is clear is that they kept their conversion a secret from Lea's Orthodox mother, Bella Salomon. Whether they discussed their new faith with Goethe in Weimar, the family's next destination, is impossible to determine. In any event, Felix was once again the center of attention, as the septuagenarian poet bid him awaken "all the winged spirits" that had slumbered in Goethe's piano since Felix's first visit the year before. For hours Felix entertained the Weimar circle, playing the young psalmist David to Goethe's Saul, but, Lea informs us, the éminence grise also received Fanny, who "had to play a good deal of Bach to him" and indeed performed her Goethe settings with his approval.[29] Among the auditors was Adele Schopenhauer, mother of the philosopher, who commemorated Fanny's musicianship with a delicate silhouette prepared for her album. It depicts the god of love brandishing an arrow and lyre, and offers this explanation: "Eros had lost his bow; his muse loaned him a lyre and, drawing its strings as a cord, he shot with it. Since then several tones, like arrows, have struck the heart."[30]

ii

Returned to Berlin, Fanny performed "beautifully and with polish" Felix's Piano Concerto in A Minor at a gathering Zelter organized on October 22.[31] But this private affair was well removed from Felix's public reading of the same work early in December at a formal concert of Anna Milder-Hauptmann, prima donna *assoluta* of the Berlin opera and the singer for whom Beethoven had created the role of Fidelio. A short *Übungsstück*, or etude, in C major recorded on November 6 (H-U 53) shows that Fanny continued to refine her piano technique. The piece offers a brisk study in cascading staccato chords exchanged between the hands.[32] But undoubtedly her principal concern was reuniting with Wilhelm, who by drawing the family's portraits now entered, at least mentally, "into the circle to which he wished to belong."[33] Thus on her birthday, November 14, he inscribed a sketch of the curly-haired Felix, and presumably for this occasion completed as well an idealized drawing of Fanny Cäcilia as the patron saint of music, Cecilia, whose feast day fell eight days later. In a robe and barefoot, Fanny appears with a floral wreath in her hair and holds an unrolled scroll of music, as three angels peer over her shoulders (figure 3.1).

Concurrently Fanny deepened her relationship with Luise Hensel, the artist's sister, who, having declined matrimonial proposals from the poets Wilhelm Müller and Clemens Brentano and from Fanny's piano teacher Ludwig Berger, had abandoned her father's faith in December 1818 to embrace Catholicism and to prepare for a life of asceticism and charities. Luise actively urged her brother Wilhelm to convert, a temptation, we shall see, that soon enough caused a crisis in the Mendelssohn household. The driving force in Luise's life seems to have been an unresolved tension between transitory sensual cravings and a more deep-seated spiritual longing, a tension often foregrounded in her poetry. After returning from the Swiss sojourn, Fanny set two of Luise's poems, one of which, "Die Sommerrosen blühen" (H-U 57), begins with this sensual image marking the passage of time:

FIGURE 3.1. Fanny Mendelssohn Bartholdy as Cecilia,
patron saint of music, 1822, pencil drawing by Wilhelm
Hensel (Berlin, Mendelssohn Archiv, BA 188,7)

Die Sommerrosen blühen	Summer roses are blooming
und duften um mich her,	and wafting fragrantly around me,
ich seh' sie all verglühen,	I see them all dying away,
will keine Blumen mehr.	I'll have no more flowers.

The transitory quality of beauty is a common enough poetic metaphor, but
here the summer roses have been read recently as symbolizing the "unbearable
passivity of women's lives" and Luise's self-identification with the roses.[34] As it
happened, Luise had written her verses in 1813 or 1814 to mark her separation
from Wilhelm, then experiencing combat in the Napoleonic wars.[35] By composing the song in December 1822, Fanny, in effect, now assumed the poetic

persona, just months before Wilhelm's departure for Italy and the beginning of a new five-year separation.

At the end of the year Fanny's relationship with Wilhelm in fact took a decisive turn when he pressed his suit more earnestly. On Christmas Eve he gave her a new volume of verse by his friend Wilhelm Müller, *77 Poems from the Posthumous Papers of a Traveling Waldhornist*, a six-part anthology that included *Die schöne Müllerin*, a reworking of the *Liederspiel* that Müller, Wilhelm, and Luise Hensel and their friends had performed in Berlin in 1816. If in Müller's eyes the fair miller's daughter of the cycle had been a literary transformation of his beloved Luise, for Wilhelm the poems now barely contained his own longing for Fanny. And so, as if to impersonate the poet, he added to the volume a new title page, with Müller's portrait and this dedicatory poem to Fanny, "signed" below with Wilhelm's own portrait:

Dies Buch voll Lust und Wehmuth	This book full of joy and melancholy
im bunten Liedertraum	in a motley dream of lieder
an Deinen Weihnachtsbaum	I hang in quiet humility
hang' ich in stiller Demuth.	on your Christmas tree.
Und hätt ich es gedichtet	And if I had created it,
Du Holde, glaube mir,	Thou dear one, believe me,
so spräche viel von Dir,	it would speak much of thee,
war viel an Dich gerichtet.	much of it would be for thee.
Sey Dir denn zugeeignet,	May its contents, then,
was es enthält in sich,	be dedicated to thee,
und zum Beweis hab' ich	and as proof
mich selber unterzeichnet.[36]	I myself am signatory.

But Wilhelm had not reckoned on Lea intercepting his amorous sentiments, expressed with the familiar *du*. On Christmas Day she returned the gift, accompanied by some gently admonitory lines: "I didn't want to disturb the joy of last evening by observing that I don't find it appropriate for a young man to send his portrait to a young maiden, regardless of how it is veiled. Tender, reverent ladies' knight, excuse this perhaps all too matronly motherliness. I'm returning your friend's poems, so that, deprived of their decoration, Fanny may willingly and freely receive them again from you."[37]

Wilhelm seems to have obliged, for early in 1823 Fanny found inspiration in several poems from Müller's volume.[38] Her first three selections, "Die liebe Farbe" ("The Beloved Color," H-U 62), "Der Neugierige" ("The Curious One," H-U 59), and "Des Müllers Blumen" ("The Miller's Flowers," H-U 60), are from *Die schöne Müllerin* and, as it happens, also figure in Schubert's familiar song cycle of 1824. Readers may recall that in Müller's cycle—to be read, the poet specified, in winter—a wandering lad becomes infatuated with a fair miller maid who scorns him in favor of a hunter; at the end, the lad drowns himself in a brook. Coursing through the cycle is the meandering image of the stream, the natural life force that has brought the lad to the miller maid. In "Der Neugierige" he turns to the personified stream to ask whether his love is reciprocated, a question no flower, no star can answer, for they cannot tell him what he "would so happily hear."

Schubert's solution was to opt for a through-composed setting, with a change of texture and meter midway when the lad addresses the stream— here the piano introduces a flowing, murmuring accompaniment—before another shift to recitative style as he ponders alternately the positive and negative answers to his question. Musically Fanny's setting is far less assuming than Schubert's, for she produced a highly compressed, strophic setting just eighteen measures in length, with the stanzas linked by a brief recurring piano transition and, significantly, without water imagery in the accompaniment. If Schubert's conception triggered an elaborate process of musical motion and development, Fanny's vision initially impresses as circular and static, with its recycling strophes generating persistent rhythmic patterns of long-short harmonies to support the reigning trochaic trimeters of Müller's verses. What she has composed, in short, is a quasi-folk song, immediately accessible to the listener and seemingly unencumbered by artful nuances. But appearances are deceptive, for in the middle of her setting Fanny has placed an unexpected deceptive cadence, marked *forte*, with which she suddenly veers from the tonic F major to D-flat major,❸ a harmonic extravagance that in turn requires some deft harmonic maneuvering to bring us back quickly to the tonic, and to the next stanza.

The brevity and similarity of Fanny's *Müllerin* settings—all three are short, strophic, and have simple piano accompaniments—differentiate them fundamentally from Schubert's. Instead of essaying a cyclic musical narrative from the point of view of the lad, in which the piano personifies the stream and helps unify Müller's poetic images through musical means, she returns to the social origins of the poems as a *Liederspiel*, a collaborative play between poetry, music, and dramatic acting. Her model was the earlier effort of her piano teacher Ludwig Berger, whose op. 11, published in 1819, bears the title *Songs from a Social Liederspiel, Die schöne Müllerin* (*Gesänge aus einem gesell-schaftlichen Liederspiele "Die schöne Müllerin"*).[39] Like Fanny, Berger avoided the elaborate through-composed or modified strophic schemes Schubert explored in favor of readily apprehended strophic designs, many of which are quite compressed. For instance, Berger's first song, "Des Müllers Wanderlied," fills only eleven measures; when Schubert set the same poem in his cycle as "Wohin?" (no. 2), he allowed the rushing stream to consume some eighty bars of churning piano sextuplets.

That the virtuoso pianist Fanny held in check the musical demands of her Müller songs demonstrates again her predisposition toward the genre of the *Liederspiel.* Perhaps she imagined inserting herself into the playlet as the miller maid Rose, the object not only of the wandering lad, but of the hunter, the role Wilhelm Hensel had played in 1816. And perhaps for this reason, she chose to set "Die liebe Farbe," in which the lad obsesses about the color green, the hunter's color; Fanny made sure to make his presence felt by insinuating horn calls into her piano introduction. But in a moment of insecurity, she undermined her effort by yielding to Berger's "authority." "Das hat Herr Berger besser verstanden" ("Herr Berger understood this better"), she wrote on her autograph; sadly, no more *Müllerin* settings flowed from Fanny's pen.

Instead, her five remaining Müller songs from 1823 drew upon two other sections of the poet's anthology, the *Reiselieder* (*Songs of Traveling*) and mini-cycle *Johannes und Esther.* In the days leading up to Wilhelm Hensel's departure on July 20 for Italy, she began imagining their new separation by drafting "Abendreihn" ("Evening Rounds"), in which a wanderer asks the moon for a message from his beloved, and *Einsamkeit* (*Solitude*), in which he pines, "Der Wanderer geht allein, geht schweigend seinen Gang, das Bündel will ihm drücken, der Weg wird ihm zu lang" ("The wanderer goes alone, goes silently on his way; his pack oppresses him, his path is too long"). Very likely she shared these two songs with Wilhelm Müller himself, for the poet visited Berlin around this time and found everything at the Mendelssohn residence "musical."[40] In August, Fanny finished her third *Reiselied*, "Seefahrers Abschied" ("Seefarer's Farewell"); here the traveler, no longer a passive figure, attempts to traverse the distance from his lover by asking a swallow to convey a message to her.

If Fanny's *Reiselieder* barely disguise her feelings for Wilhelm—or rather, translate musically his feelings for her—two other Müller lieder touch on another, more pressing issue. From *Johannes und Esther*, a cycle of poems about a stigmatized relationship between a Christian and a Jew, Fanny excerpted and set "Gebet in der Christnacht," a Christmas prayer in the style of a pastorale, and "Vereinigung" ("Union"). In the latter, Johannes addresses Esther about the religious divide that compels their separation:

Wenn ich nur darf in deine Augen schauen,	If only I may look into your eyes,
In deiner klaren, treuen, frommen Sterne,	into your clear, true, devout orbs,
So fühl' ich weichen das geheime, Grauen	so I feel the secret horror abating,
Das Lieb' und Liebe halt in stummer Ferne.	that in muted distance restrains my beloved and our love.

In 1823 the *geheimes Grauen* that threatened Wilhelm and Fanny's future happiness was, ironically enough, the prospect of a new religious schism, as Wilhelm seriously considered embracing the Catholic faith in Rome. Now when, presumably early in 1823, he spoke with Fanny's approval to her parents about their intentions, the question of his religious faith was not broached, and innocently enough he assumed their tacit approval. They asked only that the engagement remain a secret, so as not to offend the elderly Orthodox Bella Salomon, still unaware that her daughter, son-in-law, and grandchildren were all Protestants.

In a heartfelt letter written late that year from Rome to Luise Hensel, Wilhelm revealed what happened next, when, one evening,

> [Fanny's] mother unexpectedly asked me what my views about religion were and whether it was true, as she had heard, that I desired to convert to the Catholic faith. I replied that she would have known that for a long time, since I had declared it to her daughter before professing my love. And now it was revealed that Fanny, in order not to turn her parents against me and to preserve the domestic peace, had not dared to tell them. Now the mother's wrath vented against the daughter, and she declared that, had she known this, she never would have given her permission, since it did not at all accord with her views to have a Catholic son-in-law, for Catholicism always led to fanaticism and hypocrisy.... The father, though he agreed with his wife, intervened, and the upshot was this: she did not wish to be tyrannical, and if her daughter did not change her feelings, the mother would not separate us by force, though she admitted to me freely, that if I converted she would do all in her power to convince her daughter to break off the engagement. Further, if I did not bind myself to remain true to the Protestant church, she must for the time being forbid any lengthy private meetings with Fanny and any correspondence. I stood firm, and said I could not restrict my conscience; I only promised not to take the step without further reflection, and if it happened, to tell them in good conscience.[41]

Wilhelm gave no date for the confrontation, but it may have occurred in mid-May, about two months before his departure. On May 16, Fanny wrote a turbulent piano etude in G minor (H-U 69) that, she revealed on the autograph, was her "answer to May 14." As we shall presently see, during 1823 etudes became rather an avocation for her, but this one stands out for its unusual character: it is marked Allegro agitato and displays a particularly unruly style. In the opening section the right hand has to negotiate twisting, treacherous sixteenth-note figurations punctuated by awkward leaps of the octave and tenth requiring the thumb and fifth finger to fall on black keys.◉ The left hand supports this display with a jagged bass line moving in eighth notes twice as slow. One-third into the study the hands reverse roles; then, two-thirds through, they resume the original pattern. The overall effect is of an angst-ridden *perpetuum mobile* that seems to test the stronger emotions as much as it does finger dexterity. Whatever the "question" of May 14 may have been,

Fanny was considerably distraught and disheartened at the new strain between Lea and Wilhelm. Shortly before his departure, she turned to her intimate friend Therese Schlesinger and arranged for her fiancé, Eduard Devrient, Wilhelm's traveling companion as far as Vienna, to intercede: "I know how much Hensel loves and respects Eduard, and therefore urgently request you ask him to apply all his influence to distance his friend from Catholicism, for that would be a reason, I confess to you openly, that would separate us forever."[42]

For the next five years, as Wilhelm worked as a *pittore prussiano* in Rome, he dispatched to Berlin drawings instead of love letters. Barred from communicating with Fanny, he nevertheless corresponded with Lea and Abraham, who offered encouragement even as they harbored reservations. In one letter, for instance, Lea elucidated,

> Seriously, dear Mr. Hensel, you must not be angry with me because I cannot allow a correspondence between you and Fanny. Put yourself, in fairness, for one moment in the place of a mother, and exchange your interests for mine, and my refusal will appear to you natural, just, and sensible, whereas you are probably now violently denouncing my proceeding as most barbaric. For the same reason that makes me forbid an engagement, I must declare myself averse to any correspondence. You know that I truly esteem you, that I have indeed a real affection for you, and entertain no objections to you personally. The reasons why I have not as yet decided in your favor are the difference of age [eleven years], and the uncertainty of your position. A man may not think of marrying before his prospects in life are, to a certain degree, assured.[43]

Wilhelm's prospects were indeed unsettled; to explain further her concern, Lea recalled her own situation with Abraham nearly twenty years before: "You are at the commencement of your career, and under beautiful auspices; endeavor to realize them, use well what time and favor hold forth to you, and rest assured that we will not be against you, when, at the end of your studies, you can satisfy us about your position....I must remind you that I married my husband before he had a penny of his own. But he was earning a certain although very moderate income at Fould's in Paris, and I knew he would be able to turn my dowry to good account."

But why did Lea react so strongly to Wilhelm's Catholic leanings? Two reasons—one involving some family history, the other, more practical considerations—are readily apparent. Lea surely could not get around the scandalous precedent of Dorothea Schlegel, whose relationship with Friedrich Schlegel had caused her to traverse an unconventional spiritual trajectory between the Jewish, Protestant, and Catholic faiths. Abraham and Lea's own recent conversion had symbolically completed their assimilation into the upper stratum of Prussian Protestant gentry. Now Wilhelm's temptation to convert threatened not only his career prospects at the Protestant Berlin court but also potentially the Mendelssohn Bartholdys' new social standing.

Wilhelm's letter to Luise readily betrays his struggle to come to terms with his religious identity. If during her adolescence Luise had already begun to poeticize the subjective, mystical side of Catholicism, Wilhelm would find his way in a less contemplative manner. He likened Luise to Mary of Bethany and, exchanging genders, himself to her sister Martha, who prepared Christ's meal while Mary dutifully absorbed the Savior's teachings (Luke 10): "You are Mary, who chooses the best portion. My soul is more similar to the industrious Martha, but she too loves the Lord, if only in her way, and should not chide Mary, who is raised because she humbled herself."[44] Somehow Wilhelm successfully resisted the temptation to embrace Catholicism, even at the Holy City of St. Peter, where for the next five years he studied the sacred art of the church. We shall consider his Italian sojourn further in due course, but for now leave him on his way to Rome in July 1823, and return to Fanny.

iii

No solo performances by Fanny are documented for 1823, though clearly she remained active at the Sunday musicales organized at Neue Promenade. Letters from Lea reveal that Felix and Fanny had mastered the impressive task of rendering orchestral scores at the keyboard as piano duets. The proud *Musen-mama*, as Lea described herself, enlisted the aid of Amalie Beer, mother of the composer Giacomo Meyerbeer, to find new scores challenging enough for her children to sight-read.[45] But not all of Fanny's efforts aimed at the temple of high art. For instance, in July she composed a waltz in a popular style (H-U 81)[46] for Savary, the Duke of Rovigo, a former aide-de-camp of Napoleon who had committed atrocities during the war but now aligned himself with the restored French monarchy. There is also from this time a supple, melodious Adagio in E Major for violin and piano (H-U 72),[47] which Fanny may have played with Eduard Rietz, Felix's violin teacher. Overlooked, but no less significant, is a cadenza she composed in April for the first movement of Beethoven's First Piano Concerto, op. 15,[48] a clue that she probably performed this work at a Sunday concert, and thus appeared as a virtuosa.

Other compelling evidence suggests that virtuosity and piano technique weighed heavily on her mind during this period, for in 1823 she crafted more than a dozen etudes.[49] We have already proposed that the *Übungsstück* of May 16 could have been her response to Lea's confrontation with Wilhelm. A second *Stück* in the unusual key of E-flat minor (H-U 74) bears the annotation "Im Regen" and evidently contains her impressions of a soft rain on June 5. Its melancholy, haunting textures—the right hand is split between a simultaneously sounding, drooping line in the soprano (the fifth and fourth fingers) and a circuitous, more animated counterpoint in the alto (the thumb and second and third fingers)—yield a sophisticated study in digital independence and voicing. The chromatic, inner alto part generates too some pungent, clashing dissonances against the listless soprano melody, in a manner not unlike a more famous etude in E-flat minor, Chopin's op. 10, no. 6, written a few years later.❷ Some of Fanny's other studies address more predictable aspects of piano technique by routinely treating a particular task (arpeggiated and triadic figurations, rapid passagework, hand extensions, and the like) first in one hand and then the other. But throughout one senses a tension between the purely mechanical demands of the exercises and Fanny's need to fill them with poetic, musical contents; in short, the virtuosa and the songwriter collectively left their imprint on these studies.

Though a public concert career was ruled out for Fanny, at some level her concentration on the piano etude in 1823 shows a desire to identify with the growing circle of virtuosi then competing on European concert stages. As if acknowledging her desire, Felix composed in 1823 and 1824 two substantial double piano concerti, in E major and A-flat major, which he performed with her at the family residence. In this private display of virtuosity, at least, Fanny could and did appear on an equal footing with her brother. There, too, she could mingle with the very best of the traveling virtuosi, who, upon reaching Berlin, inevitably sought the company of the Mendelssohns.

One such luminary was Friedrich Kalkbrenner (1785–1849), who arrived in Berlin in November 1823 to concertize, after having established his career in Paris and London. Impeccably attired, he later acquired a reputation as a celebrity who compromised too much with the business of music. Thus, Felix and Fanny would later discover that Kalkbrenner's piano "improvisations" had already been published, and in a memorable bon mot, Heinrich Heine would disparage the artist as a bonbon fallen in the mud. But in 1823, Kalkbrenner was well received in Berlin and feted for his intimidating octave passages, multiple trills in parallel and contrary motion, and glittery passages in thirds and sixths, all dispatched with remarkable poise at the keyboard. Constantly gauging his audiences, Kalkbrenner strove to write music with contemporary relevance; attached to one of his more fanciful later keyboard creations, *Le Fou, scène dramatique* (*The Fool, Dramatic Scene*), was a program purloined from Berlioz's *Fantastic Symphony*. (In Kalkbrenner's rendition, a young pianist "deceived in his first affections becomes mad" and "expresses on his pianoforte the various sensations he experiences.") But this striving for modernity was "merely an assumed dress";[50] for all its ostentation, Kalkbrenner's music reflected certain classical traits of the previous generation.

At the Mendelssohn residence in 1823, he became well acquainted with Fanny's and Felix's music, "praised with taste, and blamed candidly and amiably."[51] At least one composition, Felix's Double Concerto in E Major, composed as a surprise for Fanny's birthday and performed by the siblings on December 7, seems to have garnered special praise. Fanny reported to Zelter that Kalkbrenner's approval far exceeded her expectations.[52] She noted too that he played one of her etudes "very beautifully," and in her album he inscribed a brief Andante "avec mille souvenirs tendres et affectueux."[53] In return, Fanny assimilated Kalkbrenner's style by creating a challenging *Übungsstück* in D Minor (H-U 103) teeming with his trademark octaves.

Balancing this new interest in virtuosity was her increased production of lieder, which peaked in 1823, Fanny's most prolific year, with thirty-two songs. Not surprisingly, many of these display texts that thematicize the separation or loss of lovers; in the absence of letters from Wilhelm, songs provided an emotional release. Thus, along with the Müller lieder already discussed, she revisited her 1820 rendition of Goethe's *Erster Verlust* and produced a second version in October (H-U 95). Another wistful Goethe setting, *An die Entfernte* (*To the Distant One*, H-U 105), followed in December. Its opening lines—"So hab' ich wirklich dich verloren? Bist du, O schöne, mir entfloh'n?" ("So have I really lost you? Have you, beloved, escaped me?")—must have resonated meaningfully for Fanny. Here, symbolically, Wilhelm addresses the *Entfernte*, Fanny, who answers from the piano. In *Der Abendstern* (*The Evening Star*, H-U 70),[54] she exploited verses of the Hungarian poet Janos Mailáth to idealize her relationship with Wilhelm, again from his point of view:

Ich schied von ihr, es stand in tiefer Bläue	I departed from her, in the deep blue sky
der Liebe Stern, in stiller goldner Pracht.	there rose the star of love in silent, golden radiance.
Sie sprach: "Rein wie der Stern, der jetzt erwacht,	She spoke: "Pure as the star that now awakens
ist meine Liebe, die ich ganz dir weihe."	is my love that I dedicate to you entirely."

The image of the rising planet Venus inspired from Fanny a gradually climbing, arching melody that reaches its melismatic zenith on *Liebe* before gently subsiding.

Fanny's other lieder of 1823 include several settings of Ludwig Tieck, to whom Müller dedicated his *Waldhornist* poems in 1821. Between that year and 1823 Tieck published three volumes of poetry, which, if not of top quality, were still facile enough to attract composers,[55] including Fanny. Among the poems she chose was *Die Spinnerin* (*The Spinning Girl*, H-U 93), which, in contrast to Fanny's miniature strophic songs, merited an extended, through-composed setting.[56] Its text, not surprisingly, again addressed an absent lover: "And if I brood all day and spin all week, you are my only thought" ("und sinn' ich Tagelang, und spinn ich Wochenlang, bist du mein einz'ger Gedank"). Nine years before, at the same age of seventeen, Schubert had set a more fateful spinning song, Goethe's *Gretchen am Spinnrade* (*Gretchen at the Spinning Wheel*, 1814), and invented a rotating figure in the piano part to symbolize the churning wheel. In contrast, Fanny confined much of her accompaniment to simple chords. Nevertheless, she worked into the vocal part a miniature four-note figure (C–B–D–C) that, circling back on itself, recurs at various transpositions as a musical image of the wheel (example 3.2). Of considerably darker-hued quality is her song *Ferne* (*Distance*), which appeared in 1850 among the handful of Fanny's posthumous works as op. 9, no. 2. Tieck's verses introduce yet another romantic figure consigned to wandering, who asks, as he seeks his homeland, "Why do you persecute me? Why do you destroy me?" Here Fanny produced another taut, compressed miniature, just twenty-seven bars centered on a somber G minor. Despite its brevity, *Ferne* impresses for its haunting, concentrated expression and deep harmonic coloration, with strategic chromatic pitches—a wayward C-sharp, for instance—added to the vocal and piano parts to convey a sense of separation from the natural form of the minor. Notable also is Fanny's handling of register—the vocal line begins securely above the accompaniment but ultimately descends and falls below the treble arpeggiations before disappearing into the piano postlude.

Apart from *Ferne*, nearly all of Fanny's 1823 lieder remained in manuscript and awaited discovery until the late twentieth and twenty-first centuries. But another notable exception was *Die Schwalbe* (*The Swallow*, H-U 77),[57] which in 1825 afforded Fanny a brief taste of official authorship. The text was by the poetess Friedericke Robert, the "fair Swabian" (*schöne Schwäbin*), who had married the poet Ludwig Robert, brother of Rahel von Varnhagen. In 1821 Fanny and Friedericke had sung two roles in Felix's opera *Die Soldatenliebschaft*, and Friedericke soon became an intimate friend of the family; "to hear the incomparable sibling pair Felix and Fanny Mendelssohn at the piano,

EXAMPLE 3.2. Fanny Mendelssohn, *Die Spinnerin* (1823)

either alone or together," she recorded in her diary, "is one of the most beautiful joys."[58] But before meeting Ludwig, Friedericke had experienced a joyless past—an abusive marriage. Ludwig had rescued Friedericke from a brothel and "awakened her better side that slumbered within."[59]

Like *Ferne*, *Die Schwalbe* treats the theme of homesickness, but now in a bright C major; the wanderer is a swallow that has strayed too far north, away from its warm southern clime. Just fifteen bars in length, Fanny's setting is another lyrical miniature, but its concision belies its historical significance.[60] In 1825, *Die Schwalbe* appeared in *Rheinblüthen*, an annual literary almanac from the Kalrsruhe firm of Gottlieb Braun, Friedericke's brother. In this venue Friedericke, serving as editor, brought out poems of Heine, Tieck, Grillparzer, and her husband, but withheld identifying herself and Fanny as the creators of *Die Schwalbe*. Presumably Friedericke took this decision to safeguard Fanny's privacy, a procedure not unfamiliar to women authors of the period. Whether Fanny's parents approved and, indeed, whether she herself was involved in the venture remain open questions. Nevertheless, by this act, Fanny emerged, even if under a veil of anonymity, before a public readership; a minor song composed in a domestic Berlin setting now briefly reached a broader creative space.

iv

On February 3, 1824, Felix's fifteenth birthday, Zelter presided over a mock ceremony in which he declared his "apprentice" student a journeyman in the trade of music. Invoking Mozart, Haydn, and "old father Bach," Zelter exhorted Felix to continue until he became a master. A dress rehearsal of the pupil's fourth opera, *Die beiden Neffen* (*The Two Nephews*), followed.[61] Whether Fanny sang a role, participated in the chorus, or joined the 150 guests who heard the premiere at her residence a few days later is unclear, but the significance of the moment was surely not lost. Felix now symbolically approached membership in an exclusive, august brotherhood—a canonic line of German musicians—a distinction that further separated him professionally from his sister.

Still, in her own creative space Fanny continued to compose lieder and piano pieces. Songs of wandering and springtime renewal again preoccupied her and today invite us to imagine Wilhelm's masculine presence. In *Auf der Wanderung* (Tieck, H-U 111),[62] every tree whispers to the wanderer his beloved's name. In *Frühlingsnähe* (*Nearness of Spring*; Friedericke Robert, H-U 120),[63] the protagonist calls upon a new spring shoot in a meadow to tarry, "for nothing is harder than the pain of separation." And in *Mailied* (H-U 122),[64] Goethe's joyful celebration of his youthful infatuation with Friederike Brion inspired from Fanny a radiant setting in C major, with a gradually rising vocal line culminating in a cadenza and the declaration, "O Mädchen, wie lieb ich dich! Wie blinkt dein Auge! Wie liebst du mich!" ("O maiden, how I love you! How your eye gleams! How you love me!").

Represented in Fanny's piano music of 1824 are additional examples of etudelike exercises, but there are also striking signs of imaginatively new compositional initiatives within the compressed format of the piano minia-ture. One memorable example is the Allegro in C Minor (H-U 139), finished on November 13, the day before her nineteenth birthday.[65] Here, in eighty-four bars, Fanny establishes a three-part pattern of statement, departure, and return familiar in many of her later piano pieces (and in her brother's *Lieder ohne Worte*). The first section (twenty bars) introduces a deceptively elemen-tary theme—a descending/ascending C-minor arpeggiation—subsequently decorated by extraneous chromatic pitches that momentarily bend or distort the basic harmony.◉ In the middle section (thirty-eight bars) she directs her theme through a series of rapid modulations traversing no fewer than seven keys (F minor, G minor, A minor, E minor, G minor, B-flat minor, and D-flat major) before reinstating the tonic C minor in the third, concluding section (twenty-six bars). New here is the harmonic diversity of the miniature and its considerably expanded tonal palette.

Fanny's other piano music of 1824 led her beyond the short piano charac-ter piece. First, as if responding to Zelter's ceremonial elevation of her brother, she turned to "old father Bach." By December, Zelter could boast to Goethe that she had completed her thirty-second fugue. Indeed, among her works of this year are a fugal Allegro di molto in G Minor (H-U 130) and an intri-cate Gigue in E Minor (H-U 127); its winding subject, introduced in a fugal exposition, revives J. S. Bach's practice of allying the lively baroque dance with contrapuntal manipulations.

There is also the singular Toccata in C Minor (H-U 114), fully 296 mea-sures in length, in which Fanny gives uninhibited expression to her Bachian ruminations and, as it were, dons a powdered wig.[66] Marked *einstimmig* (in one voice), the composition is anchored by a low bass note, above which the pianist begins to interweave through hand crossings a florid eighth-note line, the "single" voice identified by Fanny that nevertheless carries multiple lay-ers of harmonic meaning. Occasionally, the left hand returns to the lower register to sculpt the bass line beneath the flowing eighth notes in the treble, which impress as another Bachian conceit, a compound melodic line implying several voices, so that the whole can be analyzed as simulated three- and four-part harmony. Fanny's Toccata is in fact an example of a specialized technique applied by J. S. Bach in a variety of works—the solo cello suites and solo violin sonatas come to mind, as do stretches of the celebrated Toccata in D Minor (BWV 565)—in which a compacted harmonic (vertical) texture is made to unfold over time in a purely melodic (horizontal) manner. Fanny may well have had in mind a similar example by Bach's son Carl Philipp Emanuel, the so-called Solfeggio in C Minor (Helm 220, 1770), which shares its key with Fanny's piece and literally presents "one line" unleashed in a profusion of sixteenth notes (example 3.3).

Distinguishing Fanny's Toccata, apart from its unabashed baroque features, is her successful handling and structuring of its extended musical space. This is not the composition of a songwriter content to produce short, strophic lieder. Despite its fantasia-like, improvisational qualities—the middle section bears Fanny's instruction, "Hier kann der Vortrag freier werden" ("Here the performance can become freer")—the Toccata adheres to a clear, three-part plan (*ABA'*), in which the outer portions, moving in eighth notes (example 3.3a), tend to dwell on the lower and middle registers of the instrument, while the contrasting middle section, shifting abruptly to animated sixteenth notes, spans a broader range and climbs, in a written-out cadenza, into the highest register. The protracted cadenza, with chromatic arpeggiations swirling above a prolonged pedal point in the bass, again returns us to J. S. Bach and perhaps to the celebrated harpsichord cadenza in the Fifth Brandenburg Concerto, one of the works that Fanny's aunt Sarah Levy had performed at the Singakademie some twenty years before.

Why did Fanny's attraction to Bach reach a new level of intensity in 1824? To some extent, the Toccata was her response to Felix's immersion in Bachian complexities, her attempt to ally her creative voice with the dignified German tradition so esteemed by Zelter and the Mendelssohns. For in 1824 Bach

EXAMPLE 3.3.   (a) Fanny Mendelssohn, Toccata in C Minor (1824); (b) C. P. E. Bach, Solfeggio in C Minor (1770)

(a)

(b)

was very much a topic of discussion in her family. Probably early that year Felix received from his grandmother, Bella Salomon, a remarkable musical treasure, a copy of Bach's St. Matthew Passion.[67] Though Zelter had tinkered with this colossus of musical Protestantism and rehearsed a few portions at the Singakademie, the work had virtually disappeared after its Leipzig premieres in the 1720s from the German cultural consciousness; indeed, a century later, Bach was generally dismissed as "an unintelligible musical arithmetician."[68] As is well known, over the next few years, Felix began studying the score in earnest with his circle of friends and in 1829, at age twenty, accomplished a feat inconceivable to Zelter—a triumphant public performance of the Passion, the event that gave forceful impetus to the Bach revival. Of course, as a member of this exclusive circle, Fanny would have become intimately familiar with the sublime grandeur of Bach's score, a work, as we shall see, to which she returned later in life (see p. 280).

If Bach was one link for Fanny to the brotherhood of German musicians, a second was Beethoven, a composer, though conspicuously omitted in Zelter's pantheon, with whom the siblings struggled during the 1820s to come to terms. In 1824 Felix effected that rapprochement in his First Symphony, op. 11 in C Minor, a composition with clear, seemingly inevitable ties to Beethoven's Fifth Symphony. Fanny chose a more indirect approach, through a singularly wrought movement for piano solo, the *Sonata o Capriccio* in F Minor (H-U 113),[69] which she finished on February 5, two days after Zelter's dubbing of her brother.

The enigmatic title betrays Fanny's struggle over the generic identity of her creation, which she evidently viewed as a hybrid of the weighty traditions of the piano sonata and lighter diversions of the capriccio. But at first glance her invocation of the sonata seems strained. The external shape of the movement—a short Adagio introduction, an elongated Andante sostenuto interrupted by an explosive Allegro molto, and a resumption of the Andante, all centered in F minor—reflect little of the sonata principle, traditionally dependent upon tonal contrast and thematic development. And Fanny's determined massing of tonic sonorities—Felix playfully labeled the work "your 1000-part piece in F minor" (*dein 1000stimmiges Stück aus f moll*)[70]—generates a certain gravitas at odds with the quirky qualities of a capriccio. Be that as it may, the subdued character of the opening—a good part of the Andante lies in the low, dark register of the piano—and its static harmonies are familiar enough and find their source in Beethoven's *Appassionata* Sonata op. 57 (1805), as it happens, in the same key.◉ Indeed, the opening harmonic progression of Fanny's Andante, four measures in F minor followed by four in D-flat major, strikingly alludes to a texturally and harmonically similar passage from Beethoven's first movement, though now Fanny replaces his eruptive Allegro with an expressive Andante, as if to suggest a receding memory or rehearing of the model.

Her major work of 1824, the Piano Sonata in C Minor (H-U 128),[71] leaves no doubt about its generic identity. Here we encounter her first full-length, three-movement sonata, composed in Berlin after Felix's departure with Abraham in July 1824 to the resort Bad Doberan, near Rostock and the Baltic. An estimable work that deserves revival, it shows considerable advances in the treatment of sonata form, sophisticated and varied thematic techniques, and a harmonic richness that stamps Fanny's work as anything but conventional. In the monothematic first movement, built upon a melancholy theme that descends, steplike, from the soprano register,◉ she now establishes in the exposition the expected tonal contrast between C minor and E-flat major, but then further embellishes the second tonality through an imaginative excursion to a remote G-flat major. After the conventional repeat of the exposition, the development begins by momentarily retracing the opening bars, as if initiating a second repetition of the exposition, a ploy Brahms would later use in the first movement of his Fourth Symphony (1886). At the recapitulation, Fanny subtly adjusts the theme, as if now to promote its development rather than literal repetition, and in the coda goes even further, subjecting the theme to a bit of playful, if studious, canonic imitation.

As we shall see, haunting the piece is the extramusical topic of separation from a loved one, with Fanny's sibling bond to Felix now rivaling, as it were, her love for Wilhelm. That separation weighed heavily on Fanny at this time is clear enough from a song finished the very day she dated her sonata, July 19. In the passionate *Das Heimweh* (*Homesickness*, H-U 129) she seems either to have transferred Friedericke Robert's nostalgic verses for her Swabian homeland onto Wilhelm or projected onto the absent Felix some imagined desire for a musical reunion. Here the question of Friedericke's poem, "Was ist's, das mir den Atem hemmet?" ("What is it that inhibits my breath?"), accompanied by broken, searching arpeggiations in the piano, is answered by the refrainlike assertion, "Es ist das Heimweh!," where the arpeggiations give way to insistent, repeated chords. Then, in the postlude, the piano shifts from the minor to major, as Fanny plays on the emotional tug between the two modalities. *Heimweh* later found publication as the second member of Felix's op. 8, his first set of twelve songs, and thus, after *Die Nonne*, became Fanny's second lied reassigned to his authorship.

Fanny would have been aware of musical precedents for the trope of separation and reunion, ranging from J. S. Bach's *Capriccio on the Departure of His Most Beloved Brother* (BWV 992, *ante* 1705) to Beethoven's celebrated *Les Adieux* Piano Sonata, op. 81a (1810). Another work in this tradition left a mark on her piano sonata—Carl Maria von Weber's *Konzertstück* op. 79 for piano and orchestra, which the Mendelssohns had heard the composer premiere in Berlin in 1821. According to Julius Benedict, Weber's pupil and an acquaintance of Fanny's family, the *Konzertstück* traced in four connected movements a dramatic, if sentimental, narrative: a damsel, pining for her departed knight, imagines he has died in battle; the strains of a march announce the returning Crusaders and prepare the joyous reunion of the couple. In Fanny's Sonata in C Minor, she plays the role of the damsel, who emerges at the beginning of her second movement (Andante con moto), where we find an allusion to the opening theme of the *Konzertstück*, transposed and reworked from Weber's F minor to Fanny's more reassuring E-flat major (example 3.4). But in Fanny's finale, there is no figurative, joyful reunion; rather the concluding Presto, a loosely constructed rondo, continues to play on the topic of separation through its recurring, refrainlike theme, a spinning, careening subject that simulates the frenzied energy and emotional discharge of a tarantella. The tempestuous coda, echoes of which may be heard in Felix's *Hebrides* Overture and *Capriccio brillant* op. 22 for piano and orchestra, resolves little, as the work concludes with some strident chords and Fanny's brusque notation on the autograph, "Für Felix. In seiner Abwesenheit" ("For Felix. In his absence").

Within weeks of returning to Berlin, Felix was at work on his second Double Piano Concerto for Fanny, in the unusual key of A-flat major. Modeled on the Irishman John Field's Second Piano Concerto in the same key but exhibiting telltale Beethovenian markers,[72] the new composition formed a more imposing companion to Felix's Double Concerto in E Major written for Fanny the previous year, and now served musically to reunite the two siblings. Felix completed the score on November 12, in time to present it to Fanny on her birthday, which fell on a Sunday and thus prompted one of the fortnightly musical celebrations. For the occasion, Felix directed one of his string symphonies and appeared as soloist in Mozart's Piano Concerto in C Minor, K. 491, and Fanny performed with her brother the Double Piano Concerto in E Major. Among the audience was the Bohemian piano virtuoso Ignaz Moscheles (1794–1870), newly arrived in Berlin on one of his many concert tours, and immediately sought out by the *Musenmama* Lea to give her eldest two children finishing lessons.

EXAMPLE 3.4. (a) Carl Maria von Weber, *Konzertstück* (1821); (b) Fanny Mendelssohn, Sonata in C Minor (1824), second movement

Like Kalkbrenner the year before, Moscheles was a highly regarded, industrious touring virtuoso. He had trained in Vienna, where he had appeared in
the concerts of Fanny's aunt the baroness Cäcilie Eskeles. His composition
teacher was Antonio Salieri, who on his deathbed in 1823 implored his former
pupil to dispel the "malicious" rumor that he had poisoned Mozart in 1791 (in
Moscheles's estimation, "morally speaking," Salieri had "by his intrigues poisoned many an hour of Mozart's existence").[73] Moscheles also had considerable
dealings with Beethoven, who commissioned him to prepare the piano score
of his opera *Fidelio*; as recreation, in 1823 Moscheles made a new arrangement
of Beethoven's *Egmont* Overture. Though much of Moscheles's own music was
designed for the salon and expanding market of musical amateurs—his works
bore entertaining titles such as *Triumphal Entry of the Allies into Paris*, op. 26;
Les Charmes de Paris, op. 54; and *Bonbonnière musicale*, op. 55—he was capable
of considerable craft and took his art quite seriously. A fastidious musician, he
routinely supplemented his manuscripts with detailed instructions for their
layout and design, arguing that "if anyone affects the great genius by writing
so indistinctly that no engraver can read it, and if his music is published full
of mistakes, that fact does not make him a Beethoven."[74]

The official reason for Moscheles's visit to Berlin was an invitation from
the Prussian monarch, and the pianist obligingly gave three successful public
charity concerts. Nevertheless, the high point of his Berlin sojourn was meeting the Mendelssohns. He expended whole pages of his diary to his impressions, primarily of Felix, but also of Fanny: "This is a family the like of which
I have never known. Felix, a boy of fifteen, is a phenomenon. What are all
prodigies as compared with him? Gifted children, but nothing else. This Felix
Mendelssohn is already a mature artist, and yet but fifteen years old!...His
elder sister Fanny, also extraordinarily gifted, played by heart, and with admi-
rable precision Fugues and Passacailles by Bach. I think one may well call her
a thorough 'Mus. Doc.' [*guter Musiker*]."[75]

Presumably Fanny selected some fugues from the *Well-Tempered Clavier*,
but Moscheles's reference to Bachian *passacailles* requires more thought. In 1823
Felix had composed an untitled organ passacaglia in C minor, with twenty-
two variations on a recurring ground bass modeled on Bach's iconic example
in the same key, BWV 582. Almost certainly, Fanny performed this daunting work for Moscheles, but how did she render it—on a piano or chamber
organ, or, with Felix, perhaps on both? (As we shall see, she would use the last
option the following year, when she performed some Bach organ works for an
English visitor.) And what of Moscheles's reference to the plural form? Bach
composed only one passacaglia for organ, but he did incorporate ostinato bass
patterns into some choral works, including Cantatas no. 12 (*Weinen, Klagen,
Sorgen, Zagen*) and 78 (*Jesu, der du meine Seele*), and the Crucifixus of the
Mass in B Minor.[76] Could Fanny have known these works, and could she

have transcribed for the keyboard some of the relevant movements, prompting Moscheles to record in his diary *passacailles*?

Fanny and Felix regaled their visitor with more Bach on November 23; then, on December 3, they gathered at Zelter's, where Fanny performed the Concerto in D Minor (BWV 1052), according to Moscheles, from the "original manuscript," that is, the same source her aunt Sarah Levy had used on December 31, 1807, at the Singakademie.[77] Fanny's Bachian fugal fingers no doubt held her in good stead, so that before departing Berlin, Moscheles recorded in her album as a sign of his most "deep esteem" a conundrum-like duet, condensed onto one line of music notated with a treble clef. To derive the second voice, one turned the page upside down and read the same line of music, now inverted, and fitted with a bass clef.[78] Thus did he pay homage to the *guter Musiker*, the learned "musical doctor."

CHAPTER 4

Leipzigerstrasse No. 3

(1825–1828)

Gentlemen may laugh as much as they like, but it is delightful that we too have the opportunity given us of listening to clever men.

—Fanny to Karl Klingemann, December 23, 1827

The passing on March 9, 1824, of Bella Salomon—daughter of Daniel Itzig, matriarch of the Mendelssohns' wealth, and, in her declining years, mother reconciled through Fanny with her apostate son—precipitated a momentous event for her granddaughter. Upon reviewing the deceased's will, Lea and Abraham discovered that Bella had bequeathed a fortune of 150,000 thalers, comprising among other assets the residence at Neue Promenade and the old *Meierei*, to Jacob Bartholdy, the children of two granddaughters, and Lea's unborn grandchildren. As she wrote to her Viennese cousin on April 24, Lea was thus, for reasons that remain unclear, completely disinherited (*völlig enterbt*).[1]

As a result, the Mendelssohns could remain at Neue Promenade no. 7 only by purchasing or renting it. Instead, Abraham began searching for a new residence and found it in an eighteenth-century baroque mansion imposing enough but deteriorating from neglect—Leipzigerstrasse no. 3, near the Leipzigerplatz, Fanny's principal residence from 1825 until her death in 1847. In exchange for 56,000 thalers, Abraham received the deed for the property on February 18, 1825, from Major von Podewils, son-in-law of a minor nobleman

who had lived there since the 1770s through difficult and propitious times—
the onerous French occupation following the Treaty of Tilsit in 1807 and the
euphoric celebrations after the Battle of Leipzig in 1814.[2] By the 1820s, the
western portion of Leipzigerstrasse was fashionable, though still not fully
developed. On the south side, no. 2 was the property of the Prussian emissary
to Constantinople, while no. 4 was the site of the royal porcelain factory. In
1769, Frederick the Great had decreed that common Jews purchase defective
porcelain such as several simian figurines, acquired by Moses Mendelssohn,
that were presumably produced at the factory. No. 3, an impressive three-story
residence with a mansard roof, confronted the street with a massive depth of
15 meters and width of 59 meters, divided into three sections punctuated by
an elongated rhythm of nineteen windows. Of these, the central aperture,
adorned by a triangular pediment, opened onto a balcony. Extending behind
the main structure on either side were two symmetrical wings, each 52 meters
long, joined at the back by a *Gartenhaus* that completed a substantial rectan-
gular perimeter enclosing a courtyard (figure 4.1). The complex contained a
carriage house and stables and, in the cellar of the main residence, quarters
for the gardener and other servants. From the south side of the *Gartenhaus*,
the Mendelssohns could survey their landscaped park and several acres that

FIGURE 4.1. Wilhelm Hensel, watercolor of Gartenhaus, Leipzigerstrasse no. 3, Berlin,
1851 (Berlin, Mendelssohn Archiv, Art Resource, New York)

bordered the formal gardens of a Prussian prince. According to Theodor Fontane, near the turn to the new century the future Prussian monarch Frederick William IV had entertained himself as a boy in the gardens of the estate by climbing an accommodating yew tree.[3]

Around the middle of 1825, the Mendelssohns took up temporary quarters in the *Gartenhaus* while renovations commenced on the principal edifice. At the center of the *Gartenhaus* was a spacious *Gartensaal*, 14 by 7.5 meters. Sebastian Hensel later recalled that the ceiling, 8 meters high, had a shallow cupola in its center and bore "fantastic fresco-paintings." The *Gartensaal* became the music room and site, during the 1830s and 1840s, of Fanny's Sunday musicales, and thus her primary creative outlet. Sebastian claimed it could accommodate hundreds of guests, an exaggeration mitigated somewhat by an unusual feature: the south wall had movable glass panels separated by Doric columns, so that during the warmer months the hall became an open portico, allowing the audience to spill out onto the terraced lawns.[4] The novelist Paul Heyse, son of the Mendelssohn children's tutor, Carl Heyse, likened the *Gartensaal* to a temple in which the audience, like an attentive congregation, absorbed every pitch as if it were "a divine revelation."[5]

By the time of their move to Leipzigerstrasse, the Mendelssohns' social circle had expanded considerably. When a young medical student, G. F. L. Stromeyer, arrived in 1825 from Göttingen to finish his education in Berlin, his professors facilitated an introduction to the Mendelssohns, and he soon discovered in Fanny an excellent piano virtuoso, and a musician "not without talent" in composition. Stromeyer confirmed that while the family devoted weekdays to the children's studies, Sundays inevitably yielded to music and social gatherings: "Already before the meal at 12:00 the larger musical productions were undertaken, and at 8:00 in the evenings friends returned. There was music then too, but only Felix and Fanny played, accompanied by Eduard Rietz, the soulful violinist whom Felix loved like a brother. Then social games were played, and occasionally there was dancing. All who came were more or less committed to music, or at least had learned to conceal their other interests by remaining silent during the performances."[6] Other musicians in the children's circle included the Hamburg violinist Leopold Lindenau, who assumed an increasingly prominent role after Rietz suffered a hand injury, and the bass Franz Hauser from Cassel, whose enthusiasm for Bach drew him to the Mendelssohns in June 1825. Hauser made copies of lieder by Fanny and Felix and may have been the recipient of a baritone aria Felix completed in September, "Ch'io t'abbandano," on verses from Metastasio's *Achille in Sciro*. This eighteenth-century opera libretto, concerning the young Achilles' attempt to evade military service by hiding in female attire on the island of Scyros, piqued Fanny's interest as well. The same month she began setting for soprano and piano some additional verses, "Numi clementi, se puri, se innocenti" ("Merciful gods, so pure, so innocent," H-U 159). Instead of the piano quartet, the operatic genre of the Italian recitative and aria thus now triggered a friendly rivalry between the siblings, though Fanny's draft extended only as far as forty-six measures; difficulties she encountered with Italian prosody may have led her to abandon the effort.[7]

A figure of growing influence on Felix's and Fanny's musical tastes was the law student turned music critic and theorist Adolf Bernhard Marx (1795–1866), who had established himself early in 1824 as the editor of a new music journal, the *Berliner allgemeine musikalische Zeitung*, issued by A. M. Schlesinger, publisher of several of Felix's early compositions. Designating himself the critical spokesman for a new age of music following the eras of Bach and Mozart, Marx founded his musical manifesto on the art of Beethoven. For Marx, the Fifth Symphony contained a series of "soulful states with deep psychological truth."[8] Abraham came to believe that Marx exercised a pernicious effect on Felix, and Varnhagen von Ense, finding him coarse and obsequious, compared him to a crawling cockroach.[9] Nevertheless, Marx's views about Beethoven's middle- and late-period works and his interest in the composer's ability to depict extramusical ideas through tone painting (*Tonmalerei*) were of consequence for both Felix and Fanny, who, as we have seen, confronted Beethoven's music in 1823 and 1824. Marx recorded in his memoirs that Fanny "was closest to Felix and took the liveliest interest in his artistic studies. At the pianoforte, she lacked his skill and strength, but not infrequently she was first in tenderness and sensitivity of interpretation, especially of Beethoven."[10]

As it happened, 1825 saw the publication of Schlesinger's edition of Beethoven's technically and aesthetically most intimidating piano sonata—the *Hammerklavier*, op. 106. On her twentieth birthday Fanny received a copy from a new member of the Mendelssohns' circle, Karl Klingemann (1798–1862). An amateur poet and songwriter, Klingemann had entered the diplomatic service of the Kingdom of Hanover, created during the post-Napoleonic restoration, and arrived in Berlin around 1824 to serve as a clerk for the Hanoverian legation. Its emissary, Baron von Reden, rented eleven rooms on the second floor of Leipzigerstrasse no. 3, where Klingemann himself became a tenant in 1826, before his transfer to the legation in London late in 1827. He seems to have delighted in donning literary masks. One of his surviving poems, "Medical Consultation with My Mother" ("Ärztliche Konsultation an meine Mutter"), puts some verses about Fanny into the mouth of her younger brother, Paul:

Hör nur Fanny musizieren,	Just hear Fanny make music,
Und den melanchol'schen Ausdruck,	and the melancholy expression
Im dim., rit., smorz., musst du spüren,	in her dim., rit., and smorz., and you must feel
Dass da schmerzlich Sehnen 'rauskuck.[11]	that a painful yearning presses out.

Perhaps Klingemann was reacting to Fanny's rendition of the soulful slow movement of Beethoven's sonata, where the pianist has opportunities to attempt the most searching diminuendi, ritardandi, and smorzandi.[12]

Klingemann's most imaginative literary posturing, though, accompanied his gift of the *Hammerklavier*—a humorous, fabricated letter, predated November 8, 1825, from Beethoven to Fanny, that initially caused quite a sensation when it turned up in the estate of Sebastian Hensel in 1898. It begins, "My most worthy *Fräulein*! Reports of your efforts on my behalf have reached as far as Vienna,—a stout *Herr* with a moustache and a thin man with a Parisian accent [i.e., Wilhelm Hensel and Eduard Devrient] whose names I cannot recall relayed how you managed to keep a cultured audience there politely listening to my Concerti in E-flat and G and my Trio in B-flat, so that only a few fled the performance."[13] Klingemann's fictive prose thus reveals that by 1825 Fanny had in her repertoire Beethoven's Fourth and Fifth (*Emperor*) Piano Concerti, and the *Archduke* Piano Trio, op. 97, all substantial examples of the middle period "heroic" style.[14]

But the letter goes on to suggest that Fanny and her circle were fast becoming connoisseurs of Beethoven's more recent, abstract music that we recognize today as his intractable late style: "There is really no art in the public appreciating my first trios, my first two symphonies, and several of my earlier sonatas, as long as one makes music like the others, for what is youthful is also more common and trivial; they understand it and buy it, though I have tired of it and have made music like H[err] von Beethoven. To that end, during years of isolation in my bleak study ideas have coursed through my head that perhaps are not to everyone's liking." And so, counting among his true friends those who would understand his most recent music and fathom his "most intimate moods" (*innersten Gemüthslage*), Beethoven/Klingemann offers the *Hammerklavier* to Fanny in friendship but recommends she play it only when she has sufficient time, for it is not the "shortest" sonata, and the composer has "much" to say in it. And if her "friendship" should lack sufficient conviction, he suggests she consult the "connoisseur Marx" (*Kenner Marx*), who will willingly explicate the score. Thus Fanny began studying at age twenty one of the most difficult, and to many bizarre, works of contemporary music and pondering its unusual features: the elephantine girth of the first movement; the scherzo with its playful double counterpoint and hammering octaves; the emotionally laden, lamentlike Adagio sostenuto; and the culminating finale, a colossal, learned fugue *con alcune licenze*, that employs a most rarefied contrapuntal stratagem, the presentation of the subject in retrograde, or reverse order. Fanny—and her artistic twin, Felix, with whom she shared everything of musical significance—would thus be among the first musicians to approach the weightiest of piano sonatas and to count themselves among Beethoven's most ardent disciples.

Other music that attracted Fanny's attention was a now long-forgotten chamber work, Hummel's Piano Quintet in E-flat Minor, op. 87 (1822), which she performed with great success at the Sunday musicales. Her artistry inspired two anonymous sonnets, one possibly by Klingemann, that may support a date around the mid-1820s. Here the poet wonders whether Fanny's execution surpassed that of Hummel himself:

Warum Gefühle sich so mächtig drängen,	Why do feelings press so powerfully,
Sich formen zu dem klingenden Sonette?	And form around the sounding sonnet?
Ob Fanny,—Hummel größer im Quintette?	Whether Fanny or Hummel was the greater in the quintet?
Hört' Ihren mächt'gen Zauber selbst in Klängen![15]	Hear her powerful, sonorous magic resound!

According to the other sonnet, titled "An Fräulein M.," her performance was potent enough to cross Western cultural boundaries, perceived, that is, from a distinctly Eurocentric perspective: "A Turk, Hottentot or Moor may sit quietly, when *she* plays Hummel's quintet with that light commotion of her fingers."[16]

i

If Fanny's virtuosity challenged her male counterparts, in her short piano character pieces she explored expressive musical content. One untitled piece in G minor, finished on February 5, 1825 (H-U 144),[17] provides further evidence of her irrepressible interest in Bachian counterpoint, a trait she shared with Felix. Sixty-three measures in length, the piece is another example of a neobaroque gigue and recalls, for instance, J. S. Bach's gigue in the same key from the third English Suite (BWV 808). Both begin with a florid subject in compound meter (12/8, divided into four triplet groupings) answered by a second and third voice in a kind of mock fugato. Like Bach, too, Fanny later applies mirror inversion to the subject. But then, as if reviving from some baroque intoxication, she abandons her counterpoint three times in favor of cascading sixteenth-note arpeggiations that abruptly return us to the nineteenth century. Nevertheless, the final cadence is in G major; with its unexpected raised third (yielding a major instead of minor triad), it invokes the so-called Picardy third favored by Bach and his contemporaries.

In a subtly turned, untitled piece in F minor, also from February 1825 (H-U 145),[18] Fanny conceived a haunting melody that slowly spirals downward from the high treble above a bass accompaniment of broken chords.❷ The left-hand patterns traverse intervals of tenths, elevenths, and even twelfths, suggesting that she could negotiate wide leaps rarely encountered in Felix's piano music. Especially striking is the chromatic character of her melody, inflected with several "misaligned" pitches that create momentary dissonant clashes and lend the composition a poignant affect. Once again, this miniature evinces a harmonic richness in tension with the compressed brevity of the composition, as Fanny indulges in several harmonic excursions before returning to the tonic F minor.

In March 1825 Felix accompanied Abraham to Paris, to escort back to Berlin the recently pensioned Henriette Mendelssohn, and to consult Luigi Cherubini, the intimidating director of the Paris Conservatoire (and within a few years bane of the young Hector Berlioz), about Felix's musical prospects. At private gatherings of the Parisian elite Felix moved easily among a high-profile cluster of native and foreign musicians—the portly new director of the Théâtre-Italien, Gioacchino Rossini, the opera composers Halévy and Auber, the expatriate Englishman Georges Onslow, and Antoine Reicha, an eccentric theorist-composer who "hunted" parallel fifths; the pianists Moscheles, Kalkbrenner, Pixis, the Herz brothers, Camille Pleyel, and the fourteen-year-old prodigy Franz Liszt; the violinists Baillot, Lafont, Rodolphe Kreutzer, Boucher, and Pierre Rode; and the conductor François-Antoine Habeneck, who introduced Beethoven's symphonies to the Parisian public. But in a series of caustic reviews, Felix vented his dissatisfaction to Fanny: Maestro Rossini was a windbag, Liszt had many fingers but little intelligence, Pleyel violated the integrity of a Mozart piano concerto by adding cadenzas longer than the entire work, and Parisians displayed an appalling ignorance of J. S. Bach and Beethoven.

For her part, Fanny suggested that Felix inculcate Onslow and the *Schuhu* (pedant) Reicha with a reverence for Beethoven, specifically for his *Diabelli* Variations, op. 133, and revealed just how steeped she was in the transcendental late style of her "bucolic" compatriot. But Fanny longed too for news about Paris itself, and on April 11 berated Felix for limiting the scope of his letters to a review of French musical life: "It almost seems as if you've hardly seen anything because you've already heard about everything. You haven't uttered one syllable about the Tuilleries, the museum, the city, or your walks."[19]

Meanwhile, in Berlin, she drafted a proposal for a new amateur music society to promote instrumental music, lest it "disappear in the bad taste of the time, egotism of the organizer, and pandering to the public."[20] The stimulus for this remarkable document is not known. Dated March 17, 1825, it displays a reforming zeal scarcely less determined than Felix's critique of Parisian musical life. But there is too a concern for the practical details of the new society—the annual fees for its membership, establishing a lending library to defray costs, and organizing a public series of twelve subscription concerts—as if on paper Fanny intended to play a central administrative role. Preferring symphonies as the object of study, she envisioned that in alliance with the Singakademie the organization would eventually present "great musical performances" of Bach, Handel, Haydn, Mozart, Cherubini, and Beethoven, and thus extended somewhat Zelter's brotherhood of "old Bach," Mozart, and Haydn. But whatever role she may have desired to play was purely imaginary—deferring to the social strictures of her time, she designated the new organization for the use of men overseen by a male director. Because "women of private backgrounds shy away from appearing before an audience," the author of the proposal thus excluded herself from active participation and demurely withdrew into her insulated familial realm.

It was as a musician of "private background" that she welcomed two visitors early in April, Wilhelm Müller and his new wife, Adelheid, who sang Fanny's lieder, including *Die Spinnerin*, though the composer had to make a few adjustments to accommodate her new friend's range. Through the Müllers, at Easter Fanny met a young theologian from Dessau, Julius Schubring, who later advised Felix about the texts of his oratorios and reminisced that Fanny "was long [Felix's] equal in composition and pianoforte-playing. There existed between the two a mutual appreciation and affectionate esteem, which were certainly unusual."[21]

ii

Abraham and Felix's Parisian itinerary included stops in Weimar, where they paused in March and again in May on the return leg of their journey. Here the travelers found Goethe reposing, as his amanuensis Eckermann described him, like an aging monarch "elevated above both praise and blame."[22] He received Felix's newly published Piano Quartet in B Minor, op. 3, which Lea had asked permission to dedicate to the poet. As in 1821, Fanny could experience Weimar only vicariously through Felix's reports, though she found another, creative way to transport herself to Goethe's literary court. Between March 23 and May 5, she set four of his poems and then, after Felix's return to Berlin, another four between June and November. Among the eight lieder are her first attempt at the immortal *Wandrers Nachtlied* I, "Der du von dem Himmel bist" (H-U 147), and a dark, saturnine rendition of the scarcely less famous "Harper's Song" from *Wilhelm Meister*, "Wer sich der Einsamkeit ergibt" (H-U 162).[23] When Schubert set the latter verses in 1816 (D 478, two versions), he incorporated into the piano postlude a descending tetrachord, symbol of a lament. Whether in 1825 Fanny knew the Schubert is unclear, but she too made use of this traditional musical figure, subtly distributed in her opening bars between the vocal and piano parts, and then, midway through the song, openly stated in the bass of the piano.🔊 [24] For her through-composed composition Fanny specified a recitative-like performance style, to capture cogently the Harper's alienation and guilt about his incestuous relationship with Mignon.

Fanny's six other Goethe settings from 1825 were all inspired by the *West-östlicher Divan*,[25] the celebrated anthology seething with an irrepressible exoticism and sensuality barely contained within some 250 poems written between 1814 and 1816, and released together in 1819. Part tribute to the fourteenth-century Persian poet Hafiz, part transcultural exploration of the East through a Western lens, the *Divan* afforded Goethe a temporal and spatial escape from the physical, mental, and spiritual exhaustion of the Napoleonic cataclysm. The blending of the familiar and unfamiliar, of historical nearness and a remote historical-cultural Other, also unlocked an "inter-textual play of fantasy"[26] from which germinated some of the most compelling love poetry of all time, concentrated in the Book of Suleika, the primary source of verses Fanny selected. The fair Egyptian wife of Joseph, Suleika loves ardently but chastely Hatem, with whom she engages in a poetic dialogue. As we now know—but Fanny and her contemporaries did not—Suleika was Goethe's pseudonym for Marianne Willemer, wife of the Frankfurt privy counselor Jakob Willemer, and a talented poetess in her own right, several of whose poems Goethe silently incorporated into the *Divan*. He viewed her as an ideal artistic companion and so sought reunion in "Wiederfinden," which Fanny began setting in July (H-U 156):

Ist es möglich! Stern der Sterne,	Star of stars, what explanation!
Drück' ich wieder dich ans Herz!	Pressed against my heart again!
Ach, was ist die Nacht der Ferne	Ah, the night of separation,
Für ein Abgrund, für ein Schmerz!	Such a chasm, such a pain!
Ja du bist es! Meiner Freuden	Yes, it's you! To all my pleasure
Süßer, lieber Widerpart;	Sweet and dearest counterpart;
Eingedenk vergangner Leiden	When in thought past grief I measure
Schaudr' ich vor der Gegenwart.	How the present rends my heart.[27]

Mirrorlike, in Marianne's poem "Ach, um deine feuchten Schwingen," the West wind brings Hatem tidings of Suleika's grief over their separation. Perhaps the final stanza prompted Fanny to begin setting the poem on May 5 (H-U 150), to imagine playing Suleika to her absent Wilhelm's Hatem:

Sag ihm, aber sag's bescheiden	Tell him, though, with modest voice;
Seine Liebe sei mein Leben,	That his love is my life's essence;
Freudiger Gefühl von beiden	In them both I shall rejoice
Wird mir seine Nähe geben.	When again I feel his presence.[28]

On June 9, the composer may have had another encounter with Marianne's poem when Anna Milder-Hauptmann publicly performed Schubert's setting, "Suleika II" (D 717, 1821), dedicated to the Berlin soprano. Schubert translated the "moist wings" (*feuchte Schwingen*) of the West wind into a tremulous piano accompaniment that hovers unabated through nearly 200 measures, an estimable length that all but dwarfs Fanny's modest draft of fourteen measures.

Clearly, she remained most comfortable in approaching songwriting from the perspective of a miniaturist. In "Auch in der Ferne," Goethe's compact quatrain inspired from Fanny a convincing musical counterpart (*An Suleika*, H-U 148),[29] which required only thirty-five bars:

Auch in der Ferne dir so nah!	Even in distance you so near!
Und unerwartet kommt die Qual.	And unexpected comes the pain.
Da hör' ich wieder dich einmal,	Once more I hear your voice again,
Auf einmal bist du wieder da!	And suddenly your self is here![30]

She applied deceptively simple harmonic means to capture the dichotomy of intimacy and distance and in the process crafted a musical gem. In the opening bars, the music progresses from E-flat major to C minor on *Ferne* and returns to E-flat for *nah*, an easily overlooked, unassuming gesture of harmonic separation and nearness. Later Fanny exploits the conceit further when, midway through the song, the opening phrase returns but is prolonged by a fermata, bringing the music to a pause.❸ Turning now to the parallel minor, E-flat minor, she begins the phrase anew and this time reaches considerably further afield to C-flat major for *Ferne* to accentuate the sense of musical distance. Then, during the next several measures, the bass line ascends through a remote chromatic harmonic sequence before she reestablishes the major mode and tonic E-flat and concludes by reharmonizing the opening bars to secure once again the nearness of E-flat major. The basic pattern of statement, departure, and return already familiar in Fanny's piano miniatures thus finds an appropriate use in *An Suleika*, where she deepens the harmonic coloration through chromaticism in her search for apt musical counterparts to Goethe's amorous images.

Only one of Fanny's Suleika settings, the duodrama "An des lust'gen Brunnens Rand" (H-U 149), found its way into print during the nineteenth century—not as her work, but again under the "protective" aegis of Felix, who released the song in 1827 as the twelfth, final member of his op. 8. Goethe had designed the poem as an exchange between Suleika and Hatem, so Fanny obligingly set the verses as a duet. First, to playful, light figurations in the piano, Suleika discovers by the water jets of a fountain her initials tenderly traced by Hatem's hand. Her infatuated lover answers, "From Suleika to Suleika / is my coming and my going," and then the two sing together, reaching the climax of their parts near the end, before a short piano postlude. The three-part division follows a formula, familiar in operatic duets, that Felix later modified in his own stylized duet for piano, the *Lied ohne Worte*, op. 38, no. 6, inspired by his engagement in 1836 to Cécile Jeanrenaud.

Felix appropriated one other lied of Fanny from 1825, *Italien* (H-U 157), released in 1827 as his op. 8, no. 3. This was the celebrated song Queen Victoria sang at Buckingham Palace in 1842 (see p. 285), on which occasion Felix sheepishly disclosed his sister's authorship. A few years later, the poet A. H. Hoffmann von Fallersleben, now remembered for the nationalistic anthem *Deutschland, Deutschland über Alles*, was smitten by Fanny's melody and crafted a new poem, *Sehnsucht*, which he issued with her music in 1848.[31] During the 1840s the poet counted Felix among his acquaintances in Frankfurt, though whether the composer was then as forthright about Fanny's authorship as he had been with the queen is not known. In any event, the title page of von Fallersleben's *contrafactum* preserved the misattribution—here we learn that the poet had conceived his text after being "delighted" by the "genius of Mendelssohn's music."[32]

It is not difficult to imagine what attracted Fanny to Grillparzer's verses, inspired by his own Italian sojourn and published in 1820 with the geographically more precise title *Zwischen Gaeta und Kapua* (*Between Gaeta and Capua*). Here Fanny could align her own unfulfilled Italian *Reiselust* with the Austrian's desire to escape from the "burdens of prose" into an Edenlike "land of poetry." Two years earlier, in 1823, she had struggled to set another Grillparzer poem, this one inspired by his experiences near Gaeta after a storm. *Am Morgen nach einem Sturm: Im Molo di Gaeta* (H-U 89)[33] had initially resisted musical translation, for Fanny abandoned one incomplete draft before finishing a second, apportioned between a recitative and an arioso. The recitative begins with the piano firmly stating a lamentlike descending tetrachord, an outmoded stock figure that does not quite resonate to Grillparzer's memories of the raging elements. In contrast, Fanny's *Italien* does capture the heightened sensory stimulation of Grillparzer's second poem, expressed in its opening stanzas through a series of comparative adjectives: in Italy the plains are "more beautiful," the sun "more golden," the sky "more blue," the greenery "more green," the scents "more aromatic."

To intensify the accumulating sensory images in *Italien*, Fanny chose a strophic setting with three statements, of which the final, expanded repetition twice attained a climactic high G. The upward sweep and buoyant charm of the music❸ made a memorable impression on Felix, who recalled it, and Fanny's *Am Morgen nach einem Sturm*, when he visited Mola di Gaeta in April 1831: "Among a thousand other thoughts, Grillparzer's poem recurred to my memory, which it is almost impossible to set to music; for which reason, I suppose, Fanny has composed a charming melody on it; but I do not jest when I say that I sang the song over repeatedly to myself, for I was standing on the very spot he describes. The sea had subsided, and was now calm, and at rest;

this was the first song. The second followed next day, for the sea was like a meadow of pure ether as you gazed at it, and pretty women nodded their heads, and so did olives and cypresses."[34]

iii

On October 11, 1825, the English musician Sir George Smart arrived in Berlin. A keen observer of European musical life, Smart used tuning forks to calibrate discrepancies in orchestral pitch, and routinely timed the durations of compositions, especially Beethoven's. Prior to visiting Prussia, Smart had consulted with Beethoven near Vienna in Baden, where two years before his death the deaf composer jotted down a prophetic canon on the Hippocratic aphorism *ars longa, vita brevis* (art is long; life is short). The Englishman then proceeded to Dresden to visit Carl Maria von Weber but found the mechanical owls in a production of *Der Freischütz* wanting—not in number but in eyes sufficiently "glaring."[35] Within a day of reaching Berlin, Smart was dining comfortably with the Mendelssohns, speaking English with Lea, and recording observations in his diary, chiefly about Felix, that occasionally mentioned Fanny. Thus, we learn, when Felix performed a "clever fugue, pastorale and fantasia of Sebastian Bach," he used a chamber organ while Fanny supplied the pedal part on a Broadwood piano Abraham had purchased in Paris.[36] The siblings offered a duet arrangement of one of Felix's overtures, and Fanny performed Mozart duets with Smart, but he recorded no references to her own music.

Nor did Smart mention a watershed composition completed on October 15—Felix's Octet op. 20, generally regarded as his first masterpiece and the first major composition he finished at Leipzigerstrasse no. 3. Considerable mystery surrounds the origins of this iconic chamber work, which, with its myriad instrumental combinations extracted from the expanded complement of two string quartets, stands as the quintessential example of Mendelssohnian precocity. Nevertheless, we owe to Fanny's intimate knowledge of the score—she later recalled that she memorized his compositions before he notated them[37]—the significant revelation that the scherzo was a musical realization of the "Walpurgis Night's Dream" from Goethe's *Faust*, Part I. "To me alone he told this idea," she wrote: "the whole piece is to be played staccato and pianissimo, the tremulandos coming in now and then, the trills passing away with the quickness of lightning; everything new and strange, and at the same time most insinuating and pleasing, one feels so near the world of spirits, carried away in the air, half inclined to snatch up a broomstick and follow the aerial procession."[38] In 1843, she herself would succumb to the temptation to set the opening scene of *Faust*, Part II (see p. 293).

After celebrating a first Christmas in the newly renovated main residence of Leipzigerstrasse no. 3, the family welcomed in the new year additional members to the circle: Betty Pistor, who sang in the Singakademie, stirred the adolescent Felix's passion, and read, with Rebecka, Manzoni's sensational new novel, *I promessi sposi*;[39] the Swede Adolf Lindblad, a new pupil of Zelter; Carl Loewe, the ballad composer and music director of Stettin, who premiered Felix's *Midsummer Night's Dream* Overture in 1827; and the philologist J. G. Droysen, who tutored Felix and Rebecka in Greek up to Aeschylus. In November Moscheles again appeared on the concert stage in Berlin and "privately" celebrated Fanny's twenty-first birthday at a Sunday musicale given on November 12, 1826. During this visit he was among the first to hear Felix's new *Midsummer Night's Dream* Overture, presented by the siblings as a piano duet.[40] When an unidentified Frenchman, unversed in Shakespeare, reacted to the duet, he likened it, aptly enough, to a dream.[41]

Through most of 1826 Fanny remained in Berlin, but in June and July it was her turn to accompany Abraham to Bad Doberan. There she composed lieder, including two stylistically akin settings in G minor. In the first (H-U 176),[42] we hear Mignon's familiar lament from *Wilhelm Meister* that proved irresistible to Schubert and other composers—"Nur wer die Sehnsucht kennt, weiß was ich leide" (sometimes rendered in English as "None but the lonely heart"). Fanny suggests the pressing weight of Mignon's secret torment with falling arpeggiations in the piano and drooping chromatic lines in the voice, occasionally reversed by leaps to climactic high pitches that then, too, subside in a seemingly endless pattern of grief. In *Die Äolsharfe auf dem Schlosse zu Baden* (*The Aeolian Harp at the Baden Palace*, H-U 179)[43] she turned to a wistful poem of Friedericke Robert. Its three strophes recall a medieval vision of knights and armaments, of courtly love (*Minne*) and fidelity, all effaced by the passage of time. Here as well the vocal line tends to descend by chromatic motion and, as if responding to the text, momentarily seems to disappear when the treble part of the piano crosses above the vocal line. The intense chromaticism produces some striking harmonic excursions, as in an unexpected shift to D-flat major just bars before the end. There Fanny again resorts to the raised or Picardy third, to give the whole an antiquated, historically remote cadence. The song remained one of her favorites; in 1839 a revised version appeared with the title *Schloß Liebeneck* in the album *Rhein-Sagen und Lieder*, published in Cologne and Bonn.

In 1826 Fanny completed no fewer than nine settings of Johann Heinrich Voss,[44] whose death that year stimulated her interest in a now largely forgotten member of the Göttinger Hain (Göttingen Grove), a group of lyrical poets who in 1772 had declared their literary allegiance to Klopstock. Mainly celebrated for translating Homer—Schiller preferred Voss's version of the *Iliad* to the original—Voss had some success as a poet of natural, idyllic scenes, though later generations detected an excessive reliance on platitudinous figures of speech. Nevertheless, in the case of *Sehnsucht* (H-U 190),[45] Fanny composed music of considerable pathos to depict the apparition of the nightingale

Philomela, whose song wafts through the May fragrances like a funeral dirge to her lover. Fanny adjusted a three-part strophic setting to accommodate a transposition of the music a fourth higher for the second strophe and suffused the song with chromatic ornamental tones, the easier to mediate between major and minor forms of the tonic triad.

Some of Voss's poems were sufficiently *volkstümlich* in character to inspire from Fanny folk song–like settings, including *Der Rosenkranz* (*The Rosary*), published posthumously at midcentury as her op. 9, no. 3. She designated *Feldlied* (*Field Song*), scored for a cappella chorus, as a part-song that could be performed *im Garten*, suggesting how music making at Leipzigerstrasse no. 3 occasionally escaped the confines of the formal *Musiksaal* into the free out-doors. The simple but affecting *Am Grabe* (*By the Grave*),[46] for chorus or voice and piano, extracted a rare concession from Zelter, who had earlier treated the same verses, conceived by Voss in 1800 on the death of composer J. A. P. Schulz. Because Fanny's version was superior, Zelter admitted to Goethe in 1826 to forwarding a copy to Voss's widow as a fitting tribute to the poet's recent passing.[47]

As for Goethe, Fanny produced in 1826 a substantial duet, "Ich hab' ihn gesehen" (H-U 186),[48] in which a soprano and tenor play the roles of a *Mäd-chen* and *Jüngling* searching for and then finding each other. The extended format of the composition (seventy-seven measures) accommodates a dra-matic scene, in which first the maiden appears (D major, 6/8 time), and then the youth (D minor, 4/4 time), before the two sing together, thus reusing and expanding the formula Fanny had already applied in *Suleika*. Linked the-matically to "Ich hab' ihn gesehen" is Fanny's charming and contemporaneous rendition of *Nähe des Geliebten* (*Nearness of the Beloved*, H-U 189),[49] Goethe's "re-composition" of a 1795 poem by Friederike Brun,[50] with its refrainlike line, "Ich denke dein" ("I think of you"). Employing again the major-minor triad duality, Fanny's thoughts continued to dwell on her absent beloved, Wilhelm. Thus, she "thinks" of him in the sunlight on a shimmering sea and the moon-light that engulfs a fountain at night, two contrasting images from Goethe that find their musical counterpart in a sudden, passing turn from D major to D minor.

In her lieder of 1826 Fanny seemed content to refine her art as a min-iaturist, in contrast to Felix's broadening compositional aspirations. Never-theless, one of her songs betrays intriguing, though hitherto unrecognized, similarities to works of Felix and suggests that Fanny's twinlike compositional voice may have played a role in the formation of the Mendelssohnian style. The song in question is *Der Eichwald brauset* (*The Oak Forest Roars*, H-U 170),[51] a balladelike romance of Schiller, also set by Felix under the poet's title *Des Mädchens Klage* (*The Maiden's Lament*). The similarities between the two compositions are too numerous to pass as coincidence. Both are in a minor key (Fanny, A minor; Felix, B minor) that ultimately turns to the major, and both use the same time signature (6/8). Most compelling are the nearly identical pitch contours of the opening vocal phrases, strongly suggesting that one was a response to the other (example 4.1). Felix's composition is considerably more elaborate; through-composed, it traverses fifty-five turbulent bars, while Fanny's version, in a modified strophic arrangement, fills only thirty-six. And there are differences in the piano accompaniment to express the agitation of the maiden who has "lived and loved" and now wishes to end her life. While Felix employs sweeping, far-flung arpeggiations, Fanny resorts to tremolo-like broken chords against a detached, descending bass.

Which sibling inspired the other? Frustrating our inquiry is the lack of a dated autograph for Felix's *Des Mädchens Klage*; it appeared in print post-humously in 1866, nearly two decades after his death. In 1836, Fanny sent Felix for his birthday a volume of Schiller and noted, with a humorous reference to Beethoven's Ninth Symphony, "Of course you won't compose "Freude schöner Götterfunken" from it," but then wondered what else might "slumber

EXAMPLE 4.1.   (a) Fanny Mendelssohn, "Der Eichwald brauset" (1826); (b) Felix Mendelssohn, *Des Mädchens Klage*

(*Continued*)

EXAMPLE 4.I.   Continued

in a volume of poetry."[52] We might well imagine Felix on this occasion reading *Des Mädchens Klage*, recalling his sister's earlier setting of 1826, and then composing his own version, into which he wove some telltale allusions. Be that as it may, there is a second composition of Felix that betrays a relationship, albeit a more subtle one, to Fanny's lied—his textless *Lied ohne Worte* in A Minor, op. 38, no. 5, composed in 1837.◉ Felix's piano "song" uses the same key as

Fanny, has the same detached bass line encountered in Fanny's second stro-phe, and presents a treble melody that, as in "Der Eichwald brauset," opens out from the single repeated pitch E. There is a balladelike quality to Felix's piano piece, which intimates something of Schubert's *Erlkönig*,[53] but the con-nections to Fanny's lied point to something more substantial—a free artistic exchange between the two, in which a thematic idea, turn of phrase, or texture used by one was subsequently taken up and reworked by the other.

Because of his significant position in nineteenth-century music, most historians have viewed Felix as the dominant influence on Fanny, so that through much of the twentieth century, to the extent that scholars considered her music, she rarely emerged as more than a shadowy, epigonal figure in her brother's circle. To be sure, we shall have many occasions in this volume to acknowledge her profound stylistic debts to Felix. But a careful review of their compositions shows that musical ideas could flow between them in a recipro-cal way, with one creative spirit mirroring the other.

Thus, we should not be surprised to find further evidence of Felix's debt to his sister in a borrowing from one of her piano pieces of 1826, the highly singular Capriccio in F-sharp Major (H-U 165).[54] In a striking departure from her other piano miniatures, Fanny replaces the conventional tempo mark-ing with the comment, "Humorous and somewhat ironic" (*Humoristisch und etwas ironisch*). Indeed, the piece begins with a quirky, triplet upbeat figure that defines the tonic in a rather leisurely way, only to negate it by mov-ing abruptly to the subdominant B major. Offsetting the eccentric start of the composition is the lyrical, romantic second theme, introduced by a pas-sage with octave doublings reminiscent of the first movement of Beethoven's late Piano Sonata op. 110. Now Fanny's second theme itself impresses for its striking foreshadowing of the second theme in the first movement of Felix's Piano Sonata in B-flat Major, composed in 1827.◗ When Felix's student work was published posthumously in 1868, it appeared with the opus number 106, as if to emphasize its obvious ties to Beethoven's *Hammerklavier* Sonata, op. 106, the magisterial sonata that had preoccupied Fanny in 1825. But the clear links to Fanny's theme, of which Felix's theme impresses as a glosslike elaboration, suggest again an exchange of musical ideas between the siblings, in this instance, an exchange in which the sister took the lead.

iv

Fanny's study of Beethoven unlocked a hidden side of her creativity and encouraged her to explore sharply profiled, individualistic manners of expres-sion in her piano compositions. The signs of greater stylistic freedom and risk taking emerge even in two neobaroque piano compositions of 1826. The Etude in F Major (H-U 166),[55] nearly 200 bars in length, at first glance strikes the observer with conservative points of imitation, spun-out harmonic sequences, persistently recurring rhythmic patterns, and prolonged pedal points and octave doublings that simulate the sound of an organ and suggest J. S. Bach. But the tonal freedom of the composition and its unconventional opening—after four ponderous (*pesante*) octaves in the bass the first harmony we hear is a jarring, repeated, dissonant augmented triad (F–A–C-sharp)—give the work a harmonic individuality at odds with Fanny's baroque musings. And in the Andante con espressione in C Minor (H-U 198),[56] she takes the process even further. Etudelike, the piece requires the pianist to highlight from a disjunct, compound melodic line in the treble a theme, the initial contours of which trace a pattern familiar in a number of baroque fugues.[57] But no fugue or fugato ever materializes in her Andante, which rather takes shape as an expressive, heavily chromatic piano lied. Only the four-note subject and raised final cadence in C major are vestiges of its baroque origins; otherwise this soulful piece belongs to the nineteenth century.

In the case of the Allegro ma non troppo in F Minor, from February 1826 (H-U 167), Fanny created a piece nearly as unusual as the Capriccio.[58] The Allegro begins with a brooding harmonic sequence that passes stepwise from F minor to E-flat minor and D-flat major, a parallel progression that possibly recalls some of Beethoven's experiments. Pointing to Beethoven, too, are passages with rapid hand crossings, a manual device she would have encountered, for example, in the finale of his Sonata op. 110. But totally unexpected is the arrival, forty bars into her composition, of a courtly, dancelike Tempo di Polacca in A-flat major, a Polish reference that remains a mystery. Equally striking, and seemingly unprecedented, is the distinctive notational feature Fanny applied to her score, elucidated in an editorial comment: "This piece must be performed with many changes in tempo, but always gently, without jerking. The signs ⪇ ⪈ stand for *accelerando* and *ritardando*."[59] The instruction is striking on several counts. First, the performer is to interpret the tempo flexibly, presumably in a type of rubato—the rhythmic groupings are not literal but elastic, now pressing forward, now restrained. Traditionally used to control dynamics, the hairpins regulate instead a constantly shifting sense of rhythmic energy and abatement. Second, the question arises whether this unusual rhythmic experiment was unique to the Allegro in F Minor or representative of Fanny's general performance practice. And third, there is the equally vexing issue of the audience to whom Fanny directed her comment. Apart from Fanny, Felix, and perhaps Lea, exactly who would have performed the Allegro? And why did Fanny feel compelled to explain her notational experiment, especially if she did not intend to publish the piece?

For her reality was that music making remained firmly in the purview of her domestic life and immediate circle of friends. Granted, there were some unusual diversions; in August 1826, around the time Felix finished the *Midsummer Night's Dream* Overture, the siblings "founded" with Karl Klingemann a mock literary paper, the *Gartenzeitung* (*Garden Times*) followed during the winter months by a *Schnee- und Thee-Zeitung* (*Snow and Tea Times*), of which several "issues" were organized at the residence, in the form of Sapphic poems, aphorisms, short essays, drawings, and occasional musical entries.[60] Among the contributors were Zelter, Abraham Mendelssohn Bartholdy, and the world-renowned scientist Alexander von Humboldt. Fanny herself submitted on September 13, 1826, a Waltz in F-sharp Major (H-U 184); its intriguing title, *Westöstlicher Redaktionswalzer* (literally, *West-East Editorial Waltz*), suggests some connection to Goethe's *Westöstlicher Divan*, though the composition's purpose or message remains unclear.

According to Sebastian Hensel, during the closing months of 1826 Fanny and Felix led a "fantastic, dream-like life,"[61] with music making enlivened by playful readings of Shakespeare and Jean Paul Richter, whose unconventional *Bildungsromane*, filled with Shandyesque digressions reminiscent of Laurence Sterne, held sway over an impressionable German youth. Sebastian went so far as to designate the period the happiest time in the life of Abraham, then presiding over a distinguished Berlin house and children on the verge of fulfilling "beautiful promises." Thus, Fanny was "equal in gifts and talent" to Felix, who was now "past the period of hesitation, and on a safe way to the highest station a man can reach, well-deserved fame in art." Indeed, at the beginning of 1827 he surveyed promising new horizons: in February came the public premieres of the *Midsummer Night's Dream* Overture in Stettin and First Symphony in Leipzig, while in Berlin plans were made to mount his new opera *Die Hochzeit des Camacho* (*The Wedding of Camacho*) at the Schauspielhaus in April. What is more, in May Felix matriculated at the University of Berlin, in order to obtain, as Lea observed, the "*Bildung* so often lacking in musicians."[62]

The university was then not an option for women, so for Fanny, Felix's advancement entailed one more degree of separation from her brother. While her brother attended, along with the professoriate, fellow students, and countless other gentlemen, Humboldt's highly feted lectures on geography at the university, Fanny had access only to a second, more popular lecture series at the Singakademie, as she explained to Klingemann: "But do you know that at his majesty's desire [Humboldt] has begun a second course of lectures in the hall of the Singakademie, attended by everybody who lays any claim to good breeding and fashion, from the king and the whole court, ministers, generals, officers, artists, authors, *beaux esprits* (and ugly ones, too), students, and ladies, down to your unworthy correspondent? The crowd is fearful, the public imposing, and the lectures are very interesting indeed. Gentlemen may laugh as much as they like, but it is delightful that we too have the opportunity given us of listening to clever men."[63] Once again, Fanny asserted her need for intellectual stimulation, her need to take her place in the arena of men, if only, in this instance, as a passive observer.

When, in September 1828, Humboldt commissioned Felix to compose a cantata for an international gathering of scientists convened in Berlin, Fanny reported on the event as an outsider and commented on the peculiar scoring of the composition, seemingly intended to reinforce the male identity of the assembly: "As the naturalists follow the rule of Mahomet and exclude women from their paradise, the choir consists only of the best male voices of the capital; and as Humboldt, whose forte music is not, has limited his composer as to the number of musicians, the orchestra is quite original; it consists only of double-basses, violoncellos, trumpets, horns, and clarinets. Yesterday they had a rehearsal, and the effect is said to be good." The only thing that vexed Fanny was that "we must not be present."[64] Ruefully, she admitted that she could only watch Felix's "progress with loving eyes" and not lead him "on the wings of thought" and foresee his aim. He was now in full command of his abilities, "ruling like a general over all the means of development" art could offer him.[65]

In Abraham's view, by 1827 Felix indeed had completed his musical education, to the point that further instruction "would only fetter him."[66] Felix's lessons with Zelter—and presumably, Fanny's as well—were now discontinued. If Zelter's diminishment in the Mendelssohn household silenced one of the few authorities who could critique Fanny's music, it also freed her from her teacher's conservative musical tastes and, if anything, encouraged her to be more creative and spontaneous in her compositions. And it strengthened the interdependence of Fanny and Felix—and for Fanny, Felix's crucial role as her musical alter ego, her artistic twin. Striking evidence of the siblings' symbiotic relationship emerges in an unusual, if notorious, collaborative effort from this time, the twelve *Gesänge*, op. 8, published under Felix's name by the Berlin firm of Schlesinger in two installments—nos. 1–6 at the end of 1826, followed by the entire opus in May 1827. Of the twelve, nos. 2, 3, and 12—*Das Heimweh, Italien,* and *Suleika und Hatem* (see pp. 81, 95, and 94)—were of course by Fanny, though they appeared without attribution, so that the broader public naturally enough heard them as her brother's creations.

At first glance, Felix's silent incorporation of the songs impresses as nothing less than artistic theft, as an endorsement of a nineteenth-century social code that routinely devalued women's creativity. The transfer of authorship recalls the similar treatment of his aunt Dorothea, whose writings initially appeared under the name or "editorship" of Friedrich Schlegel, or Goethe's appropriation of verses by Marianne von Willemer. But some evidence suggests that the use of Fanny's songs was more complex than a deliberate suppression by Felix and that Fanny was not uninvolved, even if, according to her son Sebastian, she desired "nothing but modestly to remain within the bounds nature has set to woman."[67] We know, for instance, that Fanny read engraver's proofs of the music and, further, requested to see the title page before the work's publication.[68] Minimizing her own contributions, she singled out Felix's *Pilgerspruch* (op. 8, no. 5) as the best song in the collection, though she also criticized a faulty harmonic progression in the same work.[69] One has the impression that Fanny's role was considerably more than that of mere bystander, that in addition to contributing three lieder, she critiqued Felix's music, possibly even had a hand in final revisions, and advised him about the selection and order of the songs, several of which, significantly, are compact strophic settings that simulate Fanny's miniaturist art of lied composition. Felix's *Minnelied* (no. 1) and *Abendlied* (no. 9), for example, are but eighteen and seventeen measures in length. In the latter, to convey the idea of night wrapping the world in darkness, Felix indulges in an unexpected—for him unusual—harmonic turn that momentarily bends the music from the familiar tonic-dominant harmonic axis, a stratagem more characteristic of his sister. What is more, two of his songs (the *Minnelied* and *Hexenlied*, no. 8) set verses by Hölty, a poet, as we shall shortly see, who inspired Fanny herself to compose no fewer than nine settings in 1827.

Now if Fanny's contributions to op. 8 initially remained hidden from music officialdom, they were common knowledge among the family's circle of friends. And so, when A. B. Marx reviewed the publication in the *Berliner allgemeine musikalische Zeitung*, he pointedly suggested that *Suleika und Hatem* captured a form of love so pure that one might be tempted to label the lied *weiblich* (feminine) "if one did not know the composer, if there were female composers, and if ladies could absorb such profound music." Similarly, Marx detected in *Das Heimweh* a certain feminine, "languishing" quality uncharacteristic of the "manly" composer, a thinly veiled clue about that song's origins.[70] Why, then, did Felix tacitly incorporate his sister's songs into his collection? The act suggests not so much an arrant denial of her artistic genius—Felix later openly admitted that Fanny produced examples worthy of the very best German lieder (see p. 193)—as a calculated compromise: the publication of the three songs afforded Fanny an audience beyond her familiar circle in Berlin, while the suppression of her identity safeguarded the privacy of the family (here issues of class as well as gender came into play),[71] and protected her from undesired publicity. But the plan was not foolproof. After visiting Berlin in 1829, the English musician John Thomson revealed in the *Harmonicon* that "three of the best songs" were by Fanny and then added this remarkable *aperçu*: "I cannot refrain from mentioning Miss Mendelssohn's name in connection with these songs, more particularly, when I see so many ladies without one atom of genius coming forward to the public with their musical crudities, and, because these are printed, holding up their heads as if they were finished musicians."[72]

v

Song composition indeed dominated Fanny's attention in 1827 and in 1828; during those two years, she completed thirty new examples, several of which easily stand with her contributions to op. 8. Nearly half explored further the Göttinger Hain, whose close-knit literary league, modeled on Klopstock, had promoted a supple style of poetry extolling Teutonic virtues. Among its members were the already encountered J. H. Voss and his precocious friend L. C. H. Hölty, who had succumbed to tuberculosis at age twenty-eight in 1776. Fanny was drawn in particular to Hölty's odes, elegies, and ballads, sometimes Anacreontic in tone, but usually evincing the poet's longing for an idealized Laura and conveying presentiments of his death, often through the imagery of blurry, moonlit landscapes.

In two Klopstock settings, *Die Sommernacht* (*Summer Night*, H-U 209)[73] and *Die frühen Gräber* (*Early Graves*, posthumously published as Fanny's op. 9, no. 4), shimmering moonlight and a blossoming linden tree trigger memories of departed loved ones. The latter song, a compact, strophic composition, employs a slowly progressing figure that charts the lunar course by rising from the dark register of the piano above deep, somnolent bass tones. The unusual key, A-flat major, also enhances the otherworldly quality of the music. In *Die Sommernacht*, Fanny applies a modified strophic arrangement, with diverging harmonic cadences to demarcate the three strophes. Here the vocal line initially descends gently to suggest the magical dispersion of the moonlight and then, by reversing course and beginning to rise, the wafting fragrance of the linden. Recurring appoggiaturas impart a sense of passing dissonance, and in the concluding piano postlude, she plays further on the idea of loss and memory—the opening, descending pitches of the vocal pitch now reappear, transferred to the bass line, where they are drawn out one by one and obscured by the welling sonorities above.

Of the three Voss settings (H-U 205, 206, and 208), *Der Maiabend* ("May Evening") found print in 1850 as Fanny's op. 9, no. 5. Felix seems to have valued this short song of eleven measures, for he inscribed a "faithful copy" (*treue Abschrift*) to the English family of William Horsley.[74] Even more compact is Fanny's eight-bar *Sehnsucht*, a eulogy in the dark key of G-sharp minor for August Hanstein, a friend who had died of tuberculosis in June 1827. Upon hearing the setting, but unaware it was written for Hanstein, Felix later intuited its meaning by commenting how "consumptive" (*schwindsüchtig*) the piece sounded.[75]

Several of Fanny's nine Hölty settings from 1827 form a group linked musically by subtle means.[76] For instance, three—*Die Ersehnte* (*The Longed-For One*), "Kein Blick der Hoffnung" ("No Prospect of Hope"), and *Die Schiffende* (*The Boatwoman*)—have vocal lines that begin with wide, descending leaps; in several songs Fanny uses similar arpeggiated piano accompaniments;

and in almost all she experiments with a type of harmonic coloration that, responding to nuances in the poetry, frequently moves between the major and minor modes. *Die Ersehnte* offers a good example of the last technique. Here, Fanny condenses into a miniature of fourteen bars the poet's irregular three-line stanzas:

Brächte dich meinem Arm der nächste Frühling	If next spring brought you to my arm,
Tönten Vögel aus Blüten mir das Brautlied,	If birds intoned from blossoms a bridal song,
Dann hätt ich Seliger schon auf Erden Wonne des Himmels.	Then, blessed, I would already have heaven's rapture on earth.

She achieves a harmonic compression in which every chromatic pitch assumes heightened meaning. Though the music begins securely in the major mode, in the third and sixth bars she begins insinuating chromatic pitches to intimate the minor mode. The last line of the concluding strophe—"Trübe floß mein Leben, O Himmelsbotin, komm es zu heitern" ("Cheerlessly my life flowed; O heavenly messenger, come to lighten it")—reveals the poetic inspiration for the major-minor mode exchange, a deceptively simple technique that nevertheless lends the lied an undeniable depth of expression.

Fanny encountered in Hölty's poetry recurring images of springtime renewal, of natural scenes dappled by moonlight, and, above all, of longing for love. In two poems, "Kein Blick der Hoffnung" and "Sehnsucht" (H-U 192), he identified the object of his infatuation, after Petrarch, as Laura. (In real life she was Anna Juliane Hagemann, daughter of a Hanover superintendent, with whom the young poet had been utterly smitten.[77]) But even in poems that do not mention Laura, her presence is figuratively invoked. Thus, in *Die Schiffende*, which Fanny later published under her own name (see p. 210), Hölty transformed Laura into a seductive boatwoman, whose skiff sways and dances on a silver-hued pond—in Fanny's setting, against rippling, wavelike figurations in the piano. In *An den Mond* (*To the Moon*), set by Schubert in 1816, the poet imagines his lover returning to place flowers upon his grave. And in *Maigesang* (*May Song*), inspired by Shakespeare's "It was a lover and his lass,"[78] an explosion of sensual images envelops a youth's fantasies about a *Mägdlein*. In contrast to the plaintive G minor of *An den Mond*, Fanny turns here to a bright G major, with recurring, accumulating rhythmic patterns to match Hölty's nimble imagery.

Quite apart from these lieder is the austere, brooding *Seufzer* ("Sighs," H-U 195), in which Fanny used minimal means to invoke the call of a nightingale, perceived as a plaintive sigh by the poet wandering alone in a grove but as a cheerful vocalization by eavesdropping pairs of lovers. The first and third strophes employ an unassuming six-bar vocal phrase in A minor that initially repeats a single pitch, E, embellished by a sighlike appoggiatura simulating the nightingale. Representing the wanderer's point of view, the melodically identical outer strophes lend the vocal line a hollow, hauntingly static quality. Pitch for pitch, the melody of the second strophe, representing the lovers, nearly replicates that of the first and third, but here Fanny adds a series of sharps, so that the music quickly moves from A minor to more remote sonorities, including G-sharp major and C-sharp minor, before pausing on A major.

The halting, sparing sonorities of *Seufzer* revealed to Fanny how, paradoxically, compositional restraint could engender musical and poetic intensification. The song depends for its effect upon the most simple means—the initial fixation on a pitch, for instance—and upon subtle details that one might easily overlook—the echoing sigh of the nightingale in the piano and a few deft chromatic alterations to the melodic line in the middle strophe. The result is a song of stark beauty that brings to mind other notable lieder that employ limited means to striking effect—Schubert in *Der Leiermann* (*Winterreise*, 1828) and Hugo Wolf in *Das verlassene Mägdlein* (*Mörike Lieder*, 1888), to name two examples.

Be that as it may, in 1827 Fanny discovered a poet of seminal significance for the German lied, who would inspire countless tunesmiths to generate thousands of settings and composers such as Schubert, Robert Schumann, and Wolf to transform the genre. In that year appeared the anthology-like *Buch der Lieder* (*Book of Songs*) of Heinrich Heine, at first glance an unlikely candidate for the central position he later assumed in the nineteenth-century canon of German arts and letters. Heine viewed himself as "Romanticism's harvester and gravedigger,"[79] who did not hesitate to use the stock imagery and vocabulary of an earlier generation while he maintained a "modern" critical distance from that illusory world. Trenchant irony—the poet Eichendorff quipped that nearly all of Heine's lyrics ended in "suicide"—became his most powerful tool for dismantling the romantic fictions he constructed in his poems. In Jeffrey Sammons's appraisal, this "sardonic breach of mood" at once "fascinated and bothered his contemporaries. The tone shifts back and forth from the emotional to the conversational, from the delicate to the blunt, the setting from the realm of the imagination to the banal scenes of modern society. It is all true in Heine's poetry: the feeling and the frustration, the hope and the delusion, the desirability of the beloved and her dimwitted cruelty."[80] Heine himself was all too aware of these irremediable disjunctions; in the preface to the 1839 second edition of the *Buch*, he opined, "It would seem to me that all too many lies are told in beautiful verse, and that truth shrinks from appearing in metrical garb."[81]

Fanny perceived an uncomfortable contradiction between Heine's personal manners and his poetry, which she expressed privately to Karl Klingemann in 1829: "Heine is here, and I do not like him at all, he is so affected. If he would let himself go, he would of all eccentric men be the most amiable; or if in good earnest he would keep a tight hand over himself, gravity also would become him, for he is grave too. But he gives himself sentimental airs, is affectedly affected, talks incessantly of himself, and all the while looks at you to see whether you look at him."[82] And yet, in 1827 and 1828, she set six of his poems from the *Buch der Lieder*[83] and in 1829 found herself captivated by his *Reisebilder* (*Travel Pictures*): "They contain delightful things; and though for ten times you may be inclined to despise him, the eleventh time you cannot help confessing that he is a poet, a true poet! How he manages the words! What a feeling he has for nature, such as only a real poet has!"[84]

This natural poet had come to know the Mendelssohns a few years earlier, when he matriculated at the University of Berlin from 1821 to 1823 as a law student, supported by his uncle Salomon Heine, a wealthy Jewish banker who had socialized with Abraham and Lea in Hamburg some ten years before. At the university, Heine preceded Felix in attending Hegel's lectures on the philosophy of religion and right, but a more immediate influence on the poet's development was Eduard Gans, founder of a Verein für Cultur und Wissenschaft der Juden, a society committed to addressing Jewish assimilation into European culture, that recruited a young Heine then contemplating his Jewish identity. With little difficulty we may trace Gans's enlightened agendum to the eighteenth-century project of Moses Mendelssohn; there was, in addition, another link to the family, for Gans became a serious, if unsuccessful, suitor for the hand of Fanny's sister, Rebecka. Another Berliner who may have facilitated Heine's admission to the Mendelssohns' circle was Rahel von Varnhagen, to whom he dedicated one of the six sections of the *Buch der Lieder*. Through Rahel's celebrated salon, Heine may have met Felix, whom the poet pronounced in 1822 a "musical miracle" and a "second Mozart";[85] whether Heine was then conscious of Fanny's aspirations as a lied composer is uncertain.

Why was Fanny intrigued by Heine's poetry? At least two explanations emerge. First, like other informed readers of the time, she could not have missed Heine's frequent allusions to the folk song–like art of Wilhelm Müller, a poet she had absorbed and set to music with Wilhelm Hensel's encouragement just a few years before. In 1826 Heine admitted he had found in Müller a "pure sound and true simplicity" but then qualified the debt—if Müller's poems were all folk songs, Heine conceded only that his approach to form was "somewhat folklike," while the content belonged to "conventional society."[86] Heine indeed used Müller as a foil, a way to link his own modern sensibilities to a realm of romanticized folk mythology, but in the process drew liberally upon imagery—fisher maidens, linden trees, and the like—and even distinctive phrases and rhyme patterns from Müller.[87] For Fanny, setting Heine's verses entailed in part reengaging with a cluster of themes and ideas already explored in Müller.

In addition, Fanny would have appreciated Heine's conspicuous compression of means. Many of the poems from the *Lyrisches Intermezzo* (*Lyrical Intermezzo*) and *Die Heimkehr* (*The Homecoming*)—the most celebrated parts of the *Buch der Lieder*, and the parts from which Fanny drew—fall into a few compact quatrains, well suited to her miniaturist settings and pithy musical gestures. Thus, she fitted the four stanzas of "Was will die einsame Träne" (H-U 207) into a highly concentrated strophic setting that required only twelve bars. Heine's image of the solitary, lingering tear,

Was will die einsame Träne?	Why does this lonely teardrop
Sie trübt mir ja den Blick.	Still dim my vision—why?
Sie blieb aus alten Zeiten,	From older days of sorrow
In meinem Aug' zurück.	It lingers in my eye.[88]

inspired a stripped-down, simple melodic line, initially doubled in bare thirds, without full, four-part harmony.♪ (In 1837 Felix attempted a similar setting of the poem that impresses as a reminiscence of his sister's effort.[89]) The abrupt shift in the concluding stanza,

Ach, meine Liebe selber,	Ah, love itself has flown too,
Zerfloß wie eitel Hauch!	Like an idle breath unblest!
Du alle, einsame Träne,	Go now, lonely teardrop,
Zerfließe jetztunter auch!	Oh, fly away with the rest!

in turn elicited a harmonic surprise, Fanny's response to Heine's *Stimmungsbrechung*, or rupture of mood. In the closing bars she used an altered, chromatic chord (known to music theorists as a Neapolitan sonority) to prepare the traditional dominant to tonic, or "authentic," final cadence.[90] This manipulation entailed an unexpected harmonic twist—the unusual pairing of F major and B major triads—that momentarily displaced the conventional harmonic vocabulary of the key of E minor, and revealed Fanny to have been attentive to Heine's deflating endings. Two of Fanny's other Heine settings also display musical parallels to his ironies. In *Am leuchtenden Sommermorgen* (H-U 212), in which flowers address the poet as a "pale, sorrowful man," a Neapolitan coloring again tinges the music at strategic moments. And in "Und wüßten's die Blumen," later incorporated into Felix's second collection of songs as op. 9, no. 10, Fanny hit upon a different stratagem—beginning and concluding the song with a series of unfulfilled half cadences to suggest harmonic rupture. In the first three stanzas the poet ponders how flowers, nightingales, or stars might comfort him in his distress, though, as we learn in the final stanza:

Die alle können's nicht wissen,	None knows or gives a token,
nur Eine kennt meinen Schmerz;	One only knows it best:
sie hat ja selbst zerrissen,	For she herself has broken,
zerrissen mir das Herz.	Has broken the heart in my breast.[91]

The three inconclusive half cadences of the closing bars—none attains the D minor of the key signature—leave the song figuratively unfinished and harmonically broken.

In Fanny's catalogue, Heine's texts appear twenty-six times, second in frequency only to Goethe, who dominates with forty-six, excluding three erroneously attributed poems now known to be by Marianne von Willemer. Goethe's long shadow continued to stretch over Fanny, who produced in 1827 and 1828 five new settings,[92] including one of *Wonne der Wehmuth* (*Rapture of Melancholy*, H-U 227), composed on Maundy Thursday, most likely in 1828.[93] Goethe's "Tears of Eternal Love" ("Thränen der ewigen Liebe") summoned from Fanny thirty-two measures in a bleak, stark G minor, a tonality rendered more remote by her preference for the natural, modal form of the scale and final cadence on the raised Picardy third. If thoughts of the St. Matthew Passion affected this fervent miniature, a different rapture informed her response to another of von Willemer's Suleika poems from Goethe's *Divan* (H-U 210), which struck home with a musician still trying to fill through song the void of Wilhelm's absence:

Wie mit innigstem Behagen,	You to inmost ease compel me,
Lied, empfind' ich deinen Sinn!	Song, when so your sense I hear!
Liebevoll du scheinst zu sagen:	Lovingly you seem to tell me
Daß ich ihm zur Seite bin.	That I am to him so near.[94]

Perhaps from modesty (or to fend off objections from the ever-prying Lea?) Fanny omitted one suggestive, mildly erotic stanza—"Yes! My love, your own expressions / My heart mirrored and revealed; / Like this breast, where your impressions / Kiss on kiss in me has sealed."—preferring to wrap her music instead around Suleika's idealized expression of "sweet" and "pure" poetry. But the idea of music as a powerful agent that could cross barriers and somehow communicate ideas intimated by words took root in another short poem by Goethe, "Wenn ich mir in stiller Seele" (H-U 215), which Fanny composed early in 1828.

Some mystery surrounds this composition. Its history begins with a visit Zelter made to Weimar in the fall of 1827. Upon mentioning to the aging poet Fanny's difficulty in finding poems suitable for song, Goethe copied eight lines, dated October 13, and asked Zelter to deliver them to her:

Wenn ich mir in stiller Seele	When in silence of the soul,
Singe leise Lieder vor,	Softly to myself I sing,
Wie ich fühle daß sie fehle	How I miss her whom my whole
Die ich einzig mir erkohr;	Heart hath set o'er everything!
Möcht ich hoffen daß sie sänge	Would she sing what in her ear
Was ich ihr so gern vertraut,	My full heart would fain be telling,
Ach! Aus dieser Brust und Enge	From this breast, so vainly swelling,
Drängen frohe Lieder laut.	Songs would break forth glad and clear.[95]

It is unclear whether Goethe specifically crafted these verses for Fanny or, as a Herr von Loeper imagined in the 1890s, reused older material[96]—the ardent tone might suggest, for instance, a love song for Marianne von Willemer. In any event, on October 25, Fanny dispatched her thanks to Weimar with deferential, circumspect lines: "You have paid me an honor that might make me too proud, if I did not remind myself I had done nothing to deserve it, but rather could view it as another divine gift for which one should rejoice without becoming arrogant." She continued, "If I were to succeed in finding the right music for your words, perhaps I might be allowed to view myself a less unworthy possessor of such a treasure."[97]

According to Felix's son Karl Mendelssohn-Bartholdy, out of veneration for the manuscript, Fanny never attempted to compose it.[98] But in fact she did, for an autograph manuscript dated January 19, 1828, survives in the Berlin Mendelssohn Archiv.[99] Its twenty-eight bars begin in a demure, stately D minor and then blossom into a radiant D major for the last two lines, with shifts to faster, rushing rhythms in the piano and a climax in the vocal line to suggest the jubilant lieder gushing from the poet's heart. Evidently, Fanny never sent the song to Goethe, and it seems to have languished among her manuscripts until late in the twentieth century. But there is a significant footnote to this story of a lost song. In 1891 the Schubert scholar Max Friedlaender claimed to have examined an autograph setting in Fanny's hand that expressed the yearning and pressing of Goethe's verses in a "most charming" (höchst reizvoll) way. Intriguingly, Friedlaender identified the key of the composition not as D minor but E-flat major and, further, detected allusions to Beethoven's song cycle An die ferne Geliebte, also in E-flat major. If Friedlaender's assertion is true, then Fanny may have attempted to improve her song by setting it a second time and invoking Beethoven, whose cycle uses song to transport messages to a "distant beloved." Sadly, nothing of this putative second manuscript has survived.

vi

On November 14, 1827, Fanny's twenty-second birthday, Felix presented a manuscript of his new sacred composition, Tu es Petrus, for five-part chorus and orchestra. A few weeks later came a Christmas present, the cantata Christe, Du Lamm Gottes. If Tu es Petrus treated a fundamental Catholic text (Matthew 16:18, "Thou art Peter, and upon this rock I will build my church")—according to Fanny, Felix's friends even "began to fear that he might have turned Roman Catholic"[100]—Christe, Du Lamm Gottes offered a staple of the Lutheran liturgy, the German Agnus Dei. Musically, both compositions sprang from a similar motivation—Felix's determination to explore historically remote eras and to resuscitate the rich traditions of sacred vocal polyphony: in Tu es Petrus, with its euphonious, Italianate points of imitation, the high Renaissance art of Palestrina (ca. 1525–1594), sometimes described as the *stile antiquo*; in *Christe, Du Lamm Gottes*, with its famous chorale melody sustained against dense webs of choral and orchestral counterpoint, the sacred cantatas of J. S. Bach. At Fanny's birthday a year later came a third, more recondite gift, the Advent motet *Hora est*, for four four-part choirs and organ continuo. Here Felix explored harmonic relationships typical more of seventeenth-century modality than modern tonality, and he produced in one stunning passage a radiant example of sixteen-part imitative counterpoint, a level of complexity he never again attempted.

Felix's excavation of the musical past would culminate in March 1829 with the centenary revival of the St. Matthew Passion, the watershed moment in music history that gave forceful impetus to the modern revival of J. S. Bach. Rehearsals were underway probably by the winter of 1827 with a small circle of friends,[101] who gathered initially not to prepare a public performance but rather for private edification. Fanny was undoubtedly deeply involved in these rehearsals and, indeed, might well have been subject to Hector Berlioz's later critique that Felix had studied the music of the dead too closely.[102] For in 1827 and 1828 she herself composed a series of neobaroque piano pieces that chronicle her own creative reaction to Bach's music in general, and the St. Matthew Passion in particular. In chronological order, these efforts include a *Fugata* in E-flat Major (H-U 193, January 1827), a *Klavierbuch* in E Minor with six pieces (H-U 214, most likely finished by December 1827), and an untitled movement in E minor (H-U 216, January 1828).[103] Here we find Fanny's Bachian sympathies fully aligned with Felix's historicist leanings and, further, some fascinating examples of the siblings' continuing musical exchanges.

In August 1826 Felix had borrowed from the recitative "Wahrlich ich sage euch," the moment in the St. Matthew Passion when Christ prophesies his betrayal,[104] to fashion a subject for a contemplative fugue in E-flat major. Coincidentally or not, the subject of Fanny's *Fugata* shares not only its key, E-flat, but also its first three, descending pitches with Felix's fugal subject, and thus may have been a response to her brother's composition. Be that as it may, she crafted a rather academic double fugue of nearly 200 bars, teeming with entries of the subject, and unfolding as well a second subject in faster, ascending notes before combining them in a culminating conclusion.

In the case of the *Klavierbuch e-moll* (an appendage-like piece from 1828), Fanny sought to recreate the tonally circumscribed sound world of Bach's baroque keyboard suites. Placing all seven pieces in the key of E minor,[105] she also invoked the introductory, E minor chorus of the St. Matthew Passion, the lamentlike "Kommt, ihr Töchter, helft mir klagen" ("Come, ye daughters, help me weep"). The spirit of Bach's music informs, for instance, the opening *Praeludio* of the *Klavierbuch*, where we encounter solemn pedal points, protracted harmonic sequences, and a telltale final cadence with the raised Piccardy third on E major, also employed by Fanny in the deeply expressive

Largo of the fourth movement, the structural center of the collection. Another element from Bach's monumental chorus—the descending lament tetrachord sketched by the first violins at the beginning—appears to have left its mark on Fanny's project as well: descending chromatic motion infuses not only the second movement *Fuga*, but the following, giguelike Allegro di molto and concluding Toccata. This last movement, which begins as a severe fugue, evinces a starkly dissonant, disjunct style far removed from the melodious warmth of Fanny's lieder. Midway through the Toccata, in emulation of Bach's cerebral mysteries, she upends her opening theme and begins presenting it upside down, in mirror inversion. Yet another clear link to the Thomaskantor is the pairing of the Toccata with the preceding fifth movement, marked *Praeludio*, and, further, the derivation of thematic relationships between the two—thus, the spinning, circuitous sixteenth notes of the *Praeludio* generate the essential contours and intervallic relationships of the Toccata subject, so that the two movements are thematically related. Not surprisingly, the technique is reminiscent of the *Well-Tempered Clavier*, in which Bach occasionally worked into a prelude adumbrations of the succeeding, paired fugue in the same key.

Like the fifth and sixth movements of the *Klavierbuch*, Fanny's opening *Praeludio* and *Fuga* are also linked, but now by means of the instruction *attacca*, so that they are literally connected. The *Fuga* does not disappoint Bachian devotees—there are ample examples of specialized techniques such as *stretto* (with overlapping entries of the subject), and one of mirror inversion; and in the latter half of the piece Fanny hints at a third technique, diminution, by which she begins recasting the subject, with some modifications, in proportionally faster rhythmic values.

Fanny's *Fuga* also reveals, finally, just how closely she shared her Bachian enthusiasm with Felix; on June 16, 1827, he dated his own piano fugue in E minor, on several counts suspiciously similar to Fanny's. Indeed, a comparison of the two compositions uncovers another sibling musical exchange. Felix's fugue (later published as his op. 35, no. 1) describes an unusual musical trajectory. Its Andante subject—brimming with disjunct, dissonant intervals, not dissimilar to Fanny's subject (example 4.2)—later reappears in mirror inversion; then, Felix introduces a faster countersubject in sixteenth notes as the tempo shifts gradually to Allegro con fuoco, marking his composition as an early example of the so-called accelerando fugue. In the climactic culmination, a dissonant, unstable diminished-seventh arpeggiation gives way to a majestic, freely composed chorale in E major, of which the bass line, doubled in octaves, simulates the effect of an organ pedal part. Felix thus allies his fugue with another Bachian genre, the chorale arrangement, and lest the listener miss the gesture, even alludes in his peroration to that stalwart Protestant hymn, "Ein' feste Burg ist unser Gott" ("A Mighty Fortress Is Our God").

Julius Schubring informs us that Felix composed his fugue in memoriam to August Hanstein, the same friend for whom Fanny had written the Voss

EXAMPLE 4.2.   (a) Fanny Mendelssohn, *Fuga* in E Minor (1827); (b) Felix Mendelssohn, Fugue in E Minor, op. 35, no. 1 (1827)

(a)

(b)

setting *Sehnsucht* in July 1827.[106] According to Schubring, the fugue traced the course of Hanstein's final illness and death throes and, at the chorale, spiritual release. Schubring's account might explain the unusual structural features of Felix's fugue, but it does not mention that some of them are clearly present in Fanny's *Fuga*. In particular, in the final section, after the shift to faster rhythmic values in diminution, she writes *sempre accelerando*, a climactic point at which the strict contrapuntal rigor breaks down, as it does in Felix's fugue, into a sweeping series of dissonant, diminished-seventh arpeggiations. True, Fanny does not employ a chorale, but in the closing bars we encounter a similar broadening of tempo, as her fugal subject is summarized in four-part harmony against a bass line doubled in octaves. All in all, the many parallels—two E-minor fugues on disjunct, chromatic subjects, accelerando passages, climactic diminished-seventh sonorities, and the like—suggest either that both fugues were written to commemorate Hanstein's death or that one was a response to the other. We can comfortably date the entire *Klavierbuch* as no later than the end of 1827, but exactly when she composed her *Fuga* is unknown, and so too the direction of influence between brother and sister in this case remains unclear.

In any event, the music of J. S. Bach held Fanny in good stead throughout her life, as it did Felix, in a much more public way, throughout his career. The sister who at age thirteen had committed much of the *Well-Tempered Clavier* to memory for the delectation of her parents now absorbed the intricacies

EXAMPLE 4.3. Fanny Mendelssohn, sketch for fugal subject (1827)

of Bach's style into her maturing compositional style. How far Fanny was prepared to enter into the high temple of baroque counterpoint is evident from one final sketch recorded at the end of her *Klavierbuch*—the opening of yet another fugue in E minor. Its recherché subject, which begins by spelling a whole-tone scale and thus exceeds the conventional limits of E minor,[107] was considerably more abstruse and experimental than any fugal subject Felix attempted (example 4.3). But she pulled back from the brink, deferring to Felix's engagement with the St. Matthew Passion, to allow the Bachian phoenix, as she would describe it, to rise again.

CHAPTER 5

Becoming Frau Hensel

(1828–1830)

You must love him without end, between the three of us everything must be perfectly proper and harmonious and true—then in this world I will have no unhappy moments.

—Fanny Mendelssohn Bartholdy to Wilhelm Hensel, February 20, 1829

For five years Wilhelm Hensel had pursued an elusive goal in Rome—to process "all that was curious and informative" as he completed his training and strove to produce work worthy of an artist[1]—not impromptu portraits and occasional almanac illustrations, but durable paintings on grand historical, biblical subjects. The path to finding his identity had not been easy or direct; continually pressed by financial straits, he struggled to provide for his mother in her declining years, and he was compelled to work in Italy without being able to share his experiences with Fanny. Indeed, by October 1828, the end of his Italian tenure, prospects for marrying her must have seemed as uncertain as on the eve of his departure in July 1823.

Upon leaving Berlin, Hensel had followed an itinerary that led through Prague and Vienna to Rome. Armed with a letter of introduction from Zelter, he met Goethe in the Bohemian spa of Marienbad (Mariánské Lázně) and there drew the eminence's portrait. But the result did not impress, for, according to the poet, it bore little resemblance to himself. Hensel tended to idealize his subjects beyond recognition, to the point that he sometimes had to reveal their identities.[2] What was more, by pursuing an "erroneous" path Goethe had observed in the arts for some twenty years, the young artist had become stuck in the "shallow dilettantism of the time by seeking a false foundation in antiquity and patriotism, and embracing a debilitating form of piety."[3]

When Hensel attempted to correspond with Fanny, Lea intercepted and answered his letter. She had not yet decided in Hensel's favor, she reiterated, because of the discrepancy in age (he was eleven years older than Fanny) and the uncertainty of his future career. "Fanny is very young," she wrote, "and, Heaven be praised, hitherto has had no concerns, no passion. I will not have you through love-letters transport her for years into a state of consuming passion and a yearning frame of mind quite foreign to her character, when I now have her before me blooming, healthy, happy, and free."[4] One wonders if, over the next few years, Lea would take in the full import of the song texts Fanny chose to set, many of which, of course, explicitly dealt with the idea of *Sehnsucht*.

In return for his stipend from the Prussian exchequer, Hensel was expected to produce faithfully executed reproductions of Roman and Italian art for instructional use in the Berlin Academy of Arts. But, as with many artists finding themselves in the Eternal City, diversions soon distracted him from his assignment. Among his first Roman contacts was Lea's brother Jacob Bartholdy, then serving as the Prussian general consul and residing in the Casa Bartholdy atop the Spanish Steps. A discerning art aficionado, Bartholdy had amassed an impressive collection of antique vases and miniature sculptures; but his main distinction was to commission four of the so-called Nazarene painters, including Dorothea Schlegel's son Philipp Veit, to prepare frescoes in his drawing room on the theme of Joseph and his brethren. Still, the Nazarenes' Catholicizing tendencies disturbed this Prussian Maecenas, who had remained a staunch Protestant since his conversion in 1806; recent research has confirmed that in 1819 he published anonymously an unfavorable critique of the movement in the *Augsburger Allgemeine Zeitung*.[5]

Around the time of Hensel's arrival, Bartholdy conceived the idea of an album to celebrate the union of the Prussian crown prince (the future Frederick William IV) and Princess Elizabeth of Bavaria, to which the colony of German artists in Rome would contribute. Hensel's offering was a stylized drawing of the Wedding at Cana. While Christ performs his first miracle in the left foreground, we are drawn to likenesses of the royal couple at the center of the feast, attended by tightly compacted figures on the right of Bartholdy and sixteen of the contributing artists, including, in profile, Hensel.[6] Bartholdy did not think much of a potential union between his niece and Hensel or, indeed, of the artist's talents—in Bartholdy's view, Hensel would probably never amount to much. For his part, Hensel maintained his ties to Fanny's uncle and, when he died in July 1825, the artist sketched the deceased's portrait and corresponded regularly with Lea and Abraham about settling the estate. Hensel assisted in drawing up an inventory of Bartholdy's sizeable art collection and prepared a report about the feasibility of shipping the frescoes to Berlin.

In August 1824 Karl Friedrich Schinkel, the celebrated architect of the rebuilt Schauspielhaus and other neoclassical edifices in Berlin, arrived in Rome and found in Hensel a changed man, whose art was now shedding traces of excessive sentimentality and piety.[7] By this time Hensel was preoccupied with two significant royal commissions from Berlin that would dominate the duration of his Roman sojourn. First, he began copying, with the same dimensions, Raphael's imposing final work, the *Transfiguration* (1517–1520), a Renaissance masterpiece that had recently experienced the vicissitudes of war and politics. In 1797 Napoleon had ordered the treasure sent to Paris; after his abdication, it was returned to Rome in 1816, and by 1824 was hanging in the *pinacoteca* of the newly installed pope, Leo XII. Hensel's task was formidable on two counts. The grimy condition of the painting necessitated a thorough cleaning, which exposed "a quantity of details hidden under the crust of the dirt of centuries,"[8] and revarnishing, and the monumental size (13′4″ × 9′2″) challenged him to work on a scale that dwarfed his previous essays.

To copy Raphael was a time-honored tradition; in contrast, the Prussian monarch's second commission, for an original painting to serve as an altarpiece, required Hensel to tap his own inspiration. The subject, Christ and the Woman of Samaria (John 4), extracted enormous effort—at least forty preparatory sketches before the completion of the canvas, in which Christ and the Samarian discuss the "living water" of Jacob's well, while disciples are seen approaching in the background.[9] For more than two years Hensel alternated between the two projects and adjusted to their conflicting demands—painstaking fidelity to an authoritative model versus artistic self-reliance. Keenly aware that his prospects as a professional artist and as Fanny's husband hung in the balance, he struggled to overcome his insecurities and nagging self-doubt. Abraham and Lea did not hesitate to offer opinions. Thus, Abraham in January 1826: "I have faith that you will succeed if you remain true to yourself. But meanwhile time passes, and I consider it essential that we soon get to see here something really substantial by you." Lea was more frank. She had heard that in deference to his critics Hensel had recast his work several times, only in the end to return to the original conception. "So, yes, understandably, in two years nothing has been finished. Who does not trust firmly in his inner voice and conviction rarely achieves anything significant."[10] At first her judgment did little to strengthen Hensel's resolve. In 1827, Frances Bunsen, the English wife of the Prussian emissary to the pope, appraised Hensel as "one of those persons who have too little specific gravity to rest on their own center, and who therefore constantly have to rely for support on some familiar fellow creature."[11]

Throughout the Roman sojourn Hensel dispatched to Berlin pencil drawings of Mendelssohn family members and thereby forged another link to Fanny's parents. In these idealized sketches, the figure of Cecilia, patron saint of music, frequently appeared. In one from around 1825, recently termed a "masterpiece of Hensel's diplomacy,"[12] Lea's likeness assumed the role of a "Raphaelic" Cecilia watching over angelic figures singing (Fanny and Rebecka) and playing a portative organ (Felix) and lyre (Paul).[13] Lea did not miss the resemblances, even though her children had "so much changed and grown, and somehow got coarse-grained" since Hensel's departure. Nevertheless, the "beauty of the group, the combination of earnestness and grace, the lovely, childlike, and yet thoughtful expression of each individual head" convinced her that Hensel had chosen in Raphael "the highest, purest of all artists" as his ideal.[14]

i

When in September 1828 the Royal Academy of Art in Berlin opened its annual exhibition, the catalogue officially listed Hensel's *Samarian at the Well* and copy of Raphael's *Transfiguration*. But public viewing of the paintings was delayed some weeks, as the artist and his artworks arrived late, in mid-October. Still, critical reactions were distinctly positive. The director of the academy, Wilhelm Schadow, detected mastery in the *Samarian*, and according to one report, in the *Transfiguration* Hensel had penetrated deeply into the ineffable Raphael, whose spirit spoke to the viewer in an instructive way through Hensel's painstaking copy. Another critic was able to read into the features of the Samarian the "earnest, gentle words of the Savior," and after twice viewing the paintings, the king, usually chary of praise, offered that the artist had not spent his time in Italy uselessly.[15] On the advice of his advisors, Frederick William III agreed to reward Hensel for his efforts, and the idea was broached of his appointment as a court painter (*Hofmaler*), a move that early in 1829 decisively advanced his courtship of Fanny.

Over the course of five years, Wilhelm and Fanny had naturally enough grown apart, and at age thirty-three the artist faced new issues in wooing her. The circle of her friends had changed and now spoke a "coterie-slang not intelligible to the uninitiated."[16] Fanny's psychological dependence on Felix had deepened and intensified even further at his impending departure in April 1829 for England. Artistically, of course, she was tied inextricably to Felix, who, at twenty, was a fully mature composer routinely publishing his music and beginning an international career. Wilhelm would have been struck by the close sibling bonds and, to the outsider, impenetrable artistic exchanges. Thus, in September 1827, while laboring over the String Quartet in A Minor, op. 13, Felix had sought Fanny's advice about whether he should work into the closing bars allusions to his love song "Ist es wahr?"[17] And when, in January 1829, Felix and Fanny rendered his new concert overture, *Calm Sea and*

Prosperous Voyage (*Meeresstille und glückliche Fahrt*), as a piano duet at their residence with dimmed lighting, the effect may have been magical, but also saddening for Fanny, who was already distressed about the imminent separation from her brother.[18]

Wilhelm found himself adjusting, too, to the changing dynamics of Fanny's social circle. Among the new members were two suitors for Rebecka's hand, the young mathematician Gustav Dirichlet and the jurist Eduard Gans, who, Fanny informs us, fought with Dirichlet "like a schoolboy,"[19] and whose liberal politics would have collided with Wilhelm's more traditional, monarchist views. Another figure new to the artist, the brilliant philology student Johann Gustav Droysen, seems to have aroused suspicions, and then jealousy. Three years younger than Fanny, Droysen possessed "knowledge far above his age" and was endowed with a "pure, poetic spirit."[20] Fanny not only took a liking to his poetry but completed no fewer than six settings in 1828 and 1829,[21] culminating in a song cycle occasioned by Felix's departure for England. Some of these texts treat rather stark themes of alienation and loneliness. Her first Droysen setting, *Geräusch* (*Sound*), was published in 1830 by Felix as the seventh of his twelve *Lieder,* op. 9, where the title was modified to the more suggestive *Sehnsucht.* As the poet listens to the receding sounds of nature and becomes aware of the silence around him, Fanny's music shifts from an unassuming D major to a more darkly tinged subdominant G minor. The idea of alienation persists more forcefully in Droysen's *Gram* (*Sorrow,* H-U 228), which displays a "peculiar ambivalence toward nature—longing admiration mixed with an injured sense of alienation, even rejection."[22] Here images of sun-filled flowers and glistening dew prompt only the despairing, refrainlike answer, "Ach, ich bin einsam" ("Ah, I am alone"). Again, Fanny captures the sense of ambivalence by turning nearly identical vocal phrases first toward A-flat major and then F minor.

One other Droysen setting, the duet "Schlafe du, schlafe du süß" ("Sleep, Sleep Sweetly," H-U 233),[23] merits further consideration. Fanny composed it on April 11, just after Felix had departed for England and, most unusual for her autographs, added a detailed note about a traveler lulled to sleep on the ocean by the gentle action of the waves. While he dreams, two mermaids appear and sing the lullaby-like duet, into which Fanny embedded allusions to Felix's own music, and further enriched a web of intertextual references (example 5.1a–b). The key, E major, and gently undulating patterns of the opening bars recall unmistakably the music of another dream, Felix's *Midsummer Night's Dream* Overture of 1826—specifically the serene music of the coda (for Puck's epilogue) that, as it happens, borrows musically from the Mermaid's Song in the second act of Weber's final opera, *Oberon.*[24] In Fanny's duet, the traveler of course is Felix; the two mermaids (soprano and alto), Rebecka and Fanny.

Such was the heightened musical and intellectual environment into which Wilhelm returned. As he endeavored to take his place in the family,

EXAMPLE 5.1.　(a) Fanny Mendelssohn, "Schlafe du, schlafe du süß" (1829); (b) Felix Mendelssohn, *A Midsummer Night's Dream* Overture, op. 21 (1826)

he would have found one of the century's great polymaths, Alexander von Humboldt, scrupulously recording magnetic measurements in a copper hut newly erected in the Mendelssohns' gardens, and Felix, with Fanny, immersed in exhausting rehearsals for the St. Matthew Passion. Hensel's first opportunity to reclaim her attention probably came on Fanny's twenty-third birthday, though there was considerable competition. We have already mentioned that on November 14, 1828, Felix presented the manuscript of his motet *Hora est*, a composition only connoisseurs such as Fanny could have fully plumbed. She tells us that he also gave her some new piano compositions, including a short character piece, notated in her album and titled simply "Lied." In a letter to Klingemann, Fanny described this offering as a *Lied ohne Worte* (song without words),[25] and thus designated a new genre of piano music that later became inseparably linked to her brother's name. Marked "Espressivo & Allegro," Felix's miniature is indeed suffused with a songlike lyricism that fittingly pays tribute to the style of Fanny's texted lieder and almost invites the listener to contrive and superimpose a poetic text,[26] as does an untitled *Lied ohne Worte*–like piano piece in E major that Fanny herself crafted on February 7, 1829 (H-U 229).[27] There is indeed some evidence that the siblings may have collaboratively devised texts for their piano pieces. In 1838 Fanny compared Felix's piano songs to the then-fashionable technique of Liszt and other virtuosi of transcribing texted songs for the keyboard alone, and then reminisced: "Dear Felix, when text is removed from sung Lieder so that they can be used as concert pieces, it is contrary to the experiment of adding a text to your instrumental Lieder—the other half of the topsy-turvy world.... But shouldn't a person think a lot of himself... when he sees how the jokes that we, as mere children, contrived to pass the time have now been adopted by the great talents and used as fodder for the public?"[28] However we interpret this intriguing statement, we may yet discover that the origins of Felix's *Lieder ohne Worte* lay in a musical-literary game he played with Fanny during the 1820s, another example of artistic exchanges between the two.

Among Abraham's birthday salutations for Fanny was a letter that exhorted her to prepare for her "real calling"—the "state of a housewife." Women, he wrote, had to confront a "difficult task"—the "constant occupation with apparent trifles, the interception of each drop of rain, that it may not evaporate, but be conducted into the right channel, and spread wealth and blessing."[29] Perhaps Wilhelm would have concurred, even as he celebrated that day with a different kind of offering, a pair of ornamental shears accompanied by this poem:

Eine Scheere, nach der Sage	According to the sage
Schnitt den Lebensfaden ab.	a shear cuts off life's threads.
So verstehst Du sonder Frage	So you grasp the special question,
Wie ich Dir die Scheere gab.	How I gave you the shear.
Mehr als Kron' und Scepter reden	More than a crown or scepter
Soll sie von der heilgen Macht	it should speak of the sacred power
Die oft meines Lebens Fäden	that often assigns to you
Immerdar Dir zugedacht.	the threads of my life for all eternity.
Bleiben, Pilgern, Leben, Sterben,	To remain, wander, live, or die,
Fremde oder Vaterland,	in exile or the fatherland,
Glück verlieren—und erwerben	to lose hope and regain it—
Ruhn fortan in Deiner Hand![30]	all rest henceforth in your hand!

On Christmas Day, Wilhelm brought other presents—for Felix, a pocket diary for his trip to England, for Rebecka, a star-shaped diary, and for Fanny, a miniature Florentine album in the shape of a heart, with scalloped gilded pages, in which he inscribed: "This little book is very like the heart, / You write in it joy or sorrow."[31] Here, for the next few years, Fanny would record musical sketches, while her fiancé, then husband, contributed poems and drawings surrounding important events in the couple's lives.

Among Fanny's first entries is a cryptic musical notation,◉ dated January 3, 1829, with the accompanying caption "largo forte/Felix!!"[32] The six pitches, all in half notes, are an early version of a passage from Felix's *Reformation* Symphony, op. 107—specifically, the arching flute melody in bars 47 ff. of the finale (A–A-sharp–B–E–D–C-sharp). It is part of the sustained orchestral crescendo◉ that, following the introductory strains of the chorale "Ein' feste Burg ist unser Gott," leads to the main body of the movement, the Allegro maestoso. But Fanny's entry raises more questions than it answers, for Felix did not complete the score of his symphony until May 1830. By early 1829 he had already begun to share preliminary ideas for his "church symphony" (*Kirchensinfonie*), as he called it, with his sister, and she may have notated the passage in response. But alternatively, there is the possibility that she herself conceived the phrase and that Felix subsequently revised and worked it into his symphony. Fanny's Florentine album, in short, may record evidence of a musical exchange long effaced by the passage of time.

ii

As if she sensed the precipitous turn 1829 would take, Fanny began early in the New Year to keep a diary (figure 5.1). Her *Tagebücher*, published in 2002, offer with a few gaps a critical new source for the remaining nineteen years of her life and henceforth will become our familiar companion. Her writing style has been described as pragmatic and down-to-earth;[33] she relies upon compact, abbreviated statements to chronicle the newsworthy players and events of her family's circle and not infrequently records her impressions with a certain journalistic detachment. Thus, after a portentous announcement in her first entry (January 4)—"the commencement of the second half of my life stands before me"[34]—she launches into a bulletin-like summary of current European events—the Greek War of Independence; troop movements in Russia; the yellow fever in Spain; anarchy in Portugal; England and the Irish question; and the struggle between *Jesuitismus* and *Ultraismus* in France— before "returning" to the smaller, intimate stage of Leipzigerstrasse no. 3. Her interest in external world events runs like a broken thread through the diaries, intermittently framing the record of Fanny's private, domestic life and highlighting the opposition between the public and private spheres fundamental to our understanding of her life and work.

Rarely does Fanny commit to her diary opinions about her own compositions and musical activities, and seldom does she peel away the veneer of objectivity to expose her deeper feelings, though when she does, the admissions are inevitably telling. One example is her entry for January 22, designated "the beginning." That evening, we learn, Lea treated Wilhelm rather shabbily and put Fanny into the foulest of moods (*übelste Laune*); then, as Gans was

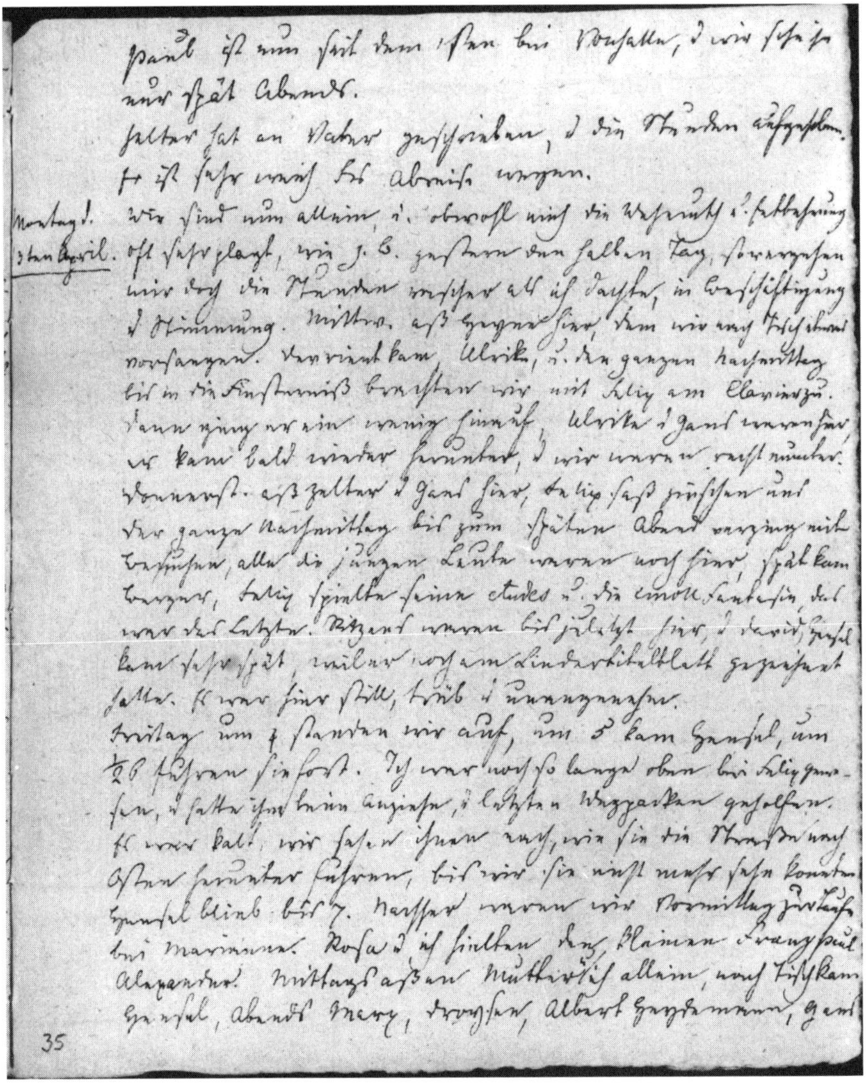

FIGURE 5.1. Fanny Hensel, Tagebuch, entry of April 13, 1829 (Berlin, Mendelssohn Archiv, Depos. Berlin 500,22)

reading poetry to the assembled company, Alexander von Humboldt burst in with the news of Wilhelm's nomination as a court painter (*Hofmaler*). But the drama of the following day elicited from Fanny only this dispassionate report: "Early the next morning I was copying the score of a Handel aria. Somewhere around 12 Hensel came; I was already downstairs, and went back to my room where I remained with Reb[ecka], while H[ensel] spoke to the parents in the grey room. After I had dressed, I read geography with Beckchen. After about a half hour H. came out and in a few minutes we were united. We went in and found mother surprised, shocked by the speed of the decision, and unable to repeat her consent. Father was at once very happy and content, and somehow or other, we brought mother around."[35] That evening, so as not to cause further friction, the couple secretly informed their friends. Wilhelm, however, was moved to poetry, and penned some verses—titled, with some relief, "What I actually sang today on the street into the air"—about a new springtime bursting inside him in the middle of the severe Berlin winter.[36] On February 4 the two were alone together for the first time and now, finally, resumed corresponding, after a hiatus of several years.

But this euphoria was short-lived. Even Sebastian Hensel, who usually depicted members of his family as emotionally centered and well-balanced, later alluded to tensions:

> Fanny's letters during the engagement...are of a truly pathetic, heart-moving beauty. Every morning Hensel's servant came, bringing and taking back a short note of greeting, often of serious purport: all the struggles of two conscientious natures are reflected in them as in a mirror. Only *her* letters have been preserved: with characteristic energy, she refuses to sacrifice her brother to the jealousy with which Hensel in the beginning regarded her love for him, but she consents to give up her friends and even her art. The claims of the present often disturb her; but when she is alone in the quiet of night, along with the ideal image of her beloved, such as her mind's eye was wont to see it during the years of separation, she feels in harmony with herself, and image and reality gradually become no longer two but one.[37]

Sebastian Hensel to the contrary, some of his father's letters have survived, and their recent publication with Fanny's as the *Brautbriefe*,[38] along with several revealing entries in her diary, offer a more candid account of this tumultuous period in the lovers' lives. Thus, Wilhelm's very first letter provoked a *kleiner Streit* (little spat), and we read of "frustrating" conversations with him and, in March, "a very unpleasant scene with mother about our marriage" that left Wilhelm utterly inconsolable. "One cannot," Fanny confided to her diary, "imagine Hensel's anxiety."[39] Through all the upheaval she emerges as the consoling, nurturing member of the partnership; Wilhelm as emotionally distraught, given to bouts of jealousy and insecurity, and needing reassurance. The most combustible flash point was the opposition of Lea, who, mindful of her patrician background, probably viewed Wilhelm as unworthy of her daughter. "You will feel with me that my relationship with your parents is not as it should be," he writes, but when he proposes confronting Lea, the pragmatist Fanny replies: "Mother is no friend of explication. You speak your words into the wind, and when they are spoken, they are forgotten."[40]

Two other issues surface in the *Brautbriefe*. In a letter of February 20, Fanny broached the unusual intimacy of her relationship with Felix, whom Wilhelm no doubt perceived as an artistic rival for her affections: "Last evening Felix composed, and his eyes were beautiful. There is something peculiar to his eyes; in no other person's eyes have I perceived a soul so directly. You must love him without end, between the three of us everything must be perfectly proper and harmonious and true—then in this world I will have no unhappy moments. If you really love each other, I will be content with my relationship to you both."[41] Wilhelm concurred: "So your love will not be divided between us; each may have it completely, and we three will be a pure mirror of unity."[42]

But Fanny's other friends, in particular Droysen, continued to arouse Wilhelm's jealousy. Matters came to a head when, having set several of Droysen's poems, she made plans to compose another for her parents' silver wedding anniversary in December 1829. Just weeks before her own wedding in October, to appease Wilhelm, Fanny decided to return Droysen's text and even went further: "I will no longer compose for voice, at least nothing by poets I personally know, certainly least of all Droysen. Instrumental music remains to me; I can confide to it what I will, it is discreet." And then, quoting Jean Paul Richter, "art is not for women, only for maidens; on the threshold of my new life I will take leave of the child's playmate." To his credit, Wilhelm rejected these draconian measures and insisted that the "unlimited practice" of Fanny's art remain a precept of their relationship. She would not abandon her childhood fancy, and together they would prove Jean Paul wrong.[43]

Nevertheless, Fanny never finished another text by Droysen; instead, Hensel's lyrics figure more and more prominently in her music from 1829 and 1830. First among these works was the choral song *Nachtreigen* (*Night Rounds*, H-U 237),[44] composed as a surprise for his birthday (July 6) after Fanny playfully deluded him into thinking it could not be set to music. Requiring an expanded, eight-part mixed chorus, *Nachtreigen* fills fully 200 measures, allotted in three sections for the female and male complements, and then the entire ensemble, for which Fanny planned a culminating and chromatically involved fugato.[45] Somewhat reminiscent of Schiller's *An die Freude* (*Ode to Joy*), the poem celebrates a supreme deity and the power of love,[46] but what also stands out in the composition is Fanny's decision to allude to Felix's music—the first few pitches of the soprano part clearly cite the principal theme of the first movement of his String Quartet in E-flat, op. 12, and thus provide an example of what Christopher Reynolds has termed *texting*, the "reuse of instrumental music as the basis of a song or choral work."[47]

In 1830, Wilhelm's poems would inspire two other examples of texting. First, in *Genesungsfeier*, celebrating Rebecka's recovery from the measles (H-U 252),[48] Fanny quoted the key and opening pitches of Felix's *Geständniss*, op. 9, no. 2,◐ a song, in turn, that had reused material from his own *Frage*, op. 9, no. 1. Then, in the *Frühlingslied* of November 1830 (H-U 255),[49] she replicated the key and opening pitches of the overture to Felix's *Singspiel, Heimkehr aus der Fremde*, op. 89, once again bringing together Wilhelm's poetry with the siblings' music, so that all reflected each other in Wilhelm's "mirror of unity." But two other settings finished around the time of their wedding assumed a more private character. In "Schlafe, schlaf!" (H-U 241), sent by Wilhelm to Fanny with an announce-ment of their wedding banns, and "Zu deines Lagers Füßen" (H-U 245),[50] the poet's subject is the sleeping Fanny; he appears at the foot of her bed in a dream-like state of yearning (*Sehnsuchtstraum*). When she set "Schlafe, schlaf," either Fanny or Wilhelm doctored some of the verses—the more suggestive "Wie sich Mund an Mund bekannten / Und die Herzen einig brannten" ("How mouth to mouth they confessed / and their hearts flamed in union") became "Wie sich Lipp' an Lippe fragten / und die Herzen eines sagten" ("How lip to lip they asked, and the hearts spoke as one"),[51] rendering the music more decorous for performance.

On Midsummer's Day, June 24, 1829, as Felix was preparing to direct the London premiere of his *Midsummer Night's Dream* Overture, Fanny and her intimate circle, now dubbed "the wheel" (*das Rad*), gathered in the garden behind her residence. In a mock performance, Rebecka and Fanny simulated the two flutes that begin Felix's celebrated work, and later, in a bit of playful ceremony, Wilhelm was initiated into the group beneath an opened umbrella.[52] His contribution, in turn, was to represent the company in a drawing of a wheel, sent to Felix in August (figure 5.2). Fanny described the concept as a self-evident, collective "moral person" but then obligingly explicated its mysteries.[53] The indi-viduals of the clique form the spokes around the center, occupied by a crouch-ing, diminutive Felix, who suggests perhaps some embryonic, homunculus-like creative force. In Scottish attire, he plays an oboe and is surrounded by dolphins, encircling him like the Arion of Greek mythology. Though separated by the water, the music spills over to the occupants of the larger wheel, one of whom, Albertine Heine (future wife of Fanny's brother Paul), dances at the 7 o'clock position a galop with Felix's empty shadow. At 12 o'clock Fanny and Rebecka appear, holding a sheet of music (the music Felix is playing?) and entwined so that their lower extremities resemble fish otters (Felix's nickname for his sis-ters). Several figures are arranged in pairs—for example, Fanny's brother Paul, to whom Auguste Wilmsen extends a flower (3–4 o'clock), and Droysen, connected to Minna Heydemann by a spool of yarn (9–10 o'clock). But quite apart from this merry coterie is Wilhelm; linked to Fanny by a chain, he remains tethered to the outer perimeter of the wheel (11 o'clock) and resists the centrifugal force that might hurl him away. In counterpoint to Felix's Arion, who charmed the dol-phins, Wilhelm plays Ixion, bound for his misdeeds to a wheel by Hermes, and destined, in Ovid's phrase, at once to pursue and flee from himself.[54] The droll symbolism seems clear enough: Wilhelm remains the outsider, still attempting to join the group as it turns around Felix, the cynosure of Fanny's life.

FIGURE 5.2. Wilhelm Hensel, *Das Rad* (*The Wheel*), pencil drawing (Berlin, Staatliche Museen Preussischer Kulturbesitz, Nationalgalerie)

iii

At the center of Felix's life during the early months of 1829 were the preparations for the revival of the St. Matthew Passion. According to Eduard Devrient, who sang the role of Christ, Felix had to overcome the opposition of Zelter, convinced that the public could not comprehend Bach's solemn masterpiece.[55] Choral rehearsals began on February 2, the day before Wilhelm gave Felix on his twentieth birthday Jean Paul's novel of adolescent awakening, *Flegeljahre* (*Fledgling Years*). A month later, the orchestra joined the chorus of 158, among whom Fanny participated as one of thirty-six altos.

On the evening of March 11, before a packed hall at the Singakademie—a thousand Berliners had to be turned away[56]—Felix gave the downbeat for the opening choral lament and, in Fanny's memorable image, the colossal score again hovered above the ashes of the past, phoenixlike, and was reimplanted in the German musical consciousness, some 100 years after Bach's first performances in Leipzig. In attendance were the elite of Berlin—among them the Prussian court, Schleiermacher, Hegel, Rahel von Varnhagen, the court composer Spontini, Heinrich Heine, and Zelter, who took his place in the audience with "exemplary resignation."[57] Owing to demand, Felix directed a second performance on Bach's birthday, March 21; a third, led by Zelter on Good Friday, followed after Felix's departure for England. The reverberations were immediate—Felix and Devrient (in a phrase Devrient ascribed to Felix, "a Jew and an actor") had reclaimed the seminal work of German musical Protestantism and given a dramatic new force to the modern Bach revival. Henceforth, Felix's Bachian preoccupations—evidenced by his predilection for fugues and chorales, and thick chromatic part writing in his music—signaled not only his musical but spiritual faith. His assimilation into Prussian high society as a Mendelssohn Bartholdy, a *Neuchrist*, was now seemingly complete.

There is a certain poignancy that Fanny, whom Felix affectionately dubbed his "old [Thomas]cantor," shared this experience from the half public, half anonymous body of the chorus. According to her diary she took her place among the "strongest" altos, from where she had a clear view of Felix. But she remained a fervent Bach disciple no less devoted than her brother. And so, during the week of the revival, on March 14, she composed a *Präludium* in A minor with telltale signs—ascending and descending chromatic lines that slowly converge against each other in a rich counterpoint reminiscent of Bach's Passion. Fanny's prelude spills over into the opening of what would have been a fugue on a particularly angular, dissonant, and Bachian subject.[58] But it breaks off after only three bars, the vestiges, perhaps, of her plan to write an *ernsthaft* (serious) fugue.[59]

While Berliners were rediscovering their Lutheran musical roots, an apparition of a different sort materialized. The Italian violinist Niccolò Paganini took the Prussian capital by storm with a series of concerts between March and May. Commanding inflated ticket prices, this sensational virtuoso performed in the Schauspielhaus, where he dazzled audiences with inconceivable technical feats—rapidly alternating pizzicato and staccato passages (with and without the bow); double, triple, and quadruple stops that rendered playable complex passages in harmony; insuperable chains of trills, octaves, and tenths; and applications of eerie harmonics. His macabre, gaunt appearance convinced many that a satanic influence was present (Fanny found Paganini the "embodiment of the devil"[60]) and for some, his unprecedented brinksmanship approached if not transgressed the line separating good taste from the hyperbolic, the beautiful from the bizarre.[61] For Fanny, he was an "unnatural, wild genius" who had the "appearance of a crazed murderer, and the movements of a monkey."[62] On two occasions Paganini dined at Leipzigerstrasse no. 3, where Fanny played for him, the violinist signed her album with a brief musical sketch,[63] and Wilhelm drew his portrait. There were spirited debates about Paganini's searing brand of virtuosity that left Fanny ambivalent. Still, she caught some of the musician's flair and demonic quality in her Presto in A Minor (H-U 239), a madcap scherzo for piano composed in August 1829, and teeming with crisp arpeggiations simulating the rapid, skittering brushwork of Paganini's bow.[64] Fanny thus joined other celebrated pianists, including Robert Schumann, Liszt, and Brahms, in emulating the Italian's vaunted violin technique at the keyboard.

When not contemplating contrasting poles of divine and diabolical music making, Fanny inevitably turned her thoughts to Felix, whom Klingemann greeted in London on April 21, the beginning of a gentleman's grand tour—three years of travel underwritten by Abraham. This time the separation was particularly difficult for Fanny, and she lost no opportunity to promote the sibling bond and, from afar, to tend to her brother's needs. Thus, she arranged to send parts of Felix's scores to London as he planned his debut at the Philharmonic, responded favorably to his first sketch for the *Hebrides* Overture, and dispensed some sisterly advice, cautioning him when Abraham suspected his son was deliberately using abroad the name Mendelssohn instead of Mendelssohn Bartholdy.[65]

Fanny's very first letter to London invokes, appropriately enough, the jubilant coda of Felix's *Calm Sea and Prosperous Voyage* (*Meeresstille und glückliche Fahrt*) Overture, in which fanfares of three trumpets symbolically greet the arrival of the vessel in port.[66] By this time she too was turning to music, in order to reexplore the trope of separation and reunion. If in 1824 she had written a piano sonata (see p. 81), in 1829 her efforts coalesced into an impressive, hauntingly beautiful song cycle on new poems of Droysen, the first of which, brought to her on the day of Felix's departure, immediately elicited a melody from her.[67] By mid-June Fanny had completed six lieder,[68] and forwarded to London a fair copy inscribed "An Felix, während seiner ersten Abwesenheit in England 1829" ("For Felix, during his first absence in England 1829"), and fitted with vignettelike drawings by Wilhelm. They include, on the first page, at least two visual allusions to Felix's music—a grape trellis, from the family garden, that figures in Felix's love song "Ist es wahr?" (op. 9, no. 1, reused in his String Quartet op. 13) and, at the bottom of the page, a boat bearing the siblings from "the grey past into the golden future,"[69] another reference to Felix's *Prosperous Voyage* Overture.

Droysen's six poems sketch a narrative of departure and return, mostly from the point of view of the pining sister. In the first, "Lebewohl" ("Farewell"), Fanny fantasizes about stealing into Felix's dreams; in the second, spring tulips and clematis fail to cheer her, and a bird secretly grieves in a linden tree; and in the third and fourth, she begins to daydream about his return. The fifth, a pseudo-Scottish folk song, shifts our attention to the Highlands, where Fanny desires to join the roaming Felix on a secluded island, perhaps an allusion to the second canto of Sir Walter Scott's *Lady of the Lake*, in which Helen and her father take refuge on an island in Loch Katrine. The sixth poem, "Wiedersehn" ("Reunion"), then closes the cycle with the joyful homecoming. Now the piano accompaniment falls silent and a seemingly weightless a cappella trio—soprano, alto, and tenor—give voice to their glorious future together. Presumably the three parts are for Rebecka, Fanny, and Felix; significantly, there is no musical role for the newest member of the wheel, Hensel, who, as illustrator of the cycle, stands apart from the principals.

By titling her offering *Liederkreis*—literally, circle of songs—was Fanny alluding to an inner circle of Wilhelm's wheel? As it happens, the first song begins with the sustained pitch E in the piano bass, and the cycle as a whole concludes with an E-major sonority, suggesting a musical circling. But the title *Liederkreis* also underscores Fanny's interest in unifying Droysen's six poems into a coherent musical cycle. We may perceive several layers of organization that connect the six miniatures, ranging in length from thirteen to thirty-two bars. First, there is the clear key scheme, which proceeds from the neutral A minor to sharp keys and alternates between minor and major tonalities (A minor–E major–E minor–B minor ending in B major–B minor–E major). Second, Fanny crafted into the cycle harmonic links between the individual songs; for example, nos. 1 and 2 end with half cadences that elide seamlessly with nos. 2 and 3; the final E minor sonority of no. 3 returns as an upbeat to no. 4, and so on. Operating on a different level are Fanny's allusions to Felix's compositions, underscoring again the siblings' musical bonds. No. 5 (June 2, 1829) shares its key and style with Felix's song *Wartend* (*Waiting*, op. 9, no. 3), as it happened, set to a text by Droysen that Felix had composed in April, shortly before his departure.[70] And no. 6 begins by quoting a phrase from Felix's so-called *Scottish* Sonata, op. 28, thus subtly linking the trio with the memory of the Highlands in no. 5 (example 5.2a–b). Fanny confessed the borrowing in a letter to Felix and playfully asked him to indulge her "naïveté," for she knew "very well where it originated and you do too, but that is precisely the joke."[71]

The poet Droysen was suitably enough impressed by Fanny's music to propose another cycle, based on the Loreley saga and constructed "with a certain inner connection" between the lieder.[72] Wilhelm was to collaborate on the poems, but the project appears not to have advanced far, and nothing of Fanny's music for it has survived. Meanwhile, from London, where a captivated Felix sang through the *Liederkreis*, came a glowing reaction. Felix found in the songs the most beautiful music one could conceive on earth, "the inner, most inner soul of music," worthy of only the most select audience.[73]

EXAMPLE 5.2. (a) Fanny Mendelssohn, *Liederkreis* no. 6 (1829); (b) Felix
Mendelssohn Bartholdy, *Scottish* Sonata, op. 28 (1828)

(a)

(b)

If Fanny utterly idolized her brother, Felix recognized Fanny's rare talents as a
songwriter, even if he remained unwilling to share her genius with the broader
public.

Through much of the eight-month separation Fanny became increasingly
enamored of a new portrait of Felix by Wilhelm, which she described for
Klingemann: "A beautiful keepsake we have of him, his portrait by Hensel,
three-quarter life-size, the likeness perfect—a truly delightful, amiable picture. He is sitting on a garden bench (the background formed by lilac-bushes
in our garden), the right arm reposing on the back of the bench, the left on his
knees, with uplifted fingers. The expression of his face and the movement of
his hands show that he is composing."[74] Over the following weeks, this painting loomed larger and larger in Fanny's life. She placed it above the fireplace
in her music room, so that he watched over her as she played the piano, and
even kept a preliminary sketch of the painting on her desk. In an example of

life imitating art, Hensel had a similar bench made for the garden. By mid-June, Fanny and Rebecka were spending hours before the painting, waiting for it to move them. This sibling adulation culminated on June 29, with Fanny lost in reverie about Felix's motet *Hora est*: "I've been alone for two hours, at the piano, which sounds especially nice today, playing the *Hora*. I get up from the piano, stand in front of your picture, and kiss it, and immerse myself so completely in your presence that I—must write you now."[75]

A few days later, Wilhelm was compulsively retouching one of Felix's hands in the painting, for which Fanny herself posed. But when Wilhelm dispatched to London a portrait of Fanny—one of six taken in 1829—the siblings reacted negatively. Wilhelm had adorned her head with a floral wreath, and Fanny feared people would imagine she was "born with such a contraption."[76] For Felix, Fanny's portrait was beautiful, but he did not care for it: "I see how splendidly it's drawn, how closely it resembles her. But in the pose, clothing, gaze, in the totally sibylline, prophet-like quality of the adoring exaltation, my cantor is not present. In her case the exaltation doesn't point upwards, but inwards, and doesn't manifest itself in the outstretched arms or the wild wreath of flowers, because anyone can see that at first glance! But he must not, and instead only gradually become aware of it. Don't take it badly, *Hofmaler*, but I've known my sister longer than you, carried her in my arms as a child (Exaggeration), and am now a regular, ungrateful bear at times."[77] Still, through her relationship with Wilhelm, Fanny somehow found herself becoming closer to Felix: "Hensel is a good man, Felix, and I am content in the widest sense of the word, happier than I ever imagined possible. For I dreamed and feared that such a relationship would tear me away from you, or rather alienate us, but it is, *if possible*, just the opposite."[78] And to Wilhelm's sister Luise, Fanny wrote: "I absolutely cannot imagine possessing a heart so narrow that a brother or a woman friend must cede first place to the beloved, as if it were a house whose rooms were all partitioned."[79] Wilhelm concurred: "fraternal love does not need to make room for another; this proves that true love already contains something divine, unlimited, and infinite while still on earth. That is why we consider it a preparation for the hereafter."[80]

iv

Among the rare descriptions of Fanny's art from 1829 is an account by the young Scottish musician John Thomson (1805–1841), who arrived in Berlin in August, bearing eagerly awaited reports of Felix's activities in Edinburgh. Thomson became quite familiar with Fanny's music, and later recollected their meeting:

> Miss Mendelssohn is a first-rate piano-forte player, of which you may
> form some idea when I mention that she can express the varied beauties

of Beethoven's extraordinary trio in B-flat [the *Archduke* Piano Trio, op. 97]. She has not the wild energy of her brother, but possesses sufficient power and nerve for the accurate performance of Beethoven's music. She is no superficial musician; she has studied the science deeply, and writes with the freedom of a master. Her songs are distinguished by tenderness, warmth, and originality: some that I heard were exquisite. Miss Mendelssohn writes, too, for a full orchestra by way of practice. When I was in Berlin she had, for this purpose, begun to *score*, for a modern orchestra, one of Handel's oratorios, and shewed me how far she had advanced![81]

Exactly what Fanny's Handelian project was remains unclear. Early in 1829 Felix had undertaken to arrange *Acis and Galatea* for the Singakademie in a modern scoring for double-wind orchestra, and perhaps in response she took up a similar exercise, in order to gain experience in orchestration. Her diary reveals that on January 23 she scored an unidentified *Händelschen Arie*, but more curious is an entry for New Year's Day: "Felix worked for several evenings downstairs on *Acis and Galatea*, which I have translated; I too am now finished with it."[82] Felix's manuscript score, dated January 3, confirms that he set the text of Handel's pastoral masque (1718) from the original English of John Gay into German, and, indeed, some of the German words are in Fanny's hand. Nevertheless, the cover label for the manuscript attributes the work solely to "Felix Mendelssohn Bartholdy";[83] there is no reference to Fanny's role as translator. If she indeed rendered the text into German, then another mystery remains—when did she achieve sufficient fluency in English to complete the task? Of her immediate family members, only Lea spoke English; perhaps in anticipation of Felix's journey she began instructing her children, an assumption possibly supported by a revelation Fanny made in 1833 to Mary Alexander, daughter of a Scottish laird: "I wish I could answer appropriately...in English, but I have no talent for languages, and English I did not learn anyway until I was a grown-up girl, and because of this inefficiency a constant target for my brother's and sister's ridicule. On the other hand Felix in those days did speak the English language possibly even worse than myself."[84]

Further research may yet shed more light on this mystery, as it may on another, no less intriguing. Fanny's diary informs us that on April 10, 1829, hours after Felix had departed for England, she played a piano work identified as her *Ostersonate* (*Easter* Sonata). On August 19, at the conclusion of the walking tour of Scotland, Felix introduced the first movement to his companion Karl Klingemann in a most unlikely venue, aboard the American vessel *Napoleon* anchored in Liverpool harbor, where they found a mahogany Broadwood piano.[85] Presumably, Felix was playing from memory; in any event, Fanny's score has not come to light, and the catalogue of her music officially lists the

Ostersonate (H-U 235), dated early 1829, as lost. That might be the end of the matter, were it not for a 1972 recording by the French pianist Eric Heidsieck of a piano work attributed to Mendelssohn—the program notes make clear that Felix, not Fanny, is meant—and identified as a *Sonate de Pâques, en la maj. (1828)*—that is, an *Easter* Sonata in A Major (1828).[86] According to the French scholar Françoise Tillard, the unsigned manuscript of this work is sequestered in private ownership.[87] Could this source in fact be Fanny's missing sonata?

Until the manuscript surfaces for examination we cannot say for sure, but it seems unlikely that Felix composed this work—no reference to an *Easter* Sonata from his pen has surfaced in his correspondence or that of his friends. On the other hand, if we judge from the recorded music, the *Sonate de Pâques* sounds suspiciously like Fanny Hensel. Its four movements—Allegro assai moderato, Largo e molto espressivo, Scherzo, and Allegro con strepito—betray all the hallmarks of her style. The warmly lyrical first movement, with its flexible modification of sonata form, expressive ornamental turns, passages in contrary thirds, and lines that climb to the uppermost treble register, show the composer to have been a devoted student of the late Beethoven sonatas, as we know Fanny was. The deeply pensive second movement, in E minor, turns to Bach for inspiration and seems cut from the same cloth as the austere pieces of her *Klavierbuch e moll* discussed earlier. The middle of the movement introduces a tortuous, chromatic fugue on a lamentlike subject, and at the end there is a brief passage in recitative style that calls out for words and seems drawn from the St. Matthew Passion. In contrast is the Scherzo in E Major—light, airy, and propelled by crisp staccato arpeggiations, it is an intermezzo in a manifestly Mendelssohnian idiom that distracts us from the serious, high style of the preceding movement. Adding support to Fanny's authorship of the sonata, the scherzo begins with a theme that strikingly anticipates the movement "April" from her piano cycle *Das Jahr* of 1841 (see p. 283).

The weighty finale clarifies the programmatic message of the *Sonate de Pâques*. Dramatically conceived, and in a heightened, dissonant style, the Allegro con strepito is evidently meant to depict the crucifixion of Christ; the agitated tremolo-like figures in the low bass, for instance, may refer to the earthquakes of Matthew 27:51. The idea of resurrection is made clear by an unambiguous use of Christian symbolism for the transfiguring coda of the sonata, announced by a solitary, bell-like A major chord, which quietly ushers in the chorale *Christe, Du Lamm Gottes*—the Lutheran Agnus Dei. We hear in succession the three phrases of the melody, each presented in a simple chordal style, and separated by free interludes, progressively removed from the accumulated dissonance of the finale. Toward the end, the chorale is repeated in a higher register, thus coupling the resurrection with a vision of Christ as the lamb of God, the perfect sacrifice.

The appearance of the chorale offers one more piece of circumstantial evidence pointing to Fanny's authorship of the work. As we have seen, at

Christmas 1827 Felix had finished for her a cantata based on the very same chorale. Its three statements of the *cantus firmus* include one in which the sooth-
ing melody is superimposed above a dissonant, chromatic fugue. One might
imagine Fanny choosing to end her sonata by quoting the familiar melody her
brother had recently treated. According to this scenario, then, Fanny's *Ostersonate* could have been written partly in response to Felix's cantata, another
example of the sibling exchange. In the end, regardless of who composed the
Sonate de Pâques, it is an impressive work that awaits further rediscovery and
consideration. If, in fact, it is Fanny's missing *Ostersonate*, then we may add to
her catalogue a substantial composition that probes well beyond the boundaries of her miniature lieder and character pieces and reveals a determined effort
to confront composition on a larger scale, and its dominant blueprint in the
1820s—sonata form.

Presumably a similar impulse motivated the creation of two chamber
compositions, the *Sonata o Fantasia* in G Minor and Capriccio in A-flat
Major for cello and piano (H-U 238 and 247),[88] which Fanny finished in the
fall of 1829 for her brother Paul, an accomplished amateur cellist. The former
(160 bars) pairs a dolorous Andante in G minor with a fast movement in
the major that initially observes the trappings of a sonata-form exposition,
with two contrasting yet related thematic groups. But Fanny interrupts the
development by briefly recalling the Andante, *in modo di fantasia*, and in
lieu of a recapitulation, proceeds to an abridged coda, yielding a truncated
movement. The alternation of slow and fast sections, use of reminiscence,
and flexible approach to the sonata principle recall Beethoven's Cello Sonata
in C Major, op. 102, which may have provided a model.[89] In the Capriccio
(175 bars), a *Lied-ohne-Worte*-like Andante in A-flat major frames a turbulent
Allegro di molto in F minor. Here she comes closer to producing a full-
fledged example of conventional sonata form, though her inspiration flags in
the effort. Notwithstanding the warmth of the Andante, the material of the
Allegro impresses as routine and somewhat stale, and the working out of the
argument stiff and forced.

Fanny explored a quite different vision of sonata form in three movements drafted for a piano sonata announced to Felix in late September, a few
days before her wedding (H-U 246).[90] The origins of this project date back to
May, when she recorded in her Florentine diary four bars for the opening of a
Scherzo in C minor. Its repeated notes, grace-note figures, and 6/8 meter suggest a whimsical response to the *campanella* finale of Paganini's Violin Concerto op. 7, then ingratiating itself among Berlin audiences.[91] In November,
Fanny expanded and fleshed out the scherzo, drafted a preceding Adagio in
E-flat major, and linked the two by an attacca sign. For the third movement
she conceived a lush Largo molto in A-flat major, but then paused. Though
the manuscript contains a few notations for the trio of the scherzo and a finale,
she was unable to complete the piano sonata. Instead, the project languished

for five years, until she reused the first two movements in her String Quartet in E-flat Major (H-U 277), for which she composed a new third movement and finale.

We shall consider the string quartet in due course (see p. 179). Of particular note in the three 1829 piano movements is their relative formal freedom and relaxed tonal definition. Thus, the Adagio in E-flat major actually begins by touching on C minor, with a series of harmonic digressions that delay and significantly postpone the attainment of the true tonic key, in the process challenging and reformulating the sonata-form concept. Instead of first establishing E-flat major and then departing from and returning to it, as traditional sonata form stipulated, Fanny initially searches for the tonic, occasionally intimating it but establishing and securing E-flat only as the ultimate goal in the final section of the Adagio. Suggesting a foreshortened sonata-form movement that commences in the middle of the process, with a quasi-development section, the music projects the quality of a fantasia, a freedom it shares with the Largo molto. Though the key signature of this movement announces A-flat major as the tonic, Fanny again avoids tonal clarity—not until bar 13 is there a firm cadence on A-flat. Rather, the Largo begins with an introductory bar of four rising, overlapping entries on the dominant harmony, as if the listener has happened upon the middle of the movement. In this case, the fluid, opening gesture betrays quite clearly the source for Fanny's experimentation—it is an unmistakable allusion to the slow movement from the Ninth Symphony of Beethoven.◐

v

On September 25, 1829, Felix addressed a letter from London "for the last time" to "Fräulein Fanny Mendelssohn Bartholdy." A week before, he had lacerated his leg when his cabriolet overturned, and now he faced a two-month convalescence: weeks of stationary bed rest, a jalapic purgative to promote digestion, and the universal panacea—bloodletting—through which, the composer grumbled, all his "free and fresh ideas" trickled "drop by drop into the basin." Still, he enjoined Fanny to "live and prosper, get married and be happy, shape your household so that I shall find you in a beautiful home when I come..., and remain yourselves, you two, whatever storms may rage outside." In the end, whether he addressed his sister as Mademoiselle or Madame did not matter.[92]

From Berlin, Fanny continued to send emotionally laden letters, reassuring Felix that her love for him would not diminish and even disclosing (at the risk, she mused, of delaying his recovery) that "her crown" adorned a "new bride"—that is, that she was a virgin.[93] The morning of the wedding, October 3, 1829, Fanny penned these fervent lines, as she contemplated Wilhelm's sketch of Felix, kept religiously on her desk: "I am very composed, dear Felix, and your picture is next to me, but as I write your name again and almost see you in person before my very eyes, I cry, as you do deep inside, but I cry. Actually, I've always known that I could never experience anything that would remove you from my memory for even one-tenth of a moment. Nevertheless, I'm glad to have experienced it, and will be able to repeat the same thing to you tomorrow and in every moment of my life. And I don't believe I am doing Hensel an injustice through it. Your love has provided me with a great inner worth, and I will never stop holding myself in high esteem as long as you love me."[94] In Fanny's idealized vision, sibling and matrimonial love would thus form a perfect alliance as she became Frau Hensel. It was, perhaps, a notion no less sentimental than the floral wreaths with which Wilhelm's portraits adorned his bride.

Nevertheless, Fanny envisioned a special demonstration of that alliance, by asking Felix to compose an organ processional for the wedding. While visiting Wales in late August, he began sketching a majestic musical exordium in A major, later destined to resurface in the Organ Sonata op. 65, no. 3 of 1844.[95] But the accident in London in mid-September interrupted his work and plan to return to Berlin for the nuptial celebrations. As a result, Fanny herself took up the task and on September 28 finished a processional, her first composition for organ (H-U 242). The last time she had been near an organ was in early April, when Felix gave recitals at three Berlin churches before his departure. There is no documentation that Fanny ever had organ lessons, so her knowledge of the instrument was very likely shaped not by actual experience but by the vicarious memories of her brother's playing. Even so, her Prelude in F Major, despite some passages more idiomatic on a piano,[96] is an effective piece, alternating between stately chordal acclamations and imitative passages, and concluding with a plagal ("Amen") cadence.

Abraham recommended J. S. Bach's *Pastorella* BWV 590 for the recessional, but when Fanny could not locate the score, she was again left to her own devices. During the *Polterabend*, the evening before the wedding day, and by tradition a time of considerable merriment, a rather implausible scene unfolded in the Mendelssohn household. While Wilhelm marked the occasion by drawing a pagan scene of a satyr reveling with naked figures,[97] Fanny began composing "in the presence of all the guests,"[98] and, shortly after midnight, finished a weighty recessional in G major (H-U 243).[99] Its counterpoint is noticeably more complex than that of its pendant; the pedal part now assumes more of an integrated thematic role; and there is a dramatic, chromatic preparation for the final cadence. All in all, the piece approached the spirit of Bach, for, as Fanny wrote, it reflected an earlier age.◐

And so, to the strains of her own music, hurriedly rehearsed and performed by A. W. Grell, Zelter's assistant at the Singakademie, Fanny and Wilhelm processed and recessed on October 3, 1829, at the Parochial-Kirche, filled with relatives and friends. Her music thus reached another semipublic space, but, we may wonder, were all the congregants aware of her authorship? Fanny's diary entry is vexingly laconic. She reports only that Pastor Wilmsen's sermon was insignificant (*unbedeutend*), the church full. Afterward there were the obligatory receptions with relatives and a few "anxious hours" before Wilhelm's sisters, Luise and Minna, escorted the newlyweds to their quarters in the *Gartenhaus* at Leipzigerstrasse no. 3. As for the rest of the evening, Fanny noted wryly, *dann schweige ich* (I'll pass over the rest).[100]

Because of their discrepancy in social standing and wealth, there were financial ramifications to Wilhelm's union with Fanny, which were not lost upon Abraham and Lea. Two days before the wedding they executed an *Ehevertrag*, or nuptial agreement, with the betrothed.[101] In this document we learn that Fanny's inheritance was the considerable sum of nearly 19,000 thalers. As long as the principal remained under Abraham's management, he agreed to pay a yearly interest of 5 percent, and to guarantee an annual income of 1,500 thalers. Legally these funds remained her property, and she could dispose of them as she saw fit, without Wilhelm's consent. A potential test of this arrangement arose even before their marriage—for months, the couple had entertained the idea of traveling to Rome with her family and then separating to enjoy excursions to Naples, Sicily, and Malta. Ruefully, Fanny thought better of the plan, in large part because it would challenge parental authority: "But now I'm worried," she wrote Felix on September 21, "a feeling I can't shake—whether our parents will rightfully disapprove when we immediately go off and enjoy a costly pleasure that would, in the best case, consume an entire year's income, instead of economizing at the start of our marriage, living quietly, and fulfilling our obligations here."[102] And so the newlyweds established a respectable household in the *Gartenhaus*, with Wilhelm working on his portraits while Fanny played the piano and composed. Within a few weeks she was confiding to her diary, with the sparing efficiency of a journalist, that she was pleased with Wilhelm and her new life, that their conjugal intimacy was at first difficult and then much improved, and that her family had taken its first meal in their new quarters.[103]

At the end of the year attention shifted to another matrimonial celebration, Abraham and Lea's silver wedding anniversary. From England Felix had begun planning the musical festivities and, to that end, enlisted Klingemann's collaboration on a humorous new *Liederspiel* titled *Heimkehr aus der Fremde* (*Son and Stranger*). Its plot centered on Hermann, the son of a town mayor, who returns incognito from soldiering abroad to regain his sweetheart Lisbeth and frustrate the vagabond Kauz. The composer and his librettist cleverly worked into the drama parts for family members and their circle: Felix was to play Hermann; Rebecka, Lisbeth; Eduard Devrient, Kauz; Fanny, the mayor's wife; and Wilhelm, the elderly mayor. There was a solo cello part for Paul, a member of the orchestra, and even a concession to Wilhelm's tone deafness, for his role required him to sing only one repeated pitch, which he dispatched, to the delight of his new family, with caricature-like grimaces that perhaps did not conceal his amusia. Largely alternating between strophic songs and spoken dialogue, Felix's *Liederspiel* recalled an earlier example of domestic music making with which Felix and Fanny were quite familiar—Ludwig Berger's setting of Müller's *Die schöne Müllerin*.

After a long-awaited return to Berlin, postponed until midnight on December 7, Felix quickly organized preparations for the festivities. Workers constructed a small stage and theater within the main residence, large enough to accommodate an audience of 120, and a small chamber orchestra was engaged. While Felix put the finishing touches on his score, Wilhelm and Fanny brought to life their own contribution, a cantata-like *Festspiel* on a text that Wilhelm doctored together in one day, and Fanny set expeditiously in one week. She had intended to use only a piano to accompany the soloists, but with Felix's encouragement scored the piece with orchestra, so that the *Festspiel* marked her orchestral debut (H-U 248).[104] To ceremonial trumpet fanfares three heralds claim the stage in turn to introduce allegories of three weddings—the first, silver, and golden. As the heralds compete for attention, their music suggests a scene from comic opera, reminiscent, for example, of the three *Damen* in Mozart's *Magic Flute*. Their bickering is summarily cut short by the arrival of the three weddings, played at the premiere by Therese Devrient, Rebecka, and Fanny, adorned with roses, myrtle and diamonds, and gold leaf.[105] In three short solos, they frame past, present, and future visions of matrimonial unions. A celebratory chorus then rounds out the work, which Fanny concludes by recalling the opening fanfares. Firm pillars of a fortunate house, Abraham and Lea are renewed and united by "that which was."

According to Therese Devrient, Felix assisted with the orchestration and directed the performance,[106] which occurred on December 26 along with the premiere of *Heimkehr aus der Fremde*. As an occasional piece, Fanny's *Festspiel* breaks no new ground but relies to a considerable extent on stock figures and familiar marchlike rhythms. In a nod to Felix's "authority," Fanny seeks to recreate the buoyant élan of his *Calm Sea and Prosperous Voyage* Overture, and her final chorus quotes nearly intact a phrase from his *Humboldt* Cantata. Still, her lyrical gifts emerge in the three solos, of which the third, for the golden wedding, is the most striking. From the "clouds of the future," the alto voice briefly emerges and sings beneath suspended flutes and clarinets, watched over by a star that confides tidings shared only rarely with humankind.

Of course, Fanny had no thought of publishing her *Festspiel*; nor, for that matter, did her brother ever release *Heimkehr aus der Fremde*, as his mother urged; instead, apart from a few performances at Leipzigerstrasse no. 3, it languished while awaiting posthumous publication as op. 89 in 1851.[107] Surely impressive is the extraordinary amount of effort that Felix and Fanny put into producing what were essentially occasional works for the private delectation of the family, but nothing more. (Indeed, the silver-wedding festivities included a preliminary *Polterabend* on December 25, when there was more musical entertainment, and when Wilhelm presented a vase after his own design from the royal porcelain factory.) Only the immediate circle of family and friends shared in these lavish celebrations, in the semiprivate space where Fanny's music flourished. But after Fanny's death, Wilhelm found another way to reuse her *Festspiel*. In November 1848, just months after the revolutionary tremors convulsed Berlin, he had a formal presentation copy of the three solos prepared and delivered to the Prussian king and queen on the occasion of their silver wedding anniversary.[108] Music for one private domestic setting thus regaled another.

vi

Writing in April 1830 to the young Sanskrit scholar Friedrich Rosen, newly appointed to the University of London, Felix described his sister's "comfortable" new life in the *Gartenhaus*.[109] The rooms were amply appointed with domestic conveniences, including furniture custom made from Wilhelm's drawings. Hanging on the walls of his studio were copies of Raphael's *Transfiguration*, and upon entering the room one encountered a disarray of finished and half-finished oil paintings, chalk sketches, palettes with moist paints, and an English piano, where Fanny composed lieder and presided over the "lovely, harmonic disorder." In the evenings a small circle would gather around a table, while Wilhelm assiduously worked away at his portraits—over the span of his career, he would amass more than a thousand, eventually gathered by his son into forty-seven albums—without interrupting the animated conversation. There was considerable discussion of events in France, about to erupt in the three "glorious days" of the July Revolution, and here, at least, differing views did collide. Wilhelm, a veteran of the 1813 and 1814 Napoleonic campaigns, had stiffened in his conservative and royalist views, so that Felix, of more liberal persuasion, referred to himself as Wilhelm's "radical brother-in-law."[110] As we shall see, Fanny's politics too inclined toward the liberal persuasion, but for the moment she assumed a certain domestic coziness (*Behaglichkeit*), of which her younger brother, reaffirming their father's mores, could only approve.

When Fanny discovered she was pregnant, her "house motherliness" (*Hausmütterlichkeit*), as Felix described it, took on a new dimension. On March 6, for the first time she felt the stirrings of life within her and confided to her diary her new sense of intimacy with Wilhelm.[111] For his part, that very day Wilhelm entered into Fanny's heart-shaped diary a miniature drawing—over a slumbering infant nestled in the petals of a flower, a winged fairy dangles a butterfly, as if to endow the fetus with a soul. Fanny's thoughts turned to composition, and on March 18, she recorded the trappings of a song, with a stave for a vocal part and two staves for the piano accompaniment.[112] But there was no text, as if the gestating composition had not yet been born. A few days later she composed a severely chromatic prelude in A minor (H-U 251),[113] and here too we encounter a paradox. Notated on systems of two staves, the prelude suggests a piece for piano, though only with difficulty can that instrument accommodate Fanny's thick textures. Rather, the octave doublings of the bass and exchanges of material between the two hands suggest that she had in mind here an organ prelude. A few weeks after her wedding, she in fact had begun but then abandoned an organ prelude in G major (H-U 244),[114] filled with baroque ornaments and invertible counterpoint reminiscent of Bach, as if she wished to perpetuate the reverberations of her own wedding music.

Meanwhile, Felix put the finishing touches on his second volume of songs, the twelve *Lieder*, op. 9, published in 1830 in two installments titled *Der Jüngling* (*The Youth*) and *Das Mädchen* (*The Maiden*). The gendered division bore a special, though private, meaning, for embedded in the second half of the opus were three of Fanny's songs, *Sehnsucht* (H-U 219), *Verlust*, and *Die Nonne* (see pp. 110 and 57–58), and three in which Felix adopted a feminine persona. If Felix is the idealized youth of the first half—in no. 6 he symbolically departs, to the opening motive of his *Calm Sea*, from the land of his youth—Fanny is his idealized counterpart in the second. Some parallels between the two halves strengthen the associations. For instance, nos. 4 and 8 are songs of springtime renewal, and, more specifically, nos. 3 and 9 (*Wartend* and *Ferne*) treat the topic of travel abroad and a homecoming, clear enough autobiographical allusions. Once again Fanny's authorship was suppressed in the publication in order to "protect" her privacy, but the omission does not tell the entire story. Fanny, it seems, was intimately involved in compiling the opus. From Glasgow in August 1829, Felix had authorized her to begin selecting songs for the opus according to her own discretion, either from his or her compositions.[115] Thus, she may have had a voice in shaping the opus and in seeing it through the press, only to remain concealed behind her brother's official, public voice. Indeed, when, decades later during the 1870s, the first collected edition of Felix's music began appearing from Breitkopf & Härtel, Fanny's contributions to op. 9 (and op. 8) were still unidentified, even though by then musicians in the know were aware of the true state of affairs.

Felix was eager to resume the next leg of his grand tour, which would take him to Munich, Vienna, and then Italy, but in mid-March 1830 Rebecka contracted the measles, followed in turn by Felix and Paul. For several weeks the family endured quarantine, with Rebecka and their parents separated from Felix, Paul, and the Hensels, so that communication between the ill and convalescing was limited to droll written notes. On April 17 the quarantine was lifted, but not until May 13 did Felix depart, and only after completing the score of his *Reformation* Symphony, which, Fanny reported, he rendered at the piano three times the day before.[116]

This time Fanny coped with the fraternal absence by studying Bach cantatas. She was quite taken with *Es erhub sich ein Streit* (BWV 19), for the feast of St. Michael, and wrote to Felix that "the old man really liked to rage"[117]—a reference to Bach's clashing counterpoint and militaristic trumpets and drums to depict the archangel's struggle with the satanic dragon. But on May 24, at the beginning of her expected two-month lying-in, her own travails unexpectedly began. That night she experienced a physical mishap, possibly a rupture of the amniotic sac, throwing the pregnancy and her health into jeopardy. For three worrisome weeks her family tended to her before she went into labor on June 14, and two days later gave birth prematurely to her son, so weak and frail that few believed he would survive. In the heart-shaped diary Wilhelm sketched for a second time the fairy and child motive; now angel-like, the protecting spirit fends off a sinister bat, while the infant lies awake in the flower.[118]

From Munich an increasingly alarmed Felix sent solicitous letters. At the time, he was socializing with members of the Wittelsbach court of King Ludwig I and appearing at soirées of the Bavarian aristocracy. When a countess praised "Felix's" lied *Italien* as *ganz entzückend* (totally charming) and he wholeheartedly concurred, he had to excuse his vanity by revealing Fanny's authorship.[119] Another distraction was a svelte, blue-eyed pianist, Delphine von Schauroth, with whom he played duets and flirted, but she could not replace the musical bond to Fanny:

> It suddenly came into my mind that we have a young lady in our garden-house whose ideas of music are somehow of a different kind, and that she knows more music than many ladies together, and I thought I would write to her and send her my best love. It is clear that you are this young lady, and I tell you, Fanny, that there are some of your pieces only to think of which makes me quite tender and sincere, in spite of all the insincerity that forms a social element in South Germany. But you know really and truly why God has created music, and that makes me happy. On the piano you are pretty good also, and if you want somebody to love and admire you more than I do, he must be a painter and not a musician.[120]

A few days later, on June 14, Felix wrote again, after receiving another discouraging report about Fanny's health.[121] This time he kept his words to a minimum and, turning instead to music, appended a short piano lied, a fragment of fifteen bars that reflected the style and miniature dimensions of Fanny's piano pieces. There was nothing new in the music, he confessed, but Fanny would recognize his name. Its key, A major, and dotted rhythms recall Felix's love song, *Frage*, op. 9, no. 1, and a cadence near the end seems extracted from the close of *Geständniss*, op. 9, no. 2. But the final gesture, an open-ended half cadence marked *pianissimo* and *dolce*, unmistakably reproduces the conclusion of the second song from Fanny's *Liederkreis*, her lament on Felix's departure in 1829.❷ Droysen's text asks why the sweet fragrances of May are now so dreary and addresses a bird that secretly grieves in a linden tree. Felix now reversed the scenario, to express his heartfelt concern for his sister, and to align his musical inspiration with hers, so that the conclusion of his lied led directly into her *Liederkreis*.

After learning the news of the birth, Felix wrote a giddy, congratulatory letter on June 23—"we have all been promoted," he observed—but it was to be shared with Fanny, he instructed Lea, only if her health improved; otherwise, it could be burned.[122] Then, when he learned Fanny was out of danger, he sent a third letter,[123] into which he copied a longer piano lied. "Half anxious" and "half joyful," it begins in an agitated B-flat minor, with frenetic, palpitating chords, but eventually turns to a joyful conclusion in the major, thus playing on the minor-major dichotomy that Fanny had used so often in her songs and piano works. Felix later revised the piece and published it as his *Lied ohne Worte*, op. 30, no. 2, without, of course, any reference to its private message.

Against considerable odds, Fanny and Wilhelm's son gained weight and thrived, so that by early August Fanny could describe him as a "chubby, splendid, healthy boy."[124] His earliest weeks coincided with the outbreak of revolution in Paris, and to show her solidarity with liberal-minded reformers, Fanny sewed into her son's garments tricolored ribbons, much to Wilhelm's dismay.[125] But their son would grow up in a largely sheltered, ideal atmosphere of art, never far from his mother's piano or his father's easel. His name would be not Wilhelm, but Felix Ludwig Sebastian Hensel, after Frau Hensel's three favorite composers—her brother, Beethoven, and J. S. Bach.

CHAPTER 6

Secret Aspirations

(1830–1833)

I have commanded Fanny to play something considerable for him, for she plays like a man.

—Zelter to Goethe, February 1831

For six weeks after giving birth, Fanny's bed rest continued. Though inspired to compose, she remained weak from the ordeal and oppressed by headaches, and Wilhelm dissuaded her from working. But when her health returned near the end of July 1830, a creative drought beset her, and she voiced her frustration to Felix.[1] Months later, he was still gently upbraiding her from Rome in a patronizing but brotherly tone: "But seriously, the child is not even half a year old, and you really wish to have ideas other than Sebastian? (Not Bach.) Rejoice that you have him there; music remains silent if there is no place for it.... Nevertheless, I wish for your birthday whatever your heart desires; I would wish you half a dozen melodies, but that will not help."[2] And then, having reminded Fanny of her maternal role, Felix announced the completion for her birthday of his new setting of Psalm 115 on the Vulgate text, *Non nobis Domine* ("Not to us, O Lord, but to your name give glory"). She already knew the opening, but the last chorus, he thought, would especially please her.

For the moment, the creative separation between the siblings intensified; now Felix expected Fanny's own muse to lie dormant, even though he had fashioned the new psalm to appeal to the sophisticated tastes of a fellow musician in arms. His letters continued to do double duty, addressing, as he wrote on her birthday in 1831, his beloved *Schwesterlein und Musiker* (little sister and musician). And so he informed her of plans to revise the *Hebrides* Overture, the early version of which dissatisfied him—she was to imagine differently the noisy conclusion of the exposition, admittedly lifted from his *Reformation* Symphony.[3] From Milan in July 1831, he praised Fanny after visiting Dorothea von Ertmann, the sensitive pianist to whom Beethoven had dedicated his Sonata in A Major op. 101, and who reminded Felix of his sister, though Fanny nevertheless was "far superior."[4] Then, in November, he shared with her a Bach chorale setting for organ newly discovered in Frankfurt and suggested she read through the piece with Rebecka: "When at the end the chorale melody begins to flutter and ends up in the air and all resolves itself in the music—that is quite divine."[5] Clearly, Fanny remained Felix's artistic confidante, privy to his innermost musical thoughts.

For a second time, his travels prevented him from attending a significant event in Fanny's life—the baptism of his nephew, which occurred on August 22, 1830. The godparents were the sculptor C. D. Rauch and Zelter, invited by Fanny to stand in for Felix, even as she unsuccessfully urged him to offer a symbolic presence by sending the A major organ composition he had promised for her wedding.[6] For a while, Fanny even pursued a fleeting hope of bridging their physical separation. Wilhelm had conceived the idea of establishing a Prussian academy at Rome,[7] after the model of the French academy, and sought royal funds to subsidize another Italian sojourn. But this time the king was not magnanimous, and there were other obstacles, including the opposition of their parents and the health of Sebastian, who, Wilhelm conceded ten days after his son's birth, was still the "smallest wight on earth."[8]

Another unsettling factor was the suddenly destabilized European political landscape. At the end of July transpired the *Trois Glorieuses*, the three-day revolution that summarily toppled the venal reign of the Bourbon king, Charles X. Abraham, then on business in Paris, sent back starkly contrasting bits of "dry intelligence." Two weeks before the revolution, he was visiting "the most marvelous monument wealth has ever, anywhere erected to its own greatness," the stock exchange (*Bourse*), not only "accessible to ladies, but actually frequented by them." But then, the fighting prompted this mind-numbing disclosure: "A cabman who drove me one of these days told me that on the dreadful Wednesday when he and a number of citizens fought in the Rue St. Honoré, several children from twelve to fourteen years of age armed with sticks had mingled in the crowd. He asked their leader, 'Malheureux, que fais-tu ici; tu n'as pas même d'armes.' ['Unhappy child, what are you doing here; you don't even have any weapons.'] 'J'attends que tu sois tué, pour prendre les tiennes' ['I'm waiting for you to be killed, to take yours'], was the answer, which could not be the invention of a cab-driver. It made me shudder, and I know nothing like it."[9] In her diary, Fanny noted that in nearly every state or country there was unrest to a larger or smaller degree,[10] all seemingly precipitated by the French seizure of Algiers in early July. Once again world events contrasted with the new tranquility of her married life.

Not surprisingly, Fanny's musical productivity declined sharply in the months after Sebastian's birth. When she did return to composing, in October 1830, she tried her hand at a new genre, the piano fantasy (H-U 253).[11] The result was 178 bars of contrasting tempi, moods, tonalities, and textures, a multisectional work resembling an improvisation at the keyboard. Here Fanny explores a free succession of ideas, beginning with a stately Adagio in A-flat major and concluding with a light Allegro vivace in E-flat major. Connecting the two are three sharply profiled passages—an Andante amoroso in E-flat on a subject recalling the aborted Sonata in E-flat (H-U 246); a turbulent, swirling Allegro di molto, centered on G minor and marked *con fuoco* (with passion), that eventually dissipates into a cadenza-like recitative; and an Andante in A-flat major, based on some sustained chords that modulate to E-flat and lead into the Allegro vivace. Through-composed, the Fantasia alternates between slow and fast passages in a way reminiscent of the *Sonata o Fantasia* for cello and piano (H-U 238). The sense of tonal latitude and structural freedom is evident at once in the Adagio, which quickly abandons the putative tonic, A-flat major, via a descending scalelike line in the bass in favor of C major, supported by a *pianissimo* tremolo. Here the music pauses, before Fanny begins afresh, this time with a passage in two-part imitative counterpoint, interrupted in turn by the new tonality and thematic material of the Andante amoroso. The spontaneous flow of ideas and use of interruption, digression, and recall are all features that Fanny would later explore in several large-scale works, including the String Quartet (1834), piano cycle *Das Jahr* (1841), and Piano Trio (1847).

Fanny finished two other compositions in 1830, two short lieder on texts of Ludwig Tieck and Wilhelm in November; a third song, possibly also on Wilhelm's verses, followed probably early in 1831. The *Minnelied* "Treue Liebe dauert lange" ("True Love Lasts a Long Time," H-U 254) is the last of eighteen poems Tieck interpolated into a novella about the chivalrous romance of the knight Peter of Provence and the fair Magelone. Fanny set the verses in a disarmingly simple style, with recurring trochaic patterns and dronelike effects to suggest a distant, medieval era. (The same text later served as the concluding, much more elaborate, romance of Brahms's cycle, *Die schöne Magelone*, op. 33, of 1869.) What attracted Fanny to the *Minnelied* may have been Wilhelm's concurrent project of illustrating several of Tieck's writings.[12] Another suggestion of the newlyweds' collaboration is the vibrant *Frühlingslied* "Blaue, blaue Luft" ("Blue, Blue Sky," H-U 255),[13] in which Fanny captured Wilhelm's images of spring flowers quivering in the sunlight with restless A major piano figurations, interrupted only by the suggestive question, "Mädchen, wohin?" ("Whither, maiden?"). Stylistically quite similar is "Der Schnee, der ist geschmolzen" ("The Snow, It Has Melted," H-U 256),[14] though here spring is a *böser, süßer Traum* (wicked, sweet dream), a prologue, in the annual cycle of the seasons, to winter. In response, Fanny dampens the vibrant music in G major by turning to the minor and by concluding with a half cadence that effectively leaves the composition harmonically incomplete, and thus open ended.

As a newly appointed *Hofmaler*, Wilhelm was keen to establish a studio where he could paint and train his students. When he was unable to locate suitable space in Berlin, Abraham offered to renovate the *Gartenhaus*. Breaking through walls and adding larger windows on the courtyard side, workers created a newly expanded space illuminated by the northern light preferred by artists.[15] Wilhelm began using his new atelier in January 1831; a few months later, a second room for his students was ready as well. The newlyweds welcomed these improvements, as Sebastian's arrival had rendered their quarters somewhat constrained: "For the entire summer, since Sebastian's birth, Wilhelm slept in the yellow room, and I with the wet nurse and child in the bedroom. Even though I frequently visited him early in the evening, and afterwards spent entire nights with him, it was still a great sacrifice for us not to be always together, and we were really happy when Wilhelm occupied his newly constructed atelier in January, yielded his former room to our child, and returned to his old room."[16] In recognition of his rising status as an artist, Wilhelm was appointed professor at the Berlin Academy of Arts in July 1831. For the next fifteen years he offered instruction from his atelier, where, all told, twenty-one students (twenty men and one woman) became his disciples. By the fall of 1832 they were beginning to show their work—chiefly portraits and genre paintings—at the annual Academy, and well before then had become familiar figures in the Hensels' household, where they celebrated Christmas together in 1831 and earned a brief entry in Fanny's diary: "The pupils made a fine procession. It really pleases me to see the young people here, and to take them into our circle. I believe that is the surest way for them to form bonds, and to have an edifying effect on them."[17]

Meanwhile, a new domestic drama erupted. In February 1831 Rebecka announced her intention to marry Peter Gustav Lejeune Dirichlet (1805–1859) and consequently had to run Lea's matronly gauntlet. When Alexander von Humboldt introduced the young mathematician to the Mendelssohns in 1828, he already had some impressive credentials. Dirichlet had studied with Ohm, formulator of the law of electric resistance, attended lectures in Paris by leading French mathematicians such as Fourier and Laplace, pored over the *Disquisitiones Arithmeticae* of C. F. Gauss, and begun his own teaching career at the University of Breslau (Wrocław) in Silesia, before assuming a position in Berlin, where his students would include Bernhard Riemann, author of a path-breaking essay on prime number theory in 1859.

Fanny recorded in her diary the calm before the storm—initially, Lea had not reacted as strongly as the siblings feared—and then the storm. We are not quite sure why Lea chose to depict Rebecka's future with Dirichlet in "the most dreadful colors" (*mit den schrecklichsten Farben*),[18] or why Abraham's objections to the proposed union gradually stiffened—intellectually, Dirichlet could certainly hold his own among the Mendelssohns, later generations of whom boasted several notable mathematicians.[19] Presumably, the sticking points concerned issues of class or economic background. In any event, the matter dragged on until November 1831, when the engagement was finally announced. It appears that Fanny and Wilhelm stepped in to reassure Dirichlet and to help smooth the way to the couple's wedding in May 1832. They took up their new quarters in the *Gartenhaus* at Leipzigerstrasse no. 3, in the wing opposite Fanny and Wilhelm.

Within a few years, Dirichlet had presented in Berlin an essay generally viewed as marking the beginning of analytic number theory. He demonstrated that an arithmetic progression generated by repeatedly adding a whole number to another lacking a common factor contains infinitely many prime numbers.[20] Fanny's new brother-in-law exhibited all the eccentricities of mathematical genius, and an unusual lecture style, as described by one of his English students in the 1850s: "What is peculiar in him, he never sees his audience—when he does not use the black-board at which time his back is turned to us, he sits at the high desk facing us, puts his spectacles up on his forehead, leans his head on both hands, and keeps his eyes, when not covered with his hands, mostly shut. He uses no notes, inside his hands he sees an imaginary calculation, and reads it out to us—that we understand it as well as if we too saw it."[21] Dirichlet's career remained centered in Berlin until 1855, when he was called to Göttingen, to fill the vacancy created by the death of his idol Gauss, viewed by many as the reigning mathematician of the century.

While Dirichlet was finding his place within the Mendelssohn family, Fanny was reorganizing the biweekly Sunday concerts at Leipzigerstrasse no. 3. On February 8, 1831, she wrote of her plans to Felix, then absorbing the encrusted traditions of Catholic polyphony in Rome while he composed Lutheran chorale cantatas (Berlioz, who met Felix during his Roman sojourn, later noted that he "believed firmly in his Lutheran faith").[22] Unfortunately, Fanny's letter is lost, but we have Felix's positive reply of February 22:

> I cannot tell you, dear Fanny, how much I am delighted with your plan about the Sunday music. This idea of yours is most brilliant, and I do entreat of you, for Heaven's sake, not to let it die away again; on the contrary, pray give your traveling brother a commission to write something new for you. He will gladly do so, for he is quite charmed with you, and with your project. You must let me know what voices you have, and also take counsel with your subjects as to what they like best (for the people, O Fanny, have rights). I think it would be a good plan to place before

them something easy, interesting, and pleasing,—for instance, the Litany of Sebastian Bach. But to speak seriously, I recommend the "Shepherd of Israel" [i.e., J. S. Bach's cantata, *Du Hirte, Israel, höre*, BWV 104] or the "Dixit Dominus" of Handel. Do you mean to play something during the intervals to these people? I think this would not be unprofitable to either party, for they must have time to take breath, and you must study the piano, and thus it would become a vocal and instrumental concert. I wish so much that I could be one of the audience, and compliment you afterwards.[23]

From these comments we may infer that Fanny conceived her concerts to showcase choral music and that Felix urged her to offer piano and instrumental chamber works in the "intervals" between choral compositions.

No documented programs from 1831 survive, and it is unclear exactly when Fanny revived the series. That may have been as early as February, when Zelter, noting privately to Goethe that "she plays like a man," "commanded" her to perform "something considerable" (*was erkleckliches*) for a visitor from Edinburgh at a Sunday musical gathering.[24] Be that as it may, in May, the Hensels made a brief excursion to Dresden, where they visited Fanny's cousin Josephine Benedix,[25] and admired the treasures of the royal Saxon art galleries, which housed masterpieces such as Raphael's *Sistine Madonna* and Titian's *Tribute Money*.[26] Presumably the concerts resumed after their return to Berlin; a laconic entry in Fanny's diary for October 4—"My Sunday musicales prosper much, and give me great joy"[27]—is the only tantalizing reference we have from her hand. Nevertheless, the concerts clearly had a decisive influence on Fanny's development as a composer, for in 1831 she finished three sacred cantatas for soloists, chorus, and orchestra, all premiered at the family residence. They included *Lobgesang* (*Hymn of Praise*, February 6–June 14), for Sebastian's first birthday; *Hiob* (*Job*, ca. July–October 1), for the couple's second wedding anniversary; and what is now known as the *Choleramusik* (October 9–November 20), to mark the cessation of the cholera epidemic in Berlin. A fourth work, a dramatic scene for soprano and orchestra on the myth of Hero and Leander (December 21, 1831–January 21, 1832), followed early in the New Year. Large-scale vocal compositions thus suddenly dominated Fanny's creative efforts, as she abruptly moved from the miniature piano pieces and lieder that had preoccupied her in earlier years. Though there is no evidence that she intended to seek a broader audience by publishing the cantatas (nor were they intended for liturgical use), their concentration in 1831 marked a turning point in her career as a composer. The public nature of the cantatas—the plural musical forces of soloists, a chorus, and orchestra—contrasted markedly with the private, diarylike character of Fanny's piano pieces and lieder and denoted a new stage in her gradual progression toward becoming a professional composer.

i

The first cantata, *Lobgesang* (H-U 257),²⁸ readily betrays Bachian roots. In five movements, it comprises an orchestral pastorale; a chorus on verses from Psalm 62 ("For God alone my soul waits in silence"); an alto recitative on John 16:21 ("When a woman is in labor, she has pain"); a soprano aria on verses from Johann Mentzer's hymn "O that I had a thousand tongues to sing His praises" ("O daß ich tausend Zungen hätte"); and a chorus employing additional verses from the hymn and citing a melody composed for it in the eighteenth century by Johann Balthasar König. In short, the organization of the composition, in which choral movements frame a paired solo recitative and aria, recalls the familiar trappings of a Bach cantata.

To honor her son, Fanny invoked the elder Sebastian in the opening Pastorale. As scholars have noted, this instrumental movement traces its ancestry to Bach's Cantata no. 104 (*Du Hirte Israel, höre*, 1724), well known to Fanny and Felix, and the second part of the *Christmas* Oratorio (1734). Both begin with instrumental pastorales that, like this Pastorale, are in G major.²⁹ The ties to the *Christmas* Oratorio are especially compelling ●—we might cite the lilting trochaic rhythms, extended pedal points, and distinctive scoring that sets in relief against the string background flutes and oboes, associated since the seventeenth century with shepherds and Christmas Eve. Fanny thus celebrated her son's birth by placing it in the context of Christ's Nativity.

With the second movement, the chorus "Meine Seele ist stille zu Gott," Fanny broadened her musical borrowings. Tripartite in structure, the chorus begins with block harmonies accompanied by gently pulsating tremolos in the orchestra. At "Denn er ist meine Hoffnung" ("from him comes my salvation"), changes in texture and meter accommodate a new figure distributed among the choral parts, which seems to recall the opening choral lament of Handel's *Israel in Egypt* ("They oppressed them with burdens"). Then, in the third section, "dass mich kein Fall stürzen wird" ("I shall never be shaken"), Fanny introduces an ascending leap in the bass that briefly brings her score close to the opening movement of Felix's Psalm no. 115, *Non nobis Domine*—as we have seen, his salutation for her birthday in 1830.³⁰

That Fanny specified an alto for the following recitative might suggest that she herself sang the part at the premiere. Its text uses the metaphor of childbirth to convey the idea of pain turning into joy. Sebastian's birth is thus again allied with profound Christian symbolism—in John 16:21, the disciples' pain at Christ's departure and death that gives way to their joy at the Resurrection and Second Coming. The next, celebratory movement expresses that joy in a brightly hued aria possibly conceived for Fanny's friend, the soprano Pauline Schätzel. In A major, and embellished by prominent passages for solo violin, the aria seems descended from the *Laudamus te* (We praise you) from the Gloria of J. S. Bach's monumental Mass in B Minor, another A major soprano aria with an especially florid solo part for violin. But stylistically Fanny's aria is more eclectic than neobaroque and exhibits too, for example, turns of phrase indebted to Haydn's *Creation*,[31] and a contrasting central part in C major well removed from the Thomaskantor's influence.

Still, the choral finale returns us to the involved, contrapuntal sound world of Bach's cantatas. Over a bustling, energetic bass line, Fanny presses into service as a *cantus firmus* König's chorale melody and presents it phrase by phrase in the altos, separated by brief, freely composed choral interludes. In the second half of the movement, fanfarelike figures add to the jubilation, and all four choral parts take up the chorale melody in imitative counterpoint. Its final phrase appears in block, chordal style in longer note values, as if affirming its identity as a chorale, while the moving bass line disperses its energy by ascending into the violins. The work closes with an open-spaced D major chord, balanced to favor the high register of the orchestra.

For all its charming qualities, *Lobgesang* betrays Fanny's inexperience with orchestration, which Felix did not hesitate to point out in a critique sent to Berlin from Paris at the end of 1831. Here he singled out the Pastorale and chided Fanny for pitching the horns too high, the oboes too low: "What the deuce made you think of setting your G horns so high? Did you ever hear a G horn take the high G without a squeak? ... And at the end of the introduction, when wind instruments come in, does not the following note 𝄞 stare you in the face, and do not these deep oboes growl away all pastoral feeling, and all bloom? Do you not know that you ought to take out a license to sanction your writing the low B for oboes, and that it is only permitted on particular occasions, such as witches, or some great grief?"[32] Despite all the "beauties" of the A major aria, Fanny had "overloaded" the voice with too many additional parts, obscuring its "delicate intention" and "lovely melody." And Felix took exception to the choice of texts for the choruses, which he found too general—they were "equally suitable for church music, a cantata, an offertorium, etc." Fanny's choruses, in short, could have been the work of "any other good master," not because of her music per se, but because the poetry did not impose "any particular music." For Felix, "not everything in the Bible," even if it suited the theme, was "suggestive of *music*."[33]

The premiere of *Lobgesang* fell on Wilhelm's birthday, July 6, 1831, before a "select audience" at Leipzigerstrasse no. 3.[34] By then, Fanny was probably at work on her next cantata, *Hiob* (H-U 258), finished on October 1 for the couple's second wedding anniversary.[35] To confront the central issue of theodicy—the reconciling of evil with God's goodness—she drew texts for the three movements from Job: 7, 13, and 10—that is, from Job's dialogues with his friends, in which, after a seven-day silence, he questions the undeserved calamities visited upon him and addresses God:

1. Chorus (Job 7:17–18)

What are human beings, that you make so much of them, that you set
　　your
mind on them,
visit them every morning, test them every moment?

2. Arioso (Job 13:24–25)

Why do you hide your face, [and count me as your enemy]?
Will you frighten a windblown leaf and pursue dry chaff?

3. Chorus (Job 10:12–13)

You have granted me life and steadfast love, and your care has
　　preserved my spirit,
Yet these things you hid in your heart; I know that this was your
　　purpose.

Fanny thus chose not to treat the culminating theophany (Job:38–42), in which God confronts Job with the divine questions from the whirlwind, before ultimately restoring his fortunes and blessing his "latter days" more than his beginning. Still, the rising emotional trajectory of *Hiob*, which progresses from the dark G minor of the first movement to the radiant G major of the third, while critically rearranging the order of the texts, is one of sorrow and affliction turning to joyful acceptance, even if, like the Old Testament book, the cantata unfolds largely as a series of resounding questions.

Fanny's opening movement betrays at the outset ties to her brother's cantata-like Psalm 115.🔊 Both works begin with choral movements in G minor prefaced by brief orchestral introductions. Both are marked *forte*, with strong downbeats in the bass that support suspiciously similar rising motives in the violins. (Indeed, the first six pitches of Fanny's motive nearly replicate the beginning of Felix's.) But, as if to assert her independence, Fanny departs soon enough from the fraternal model. While Felix's passage remains anchored on the tonic G minor, Fanny's beginning digresses harmonically: she questions, as it were, the primacy of G minor by quickly redirecting the music to C minor, F major, and B-flat major before returning to G minor for the choral entry.

First the sopranos question, "Was ist ein Mensch," with an angular figure imitated, in turn, by the tenors, altos, and bass. Riven by disjunct leaps, their motive is a reformulation of an old baroque fugal subject,[36] but Fanny's purpose here is not to write a strict fugue. Instead, the music accommodates a harmonic ebb and flow that, as in the beginning, carries us through a series of searching tonal regions. At "Du suchest ihn täglich heim" ("You set your mind on them") the tempo intensifies to *poco più vivace*, as Fanny introduces a new, compact motive, led through a sequence of rising chromatic harmonies.

Its insistent rhythmic patterns usher in the final section of the movement, which restores the music and text of the opening. Initially, it seems, we have returned as well to the tonic key of G minor, but Fanny masterfully undercuts our expectation of tonal closure, first by substituting the major form for the minor, then by inserting a false cadence on a dissonant chord, and finally, in the last three bars, by employing G major in an incomplete "half" cadence that leaves the music unanswered, as it prepares instead the C minor of the next movement, an Arioso for four soloists.

The dramatic half cadence, marking the final choral statement of the question "Was ist ein Mensch," is significant for another reason. It appears to borrow a passage from J. S. Bach's funeral cantata *Gottes Zeit ist die allerbeste Zeit* (no. 106, ca. 1707) that, like Fanny's passage, employs a half cadence to introduce a central slow movement in C minor.[37] Known as the *Actus tragicus*, this cantata became a favorite of Felix and Fanny after its publication in 1830.[38] Its bipartite subject matter—summarized by Alfred Dürr as "death under the Law and under the Gospel," by Hans-Joachim Hinrichsen as a progression from the suffering of mortal frailty to hope[39]—possibly influenced Fanny's conception of *Hiob*, so that some scholars even view Bach's cantata as a model for Fanny. Be that as it may, the soprano figure of the second movement ("Why do you hide your face?"), falling against sobering tremolo chords in the strings, recalls another work of Bach, the "Et incarnatus est" from the Credo of the Mass in B Minor. The images of the leaf and chaff drew from Fanny two fresh motives. One leads to another questioning half cadence; the other, to the returning tremolo chords, and an eerily serene cadence on C major, the first significant structural break and caesura in the work.

Standing quite apart is the joyous third movement (Vivace), which clarifies and stabilizes G major as the ultimate tonic—the musical answer, as it were, to the composition's probing questions. Fanny assigns the four half verses of Job 10:12–13 to as many distinctive subjects, apportioned one by one to the tenor, alto, bass, and soprano. Of these the first is a reworking of and response to the "Was ist ein Mensch" motive of the first movement (example 6.1). Much of the Vivace explores combinations of the four subjects, which venture harmonically further and further afield before a timpani roll underscores the return of G major, and with it the first subject, now associated with God's "steadfast love"—for Fanny, apparently, the answer to the riddles of the Book of Job. After ceremonial orchestral chords, the final bars of the cantata broaden into a stately Lento and articulate the first, fully satisfying authentic cadence in G major.

Why did the tribulations of Job form the subject for Fanny's second cantata, performed on her second wedding anniversary? The answer was probably the inexorable advance of the "Asiatic hydra"—cholera—which, Fanny noted on July 19, was already ravaging eastern Europe as far west as Danzig (Gdańsk).[40] As early as June the Prussian monarch had appointed a commission to consider countermeasures, such as cordoning off areas and fumigating

EXAMPLE 6.1. Fanny Hensel, *Hiob* (1831), first movement

buildings, but also more dubious means—clipping the wings of birds and allowing smoking of tobacco so as "not to remove protection from those who believe this to be effective against cholera."[41] But these efforts proved utterly futile against the progress of the epidemic, caused by a waterborne bacterium not yet comprehended by medical science. In August came the first confirmed cases in Berlin, and in 1832, Felix, barred by his parents from returning to Berlin, contracted a mild infection in Paris. Fanny and her family in Berlin were largely spared the disease but witnessed its destructive fury, which affected some 2,200 citizens, of whom almost 1,400 perished, many within hours of falling ill. The mortality rate peaked at the end of September 1831 before declining dramatically in the next two months;[42] among the last victims was Fanny's aunt Henriette (Jette) Mendelssohn, who died on November 9.[43]

Between October 9 and November 20, Fanny worked on her third cantata (H-U 260), the score of which she left untitled. Because of its expanded dimensions—thirteen movements requiring four soloists, a chorus divided into as many as eight parts, and an orchestra buttressed by trombones—upon its twentieth-century revival it was first thought to be an oratorio.[44] But Fanny alluded to the *Choleramusik* in her diary, and some of its parts, rediscovered only as recently as 1996, bear the title *Cantate nach Aufhören der Cholera in Berlin, 1831* (*Cantata after the Cessation of the Cholera in Berlin, 1831*), enabling the definitive identification of the score.[45]

The idea of a calamity visited upon mankind links the *Cholera* Cantata to *Job* and explains the choice of key for the solemn opening movement—G minor—the key that also inaugurates *Job*. Fanny conceived the beginning of the cantata for orchestra alone (example 6.2)—it is a voiceless lament, suffused with intense dissonant harmonies, plaintive motives in the oboe and clarinet, solemn trombone sonorities, diverging chromatic lines, and, above all, the descending chromatic tetrachord—a symbol since the seventeenth century of the musical lament, and a figure invoked at the opening of Bach's St. Matthew Passion.

Fanny's foreboding musical prelude sets the general affect of the score, given its first verbal definition in the following alto recitative. Introduced by stately fanfares, and playing the role of a herald, she announces that God has summoned the living to judgment:

EXAMPLE 6.2. Fanny Hensel, *Choleramusik* (1831)

> Hear this, all you peoples;
> give ear, all inhabitants of the world, [Psalm 49:1]
> the mighty one, God the Lord, [Psalm 50:1]
> speaks and summons the earth
> from the rising of the sun to its setting.
> He calls to the heavens above [Psalm 50:4]
> and to the earth, that he may
> judge his people.

Though this recitative delivers a unified message, Fanny culled it together from nonconsecutive verses of two different psalms, characteristic of her approach in fashioning the libretto. Unlike Felix's later oratorios, *St. Paul* and *Elijah*, each largely shaped by narrative accounts in Acts and 1 Kings, or his large-scale psalm settings, each defined by consecutive verses of individual psalms, Fanny created the *Cholera* Cantata for a particular contemporary event, the epidemic of 1831, which necessitated finding and stitching together in an ad hoc manner relevant but otherwise unrelated scriptures.[46] Whether she acted alone or collaborated with her husband in this endeavor is unclear.

Be that as it may, the *Cholera* Cantata traces a rising trajectory familiar already in *Job*, of despair over adversity yielding in the end to the joyful praise of God. As Annegret Huber has convincingly argued, the cantata projects a narrative that unfolds in a symmetrical, three-part musical design.[47] In the first part (nos. 1–5), the alto herald yields to an arioso for bass solo (no. 2), who, prophetlike, delivers God's judgment: "I reared children and brought them up, but they have rebelled against me" (Isaiah 1:2); "I beat them fine, like dust before the wind" (Psalm 18:42); "they will go to the company of their ancestors, who will never again see the light" (Psalm 49:19). A short soprano recitative—in contrast to the alto and bass, she sings against high woodwinds, suggesting perhaps the part of an angel—delivers the finality of the judgment, and its effects are immediately evident in the dramatically charged *turba* chorus of no. 3, which reinvigorates the dissonant language and unstable G minor tonality of no. 1. There is no recourse for the faithlessness of the afflicted (alto recitative, no. 4), so that "in a moment they die" (soprano recitative, no. 5), a verse from Job 34:20 that at once alludes to Fanny's earlier cantata and also to the terrible suffering of the cholera victims in Berlin.

We now reach the crux of the cantata (nos. 6–10) and the tribulations of the living, from the collective viewpoint (the chorus in nos. 6, 9, and 10) and the individual experience (tenor aria of no. 8). In no. 6 Fanny suggests a Protestant reading by adding a chorale melody, superimposed above the chorus, which delivers verses from Psalm 84:10 ("Behold our shield, O God") and Isaiah 9:12 ("For all this his anger has not turned away"). Her choice of chorale is "O Traurigkeit, O Herzeleid" ("O Sadness, O Heartfelt Grief"), a familiar seventeenth-century Passion hymn by Friedrich von Spee, set to music by

Johann von Rist, and also known to Fanny through C. P. E. Bach's collection of his father's chorale harmonizations. Two features are especially striking about this addition. First, Fanny altered the text, replacing its reference to Christ's death ("Gottes Vaters einigs Kind wird zu Grab getragen" ["God the Father's only son is borne to a grave"]) with a more general statement about human mortality ("Was der Herr zum Leben schuf, wird ins Grab getragen" ["What the Lord brought to life is borne to a grave"]). And second, the distinctive texture of the chorale suspended above the chorus alludes to "O Mensch, bewein' dein' Sünde gross" ("O man, bewail your great sin"), with which the first part of the St. Matthew Passion concludes, once again marking Fanny's cantata as a response to the nascent Bach revival.

In no. 7, the individual voice emerges in a tenor aria on texts drawn from Psalms 88 and 6. "I suffer your terrors, I am desperate," he sings, in an agitated style that straightaway recalls Tamino's initial entrance in Mozart's *The Magic Flute (Die Zauberflöte)*, "Zu Hilfe! Zu Hilfe!" ("Help, help!").[48] There Tamino flees from a dragon, not the wrath of God, but nevertheless Fanny chose to draw a parallel between her cantata and the opera, a morality tale of good versus evil. No. 8, a soprano recitative, brings the first words of consolation and encouragement, selected from Psalm 91: "He will cover you with his pinions, and under his wings you will find refuge." There then follow two choruses (nos. 9 and 10), a *Trauerchor* in which the living lament the dead, withered like grass and scattered like flowers (Isaiah 40:7) and a *Chor der Seligen* representing the departed. The *Trauerchor*, cast in the G minor with which the cantata began, forms the emotional core of the work and offers impressive, heartfelt music for eight-part chorus, divided first between the female and male parts, and then combined into one expressive ensemble. The *Chor der Seligen* invokes the familiar scripture from 2 Timothy 4:7, "I have fought the good fight," but with unfamiliar music—an imaginary, unearthly, and freely composed chorale (example 6.3), which now turns the music for the first time toward C major, the ultimate goal of the composition.

EXAMPLE 6.3. Fanny Hensel, *Choleramusik* (1831)

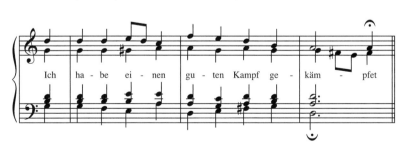

Two short recitatives (soprano, then bass) prepare the third, final section of the cantata—the people's reconciliation with God, and the implied lifting of the epidemic. After the call by the bass prophet to atone ("I reprove and discipline those whom I love. Be earnest, therefore, and repent," Revelation 3:19), the chorus begins its penance in a fugue (no. 11), the strident subject of which brims with dissonant leaps for the text, "For we are suffering because of our own sins" (2 Maccabees 7:32). Fanny conveys the approach of the Lord in three recitatives for soprano, alto, and bass, with a medley of texts from Psalm 145, 1 Peter, Isaiah, and, finally, the Book of Revelation ("See, I am coming soon; my reward is with me"). The culminating, celebratory chorus (no. 13), in a buoyant C major, juxtaposes verses of praise from several psalms, chief among them no. 150, with its injunction to use all manner of instruments, to which Fanny responds with timpani, trombones, winds, and strings (including pizzicato strings to depict the psaltery and harp). The last line of text—"Alles was Odem hat, preiset den Herrn" ("Let all that breathes praise the Lord!")— brings the cantata to a triumphant close with the same text Felix would use in 1840 to conclude his cantata-like *Lobgesang* Symphony, op. 52.

On many counts, the *Cholera* Cantata is a remarkable achievement. True, Fanny occasionally covers the voices by overscoring, though she shows also increased sophistication in blending and varying instrumental colors. But most impressive is how she rose to the challenge of large-scale composition, by imposing over a stretch of music exceeding half an hour in duration a taut, unified design. Much of the work is through-composed and harmonically connected and anticipates Felix's experiments in his first oratorio, *St. Paul*, begun in 1834. The cantata's thirteen movements are thus not independent or self-sufficient, but parts of a greater, unified whole. Emphasizing this feature, Fanny periodically recalls a plaintive motive from the orchestral introduction, which reappears in nos. 4, 7, and 10. And finally, unifying the composition is a carefully coordinated tonal plan that traces an elemental progression from the G minor of nos. 1, 3 and 9, associated with dissonant, unstable chromatic harmony, to the stable, diatonic C major of the finale. Connecting the two is G major, appearing at the beginning of the imaginary chorale in no. 10, and then in the soprano recitative of no. 12. Through this modal shift from G minor to G major, Fanny clarifies G as the dominant, so that on the macro level her composition describes an overarching dominant to tonic, or V–I, cadence in C major. The cantata is thus not the work of a miniaturist songwriter but of an ambitious composer contemplating dramatically expanded horizons.

ii

The *Cholera* Cantata received its premiere at the Mendelssohn residence on Abraham's birthday, December 10, 1831. According to Fanny, its hopeful

message prompted him to reconcile with Adolf Bernhard Marx,[49] the opin-
ionated music theorist who had wreaked a "pernicious" influence on Felix,
or so Abraham had thought. Celebrating Christmas that year, her family was
grateful for surviving the epidemic; they had lost dear friends, and indeed
the New Year brought further misfortune—on January 22, the death of the
violinist Eduard Rietz, for whom Felix had composed the Octet and who now
succumbed at age twenty-nine to tuberculosis. A few days later Fanny set a
poem by Wilhelm, "So soll ich dich verlassen" ("So Should I Leave You"),
quite possibly in memoriam to the musician. She designed its drooping,
A minor strains as a duet for tenor and soprano (H-U 264),[50] in which the
tenor assumes the role of the departing friend, and the soprano promises to
preserve his memory.

When Fanny's friend the soprano Ulrike Peters fell ill, the composer again
turned to music and quickly conceived for the musician the dramatic concert scene *Hero und Leander* (H-U 262), orchestrated in January 1832 before
her death in February. Here Fanny took another bold step by producing an
impressive example of her talents in dramatic composition and effectively
approaching the opera house. Wilhelm contributed the text, about the fabled
Greek lovers separated by the Hellespont. Every night Leander swims the strait
from Abydos, guided by a torch lit by Hero, priestess of Aphrodite at Sestos.
But one night, a storm extinguishes the beacon, Leander drowns, and Hero,
plunging from a cliff above the waters, joins him by suicide. Unlike Ovid,
who had treated the subject in his *Heroides* as an exchange of letters between
the lovers, or the Austrian dramatist Grillparzer, who fashioned a five-act play,
Wilhelm produced a dramatic monologue from the point of view of Hero,
rather along the lines of Schiller's ballad *Hero und Leander* (1801). Indeed, the
two poems share several images—dolphins sporting in the placid waters, the
coursing sun likened to the fiery chariot of the sun god Apollo, and birds fleeing the advancing storm.

Fanny's music alternates between recitative and more structured, arialike
passages. There are intimations of her brother's *Calm Sea and Prosperous Voyage* Overture (1828) in broad, open-spaced orchestral sonorities and wavelike
arpeggiations in the strings, and examples of romantic tone painting, as in
her use of the cellos to depict the night. The approaching tempest inspired
an extended orchestral interlude, reminiscent of the dramatic storm in the
fourth movement of Beethoven's *Pastoral* Symphony. To heighten the musical tension, Fanny expands the range of the orchestra to accommodate a shrill
piccolo and murky tessitura of a serpent, a distinctive bass wind instrument
related to the cornet family. (Commonly used in eighteenth-century religious processions and military bands, the serpent briefly found favor in early
nineteenth-century orchestral music, including Felix's *Calm Sea and Prosperous Voyage*.) Fanny's composition ends with an abrupt coup de théâtre. After
the horrified Hero watches her lover drown—"Weh! Er sinkt," she sings,

plunging nearly two octaves—she proclaims, "Ich folge" ("I follow"), and the music simultaneously brightens to C major, with a sweeping wavelike figure followed by descending wind chords and plummeting diminuendo (example 6.4). In effect, the work ends by returning to its opening vision of a serene, all-encompassing sea.

Among Fanny's more unusual musical projects of this time was a piano composition titled *Das Nordlicht* (*Northern Lights*, H-U 263), for which she recorded some sketches and an incomplete draft dated January 24.[51] A fantasia-like experiment, it was her attempt to capture at the keyboard the mysterious, ethereal qualities of the aurora borealis, visible in Berlin for several months during 1831. Only sixty-eight bars survive, but they suffice to reveal a far-flung chromatic modulation from B-flat minor to F-sharp minor. For much of the fragment Fanny specified a *pianissimo* dynamics level and also applied the technique of open pedal (*senza sordino*)—that is, raising the dampers to allow the sonorities to well together in a soft, dissonant blur.

One wonders how Wilhelm reacted to this atmospheric tone painting, well removed from the Bachian and Handelian ruminations of Fanny's three cantatas. At the time, he was engaged with what proved to be his most signifi-cant work, *Christus vor Pilatus* (*Christ before Pilate*), depicting the judgment

EXAMPLE 6.4.   Fanny Hensel, *Hero und Leander* (1831)

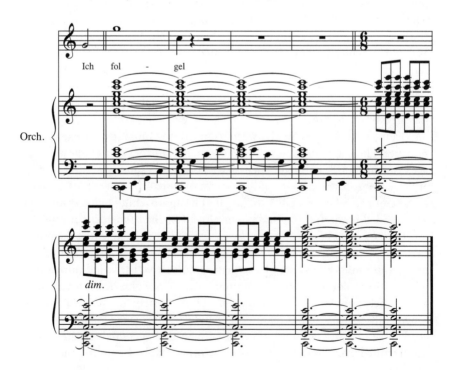

scene in which the Roman governor washes his hands of Christ's crucifixion (Matthew 27:24–25). In August 1831, an imposing canvas fifteen feet high and nineteen and a half feet wide was placed in Wilhelm's studio.[52] Eventually it would accommodate a crowded scene teeming with more than fifty figures, including Christ, St. John, the high priest Caiaphas and Pharisees, Roman lictors and soldiers, and the *turba*, among whom Wilhelm would place a mother and child modeled upon Fanny and Sebastian. In August the artist began the first of 100 preparatory sketches for the composition, but not until late February 1832 did he apply paint to the canvas,[53] which slowly took shape for two more years.

While Wilhelm commenced his painting, Fanny was undertaking another large-scale composition, the Overture in C Major (H-U 265),[54] her only orchestral essay. Written most likely between March 29 and May 1832,[55] it apparently had to wait two years for its premiere at her residence, in 1834. The stimulus for the work is unknown, but its stylistic debts are clear enough—the overture approaches the sound world of Felix's *Calm Sea and Prosperous Voyage* Overture (in particular, in an ascending scalelike passage reminiscent of the coda of *Prosperous Voyage*; and in the accompaniment to the second theme, arpeggiations in the celli and later low clarinet that are suspiciously aquatic). In addition, Fanny's score renews the formal plan of Felix's concert overture, in which a slow introduction (Andante) proceeds via a transition to a fast movement in sonata form (Allegro di molto). (The instrument that links the two sections, a solo flute, recalls Felix's use of woodwinds to announce the return of the wind at the beginning of *Prosperous Voyage*.) What is more, Fanny also occasionally employs a brass fanfare not unlike the opening figure of his *Trumpet* Overture of 1826, also in C major. But other influences are at work too: the sweep and dramatic pacing of Fanny's composition capture the élan of Carl Maria von Weber's overtures, and the extended crescendi, culminating stretto, and emphatic final chords invoke the end of Beethoven's Fifth Symphony.

To invoke a festive character, Fanny scored for four horns instead of the traditional two. Together with the trumpets and drums, they usually play fanfare figures and function as *Lärminstrumente*, that is, "noise instruments" devoid of melodic significance.[56] But on the whole, we sense in Fanny's score a newfound confidence in orchestration. There is colorful writing for the woodwinds, and an effective surprise a few bars before the reprise, in which the infectious, driving first theme prematurely appears in the trumpets, an example of the so-called false reprise.♪ And once again, Fanny enriches the tonal plan by supplementing the tonic-dominant axis (C major–G major) with a third, unexpected key, B-flat major, introduced early in the Allegro di molto, as if to challenge the authority of the tonic C major.

Despite Fanny's remarkable productivity in 1831 and 1832—in little more than a year she completed three cantatas, a concert scene, and an overture—she had to contend with continuing stresses in her family's lives. From London, her brother Paul reported the insolvency of his employer, a financial firm in which Abraham had invested, causing substantial losses. Scarcely had the cholera abated and the Mendelssohns mourned Rietz before news arrived of Goethe's passing in March 1832, followed, only two months later, by his *Duzbruder* Zelter. Suddenly, Fanny's favorite poet and her former composition teacher, her links to eighteenth-century German literary and musical traditions, were gone.

There was mounting concern too about Felix, who contracted cholera in Paris but recovered, tended by the mother of Marie Bigot, with whom Fanny and Felix had studied piano in 1816. In the French capital, where the very order of society was threatened, Felix wrote, one thought not about music, but colic. On Rebecka's birthday, April 9, he revealed that Kalkbrenner, intent upon visiting Berlin, had inquired about Fanny's musical activities. But he had intrigued against Felix in French musical circles, and the once formidable virtuoso now struck Felix as a charlatan. Should Kalkbrenner appear in Berlin, Felix advised Fanny to show him one of her sacred cantatas, which would put him to flight at once.[57]

In London, where Felix arrived in late April, his health recovered fully, hastened by joyful reunions with Moscheles and Klingemann. On May 14 came the premiere at the Philharmonic of the *Hebrides* Overture. At St. Paul's and other venues Felix played voluntaries for services, improvised, and introduced the complex organ works of J. S. Bach to a public unaccustomed to its demanding pedal parts. And Felix had contact with William Ayrton, the conservative music editor who had recently published Fanny's Ave Maria in the *Harmonicon*, the first public occasion when her music appeared under her own name. One of Felix's final tasks in London was to arrange for the publication of his first six *Lieder ohne Worte*, op. 19, which appeared later that year from Novello, not with the familiar title *Songs without Words*, but as *Original Melodies for the Pianoforte*. These lyrical, songlike pieces renewed his stylistic contact with the intimate piano miniatures of his sister.

By late June 1832 Felix returned to Berlin, after an absence of more than two years. He found his brother-in-law priming the canvas for *Christus vor Pilatus*, and his two-year-old nephew, "Bapsen," articulating his first few words. Fanny welcomed Felix by copying into his diary her own *Lied ohne Worte*, playfully titled "Duett für Tenor und Sopran, mit den Fingern zu singen" ("Duet for tenor and soprano, to be sung with the fingers," H-U 269).[58] This unpublished piece features melodic lines doubled in consonant thirds and sixths, presumably to represent the reunited brother and sister, though Fanny's vocal range was that of an alto. According to her diary, during that summer the "best harmony" (*beste Eintracht*) governed the Mendelssohn residence, though Felix vigorously debated politics with Abraham on a daily basis.[59]

Among Felix's new compositions Fanny eagerly examined was the first draft of the cantata *Die erste Walpurgisnacht* (*The First Walpurgis Night*). Its text, a ballade by Goethe, treated the conflicts between early Christian missionaries and Druids and inspired from Felix a colorful, provocative score that ranked high among Fanny's favorites. No doubt she reciprocated by sharing with Felix her new overture, *Hero und Leander*, and sacred cantatas. But she undertook no new major compositional projects, as she was now advanced into her second pregnancy. The catalogue lists only the short *Wiegenlied* (*Lullaby*, H-U 266, September 14, 1832), on some tender verses—presumably by Wilhelm—singing of a *Knäblein* waking to his mother's voice, a reference to either Sebastian or the unborn child. Fanny's artistic voice now fell silent, for late in September, her pregnancy again took a difficult turn, and she was confined to bed rest. This time there was no joyful outcome, as she confided to her diary: "From the end of September on I was confined to bed rest, and now began a very sad time for me.... On November 1, I delivered a dead baby girl."[60] Her health prevented her from welcoming Ignaz Moscheles, who spent two weeks in Berlin in October, and she had to forgo as well the annual academy exhibition, where Wilhelm's students made their debut, and the first two of three charity concerts Felix gave in November, December, and January.

The ostensible purpose of these concerts was to support the widows of deceased members of the royal Prussian orchestra. But Felix also designed his appearances as composer, pianist, and conductor to promote his campaign to succeed Zelter at the Singakademie. On January 22, 1833, the 240 members convened to elect the new director. Presumably Fanny attended and heard the results—88 votes for Felix, 4 for Zelter's pupil Grell, who had played at Fanny's wedding, and 148 for Carl Friedrich Rungenhangen, Zelter's assistant and Felix's senior by thirty-one years. Eduard Devrient later suggested that bias against the composer's Jewish name played a role in his resounding defeat.[61] When Felix was offered an assistant directorship as a consolation prize, the family severed its ties to the Singakademie. Fanny passed over the incident in her diary and instead returned to chronicling her domestic life. Thus, we read about the celebrations of her parents' and brother's birthdays—for her mother, in March 1833, Fanny arranged a masquerade, in which Felix played Frederick the Great and Fanny, J. S. Bach.

iii

This private, entertaining role-play contrasted with the reality of early 1833, when, as Felix put it, he lived contentedly for a while in Berlin like asparagus, doing nothing.[62] Her health impaired, Fanny had been unable to sustain the Sunday concerts and also fell into a fallow period, as Felix explained in a letter to Klingemann: "But Fanny's piano playing has suffered, since she has practiced far too little; she's lacking encouragement here and interest in it. But that's really quite dreadful, for otherwise everyone is happy to hear something so beautiful, and here one first has to ask her to play."[63] Felix now took the initiative—late in January he revived the Sunday concerts, to encourage Fanny and to please his parents. Lea later reported to her Viennese cousin that he extracted from Fanny a solemn promise not to allow the concerts to languish,[64] a commitment she observed for much of the remainder of her life.

The programs of early 1833 have not survived, but they seem to have had their intended effect—on May 15, 1833, Fanny performed Gluck's opera *Orpheus*,[65] presumably *Orphée et Eurydice*, the French version of 1774. There was no question of a fully staged production, with orchestra and sets; rather, she directed the performance in the music room of the *Gartenhaus* and accompanied the singers from the piano. As it happened, May 15 was a Wednesday, so the event, attended by an invited audience of sixty,[66] fell outside the biweekly Sunday concerts. By then, Felix had left Berlin, first for Düsseldorf, where he was courted to become the municipal music director, and then for his third and fourth sojourns in London, where the *Italian* Symphony received its premiere.

Once again, the family circle at Leipzigerstrasse no. 3 changed. Felix's departure was replaced by the return in May of his younger brother Paul, secretly engaged to Albertine Heine, and now the third sibling to encounter parental disapproval—in this case, of Abraham, who had quarreled with Albertine's father, a banker. In April Fanny and Wilhelm were joined by the painter's sister Luise, who lived with them in the *Gartenhaus* until 1838. A pious Catholic, Luise soon felt isolated in Protestant Berlin, despite her brother's best intentions. Though "in faith and conviction a Christian," she noted, Wilhelm followed no particular denomination and attended no church. Instead, art had become his church and, along with his domestic happiness, had suppressed any "higher yearning" that had drawn him to worship a few years before.[67]

Through the summer of 1833 Fanny lived quietly, playing chamber music with the violinist Ferdinand David,[68] for whom Felix later composed the Violin Concerto in E Minor, op. 64 (1844), often judged the most perfect example of the genre. In July, the family was augmented by the birth of Rebecka's first child, Walter Dirichlet. Meanwhile, Wilhelm advanced steadily on his monumental work, *Christus vor Pilatus*, and completed dozens of sketches for the crowded figures. According to A. B. Marx, in a rush of inspiration, the artist drew many of them after Polish Jews, who served as models, and then reconfigured and transferred the conceptions to the canvas.[69] On July 12 he began work on the head of Christ and, about a month later, on the figure of Pontius Pilate, for whom a Catholic priest agreed to pose, but only, Fanny recorded, if his identity was suppressed.[70]

At this time, she slowly returned to composition and finished two new lieder in August, settings of Goethe's *Gegenwart* (*Present*, H-U 270) and Hölty's "In die Ferne" ("In the Distance," H-U 271).[71] The latter, twenty-one bars in length, recalls her earlier miniature settings and captures within its small frame a compelling sense of tonal proximity and distance—the text reads, "You in the distance, be so near to me, like the stars, far and near to me." Much of the song lies comfortably in the orbit of its tonic key, G minor; yet, a few bars before the end, Fanny suddenly veers off into a series of chromatic harmonies that briefly test the tonal boundaries and postpone the expected cadence. In contrast, *Gegenwart* offers an expansive setting of sixty-nine bars, to accommodate vibrant images of the poet's lover. Everything, the verses begin, announces her: she follows the course of the sun, she is a rose among roses, a lily among lilies; she stirs the heavenly bodies to dance with her, and her radiance outshines the moon. Through the succession of images the music subtly interacts with the text—there are whirling figures for the dance, a turn to dark, minor-keyed sonorities for the moon, and palpitating cross-rhythms for the closing sections. Epigrammatic compression now yields to a more expansive space, as Fanny enlarges the setting to embrace broader musical gestures.

On September 1, 1833, Fanny inaugurated the fall concert season at her residence and for the first time validated her efforts by recording the details in her diary, in order "not to lose them."[72] Here we find the programs for five fortnightly concerts given on Sunday mornings between September 1 and October 27 (see table 6.1). The all-German repertoire included, in order of decreasing frequency: Beethoven (six performances), Weber (four), Felix (three), J. S. Bach and Mozart (two each), and Gluck, Spohr, Moscheles, and Fanny (one each). Represented were keyboard concerti (Bach, Beethoven, and Felix), chamber works (Mozart, Beethoven, Weber, Spohr, Moscheles, and Felix), and vocal music, chiefly operatic excerpts (Gluck and Weber), but also Fanny's concert scene *Hero und Leander*. The result was a mixture of eighteenth-century, early nineteenth-century, and contemporary music, not unlike the illustrious concert series Felix would direct from 1835 on at the Gewandhaus in Leipzig. Like Fanny, Felix favored German repertoire and designed his programs to connect contemporary composers to the main line of German instrumental music, extending back from Felix, Spohr, and Weber, to Beethoven, Haydn, Mozart, and J. S. Bach. Like the Gewandhaus series, Fanny's concerts promoted the refinement of a historical German musical consciousness, a critical step in the later consolidation of the musical canon.

At the center of Fanny's concerts was the piano, from which she presided as soloist and accompanist. Significantly, in 1833 no symphonies or overtures figured in her programs, from which we may infer that no orchestra was involved. But an intriguing question remains: How did Fanny perform piano

TABLE 6.1. Fanny Hensel's Sunday Concerts, 1833

September 1	Mozart, [Piano] Quartet [K. 478 or K. 493]
	Beethoven, Piano Concerto no. 4, op. 58
	Beethoven, *Fidelio*, duets
	J. S. Bach, Concerto in D Minor, BWV 1052
September 15	Beethoven, Triple Concerto in C major, op. 56
	Fanny Hensel, *Hero und Leander*
	Felix Mendelssohn Bartholdy, Piano Concerto no. 1, op. 25 [performed by Felix]
	J. S. Bach, Concerto in D Minor, BWV 1052 [performed by Felix]
September 29	Mendelssohn, Variations for Cello and Piano, op. 17
	Weber, [Piano] Quartet [op. 5 or 11]
	Weber, Finale from *Oberon*, Act I
	Spohr, Quintet [Piano Quintet in C Minor, op. 53]
	Weber, "Mermaid's Song" from *Oberon*
October 13	Beethoven, [Piano] Trio in E-flat Major [op.1, no.1 or op. 70, no. 2]
	Mendelssohn, String Quartet in A Minor, op. 13
	Beethoven, Piano Trio in D Major, op. 70, no. 1
October 27	Mozart, Piano Trio in G Major [K. 496 or 546]
	Weber, aria from *Der Freischütz*
	Moscheles, Piano Trio in C Minor, op. 84
	Gluck, aria from *Iphigenie auf Tauris*

concerti? One possibility was that a second pianist rendered the orchestral parts. Thus, when Felix, returning to Berlin from London before commencing his new position in Düsseldorf, performed on September 15 the Bach D Minor Concerto (BWV 1052) and his own Piano Concerto in G Minor, Fanny may well have accompanied him. But another possibility may remain concealed in the now long-lost, nineteenth-century performance practice of supporting concerto soloists with string quartet or reduced ensemble accompaniment. We know, for instance, that in 1832 both Chopin and Felix observed this custom in Paris, where Pierre Baillot's quartet routinely served as an orchestral substitute in private concerts for the aristocracy.[73] And when Fanny performed Felix's *Rondo Brillant* op. 29 at a Sunday concert on February 16, 1835, the orchestral accompaniment was reduced to a "double quartet and contrabass."[74] In short, Fanny's performances in the *Gartensaal* turned works such as Beethoven's Fourth Piano Concerto, which she rendered on September 1, 1833, into intimate chamber music experiences.

In her diary and letters Fanny identified several musicians who participated in the Sunday concerts. They included the violinist Hubert Ries and cellist Moritz Ganz from the royal Prussian *Kapelle*, the tenor Eduard Mantius,
and the baritone Eduard Devrient, already familiar from his involvement in
reviving the St. Matthew Passion. A musician who now formed a close artistic
relationship with Fanny was Pauline Decker (née von Schätzel, 1811–1882),
a soprano who had sung at the Berlin Opera and Singakademie before her
marriage to a wealthy printer in 1832. Having left the public stage, she now
devoted herself to reading operas and oratorios with Fanny as her accompanist. Lea later reported that Pauline possessed a remarkable musical memory
and, like Fanny, an impressive ability to read at sight.[75]

Pauline was the featured soloist in a new composition (H-U 272) that
Fanny hurriedly produced for the Feast of St. Cecilia (November 22), about
which she reported to Felix in some detail:

> I composed a verset from the Mass of St. Caecilia in two days in such
> haste that the accompaniment hasn't been copied yet. Mother will prob-
> ably send you the text. The whole thing was arranged as a double sur-
> prise: first Decker appeared without singing, then she sang a few notes
> unseen, and last sang in full view, from memory of course. It is said to
> have made a magical, beautiful effect. This much is clear—her beauty
> so far exceeded her usual appearance that I could only place one person
> next to her, little Rose Behrend as an angel, who really, without exaggera-
> tion, looked heavenly.... Decker's costume was modeled on Raphael's
> *Caecilia* and her hair was arranged accordingly, which was very becom-
> ing. The angels wore white.... It was a charming touch to have the two
> taller girls hold some music in their hands in the manner of the angels
> in the old paintings. By the way, the entire exhibition occurred without
> the help of a single craftsman—Wilhelm and his students did it all. They
> concocted the loveliest organ in the atelier.[76]

We learn about the inspiration for this composition in an earlier letter in
which Fanny divulged her plan to have a music party on November 22, to
celebrate in tandem Felix's first concert in Düsseldorf the same day.[77] As it
happened, that evening he directed Handel's *Alexander's Feast* (1736), based
on Dryden's famous "Ode in Honor of St. Cecilia's Day." Fanny's work, titled
Zum Fest der heiligen Cäcilia and scored for soloists, chorus, and piano, was
thus her attempt to bridge musically her physical distance from her brother
by treating the same subject—appropriately enough, the saint after whom she
had been named at her baptism.

Admittedly, Cecilia, the early Christian martyr recognized in the fifteenth century as the patron saint of music, plays different roles in Handel's
and Fanny's compositions. In Dryden's ode, she appears late (and somewhat

marginally), only after Timotheus, having entertained Alexander the Great with flute and lyre playing, incites the Greek conqueror to put to the torch the vanquished city of Persepolis. If the music of Timotheus "raised a mortal to the skies," that of Cecilia, "inventress of the vocal frame," "drew an angel down." Dryden's reference is to one of the more confusing examples of Roman hagiography,[78] according to which Cecilia's ecstatic musicality—she was often shown playing an organ or silently contemplating the music of angels—was understood as an expression of her chastity and devotion to God. That Fanny knew intimately Dryden's poem is clear, for Felix enlisted her assistance in revising the 1766 German translation by K. W. Ramler, used in the Düsseldorf performance of *Alexander's Feast*.[79]

Fanny's creative approach to Cecilia was markedly different, for she produced a composition based directly on the liturgical Latin texts for the saint's Mass, including portions of the introit, gradual, and collect appointed for November 22. One wonders if the Catholicizing tendency of the composition reflected the influence of Luise Hensel, who had joined Fanny's household a few months before. Clearly another influence was her husband, whose tastes in painting, as we have seen, inclined toward Raphael. And so the decision was taken to perform Fanny's new offering as a quasi–*tableau vivant*, in which Pauline Decker, playing the role of Cecilia, wore a robe after Raphael's famous altarpiece of 1516 (Pinacoteca Nazionale, Bologna). There the saint appears, holding an inverted portative organ and looking heavenward as she listens to a choir of angelic musicians. At her feet are discarded, earthly musical instruments, and she is surrounded by other saints, including John, Paul, Augustine, and Mary Magdalene. According to Fanny, Wilhelm's students fabricated the pipes of a portative organ as a prop (presumably held by Pauline as she sang from memory), and some children dressed as angels were positioned in the performance space. One has the impression that Fanny intended to render musically Raphael's painting, to give voice to the *tableau vivant*, or living picture, by conjuring up Cecilia's divine music.

To this end, Fanny began her score with a short piano introduction set in the high register of the instrument, to depict the angelic hosts. The style of the music, with suspended pitches and carefully regulated dissonances,◉ recalls the *stile antiquo* of Palestrina, the sixteenth-century practitioner of sacred polyphony associated with the Counter-Reformation. Four soloists sing the introit text, *Beati immaculati*, drawn from Psalm 119 ("Happy are those whose way is blameless, who walk in the law of the Lord"). Then Fanny juxtaposes parts of the gradual and collect, with the bass soloist imploring Cecilia to incline her ear, and the chorus asserting in block, chordal style,

> Deus qui nos annua beatae Caeciliae Virginis et martyris tuae solemnitate laetificas, da ut quam veneramur officio etiam piae conversationis sequamur exemplo.

O God, who gladdens us with the annual commemoration of blessed Cecilia, your virgin and martyr, grant that we may venerate her in this rite and follow her example of pious actions.

At last Cecilia replies, and the music now shifts upward by step from E-flat to F major for her solo, introduced by a few bars in the high register of the piano. In the final section, *Alleluia, Gloria in excelsis*, she is joined in a celebratory Allegro by the chorus, which introduces a rising subject, against which Cecilia offers florid melismas of praise. Several features of this work, including its luminous tonal pairing of keys separated by step, bring to mind Felix's motet of 1828, *Hora est*, based on Office texts for Advent, and, according to A. B. Marx, a composition exploring the monastic rites of early Christendom.[80] Be that as it may, Fanny's work remained an occasional piece, and she seems not to have performed it again. Indeed, she left several measures of the piano part in the autograph unfinished, presumably for realization during the performance on November 22, 1833.

From Düsseldorf Felix cheered Fanny's return to music making;[81] in addition to the Sunday concerts, she was reading through operas with Pauline Decker on a regular basis, including Weber's *Oberon* and Mozart's *Don Giovanni* and *The Magic Flute*. And she found a new admirer in the singer Franz Hauser, who corresponded with her from Leipzig, where he had begun cataloguing the music of J. S. Bach. When Hauser asked for copies of her songs, she sent *Die frühen Gräber* and proposed an exchange. From time to time she would send one of her pieces, and he, in return, "ein neues Bachsches."[82]

For Fanny's twenty-eighth birthday, Felix finished a landscape painting and a major new composition, the *Fair Melusine* Overture, op. 32, which now took its place alongside his musical gifts of earlier years, all conceived for November 14, the day Felix described as "always dedicated" to his sister: "I think the overture will please you," he wrote, "and I wish I could bring it to you straightaway. To be sure, that's not possible, but you know that 14/11 is always dedicated to you; when you first encounter the score, take it away from me and keep it and play through it very often."[83] But Felix, ever the perfectionist, could not yet bring himself to part with his score, about the fabled mermaid who assumes human form while with her knightly lover. And so he continued to fuss over the music, even though, as he put it, his "fish," now "slippery and fresh," might rot in the aridity of self-criticism. Not until February 1834 did Fanny receive her present. She herself would offer some suggestions and perhaps hasten Felix's decision to recast the score, but her first reaction was the most poignant, for it again underscored the divide between two musical geniuses—one an international celebrity in Düsseldorf, the other a lady musician of leisure in Berlin—and Fanny's secret aspirations as a composer: "But to return to your fish, it's really quite a different situation from when we used to sit together at home and you would show me a totally new musical idea without telling me its purpose. Then, on the second day, you would have another idea, and on the third day you would undergo the torment of working them out, and I would comfort you when you thought you couldn't write anything more. And in the end the piece would be completed and I used to feel that I had a share in the work as well. But those lovely times are of course a thing of the past."[84]

CHAPTER 7

Youthful Decrepitude

(1834–1835)

My lengthy things die in their youth of decrepitude.

—Fanny to Felix, February 17, 1835

Near the end of 1833 a new publication unexpectedly brought the Mendelssohn family into public view and caused considerable distress in the new year. Between December 1833 and November 1834, the Goethe-Zelter correspondence was issued in six installments, less than two years after their deaths. The editor was Friedrich Wilhelm Riemer, a classicist who had tutored the poet's children and a lexicographer whom Felix had assessed dubiously in 1825: "Dictionary writing suits him well. He is wide, fat, and radiant, like a prelate or a full moon."[1] Rather indelicately, Riemer had let stand comments disparaging Fanny's family, including Goethe's criticism of Wilhelm Hensel's early paintings as shallow and dependent on the Nazarene school and Zelter's candid observation that Felix was the "son of a Jew, but no Jew." Because the aging Abraham's cataracts occluded much of his vision, the family read aloud the correspondence, "meted out by the spoonful, like medicine," Fanny bitterly wrote, and only exacerbating their dismay: "On Zelter's side, an unpleasantly awkward way of thinking predominates that we could presume him to have possessed, but which we always rationalized away. But here it's irrefutably expressed in the trappings of self-interest, egotism, a disgusting idolizing of Goethe without a true, reasoned appraisal, and the most indiscreet exposing of everyone else, which should be absolutely prevented from being published." Exposed to a private side of Zelter and Goethe she had not known, Fanny condemned Riemer's edition for having "forever spoiled the memory of a man whom I loved and would have liked to respect."[2]

Meanwhile, she threw herself into the Sunday concerts with renewed energy. We can reconstruct at least thirteen programs for 1834 in part or full from her diaries and letters, including seven clustered in the first four months of the year, four in May and June, and, after a protracted pause, two more in December.[3] Notable about the repertoire was the prominence of Beethoven—Fanny performed several piano, violin, and cello sonatas, the *Ghost* Trio, excerpts from his opera *Fidelio*, and the *Elegischer Gesang*, op. 118, a short work for four soloists and string quartet composed in 1814 in memory of Eleonore von Pasqualati, wife of Beethoven's landlord, and now in March 1834 offered by Fanny to mark the death of the Protestant theologian Schleiermacher. In May and June she presided over readings of two major eighteenth-century works, Handel's *Acis and Galatea* and Gluck's opera *Iphigenie auf Tauris*. She performed the latter at a fete honoring C. K. J. Bunsen, Prussian minister to Rome, before 100 invited guests;[4] according to Lea, Count Brühl, intendant of the Berlin Opera, observed afterward, "Yes, if only I had had such a Kapellmeister!"[5]

Presumably Fanny led these two performances from the piano. But on June 15, members of the Königstadt Theater orchestra convened at Leipzigerstrasse no. 3 to read, among other compositions, her Overture in C Major. Unexpectedly, she was obliged to conduct, as she explained to Felix: "Mother has certainly told you about the Königstadt orchestra on Saturday and how I stood up there with a baton in my hand like a Jupiter *tonans*. That came about in the following way. Lecerf [Julius Amadeus Lecerf, director of the orchestra] had his scholars play and smashed his finger to pieces in the process, then I went out and brought your white little baton and handed it to him. Later my Overture was played and I sat at the piano, then the evil in the form of Lecerf whispered to me to take the little baton in my hand. Had I not been so horribly shy, and embarrassed with every stroke, I would've been able to conduct reasonably well."[6] And so, Fanny briefly assumed the role of the nineteenth-century orchestral conductor, which she figuratively compared to Jupiter the Thunderer, an epithet for the indomitable Roman god familiar from classical mythology. Fanny's shyness notwithstanding, the Overture was not her only work given on the concert series in 1834; on March 2, she programmed two duets and the 1823 lied *Die Spinnerin*, and on April 6, Pauline Decker again sang *Hero und Leander*. As performances of Fanny's music began to accumulate, she slowly but surely began to emerge—but only to those fortunate enough to attend—as a composer with her own voice.

We can identify some musicians who participated in Fanny's concerts as an uneven mixture of amateurs and professionals. Supporting Pauline Decker's role of Leonore in extracts from *Fidelio* were several Berlin *dilettanti* Lea described as "unmusical" and Fanny more charitably as "fair"[7] (but at least one amateur participant, Fanny's brother Paul, was from all appearances an accomplished cellist). Still, the concerts also drew, magnetlike, an increasing number of professional musicians—and celebrated virtuosi. Among them were Amalie Hähnel, a Viennese mezzo-soprano who had debuted in Berlin in 1831; Anton Bernhard Fürstenau, Carl Maria von Weber's principal flutist in Dresden; the cellist Moritz Ganz and violinist Hubert Ries, both well-established chamber musicians in Berlin; and Charles Philippe Lafont, a leading exponent of the French violin school who had enjoyed a high-profile concertizing career, though, as Fanny realized, Paganini's radical new approach to the instrument overshadowed the Frenchman's polished playing.[8] Then there was Ferdinand David's sister, the pianist Luise Dulcken, who in 1828 had settled in London, where she presided over her own series of soirees and appeared at the Philharmonic as a soloist (Dulcken would later give the English premiere of Chopin's second piano concerto).[9] On April 6, 1834, she performed for Fanny's series Felix's Piano Concerto in G Minor, op. 25, accompanied, Lea reported, by a small ensemble of string players.[10] Fanny judged the interpretation "truly remarkable," praised Dulcken's strength and rapidity of motion as phenomenal, and noted that she played as if shaking "fire from her fingers."[11]

At the concert series Fanny eagerly undertook a special task—to introduce Felix's new compositions to the Berlin circle, and so to play another masculine role—if not of Jupiter *tonans*, then of the newly established, fashionable music director of Düsseldorf. Thus, in February 1835 she introduced Felix's *Rondo brillant* op. 29, in June 1834 planned to perform his *Ave Maria*, op. 23, no. 2, and on the last concert of that year (December 28) played some *Lieder ohne Worte* and fugues received from him just days before, probably as Christmas gifts. The public, she wrote, "was extremely delighted." Having tested these pieces before an audience, she sent Felix suggestions for revisions—among them, changing a note in a *Lied ohne Worte* and shifting a passage an octave higher in the Fugue in F Minor, op. 35, no. 5.[12] These alterations were minor enough, but the correspondence of 1834 shows too the real depth of the siblings' musical relationship, and the frankness, at times a critical edge, of their exchanges. Thus, she challenged his decision to set some *Volkslieder* for a cappella choir and questioned some modulations in the development of the *Fair Melusine* Overture.[13] And when Felix revised the slow movement of the *Italian* Symphony and retouched its haunting, opening modal melody, Fanny objected, after reading through the music with Rebecka at the piano: "I don't like the change in the first melody at all; why did you make it? Was it to avoid the many a's? But the melody was natural and lovely. I don't agree with the other changes as well; however, I'm still not familiar enough with the rest of the movement to be able to render a reasonable judgment. Overall I feel you are only too ready to change a successful piece later on merely because one thing or another pleases you more then.... Bring the old version along when you come and then we can argue about it."[14] For whatever reason, Felix never managed to release the *Italian* Symphony, which appeared after his death as his op. 90. But in 1834, Fanny's critical role did bear immediate, practical benefits when the publisher Schlesinger asked her to proofread a score of Felix's First Symphony, op. 11: "I looked through [the corrections], but am so afraid of scolding that I would rather give you a little trouble than burden myself with pangs of conscience. Therefore I responded that I would send them to you first. Why? Because there are mistakes in the manuscript that are unique and so fatuous that I still can't grasp them all."[15]

In the same letter Fanny revealed that "out of empathy" she had composed some lieder, but "unfortunately nothing major." The new songs included three on texts of Heine (H-U 274, March–April) and her first settings of his nemesis, Count August von Platen-Hallermünde (H-U 275 and 276, May), the German expatriate poet then spending a literary exile in Italy. What attracted Fanny to Platen is unclear, but there can be little doubt she was aware of the controversy engulfing him. Son of an impoverished nobleman, Platen wrote patently homo-erotic verses with idealized classical allusions, and sensuous *ghazals* modeled on the fourteenth-century Persian poetry of Hafiz; much of Platen's work was a thinly veiled sublimation of his own homosexuality. In 1829 Heine launched a vitriolic, explicit attack in *The Baths of Lucca*, and in a review the same year Ludwig Robert, well known to the Mendelssohns, decried Platen's projection in his poetry of an "unfeminine femininity in the feeling of friendship."[16] Be that as it may, Fanny set two of his poems in 1834. One, the ballade *Der Pilgrim vor St. Just* (H-U 275), concerned the Holy Roman Emperor Charles V (1500–1558), who in 1556 abruptly abdicated and retired to the Spanish monastery of St. Yuste. Fanny captured the semblance of the imperial reign in stately dotted rhythms and solemn octave doublings in the bass of the piano accompaniment. But quite in contrast was her other Platen setting (H-U 276), the text of which perhaps could have prompted Robert's critique:

Wo sich gatten	Where are joined
jene Schatten	those shadows
ueber Matten	above the meadows,
um den Quell,	by the stream,
reich an losen	rich in loose
Hagerosen,	hedge roses,
kommt zu kosen,	come quickly,
Brüder, schnell!	brothers, to caress!

Platen's nimble verses referred to the sons of the muses (*Musensöhne*) entwined and tied to one another. In a similar way, Fanny linked the vocal and piano parts of her song. Marked *Rasch und anmutig* (Fast and gracefully), it unfolds as a series of brisk eighth-note chords, in which the soprano part of the piano doubles the vocal melody.◉ If *Der Pilgrim vor St. Just* required a bass part for the imperial role, Fanny set "Wo sich gatten" for soprano and piano, in a light, elfin style recalling her brother's scherzi, and emphasizing, perhaps, Platen's perceived femininity. But Fanny's tripping, delicate chords seem innocent enough; apart from a few, fleeting chromatic pitches, there is little to suggest a deeper level of reading, such as Schubert apparently applied in his 1821 setting of Platen's "Du liebst mich nicht," the verses of which allude to the myth of Narcissus as a symbol for the poet's sexual preferences.[17]

Though Platen inspired Fanny in 1834, she remained more or less ambivalent toward Heine's lyrics, except, as she put it, when he abandoned his "ironic conceit."[18] But in 1834 an external stimulus prompted her return to Heine. That year she received English translations of three Heine poems by Mary Alexander, daughter of the deceased Scottish laird Claud Alexander, who had made fortunes in the East India Company and then the nascent British cotton industry. In 1833 Felix and Abraham had met the Alexanders at their fashionable London residence in Hanover Terrace, and Mary, like Fanny about three years older than Felix, had fallen for him.[19] She began studying German and translating lyrics from Heine's *Buch der Lieder*, with the expectation that Felix would set them. He did not, but Fanny took up the challenge and arranged three of the poems (nos. 1, 4, and 27 from the section known as *Die Heimkehr* [*Homecoming*]). These were her first English settings, and she conceived them as a miniature cycle, to which she imparted "a kind of unity, as much as possible," and for which Wilhelm "drew a little arabesque" on her autograph copy sent to London.[20]

She achieved that unity in part through her choice of keys, by framing the central song in C major by two, similar in mood, in G minor, of which one seems to have impressed Felix deeply.[21] But Fanny also imposed a new poetic unity independent of Heine's conception by responding to the second quatrain of no. 1—"When children in the dark are left / and there perforce must stay, / to still their little trembling hearts / they sing a merry lay"—and then interpreting the second song, no. 4, as the lay, as if it were "really going to be sung":[22]

> I wander through the wood and weep,
> the thrush sits on the tree and gladly chirps
> and sweetly sings:
> what ails it now with thee?
> The swallows, who thy sisters are,
> can answer thee right well,
> for in their nests, ah! happy they,
> by my love's house they dwell.

Following this sprightly setting, with clipped treble chords to depict the chirping, was the more sobering rendition of "Was will die einsame Thräne" ("What Means the Lonely Tear"), a poem that also inspired Robert Schumann, who in 1840 would include a setting in the wedding cycle *Myrthen*, op. 25, for his new wife, Clara. Like Robert, Fanny seized on the image of the solitary teardrop, which slowly descends, lamentlike, in the vocal line.

Only two other instrumental compositions date from 1834. The first is the well-crafted, though still unpublished piano Fugue in E-flat Major (H-U 273), which we might mistake for one of Fanny's Bachian ruminations.● But the construction of its fugal subject—it describes a distinctive rising sequence of alternating fourths and tritones[23]—and the use, midway through the composition, of diminution to impel the fugue forward with faster rhythmic values, suggest that Fanny had another model in mind—the fugal finale of Beethoven's Piano Sonata in A-flat Major, op. 110 (1822).● This celebrated accelerando fugue, which employs a subject of rising, interlocked fourths and subsequently displays diminution and double diminution, fascinated not only Fanny but her brother as well. Early in January 1835, Felix composed a piano fugue in A-flat major, ultimately published as his op. 35, no. 4, in which he considerably strengthened and clarified the allusion to Beethoven's subject.● Felix's fugue may well have been in response to Fanny's, with which he could have become familiar in September, when he visited Berlin for several weeks, before the start of the Düsseldorf concert season. In short, the two fugues, probably written in response to op. 110, attempted a rapprochement with Beethoven's late style, and in this particular sibling exchange, Fanny may have taken the lead.

Admittedly, during the previous decade, Felix had already engaged Beethoven's music in a series of compositions culminating in the two string quartets, opps. 13 and 12 (1827 and 1829). Writing to Felix, Fanny observed that her brother had successfully worked his way through Beethoven's late style and "progressed beyond it," while she "remained stuck in it, not possessing the strength...necessary to sustain that tenderness."[24] Turning her critical gaze inward, she then made this remarkable statement: "It's not so much a certain way of composing that is lacking as it is a certain approach to life, and as a result of this shortcoming, my lengthy things die in their youth of decrepitude; I lack the ability to sustain ideas properly and give them the needed consistency. Therefore lieder suit me best, in which, if need be, merely a pretty idea without much potential for development can suffice."[25]

Fanny thus felt keenly the tension in her music between the brief, epigrammatic art song, in which she could compress musical meaning into a few, "pretty" ideas, and her attempts at larger compositions, with all the requisite trappings of thematic development and formal elaboration. Her embrace of large-scale composition in the cantatas, overture, and *Hero und Leander* had clearly moved her closer to the elusive goal of establishing her separate identity as a composer and yet, by bringing her nearer to the very public world of her brother, now led to potential conflict with him. Matters indeed came to a head in the fall of 1834 when she completed between August 26 and October 23 one of her most ambitious works, the String Quartet in E-flat Major (H-U 277, figure 7.1). This was the composition, as we shall see, that prompted Felix to write a critique in January 1835, to which Fanny replied with the self-deprecating comments cited above.

FIGURE 7.1.   Fanny Hensel, autograph manuscript of the String Quartet, first movement, 1834 (Berlin, Mendelssohn Archiv, Ms. 43)

i

The origins of the quartet lay in Fanny's abandoned piano sonata of 1829 (see p. 138). She now revived its first two movements, substituted a new Romanze for the original Largo, and composed a whirlwind finale to complete an expanded, four-movement plan. What role, if any, Felix played in her decision to convert the sonata into a string quartet is unclear, but the issue of generic identity (which later would haunt another composer, Brahms, who reconceived several works in different scorings) bears substantively on our understanding of the composition. By reconfiguring the work as a string quartet, Fanny strengthened the telling allusion of the opening bars to the quartets of Beethoven and thus made her contribution to the august tradition of the Austro-Germanic genre. Indeed, Fanny's quartet, published only in 1988,[26] some 150 years after its composition, now stands among the very first significant examples of the genre by a woman.[27]

In turning to Beethoven, Fanny was drawn particularly to the *Harp* Quartet, op. 74 of 1809, in the same key as her quartet. This work from Beethoven's middle period had earned its name from the use of harplike pizzicati exchanged among the instruments in the first movement. But what intrigued Fanny was the remarkable slow introduction (Poco adagio, twenty-four bars), a tonally shifting, ambiguous preamble that did not so much define the tonic key of E-flat major as encircle it with related harmonies, including A-flat major and F minor. Borrowing the rhythmic motive of Beethoven's opening phrase (half note, dotted quarter note, eighth note: ♩♩.♪), Fanny adapted it to generate an opening slow movement (Adagio ma non troppo, seventy-seven bars), much of which was deliberately left tonally ambiguous—in a sense, she reread and expanded Beethoven's slow introduction to produce a separate, free-standing movement (example 7.1). Thus, the

EXAMPLE 7.1. (a) Beethoven, *Harp* Quartet, op. 74 (1809), first movement; (b) Fanny Hensel, String Quartet in E-flat Major (1834), first movement

very first sonority of her work is C minor, not E-flat major, and within a few bars the subdominant A-flat major appears as a momentary point of stability. A good portion of the movement in fact lingers in F minor and F major, which ultimately proceed through the dominant B-flat major to the tonic. When E-flat major is finally reached, Fanny inserts a bar of rest to articulate its presence, allowing the elusive sonority to resonate briefly. The closing bars return us to the opening gesture, now completed through the first—and only—full cadence in E-flat major.

There is a clear logic to Fanny's goal-oriented, tonal conception, as summarized in table 7.1: instead of a conventional beginning in the principal key, she initially transports the listener away from the tonic and initiates a harmonic descent by thirds; then, by moving up a chain of fourths, finally attains the tonic. But in creating a free, formally diffuse movement that resembles a fantasia, Fanny disregards the norms of the prevalent instrumental blueprint of the day—sonata form—with its customary ternary division into an exposition (statement), development (departure), and recapitulation (return). Instead, the opening of the movement seemingly situates the listener in the development, and indeed we can describe much of the movement as a development-like (and Beethoven-like) process of searching for the tonic. When it finally emerges, we have the sense, to be sure, of arriving at a recapitulation, but it is, perhaps, a recapitulation of material implied, not previously heard, for in fracturing and telescoping the sonata-form process, Fanny has essentially curtailed much, if not all, of the traditional exposition.

Standing in contrast to the formal ambiguity of the first movement is the scherzo in C minor, which falls into a readily apprehended three-part *ABA* form, with a contrasting trio in the major. There is a slightly demonic quality in the opening section, performed for the most part at a hushed dynamics level and riven by wide leaps and briskly alternating pizzicati and arco brush strokes (example 7.2a). The boisterous C major trio begins as a mock fugato (example 7.2b) and possibly invokes Beethoven's humorously wooden display of counterpoint in the scherzo of the *Harp* Quartet (coincidentally or not, also in C minor, with a C major trio). But the distinctive melodic and rhythmic

TABLE 7.1. Fanny Hensel, String Quartet in E-flat Major (1834), Tonal Plan of First Movement

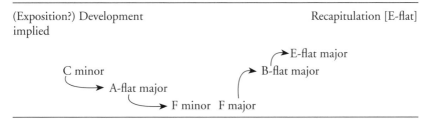

profiles of Fanny's ascending subject point to another Beethoven composition surely on her mind—the C major trio of the C minor scherzo of the Fifth Symphony (1808, example 7.2c). Like Beethoven, Fanny quickly abandons all artifices of the fugue: her trio follows an unpredictable, wayward course that reaches a fortissimo climax in F-sharp minor, the key most distantly removed from C major, before reversing its harmonic peregrinations and returning, through a diminuendo and ritard, to the C minor of the opening. An especially effective touch is the *pianissimo* conclusion of the movement, in which two pizzicato C major chords offer a fleeting reference to the trio.

If we judge by the key signature of two flats, Fanny conceived the deeply felt Romanze in G minor, yet here again, the putative tonic sonority is little in evidence. Supplanting the G minor triad are several recurring G major sonorities that pull the music toward C minor and thus skirt around the tonic. Fanny never attains a cadence on G minor, thwarted throughout the movement by deceptive progressions. Indeed, the final cadence comes to rest on G major, intensifying the sense that the real tonic, if implied, is missing. Meanwhile, Fanny gives thematic definition to the movement through its opening, poignant melody, impelled by persistent, repeated pitches and sighlike gestures. The dissonant, highly unstable middle section is harmonically free, with remote excursions to A-flat minor and B minor that distinguish her music from the harmonically more restrained style of her brother. The reintroduction of repeated chords ushers in the recapitulation, where the melody now appears transferred to the high, rarefied register of the ensemble; the Romanze ends with the first violin ascending to a high G, supported by a *pianissimo* major chord.

Fanny's first three movements thus use tonality in an expressive way that further separates her from the eighteenth-century traditions in which Zelter had trained her and Felix. She deemphasizes the keys of the three movements so that the tonal hierarchy rests more on harmonic associations and implications than on conventional, dominant-to-tonic cadential gestures. Not so the finale (Allegro molto vivace), which definitively asserts E-flat major in a brilliant, *perpetuum mobile* display that takes the form of a rondo (*ABACABA*). The cascading first theme, doubled in thirds by the two violins, serves as a refrain that periodically returns to reassert the tonic triad and, in the closing bars, emphatically gives tonal closure to the entire work.

As we have seen, the impetus for Fanny's tonal experimentations in 1834 was her study of Beethoven. In the string quartets and piano sonatas of his middle and late periods, she found new, flexible approaches to classical forms and tonal organization. Beethoven acted as a liberating force for Fanny as she struggled to produce a large-scale work in a major instrumental genre— a work, as we shall see, that her brother judged too innovative. Nevertheless, she also acknowledged in her composition what she later termed Felix's "demonic influence." Not surprisingly, embedded in all four movements are

EXAMPLE 7.2. (a) Fanny Hensel, String Quartet in E-flat Major (1834), Scherzo;
(b) Trio; (c) Beethoven, Fifth Symphony (1808), third movement

clear enough allusions to Felix's music, as if Fanny chose in part to respond to Beethoven vicariously through her brother's music.

The first few bars alone afford two examples. While Fanny's rhythmic motive mirrors that of Beethoven's *Harp* Quartet, it also reflects the opening of Felix's String Quartet in E-flat Major, op. 12 (1829), his own reaction to the same work (example 7.3a). But in addition, Fanny alludes to the beginning of her brother's *Meeresstille und glückliche Fahrt* (*Calm Sea and Prosperous Voyage*) Overture (1828) by retracing in the first violin the characteristic descending, four-note motive heard at the outset of the overture in the submerged contrabass (example 7.3b).[28] Not quite a literal quotation, Fanny's borrowing extends Felix's motive by one pitch. Her reference to *Calm Sea* is an appropriate choice, for at the suggestion of A. B. Marx, Felix composed his overture as a purely instrumental reflection on Beethoven's *Meeresstille und glückliche Fahrt*, op. 112 (1822), a cantata-like setting for chorus and orchestra of Goethe's celebrated poems.

In the case of the second movement, Fanny produced passages that could almost be mistaken for Felix's trademark scherzando style, were it not for the harmonic freedom and blurring of tonal definition. Some passages indeed come close to the ethereal, gossamer textures of the scherzo from Felix's Octet. Similarly, the close of Fanny's Romanze uses a distinctive harmonic progression suspiciously similar to that applied by Felix to conclude the slow movement of the Octet.[29] For her finale, Fanny turned from Felix's chamber music

EXAMPLE 7.3.   (a) Felix Mendelssohn, String Quartet in E-flat Major, op. 12 (1827); (b) Felix Mendelssohn, *Meeresstille und glückliche Fahrt*, op. 27 (1828)

(a)

(b)

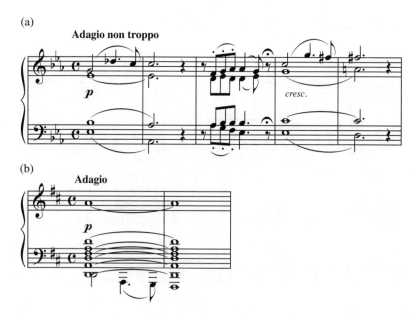

to his *Scottish* Fantasy for piano, op. 28, borrowed its churning Presto subject from the finale in F-sharp minor, and reworked and transposed it to a considerably brighter E-flat major (example 7.4a–b).

Whether the siblings discussed these references is not known, but Felix did disapprove of the tonal latitude and formal freedom of Fanny's conception. After playing through a copy of the quartet, he offered some fraternal advice on January 30, 1835:

> My favorite movement is still the C-minor Scherzo, but the theme of the Romanze also pleases me greatly. If you will permit me a small critical comment, then that concerns the style of the whole or, if you like, the form. I would prefer that you pay more heed to a definite form, namely in the modulations. It is admittedly fine to shatter such a form, but in that case, the [thematic] contents must shatter it, through inner necessity. Otherwise, through such a new, unusual treatment of form and

EXAMPLE 7.4.   (a) Fanny Hensel, String Quartet in E-flat Major (1834); (b) Felix Mendelssohn, *Sonate ecossaise*, op. 28 (1828)

modulation the piece becomes only less defined, and dissolves. I have detected the same error in several of my newer things, and therefore speak from some experience, though I do not know if I could do any better.[30]

Felix praised the tonal swaying (*Wanken*) between E-flat major and C minor at the outset of the quartet as *schön*, but the subsequent persistent appearance of F minor in the first movement and some tonal ambiguities in the second and third convinced him that Fanny had mistakenly embraced a mannerism (*Mannier*). For Felix, tonal clarity was an imperative, and form enhanced that clarity. "Don't consider me a Philistine," he insisted; "I am not, and believe I am right in having more respect than before for form and proper craft, or however one calls the trade terms. Just send me soon something nice, for otherwise I'll think you have struck me dead as a critic."

What Fanny sent in her next letter was a healthy dose of her own criticism, though not, she assured him, "a tit-for-tat action": on February 17, 1835, she took him to task for his sacred chorale cantata, *Ach Gott vom Himmel sieh' darein* (1832). Fanny noticed that its last movement began in F-sharp minor but then moved to A minor and C major, even though in her estimation Luther's paraphrase of Psalm 12 ("Help, O Lord, for there is no longer anyone who is godly") demanded "an extremely constant and steadfast musical setting in the hymn." Furthermore, in the arias of Felix's sacred works, Fanny pinpointed a quality she was tempted to label a mannerism, an "overly simple" and "somewhat childish" style.[31] Felix, too, it seems, was susceptible to tonal vagaries and mannerisms. But then, as if to deflate his criticism of her quartet, she announced, "I've composed a soprano aria that you would like better than my quartet in terms of its form and modulations. It's rather strictly handled, and in fact I had finished it before you wrote me about the quartet."[32]

The work in question was *Io d'amor, oh Dio, mi moro* ("I Die of Love, Oh God," H-U 279), on a text from Metastasio's *La ritrosia disarmata* (*Prudery Disarmed*, 1759).[33] Curiously, its first line replicates that of an aria from *Didone abbandonata*, (1724), the far more celebrated libretto that had established Pietro Metastasio as a leading Italian court dramatist. Set by dozens of eighteenth- and nineteenth-century opera composers, and inspiring instrumental compositions from the violinist Tartini and pianist Muzio Clementi, *Didone* told the tragic tale from Virgil's *Aeneid* of the ill-fated Dido, queen of Carthage. After she falls in love with the Trojan Aeneas, he abandons her to found Rome and fulfill his destiny. Metastasio adapted Virgil to permit the queen's sister to profess her own infatuation with Aeneas in the third act, when she sings *Io d'amor*. Though Fanny was likely familiar with *Didone abbandonata*, the text she actually used in her concert aria is from a minor cantata libretto of Metastasio, set in two quatrains of *octonarii*, the eight-footed lines preferred by the poet.

What led Fanny to create her work remains a mystery, though sibling rivalry was likely a compelling motivation. In 1834 Felix had composed for the London Philharmonic the concert scene *Infelice*, on texts, as he put it, of the "most beautiful nonsense"[34] drawn from four libretti of Metastasio;[35] significantly, the subject concerns another abandoned lover. Felix could have shared his score with Fanny when he visited Berlin in the fall of 1834, and in response, Fanny could have then taken up the challenge of composing her own Metastasian aria. Like Felix, she paired a cavatina-like slow section ("Io d'amor") with a faster, agitated Allegro ("No, sì barbaro non sei, hai pietà de' mali miei"; "No, you are not so heartless; you pity my misfortunes"). That Fanny was indeed heavily invested in the project is confirmed by the autograph sources. After drafting the work in E-flat major with piano accompaniment, she prepared a revised score in C major, now expanded to accommodate a culminating, concluding stretto, and, what is more, invested the time to orchestrate the accompaniment. The transposition a third below, the conspicuously virtuosic character of the music, and the orchestration all suggest that she designed the work for a particular soprano, perhaps Pauline Decker, to perform on the Sunday concert series. And yet, there is no evidence that Fanny ever heard the work with orchestra; indeed, if and when it was performed during her lifetime remains unknown. In any event, this worthy composition deserves further scrutiny and revival. If tonally less adventuresome than the String Quartet, the aria at times evinces (like Felix's *Infelice*) a Mozartian clarity and displays passages tinged by chromaticism that lend the music an emotional depth.[36] And the orchestration, to judge from the first commercial recording of 1993,[37] now shows the hand of a skilled composer.

ii

Late in September 1834, the public was at last able to view Wilhelm's monumental painting *Christus vor Pilatus* at the annual Berlin Academy of Arts exhibition. Three years of arduous work had taken a toll on the artist, as Fanny divulged to her English friend Mary Alexander: "his health has suffered a great deal lately through the great strain—especially when working on the lower part of the picture, where he has to paint permanently in a bent position or sitting on the floor...and on all the rest of the picture on a ladder in a most uncomfortable position."[38] In her diary Fanny recorded the harried final preparations—how twelve men were required to transport the unwieldy canvas through the streets of Berlin; how it nearly suffered serious damage as it made its cumbersome way up a flight of stairs; and how, finally, the mounted painting occupied nearly an entire wall in one of the exhibition rooms.[39]

Sadly, early in the twentieth century, fire would consume the painting; a surviving, preliminary oil sketch provides only an inadequate representation of its enormous scope and size.[40] One of its most fervent admirers was Wilhelm's father-in-law, who penned a description for Mary Alexander, though his own vision was then seriously impaired and his eyes extremely sensitive to light.[41] From Abraham we learn that the canvas measured an imposing fifteen feet in height and nineteen and a half feet in length. Fitted into this sesquipedalian space were more than fifty figures capturing "the moment when the Savior awaits the sentence of his judge, Pilate," surrounded by "lectors and representatives of all the nations under Roman rule." In the middle, on a raised platform, appeared the life-sized Christ surrounded by his accusers, including the Jewish high priest. To the right were Roman soldiers and a crowd, one of whom was a woman holding up her child to the bound Christ; to her Wilhelm ascribed the controversial text from Matthew 27:25, "his blood be upon us and upon our children," a cry taken up by the seething mob. Opposite her on the left, and completing a triangle with the figure of Christ, sat Saint John, "overwhelmed by pity and grief." Though Abraham did not draw the comparison, Wilhelm conceivably calculated the whole scene to recall the dramatic power of the *turba* choruses of the St. Matthew Passion, and thereby connected visually his "vast and noble enterprise," as Abraham described it, with Bach's monumental score revived by Felix and avidly studied by Fanny.

In his letter to Mary Alexander, Abraham dwelled on the artist's depiction of Christ; it avoided the "Byzantine type (petrified and incomprehensible)" and "the gentle languor which almost every modern thinks fit to portray in Christ's features." Instead, Wilhelm "represented him as he could and must have been—a Jew by origin, but leaving all that far behind him as he followed the divine call; severe but calm, and even at that moment, supreme; bound but triumphant." Indeed, Abraham could not recall having seen any representation of Christ "in so poetic and at the same time so truthful a manner."[42] Two other figures on the canvas elicited Abraham's scrutiny—a "woman on the right, holding her child in her arms," who mourned "Christ's situation, and the stupid and fanatical blindness of all who surround him." Abraham revealed the source of these figures: Wilhelm had modeled them on Fanny and Sebastian, and Sebastian's face was "particularly life-like and charming" (figure 7.2). As Cordula Heymann-Wentzel has recently suggested, Wilhelm appears to have underscored in the painting Fanny's separation from the crowd—in the surviving oil sketch, the figures of Christ, Fanny, and Sebastian are highlighted. Fanny appears, in effect, as a Madonna with child, giving expression to her Christian faith and perhaps linking the painting to her own *Lobgesang* Cantata written on the occasion of Sebastian's first birthday.[43]

As Wilhelm and Fanny waited anxiously for news of the painting's purchase, the first few reviews began to appear. On the whole, the response was positive, though no one, it seems, was prepared for the gargantuan size of the work. *Pace* Abraham, the *Vossische Zeitung* found the mouth of Christ too

FIGURE 7.2. Fanny and Sebastian Hensel, oil painting by Wilhelm Hensel, 1834 (Mendelssohn Archiv, BA 207)

small, the lower lip too defiant (*trotzig*). Similarly, Count Athanasius Raczynski later caviled about some of the figures, including the "strained" position of St. John, though conceded the painting was a significant work.[44] In March 1835 came word that the Prussian monarch had decided to acquire it for the estimable sum of 6,000 thalers,[45] and to install it in the gallery behind the altar of the Garnisonkirche, high enough to be clearly visible from the nave. There it remained for some seventy years until a 1908 fire destroyed it, Wilhelm's sole painting exhibited to the general public.

In 1835, encouraged by the king's largesse, Wilhelm contemplated travel abroad to promote his career. Already the previous year, the Hensels had

considered crossing the Channel; news of their expected arrival had prompted
Fanny Horsley, daughter of the glee composer William Horsley, to suppose
she would be awed by Fanny's "piercing eyes and 'severity', of which all who
have seen her speak with so much mystery."[46] Clearly, Fanny's reputation as a
musician to be reckoned with had preceded her, at least in private circles. But
the Hensels thought better of an English sojourn, and in the early months of
1835 turned their sights instead to Paris and its art treasures; their plans also
included an excursion to the sea resort of Boulogne, in response to a doctor's advice regarding Fanny's health. There was some discussion of exhibiting
Christus vor Pilatus in the French metropolis—the yearly Salon offered an
attractive venue—but this enterprise was deemed impractical, and the couple
settled on a more leisurely itinerary. First, early in June they visited Cologne,
to attend with Abraham, Lea, Rebecka, and Wilhelm's sister Minna the seventeenth Lower Rhine Music Festival, directed that year by Felix. The principal
work was Handel's oratorio *Solomon*, which Fanny dutifully began studying
in Berlin; in April she declared her firm intention to add her voice to the
altos. But, she playfully warned her brother, if he made a fuss over her so that
others encouraged her to play, she would not come at all, for she was still
"unreasonably afraid" of him, and did not perform "particularly well" in his
presence.[47] And so, listed among the altos as "Professorin Hensel,"[48] she joined
on Pentecost Sunday (June 7) an enormous chorus of 427 and orchestra of
179, some 600 musicians who dutifully watched "every glance" of Felix's eyes
and followed "like obedient spirits, the magic wand of this musical *Prospero*"
(figure 7.3).[49]

Traveling with Felix, the family then spent a few restful days in Düsseldorf, where he still served as the municipal music director, though he had
resigned as opera intendant and was already deep in negotiations for a new
position in Leipzig. Fanny and Wilhelm lodged at the residence of Otto von
Woringen, a musical amateur and former appellate judge and *Regierungspräsi-
dent*. His daughter Rosa, Felix noted, was already singing Fanny's lieder "very
nicely," so now he enjoined her to partake fully of the "joys of authorship in a
foreign place."[50] In Berlin, Fanny had indeed composed little that year; apart
from the concert aria *Io d'amor*, her catalogue lists as finished only the duet
"In der stillen Mitternacht" for soprano and baritone (H-U 280, February 26,
1835),[51] on the El Cid legend as retold by Herder. Here El Cid, Rodrigo, woos
Chimene, whose father he has killed. Fanny sets the scene in a dark F minor,
introduced by rolled, detached piano chords, perhaps intended as a bit of
exotic *couleur locale*.

In Düsseldorf her thoughts ranged far from eleventh-century Spain,
though she now rekindled her inspiration by exploring two new genres—the
a cappella trio and duet—associated with amateur music making in domestic settings. Heine's lyrics stimulated two miniature trios for two sopranos
and tenor, for casual performance by Rosa von Woringen and her siblings;

FIGURE 7.3. Felix Mendelssohn Bartholdy, oil painting by Theodor
Hildebrandt, 1835 (Mendelssohn Archiv, BA 136)

a compact duet from this time, "Ich stand gelehnet an den Mast" ("I Stood
Leaning on the Mast," H-U 284), later set by Felix with piano accompaniment, probably was also intended for the Woringens.[52] In the trio *Abschied*
(*Departure*, H-U 282), the voices engage in a playful chase, pursued by memories of a love never to be reexperienced. The more serious "Wandl' ich in dem
Wald des Abends" (H-U 283), from Heine's cycle *Seraphine*, inspired a collaborative effort with Wilhelm: on June 20 Fanny gave Rosa a fair autograph
copy illustrated by her husband.[53] The subject matter was familiar enough—a
"romantic" male figure trudges through a forest and sees through the breaking moonlight an apparition of his lover, depicted by Wilhelm in the upper
left margin, so that the music and text seemed to flow directly from the visual
image.

iii

On June 22 the Hensels departed Düsseldorf for Paris. They arrived a few days later in a metropolis of some 900,000 residents ruled by Louis-Philippe, the "citizen king" installed in 1830 after the abrupt overthrow of Charles X, and thus made, not born, a king. Descended from the Orléans as opposed to Bourbon line of nobility, Louis-Philippe initially held power by shuttling between the paradoxical forces of revolution and monarchy. Proclaiming himself king of the French rather than of France, he ruled not by divine right but by appealing to the politically moderate middle class, the *juste milieu*, a newly empowered economic force that eagerly supported two mainstays of "official" culture, the tradition-bound annual art exhibition at the Salon and the newly fashionable grand opera at the Opéra. The creation of the arts entrepreneur Louis Véron, and librettists and composers such as Eugène Scribe and Meyerbeer, grand opera treated dramatic historical subjects in five protracted acts made accessible through entertaining music, sumptuous set designs, and, of course, the indispensable ballet. There was an entrenched sense among audiences that the subjects, if well removed in time and place, bore relevance to contemporary events. Thus, Meyerbeer's *Robert le diable* (1831), in which the protagonist Robert is torn between a satanic father and angelic mother, was read by Heinrich Heine as an allegory about Louis-Philippe's regime and its struggle to reconcile the inherent contradiction of a citizen king who donned galoshes, carried an umbrella, and mixed with his subjects.[54] Felix, who saw the opera in 1832, was not convinced and sent a scathing review home— Robert's father was a "poor devil," and Meyerbeer's score pandered to all parties by dispensing tuneful melodies for the singers, bits of chromatic harmony for the cultured, dancing for the French, and colorful orchestration for the Germans; then, too, a midnight orgy scene set at a convent offended Felix's Lutheran sensibilities.[55] In 1835 it was Fanny's turn to judge grand opera on its aesthetic merits. After attending Auber's *Gustave III*, about the assassinated eighteenth-century Swedish monarch (a subject Verdi later treated in *Un ballo in maschera*), she reported that an entire act took place beneath a gallows. "Here the king has an assignation with his lover, here the conspirators seek to ambush him, etc. So, that is poetry! This theater really disgusted me, and if Taglioni had not danced, the entire opera would be forgettable."[56]

To ease their way into Parisian high society and artistic circles, the Hensels arrived armed with letters of introduction. Alexander von Humboldt, for one, had recommended Wilhelm as an "artist of *esprit* and outstanding culture,"[57] and facilitated his introduction to the reigning portraitist and historical painter of the Restoration, Baron François Gérard (1770–1837). Earlier in his career Gérard had legitimized Napoleon in paintings extolling the emperor's compassion and mercy;[58] the artist then committed a volte-face and served as first painter to the restored monarchy during the foreshortened, then

tumultuous reigns of Louis XVIII and Charles X. Fanny and Wilhelm visited
Gérard at his residence in suburban Auteuil and in his Parisian atelier, where
they examined sketches for his celebrated paintings, for Fanny "a seemingly
complete history of France since the Republic in figures at once attractive and
repulsive."[59] She experienced only the cream of the endless ateliers Wilhelm
visited, including those of Horace Vernet, former director of the French Academy in Rome, who, Fanny reported, wore the attire of a dancing master in
his studio, with white trousers, jacket, and a crimson scarf around his waist.[60]
Another established painter, his son-in-law Paul Delaroche, was then charting
a middle course between restrained neoclassicism and Delacroix's more urgent
manifestations of romanticism. These and other painters, along with sculptors
and architects then starting to reshape the Parisian landscape, were well com-
pensated by a patronage system that freely exploited art for political ends. But
the artistic world suffered no end of intrigues and rivalries, which may have
induced another leading historical painter, Antoine-Jean Gros (1771–1835), to
commit suicide by plunging into the Seine from the Pont de Neuilly, so that
Wilhelm could only attend his funeral and mourn his loss.

Inevitably, the absent Felix became the cynosure of conversation; Fanny
found that she traveled more as a sister than as her own person.[61] Nevertheless,
the firm of Erard et frères placed a piano at her disposal,[62] and Felix recommended her lieder to Madame Kiéné, mother of Marie Bigot, with whom
Fanny and Felix had studied piano in 1816. But Felix was careful to clarify that
music played a supporting role in his sister's life:

> It will make you happy to get to know my sister again, for she is an excel-
> lent woman; her whole nature is so gentle and calm and still so full of
> life and passion that she will certainly become dear to you. At the same
> time her musical talent is so magnificent, that if you want to hear music
> at all now, you will certainly let her play for you often and with pleasure.
> It makes me sad, that since her marriage she can no longer compose as
> diligently as earlier, for she has composed several things, especially Ger-
> man lieder, which belong to the very best which we possess of lieder;
> still, it is good on the other hand, that she finds much joy in her domes-
> tic concerns, for a woman who neglects them, be it for oil colors, or for
> rhyme, or for double counterpoint, always calls to mind instinctively the
> Greek from the *femmes savantes*, and I am afraid of that. This is then,
> thank God, therefore not the case with my sister, and yet she has, as said,
> continued her piano playing still with much love and besides has made
> much progress in it recently.[63]

Too much double counterpoint could interfere with Fanny's domestic respon-
sibilities, could disturb the equipoise of a lady of leisure, even if she happened to produce songs rivaling the very best examples of the genre, no faint
praise from a musician of Felix's stature. Perhaps half seriously, half jestingly,

he alluded to Molière's learned women who, in the celebrated comedy from 1672 *Les femmes savantes*, swoon over the pedant Vadius, merely because he knows Greek. Of course, Fanny had been exposed to Greek, and she certainly understood the finer nuances of double counterpoint. Nevertheless, as far as Felix was concerned, in social circles she remained first and foremost Frau Professorin Hensel, even though, as he fully knew, there had certainly been other learned women in their family—their aunt Dorothea Schlegel, their great aunts Sarah Levy and Fanny von Arnstein, and their mother, Lea, who had secretly read Homer in the Greek and made a practice of performing the *Well-Tempered Clavier*.

There was thus no question of Fanny appearing in the French public as pianist or composer; nor did she seem to have played an active role in the salons of nobility, venues Felix had frequented during his Parisian sojourns. Nevertheless, she reacquainted herself with the violinist Baillot, and came to know well Chopin, another musician who had specialized in miniature character pieces for piano. The Pole played for her at least three times, much to the enjoyment of Fanny, who confirmed that Felix impersonated Chopin "splendidly."[64] Details of the meetings are not known, but Fanny was probably among the first to hear some of his larger solo piano works—the *Fantaisie-Impromptu*, for instance, dates from 1834, and in 1835 he began drafting his first Scherzo and Ballade, opp. 20 and 23, compositions considerably more substantial than the intimate mazurkas Felix found somewhat mannered.[65] Nevertheless, Fanny harbored one reservation about Chopin's playing, tending to reinforce the then-current view of the frail, consumptive Pole as the Ariel of the piano: "I can't deny that his playing lacks one major component—namely power—which must be part of the total artist. His playing is not characterized by shades of grey, but rather by shades of rose, and I wish it would bite back sometimes! He is a charming man, however, and either you're mistaken or I expressed myself incorrectly if you think that his idylls haven't delighted me."[66] Presumably, in contrast, Fanny's own playing did "bite back."

On much less secure ground were Fanny's interactions with her distant relative Meyerbeer, whose brother had married her cousin Betty Meyer. When the Hensels committed the faux pas of not paying Meyerbeer their respects, the celebrity forced the issue, as he explained to his wife: "Today I also called upon Professorin Hensel (Fanny Mendelssohn), here with her fool [*Schaute*] of a husband. He was so uncivil not to pay me a visit, and just because of that I went to see them. They were very remorseful; still, their icy civility chilled me despite the July heat. Fanny's plainness is indescribable. Despite her *permanent* plainness, two years ago she appeared in comparison rather like a Venus."[67]

In Paris the Hensels resided in a *hôtel* on the Rue Louis le Grand, not far from the Place Vendôme, in the center of which stood Napoleon's column erected from canon captured at the Battle of Austerlitz in 1806 and then reforged. Among the Hensels' immediate circle was Auguste Leo, a German who had worked in the Mendelssohns' bank and served as their Parisian agent as Auguste Léo. His residence was a meeting point for Germans visiting and living in Paris; though Heinrich Heine dismissed it as a "gossip booth" (*Klatschbude*),[68] Léo was nevertheless prominent enough to merit the dedication of Chopin's Polonaise in A-flat Major, op. 53 (1843), destined to become a familiar warhorse in the piano repertoire. Among the Germans the Hensels encountered was a figure already familiar from Berlin, the physician Johann Ferdinand Koreff (1783–1851). A friend of E. T. A. Hoffmann and Heine, Koreff had produced a volume of poetry in 1816 but became established as a practitioner of animal magnetism (mesmerism), first at the University of Berlin, where he joined the faculty in 1817, and then at Paris, where he moved in 1822. When Wilhelm fell ill, Koreff treated him for a liver ailment; still, Fanny found him overly affected, an "incorrigible windbag."[69]

For five weeks the Hensels absorbed French art, music, culture, politics, cuisine, and fashions. At the Académie libre des Beaux Arts, Wilhelm delivered a lecture on majolica, the opulent, enameled Italian Renaissance pottery he had studied while cataloging Jacob Bartholdy's art collection in Rome. Published in 1836 in the society's *annales*,[70] the lecture earned his appointment as a corresponding member. Wilhelm was also in high demand for his portraits—Fanny noted that he could execute as many drawings as he wished[71]—and received several commissions from prominent aristocrats. Among them was the Countess de Sainte-Aulaire, wife of the French ambassador to Austria, and the Duchess de Broglie (1797–1836), daughter of the famous writer Madame de Staël (1766–1817) and wife of the third Duke of Broglie (1785–1879), who served as a French minister and indeed in 1835 led the cabinet. Notwithstanding his loyalty to the peerage, the duke threw his lot in with liberals known as the *doctrinaires*, who sought to dampen the influence of ultraroyalists. His daughter Louise, who had piano lessons with Chopin, became upon her marriage in 1836 the Countess d'Haussonville. She was later the subject of a polished oil portrait by Ingres; Wilhelm finished two charcoal drawings of Louise and her mother.[72] Not without reason did Fanny write to her mother, "you see, we are among grandeur" ("Du siehst, wir sind dans les grandeurs").[73]

Nevertheless, on July 28, days before their departure for Boulogne, the outside world shattered that exclusive society. From a balcony on the Boulevard du Temple, they watched the official procession of the royal family and military staff inaugurating the annual review of the National Guard. Fifteen minutes later, at the other end of the boulevard, the Corsican radical Giuseppe Fieschi and coconspirators attempted to assassinate the king, the seventh attempt on his life within a year. Fieschi had contrived to rig together twenty-three gun barrels. After they discharged simultaneously from a third-floor window and the smoke had cleared, eighteen members of the procession lay dead or dying, but the royal family was spared. One explosion from Fieschi's diabolical machine (*teuflische Machine*) had set Paris on edge; it was, Fanny wrote, as if one terrible stroke on the head had paralyzed the entire body.[74]

There had been other tremors of social unrest. In 1831 and 1834 the silk weavers of Lyon had organized strikes and an uprising to protest diminished wages; these struggles between the working class and bourgeoisie inspired Liszt to compose a militant piano piece. In her letters Fanny alluded to the ringleaders' trial that commenced in Paris in May 1835, not by a jury of peers but by the aristocratic *pairs*, a process republican sympathizers dismissed as a *procès monstre*.[75] Curiously, Fanny did not mention the remarkable proliferation of political cartoons that compared Louis-Philippe to a common fruit. Frances Trollope, mother of the novelist Anthony Trollope and a keen observer of French culture, recorded what she encountered during a visit to the Latin Quarter, as it happened, the same year Fanny was there: "Pears of every size and form, with scratches signifying eyes, nose, and mouth, were to be seen in all directions; which, being interpreted, denotes the contempt of the juvenile students for the reigning monarch."[76]

On August 6 the caricatured monarch attended a service at Notre Dame, a public act of reconciliation with the church. Behind him were diplomats and peers, a throng dense enough to impede the Hensels' view of the proceedings. But Fanny grasped the significance of the event—after recording in her diary that the music was *sehr schlecht*, she observed that the king's first visit to the cathedral signified a rupture with the Republic (*rupture à mort mit der Republik*).[77] Indeed, a few weeks later the administration promulgated repressive new laws banning representations of pears. The absurdity of the moment was not lost upon the editors of the journal *Charivari*, whose drawings were censored not because they bore any resemblance to the king, but because they depicted a "carafe that looked like the rabbit that looked like a pear that looked like *etc*."[78]

Late on the warm, moonlit night of August 6, the Hensels departed Paris. The next day they visited the square in Rouen where Joan of Arc died at the stake in 1431; the nearby cathedral, with its lacy stonework, made a "sadly ruined impression" on Fanny[79]—one of its towering spires had been struck by lightning and destroyed, its sculpted saints decapitated during the French Revolution. Around the time of their arrival Fanny and Wilhelm received news of a two-day uprising in Berlin that cost the lives of several innocent bystanders. Felix—who had accompanied his parents home from Düsseldorf to care for Lea, suffering from tachycardia—witnessed the disturbance, and Lea reported one idea for restoring the social order: "They say that somebody proposed to the king the Paris plan of dispersing the mob by the fire-engines, and that he answered in his own laconic way, 'Sure to be in bad condition.' "[80]

When the Hensels reached Boulogne sur Mer on August 9, they found more English than French spoken in a town teeming with tourists; dotting the Channel was an endless stream of smoke-billowing steamships conveying day-trippers. Accommodations were scarce, and Fanny was initially unable to begin her prescribed regimen of sea baths. But the Hensels were warmly welcomed by one English visitor, the impeccably educated translator of German literature Sarah Austin (1793–1867), then residing in Boulogne with her husband, John, and fourteen-year-old daughter, Lucie, the future Lady Duff Gordon.[81] In 1829 Felix had met Sarah in London, and presumably he facilitated her introduction to the Hensels in 1835. Daughter of the hymnist John Taylor, Sarah had married in 1820 the jurist John Austin, an ailing legal scholar who suffered from anxiety disorder and taught at the University of London for several years before publishing *The Province of Jurisprudence Determined* (1832), a study of how rulers should be chosen and why citizens should obey. Austin's immediate circle included Jeremy Bentham and James Mill. The latter's son, John Stuart Mill, had grown especially attached to Sarah, whom he habitually addressed as Mutter. Well versed in Bentham's radical utilitarianism, John Austin nevertheless advanced an elitist position—the greatest good in politics, he argued, would result from conferring power on "those most capable of making wise policy,"[82] to be determined by a scientific method.

Austin's faltering teaching prospects encouraged his wife to pursue actively the career of a professional translator. During the early 1830s her work appeared with increasing frequency, including *Characteristics of Goethe* (1833), annotated recollections of the poet by his contemporaries. Around this time she also began translating the risqué *Briefe eines Verstorbenen* (*Letters of a Deceased*), travel letters of a minor, dandylike German prince of questionable reputation, who a few years before had visited the British Isles, where he cut a seductive, Byronic figure.[83] The translator's voice now succumbed to the lover's, as Sarah, seeking escape from her hapless marriage, embarked upon a prurient, epistolary affair with the prince, even though she remained mindful that any indiscretion—such as "the vanity of showing a letter"—might destroy her, as if he had "poured poison" down her throat.[84] By the time the Austins met Fanny and Wilhelm in Boulogne, this curious platonic relationship had passed its zenith, and somehow the better part of discretion had kept it private.

While Fanny began her daily seaside cure, Wilhelm executed drawings that "instinctively" transferred to the sketch pad "fugitive" impressions of the water, a process he imagined to be similar to Fanny's and Felix's realizing at the piano an overture from a complex orchestral score.[85] Despite stimulating conversations with Sarah, existence in Boulogne became repetitive and worse, when the ceiling of their room suddenly collapsed, and when Fanny contracted an eye inflammation. Then, too, she found the security measures especially repressive, like those of an "absolute state." In order to walk on the beach, one needed two permissions from the authorities, and a third to fetch a bucket of water.[86]

According to her correspondence, the Hensels attempted to avoid Hein-rich Heine, then visiting Sarah;[87] still, on August 24, Fanny finished a setting of "Wenn der Frühling kommt" ("When Springtime Comes," H-U 286) from his *Buch der Lieder*. Here Heine comments on the singer's ability to stir mov-ing songs from deep feelings, but then, with his celebrated ironic twist, rejects lieder, stars, flowers, and all the rest, for "No matter how much you like such stuff, / to make a world they're just not enough."[88] By abruptly deflating the romantic imagery just introduced, the poet thus effectively called his own verses into question. But the rupture of mood also dampened Fanny's inspiration, so that in order to finish the song she completely rewrote the poem's ending. Her new reading recast Heine's "stuff" (*Zeug*) as *tändelnder Scherz* (dallying jest) and concluded by asserting that the lover's heart is the poet's world. Initially, Fanny's music reromanticizes Heine's images, with lilting rhythms and billow-ing arpeggiations of springtime florescence. She thus seems to follow other composers' examples, who, as Jeffrey Sammons has noted, "reimpose sincerity of feeling" upon a Heine poem "in which the truth and reliability of feeling are the very problem."[89] But Fanny provides a few hints of subsurface musical tension—she undercuts the tonic A major with some tonal excursions to minor keys, adds unexpected chromatic dissonances, and dwells on a playfully repeti-tive rhythmic figure that impresses as so much *tändelnder Scherz*.

Did Fanny share her setting with Heine? Most likely not—her exercise in poetic-musical license (her later lieder contain some other examples of her editorial hand) was probably intended for her private circle; there is no evi-dence that she ever intended to publish the song. Be that as it may, Heine may have given her in Boulogne a copy of a newly published poem, *Gleich Merlin*, which she set a few months later, in March 1836 (H-U 293).[90] Here, like Mer-lin, the poet is reduced to a vain old necromancer, ensnared by the very art he has taught his protégée, Viviane. Fanny responded with a setting displaying its own bit of magic—against ever-changing piano arpeggiations she crafted a tonally unpredictable vocal line. Thus, when Merlin is caught up in the old circles of magic (*alten Zauberkreisen*), the music turns toward F minor, only then to swerve unexpectedly to the major.

Apart from avoiding Heine in Boulogne, Fanny did find the inspiration to compose another song, an impressively concentrated rendition of Goethe's flawless "Über allen Gipfeln ist Ruh" (H-U 285),[91] and here respected the authority of the poem. Its images of forest serenity drew from Fanny somno-lent octaves in the bass and gently rustling triplets in the treble of the piano accompaniment. The final line, "Balde, ruhest du auch" ("Soon, you too will rest"), inspired a lingering, drawn-out phrase in the vocal part that slowly searched for the tonic key, E major, ultimately reached in the piano postlude that brought the listener to rest.

Among the many English tourists in Boulogne was Sophia Horsley, a daughter of William Horsley, who brought her album for Fanny and Wilhelm to inscribe.[92] Fanny was especially pleased by the arrival of Karl Klingemann; crossing the Channel early in September to spend three days in Boulogne, he met Wilhelm for the first time. From Fanny's perspective, Klingemann had not changed at all, and the old friends fell easily into lively conversations, the high point of her visit to Boulogne. Wilhelm considered returning with Klingemann to London, in order to experience firsthand the English art world, but abandoned and postponed the idea until 1838. Instead, as soon as Fanny had completed her cure, they departed Boulogne and began the return journey to Berlin.

Their route proceeded to Dunkirk and then, on a natural road of shells exposed to the sea, to the frontier of Belgium, newly independent after a brief revolution in 1830. Bruges, Ghent, and Antwerp impressed Fanny as picturesque reviews of the fifteenth, sixteenth, and seventeenth centuries. In Bruges, she wrote, with little imagination one might encounter Memling or van Eyck; in Ghent, the omnipresent bridges (Fanny counted 360) and innumerable water contrivances had frozen time, so that many streets offered the "unspoiled impression of a fifteenth-century city."[93] In each city, Wilhelm reaped a harvest of art that far exceeded his expectations—in Bruges, the lustrous, meticulous oils of Jan van Eyck and realistic mysticism of Memling; in Ghent, the inscrutable altarpiece in the cathedral, with its twenty-six hinged panels, begun by Hubert van Eyck and finished by his brother, which, when closed, depicted the Annunciation, and when opened for services, Christ the King and the Adoration of the Lamb; and in Antwerp, the powerfully sensual art of Rubens, culminating in *The Descent from the Cross*, the central panel of the altarpiece triptych in the cathedral.

Proceeding to Brussels, the Hensels dined with Eugène Verboeckhoven (1790–1881), who painted rural scenes populated by animals, and Adolphe Quetelet (1796–1874), a versatile mathematician and social scientist who in 1835 published *A Treatise on Man*, an early attempt to apply statistical probability to human affairs (one of Quetelet's innovations was the body mass index). A more notorious figure was Marquis Giuseppe Arconati-Visconti (1797–1873), who lived stylishly in a *palais* after being condemned to death in absentia in northern Italy, on account of his involvement with the revolutionary *carbonari*. Then, on September 16, the Hensel family traveled from Brussels to Mechelen via a new method—the first railway in continental Europe. Sebastian Hensel later reminisced about how incredulous Berliners later interrogated the intrepid travelers—why had they not lost their air or, indeed, burned up during the experience?[94]

After joining Rebecka and her husband in Bonn, the Hensels planned to return to Düsseldorf, but when news arrived that Wilhelm's mother was gravely ill, they started instead for Berlin. An encouraging report extended their stay in Leipzig, where Felix had recently moved to prepare for his first season as the new municipal music director. Now well advanced in the composition of his first oratorio, *Paulus* (*St. Paul*), he shared parts of the score with Fanny, who did not hesitate to offer praise but also criticism. On September 27, the Hensels were again in Berlin, just days before Wilhelm's mother died, Fanny's first experience in viewing "death and all its ritual so closely."[95] A few weeks later, the Dirichlets arrived with two unannounced companions—Felix and Ignaz Moscheles. Fanny's piano was brought over to the main residence, and for two days there was uninhibited music making. On Moscheles's request, Fanny played "several of her things" for him,[96] and Felix's rendition of a Haydn Adagio brought Abraham to tears; all but blind, he mistook his son's playing for Moscheles's, only to recognize the error and delight in the pianists' virtuoso improvisations.

While Felix resumed his new duties in Leipzig—at the Gewandhaus Orchestra the twenty-six-year-old presided over a high-profile series of twenty concerts that ran each year from Michaelmas to Easter—Fanny continued her own concerts in the *Gartenhaus*. The line separating the siblings' public and private artistic domains was underscored on November 9, when Felix conducted in Leipzig the premiere of Clara Wieck's piano concerto. Had Fanny written a concerto, no such public performance would have occurred, because of class, not gender issues. As the daughter of Friedrich Wieck, a middle-class piano pedagogue, Clara could pursue a public career as a composer and pianist, and Felix stood ready to support her; Fanny, as a lady of leisure and member of an assimilated, upper-class Jewish family that guarded its privacy, could not. Nevertheless, those fortunate to hear her in Berlin were not chary of praise, including one Herr Limburger, a Leipzig music connoisseur who, after taking in Fanny's rendition of Cramer etudes, declared she "ought to be a traveling artist" and would "kill every one else" with her playing.[97]

In May 1835, before singing in Handel's *Solomon* in Cologne under Felix's baton, Fanny had performed in the *Gartenhaus* excerpts from another Handel oratorio, *Samson*, which elicited from Lea the comment that her daughter's rehearsal technique, conducting, and accompanying were truly a "rare phenomenon among women."[98] Now, on November 15, she programmed two challenging cantatas of J. S. Bach, *Herr, gehe nicht ins Gericht* (BWV 105) and *Liebster Gott, wann werd ich sterben* (BWV 8), with a fortified chorus and four seasoned professional soloists—Pauline Decker, Auguste Thürrschmidt, Heinrich Stümer, and, visiting from Leipzig, Franz Hauser. In the estimation of Abraham, impressed by the solemn, dissonant counterpoint of *Herr, gehe nich ins Gericht* ("Enter not into judgment, O Lord," Psalm 143:2) and its depiction of trembling sinners, she achieved a level too high to be sustained. *Liebster Gott, wann werd ich sterben* ("Dear God, when will I die") proved more immediately pertinent. The day of the concert, Abraham had a heated argument with Karl August Varnhagen von Ense about the Junges Deutschland (Young Germany) movement, whose adherents, associated with the émigré Heine, were about to face prosecution in Prussia for blasphemy. Within a day or two,

Abraham was suffering from a persistent cough; he took to bed, and after a brief illness died on November 19. Hours later, Wilhelm departed for Leipzig to break the news to Felix and accompany him back to Berlin for the funeral on November 23.

After the initial shock of the loss, Fanny devoted several pages of her diary to Abraham's final days; her usually reserved, compressed style gave way to a prolix outpouring of prose as she began grieving—how her father had taken pleasure in a sketch for Wilhelm's next painting, depicting Miriam's hymn of praise after the crossing of the Red Sea; how Fanny had divided her time between reading to him and playing Gluck's *Iphigenie* for Hauser, so that, as Abraham said, they shared the "prize," like Timothy and Cecilia in Dryden's *Alexander's Feast*; how, after Fanny and other family members had announced themselves, he replied, "I cannot help you; you cannot help me"; how, finally, on the morning of the nineteenth, he had said he would try to sleep. At that moment, Fanny recorded, death entered the room: "So beautiful, unchanged, and calm was his face that we could remain near our loved one not only without sensation of fear, but felt truly elevated in looking at him.... It was the end of the righteous, a beautiful, enviable end, and I pray to God for a similar death, and will strive through all my days to deserve it, as he deserved it. It was death in its most peaceful, beautiful aspect."[99]

There was no joy at Leipzigerstrasse no. 3 that Christmas. When Felix returned from Leipzig for the holidays, Fanny found him inconsolable, silent, and closed to the world; she determined, with Wilhelm, that it was time for her brother to marry.[100] They had lost the dominant male authority figure in their lives. Felix's response was to redouble his efforts to complete *Paulus*, as Abraham had urged; Fanny's, to cancel her concerts in the *Gartensaal*, including her own performance of Felix's first Piano Concerto, op. 25. Ruing Felix's seven-year separation from his family, she also put away her diary. For the next three and a half years she lacked the resolve to continue her chronicle; in the interim, music would do double duty.

CHAPTER 8

Demonic Influences

(1836–1839)

I don't know exactly what Goethe means by the demonic influence,...but this much is clear: if it does exist, you exert it over me.

—Fanny to Felix, July 30, 1836

Fanny remembered the wintry opening of 1836 as "monotonous, sad, and quiet."[1] Mourning her father's death, she cared for the widowed Lea with Rebecka, who moved into the family residence with her husband. Another, deeply felt loss preoccupied her—the ongoing separation from her brother. Since 1829, Fanny had seen but little of him and had few opportunities to witness his meteorlike rise to fame. Dejectedly, she wrote from her living room, "it doesn't quite feel like home because you aren't familiar with it, and it's necessary for you to know everything in my life and approve of it."[2] Musically, she still depended on Felix, and rehearsing parts of *St. Paul* in Berlin to honor him on his birthday and playing through a duet arrangement of the *Melusine* Overture with Rebecka reminded Fanny of her need for his approval.

During her last visit to Leipzig, Felix had intimated that sacred music was not her forte, and upon returning to Berlin, with some urgency she had reviewed her cantatas, which now triggered feelings ranging from boredom to exuberance.[3] Surely Fanny did not lose the irony when she sent to Leipzig her own opinions about the first part of Felix's sacred oratorio, praising much yet criticizing some recitatives as too modern. She was keenly aware of Felix's lack of reciprocation: "I'm also very sad, truly not out of vanity, that I haven't been able to be grateful to you in such a long time for liking my music. Did I really do it better in the old days, or were you merely easier to satisfy?"[4]

Felix did his best to repair the damage: "I assure you, I'm thankful for everything you create. If two or three things, one after the other, do not impress me the same as your other pieces, the reason, it seems to me, is not terribly profound. Recently you have composed less than in earlier times, when an unsuccessful lied or two was dispatched quickly, and followed by others in quick succession, so that we both thought little about them or about why they didn't please us, had a good laugh instead, and then moved on."[5] Indeed, since Boulogne, Fanny had written relatively little, only a few a cappella, miniature settings, mostly conceived in February 1836, of Goethe, J. G. Jacobi, and Platen, and one strophic lied on a text by Platen.[6] At least two, the trios *Frühzeitiger Frühling* and "Wie Feld und Au," offered images of springtime and summer compelling enough to pique Felix's interest, for he later set the same texts for a cappella mixed and male chorus,[7] and, indeed, in his *Frühzeitiger Frühling*, arguably alluded to the opening of Fanny's trio. Two of her other settings, the trio *Winterseufzer* (*Winter Sigh*) and solo lied "Wie dich die warme Luft" introduce another season—winter—to intone her grief. *Winterseufzer* actually begins by reusing the opening bars of "Wie Feld und Au," as if to link musically winter to summer; Platen's poem begins by contrasting the clear, blue heavens with the frozen earth. In "Wie dich die warme Luft," balmy, warm breezes seem to dissipate all the sorrows that plague the soul. "But wait," the final stanza reads, "until winter approaches, / until all lies rigid and desolate, / and frost and snow on flowers and fields / turn you to melancholy." Fanny compressed her music into fourteen succinct bars, but tellingly neglected to copy down the title of Platen's poem—*Aufschub der Trauer* (*Postponement of Mourning*).

In March she accompanied Lea to Leipzig to witness a public recognition for her twenty-seven-year-old brother—the conferring of an honorary doctorate by the university. The citation lauded Felix as a *vir clarissimus*—a "most illustrious man"—for his signal contributions to the art of music. Fanny did not record her impressions of the ceremony or, indeed, of her visit, but we learn from Felix that she appeared privately as a pianist, much to his delight and that of music-loving Leipzigers.[8] He arranged a private reading at the Gewandhaus for Fanny and Lea of the *Melusine* Overture,[9] so that she could experience firsthand the orchestral nuances, including the *pianissimo* trumpet calls that enthralled Robert Schumann, of a work she knew primarily as a piano duet. Mother and daughter also attended the twentieth and final concert that capped Felix's first Gewandhaus season before returning to Berlin a few days later.

Late in April and early May, Fanny returned to Goethe's poetry and produced in quick succession three duets for two sopranos and piano (*März*,

April, and *Mai*) and a solo version of *Neue Liebe, neues Leben* (*New Love, New Life*).[10] The most substantial composition was the last, a through-composed setting of Goethe's celebrated poem about the ambivalent nature of love (and his conflicted relationship in 1775 with Lili Schönemann). Here the poetic persona asks the heart what troubles it, and then vainly resists powerful emotions binding him to his lover against his will. Fanny's music, which takes its rightful place among settings by Zelter, Reichardt, and Beethoven, begins with a buoyant, descending melodic line that adroitly captures the nimble rhythms of Goethe's alternating feminine and masculine verses. In contrast to the expanded frame of this song—it occupies fully seventy-seven measures— Goethe's three poems about the transition from winter to spring elicited from Fanny more compact settings that, taken together, comprised a miniature musical cycle of the very months she was then experiencing and, as it were, symbolically replaced the diary she had set aside after Abraham's death. That she had in mind a musical cycle is clear enough from the related keys of *März, April,* and *Mai* (G major, C major, and C major); the similar block, chordal style of the first two; and the systematic broadening of meter from 2/4 for *März* to 3/4 for *April* and 4/4 for *Mai,* in which the warm springtime breezes prompted some tone painting in the accompaniment—an ingratiating rustling in sixteenth notes that persists throughout the lied.

Dwarfing these relatively modest compositional aspirations was Felix's most ambitious effort to date—the completion of his first oratorio, *Paulus,* for the Lower Rhine Music Festival scheduled that year in Düsseldorf. When Paul and his wife planned to attend, Fanny decided to join them and set out for Frankfurt. There they visited the septuagenarian Dorothea Schlegel before proceeding to Coblenz, Cologne, and Düsseldorf. Again taking her place among the altos, Fanny now came to know in rehearsal the second part of the oratorio. Like the first part, it offered a blend of historicism—neobaroque fugues and chorales—and modern orchestration and romantic lyricism, all calculated, as Abraham had advised his son, to combine "ancient conceptions with modern appliances."[11]

On Pentecost Sunday (May 22), before an audience of a thousand packed into the Düsseldorf Rittersaal, Fanny emerged briefly from the chorus of 364 to perform an unanticipated role during the premiere. When one of the false witnesses against Stephen (Acts 6:13) lost his musical way early in the first part, she stepped forward and sang the correct notes to help him regain his bearings, before retreating into the anonymity of the chorus. This spontaneous gesture brought her briefly into the public world of her brother, who afterward quipped that at least the blemish was the fault of a false witness, and not the martyr.[12]

On the second day (May 23) the featured work was Beethoven's Ninth Symphony. Still relatively unknown in 1836, it inspired a terse but compelling summary from Fanny: "A gigantic tragedy, with a conclusion meant to

be dithyrambic, but falling into the opposite extreme—the height of bur-
lesque."[13] The next day Felix hastily organized a third, impromptu concert;
just two hours before, Fanny recorded in her diary, he had not yet chosen the
program.[14] It would include Beethoven's first two *Leonore* Overtures, a reprise
of selected movements from *Paulus*, and, when a soloist became indisposed,
on the spur of the moment Beethoven's formidable *Kreutzer* Sonata, rendered
by Felix and Ferdinand David.

Felix's triumph as composer, conductor, and pianist was complete. *Paulus*, published in the fall of 1836 and then premiered in 1837 in England as *St.
Paul*, decisively secured his international standing and soon was reverberating
in Germany, Denmark, Holland, Poland, Russia, Switzerland, and the United
States. Rarely, Fanny observed, had a work found its way in the world so
quickly.[15] She had experienced this resounding success vicariously from the
chorus, and with her acute ear marveled at the beauty of the score—how,
for instance, in the orchestral overture, with its solemn strains of the chorale
Wachet auf, Felix had replicated perfectly the sound of an organ.[16] But she also
maintained a critical edge and challenged tenaciously his decision to remove a
lively heathen chorus from the second part before releasing the score in print:
"[Felix]," she recorded, "would have none of it, and became really angry, since
I wouldn't desist at all. But today I still think I was right. The chorus was
lovely, and appropriate where it stood; Felix made an unnecessary sacrifice."[17]

i

From Düsseldorf, Fanny, Paul, and Albertine traveled in a coach laden with
gold for one of Paul's clients and thus hastened their return to Berlin, where
they found Rebecka slowly recovering from a miscarriage. As Fanny resumed
her domestic routine, she determined that "for a woman there can be no pleasure trip without her husband and child" and vowed never to separate from
Wilhelm and Sebastian again.[18] Fanny had begun educating her son, who was
reared without siblings or playmates in an "ideal artistic atmosphere," as he put
it—that is, he spent most of his time in his father's studio and mother's music
room. It was a childhood that offered advantages and disadvantages, as he later
recalled in his memoirs, released in 1904: "I was spared constant contact with
uncultured nannies, an ideal artistic atmosphere surrounded me, and it was
not at all immaterial to me whether my youthful eyes focused on Struwelpeter
[*Slovenly Peter*, a popular children's book from the 1845] or Raphael's loggias,
my ears on popular hurdy-gurdy tunes or fugues by Bach."[19] The drawback
for Sebastian was that he did not experience "life with other children"—until,
that is, he was sent to the Liebesche Schule to begin his formal education. But
this institution fell short of the parents' expectations and soon became known
in their household as the Libysche Wüste (Libyan Desert).

After returning from the premiere of *Paulus* in Düsseldorf, Fanny began rehearsing the first part of the oratorio with an amateur chorus and mounted a performance on June 19, 1836, her first Sunday concert since November; among the soloists were Pauline Decker and Franz Hauser. But further rehearsals and concerts that summer diminished to a handful, and by November, she was acknowledging to Felix that her performances had fallen into a slump since their father's death.[20] Vowing to remedy her "musical apathy," she directed early in December Felix's three motets, op. 39, and a psalm setting, most likely his Psalm 115, op. 31. The soloists included the sopranos Pauline Decker and Rosa Behrend and alto Auguste Thürrschmidt.

Meanwhile, Fanny returned to composition, this time encouraged by Karl Klingemann. Her response, in July, betrayed her underlying insecurity and frustration as a composer: "I enclose two pianoforte-pieces which I have written since I came home from Düsseldorf. I leave it to you to say whether they are worth presenting to my unknown young friend, but I must add that it is a pleasure to me to find a public for my little pieces in London, for here I have none at all. Once a year, perhaps, some one will copy a piece of mine, or ask me to play something special—certainly not oftener; and now that Rebecka has left off singing, my songs lie unheeded and unknown. If nobody ever offers an opinion, or takes the slightest interest in one's productions, one loses in time not only all pleasure in them, but all power of judging their value." Felix, Fanny continued, was a "sufficient public" for her, but because he was rarely in Berlin, she was left to her own devices: "But my own delight in music and Hensel's sympathy keep me awake still, and I cannot help considering it a sign of talent that I do not give it up, though I can get nobody to take an interest in my efforts. But enough of this uninteresting topic."[21]

In these powerful lines Fanny thus revealed the strong sense of creative isolation she must have felt. Driven to compose by an internal drive, not by the demands of a publisher or public, she crafted her works with relatively little reinforcement and, evidently in 1836, with little in the way of a receptive audience, beyond Wilhelm and the occasional friend. Significantly, she penned these candid thoughts not to Felix, but to Klingemann in London, not the first time she had confided to that family friend. Thus, in 1829, on the occasion of her engagement to Wilhelm, she had written to Klingemann: "But the way the lords of creation remind us every day and all day of the weaknesses of our sex, might make us disclaim and forget both our shortcomings and our privileges, which would only make the matter worse."[22] In 1829 Fanny did not identify the "lords of creation," and we can only speculate about the particular "matter"—whether, for example, it involved Felix—but by 1836, as we shall shortly see, she was very much aware of the special power he held over her.

The two piano pieces Fanny sent to Klingemann in 1836 were a scintillating Prestissimo in C Major and passionate Allegro agitato in G Minor (H-U 299 and 300). Along with a *Lied-ohne-Worte*-like Allegretto grazioso in

B-flat Major finished before her departure for Düsseldorf (H-U 294), these pieces—the "uninteresting topic" of Fanny's letter to Klingemann—inspired an extended series of piano compositions that would mark a significant way station in her gradual progression toward becoming a professional composer. By the end of July, she was ready to inform her brother, to whom she now deferred as a student: "As the strict schoolmaster has ordered, I've continued to compose piano pieces, and for the first time have succeeded in completing one that sounds brilliant. I don't know exactly what Goethe means by the demonic influence,... but this much is clear: if it does exist, you exert it over me. I believe that if you seriously suggested that I become a good mathematician, I wouldn't have any particular difficulty in doing so, and I could just as easily cease being a musician tomorrow if you thought I wasn't good at that any longer. Therefore treat me with great care."[23]

The concept of the demonic had figured prominently in Goethe's works, especially in the closing sections of his autobiographical *Dichtung und Wahrheit* (*Poetry and Truth*), where the poet wrestled with an irresistible, demonic *Wesen* (presence), inherently neither good nor evil, that had profound impact on human behavior. Goethe found the demonic in world events—the great Lisbon earthquake of 1755,[24] the reigns of Frederick II and Napoleon, and the sweeping revolutionary forces that had fundamentally transfigured Europe during his long life. For Fanny, the demonic affected her private, musical world; like some *poeticus furor*, it evidently came over her when, following her brother's advice, she composed piano instead of choral music. To her mind, Felix was the source of this power, and the sibling bond could not be severed. And so, when he inquired in October whether she had composed anything new, she immediately replied, "a half-dozen piano pieces, as per your instructions.... If you have time, play them through sometime or have one of your students play them, and let me know what you think. I bear such a great similarity to your students that I always find it most profitable if you tell me to do this or that. In the recent past, I've been frequently asked, once again, about publishing something; should I do it?"[25]

In effect, Fanny had reversed roles. Formerly her brother's Minerva, his *Kantor*-like impersonator of J. S. Bach, she now compared herself to his students and deferred to his authority, as if, after Abraham's death, the younger brother had assumed the paternal role. And yet, the "demonic" influence also led her inevitably to challenge the social code of the leisured class: in October 1836 Frau Professorin Hensel wondered, should she release her music in print? It may be that a Berlin *Musikhandler* pressed the question; if so, a likely candidate would have been Adolf Martin Schlesinger, whose firm had brought out Felix's first three *opera* in the 1820s and surely would have been aware that the music of Fanny, the sister of an international celebrity, was marketable. In any event, Felix initially downplayed the issue—in his birthday salutation of November 14, he thanked Fanny for the piano pieces, noted how rare it was for new music to please him "through and through,"[26] and praised two in particular, the Allegretto grazioso in B-flat Major and Andante in G Major (H-U 301).[27] But, he admitted, he still held his "old reservations" about Fanny's intentions to publish, though he did not specify what they were.

Be that as it may, at first Fanny was delighted with his response: "You can therefore imagine," she wrote, "how happy I am that you're pleased with my piano pieces, for it leads me to believe that I haven't gone totally downhill in music."[28] But she remained in a quandary about temptations to publish, and compared her dilemma to that of Buridan's ass, the medieval animal that starved when it was unable to choose between identical bales of hay: "With regard to my publishing, I stand like the donkey between two bales of hay. I have to admit honestly that I'm rather neutral about it, and Hensel, on the one hand, is for it, and you, on the other are against it. I would of course comply totally with the wishes of my husband in any other matter, yet on this issue alone it's crucial to have your consent, for without it I might not undertake anything of the kind."[29]

For several more months, she dwelled on the piano pieces, to which she added a few more—by late 1837, they would number eleven.[30] In the interim, Lea attempted to resolve the issue. Her unpublished letter of June 7, 1837, to Felix reveals the inner dynamics of the Mendelssohn family, as the former *Musenmama* now interceded on behalf of her daughter. Usually propounding patrician views that reflected the family's favored position in Berlin society, to her credit Lea instead supported Fanny's need for recognition:

> On this occasion permit me to pose a question and request. Shouldn't she publish a selection of her lieder and piano pieces? For about a year she has written, especially in the latter genre, many really excellent examples, perhaps not without having in mind some ideas from your first few *Lieder ohne Worte.*... All that holds her back is that you have not called upon or encouraged her to do so. Wouldn't it be reasonable for you to cheer her on and take the opportunity to secure a publisher?...I can assure you that she performs these piano pieces well, that they inevitably please, and that they completely disown her earlier manner that was somewhat dry, in a similar style, and of the same hue.[31]

But Felix refused to act as primary agent in the enterprise and, in a private letter to Lea, not to be shared with Fanny and Wilhelm, laid out his reservations, here quoted at length:

> You write to me about Fanny's new pieces, and say I should encourage her and find her an opportunity to publish them. You praise her new compositions—not really necessary, for they please me to the bottom of my heart; I consider them lovely and splendid, and surely know from whom they come. Also, I hopefully don't need to say that as soon as she

decides to publish I will spare no effort, to the extent I can, to find her opportunities. But to *encourage* her to publish I cannot do, since it runs counter to my views and convictions. Earlier we spoke at length about this subject, and I still hold the same opinion—I regard publishing as something serious (it should at least be that) and believe one should do it only if one is willing to appear and remain an author for one's life. That means a series of works, one after the other; to come forward with just one or two is only to annoy the public.... Fanny, as I know her, has neither enthusiasm nor calling for authorship; then, too, she is too much a *Frau*, as is proper, raises Sebastian and cares for her home, and thinks neither of the public nor the musical world, nor even of music, except when she has fulfilled her primary occupation. Allowing her music to appear in print would just stir her up in that, and I can't get used to the idea even once. Therefore I will not encourage her, please excuse me. But show these words neither to Fanny nor Hensel, who would think ill of me or misunderstand—rather, say nothing about it. If Fanny's own drive or desire to please Hensel leads her to publish, I'm prepared, as I said, to help her as much as I am able, but to encourage her to do something that I don't think is right, I cannot do.[32]

For the moment, Felix had the last word; neither Wilhelm's support nor Fanny's inner drive was sufficient to prevail, and she gave up the idea of publishing the piano pieces. All remained in manuscript for 150 years, save one—the Andante in G major, praised by Felix. Eventually Fanny did release it, around December 1846, as the second of her four piano *Lieder*, op. 2, just months before her death.

ii

If we paint Felix in a benign light, he was sincerely attempting to protect his sister from the pressures of a fully committed, public career; if we invoke other shades, he was shortsightedly or even deliberately subordinating her artistic fulfillment to the patriarchal mores of gentrified Prussian society. Lea's views show flexibility in her expectations for Fanny, while Felix adheres to the then-common notion of women as idealized, incorruptible keepers of the domestic hearth. His voice echoes those of his aunt Henriette, who in 1818 had been distressed by Fanny's exertion in performing the *Well-Tempered Clavier*, and of Abraham, who early on had stipulated that music would be an ornament to her life, not its foundation.

Of course, despite her professed neutrality regarding publishing, by 1836 and 1837 Fanny's compositional aspirations had widened well beyond the realm of musical ornaments. What is more, the manuscripts document just how far she was willing to pursue at this point in her life the idea of public authorship, just how close she came to choosing between the proverbial bales of hay. For sometime after finishing the eleven pieces, presumably late in 1837, she arranged ten into a numbered sequence—not according to dates of composition but, significantly, according to musical criteria: key relationships. That is to say, she made a separate editorial pass through pieces composed independently between April 1836 and November 1837, as if to prepare them for publication. Indeed, this must have been her intention, for the manuscripts also contain engraver's markings, inserted to specify the layout of the music in preparation for its publication.[33] In short, Fanny's discussions with Schlesinger or another firm must have advanced considerably before she abandoned the project.

There may be some corroborating evidence in a publication Schlesinger released in Berlin early in 1837, an album for the year 1836 titled *Neue Original-Compositionen für Gesang und Piano*. It contained Fanny's 1827 Hölty setting *Die Schiffende* (H-U 199; see p. 107), issued under her name alongside Felix's duet "Wie kann ich froh und lustig sein" and, as it happened, marked the first and only time the siblings' music appeared together in print.[34] Felix was now among the first to congratulate her: "So, then, do you know, Fenchel, that your A-major Lied in Schlesinger's album is making a sensation here? That the new musical journal (I mean its editor [Robert Schumann],...) is wild about you? That everyone says it is the best piece in the album?...Are you a real author now, and does that please you?"[35] On March 6, Felix took a significant further step—he performed the song at a Gewandhaus benefit concert for the soprano Henriette Grabau and then reported at length to Fanny:

> You know what my opinion of it has always been, but I was curious to see whether my old favorite, which I had only heard hitherto sung by Rebecka to your accompaniment in the gray room with the engravings, would have the same effect here in the crowded hall, with the glare of the lamps, and after listening to noisy orchestral music. I felt so strange when I began, your soft, pretty symphony imitating the waves, with all the people listening in perfect silence; but never did the song please me better. The people understood it, too, for there was a hum of approbation each time the refrain returned with the long E, and much applause when it was over. Mme. Grabau sang it correctly, though not nearly as well as Rebecka, but she did the last bars very prettily.

In what must have seemed to Lea a volte-face, Felix thanked Fanny "in the name of the public of Leipzig and elsewhere" for publishing the song against his wishes.[36]

Perhaps Felix supported Fanny in this instance since she had taken the decision to release *Die Schiffende*. But what of the piano pieces? They languished, even though, as an extended set of ten compositions, they represented Fanny's most substantial piano work to date by far. In scope and ambition, they assumed the dimensions of a piano cycle, not unlike those Robert Schumann produced during the 1830s, for example, the *Davidsbündlertänze* (*Dances of the League of David*) and *Carnaval*. Schumann constructed chainlike cycles from miniature character pieces, many of a distinctly lyrical quality inhabiting as much the realm of the art song as of absolute piano music. But Fanny's 1836–1837 collection differs from Schumann's cycles in at least two crucial ways. First, unlike Schumann, she did not provide colorful programmatic titles or identify an overarching, extramusical topic for her collection. To be sure, the ten pieces explore a variety of moods and emotions, now introverted (the soulful Largo con espressione in E Minor, no. 9; the songlike Allegro moderato in B Major, no. 8), now extroverted (the Allegro agitato in G Minor, no. 7; the turbulent Allegro con brio in F Minor, no. 4). But beyond the tempo markings, Fanny did not offer clues about an extramusical purpose.

Second, Fanny began by composing separate, individual piano pieces, and then hit upon the idea of arranging them into a larger musical cycle. Table 8.1 summarizes the key plan of the ten pieces and reveals their large-scale coherence: they divide into two groups of five major and five minor-keyed pieces, with the major favored in the first half; the minor, in the second. Furthermore, the first eight pieces show a symmetrical tonal design centered on the F minor and F major of nos. 4 and 5, and radiating outward with C major and C minor (nos. 3 and 6), G major and G minor (nos. 2 and 7), and B-flat major reinterpreted as B major (nos. 1 and 8).

Aside from these relationships, which betray Fanny's efforts to achieve a large-scale coherence, the ten pieces show her interest in expanding the miniature dimensions of individual pieces. At least two exceed 200 measures in length, and several exhibit formal processes that replace a simple ternary design (*ABA'*) with more complex applications of sonata form. In comparison to Felix, Fanny appears more willing to explore relatively far-flung harmonic realms, as in no. 7, where in the space of a few bars she modulates rapidly from A-flat minor to D minor. Among her most impressive achievements is no. 9,

TABLE 8.1. Key Sequence of Fanny Hensel's Set of Ten Piano Pieces, 1836–1837 (Mendelssohn Archiv, Ms. 44)

B-flat	G	C	f	F	c	g	B	e	f-sharp
1	2	3	4	5	6	7	8	9	10
H-U 294	301	299	304	303	321	300	313	322	308

EXAMPLE 8.1.   Fanny Hensel, Largo con espressione in E Minor (1836)

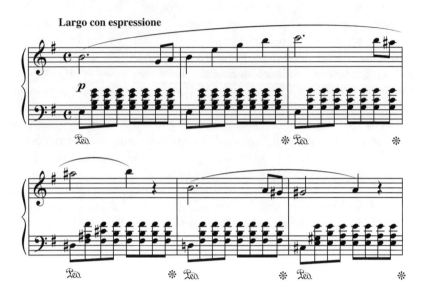

a lamentlike Largo con espressione suffused with chromaticism, in which an ascending melody slowly unfolds above a descending chromatic bass line and achieves a melancholic intensity reminiscent of Chopin (example 8.1).

As Lea recognized, Fanny's keyboard style was sometimes quite close to that of Felix's *Lieder ohne Worte*. What is more, in the final piece, no. 10 in F-sharp minor, she frankly acknowledged her debt by adapting for the principal theme the opening of a piano work by her brother in the same key, the *Scherzo a capriccio*, composed in 1835.☉ The tripping, descending staccato passagework of Felix's trademark elfin style now underwent metamorphosis, as Fanny prescribed legato slurs and positioned the reworked theme above a murky tremolo in the bass. But as if to underscore the sibling bond, Fanny identified her finale as a capriccio and thus specifically linked it to the genre of her brother's composition. Significantly, Fanny's capriccio was the only piece of the ten to merit its own title.

While the borrowings of a self-proclaimed "student" of Felix should not surprise us, the issue of Fanny's stylistic dependence is nevertheless more complex. For we can now show that on at least two later occasions, Felix himself borrowed from Fanny's unpublished set of pieces. In March 1839 he composed a *Lied ohne Worte* in G minor, subsequently released as op. 53, no. 3, and near its opening incorporated into the theme a brief passage suspiciously close to some bars from her Allegro con brio in F Minor (no. 4).[37] A few years later, in January 1844, he drafted a *Lied ohne Worte* in G major, eventually published as the first piece of the fifth volume of *Lieder ohne Worte* op. 62, dedicated to Clara Schumann. Here the allusion—to the opening theme of Fanny's Andante in G Major (no. 2)—is more subtle, but no less telling, for it appears at the very beginning of Felix's piece. He took the first eight pitches of his sister's theme, retouched them rhythmically and metrically, and made other adjustments, among them devising a new accompaniment in rising arpeggiations.[38] Whether the process was deliberate or unconscious, whether Felix set out to model his theme on Fanny's or somehow recalled her melodic phrase from his vast musical memory is unclear, but the similarity is too striking to pass as coincidence. In these two instances, it seems, we may speak of a stylistic interdependence between the siblings, as they practiced a common Mendelssohnian style.

Indeed, like artistic twins, the siblings could replicate with unerring fidelity each other's inspirations, and so bridge musically, as it were, the distance between Berlin and Leipzig. This was perhaps Fanny's unconscious motivation when, in March 1837, she finished a *Lied-ohne-Worte*-like Andante con espressione in B-flat Major (H-U 314).[39] Later that spring, she received a copy of Felix's newly published *Six Preludes and Fugues* for piano, op. 35. When in June she read through for Lea her brother's sixth prelude—as it happened, also in B-flat major—mother and daughter made a startling discovery: the two independently composed pieces were eerily similar (example 8.2). According to Lea, Fanny feared she could never publish her piece without being accused

EXAMPLE 8.2.   (a) Fanny Hensel, Andante con espressione in B-flat Major (1837); (b) Felix Mendelssohn, Prelude in B-flat Major, op. 35, no. 6 (1836)

(*Continued*)

EXAMPLE 8.2.   Continued

(b)

of plagiarism: "She will make a few changes for herself," Lea wrote to Felix, "but she intends to send you the original manuscript so that you too can observe the correspondences."[40] After receiving Fanny's piece, Felix confided to his sister:

> Yesterday I received your Prelude No. 6 in B-flat major to my Fugue in B-flat major; really, it is the same inside out, and the similarities captivated me. Isn't it peculiar how musical ideas sometimes seem to fly about in the air, and land here and there? In this case, it's not merely the same figures, motion, and form that astonish me, but namely certain details that appear not at all to lie in the theme (*i.e.*, in the notes), but nevertheless are there (*i.e.*, in the mood), and replicate themselves so conspicuously in each of us. For example, the *forte* passage in C minor that appears in your piece in octaves and moves to D-flat major, and then the *piano* repetition at the end. It's simply too wild—and, it's lovely that our ideas remain so close.[41]

iii

As it happened, Fanny had composed her prelude on March 28, the day her brother married Cécile Jeanrenaud, daughter of Auguste Jeanrenaud, a Huguenot pastor, and Elisabeth Souchay Jeanrenaud, a member of a wealthy Frankfurt merchant family. The ceremony took place at the French Reformed Church in Frankfurt; conceivably, the organ processional used was the very one Felix had drafted in England for Fanny before his accident prevented him from attending her wedding in 1829. None of Felix's family members from Berlin came to witness the ceremony. Weather conditions were difficult; Lea had ongoing health concerns; Paul was in negotiations to acquire a Hamburg bank; and Fanny and Rebecka were pregnant. Confined to bed rest, Fanny suffered her second miscarriage only days after finishing her prelude. In the face of this adversity, her composition, with its close connections to her brother's prelude, was perhaps in some sense her way of completing a new triangular relationship with her brother and sister-in-law.

Abraham once quipped that his son's "censoriousness" (*Mäkelei*) would likely prevent him from finding a suitable wife or an opera libretto.[42] As if partially to address this criticism, Felix had become smitten with Cécile after meeting her in May 1836 in Frankfurt, where he deputized for the ailing choral director J. N. Schelble for several weeks. A member of the chorus, Cécile was said to have "luxurious golden-brown hair," a complexion of "transparent delicacy," and the "most bewitching deep blue eyes," with "dark eyelashes and eyebrows."[43] Not until July did Felix mention her in his letters to Berlin, though within a few weeks Fanny was already playing Sancho Panza to her brother's Don Quixote and urging him on: "your lovely young lady from Frankfurt arouses my interest not inconsiderably. You wouldn't believe how I wish for your marriage; I sincerely feel that it would be best for you. If I were Sancho I'd cite an entire list of maxims to hasten a favorable decision: 'nothing ventured, nothing gained,' 'fortune favors the brave,' 'grab the bull by the horns,' 'strike while the iron is hot,' and many others that are not suitable here."[44]

To test his affection for Cécile, Felix undertook a "cure" at the Dutch resort of Scheveningen; then, upon returning to Frankfurt, he proposed and was accepted early in September. What was supposed to be a guarded secret quickly became the gossip of Frankfurt society, and Fanny, impressed by accumulating reports of Cécile's beauty, now pressed for an opportunity to meet her before the wedding—to see her, as Fanny put it, as a maiden.[45] In the meantime, she answered Felix's invitation to contribute several songs to a Christmas album for Cécile. Among them were two already published, *Suleika und Hatem* (released in 1827 as Felix's op. 8, no. 12) and *Die Schiffende*; and two unpublished, *Nacht*, a Heine setting from 1828 (H-U 225), and the newly composed "Ach! Um deine feuchten Schwingen" (H-U 306), on verses by Marianne von Willemer silently incorporated by Goethe into the Suleika section of his *West-östlicher Divan*. Sixteen measures in length, *Nacht* was in response to Felix's request for a "truly melancholy, short" song;[46] the new "Suleika" setting initially gave Fanny some pause, for she feared that Felix had already chosen it himself for the album[47] (in fact, he set the poem in 1837 and published it as the *Gesang* op. 34, no. 4). Its sensual lyrics—here Suleika invokes the moist West Wind to bring tidings to her lover, to tell him "his love is my life's essence"[48]—left little doubt as to its purpose. Fanny captured the wind in gently ascending piano arpeggiations, initially dampened by the una corda pedal and then, for the last verse, made more ardent through a crescendo effect; occasionally the arpeggiations lap over the vocal line and create a sustained effect of breathless agitation.[49] This sensitive setting shows too an imaginative treatment of harmony, as early on Fanny diverges from the tonic B-flat major to touch, but only fleetingly, on A-flat major, C minor, and E-flat major, and thereby achieves a certain harmonic restlessness. Adding a visual reference to the composition, Wilhelm contributed a vignette in the upper left portion of the first page, where a Cécile-like figure idealized as a Persian princess appears, framed by suggestive budding flowers, and plays a lute inclined to match the diagonal trajectories of the arpeggiations in the music.[50] At least one post-structuralist scholar has recently read this presentation autograph as a blending, from female and male points of view, of exoticism, eroticism, and femininity.[51]

For much of 1837 a domestic drama played out in letters between Berlin and Leipzig, as Fanny's desire to meet her new sister-in-law was repeatedly frustrated. Plans for Cécile to visit Berlin in February fell through when her mother became ill. Well advanced in pregnancy, Fanny was unable to attend the wedding in March, though a week or two before Lea braved inclement weather to travel to Leipzig for a performance of *Paulus*, and on the occasion met Cécile and her mother. According to Fanny, Lea returned to Berlin "totally charmed" by her new daughter-in-law.[52] Prospects for Fanny meeting Cécile did not improve when, after a honeymoon in the Black Forest, the newlyweds spent the summer in Frankfurt and on holiday in Bingen before Felix departed for England in September to conduct *St. Paul* and premiere his new Piano Concerto in D Minor. Moreover, Fanny sensed a new "alienation" from her brother: "If you think back to the time when we were constantly together, when I immediately discovered every thought that went through your mind and knew your new things by heart even before they were notated, and if you remember that our relationship was a particularly rare one among siblings, in part because of our common musical pursuits, then I think you'll admit that it's been an odd deprivation for me the past year and a day to know that you're happy in a way I've always wished for you, and yet not meet your beloved, now your wife, even one time."[53] Fanny found it peculiar to encounter Felix's new works first in published form, impelling her to evaluate their composer as Mendelssohn, not her brother.

When in July Felix sent two canonic puzzles for her delectation, she reverted momentarily to her role as Thomaskantor and dispatched solutions to Leipzig.[54] Her letters referred to the railroad and telegraph, then slowly but irreversibly changing the German landscape, as two modern technologies that might shorten distances and enhance sibling communication. But by October, she was pointedly writing to Cécile:

I am eagerly looking forward to Felix's concerto. Will it be printed soon, so that we may have it? When I see Felix's works for the first time in print, I look at them with the eyes of a stranger, i.e. criticize them without partiality; but it always makes me sadly recall the time when I used to know his music from its birth. It is so different now, and what a pity it is that fate should have decreed that we are to live so far apart, and that he should have had a wife these eight months whom I have never seen. I tell you candidly that by this time, when anybody comes to talk to me about your beauty and your eyes, it makes me quite cross. I have had enough of hearsay, and beautiful eyes were not made to be heard.[55]

Determined to force the issue, Fanny decided to visit Felix and Cécile in Leipzig and for two weeks took the measure of her sister-in-law. Cécile impressed Fanny as she did everyone else—she was "cheerful, calm, lovely, refreshing," though Fanny initially found her beauty less pronounced than expected, and perhaps not to her advantage.[56] Still, Cécile undoubtedly exercised a calming, positive influence on a sensitive spouse given to bouts of irritability. Cécile did not spoil him, but treated his capriciousness "with an equanimity" that might eventually even cure him of his disagreeable moods.[57]

iv

In a year of separation, at times alienation, from her brother—Felix's marriage had redefined the sibling relationship, and his refusal to endorse publication of his sister's piano cycle had dampened her confidence as a composer—Fanny elected to reinvigorate her Sunday concerts, which now entered a brilliant phase. Her main efforts went to mounting not one but two performances of *Paulus*, in January and June 1837. The first took place in a large salon room of the main residence cleared out to accommodate an audience of 100. From the piano she directed a chorus of about thirty, and soloists including Pauline Decker. Attending the rehearsals was Ludwig Berger, with whom Fanny rekindled an old student-teacher relationship. Then, with the warm June weather the venue moved to the *Gartensaal*, where "Felix's worthy sister of the muses," as Lea described her,[58] marshaled an expanded choral complement of fifty, reinforced by a cello and double bass supporting the bass line. On this occasion, Rebecka performed the overture with Fanny as a piano duet. Refreshments were served, and 100 printed copies of the libretto set out for the guests, who now swelled to 300, after Fanny allowed the musicians to invite acquaintances outside the Mendelssohns' immediate circle.[59] What originated as a private event thus assumed trappings of a public music festival, as total strangers mingled in the residence, filled to capacity so that the singers had difficulty finding standing room.[60]

Fanny was the conduit—in effect, Felix's agent—through whom *Paulus* first reached Berlin. Not until September 1837 was the work publicly presented in Berlin, and almost surely some of the musicians for that performance first became acquainted with the oratorio at Fanny's residence. Meanwhile, she continued to perform Felix's music, along with works by Bach, Handel, and Beethoven, in the *Gartensaal* in July. Then, in September, the visit of Ferdinand von Woringen, a passionate amateur tenor, and his music-loving family gave fresh impetus to her concerts, for several weeks collapsed into a weekly instead of fortnightly schedule.

The repertoire included portions of, or perhaps complete performances of, three major oratorios—*Paulus* and Handel's *Judas Maccabaeus* and *Samson*, along with "countless Lieder, arias, and duets of serious and light genres."[61] Two more concerts of Bach, Haydn, Beethoven, and Mendelssohn followed in November, after Fanny's return from meeting Cécile in Leipzig. The climax of the series then occurred on December 3, with the appearance of the young Belgian violinist Henri Vieuxtemps, fresh from his Gewandhaus debut under Felix in Leipzig, and about to appear publicly on the Berlin concert stage. Already known for a concerto rivaling Paganini's in difficulty, the virtuoso now turned his attention with Fanny and the cellist Moritz Ganz to an intimate chamber work, Beethoven's *Ghost* Trio, op. 70, no. 1. The program also included an aria from Mozart's cantata *Davidde penitente*, sung by Pauline Decker, for whom Fanny composed a long cadenza that created a sensation before an audience again numbering over 100.[62]

On December 17, Vieuxtemps returned for Fanny's final concert of the year and showcased his formidable technique in a set of variations. He also gave one of the first readings of Felix's new String Quartet in E Minor, op. 44, no. 2; for the occasion, Paul Mendelssohn Bartholdy appeared as cellist. Carl Maria von Weber was well represented with a piano quartet that featured Fanny, and with selections from his operas *Euryanthe* and *Oberon* sung by Decker. The remaining offering was a Chopin etude, performed by Johanna Mathieux (1810–1858), who is better known today from her second marriage as Johanna Kinkel.

In July 1836 Dorothea Schlegel had introduced this aspiring pianist and composer to Felix in Frankfurt. Impressed by Kinkel's talent, he encouraged her to continue studies in Berlin, where she soon joined Fanny's musical circle. Kinkel led a difficult, at times tumultuous, life. An abusive marriage, which she left in 1838, fortified her determination "to show that women's capabilities were equal to those of men."[63] She began her career as a pedagogue and composer of lieder before assuming a post as choral director in Bonn and challenging conventional gender roles. There she married the Protestant theologian and art historian Johann Gottfried Kinkel and began writing musical stories and editing a belletristic journal designed for "non-Philistines." Her husband's political activism during the Revolution of 1848 led to a death sentence; Johanna managed to have it commuted to life imprisonment and then organized his escape in 1851 to London, where she joined him and other liberals in exile, produced an autobiographical roman à clef, and lectured about music. In 1858 she fell from a window to her death, either by accident or suicide. She left in her estate comic *Singspiele* and dozens of supple, melodic lieder, some of which garnered Fanny's praise, and some of which espoused revolutionary and democratic texts. But when Schumann's *Neue Zeitschrift für Musik* referred to the "tenderness" of compositions by women and requested a song from Johanna, she exacted some revenge by sending her "rowdiest" drinking song for male choir.[64]

Between 1836 and 1839 Johanna was a regular member of Fanny's musical circle. Her little-known memoirs offer a compelling eyewitness account of the Sunday concerts, which, she found, offered the "most select music" then available in Berlin. Fanny encouraged Johanna to perform piano duets with her and piano solos in the concerts and thereby helped promote her career. Johanna also disclosed that the rehearsals, led by Fanny from the piano, ordinarily took place on Saturday evenings, and that only "very seasoned" (*sehr geübte*) singers participated in the concerts, held Sundays between 11 and 2 o'clock before a full audience. Nearly every famous musician who visited Berlin, Johanna recalled, either performed at or attended Fanny's Sunday concerts, to which the elite of Berlin society routinely sought invitations. But beyond the glitter of society and the wares of virtuosi who visited the *Gartensaal*, what impressed Johanna most were Fanny's own performances and style of conducting:

> She seized upon the spirit of the composition and its innermost fibers, which then radiated out most forcefully into the souls of the singers and audience. A *sforzando* from her small finger affected us like an electric shock, transporting us much further than the wooden tapping of a baton on a music stand. When one saw Fanny Hensel perform a masterpiece, she seemed larger. Her forehead shone, her features were ennobled, and one believed in seeing the most lovely shapes.... No common feeling could have possessed her; she must have been contemplating and breathing in the realm of the sublime and beautiful. Even her sharp critical judgments shared with close acquaintances were founded on ideals she demanded from art and human character alike—not on impure motives of exclusion, arrogance and resentment. Whoever knew her was convinced that she was as ungrudging as she was unpretentious.[65]

Sadly, Johanna left no account of Fanny's own music, perhaps because it played a relatively minor role in the Sunday concerts of the late 1830s, when Johanna was in Berlin. But at least two new compositions finished around September 1837—a terzetto for soprano, alto, tenor, and piano on a text by Franz von Woringen (H-U 319) and a duet for soprano, tenor, and piano (H-U 320)—were likely among the "countless lieder" performed by Ferdinand von Woringen when he visited Leipzigerstrasse no. 3. The latter, a passionate, through-composed love duet on an unknown text ("Sprich, O sprich, wird Liebe mahnen"; "Speak, O Speak, Love Will Remind Thee"), is especially well-crafted, with its persistent piano pedal points in the inner voice, alternating presentation of soprano and tenor apart and then together, and harmonic variety and depth of expression.[66]

Fanny's other songs of 1837 included a *Wanderlied* (H-U 317),[67] a fine Goethe setting eventually incorporated into her op. 1 in 1846. In the poem, the wanderer's song, a call to self-actualization through love, resounds from the mountains and hills, and Fanny responds with *Augenmusik* (music for the eye)—a sharply profiled, rising and falling arpeggiated figure that runs in the piano part unabated throughout this energetic miniature. Less predictable than Fanny's return to Goethe was her new interest in the poetry of Lord Byron, of which she completed three settings between December 1836 and the summer of 1837. They were an outgrowth of her English studies in 1834, when, reading his verses with an instructor, she succumbed to their irrepressible "magnetic force."[68] Two years later, in December 1836, she set Byron's verses "for music," "There be none of beauty's daughters," with the intention of sending the song as a gift to Cécile (H-U 307).[69] Having conceived a mental sketch, she visited a Berlin music store only to happen upon Felix's new setting of the same poem, and thus made another uncanny connection to her absent musical twin.[70] Both settings are through-composed and follow a model of statement, departure, and return, elaborated more fully in Felix's composition into something approaching a small sonata form.[71] Fanny seized on Byron's image of the beloved as "music on the waters" that causes the "charm'd ocean's pausing," and worked into the piano accompaniment flowing arpeggiations to impel gentle cross-rhythms against the poem's ingratiating rhythms. For two other Byron settings, "Bright Be the Place of Thy Soul" (from the *Hebrew Melodies*) and "Farewell!" (H-U 318 and 316),[72] she employed simpler strophic treatments, yet achieved in the recurring refrain of "Farewell!" a tonal ambiguity reminiscent of the first movement of the String Quartet from 1834. In both works the tonic E-flat major is diverted to C minor; not until the closing bars does Fanny resolve the tension and achieve tonal clarity.

One other poet captured Fanny's imagination in 1837 and, indeed, well into 1838—Heine, whom in real life she had religiously avoided after a chance encounter in Boulogne in 1835. No fewer than five lieder and six duets (one lost) date from this period, drawn mostly from the *Lyrical Intermezzo* of the *Book of Songs*, that wellspring of so many German art songs, including Robert Schumann's celebrated 1840 cycle, *Dichterliebe*.[73] Fanny in fact set several of the same poems, but in each case as a duet for two sopranos and piano. In place of the dreamy miniature that would inaugurate Schumann's solo cycle, she turned "Im wunderschönen Monat Mai" (H-U 323) into a nimble spring song, with crisp, driving rhythms to capture the sense of anticipation and longing. "Aus meinen Tränen" and "Wenn ich in deine Augen sehe" (H-U 327 and 329) are linked through their common key (G minor), thematic material, meter (6/8), and tendency to pair the voices in parallel thirds. Cut from the same cloth, they suggest that Fanny gave some thought, as Schumann did a few years later, to exploring a cyclic treatment of Heine's verses. One other feature of "Wenn ich in deine Augen sehe" is noteworthy: Fanny separated its two strophes by a piano interlude that Felix later appears to have recalled in the Scherzo of his *Lobgesang* Symphony (1840), also in G minor. Unfortunately, only a few bars of a fourth duet, "Hör ich das Liedchen klingen" (H-U 326) survive, so we cannot ascertain fully how Fanny translated into music the protagonist's recollection of his beloved's melody, which would become in Schumann's poignant setting a chromatic symbol of "intolerable grief" (*übergrosses Weh*).

Of the remaining Heine settings, Fanny realized two as short, a cappella soprano duets, "Die Mitternacht war kalt" and "So hast du ganz und gar vergessen" (H-U 309 and 324), and connected them, once again, through shared thematic material, key, and meter. The five solo lieder, composed between January 1837 and September 1838, offer some of her most exquisitely crafted examples of the genre. Two betray again how Fanny could challenge through her compositional voice the authority of Heine's texts, in one case through an act of omission, in another, of commission. In "Ach, die Augen sind es wieder" (H-U 325) she captured the speaker's passion for his lover's eyes, lips, and voice in palpitating piano chords. But she curtailed the last stanza,

Von den weißen, schönen Armen	Yet in arms so white and soft where
fest und liebevoll umschlossen,	love should glow and passion redden,
lieg ich jetzt an ihrem Herzen,	now I lie upon her bosom
dumpfen Sinnes und verdroßen.	unresponding, cold, and leaden.[74]

and effectively removed the poet's ironic twist. In the case of "Warum sind denn die Rosen so blaß" ("Why, Then, Are the Roses So Pale?," H-U 312), published in 1846 as her op. 1, no. 3, the intervention involved just three words, yet produced a most striking revision.[75] She replaced Heine's trenchant image of a malodorous corpse (*Leichenduft*),

Warum steigt denn aus dem Balsamkraut	Why rises from the balsams
hervor ein Leichenduft?	the odor of a corpse?

with the fragrance of wilted flowers (*verwelkter Blütenduft*),

Warum steigt denn aus dem Balsamkraut	Why rises from the balsams
verwelkter Blütenduft?	the fragrance of wilted flowers?

and thus rejected Heine's mood-shattering cynicism in favor of reinforcing the central poetic image—faded roses symbolizing abandoned love (example 8.3). Curiously, when a few years before Felix had begun setting the same poem,

EXAMPLE 8.3. Fanny Hensel, "Warum sind dann die Rosen so blaß?," op. 1, no. 3 (1837)

he proceeded only as far as the word *Leichenduft* before abandoning his own effort. Stylistically, the siblings were not far apart in their approaches to the poem, though Fanny does not seem to have known Felix's fragment. Each chose a minor key and 6/8 meter, and each responded to Heine's probing questions by positioning a series of open-ended, harmonic questions on the dominant. Fanny developed the technique further—she persistently destabilized the tonic key, A minor, so that it appears in a secure, root position in only six of the forty-one measures of her lied. The singer's haunting melodic strains thus searched for musical closure and paralleled the poetic search for answers to the jaded lover's pressing questions.

Fanny's three other Heine lieder from 1837 and 1838 respect the authority of the texts, even as her music betrays distinctive ways in which she interprets and shapes the poems. In "Ich wandelte unter den Bäumen" ("I Wandered among the Trees," H-U 334), a rejected male recalls in forest solitude the singing of his lover (stanza 1), imitated by birds (stanza 2), and in turn provoking a dialogue (stanzas 3 and 4) in which the protagonist accuses them of stealing his sorrow. Early on, Fanny insinuates into the vocal part a few simple ornaments and then, during the dialogue, transforms them into more florid trills. The musical onomatopoeia thus develops the topic of birdsong as a separate gesture (and second level of musical meaning) that is subtly subsumed into the composition. "Das Meer erglänzte weit hinaus" ("The Sea Was Shimmering Far Away," H-U 335), which Fanny most likely did not yet know from Schubert's rendition in *Schwanengesang* (1828), inspired a barcarole-like composition. Indeed, the doubling of the melody in parallel thirds and 6/8 meter bring her song firmly into the evocative realm of Felix's piano *Venetianische Gondollieder* from the *Lieder ohne Worte*, as do details in Fanny's piano part— the lapping arpeggiated bass and the atmospheric use of dampened diminished-seventh sonorities to suggest fog, for example. Fanny thus romanticized Heine's unspecified seaside, where lovers' tears are first shed and by the end of the poem compared to poison, by relocating the scene to Venice, on which she would first set eyes in 1839.

Finally, in *Fichtenbaum und Palme* (H-U 328), Fanny designed her setting to reinforce but also reinterpret Heine's compact binary division between the northern fir and eastern palm tree:

Ein Fichtenbaum steht einsam
im hohen Norden auf kahlen Höh!
Ihn schläfert, mit weisser Decke
umhüllen ihn Eis und Schnee.

A fir is standing lonely
in the North on a bare plateau.
He sleeps; a bright white blanket
enshrouds him in ice and snow.

Er träumt von eine Palme,
der, fern im Morgenland,
einsam und schweigend trauert
auf brennender Felsenwand.

He's dreaming of a palm tree
far away in the Eastern land
lonely and silently mourning
on a sunburnt rocky strand.[76]

We hear two contrasting types of music—first a Lento in 4/4 meter, with static, frozen pedal points in the lower piano, centered firmly on E-flat major; then, as E-flat is redefined as D-sharp, permitting an abrupt shift to B major, a flowing passage in 2/4 meter, repositioned in the upper register of the piano, with faster, less stable harmonic patterns for the sun-drenched, solitary palm.● Two short, four-line stanzas sufficed for Heine to depict the West-East division, but in Fanny's lied, the opening music in E-flat major returns, with the pedal points now shifted to a higher register, as the singer repeats Heine's second stanza. In effect, she imposed on Heine's binary pair (*AB*) a ternary division, so that the overall shape became *ABA'*—we begin with the wintry pine, shift to an exotic depiction of the palm, and then conclude, as it were, with the pine's memory of the palm, as if Fanny's music effectively added a third stanza to the poem.

v

During the winter of 1838 there was "regular music" at Leipzigerstrasse no. 3, and Fanny, pleased with her efforts, took the time to write down the repertory.[77] Though this document has not come to light, we can trace at least four concerts in January and February that attracted audiences large enough to fill completely three rooms and even half of one bedroom in the main residence.[78] According to Fanny's aunt Hinni Mendelssohn (wife of Abraham's brother Joseph), these concerts assumed more and more "epic" proportions, so that the "entire [Berlin] musical world, along with the privileged and elegant, pressed for admission."[79] Unquestionably the highlight was a reading of Mozart's opera *La Clemenza da Tito* on January 21, when three of Fanny's familiar soloists—Decker, Curschmann, and Fassmann—joined the newly arrived English star soprano Clara Novello, who had just created a sensation under Felix's baton at the Gewandhaus. Traveling with her father, music publisher Vincent Novello, the priggish Clara played the role of the prima donna to excess, though in Leipzig Felix had excused her on account of her "purity of intonation" and "thoroughbred musical feeling."[80] Fanny found her stage presence somewhat wanting, and so, when she gave her Berlin debut at the Schauspielhaus, Clara appeared with Fanny's jewelry, a fan from Rebecka, and a bouquet from Paul.[81]

As the lines between private and public became increasingly blurred, Fanny moved decisively toward and then briefly onto the public concert stage. When the Singakademie mounted a performance of *Paulus* in January, she was actively consulted during the rehearsals and able, as she wrote her brother, to "avert great disaster for the noble apostle." The Mendelssohns had not been to the Singakademie since Zelter's death in 1832, and she now encountered "all sorts of living and deceased ghosts." She vetoed a proposal to double the organ part with a tuba, not yet a common orchestral instrument, for the instrument was a "monstrosity" that transformed "all passages in which it appears into drunken beer brewers." There were also issues with tempi: "I thought to myself, 'If you were only up there, everything would be fine.' Lichtenstein sat next to me and heard my sighs. They started 'Mache dich auf' at half the right tempo, and then I instinctively called out, 'My God, it must go twice as fast.' Lichtenstein invited me to show them the way but told me that Schneider, the music director, had assured them that one cannot be ruled by a metronome marking. Then I assured them that they could be ruled by my word, and they had better do it, for God's sake."[82]

Another opportunity to deputize for Felix came on February 19, when Fanny performed his Piano Concerto in G Minor at a charity concert at the Berlin Schauspielhaus. Though the occasion marked her public debut at age thirty-two, the concert merited only a brief mention in her diary. But her letters and some press reports preserve vivid impressions of this unusual event, in which Fanny appeared with leisured musical dilettantes: "Last week," she wrote to Karl Klingemann, "the fashionable world was in great excitement about a charity concert—one of those amateur affairs where the tickets are twice the usual price, and the chorus is composed of countesses, ambassadresses, and officers. A woman of my rank was of course pressed to play, so I performed in public for the first time in my life.... I was not the least nervous, my friends being kind enough to undertake that part of the business for me, and the concert, wretched as the program was, realized 2500 thalers."[83]

The program, a jumbled musical farrago in which Felix's concerto appeared among operatic overtures and arias, duets, and a Hungarian anthem, struck Fanny as an ill-conceived menu. It was, she mused, "as if one were to arrange a dinner in the following way: soup—sugar water; steak—a piece of candy; vegetables—a meringue; fish (...); roast—a piece of sugar; and for dessert—all of the above."[84] Then, too, Fanny found in the antics of the blue-blooded amateurs a "wealth of trivial vanities, grand claims, and considerable unpleasantness.... Such dilettantes are wilder than a pack of horses once they unleash their bestiality."[85] But, to protect their privacy, they remained largely unidentified in the press reviews. Indeed, in two Berlin newspapers, the *Spenersche* and *Vossische Zeitung*, where Fanny's performance was lauded, she was identified not by name but as an "excellent dilettante, intellectually and naturally related to the composer," and a "most accomplished lady." The two leading Leipzig music journals, the *Allgemeine musikalische Zeitung* and Robert Schumann's *Neue Zeitschrift für Musik*, described her as "a sister" and "a blood and intellectual relative" of the composer.[86] And so Fanny briefly emerged on the public concert stage, not, to be sure, as a celebrated virtuoso like Clara Novello, but as an apparition that all too soon abruptly withdrew from the limelight of public scrutiny. In this instance, at least, she did enjoy the approval of her brother, who wrote in anticipation, "You are playing in a concert. *Bravississimo*. That's fitting and splendid; if only I could hear it."[87]

There was, of course, no opportunity for Felix to visit Fanny in February. The Gewandhaus season was in full swing, and early in the month, Felix and Cécile's first child, Carl, was born. The proud parents arranged his baptism for March 15, Lea's birthday, but for reasons that are unclear, only Paul and his wife, Albertine, traveled to Leipzig to stand as godparents. Then, with the conclusion of the concert season in April, Felix, Cécile, and Carl made the twelve-hour journey to Berlin, so that at last Rebecka could meet her sister-in-law. Fanny prepared Felix in advance by confessing that she had not composed a "single note" that winter and scarcely remembered the sensation of writing a song. And then, in a self-deprecating tone, she wrote: "But what does it signify? I am not a hen to cackle over my own eggs, and not a soul dances to my piping."[88] Nevertheless, there now followed several recuperative weeks that Fanny recalled as a *schöne Zeit*,[89] when most of her family was finally reunited. Felix brought several Bach cantatas for his Thomaskantor to examine, and there was much music making, though strictly of a private, domestic kind, while her brother kept a low profile. Among the likely participants was the mezzo-soprano Pauline García, then in Berlin at the start of her career after the untimely death of her older sister Maria Malibran, who had died from complications following a horse-riding accident. Fanny did not keep her diary during this period and left no account of May 1838; nevertheless, it does not seem far-fetched to imagine García contributing to the casual musical life of Leipzigerstrasse no. 3. In any event, late in May, the idyll was broken: Felix left for Cologne to direct the twentieth Lower Rhine Music Festival, and soon thereafter Wilhelm departed for London to immerse himself in the English art world, and to seek new commissions.

vi

After the French sojourn of 1835, Wilhelm had begun a new painting on the subject of Miriam's hymn of praise celebrating the miraculous crossing of the Red Sea (Exodus 15:19–21). With the pyramids in the distant background, it depicted a train of festively clad Israelites, directed by Moses from an elevated rock and led by three women musicians—Miriam playing a timbrel; a second musician (Wilhelm modeled her hands on Fanny's) plucking a harp; and a third holding two cornetto-like wind instruments.[90] On her birthday that year, Fanny received a preliminary sketch for the painting; all but blind, her father struggled to make out its form and features shortly before his death, so that, Fanny soberly recorded in her diary, it was the last object he perceived.[91] A year later, Wilhelm successfully exhibited the completed painting at the annual Berlin exhibition and sold it, and then took up another biblical subject,

Christ in the wilderness. By the time he finished it, on May 13, 1838, Wilhelm had repurchased the painting of Miriam; two weeks later, he departed with the two canvases for Hamburg.

The beginning of the journey was not auspicious. A driving rain nearly ruined his work, which he likened to carefully packed eggs,[92] but he pressed on and made a difficult crossing of the Channel, delayed when his ship ran aground on a sandbar. In London, Klingemann, accustomed to greeting Wilhelm's celebrity brother-in-law, welcomed instead an artist whose work was as yet unknown in the British Isles. At first, Wilhelm frequented a social circle familiar to Felix—he attended concerts with Klingemann and Ignaz Moscheles, and visited the Horsley family, to whom he brought several piano compositions from Fanny, which soon made their way to Moscheles. Horsley's daughter Sophie, at most a skilled amateur, announced her intention to learn every piece and then bestowed on the manuscripts the "highest praise" then imaginable in English society—it was "impossible to fancy your music to be written by a lady,...for in general there is no thing masterly or original in women's compositions."[93]

Wilhelm did not encounter such stereotypes. Armed with letters of introduction from Berlin, he easily made new social connections, strengthened by his decision to secure respectable, if expensive, lodgings at Golden Square 17 near Regent St. Like Felix before him, Wilhelm avidly played the German tourist. He was among the curious throng that gathered on June 4 to witness the opening of the Great Western Railway, then the "most complete railroad,"[94] though probably he did not experience the disquieting passage on the Vulcan or North Star, the two trains that traversed the initial stretch from Paddington to Maidenhead. But soon eclipsing the advent of the dynamic new technology was the singular, gala event of the summer—the coronation on June 28 of the young queen, Victoria. Accompanying Lord Sandon, whom Wilhelm had met in Rome some ten years before, the artist enjoyed a coveted position near the entrance to Westminster Abbey, where he took in all the pageantry— peers and peeresses arriving in ornate carriages, some to applause, others to jeers; "dressed-up modern *cinquecento* halbediers," whose cheeks and noses were redolent of beef and "tales of whisky and claret"; and finally the "golden, fairy-like carriage—supported by Tritons with their tridents, and surmounted by the great crown of England," from which descended the eighteen-year-old Victoria in all her medieval finery.[95]

The coronation posed a practical drawback for Wilhelm: because London art dealers were preoccupied with marketing mementos of the coronation, he could not find an engraver to reproduce his paintings and drawings. Nevertheless, he was soon sharing his work with prominent patrons and filling an album with portraits. Lord Egerton, whose art collection boasted examples of Raphael and Titian, commissioned a painting on an English historical subject, which Wilhelm found in Byron's *Childe Harold's Pilgrimage*, canto III, stanzas

21–23, a depiction of the ball given by the Duchess of Richmond in Brussels the day of the Battle of Quatre Bras, during the Waterloo Campaign of 1815. Wilhelm captured the height of the festivities just at the moment the Duke of Brunswick first heard the distant "canon's opening roar," "caught its tone with Death's prophetic ear," and "rush'd into the field, and, foremost fighting, fell."[96] The subject accorded with Wilhelm's desire to invest historical events of his own lifetime with sufficient gravitas so that they could stand with art depicting the history of earlier centuries.

When a second patron, the Duchess of Sutherland, requested a copy of *Miriam*, the artist took a calculated risk and declined, even though he fully realized that in all likelihood, no one had ever refused the duchess. Because he could not "repeat himself," she settled instead for a painting of a shepherdess in the land of Goshen. But of greater significance, the duchess brought Wilhelm's work to the attention of the queen, who on August 18 received the artist in Buckingham Palace, where with no small trepidation he exhibited *Miriam* and *Christ in the Wilderness* in a gallery filled with Rubens, Van Dycks, and Rembrandts. Quite taken with "the two very very fine pictures by a German painter, called Hansel [*sic*],"[97] Victoria considered purchasing *Miriam* but demurred, lest the acquisition cause complications with English artists (Wilhelm later sent her the painting as a gift). Still, the new monarch extended her generosity in other ways, by permitting Wilhelm access to see the art treasures in her private chambers at Windsor Castle and by allowing him to study and copy the Raphael cartoons at Hampton Court for the Prussian king. Wilhelm had advanced the idea as a means of extending his London sojourn, but the plan fell through, and the outbreak of a measles epidemic in Berlin convinced him to return in September to his family.

Meanwhile, after directing the music festival in Cologne, Felix had traveled to Berlin in June and shared with Fanny his new cantata-like settings of Psalms 42 and 95. During Wilhelm's absence, she suspended the Sunday musicales, and Felix and Cécile now quietly took up the "double counterpoint" of music and painting normally practiced by Fanny and Wilhelm.[98] For Felix, this meant putting the finishing touches on his three string quartets op. 44, though the elegiac opening melody of what would become the celebrated Violin Concerto in E Minor op. 64 began haunting him as well. Not for several years had Fanny and Felix been together at the family residence for a prolonged period, and their reunion during the summer of 1838 had a positive effect, so that she too contributed to the familial counterpoint. Among her offerings was a new Hölty setting, *Mainacht* (*May Night*), issued posthumously in 1850 as her op. 9, no. 6, which featured impressionistic, blurred arpeggiations and hand crossings to suggest softly dappled moonlight.[99] Fanny also completed three substantial piano compositions (H-U 330, 332, and 333), which in length and treatment of sonata form impress as a continuation of the piano cycle of 1836 and 1837.

Two of these pieces, the Andante con moto in E Major and Allegro molto vivace in E-flat Major, begin with clear enough allusions to the world of the German art song—they feature lyrical soprano melodies with chordal accompaniments, as if inviting the listener to supply the missing text.[100] But in due course they turn toward distinctly pianistic idioms, with more insistent sixteenth-note repetitions, tremolos, and bravura octave passages. In short, the music betrays Fanny's new engagement with virtuoso display, an issue surely raised by Felix's presence, but also one that had preoccupied her for some time, as she came to terms with the changing musical landscape of the 1830s—the decade of Liszt, Thalberg, and countless other concertizing pianists. Like Felix, Fanny was keenly aware that the virtuoso wars were fundamentally transforming piano technique. Her first reaction was to minimize her own efforts; to Klingemann she confided, "my playing seems to me quite antiquated after hearing those modern wizards and acrobats, and I shrink back more and more into my nothingness."[101] When Felix got wind of these sentiments, he objected to Lea: "I feel rather provoked that Fanny should say the new pianoforte school outgrows her. This is far from being the case; she could cut down all these petty fellows with ease. They can execute a few variations and *tours de force* cleverly enough, but all this facility and coquetting with facility no longer succeeds in dazzling even the public."[102]

In February, Fanny had vicariously experienced her brother's elegant style of virtuosity when she performed publicly his first piano concerto. Several months later, she composed one of her most remarkable compositions, an etude in the same key, G minor (H-U 333), with sweeping thirty-second-note arpeggiations bolstered by bass octaves, and for the pianist treacherous, if rhapsodic, hand crossings—almost as if to explore further virtuoso idioms in the privacy of her residence.[103] But her etude impresses as much more than a mere technical exercise. Like the great etudes of Chopin, it has enduring musical content and offers an imaginative treatment of form and harmony. And so, after a tumultuous, *fortissimo* opening in G minor, Fanny comes to a pause, and then begins anew *pianissimo*, in B minor, a totally unexpected key foreign to the orbit of G minor. The central portion of the composition traces a series of dizzying modulations that eventually bring us back to the tonic key. Then, just as G minor reemerges, Fanny springs her greatest surprise—the rushing arpeggiations give way to a reflective, interpolated passage that cites material from the first movement of Felix's second piano concerto, op. 40, composed in 1837 for the Birmingham Musical Festival and obviously very much on Fanny's mind in the summer of 1838 (example 8.4). The quotation yields to a few, freely composed bars, as if Fanny were here improvising on Felix's theme; then, the rushing arpeggiations resume and bring the composition to its boisterous end in G minor.

What should we make of this striking parenthetical passage from Felix's op. 40? First, it is autobiographical. Fanny is relating her etude to the music

EXAMPLE 8.4. (a) Fanny Hensel, Etude in G Minor (1838); (b) Felix Mendelssohn, Piano Concerto no. 2 in D Minor, op. 40 (1837)

of her brother, in much the same way as Robert Schumann incorporates into the last movement of his contemporaneous *Noveletten* op. 21 a quotation from a nocturne by Clara Wieck, which intrudes, according to the score, like a "voice from afar" (*Stimme aus der Ferne*). Second, in Fanny's etude (and Schumann's piano cycle), the quoted material serves as a structural interruption. Like Fanny, Schumann continues by freely extending Clara's theme, as if he too were improvising or fantasizing on the extraneous, quoted material before resuming the composition at hand. In each example, the use of quotation opens up the conventional framework of the composition; in Fanny's case, what begins as an etude briefly assumes the character of a musical diary, as she relates her private "career" as a pianist to the very public, international world of her brother.

vii

The outbreak of the measles compelled Felix and Cécile to depart for Leipzig, in an effort to safeguard their infant son's health. There they themselves contracted the disease, so that Felix was unable to conduct the opening concert of the Gewandhaus season. Meanwhile, tragedy visited the family in Berlin: Rebecka's infant son, Felix, fell ill and in November succumbed to measles. Hastening to Berlin, his uncle found Rebecka suffering from a nervous disorder and so delirious that she had to be restrained in bed.[104] Wilhelm, returned from London, endeavored to comfort her by drawing idealized images of the deceased child.

There was no question of Sunday concerts that fall, though Fanny managed to compose another Hölty setting, the duet *Blumenlied* (*Flowers' Song*, H-U 336),[105] and two impressive piano pieces. Like a presentiment of Venice, the *Notturno* in G Minor (H-U 337)[106] begins by alluding with barcarole-like rhythms and doubled melodic thirds to Felix's *Venetianisches Gondellied* in G Minor, op. 19, no. 6, but then expands into a substantial, intense composition that easily dwarfs the miniature dimensions of its fraternal antecedent (example 8.5). Through an imaginative use of register Fanny masterfully creates contrasting timbral effects, ranging from the darkened, murky depths of the piano to the radiant, translucent clarity of the high treble. Paralleling this contrast is a deft manipulation of tonality—while much of the composition is submerged in a chromatically charged G minor, near the end, as delicate sixteenth-note figurations climb into the treble, the music breaks through to a quiet, translucent close in G major. Quite a different affect is explored in the Allegro di molto in D Minor (H-U 338), finished in December 1838.[107] Etudelike, this turbulent composition surely betrays with its downward spiraling triplets and unabated energy some external stimulus, perhaps Rebecka's prolonged disease and suffering. From the opening, refrainlike subject, which

EXAMPLE 8.5. (a) Fanny Hensel, *Notturno* in G Minor (1838); (b) Felix Mendelssohn, *Venetianisches Gondellied*, op. 19, no. 6 (1830)

occurs four times, Fanny spins a lengthy, propulsive movement in rondo form. Several stylistic features suggest that she may have had in mind here a stylized tarantella, the south Italian dance traditionally associated with tarantism—the hysterical behavior allegedly caused by the bite of the tarantula. Be that as it may, the powerful conclusion of the composition, with cascading, broken triplet chords that ultimately reverse direction and climb to the highest register, left a clear mark on Felix, who in 1839 used a suspiciously similar device to end the first movement of his Piano Trio in D Minor, op. 49.

Five more compositions—two piano pieces, two solo lieder, and one duet—flowed from Fanny's pen in the early months of 1839. The Allegro grazioso in B-flat Major (H-U 339),[108] an etude for the right hand, bristles with challenging lines in doubled sixths and other intervals. In contrast, the Allegro assai in A-flat Major (H-U 342), which Fanny published in 1847 as her op. 4, no. 1, is another lyrical *Lied ohne Worte*, with a singing treble line marked *ben legato*. Its fourth bar displays a descending motive resembling a figure in Felix's *Lied ohne Worte* of February 1839 in the same key, op. 53, no. 1, though whether the similarity is coincidental or something more deliberate is uncertain. On the other hand, Fanny's duet *Verschiedene Trauer* (*Different Griefs*, H-U 341),[109] on a text by the Viennese poet Anastasius Grün, begins with a short recitative that seems to adumbrate the beginning of "O Thou that maketh thine angels' spirits" from Felix's second oratorio, *Elijah*, of 1846.[110] The two remaining lieder include *Sehnsucht* (H-U 340),[111] in which she interprets Goethe's poem of a lover's yearning by beginning the composition in A minor and ending in C major; paralleling this tonal experiment is one of form—a modified strophic structure in which Fanny gradually alters details of the recurring music for the five stanzas. The result is a song some 120 measures in length that easily exceeds the dimensions of her typical vocal miniatures, such as "Du bist die Ruh'" ("You Are Peace," H-U 343) of May 1839, a poem Schubert had set in 1823 (D. 776). In a luminous, largely consonant B major, Fanny here reverted to a simple strophic design, with the music of the first sixteen bars repeated for a total of thirty-two, to respond to Rückert's vision of a peace that quiets yearning and pain. Fanny thought well enough of her effort to include the song as the fourth of six planned for her *Sechs Lieder* op. 7, released a few months after her death in 1847.

By February 1839, Fanny was prepared to resume her Sunday concerts and began presenting three, with repertoire drawn from Gluck, Beethoven, Rossini, and her brother. The principal attraction was another star singer, the English alto Mary Shaw, who, like Clara Novello the year before, had triumphed at the Gewandhaus before arriving in Berlin. Under Fanny's direction, Shaw participated in two concert readings of parts of Gluck's *Alceste* and *Iphigenie in Aulis*. At least two other virtuosi visited the Mendelssohn residence, though they did not perform on the series: the French flutist Drouet, for whom Felix and Fanny had played as children eighteen years before (p. 48) and whom Felix now enjoined Fanny to help secure a "crowded" public venue;[112] and a celebrated musician who already had accomplished all that could be desired," because he did not "pretend to be anything" other than what he was, "a brilliant virtuoso"—Sigismond Thalberg.[113] Regrettably, Fanny did not record detailed impressions of this fashionable musician, though she did take the trouble to acquire copies of compositions in his repertoire before hearing him play. Thalberg, who had engaged in a highly touted pianistic duel with Liszt in 1837, seems not to have impressed Fanny in 1839,[114] though she later imitated a special effect popularized in his elegant piano transcriptions and arrangements—the so-called three-hand technique, in which a melody played by the thumbs in the middle register of the piano was surrounded by material assigned to the other fingers above and below, to create the illusion of three hands at the keyboard.

For some time, Fanny and Wilhelm had considered returning to England. But owing to Wilhelm's delay in finishing his commission for the Duchess of Sutherland and Rebecka's weakened health, they abandoned the plan. Instead, at the end of June Fanny accompanied her sister to the western Pomeranian sea resort of Heringsdorf on the island of Usedom. Their "cure" consisted of several weeks of daily bathing—that is, being buffeted by the rough waters of the Baltic—and singing Fanny's a cappella duets, of which one from this time, "Strahlende Ostsee" (H-U 344), survives.[115] Returning restored and refreshed to Berlin in August, Fanny joined Wilhelm in planning to fulfill a long-cherished dream—an extended sojourn in Italy. There, she would resume her familiar double counterpoint of music and art, but in unfamiliar, magical realms.

CHAPTER 9

Italian Intermezzo

(1839–1840)

Do you recognize your daughter, dear mother, frolicking away for hours in the midst of this turmoil, and in a noise which can be compared neither to the roaring of the sea nor to the howling of wild beasts, being like nothing but itself?

—Fanny to Lea Mendelssohn Bartholdy, Roman Carnival, 1840

The long anticipated journey *nach Süden* began on August 27, 1839, by the most modern contrivance, the railroad, transporting Fanny, Wilhelm, Sebastian, their cook, and provisions from Berlin to Potsdam, but no further. Then, by time-honored coach they proceeded to Leipzig, and for a week shared their domestic routine with Felix, Cécile, and "Carlchen." While Wilhelm made an excursion to the Dresden art galleries to meet the writer Ludwig Tieck, there was music making with Felix and Ferdinand David, concertmaster of the Gewandhaus. Fanny found her brother's newest compositions, including the Piano Trio in D Minor, op. 49, "very splendid" (*sehr großartig*) but left in her diary no trace of her own participation. The young Bohemian pianist Alexander Dreyschock, then appearing in Leipzig, impressed Fanny as a "hell of a chap" (*Tausendsasa*), though he had a tendency to wheeze and could be "unpleasant" (*unerquicklich*).[1] She attended a Gewandhaus concert devoted entirely to the music of the pianist, becoming known for the rapid octaves of his dexterous left hand.[2] (Dreyschock later won fame for his trademark rendition of Chopin's "Revolutionary" Etude, in which he dispatched the tumultuous sixteenth notes of the left hand in octaves.)

Since the Leipzig visit resembled a cozy extension of Fanny's life in Berlin, she regarded her family's grand tour, the cultural pilgrimage that for centuries had induced trans-Alpine, European elite to absorb the artistic treasures of Italy, as properly commencing only with their departure on September 4. Proceeding through Erlangen, where they missed meeting the poet Friedrich Rückert (Fanny had set his "Du bist die Ruh'" earlier that year), they reached Nuremberg and consumed a day visiting the spire-capped Artesian well (*schöner Brunnen*), the Gothic St. Sebaldus Church with its hagiographic shrine by the master sculptor Peter Vischer, and the baroque St. Egydien Church, where they admired Anton van Dyck's *Mourning of Christ*. From atop the cathedral in Regensburg they found a commanding view of that city, the Danube, and the Walhalla, a peculiar neoclassical conception under construction, so that its "colossal scaffolding of boards" reminded Fanny not so much of its model, the Parthenon, as of Noah's ark. Conceived by the philhellenic Wittelsbach king of Bavaria, Ludwig I, the Walhalla was designed as a repository for busts of eminent "Germans," loosely construed to include Dutch, Flemish, Anglo-Saxon, and Scandinavian figures—statesmen, composers, artists, and, of course, royalty. When it opened in 1842, its denizens comprised nearly 100 figures commemorating some 1,800 years of history.[3]

The patently nationalistic notion of a Greek temple bearing the name Walhalla, like some contrived elision of Greek and Norse mythology, was incongruous to Fanny, and she questioned too Ludwig's ambitious building projects. The whole of Bavaria, she wrote, impressed as "one large box of bricks, with which the fanciful child living in Munich amuse[d] himself as he like[d]."[4] The king's overarching project was to assert the Germans' historical eminence by linking their cultural heritage to the timeless perfection of Greek statuary and art. To that end, he commissioned new museums (the Glyptothek for Greek and Roman sculpture, the Pinakothek to house his priceless collection of German and Flemish art), churches (the neo-Byzantine Ludwigskirche on the Ludwigstrasse), and strategically placed triumphal arches, all of which dramatically transformed the urban landscape of Munich.

Like a modern-day Maecenas, Ludwig had attracted to his capital accomplished artists to advance his vision, and for two weeks in September the Hensels socialized with them. Presiding was the former Nazarene painter Peter Cornelius—according to Fanny, "very interesting and intelligent, but cutting to the quick, one-sided, and occasionally almost rough"[5]—who had decorated the domed interiors of the Glyptothek with murals of "Greek gods and heroes as prefigures of the Christian message."[6] When Fanny visited the Ludwigskirche, she found the artist engaged on a colossal undertaking, its scope greater than its beauty (*mehr groß als schön*)[7]—the chancel ceiling painting of the Last Judgment, which when completed exceeded the formidable dimensions of Michelangelo's Sistine mural. Among Cornelius's circle were the sculptor Ludwig Schwanthaler and academic painter Heinrich Maria von Hess, and two colleagues whose official work was perhaps not so much art as propaganda for the regime—the former Nazarene Julius Schnorr, commissioned to decorate rooms in the royal residence with paintings on the Nibelungen saga; and Wilhelm Kaulbach, whose *Apotheosis of a Good King* (ca. 1840) would offer a transfigured vision of Ludwig I that "almost mock[ed] the sincerity of Cornelius's *Last Judgment*."[8]

Fanny admired the diversity of art she encountered in Munich—painting, fresco, architecture, sculpture, stained glass, and porcelain—and she dutifully studied Felix's favorite paintings in the Pinakothek, before being overwhelmed by two galleries brimming with ninety-five works of Rubens. Munich offered another fleeting connection to Felix—Delphine Handley, whom he had known before her marriage to an English clergyman as Delphine von Schauroth (see p. 144), an attractive, accomplished pianist, "slim, blond, blue-eyed, with white hands, and somewhat aristocratic."[9] In 1830 and 1831 Felix had played duets and flirted with Delphine in Munich and dedicated to her his hastily composed Piano Concerto no. 1 in G Minor.[10] Now, in September 1839, Fanny was genuinely impressed by Mrs. Handley's improvisations, and she found the pianist's private reading of the concerto surpassed only by Felix[11]—no small praise, for Fanny herself had performed the work on her Berlin debut in February.

In 1830 Felix had journeyed from Munich to Vienna before proceeding to Venice, where he formed his first impressions of Italy. Instead, Fanny and Wilhelm now traversed the Austrian Tyrol and crossed into Italy via the Stelvio Pass. Along the way, they passed Hohenschwangau, a romantic medieval castle recently restored in Gothic style by the Bavarian crown prince. On a nearby Alpine lake Fanny observed swans resembling "floating stars on the dark-green water," a striking image she likely recalled when, within a year, she composed the wistful *Schwanenlied* on a Heine text. By paying a florin, the travelers crossed the Austrian border unimpeded and, pausing for the night at the foot of the daunting snow-capped peaks looming before them, steeled themselves for the ascent the next day, "ten hours of uninterrupted up-hill work."[12] In the 1820s engineers had arduously cut dozens of hairpin turns into the slopes to reach the summit, Santa Maria, which at 2,757 meters impressed Fanny for its utter desolation. Drinking a toast to their family's health, they surveyed the panorama before them. Only Sebastian, who had read that all of Italy had appeared to Hannibal's exhausted army when the Carthaginians crossed the Alps, was disappointed not to discern the boot of Italy and Sicily before the uneventful descent to Bormio.[13]

At Lake Como, Fanny's world was transformed; here, she wrote, she beheld Italy for the first time—the forbidding Alpine scenery yielded to lush subtropical vegetation and terraced gardens with a profusion of southern plants—lemons, oranges, roses, luscious figs, and "gigantic aloes growing out of the walls."[14] Arriving in Milan on September 30, they paused for a week when Sebastian fell ill with chicken pox. With "a maw like an ostrich" the tourists "consumed" the cathedral and its multitude of fretted spires,[15] later in the century described by Mark Twain as "a fairy delusion of frostwork that might vanish with a breath."[16] At the Brera Fanny admired Raphael's *Wedding of the Virgin (Sposalizio)*, as Felix had before her; in Fanny's estimation, Raphael was the only artist to achieve a mature style "through love and tenderness, not storm and struggle."[17] But a performance at La Scala did not please: the singers were mediocre, the ensemble good only because the same work had been given a "million times," and the ballet dreadful—all in all, a "conglomeration of absurdity and indecency."[18] And after viewing da Vinci's *Last Supper* in the refectory of Santa Maria delle grazie, Fanny could only record this sobering assessment: "It must have been a wonderful painting. Engravings do not nearly do it justice. But it is in wretched condition, with horse stalls nearby, and the marvelous old building is in disrepair and used as a barracks."[19]

From Milan, the Hensels proceeded in quick succession to Brescia, Verona, Vicenza, and Padua. Everywhere Fanny encountered signs of "splendid" and not so splendid "decay"—the recently excavated Temple of Hercules in Brescia, the Grotto of Catullus at Sirmione on Lake Garda, and the Roman fortifications and Arena in Verona, where men had fought with wild beasts in the distant past, and posterity, like so many "fools of antiquity," now admired every crumbling stone.[20] In Vicenza, time leapt forward to the sixteenth century, for, as Fanny noted, "half of the city" was the work of the master architect Andrea Palladio. In Padua, Fanny found the Byzantine cupolas above the Basilica of St. Anthony bewildering but still identified with the saint after seeing in the nearby Scuola di S. Antonio Titian's frescoes on Anthony's miracles. "As soon as I become Catholic," she mused in her diary, "he will be my patron saint. He revives lifeless glass and plates—that's of use in a household."[21]

On October 12, the Hensels boarded a postal ship at Mestre and, like Felix nine years before, crossed the serene waters to Venice. "As one first approaches and sees it floating upon the water," she wrote to Berlin, "one scarcely knows which to admire most, its grandeur or its fairy-like beauty."[22] She was soon exploring the bejeweled Byzantine marvels of St. Mark—"splendid, fantastic, secretive, and wonderful" was her verdict[23]—the Doge's palace and Bridge of Sighs, which connected to dank subterranean dungeons where prisoners had been tortured, and the Rialto. Many of these landmarks were familiar from pictures—they were "old friends, only superior to my recollections of them."[24] Her first excursion with a gondola conveyed her to the roseate island of St. Giorgio, where she visited the eponymous Palladian church, distinguished by its harmonious proportions and, in the chancel, two late paintings of Tintoretto, *The Last Supper* and *The Gathering of Manna*. During the next three weeks she also explored the island of Murano, for centuries center of the prized Venetian glass industry, and the Lido, not yet the popular bathing resort that offended the Victorian John Ruskin's sensibilities, but, according to Fanny's nine-year-old son, a "small tongue of land with walls to protect Venice from the sea."[25]

In her letters and diaries Fanny alluded to an earlier German tourist, Goethe, who left an engaging account in the *Italienische Reise* of his 1786 visit.[26] Indeed, in her first letter to Berlin Fanny ceremoniously quoted and adapted Goethe's description of his own arrival in the "beaver republic" (*Biberrepublik*) from Mestre some fifty years before and revealed she owned a well-used copy of his literary travelogue, still relevant in 1839, for, in Fanny's estimation, so little had changed.[27] But she was mindful too of another, authoritative voice— that of her brother, who in September sent recommendations for the Venetian sojourn, most of which Fanny and Wilhelm followed. Thus, she was not to miss the Veroneses in the Casa Pisani, or Giorgione's zither player in the Galleria Manfrini, for which Felix instructed Fanny to compose music. And he enjoined her to visit frequently his favorite painting, Titian's *Assumption of Mary*, then installed in the Accademia, where, Fanny reported, at least 400 works of art were stored for lack of exhibition space.[28] Felix encouraged Fanny to relate her viewings of Titian's masterpiece to his own: "Think of me at *The Assumption of Mary*; notice how dark Mary's head, indeed her entire figure appears against the clear heavens, how her head is completely brown, and how there is a certain rapturous expression and effusive bliss no one would believe who has not seen it. If you do not think of me with the golden, heavenly sheen behind Mary, then stop at once. Likewise with two certain angel heads, from whom even cattle can learn about beauty."[29]

Whether contemplating the rich array of Venetian churches—the Gothic Frari in which Titian was entombed, the High Renaissance San Salvador, and the octagonal baroque Santa Maria della Salute—or sipping coffee on the Piazza, the "finest open space in the world,"[30] Fanny willingly played the tourist. But not all was idyllic. In their hotel they encountered a plague of fleas and mosquitoes; Fanny's eyelids were swollen with bites, and her hands looked as though they had been tattooed. Salvation came in new quarters generously offered by Aurèle Robert, brother of the Swiss artist Léopold Robert, whom Wilhelm had known in Italy years before that artist's suicide in 1835. Aurèle was helpful too in procuring models for Wilhelm to sketch, chiefly peasant women who wore white veils and carried jugs of water, which Fanny and Wilhelm mixed with wine in an effort to fortify their health.

Before leaving La Serenissima, Fanny composed a piano piece, the *Serenata* in G Minor (H-U 345).[31] Its key, meter (6/8), and lulling, gentle rhythms tie it to her earlier *Notturno*, though she now accompanied the sustained treble melody with staccato chords instead of blurry arpeggiations. Like the *Notturno*, the *Serenata* is thoroughly Venetian in character—no longer imagined, however, but based on Fanny's own experiences, for she allied her composition with the genre of the barcarole. A later, autograph fair copy prepared sometime after her return to Berlin in 1840 actually bears the title *Gondelfahrt*

(*Gondola Journey*) and displays a vignette by Wilhelm illustrating a gondolier transporting a woman and children on the Grand Canal, with Santa Maria della Salute in the background.[32] A few bars into the *Serenata* Fanny elided her Venetian impressions with those of Felix, by paraphrasing a telltale, rising passage from Felix's *Venetianisches Gondellied* in F-sharp Minor, op. 30, no. 6 (1835). For a brief moment, she joined her compositional voice to his and, as it were, retraced musically her brother's steps (example 9.1).

EXAMPLE 9.1.   (a) Fanny Hensel, *Serenata* in G Minor (1839); (b) Felix Mendelssohn, *Venetianisches Gondellied*, op. 30, no. 6 (1835)

i

In foul weather the Hensels departed Venice on November 4. When a car-dinal legate refused them permission to cross the Po because of high water, they turned back to Rovigo. Only after the weather deteriorated the next day, prompting Fanny to coin the bilingual term *schlechtissimo*, and after they paid an inflated fee were they able to continue on to Ferrara and Bologna, traverse the Apennines, and reach their "penultimate destination"[33]—Florence. In a city surfeited with art, Fanny opined that the "Pitti Palace and Uffizi alone might supply the world from their stores."[34] The Tribune Room of the Uffizi, then as now a magnet for art aficionados, afforded her with one glance the flawless Venus de Medici and Titian's erotically tinged, recumbent Venus of Urbino. Still, Fanny preferred another Titian she encountered in a less accessi-ble room—the seductive *Flora*, with a "white blouse and a handful of flowers, looking as much like a goddess as a scamp"[35]—and argued for its immediate transfer into the Tribune. She was dumbfounded at the lax security in the galleries—would-be artists permitted to copy masterpieces left wet palettes perilously near the originals. Fanny made the requisite visits to the cathedral and Brunelleschi's dome but generally found the churches less impressive than their Venetian counterparts—the Florentine interiors were all similar, "white and black."[36] Some relief from the crush of art was afforded by strolls in the Boboli Gardens and an excursion to Fiesole, which offered commanding, hill-side views of the city.

In the nocturnal darkness of November 26 the Hensels entered their prin-cipal destination—Rome. For thirty scudi a month they secured a comfort-able, if not extravagant, four-room apartment on the Via del Tritone, near the Piazza Barberini and Bernini's baroque Triton Fountain, not far from the Casa Bartholdy above the Spanish Steps, where Fanny's uncle Jacob Bartholdy had resided. Fanny wrote to Lea that Wilhelm and Felix's reputations supported her new lifestyle like a pair of bolsters (*Ruhekissen*), and she felt all the more obliged to honor her family.[37] Wilhelm revived old Italian contacts to ease access to the galleries and St. Peter's, and as sister of the "faultless wonder" (*monstrum sine vitio*) the music bibliophile Fortunato Santini had praised in 1830, Fanny soon attracted the attention of musical circles. Without having touched a piano in months, she made her Roman "debut" at a *sauree* (soirée) of the German violinist Ludwig Landsberg, formerly of the Berlin Königstadt Theater, and now proprietor of a music firm on the Corso.

For that occasion, she performed a Beethoven piano trio,[38] but within days had discovered another, more formal outlet for serious chamber music, the French Academy at the Villa Medici, where on Sundays the eminent painter Ingres gave concerts. In Paris he had known Fanny's brother Paul as a cellist and carefully distinguished him from Felix as *votre frère qui joue si bien de la basse*. Moving to Rome in 1834, Ingres succeeded the flamboyant Horace

Vernet as director of the Academy; the two could scarcely have been more dissimilar. Sporting a substantial beard, dark complexion, and Arabian dress, Vernet was swept up in the vogue of exoticism then impacting French painting; when Wilhelm confessed to a longing for the East, the Frenchman assured him that from Trieste he could reach Egypt in only a fortnight.[39] In contrast, Ingres relished a somewhat staid role in French art as a classicist, a conservator of timeless values rather than an innovator. His choice of music reflected the same aesthetic preferences, as Fanny revealed to Lea: "As you know, he [Ingres] is a great fiddler before the Lord, and after dinner we had trios, as is the case every Sunday. The whole French Academy were assembled, all looking thorough *jeune France*, with beards and hair *à la Raphael*, and nearly all handsome young men, whom I could not blame for longing after the flesh-pots of Egypt, in the shape of the balls Horace Vernet used to give. There is no dancing to Ingres's fiddle, for he will have nothing but ultra-classical music. You may think of us there now and then, on a Sunday evening. I thought much of Felix in that house, as you may fancy."[40]

Of Italian musical practices Fanny formed a dim opinion, as had Felix nine years before. Indeed, to her mother she admitted that since Munich not a pitch had pleased her—in Rome, the music in social gatherings was of poor quality; opera was banned during Advent; and the papal singers, if they exhibited a certain external polish, sang out of tune.[41] But she reserved her most withering rebukes for the Italian organists, whose inept playing the priests mercifully silenced while chanting the Mass, and the *pifferari*, folk musicians who descended from the Abruzzi during Advent to venerate Mary with shawms and bagpipes. If Berlioz was sympathetic enough to these rustic musicians to imitate their sound in the bucolic third movement of *Harold en Italie* (1834), Fanny found the raucous music rousing her early in the mornings the "most horrid...ever produced by human lungs and goat's hide."[42]

Just days after their arrival the Hensels watched Pope Gregory XVI process with his cardinals into the Sistine Chapel. Fanny's view was obstructed, for she had to sit with other women in the background behind a trellis, and the billowing incense and candle smoke exacerbated her nearsightedness. Nevertheless, with Wilhelm she gained access to "what few strangers are allowed to see, the private apartments of the Pope": "This tough old man of seventy-five has had all his rooms newly furnished, in good but simple taste—red damask, with green curtains—as if he means to occupy them for years to come."[43] His fifteen-year pontificate in fact lasted until 1846. In 1831, after a protracted conclave, Bartolomeo Alberto Cappellari had been chosen to succeed the sickly, short-reigned Pius VII (1829–1830), whose catafalque and solemn funeral rites Felix described in his letters from Rome to Berlin.[44] Taking his name after the legendary Gregory I, the new Holy Father espoused with one notable exception conservative views. Not just suspicious of liberal reforms, he banned railroads in the Papal States and applied a French pun to dismiss them as *chemins d'enfer* (infernal roads), not *chemins de fer* (iron roads). But on December 3, during Fanny's Roman sojourn, his encyclical *Supremo Apostolato* was read at the fourth Provincial Council in Baltimore, Maryland; its unequivocal condemnation of slavery lent the authority of the church to the growing abolition movement in the northern United States. There is no mention of this worldly event in Fanny's diaries; instead, she commented on the Stanze, the suite of receiving rooms near the pope's private quarters, where she viewed Raphael's frescos commissioned by Julius II early in the sixteenth century. Of these, Fanny was most impressed by the expulsion of Heliodorus from the Temple (2 Maccabees 3). Nearby was Raphael's *Transfiguration*, of special interest because of Wilhelm's painstaking copy for the Prussian monarch, the chief product of his student years in Rome; for Fanny, the copy did justice to the original.

As German tourists, the Hensels naturally socialized with the established colony of German émigrés in Rome. They included Count von Lepel, adjutant of Prince Heinrich of Prussia; the artists August Kaselowsky (a former pupil of Wilhelm) and Friedrich August Elsasser; and, recently arrived from Berlin, the artists Wilhelm von Schadow and Eduard Magnus. For the latter, Fanny completed a duet on some verses of Goethe she had first essayed in 1825, "Das holde Tal" ("The Fair Valley," H-U 351);[45] its idyllic A major recalls some turns of phrase seemingly borrowed from Felix's *Singspiel* of 1829, *Heimkehr aus der Fremde*.[46] Of Fanny's aloof cousin, the former Nazarene Johannes Veit, she saw relatively little, though she did mingle with two of his collaborators on the frescos in the Casa Bartholdy, Franz Catel and Johann Friedrich Overbeck. The latter was just finishing a painting for Frankfurt, *The Triumph of Religion in the Arts*, when the Hensels paid him a visit, provoking a rare marital disagreement and affording an example of Fanny's independent judgment in matters artistic:

> We went to see Overbeck's sacred picture, which struck me as dull, feebly poetical, and slightly presumptuous. . . . He has actually had the arrogance to place in a corner of the picture himself, Veit, and Cornelius, as the elect spirits of the day. *Je trouve cela colossal.* I dare say it will look better in the engraving, for it has a certain simplicity and breadth of composition which makes it easy to understand. . . . If the engraver is clever, too, he will go to the originals for the heads of the great men whom Overbeck turned into old women. I am bound to state that Wilhelm is of a different opinion, and thinks much more highly of the picture than I do; but I will bow to no authority, even his, having eyes of my own which I mean to use.[47]

Writing to Berlin, Fanny admitted she had succumbed to the "mania for antiquities"—in Rome beauty was foreign to "anything that has two legs and a whole nose," and one excluded any building "with all its pillars standing."[48]

In December alone, the Hensels visited the Church of San Paolo outside the city gates, near the traditional resting place of St. Paul; the pyramid of Caius Cestius (12 B.C.) that in Madame de Staël's estimation immured a minor bureaucrat "from the oblivion which had utterly effaced his life";[49] the Baths of Caracalla (ca. 216 A.D.); the Tomb of Scipio (ca. 280 B.C.); the catacombs on the Appian Way; and the cylindrical Augustan tomb of Caecilia Metella, wife of Crassus (ca. 80 B.C.), of whom Byron speculated, "Perchance she died in youth; it may be, bowed / With woes far heavier than the ponderous tomb / That weigh'd upon her gentle dust."[50] Relevant to more recent memory was the Protestant Cemetery, where the Hensels paused at the grave of Jacob Bartholdy, though they made no mention in their letters of those of Keats and Shelley.

As 1839 neared its end, the Hensels celebrated Christmas by fabricating a tree from cypress, orange, and myrtle branches. The papal services left Fanny unexpectedly nostalgic for Berlin—instead of a sizeable choir and orchestra, even if of average quality, a small cohort of musicians offered thin, wafting chants soon lost in the vast recesses of St. Peter's. Nevertheless, Fanny divulged to Felix that at the pope's entrance into the Sistine Chapel on Christmas Eve the musicians broke into a fugal passage, allying sacred polyphony with the centuries-old authority of the church. Perhaps, Fanny ventured, moving the German fatherland somewhat south was not a bad idea.[51] From Leipzig her overworked brother, who had not written since the birth in October of his daughter Marie, sought to align memories of his own Roman experiences with his sister's. Was she able to identify cardinals by their miters and lappets, and did papal musicians still commit horrendous parallel fifths when they added improvised embellishments? Felix had just finished playing for Ferdinand Hiller several of Fanny's piano caprices, and when they searched for snags in the music, they found none, only pure pleasure (*reines Vergnügen*).[52]

Perhaps buoyed by this encouragement, and using a rented, "played-out rattletrap" of a piano, Fanny returned to composition in February and March 1840 and quickly produced a miniature a cappella trio for Lea's birthday on verses from Goethe's *Divan* (H-U 347) plus four more substantial works—three piano pieces (H-U 346, 349, and 350)[53] and a cavatina for voice and piano on a text from Ariosto (H-U 348). If the Allegro moderato in A-flat Major impresses as a songlike *Lied ohne Worte*, the other two piano pieces pair slow introductions to extended Allegros in sonata form, not unlike Felix's own three Caprices op. 33 of 1835. Each introduction adumbrates the thematic material of the linked Allegro. Thus, a descending figure treated in imitative counterpoint (Fanny later recalled it in the opening movement of her piano cycle *Das Jahr*) undergoes transformations to generate the swirling, descending sixteenth-note patterns of the ensuing Capriccio in B Minor. In the Largo–Allegro con fuoco in G Minor, she begins with a duetlike introduction that suggests another somnolent *Gondellied*; its characteristic descending triad then serves as the upbeat for the explosive fast movement, launching an energetic theme that mirrors the contours of the Largo.

We do not know the occasion for Fanny's sole Ariosto setting, completed on March 13, 1840, "Deh torna a me," but her interest in the poet may have been stimulated when she visited Ariosto's residence and grave in Ferrara, on the way from Venice to Rome.[54] For her subject Fanny selected verses from the penultimate canto of *Orlando furioso* (1532), in which Bradamante, a female Christian knight whose lance is powerful enough to unhorse any opponent, pines for her lover, the Saracen Ruggero, imprisoned on an island by the sorceress Alcina. Ariosto's monumental epic poem, some 30,000 lines in length, had inspired baroque operas from Vivaldi and Handel, and Fanny in turn contributed a graceful if modest cavatina, the opening of which could have been written by Mozart.

The New Year brought some misfortune—for several weeks Wilhelm was incapacitated by a severe stomach ailment and unable to work. But, he assured Lea, Fanny was an excellent nurse, and a music apostle who "converted the heathen" with her performances of Haydn.[55] Happily, by the time of the carnival, Wilhelm had recuperated, so that the Hensels could lose themselves in the madcap celebrations that, Goethe had recorded, allowed everyone to be "as foolish and absurd as he wishes."[56] Indeed, little had changed since the eighteenth century on the Corso, the narrow thoroughfare appointed for the festivities, which ran from the foot of the Capitoline to the Piazza del Populo—there were the unbridled horse races, the crush of revelers seething around carriages three and four abreast, onlookers from verandas and balconies above hurling hardened confetti with abandon onto the pedestrians, and what Charles Dickens described a few years later as "every sort of bewitching madness of dress."[57] Fanny reported that many of the masks, worn partly to preserve anonymity, partly to fend off confetti missiles, were unchanged since Goethe's time, though because of her eyeglasses she could only don a veil. The culmination of the carnival was the evening of the *mocoletti*, the small candles that celebrants attempted to keep kindled even as they vied to extinguish those of their neighbors, an enterprise made challenging in 1840 by the wind, dust, and rain. "Do you recognize your daughter, dear mother," Fanny wrote, "frolicking away for hours in the midst of this turmoil, and in a noise which can be compared neither to the roaring of the sea nor to the howling of wild beasts, being like nothing but itself?"[58]

ii

In preparation for Holy Week (April 12–19, 1840) Fanny asked her sister Rebecka to send the musical examples from the 1831 services Felix had interspersed in his Roman correspondence, but only after Rebecka had transcribed his musical notation into letter names, lest Italian censors sensitive to revo-lutionary tremors somehow interpret the music as encoding a conspiracy.[59] Fanny was determined to judge the services for herself, and like Felix, she recorded her impressions, though unfortunately only a portion survives in her letters and diary.[60] The procession of cardinals on Palm Sunday was most impressive but, to Fanny's surprise, instead of verdant fronds, they bore staffs twisted and bundled together like brooms. Of particular interest was Allegri's *Miserere* (after Psalms 50 and 51), sung since the seventeenth century by the Papal Choir at Matins on Wednesday and Friday of Holy Week. A ban on copying the music (those in defiance were subject to excommunication) had added to its mystery, enhanced over the years by the accretion of florid orna-ments overlaid on Allegri's stark sonorities. According to Fanny, Allegri's musi-cal skeleton was used by the choir "as a canvas to be embroidered with their traditional and somewhat rococo embellishments." After hearing the *Miserere* in 1770, the fourteen-year-old Mozart relied on perfect pitch to prepare his own copy, and in 1831 Felix transcribed the rapturous, recurring refrain, in which the descant soars to an unearthly high C, transforming, as he observed, the boy sopranos into angels. To judge by Fanny's transcription of the same passage, in 1840 the climactic high note was at least a step lower; indeed, she writes that the choir, diminished in strength from eighty to nineteen, began in A minor and progressively lost its pitch in a gradual, unauthorized descent to somewhere between F and G minor.[61]

The musical high point of the week came on Good Friday, with its spe-cial, prescribed liturgy for the one day when a Mass was not offered. Like Felix, Fanny was intrigued by the St. John Passion of Victoria (1585), the lead-ing Spanish composer of the Counter-Reformation. It consisted of choruses for the crowd (*turba*) scenes alternating with unadorned monophonic chant. As in Bach's St. Matthew Passion, there was a narrator and a part for Christ; nevertheless, for Fanny (and Felix), Victoria's austere a cappella music lacked the monumentality and dramatic cogency of Bach's masterpiece. The repeti-tive, static cadences of the chant and "obsolete" singing styles reminded her of "ancient mosaic," but even "more stiff and death-like." After the entrance of the pope came a Latin sermon "preached with alternate pathos and rant-ing," and then a series of collects for "literally, God and the whole world," to each of which the cardinals genuflected, though they did so "like old women at a tea party." During the adoration of the cross by the divested, barefooted pope, the choir sang Palestrina's *Improperia* (*Reproaches*), and Fanny had one more opportunity to experience the sacred music of the Italian Renaissance, based not on major and minor keys but on the ancient church modes, and related only distantly to the Lutheran practices with which she was familiar in Berlin.

For another month the Hensels remained in the Eternal City, unlike most tourists, who departed after Easter. The couple made an excursion to Tivoli to see the celebrated cascading waterfalls and fountains of the Villa d'Este, which later inspired a scintillating piano piece by Franz Liszt; Fanny composed a trio to a hastily improvised text of Wilhelm, though it has not survived.[62] Of course, there was no end of Roman villas to explore. The (no longer extant) Villa Mills, built early in the century on the southeast edge of the central Palatine, impressed Fanny as an eternal spring that defied the seasons. The "celebrated Italian transparency" of its air rendered distant objects remarkably clear,[63] a quality Fanny endeavored to capture in the translucent, nocturnelike Allegretto grazioso in E Major inspired in situ (H-U 357). As part of her plan to compile a second, musical diary, she titled this piece *Villa Mills*, though removed that heading in 1846 when it appeared as the third of the *Vier Lieder für das Pianoforte* op. 2.[64] From the late fifteenth-century Villa Mellini on the Monte Mario in northwest Rome (now an astronomical observatory), Fanny found wonderful views of the city, though the Villa Wolkonsky to the southeast, current site of the British embassy, totally enraptured her. Her diary reads, "Roses climb up as high as they can find support, and aloes, Indian fig-trees, and palms run wild among capitals of columns, ancient vases, and fragments of all kinds.... The beauty here is all of a serious and touching type, with nothing small and 'pretty' about it.... Nature designed it all on a large scale, and so did the ancients, and the sight of their joint handiwork affects me even to tears."[65]

At the Villa Wolkonsky the Hensels organized on May 20 a party worthy of Boccaccio's *Decameron*, with painting and drawing, singing of part-songs in the open air, and the playing of boccie and other games.[66] By May their circle had expanded to include the talented Norwegian pianist Charlotte Thygeson, related to the Danish sculptor Thorwaldsen; and several young laureates from the French Academy. The painter Charles Dugasseau (1812–1885) was a pupil of Ingres; the composer Georges Bousquet (1818–1854), recipient of the Grand Prix de Rome in 1838, enjoyed some success in writing sacred music for San Luigi dei Francesi, the national French church of Rome. At the Villa Wolkonsky Bousquet gave Fanny a few meditative verses from Alphonse de Lamartine's mystical *Harmonies poétiques et religieuses*, which she promptly set as a duet for soprano and tenor (*La Tristesse*, H-U 354).[67] The poet's haunting images of love and loss, which inspired a major piano work from Liszt in 1847, inform this composition, in which the saddened soul (*l'âme triste*) is compared to a sleeping star of a nocturnal sky that silences noise from its vermillion arch. Fanny set the verses in a lilting, elegiac G minor, with a contrasting section in chordal style for the "mysterious choruses" that suggest heavenly grace, a passing angel, or a pious man.

Another *pensionnaire* of the French Academy, the composer Charles Gounod (1818–1893), developed an intense dependency on Fanny, acknowledged in his memoirs as a "very clever pianist, physically small and delicate" who had "rare powers of compositions," and whose "deep eyes and eager glance betrayed an active mind and restless energy."[68] Awarded the Prix de Rome in 1839, the impressionable Gounod arrived at the French Academy intent upon steeping himself in Palestrina's sacred music; his major work of this time was a Mass premiered at San Luigi. But Fanny exploded Gounod's musical horizons by inculcating him with German music: "Thanks to her great gifts and wonderful memory, I made the acquaintance of various masterpieces of German music which I had never heard before, among them any number of the works of Sebastian Bach—sonatas, fugues, preludes, and concertos—and many of Mendelssohn's compositions, which were like a glimpse of a new world to me." The experience was nearly overwhelming for the excitable young musician: "Romantic to a degree and full of passion," Gounod seemed "quite upset by his introduction to German music. It has startled him like a bombshell, and I should not wonder if it did as much damage."[69] Fanny's diaries and letters reveal that her Roman repertoire was indeed heavily German, and accommodated the music of J. S. Bach (Concerto in D Minor, BWV 1052, and one of the triple concerti), Mozart, Hummel (Piano Quintet), a heavy dose of Beethoven (*Fidelio*, piano concerti, and especially piano sonatas, including the *Moonlight*, *Waldstein*, *Appassionata*, and perhaps the *Hammerklavier*), and her brother. One evening in May, as Gounod, Bousquet, and Dugasseau took turns sitting while Wilhelm executed their portraits, Fanny played through nearly all of *Fidelio* and four Beethoven piano sonatas, only to observe Gounod behave as if intoxicated and exclaim, "Beethoven est un polisson" ("Beethoven is a rascal").[70]

Gounod and his compatriots were also charmed by Felix's piano music; indeed, they styled themselves the *trois caprices*, after his capriccios for piano in A minor, E major, and B-flat minor, op. 33, which Fanny interpreted at the piano as three character sketches. Undoubtedly, the Frenchmen were familiar too with her new compositions, including two impressive piano pieces from April and May 1840. In the first, titled variously *Abschied* (*Departure*), *Abschied von Rom* (*Departure from Rome*), and *Ponte molle* (H-U 352),[71] she expressed her anxiety and sadness about leaving Rome, which she compared to a slow-acting poison or medicine.[72]

The Ponte molle (Milvian Bridge) over the Tiber was the last station European travelers encountered before entering or departing Rome, and it became emblematic of the Hensels' Roman memories. Fanny's piece begins with a dissonant, drooping phrase in A minor that pauses inconclusively on a half cadence, prolonged by a fermata that momentarily befuddles our sense of strict metrical time. The composer provided a valuable clue about the plaintive melody and soft, pulsating accompaniment that follows: above the soprano line she added the words "Ach, wer bringt etc.," thus identifying her inspiration as the opening of Goethe's poem *Erster Verlust* (*First Loss*), which she had twice set as a lied in 1820 and 1823 (example 9.2; see pp. 43 and 75). *Ponte molle* then recalls in its central section a happier time, represented by a turn to C major and change in meter from 9/8 to 6/4. An intensely chromatic transition leads us back to the opening material, that is, the present, so that, like Goethe's poem, the composition as a whole explores the present and past by subtly playing on our sense of musical time—of actual experience and memory. By quoting Goethe, Fanny plays too on our sense of musical genre, as her character piece encroaches more and more upon the world of the German art song.

The second piano work, *Villa Medicis* (H-U 353),[73] continued Fanny's new practice of preserving selected Roman compositions as a "kind of second diary" by naming them after her "favorite haunts."[74] In A-flat major, it begins with a majestic melody set against eighth-note chords and a bass line in sturdy octaves, Fanny's musical counterpart to the stately sixteenth-century villa on the Pincian Hill that Napoleon had acquired in 1803 and deeded to the French Academy. But a second, contrasting theme in a higher register, accompanied by sextuplet arpeggiations and a staccato bass line, diverts the music to the unexpected key of A minor and injects an element of pathos and romantic whimsy. Alternating between the two themes, Fanny gradually thickens the texture with widely flung, thirty-second-note arpeggiations that turn this piece into a something of a virtuoso tour de force climaxing near the very top of the keyboard (on the pitch f″″). After a final statement of the opening theme, *Villa Medicis* ends quietly in the middle register, with bell-like octaves in the deep bass.

EXAMPLE 9.2. Fanny Hensel, *Ponte molle* (1840)

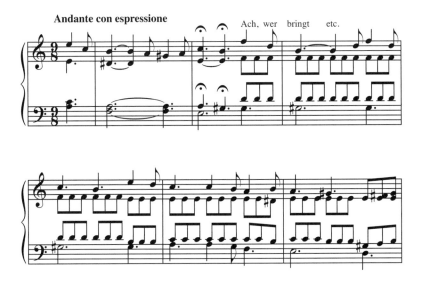

As it happened, the Hensels spent their penultimate day in Rome (May 31) at the villa, where Ingres invited them for a private farewell gathering. The gardens were closed to the public and a piano brought outdoors, and for the length of the day there was music making, first of all Beethoven violin sonatas with "Papa Ingres" to the "splash of a fountain," with "the bearded fellows [French Academy students]...lying about on the steps and pedestals of the pillars, in a state of unmitigated astonishment at our being able to enjoy ourselves in this manner from morn till dewy eve." In the evening the company reconvened in the assembly hall, where Fanny "preluded [i.e., improvised] as softly as possible" before playing the slow movement of Beethoven's Fourth Piano Concerto, the *Moonlight* Sonata, and "the beginning of the grand sonata in F-sharp minor"—possibly the transcendent Adagio of the *Hammerklavier* Sonata, or Hummel's imposing Sonata in F-sharp Minor, op. 81, which Robert Schumann had struggled to master in the early 1830s. After dinner, Fanny absorbed the magical evening from the balcony: "The stars above, and the lights of the city below, the glow-worms and a long trailing meteor which shot across the sky, the lighted windows of a church on a hill far away, the delicious atmosphere in which everything was bathed—all combined to stir in us the deepest emotion."[75] As midnight approached, there was piano music of Mozart and Felix, and part-songs, concluding with Felix's simple but affecting setting of Heine's *Auf ihrem Grab* (*On Their Grave*, op. 41, no. 4). Two lovers chattering beneath a linden tree fall silent, but know not why. The chorus was Fanny's last music in Rome.

ii

She had lived there for six months in an "atmosphere of admiration and homage"; even in her youth, she reflected, "I never was made so much of as I have been here, and that this is very pleasant nobody can deny."[76] Notwithstanding this affirmation, now she prepared to resist the allure of the city, where time and space seemingly stood still, by embarking on the final stage of the grand tour, leading to Naples, the Sorrentine coast, Amalfi, and as far south as Paestum, which Felix had reached in 1831. Departing Rome on June 2, the Hensels were joined by Bousquet as far as the Alban Hills, where they explored the seventeenth-century papal palace of Castel Gandolfo, Basilian abbey of Grottaferrata, and the ruins of Tusculum that afforded a good view of the Roman *campagna*. Climbing the Monte Cavo (3,130 ft.) on mules, they passed Campo Annibale, where according to legend Hannibal had looked down upon Rome. On the way to Genzano, the topic of conversation turned to Gounod. Bousquet revealed that his sensitive compatriot had succumbed to the influence of the Dominican Père Lacordaire, who had recruited Gounod and other young Frenchmen to join a society dedicated to applying "Christian art to convert the worldly minded." Fanny found their resolution in stark contrast to the "hideous materialism and insatiable avarice now so rampant among the French."[77]

In Ariccia, Bousquet was replaced by the Lyonais painter Pierre Bonirote, who accompanied the Hensels to Gaeta (there Grillparzer had written the poem that inspired Fanny's song *Italien*), Capua, and Naples, which they entered in the moonlight of June 5. The next day the sirocco was blowing, and from the balcony of their lodging at the Hotel de Rome they glimpsed Vesuvius at first through a thick fog, but then made out villas and villages near its base, and perceived the cone as "uncanny and awful in the midst of the glorious landscape."[78] They had a commanding view of Castellamare di Stabia and the Sorrentine peninsula jutting out to Campanella, its furthest point, and in the open sea beheld Capri, sybaritic island resort of Roman emperors and, since the "rediscovery" in 1826 of its phantasmagoric Blue Grotto, an increasingly popular tourist site. Of the environs of Naples they surveyed the Castel dell'Ovo, with its impenetrable, blocklike tufa walls rising from the diminutive islet of Megaris; the Pizzofalcone hill, site of the earliest Neapolitan settlement from the seventh century B.C.; and, rising from below, the bustling street of Santa Lucia. Anchored in the bay were three English men-of-war, appearing "as calm and majestic as if they had only come on purpose to add to the beauty of the scene."[79] In fact, the English military presence was part of a diplomatic effort to apply a "slight pressure" on the Bourbon Ferdinand II, ruler of the Kingdom of the Two Sicilies, to resolve mounting tensions concerning the Sicilian sulfur trade.

At the art museum (*Studi pubblici*), Fanny unexpectedly recognized the mezzo-soprano Pauline García Viardot, who since meeting Fanny in Berlin in 1838 (see p. 226) had made a London debut as Desdemona in Rossini's *Otello* in 1839 and married the director of the Paris Théatre italien. Several men, including Berlioz, Gounod, and the Russian novelist Turgenev, would figure in the life of this remarkable musician, but in June 1840 the newlywed was on her honeymoon and played the role of the tourist, like Fanny, who visited the museum repeatedly. There Fanny discovered an "unwieldy ragamuffin," the Farnese Hercules, among a vast collection of antiquities, all sufficient "for a complete history of art," even if not displayed artfully, as in Munich, but merely "stowed away." Artifacts from Pompeii and Herculaneum, augmented nearly daily by the ongoing excavations, captivated Fanny. There was furniture elegantly inlaid with silver, but also a thousand other practical objects that had "continued in use these 2000 years nearly unchanged." "The world did not look so very different then, after all," she concluded, "only everything had an elegance and a splendor entirely lacking in our utensils of the same kind."[80]

On Pentecost Monday (June 8) the Hensels drove by carriage to a village at the foot of Mt. Vesuvius to attend the Festival of the Madonna dell'Arco, the subject of a striking painting the Swiss artist Léopold Robert had exhibited in 1828.[81] There they experienced Neapolitan culture at its most colorful. Fanny described "hundreds of vehicles, such as Robert painted, ornamented with green boughs, handkerchiefs, and ribbons, the people in them carrying sticks like forks, from which were suspended feathers, flowers, saints' pictures, baskets, spoons, and a thousand other articles purchased at the fair near the church.... Many of the physiognomies and complexions were quite African; one girl especially, who was beating a tambourine and laughing, looked a perfect savage. In the church a man was crawling about on his knees and licking the floor—a charming penance."[82] Though Fanny did not reveal the purpose of the festivities, an earlier English tourist, who experienced the event in 1825, left a vivid account:

> In the intervals of the masses that are said by the priests the people go down on their knees, and placing their tongues on the floor, proceed in this attitude from the church door to the altar, licking the dust all the way. By the time they arrive before the virgin they are completely exhausted: they however remain on their knees (their tongues and their noses blackened with filth), till they have gone through a certain number of prayers, and then leave the church with the full assurance of having obtained the favor of the Madonna and having gained indulgence from many years of purgatory. Their throats are then cleansed in the village with abundant libations of wine, their heads decorated with oak leaves and branches of peeled nuts, that are made to hang like grapes about their hair; they are placed upon donkeys and carried home to Naples, singing drunken songs in praise of the Madonna del Arco.[83]

Imagining an ancient frieze from Pompeii, Wilhelm seized the opportunity to sketch the ribald scene, which for Fanny resembled a "bacchanalian procession," a comparison drawn more forcefully by the English tourist who had preceded them: "such a mixture of filth and piety, drunkenness and devotion, must have had its origins in the ancient Bacchanalian orgies."

Their next excursion was by water, to the islands of Procida and Ischia. On Procida, they encountered women in modern Greek attire, some of whom, it seemed, had attended the recent Festival of the Madonna dell'Arco. To disembark at Ischia, covered with an exotic profusion of aloes, figs, pomegranates, and vines, they had to ride out of the sea on mules, surrounded by a mob of *lazzaroni* "howling, shouting, and fighting for the honor of conveying us to land."[84] After a day's rest in Naples, they then set out to ascend Vesuvius on Sebastian's tenth birthday, June 16. Climbing for two hours on horseback through lush vineyards, they reached the lava flow of the previous year, still warm to the touch. At a higher altitude, the last traces of vegetation vanished, and, entering the "haunted region," they disembarked at the foot of the cone. From there Fanny and Sebastian were transported in sedan chairs for another hour in an "almost perpendicular" ascent, while Wilhelm and the guides slipped on the loose rock and hardened lava streams. Reaching the summit, they looked down upon the "diabolic mess" of the crater: "The sulfurous smell, the colors such as you see nowhere else in nature, green, yellow, red, and blue, all poisonous hues, and the ashy gray at the bottom of the cauldron, the smoke, now thick, now thin, rising from all the crevices, and enveloping everything while it conceals nothing—all this, changing with every step, made up a spectacle of horror."[85] After sunset the party began the arduous descent and in the darkness sank to their knees in ashes as they groped their way toward civilization. Toward midnight Fanny was cheered by the sight of "houses, carriages, chairs" and other "institutions" that she especially appreciated after "making acquaintance with the old gentleman and his domestic arrangements."[86]

For the next week the Hensels remained in Naples, and from their balcony they watched a romantic specter—the moon emerging from the crater of Vesuvius. Fanny had rented a piano and resumed composing, and when Bousquet arrived from Rome, he was among the first to hear her *neuen Sachen*.[87] What she played for him is unclear, though among her manuscripts are seven undated pieces likely finished during the Italian sojourn—some of them, presumably, in Naples. The sole piano composition in this group, the Allegro vivace in B Major (H-U 356), is a brightly lit work animated by constant, shimmering sixteenth-note tremolos in the inner voices; it appeared in 1847 as the second of the *Vier Lieder für das Pianoforte*, op. 6. Less significant are two Goethe settings, the male part-song "Laß fahren hin" (H-U 360) and solo lied *Hausgarten* (H-U 355), which Fanny performed for Bousquet in July, along with songs of Schubert.[88] That composer left a conspicuous mark on the singular ballad *Der Fürst vom Berge* (H-U 359), set to a fanciful poem by Wilhelm about a supernatural lord who from a mountain dais controls the flow of water to the valley below. Clearly emulating Schubert's *Erlkönig*, Fanny sought to capture a sinister mood in the piano introduction by establishing a static pedal point in the treble against rising octaves in the bass.❺ In comparison to Schubert's triangular drama between the father, son, and Erlking, Fanny's strophic setting is admittedly one dimensional; nevertheless, she later prepared a fair copy of the song for the couple's *Reisealbum*, a musical album of their Italian journey, to which Wilhelm appended an illustrative vignette.[89]

The other three compositions likely produced during the Italian sojourn indulged Fanny's abiding fascination with Heine's *Buch der Lieder*. If the part-song "Dämmernd liegt der Sommerabend" ("Dusky Lies the Summer Evening," H-U 361) betrays nothing particularly Italianate, two other songs, the duet for two sopranos "Mein Liebchen, wir saßen beisammen" ("My Love, We Sat Together," H-U 362)[90] and solo song *Schwanenlied* (*Swan Song*, H-U 358), clearly allude with their 6/8 meter, gentle trochaic rhythms, and flowing accompaniments to the genre of the barcarole. "Mein Liebchen" is among

EXAMPLE 9.3. Fanny Hensel, *Schwanenlied*, op. 1, no. 1 (1840)

Fanny's most impressive efforts and dwarfs Felix's modest solo setting of the same Heine text, *Im Kahn* (*In the Bark*), composed in 1837 for the wife of Ignaz Moscheles.[91] In a three-part *ABA'* form, the duet contrasts a lyrical framing section, in which the voices sing largely in thirds and sixths against subdued piano arpeggiations that occasionally spill over the first soprano part, with the faster central episode that depicts the passage of the boat past the *Geisterinsel* (Isle of Spirits). Here Fanny turns to the minor, with rapid staccato passagework in the piano and imitative exchanges between the voices. The setting ranks among the best nineteenth-century German duets and offers a rewarding comparison to Brahms's eerily dark setting of the same text, published in 1886 as *Meerfahrt*, op. 96, no. 4, which also revives the barcarole, albeit in a guise recalling Felix's *Venetianische Gondellieder*.

Fanny explored another watery journey in the *Schwanenlied*; cast in a melancholy G minor, its mood conjures up the *Notturno* and *Gondelfahrt* for piano solo (H-U 337 and 345). In the poem, Heine's falling star of love is mirrored by the dropping leaves of the apple tree and the singing swan that sinks into a watery grave, and in Fanny's music by subtle references in the bass line to a descending tetrachord—symbol of the lament—never explicitly stated in complete form but nevertheless felt in an intensely poignant way (example 9.3). Any number of fine details add to the allure of this composition—the mesmerizing, broken arpeggiations in the piano, the delayed climax in the vocal part, the fermata and rests for *Grab* (grave) in the second strophe, and the surprise, blurry ending in G major. The result is a magical union of great poetry and great music that shows the full range of Fanny's talents as a songwriter. Not surprisingly, when in 1846 she ventured into print with her op. 1, a collection of six songs, she chose *Schwanenlied* to introduce the opus.

iii

On June 24, the Hensels embarked in a four-oared skiff for Capri. They expected to reach the fabled island in four hours, but when adverse winds took them off course, they made instead for Sorrento and arrived badly sunburned, as if "dipped in saltpeter" and "looking almost like pickled pork." When another attempt to reach Capri failed, they turned their backs on Vesuvius and the Bay of Naples, traversed the Sorrentine peninsula, and set sail for Amalfi. Now the sea, smooth as a sheet of glass, obliged and allowed them to explore freely the coastline to Salerno. From there they traveled as far south as Paestum to see the three Greek temples, but fear of malaria encouraged them to turn north to Castellamare di Stabia. By donkey they rode to Pompeii, all the while uncomfortably eyeing Vesuvius. Nothing could be more awe inspiring, Fanny wrote, "than the aspect of this stern destroyer, still armed with the same power of doing mischief, while at his feet are the speaking witnesses of the horrid crime he committed eighteen centuries ago."[92] The ruins posed more questions than answers. Were the pits of the theaters used solely for musicians? Why was common household furniture lacking among the preserved artifacts, in contrast to the many articles of luxury? And why had the ancients not made the uncovered houses habitable again after the cataclysmic eruption?

Returned to Naples, the Hensels intended to follow Goethe's precedent and visit Sicily, but the heat proved too enervating for Fanny, and she remained with Sebastian, while Wilhelm departed by steamer on July 2. For nineteen days the artist explored Palermo and Messina, and made an excursion to Taormina, near the site of the ancient Greek city of Naxos. Wilhelm found the Sicilians "liberal, cultivated, hospitable, and wealthy" and was impressed by the display of carriages in Palermo—finer, he claimed, than in London.[93] In Palermo he encountered too the colorful annual festival of its patron saint, Santa Rosalia, thought to have saved the city from the plague of 1624, and executed portraits of Sicilian nobility. During the return voyage to Naples, despite the heaving seas, he continued to sketch among his indisposed fellow travelers.

Meanwhile Fanny consumed her time reading Bulwer-Lytton and George Sand and socializing with Bousquet and Gounod, newly arrived from Rome. She could not refuse their company, she wrote her husband, "without seeming prudish and ridiculous to the young people."[94] But Fanny took strong exception to the *Lettres d'un voyageur* of George Sand—"what a confused, eccentric, unhappy soul!" she confided to her diary. "How fatal the falseness, since one knows that a woman is writing, and that she always appears behind the mask of a man. I thought I would find much about Italy in it, but instead nothing at all."[95] More to her liking were Bulwer-Lytton's English novels, even if she preferred his *Rienzi, the Last Consul of Rome* (1834, the inspiration for Wagner's 1842 opera) to the more appropriate *Last Days of Pompeii* (1835).

Early on the morning of July 21, Fanny scanned the sea with a telescope for signs of a vessel. Not until the afternoon did a faint dot appear on the horizon and gradually relieve her mounting anxiety. For nearly three more weeks the reunited couple lingered in Naples and prepared to return to Germany. New members of their circle included the artist Wilhelm von Schadow and the retired English actor Charles Kemble and his daughter Adelaide, who had a pleasant enough singing voice, though Fanny found her "very ugly" and "abominably dressed."[96] The Duke of Montebello, French ambassador to the court of Naples and son of Jean Lannes, Napoleon's able marshal, commissioned several portraits of his family from Wilhelm, and at the duke's villa Fanny performed the Bach Concerto in D Minor on an Erard before a "very grateful audience."[97] Then, on August 11, they boarded a steamer for Genoa.

For much of the voyage the seas were unkind to Fanny; while her husband, unfazed by the elements, sketched on the deck, she remained incapacitated in her cabin. Upon arriving in Genoa, she exclaimed, "Thalatta! Thalatta!" ("The sea! The sea!"), betraying that she knew her Xenophon, though, unlike the Greek army that had surveyed the Black Sea from Mt. Theches in 401 B.C., she exulted in having the sea behind, not before, her. At the Palazzo Brignole (now Palazzo Rosso) Fanny and Wilhelm admired paintings of Titian, Van Dyck, and Rubens, including one Rubens "depicting himself and his wife surrounded by fauns and satyrs" that Wilhelm found enchanting though it was "rather too indecent" for Fanny. They also visited the Marchese Gian Carlo di Negri, a Genoese poet and patriot, who received in his villa many celebrities, including his countryman Paganini, Stendhal, and George Sand, and collected curiosities—busts of Columbus and Paganini, and the snuff box of Napoleon. Later that evening Fanny read of the misadventures of another Napoleon, the future Louis Napoleon Bonaparte, arrested in Boulogne after his failed landing and attempted coup against Louis-Philippe. "What a crackbrained and detestable man!" she recorded in her diary.[98]

In Milan Fanny perused her favorite artwork at the Brera and now found the cathedral more impressive than a year before. Proceeding to Como, the Hensels visited the composer Ferdinand Hiller, who accompanied them on a leisurely excursion around the lake. Before crossing the Alps via the St. Gotthard Pass, they spent a memorable evening on August 23 in Bellinzona, in the Italian canton of Ticino. At an inn they met an elderly gentleman who, after learning that they were bound for Berlin, inquired after Alexander von Humboldt. When Wilhelm offered to take a message to the scientist, their companion replied ruefully, "Io sono un uomo infelicemente conosciuto" ("I am an unhappily known man"). He was the Count Federico Confalonieri, condemned to death in 1824 by the Austrians for his political activism in Lombardy and then, after commutation of his sentence, imprisoned without access to family, visitors, or books at the Spielberg in Brno. Upon his release in 1835 he was deported to the United States, and had only recently received permission to return to Italy. The count had known Fanny's uncle Jacob Bartholdy; while Wilhelm sketched the count's portrait, other family connections began emerging from the conversation, so that Confalonieri soon felt like an "old acquaintance." "He seemed to me far the most remarkable man I have seen in Italy," Fanny recorded, "and to think that such is the treatment Austria bestows on men of his stamp!"[99]

When the carriage drag broke at the St. Gotthard Pass, the Hensels had to descend by foot in total darkness to the Urserenthal; the next day, as they traveled through heavy mist and rain, Fanny could recognize only limited features of the Swiss terrain she had seen with her parents and siblings in 1822, some eighteen years before. On August 27, 1840, the anniversary of the Hensels' departure from Berlin, they reached Zurich, where they learned of a political amnesty declared by the new Prussian monarch, Frederick William IV; Fanny welcomed the news as if she herself were one of the pardoned.[100]

From the raging cataracts near Schaffhausen they crossed into German territory and continued on to the Black Forest, but on a whim then made an excursion to see the cathedral in Strasbourg, just as German-French tensions were escalating over the Rhine River. Their itinerary led them to Heidelberg and Frankfurt, where they spent time with the artist Philipp Veit, son of Dorothea Schlegel and director of the Städelsche Art Institute, and the Jeanrenauds, relatives of Felix's wife. When they reached Leipzig early in September, Fanny found her brother recovering from a serious illness—possibly a stroke—suffered only two weeks before. Pale but in good spirits, he was scheduled to depart for England to conduct his new *Lobgesang* (*Hymn of Praise*) Symphony, op. 52, at the Birmingham Musical Festival. For three days, as he regained strength, he took walks with Fanny. Not until September 9 did she play for him, probably some of her compositions conceived in Italy, and the following day he reciprocated by rendering at the piano the *Lobgesang*, a symbol of musical Lutheranism, complete with a setting of the familiar chorale "Nun danket alle Gott" ("Now thank we all our God") and blending elements of the symphony, cantata, and oratorio. Commissioned for the 400th anniversary of the invention of movable type and premiered just weeks before at the Leipzig

Thomaskirche, the composition celebrated the Gutenberg Bible as the agent of the triumph of light over darkness. Despite some similarities to Beethoven's Ninth, the unified structure of the symphony impressed Fanny as *originell und tief* (original and deep).[101]

Having bid their farewells, Felix departed early on September 11 for England and the Hensels for Berlin. They had begun and concluded their grand tour in Leipzig. The serpent had consumed its tail, as Fanny observed to Lea,[102] and, having experienced the full allure of Italy, she now would face the future by reaffirming her identity as a German musician.

CHAPTER 10

Domestic Tranquility

(1840–1842)

One had always the fullest assurance that Madame Hensel said less rather than more than she felt.

—Sarah Austin

Within weeks after returning to Berlin, the Hensels found themselves stuck in the "prose" of domestic life; their familiar Berlin surroundings were no match for the poetry of Italy.[1] The accession of Frederick William IV to the Prussian throne in June 1840 had ushered in the prospect of fundamental changes, including vague promises of a constitution, but Fanny remained wary and skeptical, as her diary reveals. Invoking a divine right to rule Prussia as a Christian state, the king resorted to pseudomedieval constructs and even considered reviving the feudalistic, romantic Order of the Swan, which Fanny later dismissed as sentimental nonsense.[2] In September and October 1840, some 60,000 Berliners swore oaths of fealty to a monarch enthroned in a display of pageantry and knighthood that "shook Berlin to its core," though Fanny wondered why he had not used the opportunity to do something for the poor.[3]

When the king attempted to resolve lingering tensions with Catholics in the Rhineland, Fanny's staunch Lutheran convictions took hold: "Tetchy, out of control arrogance of Catholics in all parts of the world. The king wants to win them over through concessions, as futile an enterprise as turning ice into fire. These people are not to be converted or won; one must respond to them with utmost firmness, otherwise one is lost."[4] On the question of constitutional reform, though, Fanny was considerably more liberal minded. When the Jewish physician Johann Jacoby asserted in *Vier Fragen* (*Four Questions*, February 1841) the right of citizens to participate in the government, Fanny described his work as a "very interesting, well written, sharp, political/legal pamphlet."[5] But Jacoby's courageous activism—Felix noted that *Vier Fragen* could not have been published a year before[6]—led to its banning and the prosecution of the author for lèse-majesté. Unwilling to yield power, the king continued to vacillate for the next few years on the question of the constitution, so that Heinrich Heine was inspired to pen an acerbic rebuke in the poem *Der neue Alexander* (*The New Alexander*):

Ich bin nicht schlecht, ich bin nicht gut,	I am not bad, I am not good,
nicht dumm und nicht gescheute,	Neither a curse nor a blessing;
und wenn ich gestern vorwärts ging,	If yesterday I moved ahead,
so geh ich rückwarts heute.	Today I'm retrogressing.
Ein aufgeklärter Obskurant,	Enlightened and obscurantist,
und weder Hengst noch Stute!	Both bigoted and doubting!
Ja, ich begeistre mich zugleich	I'm equally inspired by
für Sophokles und die Knute.	Both Sophocles and knouting.
Herr Jesus ist meine Zuversicht,	I find my faith in Jesus Christ,
doch auch den Bacchus nehme	In Bacchus my consolation,
ich mir zum Trösten, vermittelnd stets	Between these two extremist gods
die beiden Götter extreme.	I seek conciliation.[7]

As if mindful of Heine's caricature, Fanny compared the Prussian state to a pilgrim intent upon reaching Jerusalem by taking one step back for every two forward.[8]

Among the king's cherished projects was the revitalization of Berlin as a center of the arts; to that end, he consulted with his ministers about reorganizing the Academy and began recruiting illustrious representatives to the capital. Ludwig Tieck was secured to direct the theater and Peter Cornelius to give new impetus to painting and sculpture. Wilhelm and Jacob Grimm, celebrated for their collection of folk tales but lately associated with liberals prosecuted as the Göttingen Seven, were rehabilitated and summoned to Berlin, and overtures were made to the poet Rückert as well. In all, the king advanced seven such invitations, though each in a sufficiently vague, indefinite manner, Fanny reported, so that the group became known as the Seven Sleepers (*Siebenschläfer*).[9] What role, if any, Wilhelm might play in this new vision remained dubious, and by May 1841, she was again imagining taking up a *Wanderstab* and returning to Italy.[10]

For some time, Wilhelm's prospects indeed remained uncertain. In October 1840, he was dispatched to the neighboring Mark of Brandenburg to arrange a *tableau vivant* for ceremonies there honoring the new Prussian monarch. The subject matter was a scene from the Thirty Years' War Schiller had treated in his *Wallenstein* trilogy (1800): the surrender of the Mark in 1633 to the imperial commander Count Wallenstein. Wilhelm left a detailed sketch in which the Bohemian commander receives his vanquished Protestant foes, while the astrologer Seni divines prophecies from an astral globe (not long after the surrender, Emperor Ferdinand II ordered the assassination of Wallenstein, whom he suspected of treason).[11] But no major commission resulted from this assignment; instead, Wilhelm continued to work on his painting for Lord Egerton of another military figure, the Duke of Brunswick, and began sketches for a new painting on the departure of the apostle Paul and Barnabas from Antioch.[12] For six years Wilhelm had not exhibited any work in Germany, and Fanny's concern about his declining visibility increased until May 1842, when the king requested the return from England of Wilhelm's *Christ in the Wilderness*, which the court subsequently purchased and had displayed in September at the annual Berlin exhibition. Also shown was the newly finished *Duke of Brunswick*, viewed publicly only weeks before in Brunswick, at the invitation of the duke's son. In Berlin, the painting garnered critical praise in the *Vossische Zeitung* for its unusual lighting effects, suggesting a harmonious blend of moonlight and artificial light that isolated the duke as he took up his sword at the incipient, muffled sounds of the battle and prepared to find his destiny as a much lamented, feted hero of the war against Napoleon.

Though the king's new vision of the arts excluded Wilhelm from a prominent position, it did include a high-profile role for his brother-in-law. To that end, in November 1840 Paul delivered an official letter to Felix in Leipzig asking if he would return to Berlin to spearhead the revitalization of music. A protracted correspondence between Leipzig and Berlin now ensued,[13] marred from the start by the royal inability to define the duties of the new position. In exchange for a generous salary of 3,000 thalers, Felix would give concerts by royal command and direct the music division of the Academy, though the particulars remained unspecified. Fanny was under no illusion that the initiative would produce the long hoped-for reunion with her brother and feared that discussions would founder, partly because of Felix's "prickliness" (*Reizbarkeit*), and partly because of the king's indecision.[14] Seeking clarification from the royal ministers, Felix visited Berlin in May 1841, all the while concealing his purpose from Lea and Rebecka, so as not to raise false hopes, even though, as Fanny wrote, the "entire city" already knew of the affair.[15] Now Felix became stuck in the prose of administrative bureaucracy and, against his better judgment, agreed to a compromise. He would return to Berlin for a trial year as a royal Kapellmeister while the Academy was reorganized. Likening Berlin to a sour apple that must be bitten,[16] Felix arrived in Berlin with his family, augmented by the birth in January of his third child, Paul, and at the end of July moved into rooms above Fanny's quarters in the *Gartenhaus*.

In the weeks following her family's return from Italy, Fanny prepared to resume her Sunday concerts. At Christmas she took delivery of a new Viennese piano that had a rich bass but thin middle register and began practicing her brother's Piano Trio in D Minor, op. 49, the composition that had prompted Robert Schumann to label Felix the Mozart of the nineteenth century. Between January and July 1841, Fanny directed at least eight concerts at her residence,[17] attended by a brilliant succession of celebrities and dignitaries, many of whose portraits Wilhelm now took the opportunity to execute—the painter Peter Cornelius, Prussian diplomat Christian Carl Josias von Bunsen, sculptor Bertel Thorwaldsen, Russian count Matthias von Wielhorsky (to whom Felix would dedicate his second cello sonata, op. 58), opera singer Giuditta Pasta, and, for a few weeks in May, Felix himself. Unfortunately, details of Fanny's programs are scarce, but among the works she performed were her brother's Psalm 114, op. 51 (January 24), with a chorus of twenty-five; excerpts from the oratorio *Judith* by Carl Anton Eckert (February 7), a young pupil of Felix with whom Fanny played Beethoven violin sonatas; the second act of Gluck's *Iphigenie auf Tauris* (May 30); and Felix's piano trio, a piano quartet by Mozart, various lieder, and the finale to Weber's *Euryanthe* (July 25). In addition, Fanny now made her second public appearance as a pianist at a charity concert of "dilettantes" presented at the Berlin Schauspielhaus on March 4, when she performed Felix's piano trio with Leopold and Moritz Ganz. As in 1838, the press again respected her privacy; the *Allgemeine musikalische Zeitung* identified her as "Frau *P.H.*" (Frau Professorin Hensel), and the Berlin *Spenersche Zeitung* mentioned her as an "extremely skilled, artistically cultured pianist," a phrase in which only the feminine form of the noun (*Pianistin*) betrayed her gender.[18] Fanny described the event as *moutarde après dîner* and at first considered offering Felix's effervescent *Serenade und Allegro giojoso* op. 43 for piano and orchestra. But the no less difficult piano trio, she explained to him, lay more comfortably in her fingers, and because she was not accustomed to performing in public, she felt obliged to choose a piece that would not unsettle her.[19]

The same month Fanny helped organize another, special performance at her residence in honor of her mother's birthday—a series of *tableaux vivants* designed by Wilhelm and realized by thirty participants. No information has come down to us about the subjects of the *tableaux*, though Fanny's contribution has survived, albeit in an incomplete, at times nearly illegible manuscript score: to introduce the "living pictures," she composed a melodrama, a dramatic scene for narrator, chorus, and piano, on a text by Wilhelm that was declaimed by Eduard Devrient (*Einleitung zu lebenden Bilder*, H-U 371). One hundred and sixty guests attended the performance in the unheated *Gartensaal*,[20] a multimedia event that explored the relationship between the musical and visual arts, and thus revisited the double counterpoint that animated Fanny's married life with Wilhelm. After a short piano introduction

that alludes to the central aria from her cantata *Lobgesang*, the scene opens
with the artist (i.e., Wilhelm) bereft of inspiration and announcing that he has
destroyed his brushes and palette. A chorus of airy spirits confronts him; they
are disembodied tones that, accompanied by Mendelssohnian elfin music in
the piano treble, seek shape and visual definition. As the work progresses, the
airy music becomes more corporeal and grounded—we hear passages in imitative counterpoint, and then one in block chordal style, as the chorus bids the
artist to engulf them with "visible beauty," to allow them to appear, ultimately
achieved by the unveiling of the *tableaux vivants*.

i

During the closing months of 1840 Fanny corresponded with Felix about an
idea she had for an opera on the *Nibelungenlied*, that hoary, revered Middle
High German epic poem about the deeds of Siegfried and Chriemhild, culminating in the murder of Siegfried and theft of the Nibelung hoard of gold
by Hagen (vassal of Chriemhild's brother Gunther), Chriemhild's subsequent
betrothal to Etzel (Attila), and her revenge on Gunther at the court of the
Huns, ending with the grisly decapitations of Hagen and Gunther. Fanny's
stimulus was the play *Der Nibelungenhort* by Ernst Raupach, a popular dramatist whose prolific pen yielded eighty-one plays between 1820 and 1840 for
the Berlin theater; *Der Nibelungenhort* reached the stage in 1828 and appeared
in print in 1834. Initially, Felix, who spent much of his career vainly searching
for the ideal opera libretto, was intrigued: "Do you know, I find your idea
about the Nibelungen luminous? It hasn't left my head, and I will devote my
first free days to reading the poem again, for I have forgotten all the details,
and retained only the general outlines and colors, which strike me as marvel-
ously dramatic."[21] For the moment, Fanny seems to have relived the uneasy
experience of competing with her brother. Writing in December, she imagined he was already further along in fashioning the libretto than she was, for
she had been able to visualize only the characters and framework of the opera,
not its segmentation into definite scenes. And there was the practical issue of
how to conclude an opera in which most of the characters were slaughtered
in the final scene. Succumbing to levity, Fanny suggested that Felix compose
a "polonaise with chorus" for the scene in which Chriemhild discovers Siegfried's corpse, and then fashion a double chorus of Huns and Nibelungs to the
nationalistic text of the *Rheinlied*, "they shall not have it" ("sie sollen ihn nicht
haben"), sung to the strains of "Ei du lieber Augustin."[22]

Traces of the Nibelung project soon disappeared in the siblings' correspondence, and there is no evidence that Fanny or Felix ever began musical
sketches. Instead, Fanny's idea languished until Heinrich Dorn composed his
opera *Die Nibelungen* in 1854, a few years after Wagner began contemplating

his own, monolithic vision of Old German–Norse mythology eventually released to the world in 1876 at Bayreuth. But if dramatic composition eluded Fanny in the sheltered Berlin of the prerevolutionary *Vormärz*, she did successfully return to her preferred, small-scale musical genres, and began producing late in 1840 and into 1841 a series of compositions that ably demonstrated her mastery of the piano character piece and art song.

Three of the piano pieces—the Allegro molto quasi presto in E Major (H-U 364), "Il saltarello Romano" in A Minor (H-U 372), and Allegro molto in A Minor (H-U 376)—date from December 1840 to June 1841; to these we may add four other, stylistically similar pieces, assigned to the period 1840–1843 in Fanny's catalogue of works—the Allegro molto vivace in G Major (H-U 365), Andante soave in E-flat Major (H-U 366), Allegro molto in G Major (H-U 368), and Allegro molto vivace in A-flat Major (H-U 369).[23] That Fanny attached special significance to this group of seven is clear on two grounds: in 1843, she included several pieces in an album of her piano music copied for Felix,[24] and in the last year of her life she incorporated four into two sets of piano pieces, op. 4/5 and 6, ultimately published in the months after her death in 1847.

Many of the piano pieces display thickened, arpeggiated textures probably deriving from the three-hand technique popularized by Sigismond Thalberg in the late 1830s, and then appropriated by Liszt and many other virtuosi, including Felix.[25] In Fanny's adaptation of the device, as in her earlier applications, each hand serves double duty: the right hand projects a singing melody above, and the left hand articulates a bass line below, while a seamless series of harplike arpeggiations simultaneously unfolds between the two. A variant texture obtains in the Allegro molto vivace in A-flat Major. Here Fanny employs hand crossings to surround the melody with rapidly repeated chords above and below. The results are challenging virtuoso passages with widely spaced arpeggiations, as in the Allegro molto quasi presto, Allegro molto vivace in G Major, and Allegro molto, that reveal Fanny's technique to have accommodated wide, awkward leaps. The sonorously enriched registers support her determined exploration of varied harmonic colorations, which expand the tonal palette of the character piece, and in the process stretch Fanny's familiar model of statement, departure, and return. Thus, in the center of the Allegro molto vivace in G Major she modulates to the most distant C-sharp minor before eventually finding her way back to the tonic. The effect of these harmonic peregrinations is at once to challenge the traditional tonic-dominant axis of tonality and to lend the music a certain harmonic spontaneity and unpredictability.

Whether Fanny had in mind specific texts or topics for these piano compositions is an intriguing issue that merits discussion. One piece, the Allegro molto quasi presto (later published by the composer as her op. 4, no. 3), begins with an anacrusis motive in the treble that outlines a traditional horn call, an

allusion strengthened as the figure descends through the course of the composition, so that it resonates more and more in lower registers associated with
the instrument. The hunting horn was a stock figure of German romantic
poetry and its wandering male protagonists, and it is, perhaps, not difficult
to imagine Fanny's Allegro as a stylized *Jagdlied* (hunting song) or *Wanderlied*
(wandering song). But in another piece, Fanny made her intentions quite
clear through a specific title. *Il saltarello Romano*, finished in March 1841,
was elaborated from a sketch recorded the year before in Rome, so that the
piano composition impresses as a reminiscence of folk music she experienced
during her Italian sojourn. Curiously, a second, fair copy of the composition
bears the title *Tarantella*,[26] after another type of Italian folk dance—one associated, as we have seen (p. 82), with the hysteria of tarantism rather than the
small leaps (*saltus*) of the saltarello. We might ascribe the generic confusion
to another decisive influence on *Il saltarello Romano*—the saltarello finale of
Felix's *Italian* Symphony (1833–1834), which shares its key (A minor) with
Fanny's piece (example 10.1) and moreover introduces toward the middle of
the movement a second dance later identified by Felix's English student William Rockstro as a tarantella.[27] Be that as it may, Fanny produced a lively,
spirited composition with whirling, dizzying melodic configurations, offbeat
accents, and zesty dissonances—all in all, an effective display piece that can
stand among the best artful imitations of Italian folk music. Not surprisingly,
she later chose to include the work as the last of her *Vier Lieder für das Pianoforte*, op. 6.

In May 1841, two months after she finished *Il saltarello Romano*, Fanny's
thoughts again turned south as she welcomed to Berlin Georges Bousquet,
with whom the Hensels had shared "heavenly days" the year before in Italy—
all "so unforgettable," Fanny mused in her diary, "like the stars in heaven."[28]
Bousquet's visit may well have prompted a remarkable marital collaboration, a
compilation of eighteen of Fanny's Italian compositions into a bound album,
to which Wilhelm contributed an illustrated title page and vignettes for the
individual works, chiefly solo lieder and piano pieces.

Titled *Reise-Album 1839–1840*, the project was finished by mid-Novem-
ber 1841.[29] It emblematizes the double counterpoint of music and painting
with which Fanny idealized her domestic life with Wilhelm. The consonant
blending of the arts is announced on the "official" title page, where Fanny
and Wilhelm jointly share authorship.[30] Beneath the title in gold lettering
Wilhelm has drawn two female figures, identified below as "Deutschland—
Italien"; here we see Germany presenting to Italy the very same *Reisealbum*,
around which the two figures revolve in circular, harmonious unity. Wilhelm
was playing on the trope of German *Sehnsucht* (yearning) for Italy, familiar in
German arts and letters of course from Goethe's poetry but also in particular from the painting *Italia und Germania* of Friedrich Overbeck (1828), one
of the Nazarene painters Wilhelm knew during his first Italian sojourn. The

EXAMPLE 10.1. (a) Fanny Hensel, *Il saltarello Romano*, op. 6, no. 4 (1841);
(b) Felix Mendelssohn, *Italian* Symphony op. 90, Finale

parallels are unmistakable: in Overbeck's painting the two allegorical female figures hold hands and are situated to suggest a harmonious coming together. Behind Germania we see a Gothic town and a hint of the Alps; behind Italia, an Etruscan villa and, in the distance, the Mediterranean. For the title page, Wilhelm has reversed the figures, so that Deutschland now appears on the left, and Italien on the right. And there is no background to distract us from the *Reisealbum*, the focal point of the drawing, into which the Hensels gathered their musical and visual reminiscences of their first Italian sojourn, now arranged to form a kind of chronological travelogue.

The inaugural composition in the album is, appropriately enough, *Nach Süden* (*Southward*), on a text by Wilhelm that Fanny newly composed in April or May 1841, possibly around the time of Bousquet's visit; the song appeared posthumously in 1850 as her op. 10, no. 1.[31] In this energetic setting the voice sings of a *Reisechor* of birds fleeing from the north to the land of "eternal flowers." Wilhelm's vignette depicts the first leg of the journey: above a train departing from Berlin to Potsdam a bird flies southward; just perceptible in the carriage behind the locomotive are the faces of the travelers. Fanny finished two versions of this song—one with welling sixteenth-note arpeggiations,[32] the other, preserved in the *Reisealbum*, with propulsive, repeated chords—to capture the frenetic motion of migrating birds, a symbol of her own *Reiselust*.

Progressing further into the album, we find next two pieces on Venetian subjects, *Gondelfahrt* (H-U 345, see p. 239) for piano solo, and, newly composed in June 1841, Fanny's first setting of the young poet Emanuel Geibel (1815–1884), who published his first volume of verse that year in Berlin. A few years later Geibel succeeded where others failed—he managed to craft an opera libretto on the Loreley legend that inspired the captious Felix to begin composing scenes before his death in November 1847 cut short the budding collaboration. But in 1841, it was Geibel's *Gondellied* that Fanny chose to set, and she produced another evocative example of this quintessential Mendelssohnian genre, for which, she wrote, she had a "particular predilection."[33] Her tuneful song, released in 1846 as op. 1, no. 6, features lapping arpeggiations in the piano treble that ultimately submerge into the bass,◉ and a brief excursion from the major to minor mode for "the air is soft like the play of love" ("die Luft ist weich wie Liebesscherz"). In Wilhelm's vignette, Fanny is serenaded by Wilhelm, who appears as a Venetian gondolier (figure 10.1).

By and large the remaining contents of the *Reisealbum* were recycled from compositions written in Italy in 1840, already discussed in the previous chapter. Seven form a group around Rome (among the vignettes are an artist contemplating Roman ruins, views from the Villa Medici and Villa Mills, and, for the travelers' departure from Rome, the Porta S. Giovanni). There then follows *Il saltarello Romano*, renamed *Tarantella* to suggest a more southern Italian clime and to introduce the next point of the itinerary, Naples, and two pieces, the Allegro molto in B Major for piano and Heine duet "Mein

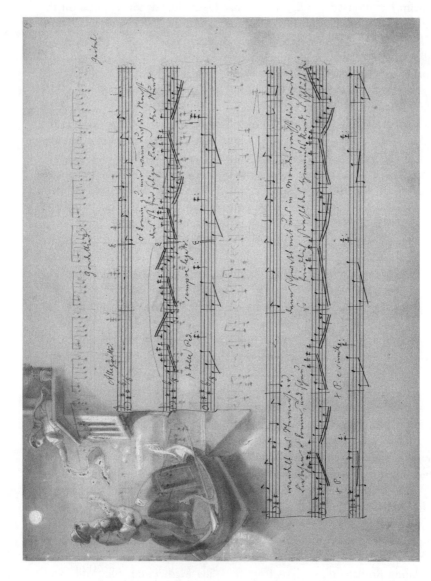

FIGURE 10.1. Fanny Hensel, autograph manuscript of *Gondellied*, op. 1, no. 6, with vignette by Wilhelm Hensel, 1841 (Berlin, Mendelssohn Archiv, Ms. 163, p. 19)

Liebchen, wir saßen beisammen," for which Wilhelm drew romantic views of Vesuvius and the magical island of Capri. Sources for the vignettes of the remaining five pieces are not all identifiable, but in at least three Wilhelm placed mountainous—possibly Alpine—scenery, while the last piece, a setting of Goethe's *Hausgarten*, completes the journey by alluding to the *Gartenhaus* of Leipzigerstrasse no. 3. The last four lines of Goethe's poem read: "And though through distant lands we love to roam / From hence we came, and here we are at home: / We turn, from all the charms the world presents us, / To this one corner, which alone contents us."[34] Writing Fanny after her return from Italy, Felix expressed the wish that Fanny would somehow preserve her "buoyant traveling spirit, while continuing to live in the quiet of home."[35]

Among Fanny's many new lieder produced during this period are two compelling Goethe settings, *Auf dem See* (*On the Sea*, H-U 382) and her second interpretation of the exquisite *Wandrers Nachtlied* (*Wanderer's Night Song*, H-U 367).[36] *Auf dem See* impresses as a response to Felix's part-song on the same text, the final member of the *Sechs Lieder* op. 41, published in 1838. Like Felix, Fanny chose the meter 6/8, began her setting with an anacrusis in the middle of the bar, and filled the composition with trochaic rhythms and block, chordal accompaniments in the piano that recall the homophony of Felix's choral song, designed for performance outdoors. As in op. 41, no. 6, Fanny's opening material later recurs as a refrain, and at one point she even appears to recall a motive from the part-song.[37] But Fanny painted with a broader brush than Felix and expanded her setting to accommodate a five-part form (*ABACA'*), in contrast to her brother's simpler three-part design (*ABA*).

The other Goethe setting, *Wandrers Nachtlied*, counts among Fanny's most evocative creations and should take its rightful place with Schubert's celebrated setting of the same poem (D 224). The wanderer's quest for "sweet peace" (*süßer Friede*) that quiets all pain and suffering elicited from her an imaginative treatment of harmonic tension and release. Thus, the tonic—A-flat major—is initially destabilized by excursions to B-flat minor and G-flat major, harmonic realms a step above and below. Then, as we hear "to what end all pain and passion?" ("was soll all der Schmerz und Lust?") and another, more fervent invocation of peace, Fanny concentrates the accumulated tension onto a critical harmonic progression that, after an unexpected rest, magically resolves two dissonant chords into the reinstated A-flat major.❸ In the closing bars the restless eighth-note rhythms that have propelled the song forward abate, and the song comes to its serene conclusion with hushed, *pianissimo* chords.

If Goethe remained Fanny's favorite poet, in the 1840s she broadened her reading considerably to include the minor thirteenth-century *Minnesänger* Otto IV, Shakespeare, and Robert Burns, and she found also a new wellspring of inspiration in several contemporary German poets she set for the first time—Justinus Kerner, Lenau, and Eichendorff.[38] The three duets on texts of the Markgrave Otto IV of Brandenburg (1238–1308),[39] which contrast images of summer and winter to treat the topic of courtly love (*Minne*), may have been in response to Wilhelm's visit to Brandenburg in October 1840. Fanny's sole Shakespeare setting, the part-song "Unter des Laubdachs Hut" (H-U 370),[40] is a sprightly rendition of Amien's "Under the Greenwood Tree" from *Twefth Night* (*Was Ihr wollt*), possibly inspired by Ludwig Tieck's readings of the bard. In the 1820s Tieck had collaborated on the completion of A. W. Schlegel's Shakespeare translations and in 1841 arrived in Berlin as the official *Vorleser* to the Prussian court; Fanny reported favorably to Rebecka about Tieck's interpretation of *Was Ihr wollt*.[41] What drew her the same year to Philipp Kaufmann's translations of Robert Burns remains unknown, but she responded with a song and a cappella duet, two wistful settings of "From thee, Eliza, I must go" and "The winter, it is past" (H-U 374 and 375).[42] Each treated the theme of lovers' separations, depicted in the song by a tonal trajectory that moves as far afield from F major as C-flat major for the lines "But boundless oceans, roaring wide / Between my Love and me, / They never, never can divide / My heart and soul from thee."

Among the new German poets Fanny set in 1841 was the Swabian Justinus Kerner, who led a double life as physician. Intent on exploring links between the physical and spiritual worlds, Kerner used regimens of magnetism to treat somnabulists and other patients deemed to be possessed by demons, and found in klecksography—the whimsical, abstract world of ink blots—"all manner of figures from the spirit-world."[43] Kerner's *Totenklage* (*Lament for the Dead*), written after the death of his brother in 1840, was an attempt to reach the supernatural world through verse. Set in a brooding E minor (H-U 384),[44] Fanny's song reaches its climax with a plummeting diminished-seventh arpeggiation in the piano as a star in the heavens answers the disconsolate poet, "He is with me."

The subject of death also informs Fanny's first setting of Lenau, *Traurige Wege* (*Sad Paths*, H-U 380, July 28, 1841),[45] in which lovers pass by the loveless crosses and stone markers of a graveyard. The music offers two contrasting textures—lush, harmonious arpeggiations in the piano that briefly skirt the major mode for a fleeting image of love resounding through a green forest; and a stark, *pianissimo* unison passage in the minor for "love without hope" (*Liebe ohne Hoffen*). In the duet *Die Sennin* (*The Dairymaid*, H-U 383),[46] on a Lenau text later set by Robert Schumann,[47] Fanny invoked the style of folk music to capture the Alpine dairymaid whose songs echo among the peaks and valleys, and awaken the rocks. Indeed, in one passage she adapted several rustic bars from Felix's *Lied ohne Worte* op. 53, no. 5, also in A minor, composed just a few months before the duet and fitted with the telling title *Volkslied* (*Folk Song*),[48] a rare example in which Felix divulged the extramusical meaning of his piano lieder.

Another new German poet who graced Fanny's songs in 1841 was Joseph von Eichendorff, a Catholic civil servant in Berlin who used his art to escape from the tedium of a bureaucratic post at the Prussian Ministry of Culture—in one of his best-known poems, *Wünschelrute* (*Divining Rod*), Eichendorff referred to the "magic word" (*Zauberwort*) of poetry that could unlock the songs immanent in all things. Often regarded as the supreme lyricist among German romantic poets, Eichendorff interpolated short poems into his stories and novels before releasing an independent collection of *Gedichte* in 1837. Three years later, during a prolific year of song composition, Robert Schumann arranged twelve Eichendorff settings into the cycle *Liederkreis*, op. 39, and in May 1840 shared some of the new songs with Felix in Berlin. Fanny was then in Italy, and exactly when she became familiar with Schumann's Eichendorff settings remains unclear; Schumann's name appears neither in her diary nor in surviving letters from this time. In any event, in the section of Eichendorff's *Gedichte* titled *Sängerleben* (*Singer's Life*) she discovered a short series of poems, *Anklänge* (*Reminiscences*), from which she selected several verses in June 1841. The result was a miniature cycle of three interconnected songs that hint at her aspirations to composition on a large scale.[49]

In the first, tautly structured strophic setting, the protagonist longs for the wings of a bird to transport him to an unknown world (example 10.2). Eichendorff's springtime vision, one of many the poet devoted to the season, blends colors and sounds in an example of synesthesia that appealed to Fanny, who responded with telling applications of chromaticism. Thus, playing on the pitches C and C-sharp, she transposed the music from A minor (triad: A–C–E) to the parallel A major (triad: A–C-sharp–E) for much of the third, concluding strophe, and in the closing bars positioned an augmented triad (A–C-sharp–F), a dissonant chromatic sonority that began to achieve some prominence in her lieder of the 1840s.

In the second and third songs, set in the related keys of E major and C major, Fanny moved from a predictable strophic structure to progressively freer, more adventurous through-composed designs. Drawn to the splendor

EXAMPLE 10.2. Fanny Hensel, *Anklänge*, no. 1 (1841)

EXAMPLE 10.3. Fanny Hensel, *Anklänge*, no. 3 (1841)

of a distant forest (*die ferne Waldespracht*), our protagonist hears songs and horn calls, two musical allusions that Fanny obligingly worked into the piano accompaniment. Then, in the ebullient third song, driven by surging sonorities in the piano, he figuratively takes flight to the forest and finds comfort in its solitude. There, in a passage framed by two pauses, the horn calls and songs no longer torment his heart. Against repeated, *pianissimo* chords to depict the horns, Fanny set two self-quotations, which function as reminiscences— a musical play, as it were, on Eichendorff's very title, *Anklänge*. Like some dreamy recollection, the first quotation offers a rhythmic transformation of the opening of Fanny's melancholy piano piece from 1840, *Abschied von Rom* (example 10.3; see p. 249). And the second recalls the opening of the first song, as the cycle briefly turns back on itself. Then the propulsive piano sonorities resume, and the protagonist takes his departure from the prosaic world and embraces the liberating poetry of the forest.

In *Anklänge*, Fanny intimates how she might have conceived a major song cycle. To our loss, she never took up that challenge, though she continued to draw inspiration from Eichendorff's poetry, and between 1841 and 1847 finished seventeen more settings. Late in her life, Eichendorff became her favorite poet after Goethe and Heine. Several of the texts Fanny chose are celebrations of spring, including two composed possibly as early as 1841, *Mayenlied* (*May Song*) and *Morgenständchen* (*Morning Serenade*), and then published in 1846 as op. 1, nos. 4 and 5. Their texts are filled with vibrant imagery of flowers, birdsong, and motion, and their piano parts palpitate with repeating chords—gentle triplets in "*Mayenlied*," more insistent sixteenth notes in "*Morgenständchen*"—that support an active treble part now doubling the vocal line, now crossing above it. Once again, all this restless stirring—for the scholar Jurgen Thym, "music in its most elementary stage"[50]—is perceived by the poetic persona in the solitude of a forest, for the romantics a magical realm of self-discovery.

By any measure, 1841 counts as one of Fanny's most productive years of song, when she crafted several examples that, in their sensitivity to text setting, imaginative harmonic treatment, and formal spontaneity, are worthy exemplars of the well-made song. It is perhaps fitting that the year she discovered in Eichendorff's verses fresh approaches to her favorite genre, she also encountered a new composer who led her to take stock of her song composition. In July Fanny acquired some recently published lieder of Josephine Lang (1815–1880), whom Felix had met in Munich a decade before. Impressed by her natural talent, he had given her counterpoint lessons, though only to teach her "what she already knew by nature,"[51] before recommending that she move to Berlin to study piano with Fanny.[52] But Lang remained in Munich, where she became a professional singer and struggled to supplement her modest income by writing and publishing songs. Lang was heavily influenced by Felix's music, but evidently never met Fanny, and probably encountered her songs only after the composer died.

Writing to Felix in July 1841, Fanny alluded to the "many novelties" she had discovered in Lang's songs. "I like them so much that I play them, and play them again—I can't tear myself away—and then finally put them aside. I've been singing them all day so that I'll remember them."[53] Ironically, just as she was immersed in Lang's music, Felix sent copies for her to examine, which prompted his musical twin, mindful of distinguishing her own creative outlook from her brother's, to respond, "I was really glad that this time fate had protected me from becoming a parrot; if I know your opinion about something, I'm always uncertain whether I'm only imitating you or actually feel the same way. I'm enjoying these pieces immensely: they're extremely musical and heartfelt, and the modulations often quite ingenious and original."

For his part, Felix deeply admired Lang's published lieder, as he did his sister's private lieder, and stood as ready to support Lang's public career as he was unwilling to promote Fanny's. To Lang's fiancé, the jurist and amateur poet Reinhold Köstlin, Felix wrote, "It is a long time since I have seen any new music so genial, or which affected me so deeply, as these charming songs; their appearance was equally unexpected and welcome, not only to me, but to all those whose predilections are in accordance with my own, who participate in my love of music, and feel in a similar manner with myself. I sent my sister a copy at the time from Leipzig, but when it arrived she had already bought one, without our ever having corresponded on the subject."[54]

Among the songs that Felix preferred was one exquisite miniature that almost certainly attracted Fanny's attention—the Lenau setting *Scheideblick* (*Parting Glance*), op. 10, no. 5:

Als ein unergründlich Wonnemeer	Like an unfathomable ocean of rapture
strahlte mir dein seelenvoller Blick!	your soulful glance radiated to me,
Scheiden musst' ich ohne Wiederkehr,	I had to depart without returning,

| und ich habe scheidend all' mein Glück | and in departing quietly sunk |
| still versenkt in diese tiefe Meer! | into this deep ocean all my joy![55] |

Into twenty-five concentrated measures Lang poured a liquid musical expressiveness and used the simplest of means to conjure up Lenau's *Wonnemeer*. First, in the piano introduction she established a slowly undulating triplet figure in the bass to create gentle, equable cross-rhythms against the prevailing common meter of the treble, where she placed a series of chords that tilt toward the subdominant F major,[56] without undercutting the static tonic C major harmony predominant throughout the song.◉ When the voice enters, it articulates short, compact phrases in a subdued, low tessitura, broken only by one expressive leap of an octave for *still versenkt*. Then the piano chords resume in the postlude and return us to the beginning. The result is a concise miniature in which every note, every subtle inflection tells—an approach to lied composition that no doubt would have found a sympathetic listener in Fanny.

ii

At the end of July 1841 Felix arrived with his family in Berlin, but without clarity about the pleasure of the king, who held his preferred composer in abeyance for several more weeks. Not until September was Felix commissioned to collaborate with Ludwig Tieck on a new production of Sophocles' *Antigone*, a timeless play that pitted the individual (Antigone) against the state (Creon's Thebes). On October 28, Fanny and family members traveled by train to Potsdam and attended at the royal palace the private premiere for the court and its privileged circle. Fanny was surprised at how in just three weeks her brother had been able to dispatch the overture and music for the *stasima*, or choral odes, to help bring "everyone clever and cultured in Berlin" closer to understanding Sophocles and to appreciating the Prussian monarch's neoclassical project.[57] No mean classicist, Felix tinkered with J. J. C. Donner's German translation used for the performance and thought about writing music in a chantlike style, with limited instrumentation to approximate the aulos, salpinx, and lyre of ancient Greek practice. But instead he elected to exploit a full orchestra to effect a rapprochement between modern musical means and the dramatic techniques of classical antiquity. A second private performance followed in November (on Fanny's birthday Felix gave her an autograph pianovocal score of the work[58]), but not until April 1842 was the general public able to hear the work in the Berlin Schauspielhaus. Eduard Devrient, who played the role of Haemon (Creon's son, betrothed to Antigone) and later reminisced about the prerevolutionary *Vormärz* in Berlin, wrote, "thus long the authorities had hesitated to bring the work before the general public."[59]

On October 13, 1841, the king conferred on Felix the title of Kapellmeister, though issued no new directives. For a few short weeks, the composer escaped the royal indecision by conducting concerts in Leipzig; when he returned to Berlin late in November, he found Fanny putting the finishing touches on a sizeable new piano cycle, *Das Jahr* (*The Year*, H-U 385), arguably her most impressive accomplishment. Felix never recorded a written opinion about the new work, a series of twelve character pieces on the months of the year and postlude, which Fanny dated between August 28 and December 23, 1841, and gave to Wilhelm as a Christmas present. Presumably, her brother shared with her privately his critical assessment at their Berlin residence.

The rediscovery of *Das Jahr* is the major milestone in our forming, post-modern critical reception of Fanny. The cycle enhances substantially our understanding not only of her music, and its layering of musical, visual, and literary elements, but of nineteenth-century piano music in general. Nearly 150 years of neglect came to an end in 1989 with the publication of the composition.[60] Remarkably, Fanny left no reference to *Das Jahr* in her diaries, though she did mention it in a letter to the painter August Elsasser—not, however, without minimizing her effort: "Now I'm engaged on another small work [*kleine Arbeit*] that's giving me much fun, namely a series of 12 piano pieces meant to depict the months; I've already progressed more than half way. When I finish, I'll make clean copies of the pieces, and they will be provided with vignettes. And so we try to ornament and prettify our lives—that is the advantage of artists, that they can strew such beautifications about, for those nearby to take an interest in."[61] Notwithstanding her modesty, Fanny did indeed prepare a second autograph copy, presumably in the early weeks or months of 1842, to which Wilhelm added illustrative vignettes. What is more, at some point the couple had this fair copy bound and fitted with an engraved title page and twelve supplemental pages interleaved between the individual pieces, on which appeared engraved verses drawn from Uhland, Goethe, Schiller, Eichendorff, and Tieck—all poets whom Fanny had set.[62] The result was a vivid synthesis of musical, literary, and visual imagery, forming, in contrast to the double counterpoint of the *Reise-Album* (see p. 265), a "triple counterpoint" that now enlivened and enriched the Hensels' artistic lives. This sumptuous second manuscript was first examined by scholars in 1993; seven years later, in 2000, it appeared in a full color facsimile.[63] In the 1840s, with the exception of family members, only a few of Fanny's friends would have known of its existence. One who did was Sarah Austin, who visited Berlin in 1842,[64] and mentioned the second manuscript in her eulogy of Fanny published in 1848: "She had composed a series of beautiful pieces of music for the pianoforte, called after the months. These were written in an album, and at the head of each month was a charming drawing illustrative of it by Professor Hensel. And all this was simple, dignified, free from the ostentation and *sensibleries* which sometimes throw doubt or discredit on such manifestations. One had always the fullest assurance that Madame Hensel said less rather than more than she felt."[65]

The painstaking care Fanny and Wilhelm lavished on *Das Jahr* underscores its central significance in the composer's oeuvre. At age thirty-six, she succeeded in producing a major piano composition—nearly an hour in length, it dwarfed Felix's efforts for the instrument—that dramatically expanded the scope of the small-scale piano pieces she had hitherto composed. The twelve *Charakterstücke*, as labeled on the printed title page, were no longer separate, independent creations but a concatenation of movements interlocked by related musical and extramusical elements and by an overarching key plan, not unlike the great piano cycles of Robert Schumann from the 1830s. That Fanny crafted the individual movements with large-scale ramifications of her cycle in mind is clear enough. First of all, there is the coordinated sequence of keys, in which she favored sharp keys in the first half, then progressed more and more to flat keys in the second, and ultimately arrived at the neutral C major in "December," and A minor in the codalike "Nachspiel." To strengthen this scheme, Fanny linked adjacent pieces through harmonic means. For example, "January" begins in B major and ends in C-sharp major, which act also as the subdominant and dominant of the key of "February," F-sharp major; that key, in turn, serves double duty as subdominant to C-sharp major, in which "March" concludes. "June" and "July" are also linked by harmonic means, and, furthermore, "January" and "February," and "April" and "May," are literally bound together by the instruction *attacca*, so that the listener perceives them too as related parts of the annual cycle, not independent miniatures.[66]

The mock printed title page of the fair copy reads *Das Jahr. Zwölf Charakterstücke für Fortepiano von Fanny Hensel* (*The Year. Twelve Character Pieces for Piano by Fanny Hensel*), all but announcing Fanny's aspiration to publish the work. Some intriguing, possibly corroborating evidence survives in the manuscripts. At least three movements come down to us either in different versions ("June") or with significantly revised passages ("August" and "December"), as if, after Felix returned to Berlin in 1841, Fanny herself contracted the "revision sickness" (*Revisionskrankheit*) that habitually plagued him while he guided his own music through the press. Compelling evidence of her intentions for the cycle, perhaps, may be found in engraver's markings notated in the first autograph, revealing that at some point someone indeed planned an edition, though whether it was Fanny or someone after her death remains unclear.

In the end, of course, she did not live to see the complete work through the press, and it disappeared into oblivion. But in 1846 she did release one movement as the second of the four *Lieder*, op. 2—her first published set of piano pieces. For this occasion, Fanny chose "September," a dark-hued composition in B minor that inspired an artful application of the three-hand technique. In the middle register of the piano, just beneath a fluid, running stream of sextuplets, she placed a pensive, songlike melody articulated mainly by the thumbs and supported by a more slowly moving bass line in octaves (example 10.4). Seventy-one measures in length, the movement observes the pattern of statement, departure, and return familiar in Fanny's character pieces—and in Felix's *Lieder ohne Worte*. But in "September" Fanny hit upon an unusual, tonally adventuresome solution that diverged considerably from Felix's more conventional approach to key relationships. Beginning in B minor, "September" modulates by thirds to the keys of D major, F-sharp minor, and—most strikingly—at the furthest remove, to B-flat minor before returning and coming full circle to B minor. Wilhelm's vignette and the poetic epigram in the fair copy, and the title *Am Flusse* (*By the Stream*) in the first autograph score, reveal the purpose of this unusual, meandering course. The vignette shows a barefooted woman sitting by a stream that washes over the sextuplets of Fanny's third measure, almost as if the water imagery of the music emanates from Wilhelm's contribution (figure 10.2). The epigram, two lines from Goethe's *An den Mond* (*To the Moon*), further elucidates the Hensels' extramusical conception:

Fließe, fließe, lieber Fluß,   Flow, flow, dear stream,
nimmer werd' ich froh.   Never will I be happy.

Unlike Schubert, who had set the poem to music in 1815, Fanny and Wilhelm may have thought of these lines after she drafted the piece, for Goethe's spondees do not fit the rhythms of Fanny's melancholy melody, which begins with a weak upbeat. Nevertheless, the poem, in which a protagonist (in the Hensels' reading, a woman) addresses first the moon and then a stream as calming, consoling natural bodies, contains in its sixth stanza lines particularly apposite to Fanny's music:

Rausche, Fluß, das Tal entlang,   Murmur, stream, along the valley,
ohne Rast und Ruh,   Without rest and peace,
rausche, flüstre meinem Sang   Murmur, whisper melodies
Melodien zu!   To my song!

As John R. Williams has noted, Goethe's stream becomes a "powerful symbol of transience and mutability" that washes away joy and sadness and, indeed, inspires the poet's song.[67] And so, in Fanny's composition, the subdued melody protrudes from the murmuring sextuplets, which pursue unabated their changing course—in Goethe's poem, the stream rages and overflows during a winter night and then, amid the erupting splendor of spring, swells its forming buds. Curiously, when Fanny published "September" in 1846, she removed all these extramusical signposts and released it as an untitled piano lied. Her public could scarcely have imagined that, far more than a miniature character piece, the composition was originally part of a comprehensive musical calendar. Fanny indeed "said" less publicly than she felt privately.

Since the appearance of *Das Jahr* in 1989, interpretations of the cycle have followed their own changing course. If the American pianist Sarah

EXAMPLE 10.4. Fanny Hensel, *Das Jahr* ("September," op. 2, no. 2, 1841)

Rothenberg and German musicologist Annette Nubbemeyer related *Das Jahr* to Fanny's Italian sojourn of 1839–1840, another German scholar, Gottfried Eberle, found correspondences between the music and Italian topics difficult to substantiate and averred that *Das Jahr* could be enjoyed as absolute music, without autobiographical encroachments. Seizing on Fanny's use of chorales in "March," "December," and the "Nachspiel," the American historian John Toews argued that at some level the cycle alluded to Felix's "cultural project" of 1829, the revival of J. S. Bach's St. Matthew Passion. And finally, the German musicologist Christian Thorau, among the first to examine the fair copy, applied structuralist musical analysis to the composition and discovered a unifying network of motives prevalent throughout the cycle—all derived from the muffled, descending bass octaves with which "January" commences.[68]

On June 2, 1841, exactly a year after she had left Rome, Fanny pondered in her diary the resumption of her Berlin life—the stimulation of the Sunday concerts, her encounters in society with celebrities such as Cornelius, Thorwaldsen, and the Grimm brothers, and, of course, Felix's return. "Berlin is now seething with interesting persons" ("aber Berlin wimmelt jetzt v. interessanten Personen"), she wrote, but then inexplicably paused, not to record another entry until April 12, 1842, when she regretted not having preserved details of the period that had now vanished.[69] Perhaps too conveniently for the modern biographer, she filled part of this nine-month gap (August–December) by composing *Das Jahr*, a process likely extended into the early months of the new year with the preparation of the second, fair-copy autograph. On one level, in short, *Das Jahr* became her substitute diary, in which poetic piano music temporarily supplanted the prosaic chronicle of the *Tagebücher*, an interpretation strengthened if we consider further Wilhelm's vignettes and the poetic epigrams. Taken together, the evidence of the manuscripts suggests that Fanny's "abstract" musical year was in fact about her Berlin life and family relationships. Of course, Fanny took center stage in this domestic musical drama, in which Wilhelm's vignettes also alluded to himself, Sebastian, and possibly Rebecka, while not surprisingly Fanny embedded into the work

FIGURE 10.2. Fanny Hensel, autograph fair manuscript of "September" from *Das Jahr*, with vignette by Wilhelm Hensel (Berlin, Mendelssohn Archiv, Ms. 155)

several clear references to the dominant musical influence on her life—Felix. We might profitably compare *Das Jahr* to Robert Schumann's *Carnaval* (1837), in which members of that composer's circle—Clara Wieck, her father, Chopin, and others—make memorable appearances, alongside the dual sides of Schumann's personality, Florestan and Eusebius, and all in the context of carnival time, which Fanny, in contrast, compressed in her cycle into "February."

Anchoring Fanny's musical calendar—and firmly setting it in the environment of Protestant Berlin—is her use of three standard chorales: "Christ ist erstanden" ("Christ Is Arisen") for Easter, placed in this year in March; "Vom Himmel hoch" ("From Heaven High") for Christmas, and "Das alte Jahr vergangen ist" ("The Old Year Now Hath Passed Away"), for the epilogue-like "Nachspiel." Prefacing the chorale in "March" is a solemn prelude, with tolling, bell-like pedal points in the lower register of the piano, a reference confirmed by Wilhelm's vignette, in which an angel rings a bell, and by the epigram from Goethe's *Faust*:

| Verkündiget ihr dumpfen Glocken schon | Do your muffled bells already |
| des Osterfestes erste Feierstunde? | Announce the first hour of the Easter feast?[70] |

When the chorale appears, Fanny sets it initially in a simple chordal style that would have been familiar to Berlin congregations, but then elaborates the melody with two variations, of which the second culminates by turning from the subdued minor to a radiant major key, with the chorale melody inverted from the soprano to the bass. In the case of "December," a blurry, *pianissimo* prelude in C minor, like an impressionistic aural snowstorm, precedes the appearance of the Christmas chorale in C major, now placed appropriately in the high register, against bell-like octaves in the bass. Finally, to mark the passage of the annual cycle, the "Nachspiel" presents in a stately A minor the chorale "Das alte Jahr vergangen ist." Here Fanny hit upon an ingenious solution: each phrase of the chorale, presented again in block, chordal style, is introduced by a few free bars of music that impress as a reminiscence of the sobering opening chorus of Bach's St. Matthew Passion. The technique of inserting free interludes reflects the performance practice of organists of Fanny's time, who would improvise short passages between the strains of congregational chorales (example 10.5). We are thus to imagine Fanny's piano transforming itself into an organ, as it provides the final commentary on the "year" just past.

If the chorales prominently situate the cycle in Protestant Berlin, other evidence relates *Das Jahr* to Fanny's family relationships. First of all, the cycle is told from her perspective; she appears in the vignette for "January" as a reclining, sleeping figure, with her left hand casually resting on the strings of a cithara, symbol of her musical inspiration. She is dreaming, as the title of the

EXAMPLE 10.5.   Fanny Hensel, *Das Jahr* ("Nachspiel," 1841)

movement in the first autograph—"Januar. Ein Traum"—and the epigram in the fair copy, four verses from Uhland, confirm:

Ahnest du, O Seele, wieder	Did you, my soul, sense again
sanfte, süße Frühlingslieder?	Gentle, sweet songs of spring?
sieh umher die falben Bäume,	Look around at the faded leaves,
ach! Es waren holde Träume.	Ah, those were fair dreams.

Uhland's poem *Im Herbste* (*In Autumn*), with its opposition of hopeful, spring renewal against the receding, lost memories of time passed, held special meaning for Fanny, who set the same poem a few years later as a part-song, published as her op. 3, no. 3 (see p. 326). But in "January," she took the initiative to create a fantasy-like dream sequence, with shifting adumbrations of material from "February," "April," "June," and "August," and thereby validated the dream as an overarching topic for the cycle. Indeed, if we leap ahead to "November," we find another epigram, this one from Ludwig Tieck's poem *Trauer* (*Grief*), that again alludes to the dream state:

Wie rauschen die Bäume	How the trees stir
so winterlich schon;	so wintry already;
es fliehen die Träume	dreams of love
der Liebe davon!	flee from there!
Ein Klagelied schallt	A lament resounds
durch Dämm'rung und Wald.	through twilight and forest.

Fanny conveyed the lament through chromatically saturated harmonies, descending musical lines, and an agitated, restless Allegro in F minor. The frequent tempo shifts—Mesto, then in succession Allegro molto agitato, Allegro molto e con brio, Adagio, and Allegro come primo—suggest again that, as with "January," she conceived "November" as a dream sequence, and that the cycle as a whole is about the perception of time—real time measured by the months and changing seasons, spiritual time measured by the Christian liturgical calendar, and the free, associative time of the subconscious. The last, of course, was the playground of romantic composers, as represented by the opium dream of Berlioz's *Fantastic* Symphony (1830) and by Felix's own "brazen dream," as he described it to Fanny—the *Midsummer Night's Dream* Overture of his adolescence (1826).[71]

And what of the other characters in Fanny's drama? Wilhelm enters in the frolicsome scherzo of "February," a carnival scene that recalls the couple's Italian experiences, as hinted by the epigram from Goethe's *Faust*:

Denkt nicht ihr seid in deutschen Grenzen	Don't think you are in German realms,
von Teufels- Narren- und Totentänzen	A merry festival awaits you
ein heitres Fest erwartet euch.	Of dances of devils, fools, and the dead.[72]

Fanny's music unfolds with crisp, rapidly descending staccato chords veering between clashing duple and triple meters (a musical technique known as hemiola); ultimately, the coursing music is checked by bell-like octaves in the bass that solemnly mark the arrival of Lent and prepare us for the bells in "March." Later, in "June," Wilhelm returns to serenade Fanny, who in the vignette listens to him from a balcony. Fanny composed two different versions of this movement. In the first, a slow introduction gives way to a barcarolle-like Andante, with Wilhelm's melody placed in the tenor voice against broken chords in the treble (Wilhelm's lute in the vignette); at the second iteration of the melody, Fanny applies the three-hand technique by enveloping the melody in a stream of triplet arpeggiations.❸ For the second version of "June," preserved in the fair copy, she removed the virtuoso display and considerably simplified the movement, in the process completely recasting the melody. The new version appears again in the tenor and is answered by the soprano, before the two sing together a *Duett ohne Worte* along the lines of Felix's *Duetto* for piano, op. 38, no. 6. Once again the 6/8 meter and lilting, trochaic rhythms allude to the barcarolle, and there is even a passage in which Fanny subtly recalls Felix's first Venetian *Gondellied*, op. 19, no. 6.

Male figures appear in vignettes for four other months—in "July" we see a shepherd; in "August" (a pastoral harvest song) a peasant blowing an alpenhorn; in "October," replete with horn calls, a hunter playing a *Waldhorn*; and in "November," a monk contemplating a tomb. Whether Wilhelm intended these roles for himself remains unclear, though certainly it is no stretch to imagine him as the hunter in "October"; twenty-five years before, Wilhelm had played the hunter in Berger's version of *Die schöne Müllerin*, and in 1823 Fanny set eight of Müller's poems from the cycle, exactly at the time Wilhelm began courting her in earnest.

Childlike figures appear in the vignettes for "April," "May," and "December." Of these, references to Sebastian seem unambiguous in "April," in which a hooded mother holds and protects her son from the "deceptive" light of the sun (the epigram is from Goethe's short poem *März*, set by Fanny as a *Duettino* in 1836; see p. 203). In perhaps the most remarkable of Wilhelm's artistic idealizations, the vignette for "December," Fanny is depicted as a winged angel carrying her son down from heaven, an all too transparent allusion to the Christmas chorale with which the movement ends, "Vom Himmel hoch."

Admittedly, some difficulties remain in overlaying autobiographical readings onto *Das Jahr*. What role Lea, Rebecka, or Paul play, if any, in the vignettes is uncertain, and Wilhelm's figures, most of which appear in rural settings and in stylized, distinctly noncontemporary garb, seem well removed from the Berlin of 1841. What, for example, do we make of the melancholy woman in "September"? Perhaps Fanny meant to represent here her sister Rebecka, whose deteriorating physical condition during the summer of 1841 led her to take a cure in Heringsdorf, followed by a "magnetic-electric" cure in Berlin in November, around the time Fanny composed "September." In her diary she described Rebecka's condition before this last resort as *ganz trostlos* (completely comfortless),[73] which might explain the second line of the epigram, "Nimmer werd' ich froh." But on the other hand, all of Wilhelm's figures could be no more than fictive personalities, quasi-literary types understood to populate Fanny's dream announced in "January."

Be that as it may, one family member left an indelible impression on *Das Jahr*. Scattered throughout Fanny's composition, like a recurring, literary idée fixe, are several unmistakable references to Felix's music.[74] We have already mentioned one passage in "June," where folded into Wilhelm's serenade is an adapted phrase from Felix's first Venetian *Gondellied*, a piano miniature he had written in Venice in 1830 as a *Duett ohne Worte*, when he was infatuated with the Munich pianist Delphine von Schauroth. The opening theme of "April" impresses as a reworking of a theme from Felix's *Capriccio brillante* for piano and orchestra, op. 22. Other movements reanimate Felix's familiar elfin, scherzo idiom, as in "February," which seems to recall material from the *Rondo capriccioso*, op. 14 for piano, an instance during the madcap carnival scene, perhaps, of the fraternal "demonic influence" Fanny had detected in 1834 (see p. 207). And, most strikingly, in "March," Fanny quotes several times, and nearly intact, a plangent bar from the *Serenade und Allegro giojoso*, op. 43 for piano and orchestra, so that Felix again figuratively intrudes upon her musical ruminations.◗

In the end, *Das Jahr* poses nearly as many questions as it answers about Fanny's creative muse in 1841 and 1842. But it remains a worthy, significant cycle from the nineteenth century that may now take its place among the major offerings for the piano of the Schumanns, Chopin, Liszt, and, of course, Felix. And, no less significant, Fanny's masterwork marks a significant advance in her inevitable progression toward becoming a professional composer.

iii

While Fanny was finishing the first draft of *Das Jahr*, Berlin was possessed by an affliction she described as *Fieberparoxismus* (feverish paroxysm).[75] Between December 27, 1841, and March 3, 1842, Franz Liszt made twenty-one concert appearances, initially at the Singakademie but then, to accommodate the swelling crowds, at the Schauspielhaus. A faddish cult that Heinrich Heine later dubbed *Lisztomanie* now besieged the pianist, as the normally rigid, stratified Berlin society succumbed to mass hysteria, a symptom, according to Dana Gooley, "of stunted spiritual and intellectual growth in monarchical Germany."[76] Felix, who had deep respect for Liszt's abilities as a pianist, privately complained to Ferdinand David about the virtuoso's unchecked musical license: "Liszt...has forfeited a good deal of respect through all the silly tomfoolery he perpetrates not only on the public (which doesn't hurt) but on the music itself. Here he has played pieces of Beethoven, Bach, Handel and Weber so wretchedly and inadequately...that renditions by average performers would have given me much greater pleasure. Here he added six bars, there omitted seven; here he made false harmonies, and later introduced other similar corruptions, and there in the most gentle passages made a dreadful *fortissimo*, and, for what I know, all pathetic nonsense."[77] It seems Fanny would have concurred with this assessment, for in 1839 she had dismissed Liszt's own music as "nonsensical and formless" and concluded, "if chaos hadn't already been invented by the good Lord before the creation of the world, Liszt could have disputed His right to it."[78] Now, in 1842, after briefly mentioning the Lisztian paroxysm in her diary, she passed over the virtuoso in favor of a violinist celebrated for imitating Paganini, the Moravian H. W. Ernst, whom she described as a "true, soulful player" (*ein wahrer Seelenspieler*). Still, according to Lea, who viewed Liszt as a "flammable bone of contention,"[79] during this period the virtuoso was "often at Fanny's."[80] Liszt did not record extended comments about Fanny's playing, but he did remember her as *une musicienne extrêmement distinguée*.[81]

Felix's presence in Berlin again drew in sharp relief the public-private divide separating the musical realms of the siblings. After completing in January his final symphony, the *Scottish* (dedicated to Queen Victoria), at the Prussian monarch's behest Felix mounted performances of *St. Paul* and the

Lobgesang with hundreds of musicians at the Schaupielhaus and Singakademie, the sites of Liszt's triumphs. Meanwhile, Fanny resumed her Sunday concerts, which according to her aunt Henriette (Hinni) were "very well attended and fashionable."[82] Details of the programs are sketchy, and only three are documented in May and June. The repertoire seems to have been exclusively German and included an aria from Handel's *Messiah*, the first part of Haydn's *Seasons*, a piano sonata of Beethoven and trio from *Fidelio*, selections from Felix's songs, *Lobgesang,* and *St. Paul*, and a movement from Fanny's *Das Jahr*.[83] Fanny was also active at smaller musical gatherings at her residence; at one, in February 1842, she managed to intimidate the young English pianist and composer William Sterndale Bennett, who recorded this account: "I went to a small music-party at Mendelssohn's where I met all his family and some other musical people. He played three pieces and then insisted on my playing. I *never was so alarmed before*; not at him, for we have played too often together, but at his sister, Mrs. Hensel. . . . I never was frightened to play to any one before, and to think that this terrible person should be a lady. However, she would frighten many people with her cleverness."[84]

Failing to conclude negotiations about the pending appointment to the Prussian court, Felix departed Berlin late in April for Düsseldorf. A few days later came news of the devastating fire that consumed one-fourth of the center of Hamburg (to flee the firestorm, Paul and Albertine had to abandon their residence there, and for a while occupied quarters above Fanny and Wilhelm at Leipzigerstrasse no. 3). While the Hensels remained in Berlin, Felix conducted the Lower Rhine Music Festival in Düsseldorf and some benefit concerts for the fire victims, and then traveled with Cécile to London. Publicly feted as conductor, pianist, and organist, he also had a private audience on July 9 with Queen Victoria and Prince Albert at Buckingham Palace, and there unexpectedly invoked Fanny. Rummaging through the queen's music, Felix came upon his first set of songs, op. 8, from which the queen selected and sang one—*Italien*—accompanied by the composer. "Then I was obliged," he reported to Berlin, "to confess that Fanny had written the song (which I found very hard, but pride must have a fall), and to beg her to sing one of my own also."[85]

From London Felix and Cécile proceeded to Frankfurt, where they met Paul and Albertine and together embarked on a Swiss vacation. Fanny's diary yields only meager information about her Berlin life during this period, when she seems temporarily to have given up composition. There is no mention in her diary or surviving letters of any new works, nor, curiously, of a significant oil portrait of her completed sometime in 1842 by Moritz Daniel Oppenheim (1800–1882).

Born in the Jewish ghetto of Hanau to the east of Frankfurt am Main, Oppenheim rose to become the premiere German Jewish painter of the nineteenth century, the "painter to the Rothschilds and the Rothschild of painters," as he was known.[86] Oppenheim reached Rome in 1821 and spent four years in Italy, where he studied with the Danish sculptor Thorwaldsen and made the acquaintance of the Nazarenes—and of Wilhelm Hensel. As Amos Elon has aptly observed, Oppenheim's paintings of German Jews and Jewish life, particularly the *Return of the Jewish Volunteer from the Wars of Liberation to His Family Living According to the Old Custom* (1834), "merge the ideals of German patriotism, Jewish piety, and cultural assimilation so common at the time."[87] In Rome, where he arrived during the Jewish high feasts, he felt instinctively drawn to the ghetto rather than the *Kunstschätzen* (art treasures) of the Vatican.[88] Received by Goethe in Weimar, Oppenheim became well known for his portraits of the Rothschilds and of Heine, Börne, and other prominent Germans. The artist eventually settled in Frankfurt, where he counted among his colleagues Fanny's cousin Philipp Veit, a son of Dorothea Schlegel. Their relationship experienced at least one awkward moment, when Veit, an ardent Catholic, inquired about Oppenheim's painting *Lavater and Lessing Visiting Moses Mendelssohn* (1856), commemorating Lavater's 1769 attempt to convince the philosopher either to convert to Christianity or justify his refusal. According to Oppenheim, "Veit confessed that he did not know exactly this episode from his grandfather's life; and I explained to him, how, as has been historically proven, Mendelssohn was then in a painful position, how he grieved at not being able to express himself as he wished and could have from his heart. Only from the Duke of Brunswick, who pressed him earnestly, did he not withhold his counter reasons. At that, Veit sighed and observed, 'Who knows how much he had to atone for!'—Otherwise Veit was a good man."[89]

What led Oppenheim to Berlin to paint Fanny's portrait in 1842 remains unclear. She appears against a beige background with spangled curls, fashionable in the 1840s, and wears a dress with a delicately embroidered collar and gold necklace, references to her family wealth and position in society. But nothing betrays her musicianship, and we do not see her hands. In contrast, some twenty years later Oppenheim would depict her brother, identified as "Felix Mendel-sohn B.," as he visited Goethe in 1830. In *Felix Mendelssohn-Bartholdy spielt vor Goethe* (1864),[90] the composer preludes at the piano while the poet listens in his Weimar music room; behind Felix is the bust of Schiller, so that the music seemingly connects the two principal figures of Weimar classical theater. Fanny, on the other hand, appears as a member of Berlin society, but nothing more.

Taking advantage of the slowly expanding railroad network transforming the German landscape, the Hensels traveled to Dresden in September 1842. For more than a week they attended the art galleries and theater, visited country estates of wealthy Saxons, and made new acquaintances. Chief among them was Carl Gustav Carus (1789–1869), a scientist distinguished in comparative anatomy, personal physician to the Saxon king, and highly skilled painter who emulated the ineffable, pantheistic landscapes of his teacher Caspar David Friedrich, the leading exponent of German romantic painting. In 1835, Carus had published a series of "letters" on landscape painting, where we find this compelling passage, which, as Hugh Honour has suggested, might pass as a description of Friedrich's iconic *Wanderer above the Mists* (1818), with its romantic, silhouetted figure, seen from behind, who contemplates a supernatural vortex of mist, craggy rocks, and distant summits: "Stand on the peak of the mountain, contemplate the long ranges of hills, observe the courses of the rivers and all the glories offered to your view, and what feeling seizes you? It is a calm prayer, you lose yourself in unbounded space, your whole being undergoes a clarification and purification, your ego disappears, you are nothing, God is everything."[91]

Early in October Felix returned to Berlin in a last effort to clarify the terms of his royal appointment. Not optimistic, he wrote Ferdinand Hiller that there was nothing worse than "traveling north in the autumn," where one ate "sour grapes and bad nuts."[92] Indeed, initial discussions did not go well, and afterward, Fanny found her brother emotionally distraught and pacing in the garden, all but ready to announce his desire to tender his resignation.[93] But then, unexpectedly, a compromise was reached during a final audience with Frederick William IV, who recognized his subject's restlessness and permitted him to return to Leipzig. In the meantime, the king's ministers began assembling the ranks of a new court chapel of select musicians. When it was ready, Felix would return to Berlin to direct sacred music and oratorios. He also agreed to compose incidental music for Shakespeare's *Midsummer Night's Dream* and the choruses of Sophocles' *Oedipus at Colonos*. Overjoyed at the unexpected turn, he broke the news to his family and then left for Leipzig, to resume his duties at the Gewandhaus. Lea and Fanny would not lose him a second time, or so it seemed.

Then, tragedy struck. At a festive gathering at the Berlin residence on December 11, Abraham's birthday, Lea suddenly fell ill; her head slumped to one side, and she reported feeling dizzy. She had suffered a stroke. Fanny recorded the grim details of the night and next morning in her diary.[94] It was "uncanny" (*unheimlich*), she wrote, how at the moment of her mother's affliction the merriment of the party fell silent, and the guests gradually dispersed. Assisted to her room, Lea slept intermittently, awakened by vomiting spells and oppressive headaches. In the early hours of the next day she slipped into unconsciousness, while her family vainly tried to warm her hands and feet, and a physician let blood from a vein, the standard "treatment" for most diseases. At 9:30 A.M. there was a slight struggle; then, in Fanny's words, "it was over" (*es war vorbei*). She found the similarities with Abraham's passing astonishing— the same time of year and day, summoning of the same physician, same death room, and Felix's arrival from Leipzig, all as if they had reexperienced Abraham's passing. But this time there was one difference. Before Lea died, Paul had written a letter to Felix, and, between concerts at the Gewandhaus, he hastily made the journey to Berlin unaware he had lost his mother. Dirichlet, dispatched to meet Felix at the train station, missed him, so that Felix arrived at Fanny's door still uninformed.

The *Vossische Zeitung* published an obituary, probably from the pen of Karl August Varnhagen von Ense, among the guests on December 11: "Her death will be deplored not only by her gifted children and near relations, but by a large circle of friends and acquaintances, for she had gathered round her a society as select as it was brilliant, and as sociable as it was animated."[95] Felix shared with his siblings the private aspects of grieving—to Fanny and Rebecka he sent the just released four-hand piano arrangement of his *Scottish* Symphony, which they would have played for Lea at Christmas in a festive house now subdued in mourning. To Paul, he ruefully observed, "We are children no longer."[96] For her part, Fanny reflected in her diary, "A happier end for her we could not imagine. Word for word it was…as she would have wished—to depart suddenly from the middle of the life she loved, in full possession of the intellectual brilliance always her lot in life, but without consciousness and medical intervention."[97] It was a death Abraham had shared, and, as Fanny prophetically wrote, she prayed every day that God would grant her.

CHAPTER II

The Joys of Dilettantism

(1843–1845)

A dilettante is a dreadful creature, a female author even more so, but when the two are joined into one person, of course the most dreadful being of all results.

—Fanny to Franz Hauser, November 24, 1843

Lamenting the darkened windows of Lea's rooms, Fanny reminisced to Felix in January 1843: "We had good times together, and, like few others, a happy childhood, and not an hour passes that I do not think back on that in gratitude. And yet our house is now so very lonely, and in particular the *Gartenhaus* is inhabited only by us, so that we shut ourselves in more than usual; and still I cannot escape shuddering whenever there is a storm, and everything rattles and clatters and clanks, as if it were collapsing together on our heads."[1] As trustee of Lea's estate, Paul expeditiously produced a financial assessment, a contribution Fanny appreciated, for, as she noted, other family members were not as inclined toward business. At first, the inheritance was appraised at roughly 60,000 thalers, but this figure undervalued Leipzigerstrasse no. 3 and was deemed too low. Fanny assumed—erroneously, as it turned out—that the residence, the familiar locus of her life and music since 1825, would be sold, for it was worth far more than the income produced from tenants. Since Fanny and Wilhelm had reaped the benefits of living there, they could not expect other family members to share its costs. Meanwhile the task of sorting through

Lea's papers fell to Fanny and Rebecka. Pondering the seriousness of reading private letters, Fanny mused in her diary, "Who of my beloved will one day read these lines? May they read everything, and may I, as the eldest, also be the first, and may my dear husband and Sebastian stand by me when I depart this life, though I still would like to have a bit more time."[2]

In Leipzig, Felix found a ready escape in the unrelenting press of the Gewandhaus season, and in plans supported by the Saxon king to open a new conservatory. The guiding spirit of the new institution, Felix served on the faculty when the Leipzig Conservatory officially welcomed twenty-four students in April 1843 (its later matriculates would include Arthur Sullivan, Edvard Grieg, and Isaac Albéniz). At Felix's invitation, Fanny traveled to Leipzig for a week in February with Rebecka and Sebastian and there experienced "many novelties in a short time." They included the First Symphony of the young Danish composer Niels Gade; his *Echoes of Ossian* Overture, patently indebted to Felix's *Fingal's Cave* Overture; and Felix's stylistically similar *Scottish* Symphony. Fanny now met Robert and Clara Schumann, who played "her husband's compositions beautifully," though they "did not seem very beautiful" to Fanny.[3] Regrettably, her laconic entry sheds no more light on her opinion of Robert Schumann, then a moody, somewhat aloof figure working largely in Felix's shadow in Leipzig, though engaged on an ambitious composition, the oratorio *Paradies und die Peri* (*Paradise and the Peri*, after Thomas Moore). In his own diary entry about Fanny, Schumann was just as terse and recorded only that the depths of her mind spoke through her eyes.[4] Whether on this occasion Fanny shared her own music with Clara and Robert remains unknown, but she likely had the opportunity, for she "heard Mme. Schumann play several times most exquisitely,"[5] and according to Sebastian soon became her friend.[6]

The other novelty Fanny encountered was Hector Berlioz, visiting in Leipzig with his mistress, the mezzo-soprano Marie Recio, and presenting two concerts of his music at the Gewandhaus. Fanny attended the second (February 23), which featured the *King Lear* Overture and the Offertorium from the Requiem. Its static, chantlike choral entries and austere orchestral counterpoint conjured up visions of a contrite humanity that for Robert Schumann surpassed "everything."[7] But most Leipzigers were not prepared for the Frenchman's flamboyant eccentricities, musical and nonmusical. The unusual demands of his scores caused nearly intractable logistical difficulties, and the Leipzig press recoiled at Berlioz's harmonic license and garish effects. In her diary Fanny unequivocally dismissed his music as nonsense (*Unsinn*) and aligned her private views with those of Felix, who had found, after meeting Berlioz in 1830, that his hyperbolic compositions needed editing. (Reacting to Berlioz's music journalism, Felix caviled that Berlioz printed "everything," and thus Felix was surprised not to find his own servants treated in the Frenchman's articles about his German tour.[8]) Berlioz and "Miss Recio" made an uncomfortable (*unbehaglich*) impression on Fanny, but another issue also concerned her: Berlioz's "odd manners gave so much offense that Felix was continually being called upon to smooth somebody's ruffled feathers. When the parting came, Berlioz offered to exchange batons, 'as the ancient warriors exchanged their armor,' and in return for Felix's pretty light stick of whalebone covered with white leather sent an enormous cudgel of lime-tree with the bark on, and an open letter, beginning, 'Le mien est grossier, le tien est simple [mine is coarser, yours is simple].' "[9]

Another observer of Berlioz was Sebastian, who recorded that during their visit the Frenchman "was up to his insane tricks."[10] Sebastian, it seems, spent a fair amount of time at his uncle's Gewandhaus rehearsals, where he encountered the timpanist Ernst Pfundt and observed at close quarters the virtuoso's eccentricities. Pfundt, Sebastian wrote, had a different kind of mallet for each required shade of expression and an incorruptible sense of musical time. Whenever he encountered several hundred measures of rest in his part, he would quietly leave the hall, consume a glass of beer, resume counting rests, and then reappear in the hall at the precise moment to "let loose" on his instrument.[11]

When not attending orchestral rehearsals, Sebastian pursued his favorite pastime—collecting beetles, an enterprise his uncle abetted by offering several unusual specimens, including a Chinese May beetle. Notwithstanding its rarity—the only other known example then was in the British Museum—the specimen evidently shocked Fanny and later, after their return to Berlin, led to some unanticipated difficulties for the young entomologist. There the director of the Entomologisches Kabinett avidly sought out the beetle and claimed it for the official collection. Deprived of his treasure, but not his enterprising spirit, Sebastian then entered into a brisk trade with other collectors, and for a while succumbed to the less than honorable side of the hobby. He discovered that he could profitably exchange inauthentic for genuine articles and soon was fabricating rare species by gluing the head of one beetle onto the body of another.[12]

Throughout 1843, Fanny welcomed several friends to the Berlin residence—the Woringens from Düsseldorf, baritone Franz Hauser from Vienna, mezzo-soprano Pauline Garcia-Viardot, and Hensel's student Kaselowsky, whom the Hensels had seen in Italy. Late in April another companion from the Italian sojourn arrived, Charles Gounod, bearing a pencil drawing from Ingres, presumably *Diva Sta. Francesca Romana*, showing the visionary fifteenth-century St. Frances of Rome.[13] "Endowed with infinite tenderness and delicacy," Gounod promptly fell ill and stayed a few weeks while Fanny nursed him back to health, before departing for Leipzig with her letter of introduction to Felix. He employed words "more precious to their recipient than all the ribbons and stars in Europe,"[14] to praise a passage from Gounod's own setting of the Requiem. Gounod's visit to Berlin, Fanny wrote, "was a great incitement to me, for I played and talked about nothing but music during the many afternoons I spent alone with him, as he generally stayed on with us after dinner."[15] Discussing Gounod's future, Fanny imagined that oratorio would prove viable in France and inspired the young Prix de Rome laureate to contemplate composing one on the subject of Judith. Ultimately nothing came of this project, but there is little doubt about "Madame Henzel's" lasting significance for Gounod—it was Fanny who introduced him to German music, to Bach, Beethoven, Felix, and, of course, her own works. According to Fanny, while Gounod was in Berlin, he heard nothing except what she played for him,[16] even though she encouraged him to take the full measure of Berlin concert life. Arguably, Fanny was a decisive influence on Gounod's forming style, which drew alternately upon Germanic counterpoint and the lyrical qualities of her songs and piano pieces.

In 1843 her own relationship with Felix benefited considerably from their increased contact, in contrast to the earlier, protracted years of separation. At Pentecost, she returned to Leipzig to attend the baptism of Felix and Cécile's fourth child, named after his father. But Felix himself now began commuting to Berlin with increasing frequency, partly to supervise the new chapel choir and consult about revisions to the Lutheran liturgy, and partly to attend to the king's commissions, including incidental music for Racine's *Athalie*; a ceremonial setting of *Herr Gott, dich loben wir alle* (Te Deum) for the millennium of the German *Reich*; another command performance of *Antigone*; and, in the fall, a production of Shakespeare's *Midsummer Night's Dream*, which required the composition of new incidental music. And so, Fanny greeted Felix in February, May, July, August, September, and October before, late in November, the composer returned to the Berlin residence with his family and possessions and took up his official post as *Generalmusikdirektor* to the court of Frederick William IV.

While Fanny's center remained Berlin, other family members traveled abroad during the summer of 1843. The Dirichlets commenced a long-planned, leisurely journey to Italy, and Wilhelm, having again visited Brunswick in April to execute portraits for the ducal court, departed for London in June. His original purpose was to deliver the completed *Duke of Brunswick* painting to Lord Egerton, but added to that task was a new commission from the Prussian king for a portrait of his godson, the one-year-old Albert Edward, Prince of Wales.[17] Once again Queen Victoria and Prince Albert received Wilhelm. Mindful that Felix had accompanied her the year before when she deigned to sing Fanny's *Italien*, Wilhelm brought more of his wife's songs, but whether the queen read through them is unclear.[18] When Wilhelm offered as a gift his painting *Miriam's Song of Thanksgiving*, the queen acknowledged the gesture in her own way: "Put out your finger," Wilhelm wrote Fanny. "I will place on it a ring with the same, fresh feeling when I gave you your engagement ring. It has a thick diamond in the middle, surrounded by two emeralds just as large, and I think it will look well on your hand. The queen gave it to me for the

Miriam painting, and since you are Miriam, I am giving it to you. As Miriam you will live in Buckingham Palace, and as Miriam you will appear on engravings, as Prince Albert has firmly promised. I am convinced that the queen, since she knows my modest hand, gave the ring with the dear intention that you should wear it. She herself chose it, as her jeweler told me today."[19] Taken aback by the royal magnanimity, Fanny confided to her diary that the ring was too lovely and valuable to wear: "really, to carry seven or eight hundred thalers on one's finger is nonsense."[20]

i

Another diary entry from 1843 reveals a quite different issue—Fanny's despair about her flagging creativity: "My own music is going dreadfully. For an eternity I have composed nothing, I have totally lost my muse, and my energies for performing too have dropped off considerably."[21] The long drought—no new music by Fanny survives from 1842—finally ended in March 1843. That month she began composing music for Goethe's *Faust*, not for the familiar first part, which inspired many composers, from Prince Antoni Henryk Radziwiłł to Berlioz, Schumann, Liszt, Gounod, and others, but for the opening scene of the second part. Here Faust, having left Gretchen to her fate, has traveled with Mephistopheles to a charming landscape (*anmutige Gegend*) where, exhausted, he falls into a deep, restorative sleep, watched over by Ariel and her elfin siblings, and awakens the next morning to a new life. In what follows, he becomes an advisor to the court of Charles V, fathers a child with Helen of Troy, and saves the German *Reich* from defeat. Goethe had begun drafting the second part in 1826 and finished it just months before his death in 1832. The opening scene and a few more installments were available to Fanny as early as 1828,[22] though when she first contemplated music remains unknown. Far less accessible than *Faust* I, *Faust* II offers compelling evidence that Goethe conceived his epic poem as a *Lesedrama* (closet drama)—it was to be read, not dramatically realized, and thus was intended for the private reader.

By composing music for the first scene (H-U 389)[23]—Fanny scored for soprano solo, four-part women's choir (and soloists), and piano—she effectively brought Goethe's verses out of the private library into the realm of "public" music making. To that end, she sent a copy to Franz Hauser and asked him to consider performing her setting with his *Singverein* in Vienna, so that she might join his "league."[24] Fanny confessed that she had envisioned the work with orchestral accompaniment but, limited by her own "dilettantism," had not orchestrated the piano part: "Actually the piece should be set with orchestra; it was so conceived, but there again you have the joys of dilettantism: first of all, I write very poorly for orchestra, and second, even if it were a masterpiece, I would always have to perform it from the piano-vocal version, and so I spared myself the effort, and the score belongs to many of my deeds that will remain unfinished."[25] Felix, it seems, had weighed in with some criticism, and Fanny finished a "much-improved" revision of the composition by mid-July 1843.[26] In turning to Hauser, she hoped to find a sympathetic judge, and at least "no fearsome Cerberus." The depth of her sense of artistic inadequacy emerged when she finally sent Hauser the score in November. Her accompanying letter contained another self-deprecating comment that underscored her conflicting needs to compose and yet subordinate her creativity to her prescribed role as mistress of Leipzigerstrasse no. 3: "Please excuse and censure all the amateurish, female snags within; a dilettante is a dreadful creature, a female author even more so, but when the two are joined into one person, of course the most dreadful being of all results. At least so far I have abstained from the printer's ink; if someone suffers, it is my friends, and why is one in this world if not to be suffered by one's friends?"[27]

Through-composed, Fanny's *Faust* music comprises several sections alternating between Ariel and the elves, who hover about Faust either in chorus or as soloists; knitting together the whole is the piano, which transports us to the supernatural realm in an introduction and provides transitions between individual sections. Most striking, perhaps, is what Fanny omitted—Faust's rejuvenating lines upon his awakening, which fill out fully the second half of Goethe's scene. Instead, we are to imagine him recumbent and asleep throughout the entire composition. As in her music for Wilhelm's *tableaux vivants* (see p. 263), Fanny has thus written "disembodied" spirit music, in this case largely in keys—E major and E minor—that occasionally bring her music close to the elfin style of Felix's *Midsummer Night's Dream* music. There is another telling sibling comparison—with the Scherzo of her brother's Octet, which, as we know from Fanny (see p. 96), had been a calculated response to the *Walpurgis Night's Dream* interlude from the first part of *Faust*. Like Felix in 1825, Fanny in 1843 dutifully observed Goethe's musical cues—just as Felix worked into his capricious music imitations of bagpipes and, at the end, the evaporating *pianissimo* puff, all present in Goethe's verses, so Fanny incorporated into her piano introduction imitations of Aeolian harps, which, Goethe advises the reader, accompany Ariel's opening song, and in Fanny's score assume the form of rippling arpeggiations in the high treble of the piano.

In an early draft of the scene Goethe apportioned the elves' material into four strophes, marking the passage of time from dusk to night, early morning, and Faust's awakening, and provided them with musical labels—*Serenade* (Evening Music), *Notturno* (Night Music), *Matutino* (Morning Song), and *Reveille* (Reveille).[28] Fanny's music observes these divisions: the choral *Serenade* in A major takes on the quality of a lullaby; the *Notturno*, in a dark C-sharp minor, is scored for four soloists; the *Matutino*, reassigned by Fanny in a moment of creative license from the elves' chorus to Ariel, turns to a restless E minor as Faust is "healed"; and the *Reveille*, with pulsating chords in the piano, reintroduces E major and near the end revives the material of the opening, so that the composition becomes a circular, self-contained whole. Its closing lines, "All things can be done by men / who are quick to see and act," prepare us for Faust's revival, but there is no "tremendous tumult announcing the approach of the sun,"[29] as Goethe specified; Fanny chose not to extend her *Faust* project further, and her composition ends quietly.

In two exquisite lieder from the summer of 1843 on texts of Goethe and Eichendorff, Fanny explored further musical twilight and night, though not from the "perspective" of elves. The lapidary "Dämmrung senkte sich von oben" ("Twilight Sank from Above," H-U 392),[30] on a late poem by Goethe, presents an image of death as a falling dusk that slowly extinguishes everything familiar (example 11.1). The inexorably weighted chromatic lines of the vocal part give way only to a brief appearance of the evening star, before all shifts into Goethe's fog-shrouded unknown. In *Nachtwanderer* (H-U 397)[31] Fanny uses various musical means—harmonically distorting augmented triads, blurring piano tremolos, and an unexpected, disorienting change in meter—to evoke Eichendorff's dreamlike state of the night wanderer.

Her other compositions of 1843 include a series of piano pieces culminating that autumn in one of her most important efforts, the Sonata in G Minor

EXAMPLE 11.1.   Fanny Hensel, "Dämmrung senkte sich von oben" (1843)

(H-U 395). At some point that year she selected twelve of her shorter key-board works and had them copied for Felix, perhaps for his birthday in February, or for Christmas.[32] The title page of this album—it reads *Clavierstücke von Fanny Hensel geb. Mendelssohn Bartholdy. Für Felix, 1843 (Twelve Piano Pieces by Fanny Hensel née Mendelssohn Bartholdy. For Felix, 1843)*—invests the appointed music with a certain authority, almost as if Fanny had thoughts of publishing the pieces and of forgoing the "joys of dilettantism" to enter the lists of public life. Indeed, two years earlier, she had already vetted several of these pieces by including them in her *Reisealbum* of 1841; and in fact no fewer than five subsequently appeared in her first three published collections of piano music, opp. 2, 4/5, and 6, issued in 1846 and 1847. One piece that survives only in the 1843 album is the Adagio in E-flat Major (H-U 396),[33] a piano lied that approaches in its tuneful lyricism and gentle, accompanying sixteenth-note figurations Felix's *Lied ohne Worte* op. 67, no. 1—as it happens, also in E-flat major, and composed in July 1843, so that the two may record another example of a sibling exchange.

Three other pieces from 1843 not in Fanny's album show different facets of her style. The Allegro molto vivace in A Major, published in 1846 as op. 2, no. 4, offers another brilliant, etudelike variant of the three-hand technique, in which she assigned a high treble melody to the third, fourth, and fifth fingers of the right hand, the bass line to the fifth finger of the left, and a stream of churning sextuplets to the remaining fingers of each.● In contrast, the less challenging Allegretto ma non troppo in E Minor (H-U 393)[34] concerns not so much virtuoso display as spinning out a monothematic sonata-form movement from a somewhat Puckish, ethereal opening subject. Some 150 measures in length, the Allegretto is dwarfed by the more ambitious Allegro agitato in G Minor (H-U 391),[35] fully 208 measures and a compelling demonstration of Fanny's abiding interest in addressing the challenges of sonata form and large-scale composition.

Once again, she adhered to no textbook model but contrived her own solution, so that traditional formal constraints could bend to the expressive ebb and flow of her music. Thus, she enlarged the exposition of the movement to accommodate three instead of two distinct thematic groups. In the first, a poignant, songlike melody in the soprano competes for our attention against a restless tenor line, while agitated triplet chords separate the two. This rich, duetlike texture then yields to a simpler, more lyrical second subject, supported by triplets in the bass. For the third group, Fanny shifts to a three-hand passage, in which cascading and rebounding sixteenth notes separate a sketch-like treble melody from the bass line. Much of the development unfolds as an intensified exploration of the first subject, building inevitably to the climactic point of arrival, the recapitulation; here the tonic G minor returns, not in its secure root position but over an unstable pedal point. In an imaginative experiment, Fanny then reverses the second and third groups before concluding with a denouement-like coda. Now the soprano and tenor lines move against each other in a chromatically grating, contrary motion, a striking texture that Brahms would later explore orchestrally in the intense opening of his first symphony (1876). Unexpectedly, Fanny's movement concludes not in G minor, but G major, supported in the final cadential gestures by augmented triads, a distinctive progression Chopin favored in several piano compositions, among them the second Scherzo, op. 31 of 1837.

Fanny's Allegro agitato could easily have served as the first movement of a sonata. Instead, it impresses as a preliminary study for her weighty, four-movement Piano Sonata in G Minor (H-U 395)[36] that followed in the autumn of 1843 but, like *Das Jahr*, remained in manuscript for nearly 150 years until its postmodern awakening in 1991. Once again Fanny left her own imprint on the hallowed genre and, in the first movement, on sonata form, the predominant formal construct of nineteenth-century instrumental music. Over a deep bass tremolo the first theme enters with a falling line in the soprano etched into a series of resolute chords (example 11.2). This thematic descent actually replicates the first bar of the Allegro agitato, but this time the melodic continuity is abruptly broken by disjunct motion, so that the theme is no longer song-like, but a sharply profiled series of dramatic gestures, cut by jagged leaps to progressively higher registers. For at least one observer, the opening "offers in miniature almost the complete semiotic code of Romantic hypermasculinity in music."[37] The bridge, which begins some twenty bars into the movement, soon departs from the tonic and passes, unconventionally enough, through remote keys (E-flat minor and B minor) before settling into the "expected"

EXAMPLE 11.2. Fanny Hensel, Piano Sonata in G Minor, first movement (1843)

second key, B-flat major. Here, the informed listener awaits the appearance of a contrasting second theme, according to standard sonata form. But Fanny deflates that expectation; instead, she extends the bridge and turns it back to the tonic, at which point the opening theme reappears above the bass tremolo, now *fortissimo*, marking the recapitulation. In effect, Fanny has foreshortened the sonata process, so that the bridge assumes the function of a quasi development. But when the bridge subsequently returns in the recapitulation in the key of G major, it projects more clearly the character of a second, contrasting theme, and so can be understood to perform a dual function.

The purpose of Fanny's telescoping of the sonata process becomes clear toward the end of the first movement, linked, like the second and third movements, to what follows. The individual movements do not stand alone but are subordinate to an overarching process and tonal scheme, here an ascending succession of keys that move first by third, from G minor to B minor (Scherzo) and D Major (slow movement), then by fourth, to G major (finale). As it happens, this scheme mirrors the descending trajectory of Felix's Cello Sonata no. 2 in D Major, op. 58, finished around June 1843, and perhaps an incentive for Fanny to write her own substantial sonata. Felix's four movements move by descending thirds, from D major to B minor and G major, and then by fourth, to D major. What is more, Felix linked his third and fourth movements through a transition, a technique that Fanny now applied to her entire composition.

Of the later movements, perhaps the most extraordinary is the eerie Scherzo in B minor, well removed in key and affect from the opening movement. Above open-fifth drones in the treble, Fanny fashions a disarming, haunting melody in the natural form of the minor, as if to conjure up a vision of folk music (example 11.3). For the middle portion, the trio, she shifts to the highest register to introduce shimmering B major tremolos into the accompaniment that gently flicker against a delicate melody above.❸ Like a fleeting vision of the sublime, the passage stands in marked contrast to the world-weary dissonance of the first movement, though the tremolo, a marker of agitation, is an element common to both. For the third movement, reminiscent of so many *Lieder ohne Worte*, Fanny reverted to her familiar *Gondellied* style, with its lilting rhythms and lapping accompaniment. The graceful melody appears first in the treble in octaves, and then descends to the tenor register, which eventually opens up to an expansive three-hand arrangement, with the melody in octaves in the high treble, the flowing accompaniment in the middle register, and, as a new element, a series of repeated notes in the low bass, yet another reference to the earlier tremolos. This enriched texture prepares us for the finale, a virtuoso tour de force in which Fanny again explores technically demanding three-hand passages, now in a rondo alternating between persistent sixteenth-note and whirling sextuplet figurations. Nearly the entire last page yields to adamantine repetitions of the tonic harmony. If the sonata, Fanny's last major

EXAMPLE 11.3. Fanny Hensel, Piano Sonata in G Minor, second movement (1843)

piano work, begins with a dramatic, assertive gesture, it concludes with massive accumulations of sonorities reminiscent of Beethoven.

Though Fanny reawakened her compositional muse in 1843, the Sunday concerts remained suspended until October, after a nearly eighteen-month pause. One reason for the hiatus was a physical symptom that began affecting her early that year, not long after Lea's death. Fanny noticed a disconcerting lack of sensation in her arms, which increased in severity during the summer; it was to be a harbinger of her own final illness. Not until late July was she able to report improvement, after some unusual treatments: "The numbness has almost disappeared, and the weakness comes and goes by fits. Galvanism did not suit me, and I am now trying bathing them in a decoction of brandy, which prescription has acquainted me with the interesting fact that in Berlin, where every third shop sells schnapps, there is no distillery, and I shall have to see where I can get the stuff. I played very well here the other day, but the next, at Mme. Decker's, worse than any night-watchman—in a word, I can no more depend upon myself now than I could at fourteen, and it is hard to become incapable before I have reversed those figures."[38] Fanny's first musical *Morgensoirée* of the year took place on October 29 and featured the premiere of her *Faust* music, along with several works by Felix—the Cello Sonata in D Major op. 58, performed by Fanny and Leopold Ganz; part-songs from his *Sechs Lieder* op. 48; and his setting of Psalm 13 for alto, chorus, and organ.[39] A second concert, probably given on November 12, was unsuccessful, but the third and last, presented on December 3, brought the abridged series to a brilliant conclusion.[40] She performed a piano trio by Beethoven and, with her recently resettled brother, a duet arrangement of the polonaise finale of Beethoven's Triple Piano Concerto. The pièce de résistance, however, was Felix's entr'acte music to *A Midsummer Night's Dream*, also rendered by the siblings as a piano duet to the "great applause" of the audience.

Only weeks before, on the king's birthday in October, the new production of Shakespeare's comedy had been premiered in Potsdam before a private audience. Fanny was in attendance to witness Felix's collaboration with Ludwig Tieck, along with an entourage of musicians from Leipzig—Ferdinand Hiller, Felix's concertmaster Ferdinand David, the Danish composer Niels Gade, and the twelve-year-old Joseph Joachim, who, Fanny wrote, was already "such a clever violinist that David [could] teach him nothing more."[41] To her sister Rebecka she sent an extended report of Felix's delectable incidental music, including the breathless Scherzo, luminescent Nocturne, and regal wedding march. If in 1826 he had first dreamed the *Midsummer Night's Dream* at Leipzigerstrasse no. 3, where he conceived the celebrated orchestral overture, in 1843 his Shakespearean reveries shifted to Frederick William's palace, Sanssouci. In conceptualizing new music for the play Felix made the critical decision to reuse elements of the overture—its rich network of motives for the elves, lovers, Mechanicals, and court of Theseus, and the magical four sustained wind chords that framed the overture, marking the passing from real to fairy time—so that the incidental music seemed inextricably woven together with the overture. Through his new score Felix in effect reexperienced his musical adolescence with Fanny, and the significance of the event was not lost on her, for she recalled "how we had all at different ages gone through the whole of the parts from Peasblossom to Hermia and Helena, 'and now it had come to such a glorious ending.' But we really were brought up on the 'Midsummer Night's Dream,' and Felix especially had made it his own, almost recreating the characters which had sprung from Shakespeare's exhaustless genius." And yet the performance was nearly too much for her to absorb, as she vividly felt the presence of her mother and indeed imagined hearing her laugh.[42]

ii

Among the new musicians to enter Fanny's intimate musical circle late in 1843 was Niels Gade, who had accompanied Felix from Leipzig for the premiere of the new incidental music. Upon hearing Fanny play at a chamber music party organized by Paul Mendelssohn Bartholdy, Gade easily rendered a positive verdict, "totally excellent" (*ganz ausgezeichnet*). The next evening, he was "totally transported" (*ganz entzückt*) at her residence by her compositions, which "for a lady," he conceded, were "really very pretty." To his parents in Copenhagen he reported, "there is much invention, skill, genius, and energy in these pieces. They say that she exercised much influence on Felix Mendelssohn's musical development. She is namely older than he. Their compositions are very similar."[43]

We cannot identify which compositions Fanny shared with Gade, though the realization that she had played a significant role in Felix's musical development must have been revelatory to the young Dane, whose own music was indebted to the rough-hewn *Volkstümlichkeit* of Felix's *Hebrides* Overture and *Scottish* Symphony. In any event, Gade returned to Leipzig before the new year, when Fanny began composing new piano compositions and lieder. Among them were an untitled piano piece in G minor (H-U 403) and an Allegro moderato assai in A Minor (H-U 405)[44] that in their modest dimensions turned back from the large-scale scope of the Piano Sonata in G Minor. On the other hand, the passionate Allegro molto in E Minor (H-U 410),[45] which featured an elegiac, descending melody superimposed upon swirling, agitated sextuplets, stretched considerably the miniature frame of the piano lied. Fanny enriched the conventional pattern of keys—her piece begins in E minor, modulates to G major, and returns to E minor before arriving in E major—with an excursion to D-flat major and with several chromatically altered harmonic progressions, and thereby gave free reign to her inspiration. The result was a composition that, as Gade had experienced in October 1843, was indeed similar to Felix's music—the E major passages, for example, recall his *Lied ohne Worte* op. 38, no. 3—but that nevertheless began to separate stylistically in its finer details from her sibling's work.

With the new year Fanny turned too to her preferred medium—the art song—and produced four, possibly five settings of Rückert, Goethe, and Eichendorff. *Zauberkreis* (*Circle of Magic*, H-U 399)[46] employs a recurring diminished-seventh sonority and breathless, palpitating chords in the piano to capture Rückert's image of beauty as a self-contained circle realized in every rose petal and the warbling of every nightingale. In *Liebe in der Fremde* (*Love Abroad*, H-U 402),[47] the piano supports with rolled, arpeggiated chords Goethe's protagonist, who nostalgically recalls a distant love affair with zither in hand. From Eichendorff's poetry Fanny selected early in January 1844 a text Felix had already composed in 1842, "Es weiß und rät es doch keiner" (H-U 401),[48] but a considerably more serious effort was her setting a few weeks later of the same poet's *Im Herbst* (*In Autumn*, H-U 407).[49] Here Eichendorff contrasts his preferred theme of dreamlike forest solitude with the soft pealing of distant evening bells that at once beckon from the protagonist's childhood and yet draw him to his grave. Fanny responds by establishing a musical dichotomy between a restless, driving figure for the journey to the forest❸ and more subdued music with repeated bass notes for the bells.

Another Eichendorff setting, *Traum* (H-U 412), may date as early as January 1844, though it survives only in a presentation copy that Wilhelm embellished with a vignette and Fanny dated in October.[50] In the vignette, we see a sleeping shepherd who in the poem dreams on a moonlit night of his distant home and family. Fanny actually compiled the text from two poems of Eichendorff titled *Erinnerung* (*Reminiscence*), from which she selected and rearranged verses of romantic nostalgia. At least two passages of the song seem to draw on works of Felix, including phrases from his lied "Es weiß und rät es doch keiner" (op. 99, no. 6) and a major composition that, as we shall shortly see, preoccupied Fanny in the early months of 1844, the cantata *Die erste Walpurgisnacht*.[51]

Well removed from the glare of Felix's public career in Berlin—for the new year he inaugurated a new setting of Psalm 91 for the Berlin Cathedral, and in the following months directed concerts for the king (including Beethoven's Ninth Symphony and a large-scale performance of Handel's *Israel in Egypt*)—Fanny quietly resumed her Sunday series. Unlike Felix, who appeared at exclusive Berlin functions and freely mingled with visiting musicians, she maintained a comparatively low profile. But when she was invited to a celebration of the octogenarian sculptor J. G. Schadow in May, she betrayed her deeper feelings by confiding to Rebecka, "As, however, it would be an unheard-of event for me to appear at a public dinner—eclipses and leap-years are frequent occurrences in comparison—I suppose something will happen to prevent my going."[52]

Thankfully, the Sunday musicales provided a creative outlet for her. The first concert of the new season occurred on February 11. In attendance were Prussian nobility, artists, and the novelist, feminist, and social critic Fanny Lewald, who in a short account made a point of confirming that Fanny's concerts brought together Berliners from dissimilar economic backgrounds. Lewald described Fanny as "small and, apart from her soulful, powerful eyes, rather homely, but she had a very sharp intellect, was well-educated and very self-determined, and as a musician evenly matched with her brother."[53] The concert program included the Piano Quartet of Carl Maria von Weber with Fanny rendering the piano, Felix the viola, and the Gans brothers the violin and cello parts; an aria from Haydn's *Creation* performed by Pauline Decker; some scenes from Heinrich Marschner's *Der Templar und die Jüdin*; and variations of Ferdinand David dispatched by the thirteen-year-old Joseph Joachim and Felix. But the two siblings offered the pièce de résistance that morning— a theme and variations for piano duet that Felix had notated only two days before. Reusing the theme and other material from an earlier variation set for solo piano (op. 83), he added several new virtuoso variations, which Fanny took page by page from his desk as he copied them and practiced at the piano.[54] On the title page of this Andante con Variazioni (op. 83a), Felix added a playful subheading in Italian, *composto per la musica delle Domeniche in casa Hensel dalla (vecchia) Vedova Felice*,[55] though why he referred to himself as an "(old) widower" remains unclear.

Perhaps Fanny suggested the idea of composing the duet; she herself finished a lyrical Allegretto in E-flat major for piano four hands late in January (H-U 406), and then, probably in response to Felix's variations, produced two additional duets in March, the Allegro molto in C Minor (H-U 408) and Allegretto grazioso in A-flat Major (H-U 409).[56] If the latter offers a limpid *Lied ohne Worte*, with hints perhaps of a *Gondellied*, the Allegro molto is a weightier piece—a turbulent sonata-form movement, albeit a movement in which Fanny again abridged and reconfigured the formal process. Thus, in lieu of a development, a short transition leads to a recapitulation compressed by the curtailment of the second theme. At times, the overly weighted exposition actually takes on the character of a development, as when Fanny unexpectedly diverts the coursing music briefly to D-flat minor and freely treats the sinuous, romantic second theme so that it appears not in the expected E-flat major, but in A-flat and then F major. Fanny's cascading sixteenth-note figurations approach the tone and affect of Felix's Piano Concerto in D Minor and the stormy overture to *Die erste Walpurgisnacht*. But occasionally her music seems to adumbrate the dramatically charged first movement of Felix's second piano trio in the same key of C minor, op. 66, sent to Fanny on her birthday in 1845, as if to extend the musical exchange between the siblings.

On March 10, 1844, Fanny presented the second Sunday concert of her series. She appeared in a favorite chamber work from her youth, the Hummel Piano Quintet, and programmed a duet from Beethoven's *Fidelio*, some songs performed by Felix and Pauline Decker, and again Ferdinand David's variations dispatched by Joseph Joachim, now no longer an "infant prodigy" but "a most praiseworthy child, and Sebastian's great friend to boot."[57] But the major work was Felix's *Die erste Walpurgisnacht*, for soloists, chorus, and orchestra rendered by Fanny at the piano. In preparation, she held three rehearsals; Felix attended only the last and, despite his sister's entreaty, declined to direct. Evidently she used a piano-vocal score of the cantata recently seen through the press by Felix, who had arranged the overture for piano duet.[58] And so, at the start of the performance, he played the overture with Fanny and assisted her in the "difficult parts" by adding "bits, now in the bass, now in the treble," before rejoining the audience. On April 14 Fanny directed the cantata again, but the second hearing did not surpass the first, which remained "the most brilliant Sunday-music that ever was."[59] The event was indeed preceded by the arrival of twenty-two carriages in the courtyard of Leipzigerstrasse no. 3 and graced by the presence of eight princesses and a young, slender man whose eyes, according to Fanny Lewald, "had something uncommonly surprising, even something overpowering about them"[60]—Franz Liszt.

During the early months of 1844, Felix's "sweetness and good temper," as Fanny reported to Rebecka, were "still [in] *crescendo*."[61] But in April, having fulfilled his commitments to the king, he departed with his family for Leipzig and Frankfurt, before embarking in May on his eighth English sojourn. We are unable to trace Fanny's concerts during this period, though we know that the last, given on June 23, concluded with a part-song of her brother.[62] She appears to have spent the summer quietly, while Wilhelm worked on a new oil painting of Wenceslaus, the hapless early fourteenth-century Roman and German emperor, for the Frankfurt town hall.[63] Most of the Hensels' friends were away for the summer, but they enjoyed at least one unusual diversion in July—the arrival of Hans Christian Andersen. The celebrated Danish author would later describe Fanny as "very similar to her brother, a true musical genius," who in appearance "shared every trait": "she was genial and lovely, had her brother's spirit and cheerfulness, played like him with a proficiency and impression that astonished."[64] For her part, Fanny reported to Felix: "*À propos*—Andersen sends his best wishes to you and especially Cécile. I know that you've heard him recite fairy tales, for I remember that Carl once cried over them (he was justified). But have you ever heard him deliver these children's tales in an incredibly ingenuous manner to nobody but adults, as I last night? That's beyond the bounds of nature and must be seen to be believed. I felt so much like a child again that I was on the verge of believing in the stork and demanding mushy food."[65] In the same letter, Fanny announced a new project, a collection of songs she was composing for a short novel (*kleiner Roman*) that Wilhelm had written for her. Conceding that Felix would easily dispatch the task—"you write as many notes in three-quarters of an hour as I do in three-quarters of a year"—she redoubled her efforts on what she described as "another small collection," a collaborative album to be embellished by Wilhelm's vignettes.[66] But how far the couple progressed is unclear, and nothing appears to have survived of the project.

Meanwhile, from Frankfurt Felix's career remained in full swing. In response to another commission from Frederick William, the composer began incidental music for Racine's *Athalie* and prepared to direct a music festival in Zweibrücken; then, in September, he finished a masterwork that had eluded him for years—the Violin Concerto in E Minor, op. 64. During his English sojourn he had agreed to assemble a collection of new compositions for organ and to that end now recalled the A major piece written in England and Wales for Fanny's wedding in 1829. But when he asked her to forward the manuscript from Berlin, a little family drama erupted, half serious and half comic. Fanny, on July 30: "I don't have the piece. I've never had the piece, and you must fashion it anew by heart, even though it will probably be quite different."[67] Felix, on August 15: "But search again in the music cabinet, in the drawer where several items of music are mixed together; there is a red, open portfolio...in which lies a pile of my unbound music in manuscript—songs, piano pieces, printed and unprinted things, and there among them you will readily find the organ piece in A major."[68] Now enlisting the assistance of Wilhelm and Sebastian, Fanny commenced a thorough search and turned up parts of Bach cantatas, but not the desired item.

On August 21, she drew a tragic mask on her stationery and filled the page with her own style of wry, self-effacing irony:

> Look, O mocking Herr Bruder! I would have worn this mask the rest
> of my life, and never let you see me bare-eyed again, if this time you
> were right. To be sure, your spectacles are quite good, but from Soden
> [near Frankfurt] they do not discern my music cabinet with unerring

accuracy. But if, when you return, you find said muttonhead in the place you described so clairvoyantly, then condemn me to some medieval punishment, perhaps to carry dogs... or ride through the streets on a donkey, though I really would rather apologize before your portrait. Moreover, the enclosed protocol, dictated to a learned jurist, attests to the enormous exertions expended to unearth the treasure. If faith could move organ preludes as well as mountains, I would have found it somewhere in my district; indeed, given your confident tone, I trod with some shame before my cabinet, and, resigned in advance, quietly contemplated whether owing to my defeat I should buy a small farm and withdraw from the world, or, stigmatized, wander further and further among my fellow men.[69]

There then followed the "official" report signed by the *Protokoll-Führer* (Sebastian), certifying that the search had indeed failed to turn up the "much discussed" composition.

Left to his own devices, Felix drew on his memory to reconstruct the composition, but now recast and expanded it by adding a learned chorale fugue in A minor, in the middle of which the sobering strains of "Aus tiefer Noth" (Luther's paraphrase of Psalm 130) appeared in the pedal part. Felix then notated the revised version and three other organ pieces in a fair copy provisionally titled *Zwölf Studien für die Orgel* (*Twelve Studies for the Organ*), which he brought to Berlin and presented to Fanny on her thirty-ninth birthday.[70] At last his sister had a copy of her wedding piece, albeit transformed into what would become in 1845 the opening movement of the Organ Sonata in A Major, op. 65, no. 3. On this issue, at least, Felix had made musical amends with his sister, though a new change in their lives now affected their relationship.

iii

At the end of September, Felix had returned alone to Berlin to gain release from the king's service. During his tenure as *Generalmusikdirektor* he had felt hindered by unending bureaucratic obstacles, by conflicts with church authorities about the role of music in the Prussian liturgy, and by the inability of the court to define a sufficiently ample sphere in which he could freely work and compose. No doubt, too, the repressive political atmosphere was particularly stifling. In her diary Fanny mentioned the "daily prohibitions, the scribbling and grinding of the government and police from all sides,"[71] and observed to Rebecka: "What a rickety concern the State of Prussia must be, if it is really in danger the moment three students form themselves into a union, or three professors publish a periodical!... The never-ending prohibitions, the meddling with everything, the system of constant *espionage*, carried on in the midst of peace and in spite of the quiet disposition of the nation, has now reached a climax which is perfectly intolerable."[72] Early in October, Felix reached an understanding with the king—in exchange for a lowered salary, the composer was no longer obliged to live in Berlin and agreed to fulfill only the occasional royal commission. Through the end of November he remained to conduct his final orchestral concerts and *Paulus*, and then departed his family home, having vowed to Eduard Devrient never again to live in Berlin.[73]

To her diary Fanny confided her reaction: "When I hear him talk about it I cannot help agreeing with him, for his motives are absolutely noble and worthy of him; but still it is a pity, and very hard for me, who enjoyed the happiness of living near him and his family so intensely. And all the music I was looking forward to!"[74] But to Cécile she admitted her distress at the suddenness of the decision, and at the greater family loss: "It is really sad that life should be passing without our being able to enjoy it together, especially after such hopes and prospects. By the present arrangement I shall completely lose sight of you and the children, and, believe me, I cannot even now think of that without tears, much as it has occupied my mind already; and believe, also, that I love you more than I can express."[75]

Having "lost" her brother a second time, Fanny now faced another family crisis. For a few months, the Hensels had received conflicting, but increasingly worrisome reports about Rebecka's health. Suffering from jaundice, she had planned to return from Italy with her husband, but when he contracted typhoid fever, they were obliged instead to winter in Florence. Their situation became more complicated when, contrary to the advice of her Roman doctors, Rebecka realized she was pregnant. Concerned by the news, Fanny and Wilhelm abruptly decided in December to travel to Italy. After Fanny recovered from a bout of nosebleed, they departed on January 2, 1845, and traveled by train and coach to Leipzig and Munich, where they paused to visit the art galleries, and then to Innsbruck and Bologna, before reaching Florence on January 19. An album decorated with vignettes by Felix served as Fanny's diary, and here she faithfully recorded her narrative of the second Italian sojourn. But somewhere during the return trip in August she lost the album and had to reconstruct her account from memory, and a few letters and drawings, after her arrival in Berlin.

Upon arriving in Florence, Fanny was shocked by her sister's appearance and disfigurement from her ordeal. The Hensels took quarters directly opposite the Dirichlets', permitting them to converse through their windows. Rebecka's health now began to improve, and she rented a piano to "unite the agreeable to the agreeable."[76] But within a week, Wilhelm made a difficult decision: unable to procure models so that he could work, he left for Rome. For the next three weeks, Fanny nursed her sister, while Gustav tended to his children and tutored Sebastian in math, Latin, and Greek. Sebastian later consigned the experience to his most dreadful memories, for his uncle, despite his brilliance as a mathematician, knew only a little Latin, less Greek, and "absolutely nothing" about teaching.[77]

Expecting her sister to deliver in April, Fanny ordered a wardrobe of clothes from Berlin. But on February 13, Rebecka went into labor, and after several anxious hours, the summoned doctor arrived nearly simultaneously with her daughter, appropriately named Florentina. For the next month Fanny managed Rebecka's household and correspondence and helped care for her niece, which led her to contemplate music of a different kind, as she explained to Felix: "I intend to lead art, which has strayed much too far from nature, back to its original path, and to this end am studying with great enthusiasm the utterances of my youngest niece as the mood strikes me. A certain degree of confusion and bad craftsmanship predominates, a *mezzoforte* muttering that promises very interesting effects in its transferal to the orchestra. When Berlioz will have placed the 50 pianos that he considers necessary, I would advise him to place a wet nurse with a nursing child who hasn't been fed for a few hours next to each. I'm convinced that the public, especially the mothers of the children, would be very moved."[78] After attending Flora's baptism on March 15, Fanny departed with Sebastian for Rome. To her dismay, she discovered that for weeks Wilhelm had been suffering in stoic silence a serious illness, diagnosed as an inflammation of the liver but probably related to recurring issues with his gallbladder. Now Fanny slowly nursed her husband back to health, until he was able to insert some reassuring verses in a letter to Rebecka. The final stanza read:

Alle Sorgen, alle Schmerzen	Earth is happy; all afflictions
sind verweht und abgethan	are with ice and snow gone by;
offen stehn die seel'gen Herzen	every breath wafts benedictions
um den Frühling zu empfahn.	from the blue and sunny sky.[79]

The Hensels resided near the Pincian Hill and Trevi Fountain and surrounded themselves, as in 1841, with German artists, chief among them Julius Elsasser, the architect Anton Hallmann, and the landscape painter Julius Helfft (1818–1894). Fanny had at her disposal a piano, though she described it as "quite out of tune, fully half a note too low, and giving out as much sound as a fur cap on a woolen blanket."[80] (A drawing by August Kaselowsky from April 1845 depicts Fanny presumably improvising at this instrument, a grand piano.[81]) Composition seems to have been far from her mind during this period; still, she happily reacquainted herself with the Norwegian pianist Charlotte Thygeson and informally read through Felix's Piano Trio in D Minor on more than one occasion. When Wilhelm's health permitted, there were visits to old haunts, including the Villa Wolkonsky, and an excursion to Albano, and new sites to explore—the Vigna Barberini on the Palatine, sixteenth- and seventeenth-century villas Poniatowsky and Ludovisi, and San Pietro in

Montorio on the Janiculum, with its High Renaissance *Tempietto* said to mark the site of St. Peter's martydom.

In mid-May, the Hensels left Rome for Florence. En route, they visited the Franciscan monastery and basilica in Assisi; Fanny later recalled the deep impression the idyllic site made as nearly powerful enough to convert her to Catholicism. "What is the empty splendor of Roman churches compared to this?" she asked in her diary.[82] Rejoining Rebecka in Florence (Gustav had departed in April to resume his lectures in Berlin), the Hensels lingered a few more weeks and admired for hours the views from the Romanesque San Miniato al Monte, though Wilhelm suffered severe burns from painting for long stretches of time in the direct sunlight.

Shortly before departing Florence in mid-June, Fanny copied from memory two movements of J. S. Bach and sent them to Julius Elsasser, along with one of her own, the wistful *Abschied von Rom* of 1840 (H-U 352). Her accompanying letter conceded that there might well be errors in her transcriptions (to the contrary, examination of the opening of the first Bach movement, the Sonatina from the cantata *Gottes Zeit ist die allerbeste Zeit*, reveals that Fanny's acute memory rarely failed her). She fully appreciated, she reassured Elsasser, the presumption of adding her compositional voice to Bach's and, indeed, only after a lengthy pause, which Fanny described as a kind of desert (*eine Art von Wüste*), did she permit herself to copy out her own composition.[83] Having accomplished this task, Fanny joined Wilhelm, Sebastian, and Rebecka and her children to commence the first leg of the return trip, traversing lush landscapes that impressed as a "continuous garden."[84] Reaching the Ligurian Sea at Pisa, they paused to experience the Luminara, the annual festival of lights in honor of Rainerius, patron saint of the city. Pressing through throngs gathered to view the glittering spectacle, they found a commanding view from a third-floor loggia from which they could trace the semicircular bend in the Arno, its palaces, quays, bridges, barges, and boats—all illuminated, along with the "remotest alleys," by means of carefully constructed scaffolds that facilitated precise placement of lighting. During the day Fanny was "vexed" by the leaning tower, "for as it is, one's eye is only distressed by it, and yet from its pure and noble proportions it might be one of the finest buildings of Italy."[85] But the strangest, most exotic experience was a visit to the nearby farm of the Grand Duke of Tuscany, where the party encountered some fifty grazing, ruminating camels, the only herd in Europe since the time of the Crusades.

Proceeding along the coast, they stopped in La Specia, not far from where Shelley's body had washed ashore in 1822 and been cremated in a grim ceremony attended by Lord Byron. Fanny did not mention Shelley in her diary, but she did refer to Byron, whose verses she had set, and who had resided in Lerici, on the left side of the gulf, which Fanny and Wilhelm made a point of visiting. On June 22 they reached Genoa, which still remained for Fanny the "summit of beauty" (*Gipfel der Schönheit*); then, after passing through

Milan and abandoning an excursion to the Lago Maggiore, they made a difficult crossing of the Splügen Pass. By mid-July they were enjoying a "family congress" with Felix and Paul in Freiburg im Breisgau, augmented by the Woringens from Düsseldorf.[86] Traveling by coach, rail, and steamer down the Rhine, the family then regathered in Soden, where for a fortnight they joined the Jeanrenauds, and where Cécile was expecting her fifth child, Lili. The Hensels managed to fit in a short visit with Fanny's uncle Joseph Mendelssohn in Horchheim. Then, having learned of Felix's firm decision to resume his former position in Leipzig, they departed Frankfurt with Rebecka and her children and reached Berlin on August 2. Though Fanny did not know it, the seven months of traveling, much of it consumed by family illnesses and celebrating the birth of her niece, was her last substantial journey. She could now return, though briefly, to the double counterpoint of her life with Wilhelm, and address forthrightly and honestly the most pressing, unresolved issue in her life.

CHAPTER 12

Engraver's Ink and Heavenly Songs

(1845–1847)

I'm afraid of my brothers at age 40, as I was of Father at age 14.

—Fanny to Felix, July 9, 1846

Not long after the Hensels' arrival in Berlin, an attenuated version of Wilhelm's Italian malady returned, and Fanny recorded in her diary a new concern—declining sales of his paintings had negatively affected their finances. But Felix's visits in August and September, and his arrival late in October to oversee two new royal commissions, soon distracted their personal lives. First, on November 1, he mounted with Ludwig Tieck at Potsdam a production of Sophocles' *Oedipus at Colonos*. In contrast to *Antigone*, which had scored early successes in Germany and England, *Oedipus at Colonos* elicited from Felix a rather spartan score, and this time the fussy efforts to produce Greek tragedy in a historically authentic style struck some reviewers as pedantic. Considerably more well received was the premiere of Racine's *Athalie* a month later at the Berlin palace of Charlottenburg. Fanny found Felix's nimble treatment of French Alexandrian verse *wunderschön*, and was soon pressing him for a copy so that she could program the work on one of her Sunday concerts.

Having sent Fanny organ "studies" for her birthday in 1844, including the reincarnated wedding processional, on her birthday in 1845 Felix presented the autograph of a weighty new chamber work—the Piano Trio in C Minor, op. 66. Whether Fanny ever performed it is unclear, though

Felix admonished that the Scherzo, teeming with rapidly repeated notes and treacherous passagework, was "a trifle nasty to play."[1] Nevertheless, there is compelling evidence that she soon enough immersed herself in the composition, for in January 1846, she produced a turbulent piano piece in the same key, the Allegro molto in C Minor (H-U 413),[2] reminiscent of Felix's dark, brooding first movement—music, as we have already suggested, that may reflect something of her earlier Allegro molto in C Minor for piano duet (H-U 408). The figurations of Fanny's solo piano piece, like those in the trio, feature sweeping arpeggiations with filled-in passing tones and other dissonant ornamental tones that create a blurring effect. Common to both movements, too, are chromatically ascending lines and colorful intrusions of the Neapolitan harmony (D-flat major). All these similarities suggest that Fanny deliberately cast her composition, which impresses as a miniature monothematic sonata-form movement, in a serious style to conjure up the affect of her brother's gift.

While Felix was visiting Berlin in the closing months of 1845, the city was transfixed by appearances of the "Swedish nightingale"—Jenny Lind—who in quick succession triumphed as Norma, Donna Anna, and Agathe in Bellini's *Norma*, Mozart's *Don Giovanni*, and Weber's *Der Freischütz*. Felix was deeply impressed by her sheer musicality, and Hans Christian Andersen became totally infatuated with her. The year before, Fanny had heard Lind's Berlin debut in *Norma*, and, though not inclined toward Bellini, assessed her radiant voice as "of the sharpest purity, which is very pleasing to hear, and exquisitely beautiful in her high register through B-flat. Her dexterity is not exactly overwhelming but certainly adequate for every large role, her trills very good, and her interpretation and expression, as much as one can tell in such a mawkish work quite strong and lovely, as is also her acting."[3] But the soprano's return to the Berlin stage in 1845 merited only a short entry in Fanny's diary—"Lind mania now for the second winter"[4]—and the two seem not to have performed together; the celebrity was in such great demand, Fanny recorded, that it was difficult to arrange to see her.[5] Regrettably, Fanny did not find occasion to compose for Lind, unlike Felix, who in 1847 would spend the last months of his life working on the opera *Die Lorelei*, with its title role conceived for the soprano.

Early in January 1846 Fanny visited Leipzig for the last time and again met the Schumanns. As it happened, she just missed the premiere of Robert's Piano Concerto in A Minor, op. 54, introduced by Clara and Felix at the Gewandhaus on New Year's Day. Instead, at a soirée hastily organized by her brother, Fanny attended a reading of Robert's Piano Quartet op. 47, with Clara at the piano; Felix may have dispatched the viola part.[6] In June, Fanny would program on one of her concerts Robert's Variations for two pianos, op. 46, toward the end of which was embedded an extended quotation from the lied "Seit ich ihn gesehen," from the song cycle *Frauenliebe und -leben*.

But Fanny was unable to muster much enthusiasm for this music, and she seems never to have engaged with his lieder. What is more, in April, she summarily rejected his oratorio, *Das Paradies und die Peri*—"But *Peri*—that is *impossible*. I can't acquire a taste for this Schumann"[7]—and later dismissed it as derived from Felix's *Die erste Walpurgisnacht*.[8] Of course, the subject, an episode from Thomas Moore's *Lalla Rookh*, was of personal significance to Fanny—in 1822, she had met Wilhelm after viewing his *tableaux vivants* and illustrations for Moore's epic poem. Robert's moody personality—he seems to have kept a low profile before Felix and Clara—likely proved a further obstacle to forming a meaningful relationship with Fanny, and in the end the two contemporaries, two of the great nineteenth-century lied composers, enjoyed but limited interaction.

In February, Felix and Cécile traveled to Berlin for the baptism of Paul's daughter, Catherine, but within days returned to Leipzig. Felix resumed his harried schedule at the Gewandhaus and prepared for a grueling schedule of commissions and concert appearances that summer—in May, Aachen, where he directed the Lower Rhine Music Festival, featuring appearances by Jenny Lind; in June, Liège, where he attended the premiere of his *Lauda Sion*, for the 600th anniversary of the Feast of Corpus Christi, and Cologne, where he participated in the German-Flemish Singing Festival, for which some 2,000 worthy amateurs massed to sing part-songs; and finally, in August, Birmingham, England, where he premiered his second oratorio, *Elijah*, often judged to be his crowning composition. Ruefully Fanny compared Felix's itinerary to "the grand style of living" in contrast to her own uneventful existence in Berlin, "our little pocket edition."[9] Indeed, in July she would lament that *Elijah* was about to be released to the world without her knowing a single note of it.[10] Nevertheless, she found some comfort in the spring that arrived early in the Prussian capital that year, with almond trees in full bloom in March, and lilacs in April.

The next month Fanny and Wilhelm celebrated the confirmation of their son on May 3, and two weeks later Fanny composed a piano piece to commemorate Sebastian's "debut" at a ball given by his parents. The inspiration for this exquisitely crafted Andante espressivo in F Major, later published as the third of Fanny's *Vier Lieder für das Pianoforte* op. 6, was a poem by Goethe:

Als ich ein junger Geselle war,	When I was a young lad,
lustig und guter Dinge,	a merry and good thing,
da hielten die Maler offenbar	the artists openly considered
mein Gesicht für viel zu geringe;	my countenance of far too little worth;
dafür war mir manch schönes Kind	still, many pretty girls

dazumal von Herzen treu gesinnt.	remained true to me in their hearts.
Nun ich hier als Altmeister sitz', rufen sie mich aus auf Straßen und Gaßen, zu haben bin ich, wie der alte Fritz, auf Pfeifenköpfen und Tassen. Doch die schönen Kinder die bleiben fern. O Traum der Jugend! O goldner Stern!	Now I sit here, an old master, they call me from the streets and byways, and, like Old Fritz, I appear on pipes and cups. But the lovely children remain far away. O dream of youth! O golden star!

In 1836 Carl Loewe had published a setting of these verses with the title *Der alte Goethe* ("The Old Goethe"), but Fanny now excerpted the final line, with its reference to a golden youth, and shaped the opening measures of her piano melody to accommodate its principal stresses, on *Jugend* and *Stern*, so that Goethe's verse is readily traceable in her piano piece (example 12.1). Another imprint is felt in the fourth and fifth bars, where Fanny reaches a half cadence with melodic contours suspiciously similar to one from Felix's *Lied ohne Worte* op. 53, no. 4, also in F major, as if Sebastian's uncle makes a brief appearance. But Fanny's Andante espressivo is first and foremost a contemplation at the keyboard of Goethe's poem, in which the idealized past and sobering present of the two stanzas are contrasted by sections in the parallel major and minor, and further distinguished by the contrasting meters of 3/4 and 9/8. After a magical transition that reverses course from minor to major, from compound to simple ternary meter, Fanny rounds out the composition by adding an abridged return to the opening, so that the whole falls into a familiar *ABA'* form. The result is a rare example of a piano lied for which she divulged a specific verbal, poetic source, again leading us to imagine that some of her other piano compositions, too, traced their origins to lyric German poetry.

EXAMPLE 12.1.   Fanny Hensel, Andante espressivo in F Major, op. 6, no. 3 (1845)

For the first time in years, during the spring of 1846 Fanny felt rejuvenated and childlike; she now fully enjoyed the garden, which became more beautiful and lush every day, "like a happiness which is always eluding our grasp."[11] Reinvigorated, she devoted her energies to reviving her concert series, which had languished for nearly two years. Between March and July she presented at least five concerts, all directed from the piano. Details of the repertoire are sketchy, but among the works performed were an old favorite of her father, J. S. Bach's cantata *Gottes Zeit ist die allerbeste Zeite* (BWV 106); a Requiem, in all likelihood Mozart's (April 26); the choruses to Felix's *Athalie* (May 10); and a triple keyboard concerto by Bach (likely BWV 1063) and the Andante and Variations for Two Pianos op. 46 by Robert Schumann (June 21).[12] Some of this information we owe to the diary of Giacomo Meyerbeer, who now overcame his earlier antipathy to Fanny and Wilhelm (see p. 194) to attend her concerts.

Exactly who joined Fanny on June 21 in the Bach triple concerto and Schumann variations remains unclear, but one of the musicians may have been Robert von Keudell (1824–1903), a talented pianist and philosophy student from Königsberg who eventually joined the diplomatic corps. A confidant and amanuensis of Otto von Bismarck, Keudell served after the unification of Germany as emissary to Constantinople and ambassador to Rome. During the winter of 1841 and 1842, he had zealously studied counterpoint in Berlin and developed a formidable technique playing Beethoven's piano sonatas, though he made no claim to being a virtuoso. In 1846, the year Keudell met Fanny, he played Beethoven's *Appassionata* Sonata for the future Iron Chancellor of Germany and his fiancée, and reportedly brought him to tears.[13] According to a less reliable account, in 1866, after Keudell arranged for Bismarck to hear a private performance of Beethoven's Fifth Symphony, the then Prussian prime minister was sufficiently stirred by the music to sign the mobilization order triggering the Austro-Prussian War.[14]

Keudell's impact on Fanny during the last year of her life was profound. He first appears in her diary on May 17, 1846, where we read, "Another agreeable acquaintance is Herr v. Keudell, who has such an ear for music as I have not met with since Gounod and Dugasseau, plays extremely well, and is altogether a very lively and charming man." To Felix, Fanny relayed that Keudell possessed the "finest feeling for music and a memory that I've seen in no one except you," and that he could recall at the piano choral works by Schubert, string quartets by Beethoven, and Felix's *Die erste Walpurgisnacht*. Not surprisingly, Keudell became a close friend of the Hensels, whom he visited on a daily basis, and in the process grew intimate with Fanny's music, in which he discovered "a treasure chest of written traditions" (*einen Schatz von Überlieferungen*).[15] By the end of July 1846 she could observe, "Keudell keeps my music alive and in constant activity, as Gounod did once. He takes an intense interest in everything that I write, and calls my attention to any shortcomings, being generally in the right too."[16] When the Hensels celebrated Christmas in 1846, they had a special album prepared for their new friend, with a dedication from Wilhelm and autographs by Felix, Fanny, Schubert, and others;[17] unfortunately, no trace of this gift survives.

Keudell looms especially large in Fanny's biography because he apparently played the critical role of convincing her late in life to begin publishing under her own name, the final step toward her artistic self-fulfillment that Felix had been unwilling to support. And so on July 9, 1846, Fanny wrote to her brother, with trepidation and anxiety, but also recognizing the prospect of finally freeing up her creativity, as this extended quote reveals:

> Actually I wouldn't expect you to read this rubbish now, busy as you are, if I didn't have to tell you something. But since I know from the start that you won't like it, it's a bit awkward to get under way. So laugh at me or not, as you wish: I'm afraid of my brothers at age 40, as I was of Father at age 14—or, more aptly expressed, desirous of pleasing you and everyone I've loved throughout my life. And when I now know in advance that it won't be the case, I thus feel RATHER uncomfortable. In a word, I'm beginning to publish. I have Herr Bock's sincere offer for my lieder and have finally turned a receptive ear to his favorable terms. And if I've done it of my own free will and cannot blame anyone in my family if aggravation results from it (friends and acquaintances have indeed been urging me for a long time), then I can console myself, on the other hand, with the knowledge that I in no way sought out or induced the type of musical reputation that might have elicited such offers. I hope I won't disgrace all of you through my publishing, as I'm no *femme libre* and unfortunately not even an adherent of the *Young Germany* movement. I trust *you* will in no way be bothered by it, since, as you can see, I've proceeded completely on my own in order to spare you any possible unpleasant moment, and I hope you won't think badly of me. If it succeeds—that is, if the pieces are well liked and I receive additional offers—I know it will be a great stimulus to me, something I've always needed in order to create. If not, I'll be as indifferent as I've always been and not be upset, and then if I work less or stop completely, nothing will have been lost by that either.[18]

By the end of July, Fanny had in hand competing offers for her compositions from two well-established Berlin firms, Bote & Bock and Schlesinger, though she still waited for Felix's reply. To her diary she confided her strengthening resolve, but also frustration at his silence: "And so I have now also decided to publish my things. Bote und Bock has made me offers that no female dilettante has probably yet received, and in addition Schlesinger even more brilliant ones. I don't at all imagine that it will continue, but rather for once am pleased that my best things will appear, since I have now finally decided to proceed. Felix, whom I notified about two weeks ago, has still not answered, which has somewhat hurt me."[19]

When Keudell, after traveling to Leipzig to meet Felix, returned to Berlin with no answer, her sense of hurt intensified. Not until August 12, just days before he left for England, did he finally offer his "blessing" in a few lines to Fanny:

> My dearest Fenchel, only today, shortly before my departure, do I, bad brother that I am, get around to thanking you for your lovely letter and to giving you my professional blessing [*Handwerkssegen*] on your deci-sion to join our guild. I herewith bestow it upon you, Fenchel; may you take joy and pleasure in providing so much joy and pleasure to others, and may you know only the joys of authorship and nothing of its misery, and may the public pelt you only with roses and never with sand, and may the engraver's ink never seem oppressive and dark to you—actually, I believe there can be no doubt about all that. Why do I only now wish that for you? It is only because of the guild, and so that I as well could give you my blessing, as hereby happens.
> The fellow journeyman tailor,
> Felix Mendelssohn Bartholdy[20]

In 1824, while Fanny had looked on, Zelter had dubbed Felix a journeyman on his fifteenth birthday and symbolically welcomed him into the brother-hood of Mozart, Haydn, and "old father" Bach.[21] Now, twenty-two years later, Felix's *Handwerkssegen* performed a similar, symbolic function, even if in a bit of paternalistic ceremony hurriedly dispatched by a "master" composer from Leipzig about to embark for England. Still, Abraham Mendelssohn Bartholdy's old judgment of 1820, that music should form only an ornament to Fanny's life, was finally set aside, as she prepared to remove the veil of anonymity she had worn during her life and to reveal her compositional identity before the broader musical public. And Felix's letter finally began the process of resolving the most painful issue in the siblings' relationship. In her diary, she recorded a somewhat halting reaction: "At last Felix has written, and given me his profes-sional blessing in the kindest manner. I know that he is not quite satisfied in his heart of hearts, but I am glad he has said a kind word to me about it."[22]

i

Fittingly, 1846 was a creatively explosive, prolific year for Fanny—arguably her *annus mirabilis*. The music she shared with Keudell included fifty-one compo-sitions apportioned nearly equally into three genres—seventeen piano pieces, sixteen lieder (a seventeenth would follow on the day she died in 1847), and, in a new departure for the composer, seventeen part-songs. In the absence of

Felix, Keudell provided encouragement and, what is more, substantive critical advice as she began selecting her best music for publication. No longer the *weibliches Dilettante*, Fanny committed to composing on a regular basis and all that it entailed—to winnowing, revising, and polishing works, and for the first time began to see her music through the press on a sustained, regular schedule. There is almost something Schumannesque about her methodical concentration on the three genres. Schumann's early career as a composer had unfolded in an equally systematic way, but over the course of a decade, with emphases on piano music for several years, then lieder in 1840 (his annus mirabilis), and the symphony, chamber music, and oratorio in 1841, 1842, and 1843. Fanny devoted 1846 to exploring and working exclusively on small-scale genres, as if she sensed the urgency to make up quickly for lost time. By composing three series of piano pieces, lieder, and part-songs, she revealed a new determination to treat her art as a disciplined craft. Her process of self-discovery as a professional composer would lead first through the smaller genres, as she began to consider the musical public beyond Leipzigerstrasse no. 3, and emerged to the public as Fanny Hensel the composer.

The majority of the piano pieces fall into the familiar category of the ternary-form (*ABA'*) *Lied ohne Worte*,[23] by 1846 well-established in the thirty-six pieces her brother had published in six sets between 1832 and 1845. Fanny persisted in describing her contributions to the genre as piano lieder, not *Lieder ohne Worte*, perhaps as if to afford herself some creative space apart from Felix. To be sure, there are the occasional similarities to his *Lieder ohne Worte*—for example, the turn of phrase in Fanny's op. 6, no. 3, mentioned earlier, drawn from Felix's *Lied ohne Worte* op. 53, no. 4; and the buoyant Allegro vivace in A Major (H-U 459), with its active soprano melody driven by pulsating triplet chords in the accompaniment, a texture reminiscent of his *Lied ohne Worte* op. 53, no. 2. But more often than not, Fanny's piano music of 1846 evinces increasing signs of stylistic independence from Felix, chiefly in her probing of dark harmonic colorations and multifarious key relationships, and in her intense applications of chromaticism to underscore the expressive qualities of the music. There is in these late compositions a strong undercurrent of wistfulness and melancholy, as if Fanny channeled into her art her stronger emotions, reminding us again, in Sarah Austin's formulation, that "Madame Hensel said less rather than more than she felt."[24]

In length the pieces range from compact miniatures in a relatively lean, if not stripped-down, spartan style, to more extravagant, extended movements encroaching on the complexities of sonata form and making virtuoso demands on the performer. To the former belong two pieces in compound meters, the Allegretto in C-sharp Minor op. 4/5, no. 2, and Lento appassionato in B Major op. 4/5, no. 4, which suggest, perhaps, further examples of *Gondellieder*, with gently rippling arpeggiations or murmuring chords in the accompaniment. In both pieces Fanny plays on subtle exchanges between the major and minor modes, and clusters toward the middle of the compositions chromatic pitches extrinsic to the key, thereby creating tonal tensions through the enriched palette of keys.

Among her most striking experiments in this vein is the lugubrious Andante con espressione in A Minor, op. 8, no. 2.[25] Here she begins modestly, with a plaintive duet in the treble gradually fleshed out to three- and four-part harmony. A few measures later, a syncopated, bell-like pedal point begins to toll in the tenor voice, as the music brightens by pivoting toward C major. A compact phrase recalling a similar passage in several of Felix's early works[26] moves the music inexorably toward a full cadence in C major, but Fanny deflects our expectation, bypasses the cadence, and continues on to the dominant E major. Now the pedal point shifts to the bass, where it tolls beneath chromatic lines that rise above, almost Bachian in their intensity. When the opening music in A minor returns, it reappears not in a secure root position, but above the syncopated dominant pitch, in effect further destabilizing the tonic. Two harmonic diversions to B minor and—more strikingly—B-flat major then take us further afield before the opening bars finally reappear above a secure pedal point on the tonic in the deep bass. The funereal affect of this music almost surely points to some extramusical stimulus; indeed, Fanny's music recalls similar tolling effects in Felix's setting of Eichendorff's *Nachtlied*, composed late in 1845 but not published until 1847, after Fanny's death, as op. 71, no. 6.◑ Invoking the topic of death, the poem refers to the extinguished day and the distant sound of bells, replicated, as in Fanny's composition, by syncopated pedal points in the bass. But Felix's harmonic palette remains comparatively monochromatic and considerably more muted than Fanny's; he described the effect of his late lieder as "grey on grey."[27] In contrast, Fanny's miniature is again marked by its unexpected harmonic turns and juxtapositions, and by the persistent destabilization of the tonic key, ultimately reaffirmed and rooted only in the closing bars.

At the other extreme in the piano music of 1846 are the Allegro molto vivace in C Major and Lied in E-flat Major (H-U 442 and 456), which run to 99 and 140 bars, respectively. Etudelike, the Allegro molto explores yet another variant of the three-hand technique, with a treble melody, now doubled in octaves, supported by rapidly descending and rebounding arpeggiations divided between the hands, and a simple bass line and chords in the left. Though Fanny chooses the most elemental, "neutral" key of C major for the tonic, she traverses a wide range of tonalities, episodelike digressions that lead us, for example, to E minor, A major, B-flat minor, G minor, C-sharp minor, and E major. Only in the concluding codalike section does she abandon this frenetic, colorful variety in favor of harmonies firmly situated in the orbit of C major. Of a considerably different affect is the Lied in E-flat Major. Like op. 8, no. 2, it begins with a muted, treble duet that calls out for words, and recalls the mellifluous a cappella duets Fanny had composed earlier for her sister, Rebecka (see p. 234). But within a few bars, chromatic, dissonant chords appear that lend the opening Andante a darker hue, and we begin to hear flowing arpeggiations in the bass, as the tempo changes to Allegro and the mode from major to minor. We now reach the core of the composition, a poignant Allegro in E-flat minor, with dramatically rising and searching melodic arabesques. Framelike, the Andante returns, first in a majestic summation and then in a truncated repetition of the opening bars, with the piano dampers raised so that the harmonies well together in a *pianissimo* blur.

A few piano pieces from Fanny's final year suggest stylistic rapprochements with Felix's music, as if, despite her professional liberation at age forty, she was indeed still "afraid of her brother." The sibling bond is perhaps most evident in the Allegro molto vivace e leggiero in B Major (H-U 414), relatively restrained in its key relationships and generally reminiscent of Felix's *Lied ohne Worte* op. 67, no. 6. But more often than not, Fanny stamps her own personality on the music, encouraging the critical ear to perceive growing evidence of her stylistic independence. Two telling examples are the Allegro moderato op. 8, no. 1 in B Minor and Allegretto in D Minor (H-U 426),[28] each of which contains clear allusions to the overture to Felix's cantata *Die erste Walpurgisnacht*, one of Fanny's favorite works of her brother. But in neither case do the allusions compromise the originality of her conception. Rather, the allusions appear, in op. 8, no. 1, as a Schumann-like digression that momentarily distracts us from the principal thread of Fanny's argument, a haunting, elegiac melody in the soprano that calls out for words (example 12.2),[29] and in the Allegretto as an incidental afterthought in the coda, where she obscures the source of the allusion through some metrical and rhythmic transformations.

In a similar way, the Andante cantabile in D-flat Major (H-U 417) begins with a graceful phrase and flowing accompaniment that, along with a half cadence a bar or two later, seem unavoidably Mendelssohnian in character. But in extending the phrase, Fanny subtly bends the music toward the relative minor, B-flat minor, setting up an ambiguity between the two keys, which compete over the course of the composition, as Fanny treats tonal relationships in distinctly more intensely expressive, uninhibited ways than her brother. In the darkened middle section, for example, she turns unexpectedly to A-flat minor and briefly explores a far-flung excursion to the rare key of B-double-flat major. Finally, the Andante espressivo in A-flat Major, published as the first of Fanny's *Vier Lieder* op. 6, begins almost as if to recall Felix's *Lied ohne Worte* op. 53, no. 1 in the same key, and, as Cornelia Bartsch has suggested in another comparison, to establish a dialogue with her brother.[30] But within a bar or two, Fanny departs from the tonic, and in the relatively confined space of sixty-one bars introduces no fewer than fourteen major and minor harmonic areas, drawn from every step of the A-flat major scale, but also including chromatically altered harmonies, such as C-flat major, G-flat major, and F-flat major.[31] This remarkable harmonic richness, subtle use of

EXAMPLE 12.2. (a–b) Fanny Hensel, Allegro moderato in B Minor, op. 8, no. 1 (1846); (c) Felix Mendelssohn, *Die erste Walpurgisnacht*, Overture, op. 60 (1843)

(a)

Allegro moderato

(b)

(*Continued*)

EXAMPLE 12.2.   Continued

(c)

exchanges between major and minor modes, and strategic placement of three increasingly high climactic pitches in the treble (bars 22, 30, and 45) lend her miniature an expressive depth and emotional shading reminiscent more of the piano music of Chopin than of her brother and, again, enable us to discern elements of Fanny's own mature, independent style.

The descending triadic melodic gesture that opens op. 6, no. 1 relates that composition to the piano music of Fanny's first Italian sojourn, including *Villa Medicis* (see p. 249), as if she sought to invest the 1846 Andante with diary-like memories of 1840, the happiest year of her life.[32] Other piano works from 1846 are more deliberately programmatic, including three that bear revealing titles. Among her most evocative creations is the *Pastorella* in A Major (H-U 425), finished on May 25, 1846, published posthumously in 1848, and anticipating with its autumnal glow Brahms's late piano pieces.◓ Firmly centered on A major, with static pedal points and drone effects, the *Pastorella* conjures up a world at peace, even though Fanny could not avoid slipping momentarily into A minor and occasionally embellishing the melody and bass lines with chromatic passing tones. Counterbalancing the tonal stability is the use of rhythmic tension—in much of the composition, she placed gentle stresses on the second of the three beats by employing a characteristic motive (quarter, dotted quarter, and eighth notes) and in the concluding coda released the built-up tension by changing the accompaniment from eighth notes to triplet figurations that climb to the highest register of the piano above fleeting horn calls in the bass.

(a)

(b)

Considerably more enigmatic than the *Pastorella* is the Lied in D-flat Major published as Fanny's op. 8, no. 3, with the intriguing, parenthetical subtitle "(Lenau)." As we shall see, between August and December 1846 Fanny composed four songs on texts by Nikolaus Lenau, but whether op. 8, no. 3 was directly related to these settings is unclear. Perhaps the piano lied was inspired by another poem of Lenau, though none has yet emerged that convincingly fits the contours of Fanny's expressive melody. At the least, the composition tests the boundaries between the abstract piano miniature and texted art song, an especially fertile ground that Fanny also explored that year in the Andante cantabile op. 6, no. 3.

In the case of the *Wanderlied*, op. 8, no. 4, a brightly hued bravura movement in E major animated by a restless melody above a torrent of churning sextuplets, Fanny alluded to an entire genre of German romantic poetry. Here the sense of wandering is conveyed through a peripatetic succession of keys,[33] but there is also a striking, recurring passage that may betray something else. Three times in the composition we hear a series of chromatically sliding harmonies that, glissando-like, swell and ebb, as if to recall a similar passage in Schubert's song *Der Lindenbaum* (*The Linden Tree*) from the cycle *Winterreise* and its celebrated traveler, who on a windswept night passes by the tree into which he has carved tender thoughts of his lover (example 12.3). Schubert's hapless, wandering protagonist seems briefly to intrude upon Fanny's composition and to invite us to imagine a text for her piano lied. That Schubert was on Fanny's mind in 1846 is supported too by the Andante con moto in E Major (H-U 452), the beginning of which appears to quote the opening bar of "Gute Nacht," the very first song of Schubert's cycle.❸ Here the wanderer, having arrived and departed a stranger, trudges wearily away from the house of his beloved. Only for the final strophe of the song, in which he takes care not to disturb her from her slumber, does Schubert turn from the minor to the major mode, an unexpected moment of arrival that briefly lightens the dark shading of the song—and may have provided Fanny with the inspiration for her Andante. In effect, Fanny reversed the trajectory of Schubert's journey by beginning in the major, before exploring through a series of chromatic episodes minor-keyed variants of the wandering theme. The result impresses as an imaginative, retrospective contemplation of Schubert's song at the keyboard, and affords another example of Fanny's testing the blurred boundaries between the art song and romantic piano music.

ii

In a bold departure from the piano pieces, between February and September 1846 Fanny produced no fewer than seventeen part-songs,[34] several of which bear corrections and drafts for alternate endings, linking their creation to revision and plans for publication. Six, in fact, appeared at the end of the year as the *Gartenlieder* op. 3, and the manuscripts of a few others are numbered, suggesting that the composer (or someone else) began culling together a second volume. The title *Gartenlieder* associates the compositions not only with the *Gartenhaus*, where Fanny's seasoned chorus rehearsed and performed the pieces (manuscript parts survive for several),[35] but also with the garden adjacent to the family residence, which Fanny found especially beautiful during the spring of 1846. Like her brother's part-songs, designated for performance outdoors (*im Freien zu singen*), Fanny's part-songs move us from the private music study of Leipzigerstrasse no. 3 to spontaneous celebrations of nature in the open air, to be shared as social, communal experiences, not private contemplations. Investing considerable creative energy into the genre, Fanny now embraced a type of composition largely associated with male composers, one that Felix had already successfully cultivated in eighteen examples published between 1838 and 1843 in his opp. 41, 48, and 59. Fanny's part-songs may be heard as a response to or dialogue with this music, and occasionally clear enough tangents emerge, as when, well into "Im Wald," op. 3, no. 6, she seemingly borrows a short phrase from Felix's op. 59, no. 6.[36] Still, as in the piano music, there are distinctive signs of her individuality, as in the *Schilflied* (*Song of the Reeds*, H-U 445) and "O Herbst" ("O Autumn," H-U 448), suffused with a tonal ambivalence between D minor and F major, so that the ambiguity of key severely tests the epigrammatic frames of the music. Fanny's deft approach to the choral ensemble shows the hand of an experienced musician well served by years of directing the Sunday concert series at her residence. Taken together, the part-songs of 1846 rank as one of her great accomplishments as a composer and show the full powers of her expressive art.

Fanny's texts celebrate the music of nature—its rustling forests, susurrant brooks, bird calls, and echo effects—and the idea of renewal through springtime, either experienced directly or imagined through a dream state. Not surprisingly, Eichendorff, that rapt, spiritually attuned poet of forest solitude (*Waldeinsamkeit*), takes precedence with seven poems teeming with sensory stimulation, followed by Fanny's husband (four), Goethe and Geibel (two each), and Uhland and Lenau (one each). Four-part writing is the norm, but in "Wer will mir wehren zu singen" ("Who Will Stop Me from Singing," Goethe, H-U 447), Fanny writes for reduced three-part chorus (soprano, alto, and bass), and in *Ariel* (on verses from the *Walpurgisnachtstraum* scene of *Faust*) begins, appropriately enough, with a transparent duet for the sopranos and altos alone, in deference to Goethe's thinly veiled allusion to Shakespeare's *Tempest*. At the other extreme is "Schweigend sinkt die Nacht" ("Silently Sinks the Night," H-U 439), in which she bolsters the four-part chorus midway by adding a second chorus, yielding an enriched, eight-part texture. A simple, chordal style of writing predominates throughout the settings, but Fanny varies her approach through various means—among them, injecting brief points of imitation between the voices, aligning the four parts in stark octave doublings, dividing them into pairs, and segregating the sopranos from the altos, tenors, and basses. And she fills her settings with effective, but not overwrought, examples of word painting, as in the drooping, chromatic lines for the weeping willows in the *Schilflied* and, at its conclusion, the unexpected turn to the major triad for the image of a glimmering evening star.

In the case of the *Gartenlieder*, Fanny shaped six of her best part-songs into a miniature cycle, unified musically by interrelated keys and meters, and textually by verses from Eichendorff, Uhland, Wilhelm Hensel, and Geibel reordered to chart an extramusical trajectory from night to day, from dream-like recollections of spring to the erupting arrival of the season. Beginning in B major, Fanny proceeds sequentially through the tonal chain of fifths to E minor (and major), A major, and D major before reversing course in the last two songs to A minor and A major. In this scheme, the two minor-keyed settings appear in the second and fifth positions, and add an element of symmetry to the tonal design. The choice of meters, too, reflects an overarching design: Fanny reserves common or 4/4 time for nos. 1, 5, and 6, while the internal nos. 2, 3, and 4 employ the compound meters of 6/8 and 9/8, with series of nimble eighth notes and trochaic patterns (♩♪).

Animating the whole cycle is the rustling (*Rauschen*) of the forest; indeed, the German word appears in all but one of the six poems, and Fanny seems intent upon allying the heightened sense of anticipation in the poetry with musical imitations of the stirrings of nature. In the first lied, *Lockung* (*Temptation*), a spectator on a balcony is tempted to eavesdrop on the "wild songs" (*die irren Lieder*) of the nocturnal forest solitude below. *Schöne Fremde* (*Distant Love*) then moves us irreversibly to the outdoors by conjuring up a bewitching vision of the night as a dreamlike phantasm—the part-song begins in a hushed *Elfenton* in E minor that yields to a brightened E major at the appearance of gleaming stars, messengers of some future happiness. The third lied, "Seid gegrüßt mit Frühlingswonne" ("Welcomed with Spring Rapture"), is set in A major, the eventual goal of the entire cycle. Here Uhland's verses concern a sun-filled spring day, or so it seems, and Fanny obliges with a buoyant setting that easily impresses as a *Frühlingslied*. But at the center of the composition, set in the contrasting parallel minor, we encounter unstable chromatic sequences that momentarily disorient our sense of key, as we realize that the images of spring are but an illusion (example 12.4):

Ahnest Du, O Seele wieder	Do you sense again, O soul,
sanfte, süsse Frühlingslieder?	those gentle, sweet songs of spring?
Sieh' umher die falben Bäume,	Look around at the faded trees,
ach, es waren holde Träume!	Ah, they were lovely dreams!

Nearly twenty-five years before, in 1822, Fanny had set Uhland's poem as an unassuming solo song (H-U 54); in 1840, when Fanny and Wilhelm prepared the fair copy of *Das Jahr* (see p. 281), they selected the verses quoted above for the epigram to the preamble-like "Januar," where intimations of spring

EXAMPLE 12.4.   Fanny Hensel, "Seid gegrüßt mit Frühlingswonne," op. 3, no. 3 (1846)

Ah-nest du____ o See-le wie-der sanf-te sü - ße___ Früh-lings - lie - der?

form part of the dreamlike free association of ideas marking the beginning of that musical calendar. In op. 3, no. 3 Fanny now gave new voice to Uhland's yearning verses, by removing them from an abstract piano cycle intended for her family's private use and releasing them in a part-song, the embodiment of shared, social music making.

In the fourth lied, *Komm* (*Come*), the nocturnal shadows do yield in a tender poem by Wilhelm to the golden splendor of a spring morning, and blooming flowers eavesdrop on the rustling of trees. All that is missing, according to the poet-spouse, is for his lover to partake of this paean to spring, and Fanny responds with a vibrant, tremulous setting animated by eighth notes and expressive leaps. Quite in contrast is the fifth lied, "Abendlich," a quiet evening song in A minor, with lean, spare textures reminiscent of the Andante espressivo op. 8, no. 2. As the world comes to rest, Eichendorff's wanderer yearns for home, and the omnipresent rustling is now perceptible only in the very depths of the forest. Not so in the sixth, concluding song, "Im Wald" ("In the Forest"), an energetic, extended setting of verses by Geibel that joyously celebrate the power of song in the open air. Toward the middle, Fanny briefly reintroduces the supernatural tone of the second lied and reverses the image of the eavesdropping listener in the opening song. Now the leaves attend the full-throated singing and willingly contribute their rustling in time to the music. As the cycle comes to its jubilant close, the poem leaves us with an optimistic thought surely not lost on Fanny—emboldened to sing in the fresh air, amid nature's springtime revival, the musician has found her voice.

iii

Song had always been the mainstay of Fanny's creative world, and it remained so in the final year of her life. Her abundant gifts as a tunesmith are compellingly evident in the very late lieder, and they betray a new depth of expression, intensity of feeling, and experimentation with unusual tonal and harmonic relationships, all within the constrained space of miniatures barely able to contain the full force of her lyrical genius. If Eichendorff's verses reign in the part-songs, Fanny's final lieder privilege Lenau with seven settings, followed by Eichendorff with four. The remainder she apportioned between Geibel with two, and Goethe, Helmina von Chézy, and Wilhelm Hensel with one each; the poet of another song, *Das Veilchen*, remains unidentified. We shall consider these last six first. The least assuming is the Goethe setting, *Erwin*, published posthumously as op. 7, no. 2. The text is from the poet's libretto *Erwin und Elmire* (1775), inspired by an episode in Oliver Goldsmith's *The Vicar of Wakefield*, and set to music as a *Singspiel* in 1776 by the dowager Duchess Anna Amalia of Weimar. It is unlikely that Fanny had access to this score, but she probably knew Mozart's popular song *Ein Veilchen* (K. 476, 1785), also drawn from Goethe's libretto, and possibly too J. F. Reichardt's *Singspiel* on the same subject (1793). Fanny's short, balladelike setting, in a chromatically tinged, melancholy G minor, leaves open the possibility that she intended to set other texts from what Goethe described as a *Schauspiel mit Gesang* (a play with song), perhaps to create a *Liederspiel* along the lines of *Die schöne Müllerin* composed some three decades before by her teacher Ludwig Berger (see p. 25).

The other five songs yield further evidence of how Fanny relaxed the strictures of classical tonality, traditionally dependent upon the tonic-dominant axis, to unlock the expressive potential of other harmonic pairings, whether of parallel major and minor tonalities, or of so-called mediant relationships, that is, keys separated by thirds. Thus, the stately "Erwache Knab'" ("Awaken, Lad," H-U 431),[37] composed on June 6, 1846, to a couplet by Wilhelm Hensel (presumably anticipating Sebastian's birthday), plays upon tonal ambiguity between D major and B minor, with the major mode associated with childhood dreams, and the latter with earthly realities, before resolving the issue in favor of the major. In *Das Veilchen* (*The Violet*, H-U 415),[38] the text likens a violet briefly blooming in the winter snow before dying to the poet's soul, also awakened by a false spring. Here the tonal ambiguity initially appears in a modal exchange, as the song, beginning innocently in the tonic G major, slips chromatically into its darker, minor form. But Fanny goes further—to capture the double-edged idea of deceptive blossoming, she also touches on altered keys a third below (E-flat major and minor) and above (B major and minor), so that the increasingly variegated tonal areas pull us further away from the tonic, while they translate musically the images of the poem. No less striking are the tonal oppositions in *Beharre* (*Persevere*, H-U 457),[39] on a poem by Helmina von Chézy, the former librettist of Schubert (*Rosamunde*) and Carl Maria von Weber (*Euryanthe*). The poem's recipient is encouraged not to abandon love, hope, faith, or even the sorrow that love brings. Set in

C major, Fanny's song employs conventional, diatonic harmonic processions, and all is quite routine, until the music abruptly veers off to D-flat major, and later E-flat major, two flat keys that again set up tonal contrasts with the neutral key of C major.

In the Geibel setting *Im Herbste* (*In Autumn*, H-U 416),[40] Fanny challenges the stability of the tonic with chromatically suffused, winding figures in the piano accompaniment to represent a solitary vine growing on a garden wall, a metaphor for the poet's preoccupation, the loss of her lover. Similar in mood, "Es rauscht das rote Laub" ("The Red Foliage Rustles," H-U 419)[41] is a somber *Wanderlied* that also treats the season of autumn, now opposed to spring, a time not of renewal but despair over a traveler's separation from his lover. The contrast again encouraged Fanny to pair two keys, here F-sharp minor for autumn and A major for the anticipation of spring, between which the music indecisively alternates. The repeated, steplike pitches in the tenor voice of the piano and the descending, interlocked fourths of the voice (C-sharp–G-sharp–A–E-sharp) unmistakably tie Fanny's lied to Felix's *Lied ohne Worte* in B Minor, op. 67, no. 5, almost as if, in discovering Geibel's poem, she determined to "recompose" her brother's piano piece from 1844 and convert it into a *Lied mit Worten* (example 12.5). This sibling exchange suggests a variant of the childhood game Fanny and Felix had played in Berlin, of adding words to their instrumental compositions, but the result reveals too just how far Fanny's conception of expressive tonality had evolved. Like Felix, she cast her composition in a ternary *ABA* form, but whereas Felix clearly segregated the tonal areas of the three sections—the *A* section is unmistakably centered on the tonic, the *B* section on the mediant—Fanny allowed a tonal ambivalence to wash over the entire song. Thus, the pensive opening in F-sharp minor turns within a few bars to A major; and in the middle section in A major, Fanny deflects a definitive cadence and instead allows the music to be pulled back into the orbit of F-sharp minor. The technique is reminiscent of the celebrated opening song of Robert Schumann's *Dichterliebe* (1840), a song of springtime that also seductively wavers between F-sharp minor and A major, though whether Fanny ever pondered the similarities or, indeed, studied that seminal song cycle is unknown.

In 1841 Fanny had first set Eichendorff to music, and in her final years she frequently found inspiration in his nature-laden poems, including, as we have seen, several that inspired part-songs in 1846. Ironically, given the siblings' intense creative relationship with Eichendorff's verses, neither she nor Felix seems to have known the poet personally well, if at all. He does not appear in her diaries or correspondence, even though he worked as a civil servant in Berlin from 1831 until his retirement in 1844. But Eichendorff and Fanny no doubt had common acquaintances; indeed, among his close friends he counted Fanny's cousin Philipp Veit, son of Dorothea Schlegel, who years before had offered advice about the young author's first novel.[42]

EXAMPLE 12.5. (a) Fanny Hensel, "Es rauscht das rote Laub" (1846); (b) Felix Mendelssohn, *Lied ohne Worte*, op. 67, no. 5 (1844)

(a)

Fanny's four late Eichendorff lieder include two she left unpublished. "Nacht ist wie ein stilles Meer" ("Night Is Like a Still Sea," H-U 453)[43] compares night to a sea that blends together pleasure and pain into its gently beating waves; Fanny's waves rise and fall in delicately detached arpeggiations in the piano that occasionally lap over, and symbolically subsume, the vocal part. "Ich kann wohl manchmal singen" ("I Can Sometimes Sing Well," H-U 451)[44] revisits the opposition of pleasure and pain, rendered musically by another series of exchanges between the major and minor modes. Though the singer may appear happy, no one suspects the deep pain concealed by the song. Here Fanny alludes to a doleful phrase from "June" in *Das Jahr*, which in turn recalls one from Felix's *Lied ohne Worte* op. 53, no. 3.[45] Quite free of the fraternal influence is *Frühling* (*Spring*), published as her op. 7, no. 3 and offering a palpitating, ebullient celebration of spring in F-sharp major that looks forward to Hugo Wolf's rapturous setting "Er ist's" from the *Mörike Lieder* (1888). The piano denotes the arrival of spring, vividly expressed in florid, recurring sextuplet figurations that flirt with pentatonic formations (i.e., mixtures of the black keys of the instrument).❷ Eichendorff's optimistic poetry also summoned from Fanny her very last composition, *Bergeslust* (*Mountain Desire*), finished the day of her death and released posthumously as op. 10, no. 5. We shall return to it in due course.

What drew Fanny in 1846 to the bleak, weltschmerz-laden verses of Nikolaus Lenau is unclear. After a disillusioning American experience in 1832, when the Austrian poet briefly joined a communal settlement of the Rappists (a German Pietist sect),[46] and lived largely in isolation on land purchased in Ohio, Lenau had returned to Europe and enjoyed initial fame and success from publications of his poetry. In 1841 Fanny set his *Traurige Wege*, a deeply melancholic poem of resignation, and the wistful *Die Sennin* (see p. 270) but then neglected his verses until 1846, when she produced in quick succession seven settings, including two extraordinary songs evincing her most ambitious treatments of tonality, *Bitte* and "Dein ist mein Herz," released as her op. 7, nos. 5 and 6. Fanny never met Lenau, though Felix briefly overlapped with him in Frankfurt in 1844, when the poet broached the possibility of collaborating on an oratorio;[47] not long after, his moodiness deteriorated into mental instability, and he was committed to an asylum near Vienna.

Occasionally, Fanny sought to brighten the gloomy shading of Lenau's verses. Thus, in *Kommen und Scheiden* (*Coming and Parting*, H-U 460),[48] she modified and softened the poem's division between the lover's appearance, as sweet as spring's first song, and parting, likened to a vanishing dream of youth. She set the two parts of the poem in a cheerful A major and lamentlike A minor, but at the conclusion briefly revived the major mode for a repetition of the final line and thus imposed a rounded ternary form on Lenau's uncompromising binary structure. In *Abendbild*, released posthumously in 1850 as her op. 10, no. 3,[49] she found the poet's vision of evening gently descending over the land euphonious enough to inspire a largely consonant setting in E-flat major, with gently rocking rhythms. On the other hand, the identically titled companion song (H-U 455),[50] in which a shepherd contemplates the sunset in prayer, summoned a darker, folk song–like setting in G minor somewhat reminiscent of Felix's *Hirtenlied* (*Shepherd Song*), op. 57, no. 2. In the case of Lenau's sonnet *Stimme der Glocken* (*Voice of the Bells*, H-U 444),[51] which explores third relationships by beginning in A-flat major, moving through a recitative in C major, and concluding in a quiet Andante in E-flat major, Fanny indulged in poetic as well as musical license. The eleventh line refers to the bells of distantly grazing alpine cows—for Lenau like fading sounds from the lost paradise of Eden. Fanny removed the alpine imagery and optimistically recast the line as "Daß aus dem Tode neues Leben blühe" ("So that new life may bloom from death"). And she recaptured the bells as a somnolent, static pedal point in the bass of the piano, where they no longer suggest a pastoral scene but the more familiar tolling of church bells.

Lenau's most plaintive verses resisted such musical and poetic retouching, and in three settings Fanny actually intensified the despairing affect of the poetry, in part by selecting unusual, chromatically saturated keys, including G-sharp minor for *Vorwurf* (*Reproach*, op. 10, no. 2), A-flat major for *Bitte* (*Request*, op. 7, no. 5), and, at the most extreme, C-sharp major for "Dein ist mein Herz" (Thine Is My Heart," op. 7, no. 6). "You complain," *Vorwurf* begins, "that dreaded melancholy creeps over you, for the forest is leafless, and migrating birds sweep over your head." Here Fanny utilized ponderous steps in G-sharp minor embellished by unrelenting chromatic pitches; only the brief turn midway to C-sharp major and the unexpected ending in G-sharp major dispel some of the gloom in this song about exhausted passion. In *Bitte*, an apostrophe to night as a dark eye that spreads its magical gaze over the poet, Fanny further confuses our tonal bearings. The supposed tonic, A-flat, is enfeebled by liberal chromatic applications that lead us within a few bars to F-flat major. The chromaticism is so intense that discerning in the nocturnal shadows whether the major or minor mode takes precedence is difficult; in the final cadence Fanny hits upon a compelling musical counterpart to the visual ambiguity, by adding a chromatic pitch to the dominant sonority, effectively blurring the traditional V–I, or dominant to tonic, cadence.

The summit of this type of experimentation is "Dein ist mein Herz," an exquisite song on which Fanny brought to bear all the subtle craft of her late style—the major-minor exchange, the expressive opening up of traditional tonality to new chromatic combinations and relationships, and the delicate interweaving and mirroring of piano and voice, all designed to heighten our appreciation of Lenau's moving poem.[52] Its first stanza reads:

Dein ist mein Herz	Thine is my heart,
mein Schmerz dein eigen	my pain, thine own

und alle Freuden	and all the joys
die es sprengen.	that burst forth.
Dein ist der Wald	Thine is the forest
mit allen Zweigen,	and all its branches,
den Blüthen allen	all its blossoms
und Gesängen.	and songs.

Set to Fanny's music, Lenau's second stanza seems directed personally toward Wilhelm, the recipient of her love songs, and, by extension, to Felix, the sibling-critic whose approval Fanny had sought her entire life:

Das Liebste was	The dearest thing
ich mag erbeuten	I may acquire
mit Liedern die	in songs that
mein Herz entführten	abduct my heart
ist mir ein Wort daß	is a word to me
sie dich freuten,	that they please you,
ein stummer Blick	a silent glance
daß sie dich rührten.	that they touch you.

On the simplest level, the music reflects the opposition of pain and joy through poignant, sudden alternations between C-sharp minor and major throughout the setting. At the end points, modal exchanges appear in the short piano prelude and in the final phrase of the vocal part and piano epilogue, where Fanny subtly insinuates the pertinent pitches regulating the mode, E-natural and E-sharp, into the tenor voice. The idea of pain is expressed as well through the generous use of dissonant appoggiaturas and descending chromatic motion, especially in the bass line of the piano, where two forms of the descending chromatic tetrachord, historically associated with grief, appear already in the opening measures. A second descending pattern emerges in the voice part for "Dein ist mein Herz"; refrainlike, this pattern appears four times in the song and forms a haunting idée fixe that unfolds a complete cycle of ever-shifting descending thirds. Beginning and ending on E-sharp (E-sharp–C-sharp–A-sharp–F-double sharp–D-sharp–B–G-sharp–E-sharp), the thirds immediately depart from the tonic C-sharp major and traverse a diffuse, variegated tonal realm (example 12.6). Anticipating Brahms's experiments with sequences later in the century,[53] Fanny's conceit serves as the springboard for subsequent harmonic excursions in her setting, including a transient though delicious arrival in C major for *daß sie dich freuten*, before the music circles back on itself and returns to the refrain. Self-reflective, Fanny's song becomes a song about the very power of song—its ability to stir and console, to move and reassure. But this song achieves its magical effect by stretching the expressive limits of tonality in 1846, to explore briefly a musical realm not envisioned by Fanny's brother. The result surely reconfirms his opinion, voiced years before to Madame Kiéné, that Fanny's songs could stand with the very best of German lieder.

EXAMPLE 12.6. Fanny Hensel, "Dein ist mein Herz," op. 7, no. 6 (1846)

iv

Living in relative seclusion at Leipzigerstrasse no. 3, Fanny privately celebrated her new creative freedom in brief diary entries, which read like bursts of optimism among the more matter-of-fact chronicling of her final year. "I feel as if newly born," she asserted in May 1846, and in June confided that she was actively composing and playing with considerably more passion than in a long time. By August, her tone remained affirming: "The indescribable feeling of well-being which I have had this entire summer," she wrote, "still continues." Finally, in February 1847 she linked her new sense of well-being directly to her new profession: "I cannot deny that the joy in publishing my music has also elevated my positive mood. So far, touch wood, I have not had unpleasant experiences, and it is truly stimulating to experience this type of success first at an age by which it has usually ended for women, if indeed they ever experience it."[54] But just months before, she had qualified her success to her old friend, Angela von Woringen, from Düsseldorf: "I'm glad that you...are interested in the publication of my Lieder. I was always afraid of being disparaged by my dearest friends, since I've always expressed myself against it. In addition, I can truthfully say that I let it happen more than made it happen, and it is this in particular that cheers me.... If they want more from me, it should act as a stimulus to achieve, if possible, more. If the matter comes to an end then, I also won't grieve, for I'm not ambitious, and so I haven't yet had the occasion to regret my decision."[55]

In the autumn of 1846, Fanny resumed her Sunday concerts. The featured work on October 11 was Beethoven's exotic music to *The Ruins of Athens*, heard by an audience that included Giacomo Meyerbeer.[56] Two more concerts followed that month and in early November.[57] The programs do not survive, but the principal work was likely Felix's cantata *Die erste Walpurgisnacht*, which, as we have seen, had left its mark on Fanny's piano music earlier that year (see p. 319). Another planned musical gathering—a "water party" with her chorus at Treptow, southeast of Berlin—failed to materialize, to Fanny's annoyance,[58] and a family scandal momentarily disturbed her well-being as well. During the summer of 1846 her cousin Arnold Mendelssohn (son of Nathan Mendelssohn) was implicated in a petty theft of a count's private papers and fled to Paris, where he sought refuge with Heinrich Heine. A man of socialist sympathies, Arnold Mendelssohn tested a politics far too liberal for Fanny; in Paris, he became a disciple of Pierre-Joseph Proudhon, the anarchist theorist celebrated for his pithy assertion that "property is theft." Fanny decried the whole affair as a "scandal of the most wicked kind."[59] The police issued a warrant for Arnold's arrest, and the incident even affected Felix, who, returning from his last visit to London, was mistaken for his fugitive cousin and briefly detained at the Belgian border in May 1847. Subsequently, Arnold returned to Germany, where he was tried, convicted, and briefly imprisoned.

For most of 1846 Fanny heard little from Felix, and by October, some seven months after his last visit to Berlin, she was chiding him that she still knew nothing of *Elijah* and resorted to discovering its name from press reports.[60] Finally, in mid-December, he arrived in Berlin for a week and enjoyed with his sister lovely days (*schöne Tagen*) relatively unencumbered by his usual overload of obligations in the Prussian capitol.[61] There were animated musical parties at which he performed his second Piano Trio in C Minor and played duets with Fanny.[62] At last, he introduced her to *Elijah*, not yet published, and already under extensive revision after its triumphant premiere at the Birmingham Musical Festival. Felix played the work at the piano, and, as we shall shortly see, it inspired a final musical exchange between the siblings.

Almost certainly, they discussed Fanny's plans for publishing her music; another, brief opportunity arose at the end of March 1847, when Felix spent a day in Berlin, the last time he saw his sister. In September and October 1846, she had forwarded to Leipzig advance presentation copies of her first two releases, the *Sechs Lieder* op. 1 and *Vier Lieder* for piano op. 2.[63] On the title pages she appeared as "Fanny Hensel geb. Mendelssohn Bartholdy" and thus now, near the end of her life, assumed status as a public author, even if she, or her publisher, chose to link the appearance of her music inextricably to her brother's name. Opp. 1 and 2 comprised ten songs and piano pieces composed years before, all almost certainly well known to Felix. Indeed, the copy of op. 2 inscribed for him bears Fanny's note, "Hier kommen einige alte Bekannte" ("Here come some old friends"),[64] as if to reassure her brother that the publication contained no new music. When, early in 1847, Felix played the pieces for Ignaz Moscheles, he found them "close imitations of [Felix's] own," but "interesting, and treated in a genuine musical spirit."[65]

Considerably more curious was the copy of op. 1 (figure 12.1). Crossing the threshold from anonymity to public authorship meant confronting old fears, and one, it seems, remained paramount. And so, Fanny sent the copy of her first official publication not to Felix, who had grudgingly given his approval of her authorship, but to Cécile,[66] and offered this explanation to her brother: "Why didn't I address my Lieder to you? In part I know why, in part I don't. I wanted to enlist Cécile as a go-between because I had a sort of guilty conscience towards you. To be sure, when I consider that 10 years ago I thought it too late and now is the latest possible time, the situation seems rather ridiculous, as does my long-standing outrage at the idea of starting Op. 1 in my old age. But since you're so amenable to the project now, I also want to admit how terribly uppity I've been, and announce that 6 4-part Lieder, which you really don't know, are coming out next."[67] From Fanny's diary, we learn that she received advance copies of the *Gartenlieder* op. 3 on Christmas Eve;[68] nevertheless, not until February 1, in time for Felix's birthday, did she dispatch a copy to Leipzig.[69] Felix's reaction to the part-songs is not known, but Cécile's acknowledgment of the *Sechs Lieder* op. 1 does

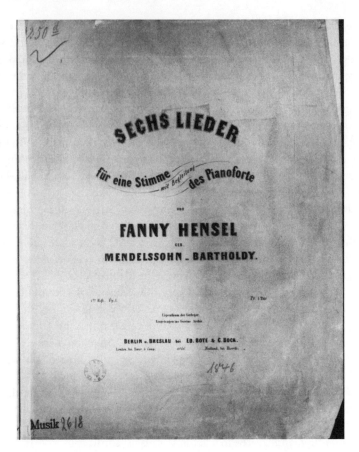

FIGURE 12.1.   Fanny Hensel, *Sechs Lieder* op. 1, title page of first
edition, 1846 (Berlin, Mendelssohn Archiv, Mus. 2618)

survive, and it betrays, perhaps, the last vestige of sibling rivalry between the
two composers: "Heartfelt thanks for the lovely Lieder, which gave me great
joy, especially when Felix sang them to us quite nicely with his wonderful
voice. I actually did let myself pick up the *blassen Rosen* ["Warum sind denn
die Rosen so blaß," op. 1, no. 3; see p. 221]. Although I haven't sung for over a
year, I view this as *my* Lied, but Felix sang the others and continually swore in
between that he wanted to avenge himself. Mother also wants me to tell you
that she is really delighted, and not at all as egotistical as Felix, who wanted to
begrudge the world something so beautiful."[70]

On February 21, 1847, Fanny made her third and final public appearance as a pianist when she accompanied a blind mezzo-soprano from Lübeck,
Bertha Bruns, in a concert of sacred arias at the Singakademie, including two

selections from Felix's *St. Paul*. Not yet accustomed to publicizing Fanny's new professional status, the press generally continued to respect her privacy, as it had for her earlier appearances as a pianist in 1838 and 1841 (see pp. 225 and 262). Thus, the *Spenersche Zeitung* referred to her as "an artistically refined amateur"; more forthcoming, the *Neue Musikalische Zeitung für Berlin* identified her as "Frau Professor Hensel."[71] But there was no reference to her new emergence as a composer, even though opp. 1–3 were recently published, and though a few weeks before she had been asked if she had composed *Auf Flügeln des Gesanges*, Felix's celebrated song (op. 34, no. 2), prompting her to compile a list of her own pieces still "floating around the world concealed."[72] She was then preoccupied with seeing through the press three more collections of piano music, advance copies of which were available from Schlesinger and Bote & Bock by early April. The *Six mélodies pour le piano*, issued as *livre I*, op. 4, and *livre II*, op. 5, and *Vier Lieder für das Pianoforte*, op. 6 juxtaposed recently composed pieces from 1846 with others drawn from earlier years. Seerlike once again, Fanny recorded in her diary, "My last three volumes have now appeared, and I fear that I have reached the end of my publishing."[73]

In the absence of Felix, the arrival of the Schumanns, who visited Berlin in February and March, provided fresh incentive for music making. At the Singakademie Fanny attended Robert's performance of his secular oratorio *Das Paradies und die Peri* and two concerts Clara gave with the mezzo-soprano Pauline Viardot. Fanny now became an intimate of Clara, another extraordinary virtuosa, but unlike Fanny a composer who had already published for many years under her maiden and married names. The two saw each other on a nearly daily basis,[74] and Wilhelm executed Clara's portrait, perhaps after a *große Soirée* the Hensels arranged on March 4 to introduce the middle-class Schumanns to the "elegant world of Berlin."[75]

For her part, Clara remembered fondly her meetings with Fanny, even if she could offer blunt opinions: "I have taken a great fancy to Madame Hensel," Clara recorded in her diary, "and feel especially attracted to her in regard to music, we almost always harmonize with each other, and her conversation is always interesting, only one has to accustom oneself to her rather brusque manner."[76] By this time, Fanny had advanced well in her last major composition, the Piano Trio in D Minor, which she may have shared with Clara. But while Clara admired Fanny as a pianist, she maintained reservations about Fanny's music and employed the same type of deprecating comment that Fanny herself had voiced before (see p. 294) and that Clara applied to her own music: "Women," Clara wrote, "always betray themselves in their compositions, and this is true of myself as well as of others."[77] As it happened, in 1846 Clara had composed her own piano trio, in G minor, op. 17; after visiting Berlin, she fully intended to dedicate it to Fanny, who unfortunately died before the honor could be bestowed.

Some mystery surrounds the origins of Fanny's trio, conceived during the winter of 1846–1847 as a birthday present for her sister, Rebecka. No autograph sources have come to light for the composition, published by Breitkopf & Härtel in 1850 as op. 11, the fourth and last of Fanny's posthumous works to appear with an opus number. Fanny premiered this *opus ultimum* on the first Sunday musicale of 1847, April 11, in honor of Rebecka, a festive occasion for which Fanny also programmed a Te Deum by Handel. Later that month she read through the trio again with Carl Eckert and an unnamed cellist.[78] Her death cut short further work on the composition, but almost surely she would have revised and released it and thus ventured publicly into chamber music; like the op. 3 part-songs, the trio represented another significant departure from her intimate lieder and shorter piano pieces. As early as July 1847, only two months after her passing, an anonymous critic who had access to the work was opining, "We [find] in this trio broad, sweeping foundations that build themselves up through stormy waves into a marvelous edifice. In this respect the first movement is a masterpiece, and the trio most highly original."[79]

For all its striking features, op. 11 evinces a conspicuous anxiety of influence, understandable in a genre to which Felix had contributed two significant examples. In choosing for her work the key of D minor, Fanny was inevitably (and deliberately?) inviting comparisons to Felix's Piano Trio in D Minor, op. 49. Thus, the principal theme of Fanny's first movement begins by retracing the rising interval of the fourth, A–D, heard at the outset of op. 49. Felix's brooding theme appears *piano* in the warm register of the cello against subdued, syncopated chords in the piano, a foretaste of the drama to come. Fanny too begins *piano*, but with a "wave" from which she builds her edifice—a rushing sixteenth-note figuration in the low register of the piano (example 12.7). From it her theme emerges in the second bar, announced by the violin and cello in octaves, and quickly rises to a *forte* level. The technique actually recalls two other compositions of Felix, the Prelude in B Minor for Piano, op. 104a, no. 2,♪ and the Overture to *Die erste Walpurgisnacht*, in which the opening themes also arise from turbulent discharges of sixteenth notes in the bass register.

Several other passages of Fanny's trio allude as well to Felix, as if, in turning to chamber music at the end of her life, she again entered into a musical dialogue with her brother and picked up threads of "conversations" they had had over the span of their lives. Thus, in the development of the first movement, she adapted the rushing sixteenth-note figurations to resemble those of Felix's Piano Trio in C Minor, op. 66, and in the coda unleashed a dramatic crescendo passage that seems to recall the first movement of his *Reformation* Symphony, also in D minor. Fanny accompanied the lyrical second theme with tremolos in the piano possibly inspired by a similar texture in the finale of Felix's op. 66, and began her finale with a cadenza-like piano passage that brings to mind the first solo entrance in the opening movement of his Piano Concerto op. 40, also,

appropriately, in D minor. And when Fanny unexpectedly turned from the minor to major mode in the closing pages of the trio and accumulated at the end radiant D major sonorities, she must have been aware that such a theatrical device resonated with the *lieto fine*, the happy ending, of Felix's op. 49.

One other allusion deserves special mention. Fanny's third movement, titled *Lied*, hints at a vocal model, and indeed readily reveals its source—the first phrase of Obadiah's aria "If with all your hearts ye truly seek me" from *Elijah* (no. 4), slightly adapted by Fanny in the piano solo that opens her movement (example 12.8). In December 1846 Felix had played the oratorio

EXAMPLE 12.8. (a) Fanny Hensel, Piano Trio in D Minor, op. 11 (1847), third movement; (b) Felix Mendelssohn, "If with All Your Hearts," *Elijah* op. 70 (1847)

for his sister in Berlin, and the aria seems to have struck her fancy, so that she decided to incorporate a reference into her trio. Four times the phrase appears in the *Lied*, first in the piano, then violin and piano, cello, and violin and piano, so that Felix's presence is firmly impressed upon our consciousness. Fanny stitches together these citations with freely composed material, like a response to or extemporized contemplation of her brother's music.

If the subtext of Fanny's trio is her musical relationship with Felix, the composition nevertheless contains powerfully expressive music and shows the hand of a musician now comfortably engaged with issues of large-scale form and structure. The many allusions to Felix's music do not so much betray a lack of originality as offer an enriching layer of complexity. Indeed, we should recall that nearly every major figure of the European musical canon exploited quotation, allusion, and paraphrase techniques—Bach, Handel, Haydn, Mozart, Beethoven, Schubert, Berlioz, the Schumanns, and, of course, Felix among them. For all the intensity of the siblings' relationship, and the masquerading, Schumannesque exchanges between them, Fanny still succeeded in finding her own creative space and in eclipsing the limitations of her miniature lieder and character pieces for piano.

To that end, she designed her trio not as four independent movements but as parts of a coordinated whole. The end points were two substantial, dramatic movements in D minor, the first in sonata form, the last a rondo—to be sure, not the textbook varieties, but applications that respected Fanny's need for spontaneity and improvisation. Thus, in the first movement, after the romantic second theme in the median F major, she inserted a lengthy episode in F minor, a parenthetical, unexpected exploration of the minor mode, before proceeding to the development section, where she pursued as her goals F-sharp minor and major, two chromatically altered forms of the mediant. And in the finale, Fanny not infrequently interrupted the haunting, refrain-like principal theme—it descends from the treble, accompanied by blurring arpeggiations that wash over it—with cadenza or recitative-like passages, as if her need for formal freedom continued to challenge conventions of rondo form. To connect the outer movements, toward the end of the finale she dramatically recalled the second theme of the first movement, and thus explored a recycling technique that, after Beethoven, would become increasingly common in the later nineteenth century.

In marked contrast are the inner movements. Linked via an *attacca* sign and related major keys (A major and D major), they inhabit the more intimate, lyrical world of Fanny's lieder. The Andante espressivo, which begins like the third movement with a piano solo, in fact falls into a ternary song form, with a contrasting middle section in F-sharp minor, another reference to the heightened role of the mediant tonality in this composition. There then follows, without a full break, the third-movement *Lied* and its unabashed reference to Felix's aria. Taken as a whole, the Trio juxtaposes extroverted outer movements conceived as musical drama with introverted, poetic inner movements, and establishes an opposition between the dramatic and lyrical, the public and private that Fanny confronted as a professional musician in the waning days of her life.

V

Fanny's last year marked the waning of the *Vormärz*, the post-Napoleonic restoration in the German states that less than a year later succumbed to the revolutionary fever of March 1848. Though committed to a rarefied world of culture, music, and the arts that Richard Wagner and others would associate with the old, absolutist order, she remained a keen, progressive observer of politics and in the closing entries of her diary clearly grasped the significance of the political drama that now began to unfold between Frederick William IV and the Prussian citizenry. As it happened, the very day Fanny premiered her Piano Trio—Sunday, April 11—the monarch convened the first "united" Diet (*Landtag*), thereby making good, or so it seemed, on a promise of a royal patent permitting representatives of the various estates to assemble in a bicameral body, and in the process inadvertently revived the aspirations of liberally minded Prussians for a constitution. But the king had no intention of granting real power to the *Landtag*; he remained wary of "the principles of popular representation," which had "laid hold of so many states and ruined them since the French Revolution."[80] As far as Frederick William was concerned, the Diet was an impotent body, to be convened or dismissed at his will. It might comment on proposed taxation or other legislation, but not render decisions. Despite these restrictions, the *Landtag* symbolized the first tangible stirrings of an alternative to autocratic rule, and its members immediately began to press the issue, even as the king disclosed in his inaugural address that he would not allow a piece of paper—a constitution—to come between the Prussian populace and Providence. In response, the Diet drafted a position paper to defend its perceived rights. When Keudell reported to Fanny that the document garnered overwhelming support, even from much of the nobility, she reflected on the last page of her diary, "That is an astonishing result.... Now politics will dominate the next time period; everything else will be impossible."[81]

There were protests in April against the scarcity of food and inflated prices in Berlin, and in her last entry, dated April 26, 1847, Fanny commented on the increasingly serious plight of her countrymen. Then, for a final time, she returned to the inner sanctum of her art and concluded her diary with a sobering assessment: "I am now having a dreadful time; nothing musical is succeeding for me—since my trio I have not written a single usable bar."[82] But by May 13, her spirits revived; when she commented to Hensel that she did not deserve her good fortune, he replied, "If you do not deserve it, who does?" The same day, she resolved her creative impasse by finishing the song *Bergeslust* (*Mountain Passion*), her final composition. After her death a facsimile of the autograph manuscript, now lost, was prepared and distributed among family members and friends,[83] and in 1850 the song appeared in print as Fanny's op. 10, no. 5. Its text, by Eichendorff, again celebrates nature, contemplated by the narrator from a commanding mountain view. There, according to the poem, "Gedanken überfliegen die Vögel und den Wind" ("Thoughts soar above the birds and wind"); incredibly, the final line reads, "Gedanken gehn und Lieder fort bis ins Himmelreich" ("Thoughts and songs are borne heavenward"). Fanny captured the idea of thoughts transformed into songs through a simple but effective conceit. In the opening bars, the piano introduces a rising melodic phrase in its tenor register to suggest the free flow of ideas. The voice then enters with its own melodic phrase, to symbolize Eichendorff's lieder (example 12.9). We hear three strophes of this optimistic, brightly hued music, in the major, parallel minor, and major modes, before the *Gedanken*

EXAMPLE 12.9. Fanny Hensel, *Bergeslust*, op. 10, no. 5 (1847)

und Lieder come together in the coda, as the voice abandons its melodic profile to double the piano melody, ultimately carried into the higher stretches of the piano.

The day after finishing the song, May 14, Fanny assembled her chorus in the afternoon to rehearse Felix's *Die erste Walpurgisnacht*, scheduled for performance at a Sunday musicale two days later. She had not proceeded far when, in the first chorus, "Es lacht der Mai" ("May Is Laughing"), she lost sensation in her hands and asked a colleague to take her place at the piano. Having experienced similar symptoms before, she declined to summon a doctor and instead rubbed her hands with vinegar in an adjoining room while she listened to the music. "How beautiful it sounds," she called out through the open door, and was on the point of returning to the rehearsal when she suffered a second, more serious attack. "It is probably a stroke, just like mother's," she reportedly said, as she was assisted to her bed. By the time her brother Paul arrived forty-five minutes later, Fanny had lost consciousness; despite the efforts of two physicians, one summoned by Sebastian, she died before 11:00 P.M. that evening.[84]

Devastated by the loss, Wilhelm struggled to sketch his wife on her deathbed, "one of his best likenesses," Sebastian later noted, but the "hardest task he ever fulfilled."[85] No doubt his final portrait of Fanny, taken sometime earlier that year, had been considerably easier to dispatch. Ironically enough, in this portrait her arms appear folded, so that her hands are concealed (figure 12.2). Instead, our attention is drawn to her large, expressive eyes and other features that seem to confirm Sebastian's final summary of his mother's "person and character":

> She was small, and had—an inheritance from Moses Mendelssohn—one shoulder higher than the other, but very slightly so. Her chief beauty was her large, dark, very expressive eyes, which did not betray her shortsightedness. Her nose and mouth were rather large, but she had fine white teeth. Her hands were those of an accomplished pianist. Her movements were quick and decided, and her countenance full of life, faithfully reflecting every change of mood. She never could disguise her feelings, and everybody soon found out what she thought of them; for while she would show her delight at seeing a dear friend immediately, if anybody approached whom she did not like wrinkles would at once form in her forehead and at the corners of her mouth.... She was very fond of the fresh air, and used to call it one of her greatest enjoyments. Her disgust with anything ugly, and her wrath with anything bad, were equally intense. She could not bear dull, insipid, vain, or shallow people, and had a few *bêtes noires*, her antipathy to whom she could not get over.... Luxury and creative comforts she was indifferent about, caring nothing for good eating and drinking, good accommodation, dress, or

FIGURE 12.2. Wilhelm Hensel, final portrait of Fanny Hensel, 1847 (Berlin, Mendelssohn Archiv, BA 44)

any articles of luxury. What she did require was intercourse with a few refined and clever people, and the pleasures of art. The love of liberty was deeply rooted in her character; and she held aloof from people who prided themselves either on their birth or their wealth. She had a great aversion to paying calls and other "social duties" and kept out of all such as much as possible. She was the most faithful and constant of friends to all she thought worthy of her intimacy, and capable of any sacrifice for their sake.[86]

Henriette Mendelssohn took some comfort in the idea that death had claimed her niece as she was occupied with her main passion, music, contented and respected by all who knew her. Henriette could not imagine a more beautiful death.[87]

On Sunday, Fanny's coffin, adorned with flowers from the conservatory of Pauline and Rudolf Decker, replaced her piano in the eerily quiet music room of the *Gartenhaus*. The following day, Wilhelm released a terse statement in the *Vossische Zeitung* about his wife's sudden passing and announced that the funeral would take place early that evening. Words now failed the amateur poet, and he could offer only the most epigrammatic of eulogies: "Her life was truth; her end, blessed."[88] Fanny was laid to rest in the cemetery of Trinity Church, near her parents. On her tombstone was later inscribed a quotation from her final song, *Bergeslust*, with the apposite words "Gedanken gehn und Lieder fort bis ins Himmelreich." Presumably the members of her chorus were among the mourners, along with relatives and the composer Giacomo Meyerbeer,[89] but not Felix, who learned of the tragedy that day in Frankfurt, where he had returned early in May after premiering the revised version of *Elijah* in London. The messenger was a brother of Paul's wife, dispatched to Frankfurt to break the news. Shrieking, Felix fell to the floor in a faint and possibly ruptured a cranial vessel, in turn hastening his own death from a stroke some five months later.

In Berlin, the musical world was in shock. The Singakademie, Zelter's former institution, where Fanny had sung with the altos until her family's resignation in 1833 (see p. 165), held a memorial celebration on May 18. Its director and former rival of Felix, Carl Friedrich Rungenhagen, commemorated her in an address to the membership, after which some choral music was performed, including "Siehe, wir preisen selig, die erduldet haben" ("Happy the man who remains steadfast," James 1:12) from Felix's *St. Paul*.[90] One month later a memorial concert was organized by "Herr D.," possibly Rudolf Decker, whose wife had served as the principal soprano soloist in Fanny's chorus; the program included the Mozart *Requiem* and selections from Felix's *St. Paul* and *Lobgesang*.[91] In the press it fell to the critic and poet Ludwig Rellstab, not an intimate of Fanny's circle, to publish her obituary, which appeared in the *Vossische Zeitung* on May 18. History has remembered Rellstab as the poet of some Schubert lieder that appeared in 1828 in the posthumous pseudo-cycle *Schwanengesang*; he was also credited with immortalizing Beethoven's *Sonata quasi Fantasia* op. 27, no. 1 as the *Moonlight*. Now through Rellstab's pen Fanny was briefly honored and remembered by a press that had left most of her life untouched. He could not resist identifying her first and foremost as the "sister of Felix Mendelssohn," who shared her considerable talents with a "famous brother"; what is more, Rellstab expended only a few words on Fanny's own music. Still, his prose communicated a heartfelt sense of mourning for an extraordinary musician who had played a vital, if largely hidden, role in the musical life of Berlin:

She had attained in music a level of refinement that not many artists professionally devoted to their art could claim. Already during her early childhood development, she was a prodigy who aroused the notice of artists. She was educated by the most worthy teachers—in composition by Zelter, in piano first by Lauska and later by Ludwig Berger, whose most distinguished pupil she became. Her artistic talents flowered and matured to the fullest, and in the most noble, tasteful direction. Neither dazzling, transient fashions embraced by the times nor pursuing the eternal, the genuine (denied her) ultimately captured and uplifted her spirit. Rather, she accomplished that in her art. For a quarter of a century and more her father's residence, later her own, was the local site for everything truly excellent in music. Since the siblings' early talents developed to the amazement of all, the elders took care to surround them with a constant, lively traffic of artists and art works. On Sunday mornings there took place (the deceased continued the custom even most recently) artistic gatherings of the rarest kind, where classical works of older times and the best of the present were heard in the most scrupulous performances, and where the audience's enjoyment was enhanced by the participation or presence of the most distinguished artists who either lived in our city or visited it. As mentioned, the deceased took over this parental custom as a sacred inheritance, and so her home remained the sacrificial altar for worshiping the best in music. That is a service for the artistic standards of our city for which we are deeply obliged![92]

Fanny's deeply rooted love of art, Rellstab continued, led her by necessity to composition, and her talents were formidable enough so that she could have embraced any of the larger, most complex forms. Instead, she published only beautiful songs (*schöne Lieder*) associated with the feminine expressions of emotion and avoided the (implied) masculine entanglements of larger forms. Presumably, Rellstab did not yet know of Fanny's piano trio, but he did understand how the mores of class and gender in patrician Berlin had limited Fanny's artistic freedom for much of her life, and he struggled somewhat to eulogize her even as he continued to respect (as had Felix) those mores. And so Fanny went to her grave with the "esteem and thanks" of many Berliners for her services to music, though far more knew precious little of the full range of her abilities as a composer and virtuoso pianist.

By the time of her death, Fanny had seen through the press her first six opera, all officially published in Berlin or available in advance copies. Op. 7, *6 Lieder für Gesang und Klavier*, was issued by Bote & Bock by September 1847. In all likelihood Fanny herself assembled and authorized the volume during her last months, and perhaps even completed preliminary editorial work. The sequence of keys—F major–G minor–F-sharp major–B major–A-flat major–C-sharp major—betrays a sophisticated understanding of relationships between flat keys and sharp keys, and uses A-flat major as the enharmonic equivalent of the more abstruse G-sharp major, dominant of C-sharp major. Put more simply, the key sequence betrays the hand of a composer, not a publisher who selected six lieder after sorting through the musical estate of the deceased. Be that as it may, with the appearance of op. 7 the first flurry of Fanny's publications came to a close. These seven slender volumes offered the first sustained public view of Fanny's music, and around them the first few threads of a fledgling critical tradition were spun in a handful of reviews that began appearing in three German music periodicals in 1847 and 1848. They included the *Neue Berliner Musikzeitung*, the house organ of Bote & Bock; and two far more influential Leipzig journals, the *Neue Zeitschrift für Musik*, which Robert Schumann had founded in 1834 and edited until 1845, and the *Allgemeine musikalische Zeitung*, the house organ of Felix's principal publisher, Breitkopf & Härtel. Most of the reviews were quite short;[93] the most substantial, appearing in the *Allgemeine musikalische Zeitung* in June 1847, ran to one and a half columns.

On the whole, the reactions were positive, but betrayed some unease at evaluating the work of a woman composer who happened to be the sister of an international celebrity. Thus, in order to praise Fanny's efforts, some reviewers chose the tack of emphasizing "masculine" aspects in her music. According to the *Neue Zeitschrift für Musik*, the op. 2 piano pieces did not betray a "woman's hand" but much more a "manly, serious, study of art," and the op. 7 *Lieder* gave evidence of a "deeper, manly, artistic striving."[94] On the other hand, some reviews damned with faint praise. For one correspondent, the op. 1 *Lieder* lacked the depth of feeling that should emanate from the soul, even if the external trappings of the music—its craft, pure harmonies, and elegant accompaniments—were faultless. And for Dr. Emanuel Klitsch, the op. 3 *Gartenlieder* expressed more charm than it did strong emotions wrung from the depths of the soul, even though he readily conceded that Fanny's part-songs evinced considerable art.[95]

Not surprisingly, the questions of Fanny's artistic relationship with Felix and her originality formed two persistent subtexts of the reviews, most of which emphasized her stylistic dependence on her brother. Thus, the reviewer of op. 7 detected a *Mendelssohn'schen* influence in no. 2 (the Goethe setting *Erwin*) and in the romantic melodic lines of nos. 3 and 6 distant traces of Robert Schumann.[96] For Alfred Dörffel, a pupil of Felix who later authored a history of the Leipzig Gewandhaus, Fanny's op. 6 piano pieces revealed her "deep relationship with the esteemed master" who had created the genre of the *Lied ohne Worte*. Dörffel could not have known the full scope of the musical exchanges between Fanny and Felix, or indeed imagined that Fanny may have had an early role in developing the *Lieder ohne Worte*; the similarity of her music to her brother's alone was sufficient reason to warrant a positive review.[97] In Dörffel's paternalistic lines we may trace the roots of one persistent assessment of Fanny's music, that it derived from her brother's familiar style, and that Fanny was an epigonous figure in Felix's circle.

The unidentified critic of the *Allgemeine musikalische Zeitung* expounded a quite different interpretation in a lengthier review of Fanny's published piano music. As if fending off Dörffel's critique, the reviewer began by asking whether after Felix's *Lieder ohne Worte* anything new could be accomplished in the genre. But examination of the first eight bars of op. 2, no. 1 in fact revealed a new, interesting musical acquaintance, and the body of the review then made the case for Fanny's stylistic independence from her brother. First, readers were assured that her compositions were not the first efforts of a musical amateur, but the mature, carefully chosen fruit of a rich artistic life. Her music depicted no strong affects, but rather truly feminine feeling. Her phrases betrayed the finest taste, and her harmonic progressions were masterful, often astonishing. What stamped the music was the exquisite voice leading that betrayed a deep understanding of the music of J. S. Bach. Felix's music displayed the same property, but one would err in dismissing Fanny as a mere imitator of Felix. Considering that the siblings were nurtured in the same music environment, the family similarities were not only to be expected, but necessary. Nevertheless, the differences were obvious to the critical eye: "Mendelssohn's manner of expression is highly precise, he would rather say too little than too much, he always builds [his compositions] on one idea and rounds out the whole in a way that is readily apprehended. Frau Hensel's lieder are more complicated; here fantasy is permitted a freer reign, the form is applied in broader strokes, and not infrequently a greater variety is achieved by means of a contrasting middle section."[98] In short, the reviewer authenticated Fanny's own compositional voice and laid the groundwork for developing a critique of her music. It was all too unfortunately cut short by her death, the Revolution of 1848, and the curtain of silence that soon descended upon her compositions, most of which were lost to history until the latter part of the twentieth century.

Epilogue

For Felix, the loss of Fanny was a crushing blow from which he never recovered. With her passing, he confided to Karl Klingemann, his entire youth had disappeared, and he found himself wandering about as if halfway in a dream.[1] To Charlotte Moscheles he wrote, "You can fancy, however, what I feel,—I, to whom she seemed present at all times, in every piece of music, and on all occasions, whether of happiness or of sorrow."[2] According to Eduard Devrient, Felix spent his final months living under the "impending sword of the angel of death,"[3] convinced that he too would succumb to a stroke. Distraught and unable to contemplate traveling to Berlin, he penned these emotional lines to Wilhelm:

> If the sight of my handwriting checks your tears, put the letter away, for we have nothing left now but to weep from our inmost hearts; we have been so happy together, but a saddened life is beginning now. You made my sister very happy, dear Hensel, through her whole life, as she deserved to be. I thank you for it today, and shall do so as long as I live, and longer too I hope, not only in words, but with bitter pangs of regret, that I did not do more myself for her happiness, did not see her oftener, was not with her oftener. That would indeed have been for my own pleasure, but it pleased her too. I am still too much stunned by the blow to be able to write as I would: still I dare not leave my wife and children and come to you, knowing as I do that I can bring neither help nor comfort. Help and comfort—how different these words sound from all I have been thinking and feeling since yesterday morning. This will be a changed world for us all now, but we must try and get accustomed to the change, though by the time we have got accustomed to it our lives may be over too.[4]

During the summer months Felix sought refuge in Switzerland, where Paul's family and Wilhelm joined him for several weeks. Initially, the composer grieved not through music but landscape painting, and produced vibrant watercolors of Interlaken, Thun, Lucerne, Montreux, and Lake Geneva. His nephew Sebastian found them to possess "a much greater freedom of handling, and force and harmony of coloring" than his earlier efforts in the medium; they were "real pictures, such as no artist need have been ashamed to own."[5] Most of the watercolors presented views of serenely idyllic Swiss landscapes, but one, of the Rheinfall near Schaffhausen, suggested something more. Its turbulent cataracts hinted at the turmoil raging within Felix, which inevitably found another outlet in his music. The String Quartet in F Minor, op. 80, drafted during the final Swiss sojourn and cast in the composer's most dissonant, disjunct style, is laden with his grief over Fanny, and indeed in 1961 was labeled by the East German scholar Georg Knepler as the "*Requiem* of an era."[6] Like the late watercolors, the score evinces a greater freedom and force of coloring than the composer's earlier string quartets. The outer movements are in an unrelenting, dynamic, agitated style, with driving string tremolos, wide leaps, and forays into the high register. The tender slow movement, placed as the penultimate third movement, seems to reminisce about the intimate, lyrical style of Fanny's lieder, while the second movement, propelled by jarring syncopations, is a macabre scherzo such as Felix imagined his sister might have composed.[7]

World-weary and disconsolate, Felix returned with his family to Leipzig in mid- September. After a week he made the difficult journey to Berlin, but the sight of Fanny's rooms, unchanged since her death, utterly unnerved him. Presumably what he saw upon entering her music study was the scene Julius Helfft captured in a watercolor drawing of 1849. There Fanny's piano appears with its lid closed, and an empty music stand behind it; adorning the walls are Wilhelm's paintings, and on a table we see Fanny's crucifix. Through windows behind it light streams diagonally over potted plants, images of life in an otherwise uninhabited room (figure E1). We know little about Felix's daily routine in Berlin during the last week of September, but it seems likely that he examined her manuscripts and became intimately familiar with the piano trio and other recent compositions. But this last visit to the family residence wiped away all the salutary effects of the Swiss holiday, and when he returned to Leipzig early in October, he was once again disillusioned and psychologically exhausted.

Presumably he brought with him Fanny's piano trio and other manuscripts to share with his principal publisher, Breitkopf & Härtel, and to arrange for their publication, in partial expiation for his guilt over earlier withholding unqualified support for her need to release her music.[8] But not until 1850—after Felix's death and the revolutionary shock waves of 1848—did the distinguished Leipzig firm bring out what became, as far as the nineteenth century was concerned, Fanny's *opera ultima*. First to appear were the *Vier Lieder* op. 8 for piano, followed by the *Sechs Lieder* op. 9, *Fünf Lieder* op. 10,

FIGURE E1. Julius Helfft, Fanny Hensel's music study, watercolor and pencil, 1849 (London, private possession)

and Piano Trio op. 11, announced as nos. 1–4 of the "posthumous works." If op. 8 seems to have featured piano pieces from Fanny's last year (two, nos. 2 and 3, cannot be firmly dated), op. 9 gathered together six songs from 1823 to 1838, while op. 10 comprised five songs from the 1840s, concluding with Fanny's very last composition, *Bergeslust*. As was the case with so much of her music, these works had been composed separately, so that Fanny probably never envisioned their appearance together in distinct sets. Felix's final service for his sister was very likely to compile opp. 8, 9, and 10, which entailed not only selecting individual piano pieces and lieder for publication but also arranging them in suitable key sequences. In the case of op. 8—B minor, A minor, D-flat major, and E major—this meant treating D-flat major as the enharmonic equivalent of C-sharp major, situated halfway between A minor and E major, and thus exploring between the last three pieces mediant relationships favored by Fanny in her later music. Third-related keys also obtained between individual songs in opp. 9 and 10. In op. 9, for instance, mediant pairings occur among the first four lieder—E-flat major to G minor, and E major to A-flat major (the enharmonic equivalent of the third above E major, G-sharp)—clear signs again that the compiler, like Fanny, remained especially sensitive to key relationships.

If Felix was responsible for promoting these final publications, he probably finished that task early in October 1847, perhaps by October 9, when he drafted his own last composition, the *Altdeutsches Frühlingslied*, op. 86, no. 6, based on an old German text. Its closing lines read, "Nur ich allein, / ich leide Pein, / ohn' Ende werd' ich leiden / seit du von mir, / und ich von dir, / O Liebste, musste scheiden." ("Only I suffer pain, I will suffer without end, since, most beloved, you had to part from me, and I from you.") Two days later, he suffered the first in a series of strokes that took his life on November 4. After solemn ceremonies attended by thousands of mourners at the Paulinerkirche, Felix's coffin was placed on an *Extrazug* that departed during the night of November 7 for Berlin. There, thousands more followed a procession to the cemetery of Trinity Church, which Felix had probably visited just weeks before, and where he was now interred, next to Fanny. The finality of death thus brought the siblings together and fulfilled a promise Felix had made to Fanny in December 1846—to celebrate her next birthday with her.[9]

i

At the time of Fanny's death, Wilhelm was at the height of his career, with sufficient commissions and demand for portraits to ensure a backlog for several years.[10] The artist's larger projects included a portrait of the Prussian king, which Fanny described near the end of her diary as a "splendid picture" that, produced during politically charged times, would certainly generate "great interest in the future."[11] Wilhelm was also engaged with a painting commissioned in 1842 for the coronation hall at Brunswick, on a subject from the Napoleonic Wars—the Bivouac of the Duke of Brunswick in 1809. To judge from a few surviving sketches, this work would have treated the military heroism of Frederick William, celebrated as the Black Duke, who briefly recaptured Brunswick from the French during the War of the Fifth Coalition. Among the jubilant citizens streaming forth to greet the duke Wilhelm intended to place likenesses of himself, Fanny, and Sebastian. The artist was already well advanced with this painting, but Fanny's unexpected death shattered his inspiration, and, according to Sebastian, "he never painted anything worth having during the fifteen years that he survived her, and never touched again the picture for Brunswick so near completion."[12]

Though in his element while painting or contriving pithy, well-turned verses, Wilhelm loathed writing letters, and so all the more compelling was the unbounded expression of grief he poured into a letter two weeks after Fanny's death to his sister Luise: "How often have I put down this sheet, or carried it from room to room in order to write to you, and then it became too difficult for me. May God, who has imposed such a colossal calamity, help all of us poor sinners! Amen. You see how that already sounds like resignation, and that at least I do not revolt against God, even if this time I must find Him so completely incomprehensible—a life so full of blessings for others, so full of joy for herself, so grateful to Him! Why, why, why so early?"[13] The bright spirit that had pervaded Leipzigerstrasse no. 3 had now departed, and Wilhelm was left to tend to its physical exterior, its trappings, which nothing, no one could reanimate. Fanny's death represented for the artist the "loss of everything, for his whole family life was destroyed."[14] Advised by his doctor to travel, Wilhelm joined Felix for a few weeks in Switzerland, considered escaping to the Orient, and visited The Hague, where he encountered Hans Christian Andersen. The Danish author recorded in his diary that Wilhelm tearfully carried with him the deathbed sketch of Fanny, and that to see a strong man so deeply moved was especially gripping.[15]

And so Wilhelm lapsed into what the novelist Theodor Fontane described as an "artistic *far niente*"—artistic idleness.[16] If Felix had grieved by turning to painting, Wilhelm now reverted to politics, to reaffirming the conservative values of a Prussian loyalist ever faithful to his king. When the barricades went up in Berlin in March 1848, Wilhelm personally escorted a princess to the royal palace. And when the king, forced to withdraw the military after the deaths of scores of citizens, authorized armed citizen patrols to reestablish order, Wilhelm took command of a newly formed corps of artists, whose principal duty was to guard the king. By November 1848 Frederick William had regained control of Berlin, but then barely survived an assassination attempt in May 1850. Wilhelm now riveted his attention on the dramatic events in the capitol and began attending the trials of political activists, revolutionaries charged with treason, and common criminals, all of whom he chronicled with courtroom sketches.

In 1851, Leipzigerstrasse no. 3 was sold to the state; within a few years, it would serve as the upper house of the new German parliament for a few decades before being razed in the closing years of the century. Wilhelm was now obliged to leave his atelier, the *Gartenhaus* and all its fading memories of music, art, and culture of a prerevolutionary age. For a while, he served on the Senate of the Royal Academy, and then began to travel, to the Bohemian spas of Marienbad and Carlsbad to seek relief for an inflamed gallbladder, to Munich where he produced fifty more portraits, and to East Prussia to visit Sebastian, who had purchased property near Königsberg. When Frederick William IV died in 1861, having ceded authority in 1858 to his brother (the future Emperor Wilhelm), Hensel made one final drawing, of the Hohenzollern monarch on his sarcophagus. It was the death of an era, as the old veteran of the War of Liberation ceded his final vision of the receding Prussian monarchy, and of his own gallant, patriotic youth. There was little left to sustain him, and his former discipline—during his married life he habitually drew when not working on a canvas—yielded to indifference and apathy. But early in November Wilhelm performed one final heroic deed: he saved a

Berlin pedestrian—whether it was a child, woman, or man is unclear—from being run over by an onrushing omnibus, and in the process severely injured his knee. In the following weeks the wound became infected, and on November 26, 1861, he succumbed, probably to tetanus.

Attending his funeral were royalty, colleagues, and former students. Felix's song "Es ist bestimmt in Gottes Rath" ("It Is Determined by God's Counsel"), op. 47, no. 4, was sung, and Wilhelm's remains too were interred in the cemetery of Trinity Church, next to Fanny and Felix, bringing together in death the "perfect" triangle that Fanny had sought in life to sustain.

ii

And finally, what of Sebastian (figure E2)? When Fanny died, he was an impressionable, somewhat sickly seventeen-year-old. He had been raised in a sheltered world of music and art. Though he never learned how to read music, he possessed a good enough musical ear and memory to enable him to sing as a boy soprano in his mother's chorus, where, after only one or two rehearsals, he was able to memorize his part.[17] He studied drawing and painting with a colleague of his father's, and for a while raised his parents' earnest hopes that he would become an artist. But in the end, the allure of art was not powerful enough to ensnare him, and by his own admission, he lacked sufficient talent.[18]

Less than a year after his mother's death, Sebastian experienced firsthand the Revolution of 1848, its brutality, its turbulent assault on the Prussian monarchy that his father had so vigorously defended, and above all, its disturbing images that no one could have conceived—dragoons firing on unarmed civilians, the surreal magic of spontaneously appearing barricades, the king forced to doff his hat before the funereal procession of coffins containing common Prussians now celebrated as heroes. Like many students, Sebastian joined the civil guard, and for several months "played soldier," as he wrote in his memoirs.[19] His aunt Rebecka now stepped in to fill the maternal void, and Sebastian also came to rely more and more on his uncle Paul for support, as Wilhelm became increasingly distant and then alienated from his son. It was, Sebastian observed, as if his father had sunk with his mother into her grave.[20] After finishing school he acquired a neglected country estate near Königsberg in East Prussia, where he married the daughter of a wealthy merchant and farmed for several years. Returning to Berlin in the 1870s, he eventually became the director of a newly established hotel consortium and managed the Kaiserhof, the city's first luxury hotel. It was a grand edifice that burned down just days after its opening in 1875, but was quickly rebuilt, and served as the site of Bismarck's Congress of Berlin in 1878, at which the European powers, Russia, and the Ottoman Empire debated the emergence of pan-Slavism after the Russian-Turkish War.

FIGURE E2.   Sebastian Hensel, pencil drawing by Wilhelm Hensel,
1860 (Berlin, Mendelssohn Archiv, BA 188,44)

When, in 1861, Sebastian had entered his father's quarters on the
Wilhelmstrasse, he found a confusion of unfinished canvases and, among
the accumulated papers and domestic debris, 1,000 pencil portraits of family,
friends, colleagues, nobility, and the European artistic and cultural elite, all
punctiliously recorded by Wilhelm over several decades. It now became Sebastian's solemn duty to organize this imposing paternal legacy into portfolios;
today, they are preserved in the Kupferstichkabinett of the Staatliche Museen
in Berlin, where they remain a priceless documentary source for anyone curious about the German *Vormärz*.[21] But Sebastian's urge to preserve his family's history extended considerably further—in 1879 he published *Die Familie
Mendelssohn 1729–1847*, a three-volume history of the Mendelssohns from the
birth of Moses Mendelssohn to the deaths of Fanny and Felix. Sebastian's

principal aim was to depict the Mendelssohns as fully assimilated, upstanding Prussian citizens who had made extraordinary, lasting contributions to German music, the arts, sciences, and finance. To that end, he exercised editorial judgment in selecting and abridging family letters and diaries, from which he quietly removed indelicate passages that might offend the living or tarnish the family image he sought to promote. Nevertheless, the result was a landmark publication that ran to many editions well into the twentieth century and was translated into English by the son of Karl Klingemann. Sebastian's work remains to this day a vital source for modern Mendelssohn scholarship and a central strand in our critical understanding of his mother, even if it emphasized her domestic roles as sister and mother over those of musician and composer.

By 1879 Fanny's memory had slipped from the consciousness of many Germans, and yet her music was not completely forgotten. Late in 1847 Robert Schumann examined the *Gartenlieder* for possible performance by his choral *Verein* in Dresden, where he had assumed the post of municipal music director. In Bonn, Johanna Kinkel, who had sung in Fanny's chorus, read the part-songs with her own amateur music society. There was sufficient interest in England to warrant two issues of the *Gartenlieder* in 1867 and 1878 from publishers that had been associated with Felix, J. J. Ewer and Novello. In the United States, the hymnist and music educator William B. Bradbury, who had traveled in Germany from 1847 to 1849, brought out the fourth part-song, *Morgengruß*, as *Morning Greeting* in *The Alpine Glee Singer: A Complete Collection of Secular and Social Music* in 1850,[22] and later the part-songs appeared in transcriptions for brass band.[23] A few other works were occasionally heard—Clara Schumann performed some lieder in Göttingen in 1855, and the pianist Otto Dressel introduced the Piano Trio to a Boston audience in 1856. That performance merited a notice in *Dwight's Journal of Music*. The reviewer found the music "full of interest and beauty" and "vigorous, so full of fire"; its "sustained strength" even surpassed some works of Felix.[24] The American composer George Chadwick, who studied at the Leipzig Conservatory in the 1870s, was even of the opinion that Fanny had written a trio as good as her brother ever produced.[25] And, of course, connoisseurs of Felix's music were vaguely aware that six of his published songs were in fact by his sister.

Still, the nineteenth century and much of the twentieth remained woefully unaware of the full scope of Fanny's oeuvre. Few would have suspected that she produced well over 400 compositions in a variety of genres, that she was an accomplished choral director, a scholar of J. S. Bach's music, and a piano virtuoso capable of rivaling her brother. The grand caesura, the nearly century and a half during which most of these accomplishments were neglected, is one of the great injustices of music history, as was Fanny's tragedy, to be struck down just as she was beginning her professional career as a composer. It will be some time yet before the new critical interpretations of her life and work are consolidated. But there is, perhaps, a modicum of comfort that Fanny's music, like a new voice from the nineteenth century, is now fully before the public. She is finally emerging from the shadowy, semipublic world she inhabited—she can now become Fanny Hensel.

Abbreviations

AmZ	*Allgemeine musikalische Zeitung*
BamZ	*Berliner allgemeine musikalische Zeitung*
GM	Karl Mendelssohn Bartholdy, *Goethe and Mendelssohn*, London, 1874
H-U	Renate Hellwig-Unruh, *Fanny Hensel geb. Mendelssohn Bartholdy: Thematisches Verzeichnis der Kompositionen*, Adliswil, 2000
JAMS	*Journal of the American Musicological Society*
LA	Felix Mendelssohn Bartholdy, *Briefe aus Leipziger Archiven*, ed. H.-J. Rothe and R. Szeskus, Leipzig, 1972
MA	Mendelssohn Archiv, Staatsbibliothek zu Berlin—Preussischer Kulturbesitz
MaHW	R. Larry Todd, ed., *Mendelssohn and His World*, Princeton, 1991
MALIM	R. Larry Todd, *Mendelssohn: A Life in Music*, New York, 2003
MDM	Margaret Deneke Mendelssohn Collection, Bodleian Library, Oxford
MF	Sebastian Hensel, *The Mendelssohn Family (1729–1847) from Letters and Journals*, 2 vols., London, 1882
MLL	*Felix Mendelssohn: A Life in Letters*, ed. R. Elvers, trans. C. Tomlinson, New York, 1986
MN	Mendelssohn Nachlass, Staatsbibliothek zu Berlin—Preussischer Kulturbesitz
MQ	*The Musical Quarterly*
MS	*Mendelssohn Studien*
NCMR	*Nineteenth-Century Music Review*
NYPL	New York Public Library
NZfM	*Neue Zeitschrift für Musik*
SBB	Staatsbibliothek zu Berlin—Preussischer Kulturbesitz
Tagebücher	Fanny Hensel, *Tagebücher*, ed. H.-G. Klein and R. Elvers, Wiesbaden, 2002

Notes

Preface

1. Felix to Madame Kiéné, June 1, 1835, Library of Congress, Mendelssohn correspondence.
2. *AmZ* 49 (1847), 382.
3. *NZfM* 33 (1850), September 3 and 6.
4. Fanny to Felix, July 9, 1846, in Citron: 1987, 349.
5. Entry in Clara Schumann's diary, cited in Reich: 2001, 216.
6. George Eliot, "Women in France: Madame de Sablé," in *Selected Critical Writings*, ed. Rosemary Ashton, New York, 1992, 37.
7. Goethe to Felix, June 18, 1825, in Karl Mendelssohn Bartholdy, ed., *Goethe and Mendelssohn*, trans. M. E. von Glehn, London, 1874, 50.
8. Wilhelmy-Dollinger: 2006, 17.
9. See further on this point Klein: 2006, 59.
10. Lampadius, 31.
11. Obituary notice, Berlin *Vossische Zeitung*, May 18, 1847.

Chapter 1

1. Bulletin of November 14, 1805; *Imperial Glory: The Bulletins of Napoleon's Grande Armée 1805–1814*, trans. J. David Markham, London, 2003, 39.
2. Thomas Hodgskin, *Travels in the North of Germany*, Edinburgh, 1820 (repr. New York, 1969), I, 202.
3. *Leipziger AmZ* 4 (1869), 207.
4. Salomon Maimon, "Recollections of Mendelssohn," in Robertson, 48.
5. [Joseph Mendelssohn,] "Moses Mendelssohn's Lebensgeschichte," in *Moses Mendelssohn's gesammelte Schriften*, ed. G. B. Mendelssohn, Leipzig, 1843, I, 17.
6. Ibid., I, 9.
7. Lavater, *Physiognomic Fragments*, cited in Elon, 49. See also Jacob-Friesen, 27.
8. Tom Wolf, *Smaragdgrün*, Berlin, 2004, 246; cited in Nieding: 2007, 110.
9. See further Nieding: 2007.

10. *MF* I, 63.

11. Ibid., I, 62.

12. Stromeyer, I, 198.

13. Marx: 1991, 209.

14. Amalie Beer to Giacomo Meyerbeer, May 18, 1816, in Meyerbeer, I, 313.

15. Samuel Butler, *The Way of All Flesh*, Harmondsworth, 1986, ch. 5. For Abraham's assertion, see Heine, 245.

16. *MF* I, 61.

17. Stromeyer, I, 198.

18. Kippenberg, 73.

19. *MF* I, 72.

20. Lewald: 1992, 47.

21. See Wollny.

22. See Oleskiewicz.

23. Thayer, 729.

24. Spiel, 329.

25. *MF* I, 36.

26. Brendel Veit to Carl Gustav von Brinckmann, February 2, 1799, in Blackwell and Zantop, 339.

27. Cited in Schlegel: 1988, cvi–cvii (n. 8).

28. See in particular, Librett, 179 ff.

29. *MF* I, 40–41.

30. Librett, 177.

31. Ibid., 122.

32. Blackwell and Zantop, 345.

33. Stern, 187.

34. Abraham to Bella Salomon, November 15, 1805, in Elvers: 1997, 17.

35. Lea to Henriette von Pereira-Arnstein, May [2], 1809, from a transcribed extract in MDM c. 29; see also Elvers: 1997, 17.

36. Therese Devrient, 329.

37. Elvers and Klein, 131–36; in 1983, the sum was estimated as the equivalent of 100,000 marks.

38. *MF* I, 72–73.

39. In the novel *Schach von Wuthenow* (1883), trans. by E. M. Falk as *A Man of Honor*, New York, 1975, 85.

40. *MF* I, 34.

41. Panwitz: 2005.

42. Klein: 2005, 111; Henriette to Lea, March 25, 1812. Henriette Maria Mendelssohn (1775–1831) was the youngest daughter of Moses Mendelssohn. See further *MALIM*, 19–20.

43. Klein: 2007a.

44. Abraham to Berlin, May 28, 1833, in *MF*, I, 289; see also I, 74, and Spiel, 276, 328, and Lea to the Swedish diplomat Carl Gustav von Brinkman, October 6, 1818, in Klein: 2007, 260.

45. Klein 2007a, 205.

46. Elvers and Klein, 160.

47. On this point see Sievers, 100, 101.

48. Elvers: 1997, 18.

49. Jacobson, 257; see also Gilbert, 315.

50. Elon, 74.

51. See further ibid., 44–45.

52. Spiel, 112–13.

53. Zelter to Goethe, October 23, 1821, in Hecker, II, 139. See also Elvers: 1997, 18, concerning the remarkable redaction of this passage, restored to its original by Max Hecker in 1913.

54. Lea to Henriette von Pereira-Arnstein, July 4, 1819, MN 15 no. 5.

55. *Wiener Zeitschrift für Kunst* 7 (1822); facs. in Klein: 1997, 65.

56. *MF*, I, 75.

57. Ibid., I, 89.

58. Sir George Grove, "Mendelssohn," in *Dictionary of Music and Musicians*, London, 1890, II, 254.

59. *MF*, I, 77.

60. Lea to Carl Gustaf von Brinkman, February 6, 1816, in Klein: 2007, 255.

61. Pope, 304.

62. March 22, 1820 [*recte* 1821], Pierpont Morgan Library, New York. Felix Mendelssohn Bartholdy: 1997, 5–6.

63. Schubring, 223.

64. Klein: 1997, 58.

65. Benedict, 6.

66. Fanny Hensel obituary notice, *Vossische Zeitung*, May 18, 1847.

67. Rellstab, 63.

68. Ibid., 79.

69. Berger to Jenny Sieber, April 21, 1822, in Siebenkäs, 233.

70. The identifying numbers used here and throughout the volume for compositions of Fanny Hensel refer to Hellwig-Unruh: 2000.

71. Youens: 1997.

72. Hellwig-Unruh: 2000, 117.

73. Zelter to Goethe, April 4, 1816, in Hecker, I, 465.

74. November 10, 1816, in Gilbert, 35.

75. Abraham to Fanny, [July 18,] 1820, in *MF*, I, 83.

76. Stern, 305.

77. Klein: 1993, 144.

78. Rebecka Meyer to Rosa Herz, March 2, 1818, in Gilbert, 39.

79. *AmZ* 20 (1818), 791; *AmZ* 39 (1837), 845–46.

80. *MF*, I, 88–89.

Chapter 2

1. Schröder: 1997; Lea to Henriette von Pereira-Arnstein, May 6, 1821, in MDM c. 29, extract; *Posthumous Memoirs of Karoline Bauer*, London, 1884, I, 220.

2. Schottländer, 155–56.

3. *AmZ* 2 (1799), 587.

4. Goethe to Zelter, May 11, 1820, in Hecker, II, 59.

5. Zelter to Goethe, March 1, 1818, in Hecker, II, 593.

6. Klein: 1993, 194.

7. Lea to Henriette von Pereira-Arnstein, May 1, 1819, in MDM c. 29, extract.

8. Lea to Henriette von Pereira-Arnstein, July 19, 1819, quoted in Filosa, 23.

9. Fanny to Zelter, August 18, 1819, cited in Klein: 1997, 69.

10. Seaton: 1981.

11. The baroque discipline of providing a bass line with figures to summarize the harmonies necessary to realize a suitable accompaniment.

12. Felix to Rudolph Gugel, November 1, 1819, in Elvers: 1963.

13. Ward Jones.

14. "Aus Berliner Briefen Augusts von Goethe (19.–26. Mai 1819): Ein Brief der Ottilie (undatiert)," *Goethe Jahrbuch* 28 (1907), 35.

15. Lea to Henriette von Pereira-Arnstein, May 1, 1819, in MDM c. 29, extract; Henriette Mendelssohn to Fanny, August 1819, in Lambour: 1986, 52.

16. For facs. of the autographs, now in SBB (MA Depos. Berlin Ms. 3 and MDM c. 21, fol. 107), see Maurer: 1997, 16, and E. Wolff: 1906, 13.

17. See *MALIM*, 50.

18. Abraham to Henriette Mendelssohn, August 9, 1819, in Klein: 1997, 42.

19. See *MALIM*, 73.

20. MA Depos. Lohs I; for a description, see Klein: 1995, 77–84.

21. As a deist Voltaire coined the imperative *écrasez l'infâme* to oppose the doctrinaire aspects of Christian orthodoxy.

22. Gourdin, 159.

23. Abraham to Fanny, July 16, 1820, in *MF*, I, 82–83.

24. MA Depos. Lohs I, 82 ff.

25. Rousseau, *The Confessions*, trans. J. M. Cohen, Baltimore, 1965, 344.

26. Ibid., 350.

27. The ◉ icon refers to musical examples that are available online.

28. Leo Damrosch, *Jean-Jacques Rousseau: Restless Genius*, Boston, 2005, 229.

29. In Hellwig-Unruh's catalogue of Hensel's music, the fragment is misidentified as an arrangement (*Bearbeitung*) of Rousseau's aria (Hellwig-Unruh, 367). But apart from the common text, the fragment bears no resemblance to Rousseau's music and may now be recognized rather as her original attempt at composition.

30. MN, 2, 12–19.

31. Lea to Henriette von Pereira-Arnstein, February 26, 1821. See *MALIM*, 65–66.

32. *MALIM*, 74.

33. Felix to A. W. Bach, May 3, 1821, in *MLL*, 4.

34. See further Schröder: 1997.

35. For an edition of the exercises, see Todd: 1983.

36. Ibid., 36–39.

37. MA Depos. Lohs I, 36.

38. Ibid., 76–77.

39. Berlioz, 74–75.

40. The imposing fugue of the *Hammerklavier* Sonata op. 106, for instance, has one perplexing passage, in which the subject appears in retrograde, or reverse order, that challenges even the most attentive listener.

41. Zelter to Goethe, December 10, 1824, in Hecker, 310.

42. MA Depos. Lohs I, 49.

43. "Schwarz ihre Brauen, / Weiß ihre Brust, / Klein mein Vertrauen, / Groß doch die Lust." ("Her eyebrows dark, her breast white, my confidence lacking, but my desire great.")

44. *MF*, I, 77.

45. Ibid., I: 79–80.

46. D. 162, 226, 259, and 296. These lieder formed part of the parcel of Goethe settings sent by Schubert to Weimar and, on Zelter's recommendation, returned unopened.

47. See further Roger Fiske, *Scotland in Music: A European Enthusiasm*, Cambridge, 1983, 80–105.

48. D. 839 of 1825.

49. *Harmonicon* 10 (1832), 2nd part, 54–55.

50. Lea to Henriette von Pereira-Arnstein, ca. June 1821, in MDM c. 29 (extract).

51. *MF*, I, 83.

52. MA Depos. Lohs I, 93–95.

53. MA Depos. Lohs I, 60–61; between January 27 and March 3, 1821.

54. Fanny to Felix, September 7, 1838, in Citron: 1987, 261.

55. *MALIM*, 75.

56. Lea to Henriette von Pereira-Arnstein, September 1821, in MDM c. 29 (extract). MA Depos. Lohs I, 45–48.

57. *MF*, I, 82.

58. Klein: 1993, 145.

59. Universitäts- und Landesbibliothek Bonn, Abtheilung Handschriften und Rara S2398 (Nachlass Kinkel, 35). I wish to thank Monika Hennemann for alerting me to this source. The theoretical key of A-sharp major, sounding enharmonically the same as B-flat major, would be notated A-sharp, B-sharp, C-double-sharp, D-sharp, E-sharp, F-double-sharp, G-double-sharp, and A-sharp, and thus contain ten sharps.

60. Zelter to Goethe, October 22, 1821, in Hecker, II, 139.

61. Letters of November 6 and 14, 1821, in Mendelssohn: 1986, 7–10; *GM*, 26. Goethe's verdict on Fanny's early lieder has not survived. The poem he wrote for her, *An die Entfernte*, attributed by Hensel to the time of Felix's 1821 Weimar visit (*MF*, I: 92), in fact dates from several years later (see further, p. III below).

62. Fanny to Felix, October 28 and November 4, 1821, in Citron: 1987, 1–2, 4.

63. *MF*, I: 75.

64. Jacob Bartholdy to Fanny, August 11 and November 16, 1821, in Lambour: 1986, 87–88.

65. Therese Devrient, 231.

66. Ibid.

67. Eduard Devrient, 3.

68. Lowenthal-Hensel: 1979, 188.

69. Lowenthal-Hensel: 1979a, 176.

70. For a reproduction, see Lowenthal-Hensel and Arnold, 26.

71. For a reproduction, see the frontispiece to *MS* 3 (1979).

72. Binder, 28.

73. Lowenthal-Hensel: 1979, 195.

74. Helmut Börsch-Supan, ed., *Die Kataloge der Berliner Akademie-Austellungen 1786–1850*, vol. I, Berlin, 1971, catalogue for the year 1816.

75. George Saintsbury, *Essays in English Literature*, London, 1896, 185–86.

76. Miriam Allen DeFord, *Thomas Moore*, New York, 1967, 47.

77. Thomas Moore, *Paradise and the Peri*, in *Lalla Rookh*, London, 1888, 118.

78. *MF*, I, 95.

79. Ibid., I, 96.

Chapter 3

1. *MF*, I, 117.

2. Heinrich Heine, "Dritter Brief aus Berlin," in K. Briegreb, ed., *Sämtliche Werke*, Munich, 1959, II, 59 (June 7, 1822).

3. Lea to Henriette von Pereira-Arnstein, October 19, 1821, cited in Klein: 2005b, 11.

4. Marx: 1865, I, 111–12; Dorn, 1872, III, 49.

5. Cited in Lambour: 2005, 272.

6. Lea to Henriette von Pereira-Arnstein, March 29, 1822, in MDM c. 29 (extract).

7. For Fanny's 1822 version, see Hensel: 2003a, 16–17.

8. An edition by Liana Gavrila Serbescu and Barbara Heller is available (Hensel: 1991).

9. See the edition by Renate Eggebrecht-Kupsa (Hensel: 1989a).

10. See further Cadenbach: 1997.

11. Felix to J. Alfred Novello, April 7, 1838, in *GM*, 191.

12. Ibid., 85.

13. Fanny to Zelter, June 4, 1822, in Klein: 1997, 70.

14. Arguing for a performance is Lea's letter to Amalia Beer of April 8, 1823: "Fanny has finally also ventured to write a larger work, and several weeks ago let us hear a quartet that really pleased," in Meyerbeer, I, 468. Presumably the work in question is her Piano Quartet, but whether she performed it with the string parts or in a rendition for piano solo is unclear.

15. Lea was actively involved in guiding her son's *Werklein* through the press. See Elvers: 1974, 48 (letter of [July] 29, 1823).

16. Hensel: 2003a, 18–19.

17. Klein: 1993, 146.

18. *MF*, I, 115.

19. Hiller, 4.

20. *MF*, I, 108.

21. Ibid.

22. Fanny to Zelter, July 19, 1822, in Heinrich Heine Institut, Düsseldorf, Sig 51.4896.

23. Fanny to Henriette Mendelssohn, August 21, 1822, in Lambour: 1990, 172.

24. *MF*, I, 110.

25. For an edition (transposed from the original A major to G major), see Hensel: 1991a, 8–9.

26. *MF*, I, 112.

27. C. H. Müller, *Felix Mendelssohn, Frankfurt am Main und der Cäcilien-Verein*, Darmstadt, 1925, 2.

28. Elvers: 1974, 49; Jacobson: 1960, 257.

29. *GM*, 35.

30. Klein: 1993, 148–49 and Abb. 4b.

31. Montgomery, 203.

32. Edition in Hensel: 1986, 1–3.

33. *MF*, I, 101.

34. Youens: 1997, 40.

35. Maurer: 1997, 88.

36. Elvers and Klein, 180–82, with facs.

37. Gilbert, 51.

38. For an edition, see Hensel: 2001.

39. For a probing discussion of Berger's "sociable" songs, see Youens: 1997, 107 ff.

40. Wilhelm Müller to Adelheid Müller, July 29, 1823, in P. S. Allen and J. T. Hatfield, ed., *Diary and Letters of Wilhelm Müller*, Chicago, 1903, 112.

41. Wilhelm to Luise Hensel, December 1, 1823, in Gilbert, 59.

42. Therese Devrient, 268.

43. *MF*, I, 102.

44. Gilbert, 59.

45. Lea to Amalie Beer, April 8, 1823, in Meyerbeer, I: 468.

46. For an edition by Judith Raskell, see Hensel: 1995e.

47. Hensel: 1989b.

48. MA, Ms. 33.

49. H-U 67, 69, 71, 74, 79, 84, 86, 88, 92, 96, 99, 102, and 103. For editions, see Hensel: 1996d, 1996a, and 1986.

50. Frederick Niecks, *Programme Music in the Last Four Centuries*, London, 1907, repr. New York, 1969, 161.

51. *MF*, I, 118.

52. Fanny to Zelter, December 9, 1823, in Klein: 1997, 138.

53. Klein: 1993, 150.

54. Hensel: 1995f, 11–13.

55. See further Roger Paulin, *Ludwig Tieck: A Literary Biography*, Oxford, 1985, 226–27.

56. For an edition see Jack Werner, ed., *Classical Discoveries*, London, 1959, no. 5.

57. For an edition, see Hensel: 2003a, 20–21.

58. Cited in Rebmann: 1989, 115.

59. Ludwig to Rahel, October 11, 1818, in Rahel Levin Varnhagen, *Briefwechsel mit Ludwig Robert*, ed. Consolina Vigliero, Munich, 2001, 181.

60. See Maurer and Huber.

61. Also known as *Der Onkel aus Boston* (*The Uncle from Boston*).

62. Hensel: 1995f, 17–19.

63. Hensel: 2003a, 25.

64. Hensel: 1995f, 21–25.

65. Hensel: 1994c, 4–8.

66. Hensel: 1996d, 20–32.

67. On the date of Bella Salomon's gift, see further *MALIM*, 123.

68. Eduard Devrient, 13.

69. Hensel: 1996d, 10–19.

70. Felix to Fanny, July 17, 1824, in Weissweiler: 1997, 23.

71. Hensel: 1991.

72. See *MALIM*, 133.

73. Ignaz Moscheles, 59.

74. Ibid., 50.

75. Ibid., 65.

76. See further the thorough study by Alexander Silbiger, "Bach and the Chaconne," *Journal of Musicology* 17 (1999), 358–85.

77. Berlin, Staatsbibliothek zu Berlin–Preussischer Kulturbesitz Mus. Ms. Bach P 234. In 1823 Eduard Rietz prepared a copy (MDM, c. 73) for the Mendelssohns, which appears in Fanny's inventory of the family's music library; see Elvers and Ward Jones, 89.

78. See Klein: 1993, 153.

Chapter 4

1. Lowenthal-Hensel: 1990, 142.

2. For a detailed study of the history of the residence, see Cullen.

3. Cited in Cullen, 35.

4. *MF*, I, 132.

5. Heyse, I, 42.

6. Stromeyer, 201.

7. See further Streicher, 243.

8. *BamZ* 1 (1824), 174.

9. Siegfried, 38–39.

10. "From the Memoirs of Adolf Bernhard Marx," in *MaHW*, 209.

11. Klingemann, 347. Dim., diminuendo; smorz., smorzando; rit., ritardando.

12. That is, passages with a decrease in dynamics, lessening of tempo, or fading away of pitches.

13. Elvers: 1997.

14. Though we can document none of Fanny's Beethoven performances for 1825, the Swedish traveler Malla Montgomery-Silverstolpe reported that at a Sunday "Matinee" on June 11, 1826, Fanny performed a concerto by Beethoven. *Das romantische Deutschland: Reisejournal einer Schwedin (1825–1826)*, Leipzig, 1912, 276; cited in Lambour: 2005, 276. According to Fanny's catalogue of the family music library, she received scores of Beethoven's Fourth and Fifth Piano Concerti as gifts from Eduard Rietz in 1825 and 1823, respectively. Elvers and Ward Jones, 91, 92.

15. MA, Ms. 63, 1, 40; see also Lambour: 2005, 274–75.

16. MA, Ms. 63, 1, 39; see Klein: 1997, 139–41.

17. Hensel: 1991a, 9–12.

18. Ibid., 13–15.

19. Citron: 1987, 9.

20. "Proposal to Establish an Instrumental Music Lovers' Association," bound with Fanny's diaries in MA Depos. Berlin 500,22. For a translation, see Tillard: 1996, 199–201.

21. Schubring, 223.

22. Conversation of June 10, 1823, in J. K. Morehead, ed., *Conversations of Goethe with Johann Peter Eckermann*, trans. J. Oxenford, New York, 1998, 2.

23. Hensel: 1993, 10–11.

24. Schubert opted for a chromatic tetrachord, descending from A through G-sharp, G-natural, F-sharp, and F-natural to E. Fanny used the natural form of the tetrachord, which in her setting appears as G–F–E-flat–D.

25. H-U 148, 149, 150, 151, 156, and 158, of which the last, "Dir zu eröffnen mein Herz," Fanny found in Goethe's explanatory comments, or *Abhandlungen*, to the *Divan*.

26. Inge Wild, "Goethes *West-östlicher Divan* als poetischer Ort psycho-kultureller Grenzüberschreitungen," in *Westöstlicher und Nordsüdlicher Divan: Goethe in interkultureller Perspektive,* ed. Ortrud Gutjahr, Paderborn, 2000, 73.

27. From John Whaley's verse translation, 327.

28. Ibid., 325.

29. Hensel: 1991a, 18–19.

30. Whaley, 295.

31. See Büttner, 104–5.

32. *Sehnsucht / Neue Dichtung von Hoffmann von Fallersleben / Composition von F. Mendelssohn-Bartholdy*, Berlin, Schlesinger, 1848.

33. Transcribed and discussed in Büttner.

34. Felix to his sister Rebecka, April 13, 1831, in Felix Mendelssohn Bartholdy: 1862, I, 139.

35. Cox and Cox, 139.

36. Ibid., 173.

37. Fanny to Felix, June 2, 1837, in Citron: 1987, 234.

38. *MF*, I, 131.

39. Reich: 1991, 260.

40. Ignaz Moscheles: 1873, 89.

41. Lea to Henriette von Pereira-Arnstein, August 1826, in MDM c. 29, fol. 59, extract.

42. Rieger and Walter, 31–31.

43. Hensel: 2003a, I, 34–35.

44. H-U 164 (*Die Schläferin*), 168 (*Der Rosenkranz*), 169 (*Feldlied*), 171 (*Am Grabe*), 172 ("Sie liebt, mich liebt die Auserwählte"), 185 (*Der Frühlingsabend*), 188 (*Marias Klage*), 190 (*Sehnsucht*), and 191 (*Neujahrslied*).

45. Hensel: 1995f, 31–33.

46. H-U 171; for a facsimile of Fanny's fair copy, see Weissweiler: 1981, 188.

47. Zelter to Goethe, June 11, 1826, in Hecker, III, 180.

48. Hensel, 1999–2002, *Duette*, IV, 17–23.

49. Hensel: 1995f, 27–29.

50. In turn based on the poem *Andenken* of Friedrich Matthisson, which Felix had set in 1823. See *MALIM*, 114–15.

51. Hensel: 1991a, 54–56. Fanny's autograph survives in the album, MA, Ms. 35, where it appears between two compositions dated March 43 and May 6, 1826.

52. Fanny to Felix, February 3, [1836,] in Citron: 1987, 198.

53. See *MALIM*, 351.

54. Hensel: 1994c, 9–16, where the date of composition is incorrectly given as 1825.

55. Hensel: 1996a, 20–26.

56. Hensel: 1994c, 26–29.

57. In its basic form, the subject would be G–C–A-flat–B-natural and may be found in related forms, for instance, in Bach's *Well-Tempered Clavier* (Fugue in G Minor, Book I), and Handel's "And with his stripes" in *Messiah*. Fanny has rotated the pitches of the subject, so that her melody takes the form A-flat–B-natural–G–C.

58. Hensel: 1994c, 20–25.

59. See further Sirota, 161–62.

60. See Klein: 1997, 52–55.

61. *MF*, I, 130.

62. Lea to Henriette von Pereira-Arnstein, ca. September 1827, in MDM c. 29, fol. 60 (extract).

63. Fanny to Klingemann, December 23, 1827, in *MF*, I, 151.

64. Fanny to Klingemann, September 12, 1828, in ibid., I, 162.

65. Fanny to Klingemann, December 8, 1828, in ibid., I, 163.

66. Eduard Devrient, 32.

67. *MF*, I, 132.

68. Fanny to Felix, February 16, [1827,] in Citron: 1987, 18; Lea to Carl Schlesinger, April[?] 1827, in Elvers: 1974, 50.

69. Schubring, 223–24.

70. *BamZ* 4 (1827), 179 (June 6, 1827).

71. See further Reich: 1991.

72. *Harmonicon* 8 (1830), 99.

73. Hensel: 1995f, 36–38.

74. Bodleian Library, Oxford, Horsley b. 1, fol. 19.

75. *Tagebücher*, 5–6.

76. H-U 192, 194, 195, 196 (published posthumously as Fanny's op. 9, no. 1), 197, 198, 199, 201, and 203. For editions, see Hensel: 2005a; Rieger and Walter, 32; and Hensel: 1991a, I, 48–53.

77. See Ernst Müller, 33–36.

78. *As You Like It*, V:3.

79. Sammons, 59.

80. Ibid., 62.

81. Draper, 3.

82. Fanny to Klingemann, March 22, 1829, in *MF*, I, 173.

83. H-U 207, 212, 213, 220, 224, and 225. The first four are available in Hensel: 2003a, I, 36–41, and II, 14–15.

84. *MF*, I, 173.

85. Heinrich Heine, "Dritter Brief aus Berlin," in *Samtliche Werke*, ed. K. Briegleb, Munich, 1959, II, 59.

86. Heine to Müller, June 7, 1826, cited in Sammons, 62.

87. See further Michael Perraudin, *Heinrich Heine: Poetry in Context—A Study of Buch der Lieder*, Oxford, 1989, 37–71.

88. From the translation in Draper, 87.

89. See Gisela Müller: 1997, 48.

90. Fanny's setting is in E minor; the altered chord of the Neapolitan is an F major triad, which then proceeds to the dominant B major and tonic E minor. The relationship between the Neapolitan and dominant, or F major to B major, breaks the conventional harmonic patterns of the song and corresponds to Heine's unexpected twist in the fourth stanza.

91. Draper, 59.

92. H-U 204, 210, 215, 226, and 227.

93. Edition in Hensel: 2002b, 17.

94. John Whaley, 339.

95. Karl Mendelssohn-Bartholdy, 24–25.

96. Friedlaender: 1891, 116.

97. Ibid.

98. Karl Mendelssohn-Bartholdy, 25.

99. For a facsimile of the song and of Goethe's verses for Fanny, see Klein: 1997, 89.

100. *MF*, I, 131.

101. Eduard Devrient, 38.

102. Berlioz, 294.

103. For editions, see Hensel: 1994c; 30–36; Hensel: 2003; and Hensel: 1996b, 26–28.

104. No. 15; see *MALIM*, 157, and Todd: 1990.

105. Two of Felix's *Sieben Charakterstücke* for piano, op. 7, published in 1827, are also in E minor and seem cut from the same, neo-Bachian cloth.

106. Schubring, 227.

107. C–D–E–F-sharp–G-sharp–A-sharp–C–B.

Chapter 5

1. Wilhelm Hensel to Minister Altenstein, February 7, 1825, in Lowenthal-Hensel and Arnold, 122.

2. Lowenthal-Hensel: 1981, 15.

3. Goethe to Zelter, August 24, 1823, in Hecker, II, 218.

4. *MF*, I, 102–3 (dated August 21, 1823, according to Lowenthal-Hensel and Arnold, 108).

5. Unpublished paper of Dr. Hilmar Frank, "Jakob Salomon Bartholdy zwischen Nazarenern und Hellenen," cited in Lowenthal-Hensel and Arnold, 110.

6. For a facs., see Lowenthal-Hensel and Arnold, 111.

7. Ibid., 121–22.

8. *MF*, I, 105.

9. For a color reproduction, see Lowenthal-Hensel and Arnold, Pl. V.

10. Abraham and Lea to Wilhelm Hensel, January 4, 1826, in Gilbert, 63, 65.

11. Letter of Frances Bunsen, October 1827, cited in Lowenthal-Hensel and Arnold, 143.

12. Ibid., 140.

13. For a facs. see Klein: 1997, 53.

14. *MF*, I, 103.

15. Lowenthal-Hensel and Arnold, 151, 154.

16. *MF*, I, 166.
17. Felix to Fanny, September 14, 1827, NYPL, *MF*, I, 136–38.
18. *Tagebücher*, 2 (entry for January 10, 1829).
19. Fanny to Klingemann, December 27, 1828, *MF*, I, 164.
20. Ibid.
21. H-U 219, 221, 228, 233, 234, and 236.
22. Benjamin, 186.
23. Hensel, 1999–2002, *Duette*, I, 22–24.
24. See *MALIM*, 164–65.
25. December 8, 1828, *MF*, I, 163.
26. For a facs., see Klein: 1993, 155 and Pl. I.
27. Edition in Hensel: 1996b, 24–25.
28. Fanny to Felix, September 7, 1838, in Citron: 1987, 261.
29. *MF*, I, 84.
30. Lowenthal-Hensel and Arnold, 156.
31. Berlin, MA, Ms. 158; see also Benjamin.
32. See Benjamin, 185.
33. Introduction to Elvers and Klein, xiii.
34. Ibid., 1.
35. *Tagebücher*, 5.
36. Lowenthal-Hensel and Arnold, 158.
37. *MF*, I, 167.
38. Helmig and Maurer.
39. *Tagebücher*, 7–9.
40. Helmig and Maurer, 147–48.
41. Ibid., 145.
42. Lowenthal-Hensel and Arnold, 160.
43. Helmig and Maurer, 155, 158.
44. For an edition, see Hensel: 1995b.
45. Fanny to Felix, June 29 and July 1, 1829, in Citron: 1987, 57, 60.
46. See further, Tillard: 1996, 164.
47. Reynolds, 88, 94–95.
48. For an edition see Hensel: 2003a, II, 20–22.
49. Ibid., II, 23–25.
50. Ibid., II, 16–17, 18–19.
51. See Helmig and Maurer, 153–54.
52. Fanny to Felix, July 1, 1829, in Citron: 1987, 59–60.
53. Fanny to Felix, August 15, 1829, in Citron: 1987, 73–75.
54. Ovid, *Metamorphoses* iv: 461.
55. See *MALIM*, 193 ff.
56. *Tagebücher*, 10.
57. Fanny to Klingemann, March 22, 1829, in *MF*, I, 171.
58. H-U 231; edition in Hensel: 2002b, 18–20.
59. Citron: 1987, 21.
60. Ibid., 36.
61. See, for instance, *AmZ* 31 (1829), 256–58.
62. *Tagebücher*, 9, entry of March 9, 1829.

63. For a facs., see Klein: 1993, 155–56.

64. Edition in Hensel: 1996b, *Klavierstücke* vol. 8, 16–20.

65. See Sposato, 26–28.

66. April 18, 1829, in Citron: 1987, 23.

67. *Tagebücher*, 14.

68. H-U 236, Hensel: 2005.

69. Fanny to Felix, June 4, 1829, in Citron: 1987, 50.

70. See *MALIM*, 202, 212.

71. Fanny to Felix, June 4, 1829, in Citron: 1987, 50; see also 51, n. 19.

72. Fanny to Felix, August 21, 1829, in ibid., 77.

73. Felix to Paul Mendelssohn Bartholdy, July 3, 1829, NYPL Mendelssohn Correspondence no. 70, cited in Hellwig-Unruh: 2000, 214.

74. Fanny to Klingemann, March 22, 1829, in *MF*, I, 170. The painting, which remained in the family's possession until the early twentieth century, is lost. For a reproduction, see Lowenthal-Hensel: 1997, Pl. 2.

75. Fanny to Felix, June 29, 1829, in Citron: 1987, 57.

76. June 11, 1829, in ibid., 55.

77. Felix to Fanny, September 10, 1829, cited in ibid., 56.

78. July 8, 1829, in ibid., 62.

79. Fanny to Luise Hensel, March 30, 1829, in Gilbert, 76; English translation in Tillard: 1996, 156.

80. Ibid.

81. *Harmonicon*, March 30, 1830, 99.

82. *Tagebücher*, 5 and 1.

83. Bodleian Library, Oxford, M. Deneke Mendelssohn Collection c. 74. The cover label reads: "Haendel Acis und Galathea aus dem Englischen des Gay ins Deutsch mit neuen Blasinstrumenten von Felix Mendelssohn Bartholdy im Januar 1829" ("Handel, *Acis and Galatea*, from the English of Gay into German, with new wind instruments, by Felix Mendelssohn Bartholdy in January 1829").

84. Fanny to Mary Alexander, October 14, 1833, in Alexander: 1979, 44. I am grateful to Peter Ward Jones of the Bodleian Library for alerting me to this passage.

85. *Tagebücher*, 14; *MF*, I, 213.

86. Cassiopée Records 369182.

87. Tillard: 1996, 154.

88. For an edition see Hensel: 1994d.

89. See Huber: 1997, 101–2. "Schreibart" und "Lebensprinzip."

90. Fanny to Felix, September 28/29, 1829, in Citron: 1987, 88. For an edition of the drafts, see Hensel: 2002b; the chronology of the work is treated in Hellwig-Unruh: 2002.

91. See Klein: 1993, 155–56; and Nubbemeyer: 1999, 102–4.

92. *MF*, I, 230.

93. Fanny to Felix, September 28, 1829, in Citron: 1987, 87.

94. Ibid., 90.

95. For the 1829 sketch, see Felix Mendelssohn Bartholdy, *Complete Organ Works*, ed. Wm. A. Little, London, 1987, II, x. See also Klein: 2001.

96. See Sirota, 183–85.

97. See Benjamin, 199.

98. Fanny to Felix, October 3, 1829, in Citron: 1987, 91.

99. Hensel: 1996c, 5–9.

100. *Tagebücher*, 24.

101. Klein: 1997, 156–59.

102. Citron: 1987, 84.

103. *Tagebücher*, 25.

104. For an edition, see Hensel: 1997; and Vana, 1996.

105. Lea to Klingemann, December 30, 1829, in Klingemann, 70.

106. Therese Devrient, 317.

107. On Felix's reluctance to release the *Liederspiel*, see Eduard Devrient, 92–93.

108. See Klein: 1987, 162; and Klein: 1997.

109. Felix to Friedrich Rosen, April 9, 1830, in Klingemann, 77–78.

110. Eduard Devrient, 97.

111. *Tagebücher*, 26–27.

112. H-U 250; see also Benjamin, 201–2.

113. Edition in Hensel: 1996b, 21–23.

114. Edition and completed in Hensel: 1996c.

115. Felix to Berlin, August 15, 1830, cited in Klein: 1997, 99.

116. *Tagebücher*, 28.

117. Fanny to Felix, May 22, 1830, in Citron: 1987, 100.

118. For a facs. see Benjamin, 203.

119. Felix to Fanny, June 11, 1830, in Weissweiler: 1997, 118.

120. Felix to Fanny, June 11, 1830, in *MF*, I, 263–64.

121. Felix to Fanny, June 14, 1830, in Sutermeister, 127 (with a facs.).

122. Felix to Fanny, June 23, 1830, in Weissweiler: 1997, 120; and Felix to Lea, June 24, 1830, NYPL.

123. Felix to Fanny, June 26, 1830, in *MF*, I, 266–72.

124. *Tagebücher*, 29.

125. Sebastian Hensel: 1904, 14.

Chapter 6

1. Weissweiler: 1997, 126.

2. Felix to Fanny, November 16, 1830, in ibid., 129.

3. Felix to Fanny, February 25, 1831, in ibid., 130.

4. Felix to Fanny, July 14, 1831, in Sutermeister, 175.

5. Felix to Fanny, November 14, 1821, in Weissweiler: 1997, 133.

6. Fanny to Felix, late July, 1830, in Citron: 1987, 107.

7. *MF*, I, 241.

8. Wilhelm to Felix, June 26, 1830, in Weissweiler: 1997, 122.

9. Letters from Abraham, July 13 and August 25, 1830, *MF*, I, 253, 256–57.

10. *Tagebücher*, 31.

11. October 19, 1830; for an edition see Hensel: 1996b, 9–15.

12. See further Lowenthal-Hensel and Arnold.

13. Hensel: 2003a, II, 23–25.

14. Ibid., 26–28.

15. For an architectural drawing of the renovations, see Cullen, Pl. 3.

16. *Tagebücher*, 32, entry of March 4, 1831.

17. Ibid., 37, entry of January 1, 1832.

18. *Tagebücher*, 31.

19. See further, Lausch.

20. That is, adding 6 repeatedly to 35 generates the progression 35, 41, 47, 53, 59, 65, etc. See Derbyshire, 95–96.

21. Ibid., 94.

22. Berlioz to Gounet et al., May 6, 1831, Hector Berlioz, *Correspondance Générale I: 1803–1832*, ed. Pierre Citron, Paris, 1972, 441.

23. Felix to Fanny, February 22, 1831, in Felix Mendelssohn Bartholdy: 1862, 11–12.

24. Zelter to Goethe, February 17–18, 1831, in *Briefwechsel zwischen Goethe und Zelter in den Jahren 1796–1831*, ed. F. W. Riemer, Berlin, 1834, VI, 141.

25. The sister of Marianne Mendelssohn, wife of Joseph Mendelssohn's son Alexander.

26. See *Tagebücher*, 33; and Lowenthal-Hensel and Arnold, 205.

27. *Tagebücher*, 35.

28. For an edition, see Hensel: 1992a.

29. Hinrichsen: 1997, 118, and 1999, 218.

30. See bars 70 ff. of Felix's Psalm 115, op. 31, no. 1, and bars 110 ff. of the second movement of Fanny's *Lobgesang*.

31. See Wolitz, 80–81.

32. Felix to Fanny, December 28, 1831, in Felix Mendelssohn Bartholdy: 1862, 314.

33. Ibid., 315.

34. *Tagebücher*, 34.

35. For analyses of the cantata, see Nubbemeyer: 1997a; Kellenberger; Hinrichsen: 1997; and Fladt.

36. In its G-minor form, the baroque prototype is D–G–E-flat–F-sharp; modern listeners will recognize its lineage in "And with his stripes" from Handel's *Messiah*, though whether Fanny was thinking of Handel or examples of the subject by J. S. Bach is unclear.

37. The bar before the Lento, "Ach Herr! Herr lehre uns bedenken" (Psalm 90:12).

38. See Hinrichsen: 1997, 121; and *MALIM*, 296, 321.

39. Alfred Dürr, *The Cantatas of J. S. Bach*, Oxford, 2005, 760.

40. *Tagebücher*, 34.

41. Richard J. Evans, *Death in Hamburg*, Oxford, 1987, 259.

42. See Barbara Dettke, *Die asiatische Hydra: Der Cholera von 1830/31 in Berlin und den preußischen Provinzen Posen, Preußen und Schlesien*, Berlin, 1995, 180.

43. *Tagebücher*, 41. The common attribution of the philosopher Hegel's death (November 14, 1831) to cholera is incorrect. See Terry P. Pinkard, *Hegel: A Biography*, Cambridge, 2000, 659.

44. The edition of the score published by Elke Blankenburg in 1999 (Hensel: 1999a) bears the title *Oratorium nach Bildern der Bibel*.

45. Hellwig-Unruh: 1996.

46. For the identification of the texts, see Kellenberger, 297.

47. Huber: 1997, 230, 232.

48. The *piano* openings, similar rising chromatic sequences, and repeated cadences in the orchestral introductions are three conspicuous features that link Fanny's aria to the Mozart.

49. *Tagebücher*, 37.

50. For an edition, see Hensel: 1999, *Duette*, vol. 5, 10–15, and also Benjamin, 208–9.

51. MA, Depos. Lohs II, 48; see also Benjamin, 204–6.

52. *Tagebücher*, 34; and Abraham to Mary Alexander, December 23, [1834,] in Alexander: 1979, 36.

53. Lowenthal-Hensel and Arnold, 188.

54. For an edition, see Hensel: 1994a.

55. Concerning the dating, see Hellwig-Unruh, 2000: 244.

56. Schröder: 1999, 168.

57. Felix to Rebecka, April 9, 1832, NYPL.

58. For a facs. of the autograph see Klein: 1997, 203.

59. *Tagebücher*, 41.

60. Ibid.

61. See also Little: 1991 for a review of the episode.

62. Felix Moscheles: 1888, 44.

63. Felix to Klingemann, February 4, 1833, in Klingemann, 109.

64. Lea to Henriette von Peireira-Arnstein, January 20, 1834, in Klein: 2005b, 13.

65. Ibid.

66. Citron: 1987, 109.

67. Binder, 259–60.

68. *Tagebücher*, 43.

69. Marx: 1865, II, 120.

70. *Tagebücher*, 45.

71. For editions, see Hensel: 1994e, 57–61, and Hensel: 1991a, 12–13 (transposed from the original key of G minor to E minor).

72. *Tagebücher*, 47–48; see also H.-G. Klein's "Chronik," in Klein: 2005b, 33–34.

73. See R. L. Todd, "Mozart according to Mendelssohn: A Contribution to *Rezeptionsgeschichte*," in *Perspectives on Mozart Performance*, ed. R. Larry Todd and Peter Williams, Cambridge, 1991, 184.

74. Fanny to Felix, February 17, 1835, in Citron: 1987, 174.

75. See Klein: 2005b, 25.

76. Fanny to Felix, November 23, 1833, in Citron: 1987, 114–15.

77. Fanny to Felix, November 2, 1833, in ibid., 115.

78. See Thomas H. Connolly, *Mourning into Joy: Music, Raphael, and Saint Cecilia*, New Haven, 1994.

79. Felix to Fanny, October 26, 1833, in Felix Mendelssohn Bartholdy: 1862, 14–15; and Fanny to Felix, November 2, 1833, in Citron: 1987, 114.

80. *BamZ* 7 (1830), 20–23.

81. Felix to Lea, November 28, 1833, NYPL.

82. Fanny to Hauser, October 1833, in Hellwig-Unruh: 1997, 218.

83. Felix to Fanny, November 14, 1833, in Weissweiler: 1997, 141.

84. Fanny to Felix, ca. November 27, 1834, in Citron: 1987, 127.

Chapter 7

1. Felix to Lea, March 13, 1825, *MLL*, 29.

2. Fanny to Felix, December 1, 1833, in Citron: 1987, 118–19.

3. See Klein: 2005b, 36–41.

4. See "Fanny by Gaslight," *Musical Times* 138/4 (1997), 30.

5. Lea to Henriette von Pereira-Arnstein, May 12, 1834, MN, 15, 80.

6. Fanny to Felix, [June 11, 1834,] Citron: 1987, 144.

7. Lea to Felix, January 24, 1834, Oxford, Bodleian Library, M. Deneke Mendelssohn Green Books III, no. 14; Fanny to Felix, January 25, 1834, in Citron: 1987, 121.

8. Fanny to Felix, November 4, 1834, in Citron: 1987, 155.

9. See Ellsworth.

10. See Klein: 2005b, 38.

11. Fanny to Felix, April 12, 1834, in Weissweiler: 1997, 161.

12. Fanny to Felix, December 27, 1834, and January 16, 1835, in Citron: 1987, 167, 170.

13. Fanny to Felix, ca. February 27, 1834, in ibid., 128–29.

14. Fanny to Felix, ca. August 1, 1834, in ibid., 151.

15. Fanny to Felix, June 4, 1834, in ibid., 141.

16. For the German text, see Paul Derks, *Die Schande der heiligen Päderastie: Homosexualität und Öffentlichkeit in der deutschen Literatur 1750–1850*, Berlin, 1990, 505; trans. in Kristina Muxfeldt, "Schubert, Platen, and the Myth of Narcissus," *JAMS* 49 (1996), 508.

17. See Muxfeldt, and, for an alternate reading, David Gramit, "Orientalism and the Lied: Schubert's 'Du liebst mich nicht,' " *19th Century Music* 27 (2003), 97–115.

18. Fanny to Felix, ca. February 27, 1834, in Citron: 1987, 128.

19. See Alexander: 1975, 74 ff.

20. Fanny to Felix, April 12, 1834, in Citron: 1987, 136. For an edition, see Hensel: 1995a.

21. Felix to Fanny, January 30, 1836, in which he refers to an "Englisches Lied aus g-moll," in Weissweiler: 1997, 212.

22. Fanny to Mary Alexander, April 7, 1834, in Alexander: 1979, 45.

23. In its simplest form, E-flat–A-flat, G–D-flat, C–F, D–A-flat.

24. Fanny to Felix, February 17, 1835, in Citron: 1987, 174.

25. Ibid.

26. Hensel: 1988.

27. Preceding her is Tartini's pupil, the Venetian Maddalena Lombardini Sirmen (1745–1818), who published six quartets in 1769.

28. Felix's motive, in D major, contains the pitches D–A–G–F-sharp; Fanny's, in E-flat major, E-flat–B-flat–A-flat–G–F.

29. Fanny: A-flat major to G major; Felix: D-flat major to C major.

30. Felix to Fanny, January 30, 1835, Berlin, MA Depos. MG 28; partly transcribed, with a facsimile, in Klein: 1997, 188–89.

31. Fanny to Felix, February 17, 1835, in Citron: 1987, 173.

32. Ibid., 174.

33. Bruno Brunelli, ed., *Metastasio*, Milan, 1965, vol. 2, 373.

34. Felix to Lea, February 19, 1834, in NYPL, no. 182.

35. *Infelice*, revised in 1843 and then published posthumously as op. 94. For the identification of the texts, see Cooper.

36. See further, Streicher, 245–46; and Schröder: 1999, 171.

37. On the Capriccio label, with Helen Kwon and the Philharmonisches Staatsorchester Hamburg.

38. Fanny to Mary Alexander, ca. August 1834, in Alexander: 1979, 48.

39. *Tagebücher*, 60.

40. See Lowenthal-Hensel and Arnold, Pl. VII.

41. Fanny to Felix, March 8, 1835, in Citron: 1987, 177.

42. Alexander: 1979, 37.

43. Heymann-Wentzel, 469–71.

44. See Lowenthal-Hensel and Arnold, 202, 204.

45. *Tagebücher*, 63.

46. Fanny Horsley to Lucy Callcott, July 21, 1834, in Gotch, 97.

47. Fanny to Felix, April 8, 1835, in Citron: 1987, 182.

48. Klingemann, 180.

49. Benedict, 25–26.

50. Felix to Fanny, May 4, 1835, in Weissweiler: 1997, 191.

51. Hensel, 1999–2002, V, 25–31.

52. H-U 282, 283, and 284; Hensel: 1995g; and Hensel: 1991b.

53. Facs. in Hellwig-Unruh: 2000, 259.

54. See further, Sandy Petrey, *In the Court of the Pear King: French Culture and the Rise of Realism*, Ithaca, NY, 2005, 107 ff.

55. See *MALIM*, 251–52.

56. Fanny to Elise and Rosa von Woringen, June 26, 1835, in Hensel: 2007, 25.

57. Halina Nelken, *Alexander von Humboldt: His Portraits and Their Artists, a Documentary Iconography*, Berlin, 1980, 159.

58. See, for instance, Robert Herbert, "Baron Gros's Napoleon and Voltaire's Henri IV," in *The Artist and the Writer in France: Essays in Honour of Jean Seznec*, ed. F. Haskell et al., Oxford, 1974, 52–71.

59. Fanny to her parents, July 7, 1835, in Hensel: 2007, 35.

60. *MF*, I, 320.

61. Fanny to Rebecka Dirichlet, July 3, 1835, in Hensel: 2007, 28.

62. Fanny to Abraham Mendelssohn Bartholdy, July 7, 1835, in ibid., 32.

63. Felix to Madame Marie-Cathérine Kiéné, June 1, 1835, Library of Congress; trans. in Sirota, 85.

64. Fanny to Abraham, July 26, 1835, in Hensel: 2007, 49.

65. Felix to Moscheles, February 7, 1835; in Felix Moscheles: 1888, 129.

66. Fanny to Felix, October 8, 1835, in Citron: 1987, 184–85. On Chopin's reception in Paris, see Jeffrey Kallberg, "Small Fairy Voices: Sex, History, and Meaning in Chopin," in *Chopin Studies 2*, ed. John Rink and Jim Samson, Cambridge, 1994, 50–71.

67. Giacomo to Mina Meyerbeer, July 6, 1835, in Meyerbeer, 468.

68. Heinrich Heine, *Lutetia*, II: 57.

69. Fanny to Lea, July 14, 1835, in Hensel: 2007, 40.

70. "Essay sur la Majorique (Majolica) ou terre émaillée," *Annales de la Société libre des Beaux-Arts* 6 (1836), 49–66; see also Lowenthal-Hensel and Arnold, 211–12.

71. *Tagebücher*, 65 (August 5, 1835).

72. See Edgar Munhall, *Ingres and the Comtesse d'Haussonville*, New York, The Frick Collection, 1985; Hensel's portraits are reproduced on pp. 22 and 26.

73. Fanny to Lea, July 14, 1835, in Hensel: 2007, 40.

74. Fanny to Abraham and Lea, August 2, 1835, in ibid., 50.

75. Fanny to Rebecka, July 3, 1835, in ibid., 29.

76. Frances Trollope, *Paris and the Parisians*, Paris, 1836, I, 152.

77. *Tagebücher*, 65.

78. *Le Charivari*, September 18, 1835, cited in Petrey, *In the Court of the Pear King*, 17.

79. *Tagebücher*, 65.

80. *MF*, I, 318.

81. See Frank, 1994.

82. Hamburger and Hamburger, 35.

83. See Frank, 46 ff.

84. Quoted in Hamburger and Hamburger, 79.

85. Wilhelm to Abraham and Lea, August 21, 1835, in Hensel: 2007, 67–68.

86. Fanny to Felix, August 15, 1835, in Weissweiler: 1997, 193–94.

87. Fanny to Rebecka, August 17, 1835, in Hensel: 2007, 58.

88. Draper, 45.

89. Sammons, 65.

90. For an edition, see Hensel: 1995f, 39–43.

91. Hensel: 1993, 13–14 (August 22, 1835).

92. Elvers: 2002, 573.

93. Fanny to Abraham, September 13, 1835, in Hensel: 2007, 62.

94. Sebastian Hensel: 1904, 1.

95. Fanny to Felix, October 8, 1835, in Citron: 1987, 184.

96. *Tagebücher*, 73.

97. Felix to Fanny, November 13, 1835, in Weissweiler: 1997, 205; trans. in *MF*, I, 334.

98. Lea to Henriette von Pereira-Arnstein, May 12, 1835, in MA 15, 80; cited in Klein: 2005b, 42–43.

99. *Tagebücher*, 77–78; *MF* I, 337.

100. Ibid., 80–81.

Chapter 8

1. *Tagebücher*, 81.

2. Fanny to Felix, January 5, 1836, in Citron: 1987, 195.

3. Fanny to Felix, February 4, 1836, in ibid., 201.

4. Fanny to Felix, January 5, 1836, in ibid., 195.

5. Felix to Fanny, January 30, 1836, in Weissweiler: 1997, 211.

6. "Der Strauß" (Goethe, H-U 287); "Wie Feld und Au" (J. G. Jacobi, though believed by Fanny's generation to be by Goethe, H-U 288); *Frühzeitiger Frühling*

(Goethe, H-U 289); "Ein Hochzeitbitter" (Platen, H-U 290); *Winterseufzer* (Platen, H-U 291); and "Wie dich die warme Luft umscherzt" (Platen, H-U 292).

7. The lieder op. 59, no. 2 and op. 50, no. 3.

8. Felix to Fanny, March 28, 1836, in Weissweiler: 1997, 218.

9. Felix to Klingemann, March 22, 1836, in Klingemann, 199.

10. H-U 295–297 and 298; see Hensel: 1999–2002, I, 14–21, and Rieger and Walter, 26–29.

11. Abraham to Felix, March 10, 1835, in Paul Mendelssohn Bartholdy: 1868, 70.

12. F. G. Edwards, "First Performances. I.—Mendelssohn's 'St. Paul,'" *Musical Times* 32 (1891), 137; see also *Tagebücher*, 82; and Polko, 68–69.

13. *MF*, II, 8.

14. *Tagebücher*, 82.

15. Ibid., 83.

16. *MF*, II, 7.

17. *Tagebücher*, 82.

18. Ibid., 83.

19. Sebastian Hensel: 1904, 14.

20. Fanny to Felix, November 16, 1836, in Weissweiler: 1997, 236.

21. Fanny to Karl Klingemann, July 15, 1836, in *MF*, II, 31.

22. Fanny to Karl Klingemann, March 22, 1829, in *MF*, I, 173.

23. Fanny to Felix, July 30, 1836, in Citron: 1987, 209.

24. See Robert H. Brown, "The 'Demonic' Earthquake: Goethe's Myth of the Lisbon Earthquake and Fear of Modern Change," *German Studies Review* 15 (1992), 475–91.

25. Felix to Fanny, October 23, 1836, in Weissweiler: 1997, 230; and Fanny to Felix, October 28, 1836, in Citron: 1987, 214.

26. Felix to Fanny, November 14, 1836, in Weissweiler: 1997, 234.

27. Fanny would eventually publish it as her op. 2, no. 2.

28. Fanny to Felix, November 16, 1836, in Citron: 1987, 217.

29. Fanny to Felix, November 22, 1836, in ibid., 222.

30. For an edition, see Hensel: 1994b.

31. Lea to Felix, June 7, 1837, in MDM, Green Books VI, 44.

32. Felix to Lea, June 24, 1837, in Weissweiler: 1997, 260–61.

33. Berlin, MA, Ms. 44, 1–70; see further the preface to Hensel: 1994b.

34. For a facsimile of the album cover, see Klein: 1997, 195–96.

35. Felix to Fanny, January 24, 1837, in Weissweiler: 1997, 244.

36. *MF*, II, 30.

37. See mm. 6–8 of the Allegro con brio (Hensel: 1994b, 29) and mm. 21–22 of the op. 53, no. 3.

38. See further Todd: 2002, repr. in Todd: 2007, 236 ff.

39. Hensel: 1996e, 10–12.

40. Lea to Felix, June 7, 1837, in MDM, Green Books VI, 44.

41. Felix to Fanny, June 24, 1837, in Weissweiler: 1997, 261.

42. Eduard Devrient, 193.

43. Polko, 60–61.

44. Fanny to Felix, July 30, 1836, in Citron: 1987, 208.

45. Fanny to Felix, November 16, 1836, in ibid., 218.

46. Felix to his family in Berlin, November 18, 1836, cited in Citron: 1987, 223 n.

47. Fanny to Felix, December 19, 1836, in ibid., 225.

48. John Whaley, 325.

49. For an edition, see Hensel: 1993, 20–23.

50. MDM, b. 2, fol. 10; for a facs., see Citron: 1987, 220.

51. Iitti, 70–74.

52. *Tagebücher*, 84.

53. Fanny to Felix, June 2, 1837, in Citron: 1987, 234.

54. Fanny to Felix, July 31, 1837, in ibid., 242–43.

55. Fanny to Cécile, October 5, 1837, in *MF*, II, 36.

56. *Tagebücher*, 86.

57. *MF*, II, 37.

58. Lea to Henriette von Pereira-Arnstein, January 27, 1837, in MN, 15, 91, in Klein: 2005b, 45.

59. Ibid., 47.

60. *MF*, II, 36.

61. Ibid., 48.

62. Fanny to Felix, December 12, 1837, in Citron: 1987, 246.

63. Iitti, 117.

64. See Ostleitner, 53–54.

65. Johanna Kinkel, "Memoiren. Hrsg. von deren Söhne Dr. Gottfried Kinkel-Zürich. VIII," *Der Zeitgeist: Beiblatt zum Berliner Tageblatt*, no. 45 (November 15, 1886), in Klein: 2005b, 68.

66. Hensel, 1999–2002, V, 16–24.

67. Hensel: 1994e, I, 9–11.

68. Fanny to Felix, November 30, 1834, in Citron: 1987, 160.

69. Hensel: 2001a, 9–14.

70. Fanny to Felix, January 27, 1837, in Citron: 1987, 230.

71. See Hennemann: 1997, 147.

72. Hensel: 2001a, 15–20.

73. The eleven are H-U 309, 312, 323–329, 334, and 335. For editions, see Hensel: 1999–2002, II, 7–18, and III, 6–7; Hensel: 1994e, 12–15; Hensel: 1993, 24–29; and Hensel: 1995f, 45–56.

74. From the translation in Draper, 107.

75. See especially Gisela Müller: 1997.

76. Heine, *Lyrical Intermezzo* no. 33, *Book of Songs*; trans. in Draper, 62 (adapted).

77. *Tagebücher*, 86.

78. Lea to Henriette von Pereira-Arnstein, MN, 15, 98, cited in Klein: 2005b, 50.

79. Hinni to her son Benjamin Mendelssohn, January 26, 1838, cited in ibid.

80. Felix to J. Alfred Novello, November 18, 1837, in Averil Mackenzie-Grieve, *Clara Novello: 1818–1908*, London, 1955, 50.

81. Fanny to Felix, February 2, 1838, in Citron: 1987, 254.

82. Fanny to Felix, January 15, 1838, in ibid., 248.

83. Fanny to Klingemann, February 27, 1838, in *MF*, II, 37.

84. Fanny to Felix, February 14, 1838, in Citron: 1987, 256.

85. Fanny to Felix, February 21, 1838, in ibid., 258.

86. Full details are in Klein: 2005a, 287–88.

87. Felix to Fanny, February 12, 1838, in Weissweiler: 1997, 283.

88. Fanny to Felix, ca. April 1838, in *MF*, II, 38.

89. *Tagebücher*, 87.

90. For a color facsimile of an oil sketch in private possession, see Lowenthal-Hensel and Arnold, Pl. XI.

91. *Tagebücher*, 80.

92. Cited in Lowenthal-Hensel and Arnold, 217.

93. Cited in ibid., 223.

94. Ibid., 219.

95. Wilhelm to Fanny, June 29, 1838, in *MF*, II, 40–42.

96. For a reproduction of the painting, see Lowenthal-Hensel and Arnold, 255.

97. From Victoria's diaries, cited in ibid., 224.

98. *Tagebücher*, 88.

99. For an edition, see Hensel: 1994e, 28–29.

100. Hensel: 1996e, I, 13–32.

101. Fanny to Klingemann, April 2, 1837, in *MF*, II, 32.

102. Felix to Lea, July 13, 1837, in ibid.

103. Hensel: 1996f, 9–16.

104. *Tagebücher*, 90–91.

105. Hensel: 1999–2002, II, 4–6.

106. Hensel: 1986, 16–20.

107. Hensel: 1996f, 17–30.

108. Ibid., II, 31–38.

109. Hensel, 1999–2002, II, 19–27.

110. No. 4 of part I.

111. Hensel: 1991a, 14–20.

112. Felix to Fanny, April 17, 1839, in *MF*, II, 47; Fanny to Felix, April 28, 1839, in Citron: 1987, 276.

113. Felix to Fanny, December 29, 1838, in *MF*, II, 47.

114. Fanny to Felix, January 6, 1839, in Citron: 1987, 264.

115. Hensel, 1999–2002, III, 10.

Chapter 9

1. *Tagebücher*, 94; Fanny to Felix, September 23, 1839, in Citron: 1987, 280.

2. *AmZ* 41 (1839), 822.

3. Today there are nearly 200, with recent additions, including Brahms in 2000, chosen by the Bavarian government; Mendelssohn is not yet represented.

4. *MF*, II, 59.

5. *Tagebücher*, 97.

6. William Vaughan, *German Romantic Painting*, New Haven, 1980, 216.

7. *Tagebücher*, 96.

8. Vaughan, *German Romantic Painting*, 218.

9. Felix to his sister Rebecka, June 25, 1830, in Judith K. Silber, "Mendelssohn and the *Reformation* Symphony: A Historical and Critical Study," PhD diss., Yale University, 1987, 225.

10. See further *MALIM*, 249.

11. Fanny to Felix, September 23, 1839, in Citron: 1987, 279.

12. *MF*, II, 62.

13. Sebastian Hensel: 1911, 21.

14. Fanny to Lea, September 27, 1839, in *MF*, II, 64.

15. Ibid., II, 65.

16. Mark Twain, *The Innocents Abroad*, 1869, ch. 18.

17. *Tagebücher*, 102.

18. Ibid.

19. Ibid.

20. Ibid., 104.

21. Ibid., 105.

22. *MF*, II, 67.

23. *Tagebücher*, 107.

24. Fanny to Berlin, October 13, 1839, in *MF*, II, 67.

25. Sebastian Hensel to his grandmother Lea, October 2, 1839, in Hensel: 2004, 39.

26. See further Klein: 2007b.

27. Fanny to Lea, October 13, 1839, in ibid., 31.

28. Fanny to Lea, October 28, 1839, in Hensel: 2004, 43.

29. Felix to Fanny, September 14, 1839, in Weissweiler: 1997, 314.

30. Fanny to Cécile, October 28, 1839, in *MF*, II, 72.

31. Hensel: 1997a, 15–21.

32. For a facs., see Klein: 2002a, 63.

33. Fanny to Rebecka, November 11, 1839, in Hensel: 2004, 48.

34. Fanny to Rebecka, November 19, 1839, in *MF*, II, 74.

35. Fanny to Felix, March 4, 1840, in Citron: 1987, 286.

36. *Tagebücher*, 112.

37. Fanny to Lea, November 28, 1839, in Klein: 2002a, 23.

38. *Tagebücher*, 115.

39. Ibid., 123.

40. Fanny to Lea, December 8, 1839, in *MF* II, 79.

41. Fanny to Lea, December 8, 1839, in Klein: 2002a, 28.

42. *MF,* II, 78.

43. Ibid., II, 79.

44. *MALIM*, 239.

45. Hensel: 1999–2002, IV, 6–13.

46. Cf. bars 4–5 of the duet and 14–15 of the Overture (Allegro di molto).

47. *MF*, II, 105.

48. Ibid., II, 83.

49. Madame de Staël, *Corinne or Italy*, trans. Isabel Hill, Philadelphia, 1973, 80.

50. Lord Byron, *Childe Harold's Pilgrimage*, 1818, IV, 102.

51. Fanny to Felix, January 1, 1840 in Weissweiler: 1997, 322, 324.

52. Felix to Fanny, January 4, 1840, in ibid., 324–35.

53. Hensel: 1999b, 3–32.

54. *Tagebücher*, 110.

55. Fanny and Wilhelm to Lea, February 4, 1840, in Klein: 2002a, 53.

56. Goethe, *Italian Journey*, trans. R. R. Heitner, New York, 1989, 390.

57. Charles Dickens, *Pictures from Italy*, ch. 10, in *The Works of Charles Dickens*, New York, 1900, 484.

58. *MF*, II, 88.

59. Fanny to Rebecka, January 10, 1840, in Klein: 2002a, 42.

60. Fanny to Rebecka, April 13, 1840, in Klein: 2002a, 81; *MF*, II, 95–98. See also Felix's lengthy letter to Zelter of June 16, 1831, in Felix Mendelssohn Bartholdy: 1862, 167–88.

61. See *MF*, II, 97, 98; and Fanny to Felix, May 1, 1840, in Weissweiler: 1997, 331.

62. *MF*, II, 106.

63. Fanny to Lea, March 14, 1840, in Klein: 2002a, 65.

64. For a facs. reprint, see Todd: 2004, 10–13. After their return to Berlin the Hensels prepared a *Reisealbum*, for which Fanny made a fair copy of the composition, this time illustrated with a vignette by Wilhelm showing a view from the villa, with the waters of a fountain spilling over onto Fanny's music and in the distance the Cestius pyramid. For a facs. see Klein: 2002a, 74–75, 81.

65. *MF*, II, 115–16.

66. Ibid., II, 112.

67. Hensel: 1999–2002, IV, 30–36.

68. Gounod, 91.

69. *MF*, II, 104.

70. Ibid., II, 108.

71. For the version known as *Ponte molle* see Hensel: 1999b, 33–36; for a facs. of *Abschied*, see Klein: 2006a, 39.

72. Fanny to Rebecka, March 30, 1840, in Klein: 2002a, 72.

73. Hensel: 1997a, 4–14.

74. *MF*, II, 103.

75. Ibid., II, 120.

76. Ibid., II, 101.

77. Ibid., II, 123.

78. Fanny to Lea, June 9, 1840, in ibid., II, 125.

79. Ibid., II, 126.

80. Ibid., II, 129–30.

81. *Pilgrims Returning from the Feast Day of the Madona dell'Arco* (Paris, Louvre). See further Albert Boime, *Art in an Age of Counterrevolution (1815–1848)*, Chicago, 2004, 225.

82. *MF*, II, 129.

83. *The Christian Guardian and Church of England Magazine for 1825*, London, 1825, 295–96.

84. *MF*, II, 132.

85. Ibid., II, 134.

86. Ibid., II, 135.

87. *Tagebücher*, 160.

88. Ibid., 174 (July 13, 1840). The diary thus contradicts Sebastian Hensel's assertion that the song was composed after Fanny's return to Berlin (see *MF*, II, 158).

89. For a facsimile, see Klein: 2006a, 50.

90. Hensel: 1999–2002, II, 28–36.

91. See Felix Moscheles, 161.
92. *MF*, II, 139.
93. Ibid., II, 144.
94. Ibid., II, 143.
95. *Tagebücher*, 170.
96. *MF*, II, 147.
97. *Tagebücher*, 182.
98. *MF*, II, 149.
99. Ibid., II, 153.
100. *Tagebücher*, 193.
101. Ibid., 196.
102. Fanny to Lea, July 22, 1840, in *MF*, II, 145.

Chapter 10

1. Fanny to F. A. Elsasser, September 25, 1840, in Klein: 2003, 130.
2. *MF*, II, 250.
3. *Tagebücher*, 198.
4. Ibid., 201.
5. Ibid.
6. Felix to Paul, March 3, 1841, in Paul Mendelssohn Bartholdy: 1868, 225.
7. Draper, 544.
8. *Tagebücher*, 207.
9. Ibid., 199.
10. Ibid., 203.
11. See Lowenthal-Hensel and Arnold, 246–47.
12. See ibid., 251.
13. See Wolfgang Dinglinger, "'Acta betreffend: Die Berufung des Componisten Dr. Felix Mendelssohn Bartholdi nach Berlin'. Briefe von und an Felix Mendelssohn Bartholdy," *MS* 14 (2005), 189–219.
14. *Tagebücher*, 199.
15. Ibid.
16. Felix to Klingemann, July 15, 1841, in Klingemann, 264.
17. Klein: 2005b, 53–55.
18. Klein: 2005a, 290.
19. Fanny to Felix, March 2, 1841, in Citron: 1987, 306–7.
20. Fanny to Felix, March 17, 1841, MDM, Green Books XIII no. 130, cited in Hellwig-Unruh: 2000, 16 n.
21. Felix to Fanny, November 14, 1840, in Weissweiler: 1997, 346.
22. Fanny to Felix, December 5 and 9, 1840, in ibid., 347, and Citron: 1987, 299.
23. For editions of H-U 364, 365, and 366 see Hensel: 1982, 13–21, 24–35; of H-U 368 and 369, Hensel: 1997b, 26–43; and H-U 372, Hensel: 2004a, 36–42.
24. *Zwölf Clavierstücke von Fanny Hensel geb. Mendelssohn Bartholdy. Für Felix 1843*, MDM, c. 85.
25. On Felix's use of the device, see my "*Me voilà perruqué*: Mendelssohn's Six Preludes and Fugues Op. 35 Reconsidered," in Todd: 2007, 199–200.

26. MA, Ms. 163, 67–73.

27. See Donald Francis Tovey, *Essays in Musical Analysis*, London, 1935–1939, repr. 1981, 393–94; also, R. Larry Todd, "On Stylistic Affinities in the Works of Fanny Hensel and Felix Mendelssohn Bartholdy," in Todd: 2007, 236–38.

28. *Tagebücher*, 202.

29. See Fanny to F. A. Elsasser, November 11, 1841, in Klein: 2003, 138.

30. See further Klein: 2006a, which contains a thorough study of the *Reisealbum* and nineteen facsimiles.

31. Hensel: 1993, 30–34.

32. MA, Ms. 46, 34–40.

33. Fanny to F. A. Elsasser, end of June 1841, in Klein: 2003, 136.

34. From the translation of Carl Klingemann in *MF*, II, 159.

35. Felix to Fanny, October 24, 1840, quoted in *MF*, II, 159 n.

36. For editions, see Hensel: 1991, 36–46; and Hensel: 1993, II, 15–17.

37. Cf. bars 53 ff. and 71 ff. of Fanny's and Felix's settings.

38. The German poet of *Waldruhe* (*Forest Peace*, H-U 379), set by Fanny in June 1841 as a trio with piano accompaniment, remains unidentified. For an edition, see Hensel: 1995d.

39. H-U 363; Hensel: 1999–2002, I, 4–13.

40. Hensel: 1989d.

41. Unpublished letter from Fanny to Rebecka, August 31, 1841, NYPL.

42. Hensel: 1995f, 58–60; and Hensel: 1999–2002, III, 9.

43. "A Biographical Sketch of Justinus Kerner, Part III," *The Spiritual Magazine* 2 (1867), 210.

44. Hensel: 1995f, 62–64.

45. Hensel: 1993, 8–9.

46. Hensel: 1999–2002, IV, 14–16.

47. No. 4 of the *Sechs Gedichte*, op. 90 (1850).

48. See bars 12–16 of "Die Sennin" (August 11, 1841) and 27–31 of the "Volkslied" (April 30, 1841).

49. H-U 378; Hensel: 1993, 41–49.

50. Preface, in *100 Years of Eichendorff Songs*, ed. Jurgen Thym, Madison, Wis., 1983, x.

51. Felix to Berlin, November 7, 1831, in NYPL, cited in Krebs and Krebs, 2006, 24.

52. On Mendelssohn's estimation of Lang, see further Krebs and Krebs, 2006, 24 ff.

53. Fanny to Felix, July 13, 1841, in Citron: 1987, 308.

54. Felix to Reinhold Köstlin, December 15, 1841, in Felix Mendelssohn Bartholdy: 1862, 278.

55. For an edition see Lang, 88–89.

56. The chords uncannily anticipate a nearly identical phrase toward the end of the Wedding March from Felix's incidental music to *A Midsummer Night's Dream*, premiered in 1843. Whether the similarity was coincidence or a deliberate allusion remains unclear.

57. *Tagebücher*, 206.

58. SPK MA, Depos. Berlin Ms. 4; see Klein: 1997, 207–8.

59. Eduard Devrient, 235.

60. Hensel: 1989.

61. Fanny to August Elsasser, November 11, 1841, in Klein: 1999, 270–71.

62. See the stimulating new study by Marian Wilson Kimber, the first to identify the sources of the twelve epigrams (Wilson Kimber: 2008).

63. Hensel: 2000.

64. *Tagebücher*, 217.

65. Austin: 427–28.

66. See further Todd: 2007, 253 f.

67. John R. Williams, *The Life of Goethe: A Critical Biography*, Oxford, 2001, 77–78.

68. See Rothenberg; Nubbemeyer: 1997; Eberle: 1987; Toews; and Thorau.

69. *Tagebücher*, 204.

70. *Faust*, I, 744–45.

71. Felix to Fanny, July 7, 1826, in Weissweiler: 1997, 48–49.

72. *Faust*, II: 5065–68.

73. *Tagebücher*, 205.

74. See further Todd: 2007c, 255 ff.

75. *Tagebücher*, 206.

76. Dana Gooley, *The Virtuoso Liszt*, Cambridge, 2004, 205.

77. Felix to Ferdinand David, February 5, 1842, in *LA*, 142.

78. Fanny to Felix, April 28, 1839, in Citron: 1987, 277.

79. Lea Mendelssohn Bartholdy to Frau Prof. Erdmann, December 28, 1841, cited in Lambour: 2007, 255.

80. Lea to Henriette von Pereira-Arnstein, MN, 15,125, cited in Klein: 2005b, 79.

81. Marie Lipsius La Mara, ed., *Franz Liszts Briefe*, Leipzig, 1899, Vol. 4, 117–18.

82. Henriette Mendelssohn to Rosa Mendelssohn, April 24, 1842, MN, 6, 2–13, 50, cited in Klein: 2005b, 55.

83. See Klein: 2005b, 56.

84. William Sterndale Bennett, February 21, 1842, in J. R. Sterndale Bennett, *The Life of William Sterndale Bennett*, Cambridge, 1907, 126–27.

85. *MF*, II, 170.

86. Moritz Daniel Oppenheim, *Erinnerungen*, Frankfurt, 1924, 75.

87. Elon, 132; see also Georg Heuberger and Anton Merk, eds., *Moritz Daniel Oppenheim: Die Entdeckung des jüdischen Selbstbewußtseins in der Kunst*, Frankfurt am Main, 1999, passim.

88. Oppenheim, *Erinnerungen*, 33.

89. Ibid., 90.

90. Jüdisches Museum, Frankfurt am Main; Heuberger and Merk, *Moritz Daniel Oppenheim*, 220.

91. Carl Gustav Carus, *Briefe über Landschaftsmalerei*, Leipzig, 1835, 29; quoted in Hugh Honour, *Romanticism*, New York, 1979, 80.

92. Felix to Ferdinand Hiller, October 8, 1842, in Hiller, 194.

93. *Tagebücher*, 213.

94. Ibid., 217–19.

95. Cited in *MF*, II, 179.

96. Felix to Fanny and Rebecka, December 20, 1842, in Weissweiler: 1997, 359; and Felix to Paul, December 22, 1842, in Paul Mendelssohn Bartholdy, 291.

97. *Tagebücher*, 220.

Chapter 11

1. Fanny to Felix, January 17, 1843, in Weissweiler: 1997, 361.

2. *Tagebücher*, 219, 222.

3. Ibid., 222.

4. Schumann, 266.

5. *MF*, II, 185.

6. Sebastian Hensel: 1904, 35.

7. Berlioz, 297–98.

8. Felix to Rebecka, October 29, 1843, *MF*, II, 220.

9. *MF*, II, 185.

10. Sebastian Hensel: 1904, 35.

11. Ibid.

12. Ibid., p. 34.

13. Fanny to Franz Hauser, May 5, 1843, in Hellwig-Unruh: 1997a, 219–20; for a facs., see Klein: 2002, 71.

14. Gounod, 124.

15. Ibid., 185–86, after the *Tagebücher*, 224–26.

16. *Tagebücher*, 224.

17. See Lowenthal-Hensel and Arnold, 263.

18. See ibid., 262, 267.

19. Wilhelm to Fanny, August 29, 1843, in ibid., 268.

20. *Tagebücher*, 231.

21. Ibid., 222.

22. Fanny to Klingemann, June 18, 1828, in *MF*, I, 160.

23. Hensel: 1998b.

24. Fanny to Hauser, February 8, 1844, in Hellwig-Unruh: 1997, 224.

25. Fanny to Hauser, November 24, 1843, in ibid., 223.

26. Fanny to Wilhelm, July 12, 1843, cited in ibid., 107.

27. Fanny to Hauser, November 24, 1843, in ibid., 222–23.

28. Hellwig-Unruh: 1997, 108.

29. From the trans. by Walter Kaufmann, *Goethe's Faust*, New York, 1961, 426.

30. Hensel: 1993, II, 12–13.

31. Hensel: 1994e, I, 20–22.

32. MDM, c. 85.

33. Hensel: 1997a, 22–25.

34. Ibid., 19–21.

35. Ibid., 4–18.

36. Hensel: 1992, 29–65.

37. Head: 2007, 74.

38. Fanny to Rebecka, July 27, 1843, in *MF*, II, 192.

39. Posthumously published as the *Drei geistliche Lieder* op. 96; concerning the repertoire of Fanny's concert, see Klein: 2005b, 57–58.

40. Fanny to Rebecka, November 15 and December 5, 1843, in *MF*, II, 232, 236.

41. *MF*, II, 216.

42. Fanny to Rebecka, October 18, 1843, in *MF*, II, 216, 218.

43. Niels Gade to his parents, October 16, 1843, in Gade, 42.

44. Hensel: 1997a, 26–33.

45. Ibid., 34–45.

46. Hensel: 2003a, II, 33–36.

47. Hensel: 1991a, 47–50.

48. Later published as Felix's op. 99, no. 6; Fanny's setting, bearing the title *Die Stille*, survives in MA, Ms. 86, 52–53.

49. Hensel: 1993, II, 36–40.

50. Hensel: 2003a, 37–40; for a facsimile of the autograph, see Hensel: 1997c.

51. See in particular bars 3–8 of *Traum* and 29–35 of Felix's op. 99, no. 6; and 25–29 of *Traum* and 74–81 of *Die erste Walpurgisnacht*, no. 1.

52. Fanny to Rebecka, May 18, 1844, in *MF*, II, 274.

53. Fanny Lewald, *Meine Lebensgeschichte*, Berlin, 1862, III, 196–201; cited in Klein: 2005b, 66–67.

54. Fanny to Rebecka, after February 11, 1844, in *MF*, II, 257.

55. MA N. Mus., Ms. 241; for a facs. see Klein: 1997, 220.

56. All three are available in Hensel: 1996.

57. Fanny to Rebecka, March 18, 1844, in *MF*, II, 260.

58. Leipzig, Kistner, published on February 1, 1844. For a facsimile of Felix's autograph of this arrangement, acquired by Tamagawa University in Tokyo in 1990, see Felix Mendelssohn Bartholdy, *Die erste Walpurgisnacht: Ballade von Goethe für Chor und Orchester op. 60*, ed. Hiromi Hoshino, Tokyo, 2005.

59. Fanny to Rebecka, March 18, 1844, in *MF*, II, 260.

60. See Hensel: 1993, II, 36–40.

61. Fanny to Rebecka, after February 11, 1844, in *MF*, II, 256.

62. Fanny to Rebecka, June 19, 1844, in *MF*, II, 287.

63. See Lowenthal-Hensel and Arnold, 282–86.

64. H. C. Andersen, diary entry, June 21, 1847, in H. C. Andersen, *Meines Lebens Märchen*, trans. and ed. Tove Fleischer, Leipzig, 1989, 486–87.

65. Fanny to Felix, July 30, 1844, in Citron: 1987, 327.

66. Ibid.

67. Fanny to Felix, July 30, 1844, in ibid., 326.

68. Felix to Fanny, August 15, 1844, MA, Ep. 105, cited in Klein: 2001, 181.

69. Fanny to Felix, August 21, 1844, Oxford, Bodleian Library, M. Deneke Mendelssohn Green Books Collection XX no. 249, cited in Klein: 2001, 182.

70. For an edition, see *Leipziger Ausgabe der Werke Felix Mendelssohn Bartholdy* series IV, vol. 8, 50–57.

71. *Tagebücher*, 235.

72. Fanny to Rebecka, September 4, 1844, in *MF*, II, 299.

73. Felix to E. Devrient, October 25, 1844, in Eduard Devrient, 255.

74. *MF*, II, 300.

75. Fanny to Cécile, November 19, 1844, in *MF*, II, 301–2.

76. *MF*, II, 311.

77. Sebastian Hensel: 1911, 46.

78. Fanny to Felix, March 4, 1845, in Citron: 1987: 332.

79. *MF*, II, 314 (March, 1845).

80. Ibid., II, 315.

81. For a facs. see Klein: 2005b, 63.

82. *Tagebücher*, 252.

83. Fanny to Julius Elsasser, June 13, 1845, cited in Klein: 1997, 143–44; for a facsimile of Fanny's transcription of the Sonatina, see p. 145.

84. Ibid., 255.

85. *MF*, II, 322.

86. Felix to Fanny, April 20, 1845, in *MF*, II, 321.

Chapter 12

1. Felix to Fanny, April 20, 1845, in *MF*, II, 321.

2. Hensel: 1986, 25–31.

3. Fanny to Felix, December 21, 1844, in Citron: 1987, 330.

4. *Tagebücher*, 263.

5. Fanny to Felix, February 2, 1846, in Citron: 1987, 341.

6. Felix to Clara Schumann, January 4, 1846, in Reich: 1994, 222.

7. Fanny to Felix, [April 11, 1846,] in Citron: 1987, 345.

8. Fanny to Felix, October 26, 1846; in ibid., 358.

9. Fanny to Felix, June 22, 1846; in ibid., 347.

10. Fanny to Felix, July 9, 1846; in ibid., 349.

11. *MF*, II, 324.

12. See Klein: 2005b, 62–64.

13. Keudell, 2, 63.

14. See further, David B. Denis, *Beethoven in German Politics, 1870–1989*, New Haven, 1996, 36–38.

15. Keudell, 63.

16. *MF*, II, 324, 325.

17. *Tagebücher*, 271.

18. Fanny to Felix, July 9, 1846, in Citron: 1987, 349–50.

19. *Tagebücher*, 265.

20. Felix to Fanny, August 12, 1846, in Weissweiler: 1997, 393.

21. Dorn, 399.

22. *Tagebücher*, cited in *MF*, II, 266.

23. They include, in chronological order, the Allegro molto in C Minor (January 22, H-U 413), Allegro molto vivace e leggiero in B Major (January 23, H-U 414), Andante cantabile in D-flat Major (February 4, H-U 417), Allegretto in C-sharp Minor, op. 4/5, no. 2 (between March 21 and May 3, H-U 420), Allegro moderato in B Minor, op. 8, no. 1 (May 14, H-U 423), Andante cantabile in F Major, op. 6, no. 3 (May 16, H-U 424), *Pastorella* in A Major (May 25, H-U 425), Allegretto in D Minor (May, H-U 426), Lento appassionato in B Major, op. 4/5, no. 4 (July 27, H-U 438), Allegro molto vivace in C Major (August 15, H-U 442), Andante con moto in E Major (October 13, H-U 452), Andante espressivo in A-flat Major, op. 6, no. 1 (November 11, H-U 454), *Lied* in E-flat Major (November 24, H-U 456), *Wanderlied* in E Major, op. 8, no. 4 (December 4, H-U 458), *Lied* in A Major (December 8, H-U 459), and two pieces for

which autographs do not survive but which likely were composed in 1846, the *Lied* in D-flat Major op. 8, no. 3 (H-U 461) and Andante con espressione in A Minor, op. 8, no. 2 (H-U 463). For editions, see Hensel: 1986, 25–45 (H-U 413, 417, 424, 426, and 459); Hensel: 1983, 41–43 (H-U 425); Hensel: 1996 (H-U 414, 442, 452, and 456); and Hensel: 2004 (op. 4/5, nos. 2 and 4, op. 6, nos. 1 and 3, and op. 8, nos. 1–4).

24. Austin, 427–28.

25. See further, Todd: 2007, 225–31.

26. Including the *Midsummer Night's Dream* and *Calm Sea and Prosperous Voyage* Overtures.

27. Ignaz Moscheles, 339.

28. Hensel: 1986, 38–41.

29. See further, Todd: 2007, 241 ff.

30. Bartsch: 1999.

31. See further, Todd: 2007b.

32. See ibid.

33. In brief, it describes a rising sequence of third-related keys—E major, G major, B-flat major, C-sharp minor, and, completing the circle, E major. See further, Todd: 2007, 223–24.

34. In addition to the six *Gartenlieder* op. 3, they include: *Waldeinsam* (H-U 428), *Morgenwanderung* (H-U 429), *Morgengruß* (H-U 433), *Ariel* (H-U 435), *Abend* (H-U 436), "Schweigend sinkt die Nacht hernieder" (H-U 439), "Lust'ge Vögel" (H-U 441), *Schilflied* (H-U 445), "Wer will mir wehren zu singen" (H-U 447), "O Herbst, in linden Tagen" (H-U 448), and "Schon kehren die Vögel wieder ein" (H-U 449). For an edition, see Hensel: 1997d.

35. For a study of the sources, see further, Wallace.

36. See Gundlach: 1999, 121.

37. Hensel: 1998c, 12–13.

38. Hensel: 1995f, 66–70.

39. Ibid., 86–89.

40. Hensel: 1994e, 41–43.

41. Hensel: 1995f, 71–75.

42. See Hartwig Schultz, *Joseph von Eichendorff: Eine Biographie*, Frankfurt am Main, 2007, 121 ff.

43. Hensel: 1993, II, 30–32.

44. Ibid., II, 33–35.

45. See bars 24–28 of "Ich kann wohl manchmal singen," the opening of the principal theme in "Juni," and bars 17 ff. of op. 53, no. 3.

46. Founders of the utopian village of New Harmony, Indiana.

47. See Michael Ritter, *Zeit des Herbstes: Nikolaus Lenau. Biografie*, Vienna, 2002, 274.

48. Ibid., 91–94.

49. Hensel: 1993, I, 38–40.

50. Hensel: 1998c, 32–34.

51. Hensel: 1995f, 77–84.

52. See also the perceptive analysis in Sirota, 202–7.

53. See, for example, the opening of the Fourth Symphony, the Intermezzo for piano, op. 119, no. 1, and the first of the *Ernste Gesänge*, op. 121.

54. *Tagebücher*, 264–66, 274; and *MF*, II, 333.

55. Fanny to Angela von Woringen, November 26, 1846, in MDM, c. 36, fols. 19–20; cited in Citron: 1987, 352.

56. Meyerbeer, IV: 119.

57. Klein: 2005b, 64–65.

58. *Tagebücher*, 267.

59. Ibid., 268.

60. Fanny to Felix, in Citron: 1987, 355. Though undated, the letter may be placed around early October 1846, based on its reference to a future performance of Beethoven's *Ruins of Athens*, which occurred on October 11.

61. *Tagebücher*, 270.

62. Ibid., 270–71.

63. They were officially announced in Friedrich Hofmeister's *Musikalisch-Literarische Monatsberichten neuer Musikalien* in December 1846. See Klein: 1997, 220.

64. MDM, 216 (6).

65. Ignaz Moscheles, 332.

66. MDM, 216 (5); inscribed, "September 1846. / Ihrer lieben Cécile Mendelssohn / Bartholdy / von Fanny."

67. Fanny to Felix, ca. early October 1846, in Citron: 1987, 353.

68. Ibid., 272.

69. Fanny to Felix, February 1, 1847; in Weissweiler: 1997, 396.

70. Cécile to Fanny, undated, Staatsbibliothek zu Berlin–Preussischer Kulturbesitz, Depositum Berlin 31; cited in Citron: 1987, 356.

71. See further, Klein: 2005a, 291–92.

72. Fanny to Felix, February 1, 1847, in Citron: 1987, 363.

73. *Tagebücher*, 275.

74. Ibid., 274.

75. Schumann (March 4, 1847), 417.

76. Berthold Litzmann, *Clara Schumann, An Artist's Life*, trans. Grace E. Hadow, London, 1913, I, 429.

77. Ibid.

78. *Tagebücher*, 276.

79. *Neue Berliner Musik Zeitung* 1 (1847), 231–32, quoted in Hellwig-Unruh: 2000, 78.

80. Frederick William IV to his brother Carl, March 19, 1847, cited in Barclay, 126 n.

81. *Tagebücher*, 275 (entry of April 12, 1847).

82. Ibid., 276.

83. For facsimiles, see Hensel: 1994e, 8.

84. For accounts of Fanny's death, see *MF*, II, 334–35; Sebastian Hensel: 1911, 59; Eduard Devrient, 291–92; Felix to Klingemann, June 3, 1847, in Klingemann, 328–29; and Henriette Mendelssohn to Benjamin and Rosa Mendelssohn, May 21, 1847, in Gilbert, 144.

85. *MF*, II, 335.

86. Ibid., II, 335–36.

87. Henriette Mendelssohn to Benjamin and Rosa Mendelssohn; see *Tagebücher*, 276.

88. *Vossische Zeitung*, May 17, 1847, in *Tagebücher*, 277.

89. Meyerbeer, IV, 243.

90. See further, *Tagebücher*, 279.

91. Hellwig-Unruh: 2000, 400.

92. Reprinted in the *Tagebücher*, 277–79.

93. For a complete list, see Hellwig-Unruh: 2000, 425.

94. *NZfM* 26 (1847), 14; 28 (1848), 88.

95. *NZfM* 26 (1847), 38, 169.

96. *NZfM*, 28 (1848), 88.

97. *NZfM* 27 (1847), 50.

98. *AmZ* 49 (1847), col. 382.

Epilogue

1. Felix to Klingemann, June 3, 1847, in Klingemann, 328.

2. Felix to Charlotte Moscheles, June 9, 1847, in Felix Moscheles, 287.

3. Eduard Devrient, 293.

4. *MF*, II, 337.

5. Ibid., II, 338.

6. Georg Knepler, *Musikgeschichte des 19. Jahrhunderts*, Berlin, 1961, II, 770.

7. Felix to Sebastian Hensel, February 22, 1847, in *MLL*, 381.

8. See also Lowenthal-Hensel: 1970, 31.

9. Eduard Devrient, 301.

10. *MF*, II, 335.

11. *Tagebücher*, 276.

12. Ibid.

13. Wilhelm to Luise Hensel, May 28, 1847, in Gilbert, 145.

14. *MF*, II, 335.

15. H. C. Andersen, *Meines Lebens Märchen*, trans. Tove Fleischer, Leipzig, 1989, 486–87.

16. Lowenthal-Hensel: 1979, 187.

17. Sebastian Hensel: 1904, 59.

18. Ibid., 52.

19. Sebastian Hensel: 1911, 68.

20. Ibid., 60.

21. Many reproductions are available in Lowenthal-Hensel: 1981.

22. On the reception of op. 3 see further, Wallace, 94 ff.

23. Wilson Kimber: 2006.

24. "Otto Dressel's Soirées," in *Dwight's Journal of Music* 8 (1856), 174 (March 1).

25. *Boston Daily Traveler*, December 10, 1892; see also Wilson Kimber: 2002, 261–62; and Wilson Kimber: 2006.

Bibliography

Alexander, Boyd, "Felix Mendelssohn and the Alexanders," *MS* 1 (1972), 80–105.

———, "F. Mendelssohn Bartholdy and Young Women," *MS* 2 (1975), 71–102.

———, "Some Unpublished Letters of Abraham Mendelssohn and Fanny Hensel," *MS* 3 (1979), 9–50.

Altmann, Alexander, *Moses Mendelssohn: A Biographical Study*, University of Alabama, 1973.

Austin, [Sarah], "Recollections of Felix Mendelssohn," *Fraser's Magazine for Town and Country* 37 (April 1848), 426–28.

Barclay, David E., *Frederick William IV and the Prussian Monarchy 1840–1861*, Oxford, 1995.

Bartsch, Cornelia, "Das Lied ohne Worte op. 6,1 als offener Brief," in Borchard and Schwarz-Danuser, 55–72 [1999].

———, "Geburtstagslieder von Fanny Mendelssohn Bartholdy: Reflexionen über das Schreiben," in *Musk und Biographie: Festschrift für Rainer Cadenbach*, ed. Cordula Heymann-Wentzel and Johannes Laas, Würzburg, 2004, 73–81.

———, *Fanny Hensel geb. Mendelssohn Bartholdy: Musik als Korrespondenz*, Kassel, 2007.

Behler, Ernst, *German Romantic Literary Theory*, Cambridge, 1993.

Benedict, Jules, *Sketch of the Life and Works of the Late Felix Mendelssohn Bartholdy*, London, 1850.

Benjamin, Phyllis, "A Diary-Album for Fanny Mendelssohn Bartholdy," *MS* 7 (1990), 179–217.

Berlioz, Hector, *The Memoirs of Hector Berlioz*, trans. David Cairns, New York, 1969.

Binder, Franz, *Luise Hensel: Ein Lebensbild nach gedruckten und ungedruckten Quellen*, Freiburg, 1904.

Blackwell, Jeannine, and Susanne Zantop, eds., *Bitter Healing: German Women Writers from 1700 to 1800: An Anthology*, Lincoln, Neb., 1990.

Borchard, Beatrix, "Leipziger Straße Drei: Sites for Music," *NCMR* 4 (2007), 119–38.

Borchard, Beatrix, and Monika Schwarz-Danuser, eds., *Fanny Hensel geb. Mendelssohn: Komponieren zwischen Geselligskeitsideal und romantischer Musikästhetik*, Kassel, 1999.

Botstein, Leon, "The Aesthetics of Assimilation and Affirmation: Reconstructing the Career of Felix Mendelssohn," in *MaHW*, 5–42.

Bridenthal, Renate, Claudia Koonz, and Susan Stuard, eds., *Becoming Visible: Women in European History*, Boston, 1998.

Brooks, Jeanice, "Nadia Boulanger and the Salon of the Princesse de Polignac," *JAMS* 46 (1993), 415–68.

Büchter-Römer, Ute, *Fanny Hensel*, Reinbeck bei Hamburg, 2001.

————, *Das Italienerlebnis Fanny Hensels, geb. Mendelssohn Bartholdy*, Essen, 2002.

Büttner, Fred, "Zwischen Gaeta und Kapua: Grillparzers Gedicht als Liedkomposition," in *Neues musikwissenschaftliches Jahrbuch* 1 (1992), 87–117.

Cadenbach, Rainer, "Vom Gang des Herankommens—Fanny und Felix wetteifern in Klavierquartetten," in Helmig, 81–92 [1997].

————, " 'Die weichliche Schreibart', 'Beethovens letzte Zeit' und 'ein gewisses Lebensprinzip': Perspektiven auf Fanny Hensels spätes Streichquartett (1834)," in Borchard and Schwarz-Danuser, 141–64 [1999].

Cai, Camilla, "Fanny Hensel's Songs for Pianoforte of 1836–37: Stylistic Interaction with Felix Mendelssohn," *Journal of Musicological Research* 14 (1994), 55–76.

————, "Texture and Gender: New Prisms for Understanding Hensel's and Mendelssohn's Piano Pieces," in *Nineteenth-Century Piano Music: Essays in Performance and Analysis*, ed. David Witten, New York, 1997, 53–93.

————, "Virtuoso Texture in Fanny Hensel's Piano Music," in Cooper and Prandi, 263–278.

Citron, Marcia, "The Lieder of Fanny Mendelssohn Hensel," in *MQ* 69 (1983), 570–94.

————, "Fanny Hensel's Letters to Felix Mendelssohn in the Green-Books Collection at Oxford," in *Mendelssohn and Schumann: Essays on Their Music and Its Context*, ed. Jon W. Finson and R. Larry Todd, Durham, N.C., 1984, 99–108.

————, "Felix Mendelssohn's Influence on Fanny Mendelssohn Hensel as a Professional Composer," *Current Musicology* 37/38 (1984), 9–17.

————, ed., *The Letters of Fanny Hensel to Felix Mendelssohn*, Stuyvesant, N.Y., 1987.

————, "Gender, Professionalism and the Musical Canon," *Journal of Musicology* 8 (1990), 102–17.

————, "Women Composers and Musicians in Europe, 1880 to 1918," *Women and Music: A History*, ed. K. Pendle, Bloomington, Ind., 1991, 123–41.

————, *Gender and the Musical Canon*, Cambridge, 1993.

————, "Mendelssohn (-Bartholdy) [Hensel], Fanny (Cäcilie)," in *The New Grove Dictionary of Music and Musicians*, 2nd ed., London, 2001, XVI: 388–89.

————, "A Bicentennial Reflection: Twenty-five Years with Fanny Hensel," *NCMR* 4 (2007), 7–20.

Cooper, John Michael, "Mendelssohn's Two *Infelice* Arias: Problems of Sources and Musical Identity," in Cooper and Prandi, 43–97 [2002].

Cooper, John Michael, and Julie D. Prandi, eds., *The Mendelssohns: Their Music in History*, Oxford, 2002.

Cox, H. B., and C. L. E. Cox, *Leaves from the Journals of Sir George Smart*, London, 1907, repr. 1971.

Cullen, Michael, "Leipziger Straße Drei: Eine Baubiographie," *MS* 5 (1982), 9–77.

Derbyshire, John, *Prime Obsession: Bernhard Riemann and the Greatest Unsolved Problem in Mathematics*, Washington, D.C., 2003.

Devrient, Eduard, *My Recollections of Felix Mendelssohn Bartholdy and His Letters to Me*, trans. Natalia Macfarren, London, 1869, repr. New York, 1972.

Devrient, Therese, *Jugenderinnerungen*, Stuttgart, 1905.

Dorn, Heinrich, "Recollections of Felix Mendelssohn and His Friends," *Temple Bar* (February 1872), 397–405.

Draper, Hal, trans., *The Complete Poems of Heinrich Heine*, Boston, 1982.

Eberle, Gottfried, "Zu Fanny Hensels Klavierzyklus 'Das Jahr,'" in *Komponistinnen in Berlin*, ed. Bettina Brand, Martina Helmig, Barbara Kaiser, Birgit Salomon, and Adje Westerkamp, Berlin, 1987, 56–64.

———, "Eroberung des Dramatischen: Fanny Hensels *Hero und Leander*," in Helmig, 131–38 [1997].

Eichner, Hans, "'Camilla'—Eine unbekannte Fortsetzung von Dorothea Schlegels 'Florentin,'" in *Jahrbuch des Freien Deutschen Hochstifts 1965*, Tübingen, 1965, 314–68.

———, *Friedrich Schlegel*, New York, 1970.

Ellsworth, Therese, "Women Soloists and the Piano Concerto in Nineteenth-Century London," *Ad Parnassum* 2 (2003), 21–49.

Elon, Amos, *The Pity of It All: A History of Jews in Germany, 1743–1933*, New York, 2002.

Elvers, Rudolf, "Ein Jugendbrief von Felix Mendelssohn," in *Festschrift für Friedrich Smend zum 70. Geburtstag*, Berlin, 1963, 93–97.

———, "Verzeichnis der Musik-Autographen von Fanny Hensel im Mendelssohn Archiv zu Berlin," *MS* 1 (1972), 169–74.

———, *Fanny Hensel, geb. Mendelssohn Bartholdy: Dokumente ihres Lebens*, Berlin, 1972 [1972a].

———, "Acht Briefe von Lea Mendelssohn an den Verleger Schlesinger in Berlin," in *Das Problem Mendelssohn*, ed. Carl Dahlhaus, Regensburg, 1974, 47–54.

———, "Weitere Quellen zu den Werken von Fanny Hensel," in *MS* 2 (1975), 215–20.

———, "Fanny Hensels Briefe aus München 1839," in *Ars iocundissima: Festschrift Kurt Dorfmüller zum 60. Geburtstag*, ed. Horst Leuchtmann and Robert Münster, Tutzing, 1984, 65–81.

———, "Frühe Quellen zur Biographie Felix Mendelssohn Bartholdys," in Schmidt, 17–22 [1997].

———, "Auch kleinste Dinge…Die Mendelssohn Bartholdys im Album der Sophia Horsley," in *Im Dienst der Quellen der Musik: Festschrift Gertraut Haberkamp zum 65. Geburtstag*, ed. Paul Mai, Tutzing, 2002, 571–73.

Elvers, Rudolf, and Hans-Günter Klein, *Die Mendelssohns in Berlin: Eine Familie und ihre Stadt*, Wiesbaden, 1983.

Elvers, Rudolf, and Peter Ward Jones, "Das Musikalienverzeichnis von Fanny und Felix Mendelssohn Bartholdy," *MS* 8 (1993), 85–104.

"Fanny by Gaslight," *Musical Times* 138/4 (1997), 27–31.

Ferris, David, "Public Performance and Private Understanding: Clara Wieck's Concerts in Berlin," *JAMS* 56 (2003), 351–408.

Fétis, F.-J., *Biographie universelle des musiciens*, Brussels, 1835–1844; repr. 1963.

Filosa, A. J., "The Early Symphonies and Chamber Music of Felix Mendelssohn Bartholdy," PhD diss., Yale University, 1973.

Finke, Heinrich, ed., *Der Briefwechsel Friedrich und Dorothea Schlegels 1818–1820*, Munich, 1923.

Firchow, Peter, trans. and ed., *Friedrich Schlegel's* Lucinde *and the Fragments*, Minneapolis, 1971.

Fladt, Ellinore, "Das problematische Vorbild: Zur Rezeption des 'vokalen Bach' in der Kantate *Hiob*," in Borchard and Schwarz-Danuser, 223–34.

Florian, Jean-Pierre Claris de, *Nouvelles*, ed. R. Godenne, Paris, 1974.

Fontijn, Claire, "Bach-Rezeption und Lutherischer Choral in der Musik von Fanny Hensel und Felix Mendelssohn Bartholdy," in *"Zu groß, zu unerreichbar": Bach-Rezeption im Zeitalter Mendelssohns und Schumanns*, ed. Anselm Hartinger, Christoph Wolff, and Peter Wollny, Wiesbaden, 2007, 255–77.

Frank, Katherine, *A Passage to Egypt: The Life of Lucie Duff Gordon*, Boston, 1994.

Friedlaender, Max, "Briefe an Goethe von Felix Mendelssohn-Bartholdy," in *Goethe Jahrbuch* 12 (1891), 77–127.

Gade, Niels W., *Aufzeichnungen und Briefe*, ed. D. Gade, Leipzig, 1894.

Gilbert, Felix, ed., *Bankiers, Künstler und Gelehrte: Unveröffentlichte Briefe der Familie Mendelssohn aus dem 19. Jahrhundert*, Tübingen, 1975.

Gotch, Rosamund Brumel, ed., *Mendelssohn and His Friends in Kensington: Letters from Fanny and Sophie Horsley Written 1833–36*, London, 1938.

Gounod, Charles, *Autobiographical Reminiscences with Family Letters and Notes on Music*, trans. W. Hely Hutchinson, London, 1896, repr. New York, 1970.

Gourdin, Jean-Luc, *Florian le fabuliste: 1755–1794*, Paris, 2002.

Gray, Richard T., *About Face: German Physiognomic Thought from Lavater to Auschwitz*, Detroit, 2004.

Gundlach, Willi, "Fanny Hensels geistliche Kantaten," *Forum Kirchenmusik* 6 (1997), 219–24.

———, "'…wie ensetzlich mausig ich mich gemacht habe…' Fanny Hensels Chorlieder op. 3," in *Festschrift zum 65. Geburtstag Günther Eisenhardts*, Potsdam, 1998, 12–26.

———, "Die Chorlieder von Fanny Hensel—eine späte Liebe?" in *MS* 11 (1999), 105–30.

———, "Über Fanny Hensels Vokal-Duette," in Fanny Hensel, *Duette, Gesamtausgabe in 5 Bänden*, ed. W. Gundlach, Kassel, 1999–2003.

Gutjahr, Ortrud, ed., *Westöstlicher und Nordsüdlicher Divan: Goethe in interkultureller Perspektive*, Paderborn, 2000.

Hamburger, Lotte, and Joseph Hamburger, *Troubled Lives: John and Sarah Austin*, Toronto, 1985.

Head, Matthew, "Cultural Meanings for Women Composers: Charlotte ('Minna') Brandes and the Beautiful Dead in the German Enlightenment," *JAMS* 57 (2004), 231–84.

———, "Genre, Romanticism and Female Authorship: Fanny Hensel's 'Scottish' Sonata in G Minor (1843)," *NCMR* 4 (2007), 67–88.

Hecker, Max F., ed., *Der Briefwechsel zwischen Goethe und Zelter*, 3 vols., Leipzig, 1913–1918.

Heckscher, Eli F., *The Continental System: An Economic Interpretation*, Oxford, 1922.

Heine, Maximilian, *Erinnerungen an Heinrich Heine und seine Familie*, Berlin, 1868.

Helferich, Gerard, *Humboldt's Cosmos*, New York, 2004.

Hellwig-Unruh, Renate, "Die 'Cholerakantate' von Fanny Hensel," *Musica* 50 (1996), 121–23.

———, "'Eigentlich sollte das Stück wohl für Orchester gesetzt seyn…': Fanny Hensels *Faust-Szene*," in Helmig, 105–14 [1997].

———, "'Ein Dilettant ist schon ein schreckliches Geschöpf, ein weiblicher Autor ein noch schrecklicheres…': Sechs Briefe von Fanny Hensel an Franz Hauser (1794–1870), in *MS* 10 (1997), 215–226 [1997a].

———, "Zur Entstehung von Fanny Hensels Streichquartett in Es-Dur (1829/34)," in Borchardt and Schwarz-Danuser, 121–40 [1999].

———, *Fanny Hensel geb. Mendelssohn Bartholdy: Thematisches Verzeichnis der Kompositionen*, Adliswil, 2000.

Helmig, Martina, ed., *Fanny Hensel, geb. Mendelssohn Bartholdy: Das Werk*, Munich, 1997.

Helmig, Martina, and Annette Maurer, eds., "Fanny Mendelssohn Bartholdy und Wilhelm Hensel: Briefe aus der Verlobungszeit," in Helmig, 139–61 [1997].

Hennemann, Monika, "Mendelsson and Byron: Two Songs Almost without Words," *MS* 10 (197), 131–56.

Hensel, Fanny, *Six Mélodies pour le Piano, Op. 4 und Op. 5*, ed. Barbara Heller, Berlin-Lichterfelde, 1982.

———, *Lieder für das Pianoforte*, Berlin, 1983.

———, *Ausgewählte Klavierwerke*, ed. Fanny Kistner-Hensel, Munich, 1986.

———, *Streichquartett Es-dur*, ed. Günter Marx, Wiesbaden, 1988.

———, *Prelude für Orgel*, ed. Elke Mascha Blankenburg, Kassel, 1988 [1988a].

———, *Weltliche a-cappella-Chöre von 1846*, ed. Elke Mascha Blankenburg, Kassel, 1988, 5 vols. [1988b].

———, *Das Jahr: 12 Charakterstücke für das Pianoforte*, ed. Liana Gavrila Serbescu and Barbara Heller, Kassel, 1989, 2 vols.

———, *Klavierquartett As-Dur*, ed. Renate Eggebrecht-Kupsa, Kassel, 1989 [1989a].

———, *Adagio für Violino und Klavier*, ed. Rosario Marciano, Kasel, 1989 [1989b].

———, *Vier Lieder ohne Worte Opus 8*, ed. Eva Rieger, Kassel, 1989 [1989c].

———, *Unter des Laubdachs Hut*, ed. Joachim Draheim and Gottfried Heinz, Wiesbaden, 1989 [1989d].

———, *Drei Stücke zu vier Händen*, ed. Barbara Gabler, Kassel, 1990.

———, *Sonate g-Moll*, ed. Liana Gavrila Serbescu and Barbara Heller, Kassel, 1991.

———, *Ausgewählte Lieder*, ed. Aloyisa Assenbaum, Düsseldorf, 1991 [1991a].

———, *Sonatensatz E-Dur, Sonate c-Moll*, ed. Liana Gabvrila Serbescu and Barbara Heller, Kassel, 1991 [1991b].

———, *Two Duets on Texts by Heinrich Heine*, ed. Suzanne Summerville, Fairbanks, Alaska, 1991 [1991c].

———, *Two Piano Sonatas*, ed. Judith Radell, Bryn Mawr, 1992.

———, *Lobgesang*, ed. Conrad Misch, Kassel, 1992 [1992a].

———, *Hiob*, ed. Conrad Misch, Kassel, 1992 [1992b].

———, *Ausgewählte Lieder*, ed. Annette Maurer, vol. 2, Wiesbaden, 1993.

———, *Three Songs on Poems by Lord Byron Composed by Fanny Hensel née Mendelssohn Bartholdy*, ed. Suzanne Summerville, Bryn Mawr, 1994.

Hensel, Fanny, *Ouverture C-Dur*, ed. Elke Mascha Blankenburg, Kassel, 1994 [1994a].

———, *Songs for Pianoforte, 1836–1837*, ed. Camilla Cai, Madison, Wis., 1994 [1994b].

———, *Six Piano Pieces from the 1820s*, ed. Judith Radell, Bryn Mawr, 1994 [1994c].

———, *Zwei Stücke für Violoncello und Klavier*, ed. Christian Lambour, Wiesbaden, 1994 [1994d].

———, *Ausgewählte Lieder*, ed. Annette Maurer, vol. 1, Wiesbaden, 1994 [1994e].

———, *Three Songs on Texts by Jean Pierre Claris de Florian*, ed. Suzanne Summerville, Bryn Mawr, 1995.

———, *Three Poems by Heinrich Heine in the Translation of Mary Alexander by Fanny Hensel geb. Mendelssohn Bartholdy*, ed. Suzanne Summerville, Bryn Mawr, 1995 [1995a].

———, *Nachtreigen*, ed. Ulrike Schadl, Stuttgart, 1995 [1995b].

———, *Hero und Leander*, ed. Elke Mascha Blankenburg, Kassel, 1995 [1995c].

———, *Waldruhe*, ed. Barbara Gabler and Tilla Stöhr, Kassel, 1995 [1995d].

———, *Music for Piano Four-Hands*, ed. Judith Raskell, Bryn Mawr, 1995 [1995e].

———, *16 Songs*, ed. J. G. Paton, New York, 1995 [1995f].

———, *Fünf Terzette*, ed. Barbara Gabler and Tille Stöhr, Kassel, 1995 [1995g].

———, *Vier Klavierstücke zu vier Händen*, ed. Irene Patay, Adliswil, 1996.

———, *Übungsstücke und Etuden (1823)*, ed. Annegret Huber, 2 vols., Kassel, 1996 [1996a].

———, *Klavierstücke 1828–1830*, ed. Annette Nubbemeyer, Kassel, 1996 [1996b].

———, *Organ Works*, ed. Calvert Johnson, Pullman, Wash., 1996 [1996c].

———, *Frühe Klavierstücke (1823/24)*, ed. Barbara Heller, Kassel, 1996 [1996d].

———, *Lyrische Klavierstücke (1836–1839)*, ed. Annegret Huber, Kassel, 1996 [1996e].

———, *Virtuose Klavierstücke (1838)*, ed. Annegret Huber, Kassel, 1996 [1996f].

———, *Festspiel (1829) "Die Hochzeit kommt,"* ed. Marilee A. Vana, Kassel, 1997.

———, *5 Klavierstücke*, ed. Renate Hellwig-Unruh, Frankfurt, 1997 [1997a].

———, *Klavierstücke 1843–1844*, ed. Renate Hellwig-Unruh, Frankfurt, 1997 [1997b].

———, *"Traum": Lied auf einen Text von Joseph von Eichendorff für Singstimme und Klavier, F-dur 1844, Faksimile des Autographs*, ed. H.-G. Klein, Wiesbaden, 1997 [1997c].

———, *Choral Music*, 5 vols., Bryn Mawr, 1997 [1997d].

———, *Eine musikalische Italienreise*, ed. Aloysia Assenbaum, Kamen, 1998.

———, *Zum Fest der heiligen Cäcilia*, ed. Willi Gundlach, Kassel, 1998 [1998a].

———, *Faust: Part II of the Tragedy: Act I—A Pleasant Landscape*, ed. Suzanne Summerville, Kassel, 1998 [1998b].

———, *Die späten Lieder*, ed. Aloysia Assenbaum, Kamen, 1998 [1998c].

———, *Duette: Gesamtausgabe in 5 Bänden*, ed. Willi Gundlach, Kassel, 1999–2002.

———, *Oratorium nach Bildern der Bibel*, ed. Elke Mascha Blankenburg, Kassel, 1999 [1999a].

———, *Vier römische Klavierlieder*, ed. Christian Lambour, Wiesbaden, 1999 [1999b].

———, *Das Jahr, zwölf Charakterstücke (1841) für das Fortepiano, illustrierte Reinschrift mit Zeichnungen von Wilhelm Hensel*, ed. Beatrix Borchard, Kassel, 2000.

———, *Acht Lieder nach Texten von Wilhelm Müller*, ed. Suzanne Summerville, Kassel, 2001.

———, *Three Songs on Poems by Lord Byron*, ed. Suzanne Summerville, Kassel, 2001 [2001a].

————, *Tagebücher*, ed. Hans-Günter Klein and Rudolf Elvers, Wiesbaden, 2002.

————, *Briefe aus Rom an ihre Familie in Berlin 1839/40*, ed. H.-G. Klein, Wiesbaden, 2002 [2002a].

————, *Drei Klavierstücke*, ed. Peter Dicke, Cologne, 2002 [2002b].

————, *Klavierbuch e-moll*, ed. Peter Dicke, Wiesbaden, 2003.

————, *Lieder ohne Namen (1820–1844)*, ed. Cornelia Bartsch and Cordula Heymann-Wentzel, 2 vols., Kassel, 2003 [2003a].

————, *Briefe aus Venedig und Neapel an ihre Familie in Berlin 1839/40*, ed. H.-G. Klein, Wiesbaden, 2004.

————, *Piano Music*, ed. R. Larry Todd, Mineola, N.Y., 2004 [2004a].

————, *Liederkreis*, ed. Suzanne Summerville, Fairbanks, Alaska, 2005.

————, *Eight Songs on Poems by Hölty*, ed. Suzanne Summerville, Fairbanks, Alaska, 2005 [2005a].

————, *Briefe aus Paris*, ed. H.-G. Klein, Wiesbaden, 2007.

Hensel, Luise, and Christoph Bernhard Schlüter, *Briefe aus dem deutschen Biedermeier 1832–1876*, ed. Josefine Nettesheim, Münster, 1962.

Hensel, Sebastian, *Die Familie Mendelssohn (1729–1847) nach Briefen und Tagebüchern*, Berlin, 1879; 15th Auf., Berlin, 1911; *The Mendelssohn Family (1729–1847) from Letters and Journals*, trans. Carl Klingemann [Jr.], 2 vols., London, 1882.

————, *Ein Lebensbild aus Deutschlands Lehrjahren*, Berlin, 1904.

Hertz, Deborah, "Seductive Conversion in Berlin, 1770–1809," in Todd M. Endelman, ed., *Jewish Apostasy in the Modern World*, New York, 1987, 48–82.

————, *Jewish High Society in Old Regime Berlin*, New Haven, 1988.

————, "Work, Love and Jewishness in the Life of Fanny Lewald," in *From East and West: Jews in a Changing Europe*, ed. F. Malino and D. Sorkin, Oxford, 1991, 202–22.

————, ed., *Briefe an eine Freundin: Rahel Varnhagen an Rebecca Friedländer*, Cologne, 1988.

Heymann-Wentzel, Cordula, "Ein ungewöhnliches Geburtstagsgeschenk: Fanny Hensels 'Lobgesang,'" in *Musik und Biographie: Festschrift für Rainer Cadenbach*, ed. Cordula Heymann-Wentzel and Johannes Laas, Würzburg, 2004, 462–71.

Heyse, Paul, *Jugenderinnerungen und Bekenntnisse*, Berlin, 1900.

Hiller, Ferdinand, *Mendelssohn: Letters and Recollections*, trans. M. E. von Glehn, London, 1874, repr. New York, 1972.

Hinrichsen, Hans-Joachim, "Kantatenkomposition in der 'Hauptstadt von Sebastian Bach': Fanny Hensels geistliche Chorwerke und die Berliner Bach-Tradition," in Helmig, 115–29 [1997].

————, "Choralidiom und Kunstreligion: Fanny Hensels Bach," in Borchard and Schwarz-Danuser, 216–22 [1999].

Huber, Annegret, "Anmerkungen zu 'Schreibart' und 'Lebensprinzip' einiger Sonatenhauptsätze von Fanny Hensel," in Helmig, 93–104 [1997].

————, "In welcher Form soll man Fanny Hensels 'Choleramusik' aufführen?" in *MS* 10 (1997), 227–45 [1997a].

————, "Zerschlagen, zerfließen oder erzeugen? Fanny Hensel und Felix Mendelssohn Bartholdy im Streit um musikalische Formkonzepte nach 'Beethovens letzter Zeit,'" in *Maßstab Beethoven? Komponistinnen im Schatten des Geniekults*, ed. Bettina Brand and Martina Helmig, Munich, 2001, 120–44.

Huber, Annegret, *Das* Lied ohne Worte *als kunstbegreifendes Experiment,* Tutzing, 2006.

Iitti, Sana, *The Feminine in German Song,* New York, 2006.

Jacob-Friesen, Holger, "Moses Mendelssohn im Bilde: Einige bisher wenig beachtete Darstellungen," *MS* 13 (2003), 9–34.

Jacobson, Jacob, "Von Mendelssohn zu Mendelssohn Bartholdy," *Leo Baeck Institute Yearbook* 5 (1960), 251–61.

———, *Die Judenbürgerbücher der Stadt Berlin: 1809–1851, mit Ergänzungen für die Jahre 1791–1809,* Berlin, 1962.

Kahn, Lothar, "Ludwig Robert: Rahel's Brother," in *Yearbook of the Leo Baeck Institute* 8 (1973), 185–99.

Karl, Frederick R., *George Eliot: Voice of a Century,* New York, 1995.

Kellenberger, Edgar, "Fanny Hensel und die Cholera-Epidemie 1831," *Musik und Kirche* 67 (1997), 295–303.

Keudell, Robert von, *Erinnerungen aus den Jahren 1846 bis 1872,* Berlin, 1901.

Kippenberg, Anton, "Ein Brief Abraham Mendelssohn an Zelter über Goethe," *Jahrbuch der Sammlung Kippenberg* 4 (1924), 72–91.

Klein, Hans-Günter, "Autographe und Abschriften von Werken Fanny Hensels im Mendelssohn-Archiv zu Berlin," *MS* 7 (1990), 343–45.

———, "'…dieses allerliebste Buch': Fanny Hensels Noten-Album," *MS* 8 (1993), 141–57.

———, "Quellen zu Werken Fanny Hensels in der Musikabteilung der Staatsbibliothek zu Berlin," *MS* 8 (1993), 159–60 [1993a].

———, *Die Kompositionen Fanny Hensels in Autographen und Abschriften aus dem Besitz der Staatsbibliothek zu Berlin—Preußischer Kulturbesitz,* Tutzing, 1995.

———, *Das verborgene Band: Felix Mendelssohn Bartholdy und seine Schwester Fanny Hensel,* Berlin, 1997.

———, "Eine postume Huldigungskomposition für Friedrich Wilhelm IV. und Elisabeth von Preußen von Fanny Hensel," in *Staatsbibliothek zu Berlin—Preußischer Kulturbesitz, Mitteilungen* (1997), 67–70 [1997a].

———, "Auch in künstlerischer Zusammenarbeit vereint—Wihelm Hensel, zeichnend, und Fanny Hensel, komponierend," *Jahrbuch Preußischer Kulturbesitz* 35 (1999), 270–71.

———, "'O glückliche, reiche, einzige Tage': Fanny und Wilhelm Hensels Album ihrer Italienreise 1839/40," in *Jahrbuch Preußischer Kulturbesitz* 36 (1999), 291–300 [1999a].

———, "Eine (fast) unendliche Geschichte: Felix Mendelssohn Bartholdys Hochzeitsmusik für seine Schwester," *MS* 12 (2001), 179–86.

———, "Similarities and Differences in the Artistic Development of Fanny and Felix Mendelssohn Bartholdy in a Family Context: Observations Based on the Early Berlin Autograph Volumes," in Cooper and Prandi, 245–62 [2002].

———, *Die Mendelssohns in Italien: Ausstellung des Mendelssohn-Archivs der Staatsbibliothek zu Berlin-Preußischer Kulturbesitz,* Wiesbaden, 2002 [2002a].

———, "Fanny und Wilhelm Hensel und die Maler Elsasser," *MS* 13 (2003), 125–67.

———, "'Alle die infamen Gefühle': Überlegungen zu Fanny Hensels Klavierstück *Abschied von Rom,*" *Jahrbuch des Staatlichen Instituts für Musikforschung Preußischer Kulturbesitz 2003,* ed. Günther Wagner, Stuttgart, 2003, 177–88 [2003a].

———, "Henriette Maria Mendelssohn in Paris: Briefe an Lea Mendelssohn Bartholdy," *MS* 14 (2005), 101–87.

———, "Fanny Hensels öffentliche Auftritte als Pianistin," *MS* 14 (2005), 285–93 [2005a].

———, *"…mit obligater Nachtigallen- und Fliederblütenbegleitung": Fanny Hensels Sonntagsmusiken,* Wiesbaden, 2005 [2005b].

———, ed., *Die Musikveranstaltungen bei den Mendelssohns—Ein "musikalischer Salon"?,* Leipzig, 2006.

———, ed., *"O glückliche, reiche, einzige Tage": Fanny und Wilhelm Hensels italienische Reise,* Weisbaden, 2006 [2006a].

———, "Sonntagsmusiken bei Fanny Hensel," in Klein, 2006, 47–59 [2006b].

———, " '…Als unsrer geistreichsten Landsleute einen': Lea Mendelssohn Bartholdys Briefe an Carl Gustaf von Brinkman aus den Jahren 1811–1822," in *Jahrbuch des Staatlichen Instituts für Musikforschung Preußischer Kulturbesitz 2005,* Mainz, 2007, 243–66.

———, "Die Mendelssohns auf der Flucht: Abraham Mendelssohn Bartholdy und seine Familie 1813 in Wien," *MS* 15 (2007), 199–206 [2007a].

———, "Fanny Hensels Italienische Reise—unter den Auspizien Goethes," in *Jahrbuch des freien deutschen Hochstifts 2007,* Tübingen, 2007, 215–23 [2007b].

———, "Rebecka Dirichlet in Rom: Die Briefe an ihre Schwester Fanny Hensel im Winter 1843/44," *MS* 15 (2007), 261–332 [2007c].

Klein, Hans-Günter, and Felix Müller-Stüler, "Das Testament von Wilhelm und Fanny Hensel," *MS* 13 (2003), 169–75.

Kleßmann, Eckart, *Die Mendelssohns: Bilder aus einer deutschen Familie,* Frankfurt am Main, 1993.

Klingemann, Karl, Jr., ed., *Felix Mendelssohn-Bartholdys Briefwechsel mit Legationsrat Karl Klingemann in London,* Essen, 1909.

Koch, P.-A., *Fanny Hensel geb. Mendelssohn (1805–47): Kompositionen—eine Zusammenhang der Werke, Literatur und Schallplatten,* Frankfurt, 1993.

Köhler, Karl-Heinz, "Fanny Mendelssohn," in *The New Grove Dictionary of Music and Musicians,* ed. Stanley Sadie, London, 1980, XII: 134.

Köhler, Oskar, *Müde bin ich, geh' zur Ruh': Die hell-dunkle Lebensgeschichte Luises Hensels,* Paderborn, 1991.

Krebs, Harald, and Sharon Krebs, *Josephine Lang: Her Life and Songs,* New York, 2006.

———, "The 'Power of Class' in a New Perspective: A Comparison of the Compositional Careers of Fanny Hensel and Josephine Lang," *NCMR* 4 (2007), 37–48.

Lackmann, Thomas, "Grenzüberschreitung und Identität: Vier Briefe Abraham Mendelssohn Bartholdys aus drei Jahrzehnten—eine Charakterskizze," *MS* 13 (2003), 35–70.

Lambour, Christian, "Quellen zur Biographie von Fanny Hensel, geb. Mendelssohn Bartholdy," in *MS* 6 (1986), 49–105.

———, "Ein Schweizer Reisebrief aus dem Jahr 1822 von Lea und Fanny Mendelssohn Bartholdy an Henriette Mendelssohn, geb. Meyer," *MS* 7 (1990), 171–77.

———, "Fanny Hensel als Beethoven-Interpretin: Materialien," *Maßstab Beethoven? Komponistinnen im Schatten des Geniekults,* ed. Martina Helmig and Bettina Brand, Munich, 2001, 106–19.

———, "Fanny Hensel—Die Pianistin: Erster Teil. Die Lehrer; Zweiter Teil. Die Instrumente," *MS* 12 (2001a), 227–42.

Lambour, Christian, "Fanny Hensel—Die Pianistin: Dritter Teil. Berichte der Zeitgenossen," *MS* 14 (2005), 269–83.

———, "Fanny Hensel—Die Pianistin: Vierter Teil. Wie Fanny Hensel ihr eigenes Klavierspiel einschätzt; Fünfter Teil. Fanny Hensel beurteilt die Pianisten ihrer Generation," *MS* 15 (2007), 247–60.

Lampadius, W. A., *Life of Felix Mendelssohn Bartholdy*, trans. W. L. Gage, 2nd ed., London, 1877.

Lang, Josephine, *Selected Songs*, ed. Judith Tick, New York, 1982.

Lausch, Hans, "'Der Mathematiker schwimmt in Wollust': Mathematik bei Moses Mendelssohn—Mathematiker in Familienstammbaum," *MS* 7 (1990), 77–106.

Ledebur, Carl von, *Tonkünstler-Lexicon Berlin's von den ältesten Zeiten bis auf die Gegenwart*, Berlin, 1861.

Lewald, Fanny, *The Education of Fanny Lewald: An Autobiography*, trans. and ed. H. B. Lewis, Albany, N.Y., 1992.

Librett, Jeffrey S., *The Rhetoric of Cultural Dialogue: Jews and Germans from Moses Mendelssohn to Richard Wagner and Beyond*, Stanford, 2000.

Little, Wm. A., "Mendelssohn and the Berlin Singakademie: The Composer at the Crossroads," in Todd, 65–85 [1991].

Litzmann, Berthold, *Clara Schumann: Ein Künstlerleben nach Tagebüchern und Briefen*, 3 vols., Leipzig, 1902–1903.

Lowenthal-Hensel, Cécile, "F in Dur und F in Moll: Fanny und Felix Mendelssohn in Berlin," in *Berlin in Dur und Moll*, ed. Felix Henseleit, Berlin, 1970, 30–32.

———, "Wilhelm Hensel in England," in *MS* 2 (1975), 203–13.

———, "Theodor Fontane über Wilhelm Hensel," *MS* 3 (1979), 181–99.

———, "Wilhelm Hensels 'Lebenslauf' von 1829," *MS* 3 (1979), 175–79 [1979a].

———, *Preußische Bildnisse des 19. Jahrhunderts: Zeichnungen von Wilhelm Hensel*, Berlin, 1981.

———, *19th Century Society Portraits: Drawings by Wilhelm Hensel*, London, 1986.

———, "Wilhelm Hensel und seine zeichnerisches Werk," in *Jahrbuch Stiftung Preußischer Kulturbesitz* 23 (1987), 57–70.

———, "Neues zur Leipziger Straße Drei," *MS* 7 (1990), 141–51.

———, "Wilhelm Hensel: Fanny und Felix im Porträt," in *MS* 10 (1997), 9–24.

Lowenthal-Hensel, Cécile, and Jutta Arnold, *Wilhelm Hensel 1794–1861: Porträtist und Maler, Werke und Dokumente*, Wiesbaden, 2004.

Marx, Adolf Bernhard, *Erinnerungen aus meinem Leben*, Berlin, 1865.

———, "From the Memoirs of Adolf Bernhard Marx," trans. Susan Gillespie, in *MaHW*, 206–20 [1991].

Maurer, Annette, "Biographische Einflüsse auf das Liedschaffen Fanny Hensel," in Helmig, 33–41 [1997].

———, *Thematisches Verzeichnis der klavierbegleiteten Sololieder Fanny Hensels*, Kassel, 1997 [1997a].

Maurer, Annette, and Annegret Huber, "Fanny Mendelssohn Bartholdys Lied *Die Schwalbe* als Musikbeilage des Almanachs *Rheinblüthen*," in Helmig, 51–57 [1997].

Mendelssohn Bartholdy, Felix, *Letters from Italy and Switzerland*, trans. Lady Wallace, London, 1862.

———, *Briefe an deutsche Verleger*, ed. Rudolf Elvers, Berlin, 1968.

———, *Felix Mendelssohn: A Life in Letters*, ed. Rudolf Elvers, trans. C. Tomlinson, New York, 1986.

———, *Briefe: Band I, 1817 bis 1829*, ed. Rudolf Elvers, Vorabdruck, Leipzig, 1997.

Mendelssohn Bartholdy, Karl, *Goethe and Mendelssohn (1821–1831)*, trans. M. E. von Glehn, London, 1874.

Mendelssohn Bartholdy, Paul, *Letters of Felix Mendelssohn Bartholdy from 1833 to 1847*, London, 1868.

Meyerbeer, Giacomo, *Briefwechsel und Tagebücher*, ed. H. Becker, Berlin, 1960, vol. 1.

Montgomery, David L., "From Biedermeier Berlin: The Parthey Diaries," *MQ* 74 (1990), 197–216.

Moscheles, Felix, trans. and ed., *Letters of Felix Mendelssohn to Ignaz and Charlotte Moscheles*, London, 1888.

Moscheles, Ignaz, *Recent Music and Musicians*, ed. Charlotte Moscheles, trans. A. D. Coleridge, London, 1873.

Müller, Ernst, *Ludwig Christoph Heinrich Hölty: Leben und Werk*, Hannover, 1986.

Müller, F. Max, *Auld Lang Syne*, New York, 1898.

Müller, Gisela A., "'Leichen-' oder 'Blüthenduft'? Heine-Vertonungen Fanny Hensels und Felix Mendelssohn Bartholdys im Vergleich," in Helmig, 42–50 [1997].

———, "'Goethe hat mich auf dieser Reise nicht verlassen': Das letzte Lied in Fanny und Wilhelm Hensels Reise-Album 1839–40," in *Jahrbuch des Staatlichen Instituts für Musikforschung Preußischer Kulturbesitz 2003*, 189–206.

Müller, Harald, "Franz Xaver Mozarts Hölty-Vertonungen und ihr kompositorisches Umfeld," *Acta Mozartiana* 45/3–4 (1998), 59–77.

———, *Ludwig Christoph Heinrich Höltys Gedichte in Vertonungen*, Bielefeld, 1998 [1998a].

Nieding, Elke von, "Versteckt in der Geschichte—Bartholdys Meierei," *MS* 15 (2007), 107–20.

Nowack, Natalie, "'Martens Mühle soll leben," *MS* 10 (1997), 247–49.

Nubbemeyer, Annette, "Italienerinnerungen im Klavieroeuvre Fanny Hensels: Das verschwiegene Programm im Klavierzyklus *Das Jahr*," in Helmig, 68–80 [1997].

———, "Zweifel und Bekenntnis: Fanny Hensels Kantate 'Hiob'—Entstehungsgeschichte und Werkanalyse," *Musik und Kirche* 67 (1997), 286–95 [1997a].

———, "Die Klaviersonaten Fanny Hensels: Analytische Betrachtungen," in Borchardt and Schwarz-Danuser, 90–119 [1999].

Offen, Karen M., *European Feminisms, 1700–1950: A Political History*, Stanford, 2000.

Oleskiewicz, Mary, "Quantz's *Quatuors* and Other Works Newly Discovered," *Early Music* 31 (2003), 485–504.

Ostleitner, Elena, "Fanny Hensel, Josephine Lang, Johanna Kinkel: Drei komponierende Zeitgenossinnen aus der Zeit Benedict Randhartingers," in *Vergessene Komponisten des Biedermeier*, ed. Andrea Harrandt and Erich Wolfgang Partsch, Tutzing, 2000, 53–60.

Panwitz, Sebastian, "Das Testament von Wilhelm und Fanny Hensel," *MS* 13 (2003), 169–75.

———, "Zur Besitzgeschichte der Mendelssohn-Häuser in der Jägerstraße 49–53," *MS* 13 (2003), 299–303 [2003a].

———, "Joseph und Abraham Mendelssohn unter Arrest: Eine Akte aus den Jahren 1811/12," *MS* 14 (2005), 77–100.

Piggott, Patrick, *The Innocent Diversion: A Study of Music in the Life and Writings of Jane Austen*, London, 1979.

Polko, Elise, *Reminiscences of Felix Mendelssohn-Bartholdy: A Social and Artistic Biography*, London, 1869, repr. 1987.

Pope, Barbara Corrado, "Angels in the Devil's Workshop: Leisured and Charitable Women in Nineteenth-Century England and France," in *Becoming Visible: Women in European History*, ed. Renate Bridenthal and Claudia Koonz, Boston, 1977, 296–324.

Rebmann, Jutta, *Die schöne Friederike: Eine Schwäbin im Biedermeier; Biographischer Roman*, Irdning/Steiermark, 1989.

———, *Fanny Mendelssohn: Biographischer Roman*, Irdning/Steiermark, 1991.

Reich, Nancy, "The Power of Class: Fanny Hensel," in *MaHW*, 86–99 [1991].

———, "Women as Musicians: A Question of Class," in *Musicology and Difference: Gender and Sexuality in Music Scholarship*, ed. Ruth A. Solie, Berkeley, Calif., 1993, 125–46.

———, ed. and trans., "The Correspondence between Clara Wieck Schumann and Felix and Paul Mendelssohn Bartholdy," in *Schumann and His World*, ed. R. Larry Todd, Princeton, 1994, 205–32.

———, *Clara Schumann: The Artist and the Woman*, 2nd ed., Ithaca, 2001.

———, "The Diaries of Fanny Hensel and Clara Schumann: A Study in Contrasts," *NCMR* 14 (2007), 21–36.

Reichenberger, Arnold G., "Federico Confalonieri as Seen by Fanny Mendelssohn Hensel," *Italica* 21/2 (1944), 61–65.

Rellstab, Ludwig, *Ludwig Berger, ein Denkmal*, Berlin, 1846.

Reynolds, Christopher Alan, *Motives for Allusion: Context and Content in Nineteenth-Century Music*, Cambridge, Mass., 2003.

Rieger, Eva, and Käte Walter, eds., *Frauen komponieren: Female Composers*, Mainz, 1992.

Robertson, Ritchie, *The German-Jewish Dialogue: An Anthology of Literary Texts 1749–1993*, New York, 1999.

Rothenberg, Sarah, "Thus Far, but No Further: Fanny Mendelssohn-Hensel's Unfinished Journey," in *MQ* 77 (1993), 709–17.

Rousseau, Jean-Jacques, *Le Devin du village*, ed. Charlotte Kaufman, Madison, Wis., 1998.

Sammons, Jeffrey L., *Heinrich Heine: A Modern Biography*, Princeton, 1979.

Schlegel, Dorothea Mendelssohn Veit, *Florentin: A Novel*, trans. Edwina Lawler and Ruth Richardson, Lewiston/Queenston, 1988.

———, *Camilla: A Novella*, ed. Hans Eichner, trans. Edwina Lawler, Lewiston/Queenston, 1990.

Schmidt, Christian Martin, ed., *Felix Mendelssohn Bartholdy: Kongreß-Bericht Berlin 1994*, Wiesbaden, 1997.

Schottländer, J. W., ed., *Carl Friedrich Zelters Darstellung seines Lebens*, Weimar, 1931.

Schröder, Gesine, "Fannys Studien," in Helmig, 23–32 [1997].

———, "Schreiben für Orchester," in Borchard and Schwarz-Danuser, 165–74 [1999].

Schubring, Julius, "Reminiscences of Felix Mendelssohn-Bartholdy [1866]," in *MaHW*, 221–36 [1995].

Schumann, Robert, *Tagebücher II*, ed. Gerd Nauhaus, Leipzig, 1987.

Schwarz-Danuser, Monika, "Mendelssohn, Fanny (Caecilie)," in *Musik in Geschichte und Gegenwart*, Kassel, 2004, Personenteil, XI, cols. 1534–1542.

Seaton, Douglass, "A Composition Course with Karl Friedrich Zelter," *College Music Symposium* 21 (1981), 126–38.

Seidel, Katrin, "Anmerkungen zu den Klavierkompositionen im ersteigerten 'Reisealbum Deutschland-Italien 1839/40' von Fanny Hensel," *Die Musikforschung* 53 (2000), 451–53.

Siebenkäs, Dieter, *Ludwig Berger: Sein Leben und seine Werke unter besonderer Berücksichtigung seines Liedschaffens*, Berlin, 1963.

Siegfried, Christina, "'Der interessanteste und problematischste seiner Freunde'—Adolph Bernhard Marx (1795–1866)," in *Blickpunkt Felix Mendelssohn Bartholdy*, ed. B. Heyder and C. Spering, Cologne, 1994.

Sievers, H.-J., "Die Familie Mendelssohn-Bartholdy in den Kirchenbüchern der Evangelisch-reformierten Kirche zu Leipzig," in *In der Mitte der Stadt: Die evangelisch-reformierte Kirche zu Leipzig von der Einwanderung der Hugenotten bis zur Friedlichen Revolution*, ed. H.-J. Sievers, Leipzig, 2000, 100–103.

Simms, Brendan, *The Impact of Napoleon: Prussian High Politics, Foreign Policy and the Crisis of the Executive, 1797–1806*, Cambridge, 1997.

Sirota, Victoria, "The Life and Works of Fanny Mendelssohn Hensel," DMA diss., Boston University, 1981.

"The Sisters of Two Great Composers," *Musical Times* 42 (1901), 56–60.

Sousa Correa, Delia da, *George Eliot, Music and Victorian Culture*, New York, 2003.

Spiel, Hilde, *Fanny von Arnstein: A Daughter of the Enlightenment 1758–1818*, trans. C. Shuttleworth, New York, 1991.

Sposato, Jeffrey S., *The Price of Assimilation: Felix Mendelssohn and the Nineteenth-Century Anti-Semitic Tradition*, New York, 2006.

Stern, Carola, *"Ich möchte mir Flügel wünschen": Das Leben der Dorothea Schlegel*, Reinbeck bei Hamburg, 1990.

Streicher, Johannes, "Per Fanny Mendelssohn-Hensel. Minima italica e altre divagazioni," in *Ottrocento e oltre: Scritti in onore di Raoul Meloncelli*, ed. Francesco Izzo and Johannes Streicher, Rome, 1993, 235–66.

Stromeyer, Georg Friedrich Louis, *Erinnerungen eines deutschen Arztes*, Hannover, 1875.

Sutermeister, Peter, ed., *Felix Mendelssohn Bartholdy: Eine Reise durch Deutschland, Italien, und die Schweiz*, Tübingen, 1979.

Thayer, Alexander Wheelock, *Life of Beethoven*, ed. Elliot Forbes, Princeton, 1969.

Thorau, Christian, "'Das spielende Bild des Jahres': Fanny Hensels Klavierzyklus Das Jahr," in Borchard and Schwarz-Danuser, 73–89 [1999].

Tillard, Françoise. *Fanny Mendelssohn*, trans. Camille Naish, Portland, Ore., 1996.

———, "Felix Mendelssohn and Fanny Hensel: The Search for Perfection in Opposing Private and Public Worlds," in Cooper and Prandi, 279–90 [2002].

Todd, R. Larry, *Mendelssohn's Musical Education: A Study and Edition of His Exercises in Composition*, Cambridge, 1983.

———, "From the Composer's Workshop: Two Little-Known Fugues by Mendelssohn," *Musical Times* 131 (1990), 183–87.

———, ed., *Mendelssohn and His World*, Princeton, 1991.

———, "On Stylistic Affinities in the Works of Fanny Hensel and Felix Mendelssohn Bartholdy," in Cooper and Prandi, 245–62 [2002].

Todd, R. Larry, ed., *Fanny Hensel: Selected Piano Music*, Mineola, N.Y., 2004.

———, *Mendelssohn: A Life in Music*, rev. ed., Oxford, 2005.

———, *Mendelssohn Essays*, New York, 2007.

———, "Fanny Hensel's Op. 6 No. 1 and the Art of Musical Reminiscence," *NCMR* 4/2 (2007), 89–100 [2007a].

———, "Fanny Hensel and Musical Style," in Todd, *Mendelssohn Essays*, 217–31 [2007b].

———, "Issues of Stylistic Identity in Fanny Hensel's *Das Jahr*," in Todd, *Mendelssohn Essays*, 249–60 [2007c].

Toews, John E., "Memory and Gender in the Remaking of Fanny Mendelssohn's Musical Identity: The Chorale in 'Das Jahr,'" in *MQ* 77 (1993), 727–48.

Vana, Marilee Ann, "Fanny Mendelssohn Hensel's *Festspiel*, MA Ms. 37: A Modern Edition and Conductor's Analysis for Performance," DMA diss., University of North Carolina at Greensboro, 1996.

Wallace, Sean Michael Hamilton, "The *Gartenlieder*, Op. 3, by Fanny Mendelssohn Hensel (1805–1847)," DMA diss., Michigan State University, 2000.

Walsh, John Evangelist, *The Hidden Life of Emily Dickinson*, New York, 1971.

Ward Jones, Peter, "Mendelssohn's First Composition," in Cooper and Prandi, 101–13 [2002].

Weber, Paul, *On the Road to Rebellion: The United Irishmen and Hamburg 1796–1803*, Dublin, 1997.

Weber, William, *Music and the Middle Class: The Social Structure of Concert Life in London, Paris and Vienna*, New York, 1975.

Weissweiler, Eva, *Komponistinnen aus 500 Jahren: Eine Kultur- und Wirkungsgeschichte in Biographien und Werkbeispielen*, Frankfurt, 1981.

———, ed., *Fanny und Felix Mendelssohn: "Die Musik will gar nicht rutschen ohne Dich": Briefwechsel 1821 bis 1846*, Berlin, 1997.

Wendler, Eugen, *"Das Band der ewigen Liebe": Clara Schumanns Briefwechsel mit Emilie und Elise List*, Stuttgart, 1996.

Werner, Eric, *Mendelssohn: A New Image of the Composer and His Age*, trans. Dika Newlin, New York, 1963.

Werner, Jack, "Felix and Fanny Mendelssohn," in *Music & Letters* 28 (1947), 303–37.

Whaley, Joachim, *Religious Toleration and Social Change in Hamburg: 1529–1819*, Cambridge, 1985.

Whaley, John, trans. and ed., *Goethe, Poems of the West and East*, Bern, 1998.

Wilhelmy, Petra, *Der Berliner Salon im 19. Jahrhundert (1780–1914)*, Berlin, 1989.

Wilhelmy-Dollinger, Petra, *Die Berliner Salons*, Berlin, 2000.

———, "Musikalische Salons in Berlin 1815–1840," in *Die Musikveranstaltungen bei den Mendelssohns—Ein "musikalischer Salon"?*, ed. H.-G. Klein, Leipzig, 2006, 17–33.

———, "Biography and Symbol: Uncovering the Structure of a Creative Life in Fanny Hensel's Lieder," *NCMR* 4 (2007), 49–65.

Wilson Kimber, Marian, "Zur frühen Wirkungsgeschichte Fanny Hensels" in Borchard and Schwarz-Danuser, 248–62 [1999].

———, "The 'Suppression' of Fanny Mendelssohn: Rethinking Feminist Biography," *19th Century Music* 26 (2002), 113–29.

————, "From the Concert Hall to the Salon: The Piano Music of Clara Wieck Schumann and Fanny Mendelssohn Hensel," in *Nineteenth-Century Piano Music*, ed. R. Larry Todd, 2nd ed., New York, 2003, 316–55.

————, "Fanny Hensel Meets the Boys in the Band: The Brass Transcriptions of the *Gartenlieder*, Op. 3," *Historical Brass Society Journal* 18 (2006), 17–36.

————, "Fanny Hensel's Seasons of Life: Poetic Epigrams, Vignettes and Meaning in *Das Jahr*," *Journal of Musicological Research* 27 (2008), 359–95.

Wolff, Ernst, *Felix Mendelssohn Bartholdy*, Berlin, 1906.

Wolitz, Stefan, *Fanny Hensel's Chorwerke*, Tutzing, 2007.

Wollenberg, Susan, "Fanny Hensel's Op. 8, No. 1: A Special Case of 'multum in parvo'?" *NCMR* 4 (2007), 101–17.

Wollny, Peter, "Sarah Levy and the Making of Musical Taste in Berlin," *MQ* 77 (1993), 651–88.

Youens, Susan, "Behind the Scenes: *Die schöne Müllerin* before Schubert," *19CM* 15 (1991), 3–22.

————, *Schubert, Müller, and* Die schöne Müllerin, Cambridge, 1997.

Index of Fanny Hensel's Compositions

Index of Felix Mendelssohn Bartholdy's Compositions

General Index